Ocean Grove National Education Assembly, Joseph Crane Hartzell

Christian Educators in Council

Ocean Grove National Education Assembly, Joseph Crane Hartzell

Christian Educators in Council

ISBN/EAN: 9783337301880

Printed in Europe, USA, Canada, Australia, Japan

Cover: Foto ©Andreas Hilbeck / pixelio.de

More available books at **www.hansebooks.com**

CHRISTIAN EDUCATORS IN COUNCIL.

SIXTY ADDRESSES BY AMERICAN EDUCATORS;

WITH

HISTORICAL NOTES UPON THE

HELD AT

Ocean Grove, N. J., August 9-12, 1883.

ALSO,

Illiteracy and Education Tables from Census of 1880.

COMPILED AND EDITED BY

REV. J. C. HARTZELL. D.D.

NEW YORK:
PHILLIPS & HUNT.
CINCINNATI:
WALDEN & STOWE.
1883.

TABLE OF CONTENTS.

EDITOR'S NOTE.

THE contents of this volume require but a word of explanation. It seemed fitting that there should be one platform in America, where once a year, Christian educators and statesmen, irrespective of section, Church, or party, could assemble to awaken and direct public sentiment in favor of enlarged National, State, and Church effort, for the education and elevation of our illiterate and degraded masses.

The Ocean Grove Association tendered the use of its auditorium, and offered to welcome as its guests all who should participate as speakers at these annual gatherings. The co-operation of the United States Commissioner of Education was readily secured, as was also that of the Corresponding Secretaries of the great Educational Societies, of the chief religious denominations of the country.

The first National Education Assembly was held in 1882, and its success proved the wisdom of the movement. The Assembly of 1883 was organized upon a larger scale, with a broader range of subjects and more speakers. Three times a day for four days great audiences attended, and an enthusiastic interest was maintained to the end. This volume contains all the addresses delivered at the Assembly of 1883, and some of the more important ones delivered in 1882. To add to its practical value, a large amount of statistical information is given from the census of 1880, and the National Bureau of Education, showing the illiterate and educational status of the United States, each State and Territory, and of the South as a section.

The addresses, in the main, are the words of workers, inspired by profound convictions and telling of results achieved in fields where they have spent years of sacrificing toil. The speakers, who hold official relations to the government or to the great denominations, have superintended the expenditure of many millions among the ignorant and poor of our land. Their information is trustworthy, and their words ought to have the greatest possible weight. Each speaker has spoken freely his own views, and the addresses are now printed as revised by their authors.

The subjects discussed are among the most intensely practical and profoundly important before the American nation. The questions of education and ignorance, and their relations to individual, social, and national well-being, are at the front, and are there to stay. The American Republic must now decide whether intelligent morality or ignorant chicanery will rule at the ballot-box—the place of supreme power in the nation. Invincible there, the Republic lives; defeated there, it dies. To educate and make moral our illiterate masses—native and foreign, Negro and Indian—is not a benevolence work simply, but one involving the very existence of the Nation, and the maintenance of every essential principle on which rests our Christian civilization. This volume contains a vast amount of information bearing upon many phases of this work, gathered by scholars and laborers from very wide fields of observation.

The arrangement of the addresses under topics, freeing the body of the book from all details of proceedings, brings together the discussions on each subject. The full Table of Contents is supplemented by a copious and carefully prepared General Index. Mr. Henry F. Reddall, of New York city, has rendered valuable assistance in the editorial work.

J. C. H.

I. EDUCATION AND MAN'S IMPROVEMENT.

EDUCATION A MEASURE OF MAN'S IMPROVEMENT.

BY HON. JOHN EATON, LL.D.,
United States Commissioner of Education.

MAN is confronted with two possibilities: he may become worse or better. Those looking on the sunset of life are apt to see the shadows of evil growing; but our day accepts the idea that man has not only gone forward with time and the course of events, here worse and there better, but that on the whole he has greater possibilities and is in better conditions. We agree with Whittier when he exclaims,

"Take heart! The waster builds again.
    A charmèd life old Goodness hath;
The tares may perish, but the grain
    Is not for death.
God works in all things; all obey
    His first propulsion from the night;
Wake thou and watch! the world is gray
    With morning light."

The instinct of life in the animal is hardly more universal than the aspiration of man for improvement; individuals, families, societies, churches, nations, races, seek for its measure. Every new scheme for the amelioration of man's condition, every ism or ology or reform, lays claim to attention on the ground of its power to improve human affairs. Great writers and orators have each advanced the claims of their favorite theme —industry, commerce, travel, poetry, history, philosophy, science, art, religion, education— each of these has performed its great part and deserves its eulogy. We disparage none; but we may say that whatever commerce, or industry, or philosophy, or religion, even, has accomplished, that only remains which has been wrought into man or his conditions by those processes of forming habits of thought or action, of growth, of nursing, or training, or instruction, which we call education. We may not pause to define this term, or lift it out of the crude notions that limit it to the book or the teacher, or that flatter every body with the idea that he knows all about it without attending to it,

and is qualified and ready to assume its responsibilities whenever he has failed in every thing else. These are evils that must be cured by the onward march of culture.

The power of education is so admitted in the best thinking of civilized nations in our day, that all men point to Sadowa and Sedan, those scenes of conflict and horrid war, and tell us that we find the cause of victory not alone in the bravery of the generals, not alone in the material of war, but in the education of the respective combatants. The nations of the earth, laden with the articles illustrative of their accomplishments, meet in the great world's fairs in peaceful contest, and compare their positions in the trades and industries, and the most considerate and thoughtful inquiry shows that not merely the investments in commercial fleets, not merely the money invested or the numbers engaged in industries, but the skill taught in the schools, determines the supremacy of their articles in the markets of the world. Moreover, inter-communication is so rapid and direct in spite of oceans and mountains, indeed of all natural barriers and of all impediments imposed by nations, that every producer is brought into competition with every other, wherever he may live on the globe, and thus the quality of each article determines its sale, and its quality is dependent upon the skill of the producer, and that skill upon his education. Thus commerce by its immutable laws daily enforces the lessons of these great contests of war and peace.

The European nations most nearly affected by these contests consuming a large proportion of the products of their energy, skill, and industry, in keeping up great standing armies to preserve the peace, and trembling all the while lest the balance of power may somewhere be disturbed and involve them in destructive war, have been most profoundly affected by this emphatic and conclusive showing that education is the greatest power at their control and the final measure of the improvement of their people. The German States, led by Prussia, first made this discovery. To the selfishness of royalty it showed how their power could be multiplied by the cultivation of each of their subjects; more children could be stronger and live longer, could think more and better, and direct the affairs of peace and war more effectively. Training, though it waked up the powers of the youth, and rendered him liable to self action, was seen to be of so great possibilities that it could be conducive to habits of submission and devotion, and that the natural and acquired potentialities of the people would, in spite of this risk, be only more effective for the hand that ruled them. A king who could make every male subject of sufficient bodily health a soldier, and, by training a few for officers, could turn his whole country into a camp for a war of seven years, or a generation, as he chose, could, by a decree, send every child to school, and by training a few teachers, could mold his whole people to his will. Thus these rulers reached the enforcement of universal compulsory education and the establishment of normal schools for the training of teachers, and, as new necessities arose, they saw in education the power to meet them. Must they have more effective weapons of war, or implements of industry, or better roads and bridges? the school must train the skilled men to make them. Was better or more clothing or food, or stricter economy, or greater care of health, needed? the schools must train the men to prepare the way and assure these results. But to the German reformers this power of education revealed a far higher purpose. The light which dawned upon them, gathering rays from all the past, had touched Italians and others, but produced the most effect in Germany. Her reformers saw that culture had been directed for the benefit of a few for man's selfish purposes in Church and State ; they and their followers in due time seemed to apprehend, in the universal application of the power of education, a figure of the universal proclamation of salvation by the blood of the Saviour. Printing came to their aid with its almost miraculous multiplication of the power of thought. Education was to be universal for a higher end than the service of man. All men must have it, not to serve their generation alone, but to honor their God. If the king or his magistrate, who was on all hands counted a servant of heaven, could build roads or levy war, he could and should build school-houses, pay teachers, and educate the children that they might not grow up for their own destruction and that of society, the State, and the Church. Out of the joint action of these diverse views came the elementary, secondary, and superior education of Germany— her volk-schools, her gymnasia and real

schools, and her universities. Their results were greatest in those states that acted with William of Prussia, so that, when his armies, with 2½ per cent. of illiterates, met those of Austria with 17 per cent. of illiterates, other things being equal, there could be no doubt who would be the victor at Sadowa.

Austria, of her twenty millions of people, had, in every ten thousand, one thousand in elementary schools, five in normal schools, twenty-eight in secondary schools, and five in universities, while Germany, of forty millions of people, had, in every ten thousand, fifteen hundred and ninety-four, or one half more, in elementary schools, one hundred and ten, or about three times the proportion of Austria, in her secondary schools, and about the same each in normal schools and universities. Austria, heeding this lesson, yielded to a liberal movement which culminated in the exhibition of 1873 at Vienna, gave greater attention to education, (even sending her soldiers to protect teachers in opening schools in certain mountain regions,) but never reached the point when there could be freedom of religious belief or declaration in her territory, and has finally yielded to a serious reaction.

Many schools were established in France in the eighth century, and the great burst of light which so moved the Germans had also a most salutary effect upon the French; but in the darkness of the St. Bartholomew massacre that portion of her people who had felt its influence most was blotted out, or, at the Revocation of the Edict of Nantes, driven from their fair land, or crushed. With them departed much of skilled industry, many citizens of high character and enlightened religious zeal, and much of wise and liberal statesmanship, greatly needed then and ever since. How much France lost may be seen in part by what was gained in this and other lands from the Huguenots. What a tale of woes and wars at home and abroad remained for France! Every thing in the minds of the leaders of the period was tried for her improvement but the sound and universal education of her people. Only that culture was attempted or allowed which was consistent with selfish or perverted schemes of Church or State. After the appalling scenes of the Revolution of 1793 they bethought themselves more seriously of education for a moment. Napoleon, in his days of supreme authority, as if knowing the power of education, tied its several parts up in one bundle and handled them for his own purposes through the head of the University of France. In the days of Cousin and Guizot, the former went to Germany to report on the progress and condition of education, and united with the latter in efforts for the universal instruction of the people. Look at the dark map of the illiteracy of France. In their day a dawning light appears in Paris and among the Vosges, gaining, against great odds, under the empire of Napoleon the Third, until the day for the end of his acting as ruler of the French, in the victory of the more cultured Germans at Sedan over his soldiers, of whom 36 per cent. were illiterate.

The republic, coming into existence as a forlorn hope among scenes of the greatest confusion and suffering, at once rested its hopes for continuance on the education of the people. Step by step, taxes for education were increased, while the great burdens of the war were borne with alacrity. Inspection was more efficient; school-houses, teachers, and text-books were improved. Through the eminent Buisson commission at Vienna and Philadelphia, and others, the progress of the world in education was brought under view for hints of possible improvement. The maternal schools so-called, dating back to the efforts of Oberlin, which received such aid from the consecrated labors of Madame Pape-Carpentier—schools that are intended to save children from death and degradation, and give them habits of betterment before the school age—have been encouraged until they care for six hundred thousand infants. Attendance at school, during the school age, has been made compulsory, and finally elementary schools, gratuitous or free. All education is emancipated from all control but that of the civil authority which directs it. A great scheme for secondary education for girls has been introduced. If a new feature of education were to be inaugurated, with most logical precision the French have established normal schools to prepare teachers for the special work proposed. Attendance on the elementary and secondary schools has greatly increased; instruction in civic and moral duties is required by law. Soon youth, thus better taught, will bear their part as citizens. Freedom of conscience is declared, and the press and pulpit are less restricted in their utterances.

Monsieur Jules Ferry, in an address to the Society of Savants, March 31, 1883, showed that the republic in France had reduced illiteracy one per cent. per annum, while it had expended more than any previous government for superior as well as elementary instruction. The superior schools that were found decaying had been revived; sixty million francs had been spent in ten years in the work of construction alone, three fifths of the amount that would be necessary to place them on a level with schools of the same grade in neighboring countries. He also observed that, in a country like France, where birth no longer conferred privileges, and where wealth was dissipated almost as soon as acquired, it was preeminently necessary for the state to assume the noble responsibilities that rank and

wealth had imperfectly sustained, and that this duty was more imperative as the constitution became more democratic, so that the state should be not merely the administrator, the police officer, the economist, but the teacher of high studies and the guardian of the ideal, amid the industrial competitions and social changes of modern life. He also urged that attention to superior instruction would go hand in hand with attention to primary and middle schools, and that a democracy having only primary schools, no matter how excellent, perfect, or imposing they were, would be a poor society and a poor democracy.

Monsieur Duruux, in an address at the laying of the corner-stone for the " Lakanal " Lyceum at Sceaux, October 6, 1882, said that formerly the founding of a city was the event most commemorated by festivities, inscriptions, and monuments, but that now the most engrossing and absorbing event, both in great cities and little villages, was the founding of a new school. It was becoming acknowledged by all every-where that intelligence is the real ruler of the world; in a republic it was not enough to conquer liberty and fully retain it, but it was necessary to learn how to control its manifestations and developments in harmony with all rights and interests; to the schools we should look for this final achievement; through the school each one is linked with others in the powerful association of modern thought; by the school only can we hope to control and finally end the agitation inseparable from the achievement of freedom.

England, early noted for her several great public schools for secondary instruction, and for her universities at Oxford and Cambridge, though holding the closest social, political, and civil relations with Germany and France, was one of the last to learn the lesson of universal and adequate education, or to venture to give the control of instruction to the civil administration. The story of her delay has a sad moral for the instruction of English pride. Brougham first gained national reputation by his endeavors to arouse public attention to the ignorant and degraded condition of the masses. Only a commission of inquiry was the result in 1816, followed by small grants, increased from year to year, to schools under the direction of Church societies. Not a few Englishmen believe that the Elementary School Act of 1870 barely saved England from violent revolution. This act, not yet every-where in the highest degree operative, has been followed with results more significant and satisfactory than was anticipated by its friends. School attendance in six years went up 75 per cent. in London, the center of the most appalling ignorance and degradation, and crime and pauperism immediately showed signs of diminution.

Scotland, that had been put in the very front rank of education by the parish schools inaugurated by John Knox, found a new forward step necessary, while the school system of Ireland, if vigorously enforced, will remove many of the evils now traceable to ignorance. Mr. Mundella, who for three years has been the administrative officer of the Council of Education, in a recent speech says that there were only two hundred thousand enrolled in the public schools of the Kingdom before the act of 1870, and that now there are four million seven hundred thousand; and, referring to the question of religious teaching, which was made a great bugbear and occasion of assault by the ecclesiastical party that opposed its passage, he calls attention to the fact that he has recently been made president of the Sunday-School Union and can speak intelligently from observation on both sides, and he declares that but one case of complaint has been made in the London Board schools which he had specially observed, and, in that case, the father and mother were not agreed; and he quotes approvingly Mr. Fountain Hartley, the great English authority in Sunday-school matters, who declares that, throughout the country, the increase of day-school education has had a most beneficial influence upon Sunday-schools. No scholars come to school better fitted to receive scriptural instruction, and the teachers, knowing the efficiency of the day-school teachers, are stimulated to increased efforts toward self-improvement and careful preparation.

Some of the colonies, like those of Australia and Victoria, were in advance of the mother country, having their public-school systems, universities, and libraries, enabling their population, though far removed from the centers of civilization, to keep step with the most rapid advances of the age.

Americans well know the lack of education in the province of Quebec and the backwardness of its people, while Ontario, under the lead of the eminent Dr. Ryerson, sought, the world over, the best things in education for its youth, and its scheme of instruction will not suffer by comparison of methods and appliances with any portion of the world. Its normal school is better furnished with aids than any other on our continent. Some of the more backward colonies have received new impulse in education since the action of the mother country, and now we have the report of the school systems of Cape Colony and the calendar of its university. Even Malta is supplied with a school system, to restore, if possible, the lost vitality of its native population. Unfortunately, the date of the emancipation of the slaves in the English colonies, the condition of education at home was most deplorable and the conceptions of its power to uplift man

were most imperfect, and, after the slaves were set free, little was done save by limited Church influence to educate and prepare them for their new condition in life. As a consequence, their progress since, either in thrift, manhood, or religion, has been most unsatisfactory. In confirmation of this statement it is enough to name the fact that very competent and trustworthy authority, in disclosing the deplorable condition of the negroes in Jamaica, informs us that 60 per cent are born out of wedlock.

India, that vast English dependency, is chiefly known to Americans as a missionary field, but the home country for a long time has acknowledged the obligations of public education. But up to the time of the Sepoy rebellion the administration of instruction, while declaring the freedom of conscience, only respected the sentiments of the natives. It carried this so far that neither text-books nor teachers were allowed except those in accord with the doctrines of the Brahmin, the Mohammedan, or the Parsee. There was no freedom for the Christian teacher or Christian text-book. But after the stormy and appalling horrors and cruelty of the Sepoy rebellion were past, and an account was taken of those who had participated in it, it was found that a very large number of them were trained in these government schools, and that less than half-a-dozen could be definitely traced who had ever had any connection with the Christian schools of the missionaries. This lesson, together with the additional attention to education at home, led to an advance step. A teacher or text-book could be Christian, though no efforts of propagandism were allowed.

But greater progress is noted: I invite your attention to some figures for 1881; first, to those indicating the extent to which people avail themselves of the provision for superior instruction. The total number presented for the university examinations in the universities of Bombay, Calcutta, and Madras was 6,810, of whom 2,984 passed, including one girl. The total number that completed courses and offered themselves for graduation in art schools and professional schools was 2,799, of whom 1,196 passed. From the official reports on public instruction in nine provinces and two native states, having a population in all of 201,064,016, we learn that on March 31, 1881, the number of students in colleges of the arts was 5,620; in colleges for professional trades, 1,497; in schools for technical or special training, 19,-847; in secondary schools for boys, 260,354; for girls, 14,486. In Bengal or Bombay, where secondary instruction is most widely diffused, it is estimated that the ratio of boys in the high-schools to the whole population is for the former one to five thousand, for the latter one to fourteen hundred. In middle schools the estimates are respectively one to sixteen hundred and sixty-six, and one to one thousand.

The primary schools in the nine provinces and two states mentioned, including those aided and those unaided by the government, but under inspection, had a total enrollment of 1,880,345, namely, 1,784,988 boys and 103,357 girls. The total government expenditure for primary schools was 2,238,797 rupees, or $873,130 93. The current reports call attention to the growing interest in education in the rural districts and among the Mohammedan population, the tendency to multiply schools for girls, and the steady increase in the number of indigenous schools brought under government inspection. With all that has been accomplished, however, it is estimated that upward of twenty-five millions of children needing primary education are uncared for, and such is the urgent need of extending elementary education among the masses of India that an educational commission has been appointed to in every ten thousand in elementary schools, take testimony in the matter and to devise practical measures for meeting the demand. The total number of scholars reported in all the schools of the nine provinces and two native states before mentioned is 2,190,197, of whom 206,832, or a little over nine per cent., were studying English.

John Bright, in his recent inaugural on the occasion of his installation last March as Lord Rector of the University of Glasgow, predicted the inevitable consequences of the education which is fostered under English rule in India as follows:

" English literature, as a matter of course where the English language is spoken, and English science—I mean science such as it appears in English books—will there find students, and with regard to religion, if we do little or nothing to spread among the natives of India the religion which we hold to be true, of this we may be well assured, that the English language and English literature and English science must necessarily break down the ancient superstitions and religions of the Indian people. If this be so, we may come to the certain conclusion that there will grow up in the minds of the natives of India the most educated and the most cultivated feelings in favor of change and of freedom. In fact, all the good that we are endeavoring to do—and it is more than we have endeavored to do in past years —all the good that we endeavor to do by education, by improved legislation, every thing that tends to lift the native a little higher, every thing of that kind necessarily must tend to give his mind feelings which, some time or other, will be hostile to the permanent subjection of his country to another country. As one of the consequences of the introduction of universal learning into India, native scholars are prepared to discuss social problems from the Indian stand-point, and to

support their views by the logic, the ethical conceptions, and the understanding of affairs which pass current in Europe."

Coming back to smaller European governments for studies illustrative of our theme, we observe that Belgium since its foundation has acted upon a scheme of education with many excellent features. Of her five and a half millions of population one thousand two hundred and seventy in every ten thousand are in elementary schools, five in normal schools, thirty-four in secondary schools, and seven in universities. Yet not far from 50 per cent. of those entering the military service are illiterate. The people and the government, dissatisfied with the results of the past, believing that ecclesiastical control of education has been injurious to its efficiency, are in the midst of a severe conflict, attempting to give civil control to the administration.

Denmark, of her two millions of people, has one thousand one hundred and ninety-five in normal schools, fifteen in secondary schools, and six in universities; and about one fifth of her population has no knowledge of reading and writing.

The Netherlands, of her four millions, has one thousand three hundred and thirty in every ten thousand in elementary schools, one in normal schools, seventeen in secondary schools, and four in universities.

Norway and Sweden, from which the United States receive a population of great promise, in their northern comparative isolation might be conjectured by those not well informed to be behind in education, but however slow their progress at times, now they are well to the front, about ninety-seven in a hundred of children of school age being under instruction; their universities and higher special schools are well attended and of a high order. They have a device called ambulatory schools, for sparsely settled regions, which might be imitated in parts of our own country. They aim to have all taught, and that by good teachers, and when the people live remote from each other four school houses are erected, say in a territory six miles square, so near the respective corners that all will be within attending distance at least one of the four terms in the year, and the teacher, who is continuously employed and who is thus paid to be well qualified, travels about for the accommodation of the young, who are compelled to be present one term, while any who can may attend all the year. The present king, when he came to the throne, wishing to show his desire to benefit his people, selected certain apparatus in physics and chemistry, and furnished them to a class of schools; and for those schools in barren sections, where the culture and manufacture of the willow is a main source of support, he prepared and furnished the schools a cabinet of apparatus used in cultivating the willow and making it into wicker work, in order that while the children learned their letters they might gain something of the skill by which they are to support themselves. It may be mentioned as a circumstance of interest to Americans that the present advancement of education is due very much to the visit to this country of Mr. P. A. Siljestrom, an eminent Swedish gentleman sent thirty years ago at the expense of his government to study our political questions, but he became interested in our education more than all else, and on his return published a stirring account of the influence and popularity of our schools, confessing that he was more affected by our crusade against dilapidated school-houses, against inefficient school-masters and faulty methods of instruction, than by many of the enterprises that are most highly lauded in history, and that to such a nation no difficulties, no dangers, are insuperable. But a recent Swedish writer, gathering up the figures which underlie the dark picture of our illiterates, and our lack of schools for their instruction, believes we have already met a difficulty too great for us to overcome.

Norway has fourteen hundred and forty-three in every ten thousand in elementary schools, and Sweden thirteen hundred and thirty-four; Switzerland, fifteen hundred and forty-two, but, like Germany, Switzerland shows a high average of education in her middle classes by her one hundred and twelve in every ten thousand in secondary schools.

Spain has of her seventeen million people only eight hundred and sixty in her elementary schools; Portugal, her neighbor on the peninsula, only four hundred and seventy-three in ten thousand; but the restrictions of ecclesiasticism cast a deep shadow over all the work of education, yet not a few progressive minds in each country, catching the spirit of the age, are beginning to move with great earnestness for the improvement of education in all its grades and departments.

The story of education in Italy taken up in its completeness has the interest of a thrilling romance. Visitors from every nation are familiar with the beggarly condition of her masses for centuries; her universities educated mainly those intended for the priesthood and the service of the state, and occasionally produced an eminent specialist. It is impossible for us to go back to the distracted condition of the diverse states and point out in detail recent progress, which, beginning in Sardinia, has taken effect throughout united Italy, so that, of her twenty-eight millions, there are now seven hundred and twenty-eight in ten thousand in elementary schools, on the average one and a half in normal schools, five in secondary schools, and three in universities. To none more than

to Cavour, fitly called the Regenerator of Italy, and one of the greatest of modern statesmen, is due the great changes in instruction which have told so favorably upon the Italians. During ten years, in which the statistics are tolerably accurate and trustworthy, it appears that illiteracy diminished about one per cent. annually. Cavour's treatment of the question pointed to his superiority over Napoleon, who showed an equally keen perception of the power of education, but was disposed to destroy that which he could not control—a conspicuous illustration of which remains in Italy. When his conquering armies reached Bologna, the seat of the oldest European university then in existence, where thousands of the most eminent of European scholars, statesmen, orators, scientists, poets, and philosophers had been educated, and found that he could not warp and wield its power at will, he laid his destroying hand upon it and annihilated it. Cavour, though he found the universities the centers of superstitions and ecclesiasticisms that would thwart the regeneration of Italy, left them to pursue their course, but bent his efforts for education toward the increase of the efficiency of elementary instruction and the establishment of industrial schools which should render the skill of the common laborer more productive, and of the higher technical schools from which there should come up men thoroughly prepared by the most scientific training to defend and administer to united Italy. Nine of those schools are still reported. In the one at Turin appears a striking incident of far-sightedness. It is well known how much land was useless for cultivation, either by its being too dry or by its being marshy and filled with water. Into the grounds of this institution waters were brought from a neighboring stream, and illustrations furnished the young students, on the one hand of the principles of irrigation, and on the other of drainage, by application of which vast barren regions were made productive, and thus the food-producing power of the country greatly increased.

Freedom of conscience is greater than ever. There are promises of a liberty more salutary and beneficial than was ever known in the days of the ancient republic, in which a new life shall come to enjoy and improve the remains of the architecture, sculpture, and memories of that Rome which once ruled the world from her seven hills.

Hungary, joined to Austria under Kaiser Joseph, has made substantially the same progress in education, but a large and increasing class is seeking for her schools every improvement.

The principalities lying along her borders have been foot-balls of contest between Russia and Turkey. Having many physical elements of progress they have hardly yet sufficient education among their peoples to undertake a direct and far-reaching line of advancement.

Greece, where Herodotus lived, whence he went forth so widely to gain knowledge of mankind and prepare the records which should fairly give him the title of " the father of history," where Homer sang for his own and all coming generations, where Lycurgus and Solon laid the enduring foundations of cities, where art and oratory reached some of their highest triumphs, where the growth of philosophy produced a Socrates who taught Plato and Aristotle, both to remain the instructors of mankind, the latter the personal teacher of Alexander the Great, who went forth from this land thus taught to conquer the world, and by his wise dissemination of the results of Grecian civilization to liberate also and advance mankind in preparation for the dawn of the Christian era. So much of this historic land as is now known as the kingdom of Greece has a university, a polytechnic school, and is struggling, under great embarrassments, to extend among the people elementary education.

Finland, though a dependency, has its university, normal school, and a fair number of elementary schools of excellent character.

The Finns sent a commission to this country to study our schools, and are now discussing some of the most advanced problems, among which is the adoption of co-education of the sexes, in reference to which they have called on this country for its experience.

Approaching Russia, and remembering how Peter the Great, seeking to improve his people, went abroad to educate himself in the learning, arts, and trades of more advanced civilizations, one would naturally expect to see some adequate and effective illustration and appreciation of the power of education, but, alas! in the district of Kostroma over ninety per cent. of the children have no education. Other districts do slightly better, but the city of Moscow sends only twelve per cent. of her children to school, and St. Petersburg, forty-one per cent. Out of the population of seventy-eight and a half millions in Russia only one hundred and fifty-one in ten thousand attend elementary schools, four normal schools, seven secondary schools, and eight universities. What wonder that Nihilism and its horrors have here their home! That portion of the population declared free from serfdom by Alexander has experienced little change, and has made the slightest possible progress on account of the absence of education; yet we should remember that some of the institutions established for special instruction and the universities and professional schools are among the rarest and best of the age, and women in some instances are admitted to all their advantages; but the tyranny of administration permits no freedom of elementary

education, the press is muzzled, neither newspapers nor books can be circulated with freedom, a meeting of teachers cannot be called without special permission, but the Bible is permitted to have some measure of circulation, and the Stundists, as they are called, are now organizing and bind themselves, like some unions of Christian people elsewhere, to devote an hour a day to the study of the Bible. Whole villages have thus been touched as by a magic power; drunkards have been saved, and criminals have forsaken their evil ways, and those who have been inspired by this new course to pursue a nobler life have now set themselves to win others.

You have already indulged me in the use of so many figures as the briefest way to treat these data that I hesitate to go further, and yet I am sure you will not permit me to leave this view of Europe without presenting in summary some figures comparing the war expenditures in these countries with those for education. The statement is prepared by Leon Donnat, a learned Belgian, and is believed to be substantially correct, and shows the amount each citizen pays for war purposes and for education, from two times to seventy-six times as much:

	For war.	For education.
COUNTRY.	Francs.	Francs.
Italy	9.05	0.80
Switzerland	5.80	5.00
Denmark	10.40	5.50
Saxony	14.15	4.00
Holland	21.30	3.80
England	22.25	3.75
Bavaria	14.15	3.00
Prussia	13.15	2.90
Belgium	8.10	2.75
Wurtemburg	14.15	2.10
Austria	8.00	1.96
France	25.85	1.85
Russia	12.23	0.16

Turkey, controlling in a semi-civilized administration what remains of the territory subject to the Moslem faith, which once gave such an impulse to activity of thought, and carried so far to the front the standards of arithmetic, algebra, chemistry, and architecture, now promotes the least possible of any form of uplifting learning, and is so weakened by the ignorance and degradation of the masses as to be known as the "sick man" among the nations.

The education of China confirms with emphasis the sentiment of our theme. A large share of her people taught in the books of Confucius, having no proper sense of religion, little knowledge of mathematics and physics, superstitiously afraid of medicine, though all expect their promotion through their attainments in learning, save in the line of royalty and military activity, and though long in possession of some of the most valuable inventions of mankind, yet this people, numbering more than any other nation populating a single country, present an absence of improvement that appears like the monotony of a dead level in human affairs.

What shall we say of Japan, possessing maritime and commercial possibilities like those of Great Britain, so long isolated from mankind and shut up to herself, yet, when opening her gates, receiving the most advanced civilization, and making education pre-eminently the agent of future progress? Her territory is divided into districts for universal education and for the establishment of secondary schools, crowned with the university; normal schools for the training of teachers are made a specialty; her commissioners and teachers are sent the world over to find the best methods, text-books, and appliances; an extensive pedagogical museum is established at her capital where teachers and educators can see and study improvements in architecture, furniture, books, and other appliances for school use. Already six hundred and sixty in ten thousand are in her elementary schools, two in her normal schools, six in secondary schools, and three in universities. Wishing to establish three additional special schools, one for business, one for general industries, and one for agriculture, she sends abroad to secure the best hints that can be afforded. No country has more effectually illustrated the sentiment of an eminent German, What you would have your people, that put in your schools.

Africa, touched only here and there by the light of modern civilization, presents one vast dark expanse, not relieved even, as in ancient times, by the learning of Egypt, so instructive in the ruins of its pyramids and monuments, cities and catacombs, that learning of the Pharaohs in all of which Moses was taught to prepare him to become the miraculous deliverer of his brethren, and to leave them that code of laws, those personal habits, those customs of society, the family, Church and State which, wrought into them and their condition by every process of education, should render them a peculiar people. It is a striking illustration of the power of education carried on for generations, and should not be forgotten here, line upon line, precept upon precept, here a little and there a little, at home and by the way, in every circumstance in which parent or society or Church or State can mold or shape the nature and character of childhood, so that while there is no evidence that the natural peculiarities of Abraham were any greater or more marked than those of the other peoples with whom he was associated, yet these other nations have communicated nothing to their descendants by which they can be distinguished, but the son of Abraham is known by his appearance as well as by certain characteristics, customs, and ideas wherever met.

Crossing the ocean to the American con-

tinent we find in the States of South America at the present date among the leaders an acknowledgment of the principles of the power of education, but their inadequate application. They obtain teachers from the United States, and would take more and would have larger commercial dealings with us if more of our youth were taught Portuguese and Spanish. Prof. Gould, who has made so renowned the observatory of the Argentine Republic by his work upon the stars of the southern hemisphere, is from Cambridge, Massachusetts. Brazil is just now holding a congress of education, at which there is an exhibition of educational appliances, drawn largely from the United States. Her worthy emperor is active in every way to promote the progress of his diversified people, and recently, in view of increasing the demand for education among the negroes as slavery passes away, has had the education of our blacks studied and reported. Brazil has one hundred and fifty-six in ten thousand of her population in elementary schools, and gives great attention to her university, principal library, and certain special forms of instruction.

In the Argentine Republic only about five per cent. of the population are found in schools, and the efforts for advanced instruction are only partially successful; her university instruction has one thousand four hundred and ninety-five students.

Chili, of her two millions of people, has, in each ten thousand, three hundred and nine in elementary schools, twenty in secondary schools, and four in universities, and has sixty thousand volumes in her national library. A large body of her enterprising citizens are urging greater activity in behalf of the education of the masses, and just now her president has recommended the separation of Church and State.

In the United States of Colombia and the states of Central America the ups and downs of social order permit no systematic or steady progress in education, but continual attempts are made to introduce the improved notions of instruction; here they succeed in elementary schools, there in normal schools, and again in the medical college. The principles of administering education by the state made universal and effective for all its children, opening up the highest opportunities for those of the lowest birth, is gaining ground in all the states of South and Central America. Mexico is thoroughly committed to this principle by its constitution and administration, yet can only make slow progress in bringing systematic education to her people out of the confusion, bigotry, and degradation of the past; but, of her ten millions of people, she is able to report three hundred and seventy-three in ten thousand in her elementary schools, and seventeen under secondary instruction.

Bringing our own country into this general review, of our fifty millions, one thousand nine hundred and thirty-nine in ten thousand are in elementary schools, five in normal schools, and forty in secondary schools.

It is impossible to canvass here the vast human experience found in ancient history in support of our proposition.

In this glance around the educational horizon, in which much has come into view that it is impossible to state, while we gain a measure of man's progress we are

I. Appalled at the improvement that remains for him to make. The great masses of mankind are untouched by the faintest gleam of advancing light, and the most advanced nations have vast necessities unmet and vast opportunities unimproved.

II. We see how the quality of education determines the quality of man's improvement, especially how dependent its results are upon freedom of person, freedom of conscience, of thought, of action.

III. We observe how public systems of education are in the nature of civil affairs, and we see how the Church fails when it undertakes to administer them as it does when it assumes to direct any other duties of the state. We are more than ever convinced that the Church furnishes the highest motives to human action by its teachings; it would make the body of man a temple for the indwelling of the Divine Spirit; it would consecrate the intellect to the highest purposes; but the Church, the organization through which these blessings are to be transmitted, is neither the family nor the state, but fundamentally apart from each, and must exert its power over them not by force, not through the forms of civil law, but after the manner of the Divine Spirit, teaching all men and by its all-pervading doctrines arousing within every man the latent possibilities of his soul, and through these appointed methods so influencing each individual that the family and state shall alike be ordered in conformity to its precepts.

IV. We discover how the efficiency of the pulpit must depend on the extent with which its efforts accord with the principles of education, and that its loss of power is due in part to the extent to which it has devoted itself to preaching, technically so-called, in distinction from educating and instructing the people in divine things. It must preach, but it must also, following its Great Head, teach all men.

V. In recognition of education as a measure of man's improvement, Sabbath-schools have been established and their great work extended around the globe, having a total attendance of 14,184,880.

VI. We observe that the final effect of all great moral movements, like those of Luther and Wesley, is determined by their educating power.

VII. It brings into striking contrast the methods of the early missions of modern times with those of the nineteenth century. The earlier missions, characterized by great self-abnegation and most triumphant heroism, did indeed bestow efforts upon childhood, but they employed the great principles of education not so much for improving the mind, or regenerating the life, or in awakening the reason, as for forming habits of thought and action and impressing beliefs and observances that might remain, while little regard was had to the strict moral and spiritual duties imposed by Christianity. But the representative of the new spirit of missions meets at a vantage all comers from other conditions of life. He seeks to imitate the Great Master in the skillful adaptations of his efforts to the conditions around him; he teaches all men; he feeds the lambs. The work is not satisfactory in any individual till his spiritual life is renovated and the whole man consecrated to the divine service and he lives a new life. The improvement of mankind through missionary labors is measured by the education of the people in countries affected by these Christian influences. Christianity is the warmth that raises the column of humanity, and the number of schools planted and pupils educated measures its height. The number of communicants at foreign mission churches outside of Europe and British America increased three and a half times from 1850 to 1880; the number of pupils increased three times in the same period. Throwing out a few countries having public schools, the ratio of increase of communicants and pupils would be almost identical. In India, where Lord Lawrence said that missionaries had done more for its benefit than all other agencies combined, the pupils in their schools have increased almost as rapidly as their Church members, notwithstanding the existence of government schools. The same is true of Burmah and Siam. These three countries had in 1880 more than one hundred thousand communicants, and one hundred and forty thousand pupils in missionary schools. In Oceanica the communicants have increased from fifty-nine thousand to one hundred and twenty-eight thousand in thirty years; pupils, from thirty-one thousand to seventy-five thousand. Here the ratios are almost identical, (2.6 and 2.4.) There are nine thousand three hundred mission schools attended by four hundred and forty-eight thousand pupils, now maintained by seventy foreign missionary societies. Nearly all of these schools are in Asia, (4,265,) Africa, (1.696,) and Oceanica, (2,522.) Over one-seventh of them are sustained by the churches of the United States.

When missionary achievements are recounted the elevation of people from ignorance is emphasized. Sir Bartle Frere testi-ties that Christianity is effecting extensive and rapid changes, morally, socially, and politically. Mr. Robert Mackenzie finds among the results of missions in South Africa that "Education is rapidly extending." Not only have schools been established by missionaries, but text-books have been provided for students and men of science. To the Chinese " Dr. Hobson has given works on physiology, surgery, medicine, chemistry, and natural philosophy; Mr. Wylie, Euclid, algebra, arithmetic, geometry, calculus, Herschel's large astronomy, and Newton's Principia; Mr. Edkins, Whewell's Mechanics and works on Western literature; Mr. Muirhead, English history and universal geography; Dr. Bridgeman, an illustrated history of the United States; Dr. Martin, Wheaton's International Law, and illustrated volumes on chemistry, natural philosophy, etc. The mission presses in India are 25 in number. During the years between 1852 and 1862 they issued 1,634,940 copies of the Scriptures, chiefly single books, and 8,604,-033 tracts, school-books, and books for general circulation. During the ten years between 1862 and 1872 they issued 3,410 new works, in 30 languages, and circulated 1,315,503 copies of books of Scripture, 2,375,040 school-books, and 8,750,129 Christian books and tracts."

The conversion of the Sandwich Islanders, their transformation from the customs and laws and degradations of pagan life to those in conformity with Christianity, is a striking illustration of the purpose and accomplishments of our modern missions, and the contrast may be further followed to advantage by tracing the early heroic endeavors in Africa, China, and among the aborigines of our own continent, and comparing them with surer results of the present day. In the light of the hour to the stranger it is one of the marvels that the United States have only just now come to treat adequately the long-disturbing Indian question.

VIII. We may learn from this survey that whatever evils we propose to remove from among men the one comprehensive means is education. If we would civilize the wild Indian, we must educate his child in the fittest and fullest significance of that term. If we would remove Mormonism, we must

educate its youth in a more liberal spirit. If we would uplift the former slaves in our midst, we must establish schools among them for universal instruction. If we would guard our land from the perils threatened by misused capital and disorganized labor or destructive communism, we must use the utmost power of education to bring every child up with a sound mind in a sound body with all powers trained for honest dealing and high endeavor.

IX. The extent to which the English language is used in this progress of education gives great encouragement to all efforts for human improvement; through that language the advance in one country in education, science, or art, or literature, may be readily communicated to all others. Every thought, every feeling, may easily encircle the globe. Most eloquently does Joseph Cook say, after his trip around the world, during which he discussed substantially the same great subjects to large audiences in Europe, Asia, and the islands of the sea: "As the growth of civilization brings us into contact with the ends of the earth, we should feel that we cannot cut ourselves off from the other side of the globe, that humanity is a unit, commercially, scientifically, socially, industrially, almost politically, to-day. In our time there are no foreign lands. Communication is so swift between country and country that no shores are distant. There can be no hermit nations; no people can live behind a screen. The mental seclusion of false faiths must be broken up. The light of the Occident cannot be hidden from the Orient."

X. Consideration of these facts prompts us to agree with the feelings of the Hebrews in reference to the teacher as shown in their traditions and in many passages of the Talmud. In one of these they tell how once in a great drought their greatest rabbis prayed and wept for rain and the rain came not, and at last a common-looking person got up and prayed to Him who causes the wind to blow and the rain to descend, and instantly the heavens began to cover themselves with clouds and the rain began to fall. "Who art thou," they cried, "whose prayers have alone prevailed?" and he answered, "I am a teacher of little children."

II. ILLITERACY IN THE UNITED STATES.

1. ADDRESS.

REV. HERRICK JOHNSON, D. D., OF CHICAGO.

As presiding officer at the third session Rev. Dr. JOHNSON spoke as follows:

MY office to-night is that of introduction. The chief and conspicuous excellence of an introduction is its brevity, and I shall therefore undertake to put that excellence into the introductions of to-night. We have come, in my judgment, to a topic that should concern and tax the best statesmanship of our time. It stands related to all the other topics in that it embraces them all. If we are to reach a solution of the Indian problem, or the Negro problem, or the Chinese problem, or the poor-white problem, we shall do it most effectually and simply by reaching the solution of this problem of the illiterate masses; for when we have solved this we have solved all the rest. Illiteracy and the illiterate are bad enough; masses of the illiterate, or "the illiterate masses," are inexpressibly bad, and this badness reaches its utmost intensity when these illiterate masses are under a free government like ours. Under despotisms illiterate masses may be well enough, for ignorance is the prop of despotism; ignorance, not in the despotism, but in the tools which despotism puts to use. And tools are things that have no rights, no duties, no responsibilities. They ought to be illiterate—intelligence is not to be mentioned in connection with them. Therefore the masses in despotisms go in droves, move in fixed grooves, are simply material to be used in wars.

But our government is "a government of the people, by the people, for the people;" the sovereign is each individual; the people is king. Woe to thee, O law, when thy king is a child. Wisdom and knowledge must characterize the governing power. And as here the masses rule, intelligence must pervade the masses. The standing peril is prevalent illiteracy. Take it in connection with the ballot-box: winging a ballot is very much like winging a bullet. It needs intelligence, aim, and knowledge of the situation. As the rifles that think carry the farthest and surest, so the ballots that think effect the best and widest results. And universal suffrage is here. Whether for good or ill, we are in for it. But it is not simply in connection with the ballot that we are to guard against illiteracy. It is in connection with the shop and the farm, and with honest labor of any sort anywhere.

One of the chief reproaches and disgraces of manhood is machine-work—that is, work with no intelligence at the helm—and therefore no improvement in methods, and no possibilities of change; the eternal see-saw of mere mechanical contrivance. If you would elevate labor, you must educate the laborer. If you would enhance the value of citizenship, you must make intelligent citizens. If you would take brawn out of the category of the merely animal and mechanical, you must put brain into the brawn. Not that the brain is to do brawn's work. The brain was made to do thinking, not to saw wood or make shoes. But the point is, that just as intelligence gets behind the saw and the hammer, we shall have better saws and better shoes. When brain guides the plow and gets mixed with the soil, a better furrow will be turned on the old farm.

Let us to-night get increased and profound convictions of the importance of solving this problem in connection with our illiterate masses. We have these masses, and they are citizens; and it is the duty of the hour for the statesmanship of our time to see to it that they are made good citizens.

2

2. ILLITERACY IN OUR GREAT CITIES.

HON. B. PETERS,

Editor "Brooklyn Times."

IN the time allotted to me this evening I have been requested to consider the question of illiteracy in connection with our great cities, the dangers it may be said to involve, and the best way to avoid these dangers.

Some twenty years ago the people of this country, as with the stroke of a pen, freed four millions of bondmen, to whom all educational advantages had not only been made impossible by their social condition, but had been positively interdicted by special statutes in every slave State.

A few years after the Negroes had been made free it was found necessary, for their proper protection, to invest them with the elective franchise. This right had not been conferred for any great length of time ere it became apparent to every clear-headed citizen of the republic that special efforts must be made by the humane and philanthropic, for the safety of the country, to advance the cause of education, not only with special reference to the class among whom these new-made voters were found, but in every Southern State, and for the benefit of the whites and blacks alike. For some years past there has been an intelligent and wide-spread movement—as the result of this recognized necessity—among the better and more thoughtful of our citizens, in private and official stations, to awaken the lawmaking authorities of the Government, in order to induce them to grant national aid to the States in which this unusual degree of illiteracy exists, for the express purpose of reducing the evil to a minimum. Senator Blair, of New Hampshire, in the United States Senate, has given persistent and intelligent support to this measure. Mr. Hayes, both while President and since his retirement from office, has paid special attention to this subject. In other and varied ways has this question been urged upon the attention of the American people, and the fact has been demonstrated that there exists a pressing necessity for favorable national action on this all-important subject. While no practical steps have been taken, so far as the granting of national aid is concerned, there are many reasons for believing that the intelligence of the country has been awakened, and awakened sufficiently on this subject to influence Congress and that, ere many years pass away, a liberal policy will be inaugurated by the Government.

In the meantime the need of the South, occasioned by the changed condition of those once held in slavery, and who were thereby kept in ignorance—springing, it is true, from a different cause, and existing on a more limited scale, but still dangerous and forbidding—has its exact counterpart in all our populous cities. In these cities there exists an increasing class that is enslaved by the most reckless vices, by lives of steady and almost unbroken debauchery, a class that is impoverished by thriftlessness, and whose progeny, by the most abject degradation—into which it is born, and in the midst of which it is doomed to exist and to grow up—is deprived of every possible advantage, not only educational, but physical, social, moral, and religious; and will continue to be deprived of these advantages, unless provided with the means to secure them at the public expense. No city has its Heights, its Fifth Avenue, or its Beacon Street, that has not, also, and not far away, its Fifth Ward, its Baxter Street, and its North End. As the population of our great cities increases, and wealth multiplies in the hands of the few, while the masses are impoverished and large numbers of them are hopelessly degraded—though it be in great proportion by the vices that are so common among the helpless mortals of our race—it is becoming more and more a pressing question of the gravest importance: *What shall be done with the children of those who are too debauched, or too poor, to care for their offspring in any proper or systematic way?* that is, *with the children of those in whom the obligations of maternity and paternity have lost their force?* We may be told that our common schools are free to all, and have been established to educate the children of the poorest citizen of the Republic. That may be very true, and yet it is no impeachment of our public-school system to say that, as at present organized, it does not, and can not, reach the children of the particular class to which I refer. It may seem startling, but it is nevertheless a fact, that there are those, and especially in our populous cities, who are too poor to send their children to our common schools, too degraded to be able to secure to their offspring the benefits of our public-school system; and this is true, no matter how free the public schools may be, as at present administered. The children of the debauched, of the ragged and hungry; of those who consume in drink, every night, all they have begged, or stolen, or even earned in the day, are placed below the reach of our public schools. How, we may ask, are the children of the vicious to be fitted for, and kept under, the influence of the public schools? A moment's reflection must convince every one that the poor and helplessly degraded cannot be reached by any ordinary common-school system such as we now have. It is as self-evident as a proposition in mathematics, that the child that is naked cannot be sent to the public schools; and that the child that is not only naked, but possibly living in a condition of starvation, or of semi-starvation, cannot be reached by the teachers who are ready to impart the rudiments or the fundamentals of an education in our public schools.

It has become well understood that the vital sources of danger to our free institutions are to be found in our great cities. While they contain a concentration of wealth, of virtue, and of thrift, these favorable conditions are counterbalanced by a concentration as well of the worst elements to be found in society. It is in our larger cities that the worst features of our modern and peculiarly American methods in politics have been developed. The corrupt "boss" system in these cities, by which crafty and unscrupulous leaders have gathered influence and power—through the unprincipled following they have been able to gather about themselves—is almost wholly owing to the criminal tendencies and the crass ignorance to which I have referred. The men who live from hand to mouth; who, like Micawber, are perpetually on the *qui vive* "for something to turn up," who drink and gamble and otherwise waste most of their time in idleness, are easily organized into mischievous cabals, or into rings; that is, into corrupt combinations of bad men, not only for the purpose of controlling the politics of a city, or a State, or to gain influence over the nation, but quite too often to promote the chances of public plunder, and in the interests of the combination. Our great cities have demonstrated, and in the most striking manner, not only the possibility, but the actual evils, of this tendency. This danger was foreseen from the earliest days of the Republic. Dr. David Ramsay, of South Carolina, in a speech delivered at an early date in our history—on the significance of our new-found liberties—foretold that the special peril to our free institutions would not come from the rural districts, from the tillers of the soil, but from our great cities, where ignorance and vice would find a special field for concentration, and where unscrupulous men might organize those given to these tendencies for corrupt and evil purposes. Charles Kingsley described both this class and this danger when he said: "We have, then, first of all, to face the existence of a dangerous class of this kind, into which the weaker as well as the worse members of society have a continual tendency to sink. A class which, not respecting itself, does not respect others; which has nothing to lose, and all to gain by anarchy; in which the lowest passions, seldom

gratified, are ready to burst out and avenge themselves by frightful methods."

It was because of these facts that a municipal *régime* like that inaugurated and controlled for so many years by Bill Tweed in New York city was made a possible thing. A writer in the last number of the *Century*, on "Caucus Reform," tells us that not in our great cities alone has this evil made itself felt, but "even in communities like many of the New England cities, where the traditions of the old town-meeting are in a great measure preserved by a wide-spread sense of public duty, which leads men of high standing and repute to attend and share in the party management, the caucus is fast drifting into the hands of wire-pullers and log-rollers, such as have brought disgrace upon the primaries of Brooklyn and New York, and the ward-meetings of Boston, Philadelphia, and Baltimore."

If the accepted maxim of modern times be true, that "as intelligence increases crime diminishes," and that as education is diffused the possibility of corrupt combinations is rendered less feasible, and therefore less likely, how are we to cope with this danger unless it be through education. And if the common schools, as now administered and limited, cannot be made to reach the children of the debauched, the drunken, and the beggared, who so largely abound in our cities, special changes need to be made to effect this object, and thus to correct, or at least to restrain, this danger to our institutions.

A writer in the *Gentleman's Magazine*, not many years ago, in discussing the "Great Towns and their Influence," traced to the chief cities of England—to Birmingham, Manchester, Bristol, Liverpool, and Newcastle-upon-Tyne—the forces in every direction that control and shape the life and policy of the British Kingdom. Is not the life of this new Republic to be sought for and found, and not for good alone, but for ill as well, in New York, Boston, Philadelphia, Baltimore, and Washington; in Pittsburg, Cincinnati, Chicago, and St. Louis? And not in these alone, but in the smaller, though in other respects equally important, municipalities, that are scattered in such important numbers over this great American continent?

Robert Vaughan, D.D., in his "Age of Great Cities," finds, in the very solidification and strength that evil secures to itself in our cities, a tendency toward "every thing opposed to individual happiness and the stability of nations." "It is there," he adds, "where faction becomes stronger than patriotism," and where men acquire the habit of "scrambling for themselves, heedless of their country, of justice, or humanity." "Nowhere else," he again declares, "does man acquire such expertness in iniquity, and nowhere else has evil so large a space over which to diffuse its pestilential influence. In the populous city this poison may be said to insinuate itself almost as through a vein. The contact with it is close and perpetual."

Those who have interested themselves in the welfare and improvement of humanity have not been ignorant of this evil, nor indifferent to its demands, as very vigorous efforts, more or less effective and intelligent, have been made for a generation or more to reach and cure it. Institutions have been established, supported for the most part by charity, to provide for this class. These institutions first took on the penal form of correction, to which young truants and incipient criminals were sent, and were known as "Houses of Refuge." They were first established in 1825. They were next called "Reform Schools," and are now generally known as "Children's Homes" or "Industrial Schools." Thus the world has gradually grown up to the idea of providing for its helpless and dependent waifs.

If I had the devising of the laws, I would lift all these places, whether known as "homes," "industrial" or "reform" schools, or by any other name, out of the category of mere eleemosynary or penal institutions. I would make them a part of the public-school system of our great cities. I would place them directly under the control of our Boards of Education, and I would provide for a special governing commission by giving to the clergymen in every city the right to meet once in every two or five years, in order to select from among the best of their citizens five wise and prudent men, whose duty it should be to devise ways and means to find suitable homes for these wards of society—these children of the State—when they had attained a suitable age, and had been sufficiently advanced in their studies. I would make the Industrial Schools a special feature and a separate department in our public-school system. I would provide for these poor, unfortunate, and helpless children, not only books and teachers, but such clothing and shelter and food as their requirements and needs might demand. I would do this, in the case of every such child, for at least two years. In the case of very young children I would do it for even a longer period. I would provide the extra means—and it ought not to require a very large amount over the sum we already expend upon our public schools—to support these institutions by levying a tax on all the street-car lines, the elevated railroads, and other corporations in our cities. If the constitutional provision regulating the question of taxation on individuals, and requiring that the rate of taxation shall be made equal upon all could, in any way, be obviated, I would also levy a special tax upon all individuals of large wealth—say upon all men worth over one million dollars in taxable assets. A tax, let us estimate, of from one

tenth of a mill to one mill, as the exigencies might demand, ought to yield, if honestly collected, the amount required. The rate, of course, would have to be determined by the amount needed and the aggregate value of the taxable possessions that might, in this way, be reached and made available for this excellent purpose. It ought to be an easy matter for a city like New York, for instance, to secure, by this means, from one to three hundred thousand dollars annually, to be expended upon the proper care and education of the waifs that exist within its borders. Other cities ought to be able to secure special sums for this same purpose, and in proportion to whatever their actual local needs might require.

I would base the justice of such an exaction upon the fact that all the corporations in this country, to whom such a law would apply, hold important and valuable franchises that were granted them by the people; franchises which, as the population and wealth of the country increases, are steadily gaining in value; and that, in fact, all men of wealth are peculiarly favored by our free institutions and enjoy rare opportunities, and have, therefore, peculiar and urgent obligations resting upon them, not only toward the poor and the children of the poor, but toward the masses of the people, and they have the very highest stake in the proper education and the moral welfare of these waifs. It is in the most direct sense to the interest of the well-to-do—the prosperous—that these waifs should be lifted out of their condition and made intelligent, law-abiding, and thrifty citizens. If any body has any interest in upholding our free institutions and in making every child born into the State a law-abiding, intelligent, and good citizen, it is the men of wealth who own the property and the stocks upon which I would lay this special and important tax. Prof. Huxley is credited with this terse remark, that "No system of public education is worthy the name, unless it creates a great educational ladder, with one end in the gutter and the other in the university." Horace Mann is said to have exclaimed, with like force, that, "In our country and in our times no man is worthy of the honored name of statesman who does not include the highest practical education of the people in all his plans of administration."

If the law of self-preservation in a free republic makes the common school and the general education of the people a necessity, how can it fail to demand, and in the most emphatic terms, the proper care of the waifs in behalf of whom I plead. The Jukes family is not confined to that branch alone so skillfully traced by the late R. L. Dugdale. It is a large family and of many branches, and to stem its growth the proper and only remedy is found in the early and judicious care of its progeny and by means of healthy moral education. If uncared for and neglected, this progeny becomes the seeds of a spreading evil. They are a sort of human caterpillar that will in due time spin themselves into cocoons, cocoons that will in turn deposit unnumbered eggs; and eggs that will in the end hatch out new batches of crime; and crime that tends to devour the flowering glory of every privilege and blessing which we now enjoy and in which our thrifty and prosperous people have so large a stake.

It is a familiar and a well-established fact—and one that conveys its significant lesson—that, since the establishment of our government, a constantly increasing tide of population, most of it of the poorer classes—though not until recently of the "assisted immigrant" variety—has been poured from Europe, for more than a century, into all our sea-port towns. This has tended to swell the class of helpless waifs of whom I speak. In due time—in a single generation—they give up the national prejudices they bring with them and most of the habits of life and thought that made them peculiar,

and, to all intents and purposes, they become Americans and good citizens, about as much so as would have been the case had they been born here and reared wholly under the influence of our institutions. Intelligent citizens attribute to our public schools the special influence that helps us so readily to absorb and assimilate our extraneously acquired populations.

Now, in the same way, it would seem to me, we ought to be able—if our industrial schools, established especially in the interest of society, were made, as I have suggested, a part of our public-school system—to recover and incorporate these children again with our better and more prosperous classes, completely assimilating them with the moral thrift and virtue of the nation. To thus save the children of the degraded and abandoned ought to be the highest ambition of a free people. To say the least, this, as an object, is worthy of the best thought of the best men of the freest nation on earth; and the wisdom and statesmanship of our country can find no higher inspiration than this affords for wise, generous, and practical legislation.

3. STUMBLING-BLOCKS, OR STEPPING-STONES?

ROBERT R. DOHERTY, ESQ.,

Assistant Editor of "The Christian Advocate," New York.

THE author of "Lacon" has pungently said, that unless a man can throw fire into his book he would better throw his book into the fire. That is quite as good a rule for the speech-maker as for the book-maker. There is, however, no need to search for rhetorical tinder to-night, or to set ourselves to the tedious task of fanning flickering flames. The facts and figures already presented on this platform should fire every patriot heart, and cause an explosion of righteous indignation against the evils of which we have heard, and against ourselves for having so long and so lethargically permitted those evils to flourish.

From the programme I learn that a distinguished statistician was expected here this afternoon, to tell us where our illiterate masses are. I wish some one could tell us where they are not! They teem, by the million, among both whites and blacks, in the sunny South. They wander in unnumbered multitude among the mushroom settlements of the Far West. They are counted by the hundred thousand even in cultured New England—the very birthplace of the common school. They spring up like thistles over all

our prairies; they are packed like the paving-stones in our great cities; they are brought across the seas by every emigrant ship from every country under the skies. Illiteracy is increasing at a rate that is simply appalling; and we are sitting with folded hands doing nothing, or, at the best, are making but fitful efforts to lop off its exuberant growth. The ax should be laid to the root of the tree—nay, the roots themselves should be wrenched from American soil, and all that ministers to their growth be at once and forever banished.

There are, doubtless, many serious obstacles in the way of the general diffusion of intelligence through the land, which cannot be removed, and which cannot easily be surmounted. Any one of us could tabulate such difficulties till all the rest grew weary. But it is not to these that I am to call your attention this evening. Other forces at work in the nation have furnished the title to this address. These forces are powerful though silent factors in the education or degradation of the masses, and may be made to help in the spread of intelligence, or to tend to the increase of illiteracy, according to our treatment of them. Incautious walking will turn the most convenient stepping-stone into a stumbling-block. It is ours to make these subtle forces stepping-stones toward enlightenment and prosperity, or stumbling-blocks, over which to fall into ruin. Let us briefly consider some of the most important of them.

I.—THE LAX APPRECIATION OF THE DIGNITY OF MANHOOD.

For much of the illiteracy in the United States we are to be pitied rather than condemned. For part of it our ancestors are responsible; much of it is the result of European misgovernment. Our attitude toward this imported ignorance, however, has been far from discreet. We have been thoughtless in our tolerance, and have allowed our liberality to run to excess. One of the great metropolitan dailies said, a few years ago, that if a man stood at the City Hall, in New York, and cast stones indiscriminately into the thronged thoroughfare, nine out of every ten men he hit would be well qualified for the office of Chief Executive of the nation. This extravagant statement is representative of a laxity of thought which is traceable in the popular discussion of all political, social, and educational questions.

Perhaps no danger is, to-day, more threatening to the enlightenment of our nation— more threatening even to its continued existence—than that which lurks underneath, that ready appreciation of the dignity of manhood which is the glory of American society and American thought. This is the one country on the round world in which —regardless of wealth and regardless of race—the idea of Burns's song is realized: "A man's a man for a' that." We feel that noble sentiment in our hearts; we announced it in our Declaration of Independence one hundred years ago; a little later, we embodied it in our Constitution; we have emphasized it in every amendment adopted since; we recognize it constantly with pride —and in this very recognition the danger lurks. Already the consequences of an inconsiderate and distorted conception of this noble doctrine are felt in a degeneration of our ideal of manhood, and—what bears more directly on the thought before us—in a light valuation of the inestimable privileges of universal education, and a frivolous depreciation of profound scholarship.

It is too late to lament the policy which has made the vote of the most intelligent man in this auditorium count no more than the vote of the most ignorant freedman or foreigner. But, thank God! it is not too late to declare open hostility to that so-called "love of liberty" which, in the great centers of our population, has

put a premium on ignorance; it is not too late to learn the wholesome lesson that equal justice to all demands intelligent and educated office-holders, and, as far as may be, intelligent and educated voters; it is not too late to devise and put into practice far-reaching measures for instructing, in at least the elements of morals and letters, the hundreds of thousands of adults who annually cast their ballots for men and measures of whom and which they know nothing. Tolerance of ignorance is as criminal and preposterous as would be the tolerance of the most pestiferous physical disease.

Another potent factor for good or for evil exists in

II.—THE EDUCATION OF OUR GIRLS.

While few topics have elicited more wordy discussion during a quarter century than that inchoate and indeterminate thing called Woman's Rights, there is, perhaps, no important subject which has called forth so little thoughtful attention as this — the most momentous question of all—How shall we best secure the highest education for our girls? Never before, in the history of the world, has there been a nation or an age in which the young women were so *much* educated as in these United States and these closing decades of the nineteenth century. The doors of our public schools are as widely opened to them as to our boys. The rapid, heated processes of our civilization tend to their profuse and abnormal development; but it is a development in characteristics which, if we are not careful, may lead to the deterioration of our race. I stand not here to champion any pet theory for or against the recognition of "sex in education." I plead, simply, that the loftiest ideals be adopted for the training of our daughters in body, in intellect, and in morals. Their education is the most sacred trust committed to this great Republic. The claims of the ignorant immigrant voters; the pressing needs, even, of the freedmen of the South, are hardly as momentous as the solemn demands made upon us by these mothers of our future generations. For, indeed, these demands include the others. By the grade of intelligence and the moral standards of these young women the future of our nation is to be molded. The sneering allusions to "the girl of the period" that we so often hear from press and platform, are unmistakable indications of a want of reverence for womanhood that is alarming. Do not lightly dismiss this thought as irrelevant to the general subject in hand—the illiteracy of our nation. A large proportion of all the maidens in the United States, who stand on the verge of matrimony and motherhood, "where brook and river meet," are utterly unqualified for the solemn responsibilities before them. Thousands of them—dusky daughters of the South, children of priest-ridden foreigners, offspring of polyg-amous Mormons—have spent the golden years of their youth outside of the educational provisions of our schools, and their descend-ants will, in the natural order of events, grow up ignorant and uncared-for; while the training of many of their more favored sisters has had so little bearing upon the duties of motherhood that it would be idle to expect to find their progeny on the side of enlighten-ment. By the intelligence and moral pur-pose of these mothers of the future, I repeat, are the destinies of the Republic to be shaped, and their fitting culture is the most impera-tive of national duties.

III.—THE PUBLIC SCHOOL AS AN INDUS-TRIAL AGENCY.

Another of the most formidable difficulties hitherto found in the way of securing universal enlightenment, lies in the inade-quacy of the public school as an industrial agency. Its value as an enlightening and civilizing agency can hardly be overesti-mated; but as a means of industrial training it is a failure. The years of study are often sadly abridged because of the poverty of par-ents, whose children must as early as possi-ble be taught the principles of their life-work—in trade, mechanics, housekeeping, or agriculture. The boy who is destined to become a bricklayer, a carpenter, or a plumb-er—the girl whose humble energies are to be expended in dairy work or dress-making—have the same rights in the shaping of the public-school curriculum as those of higher social rank. Our children are kept at the tedious study of branches which can be of no practical use to ninety-nine out of one hundred of them when school days are over. To object to the expansion of the public-school system to meet the requirements of exigencies is to ignore the logic and march of events. As long as the energies of the great majority of our boys and girls must in their maturity be tasked to provide them-selves with the necessaries of life, so long should our rudimentary schools be industrial as well as literary.

The consideration of this need of American children for an industrial training brings us to view another stepping-stone toward na-tional prosperity, which has already been turned into a stumbling-block ; a danger that stands in contrast with the need just pre-sented; a danger which is not new to the thoughtful minds of our country, but which has of late been happily phrased by an em-inent educator as

IV.—MERCANTILISM.

Guizot, in his " History of Civilization," makes the broad generalization, that "when a civilization is dominated over by some one principle, which gains complete mastery,

and develops all in subordination to itself, the civilization will either sink into immo-bility, or else will develop with astonishing rapidity and brilliancy only to decline and decay just as rapidly. On the other hand, a civilization in which no one element ever becomes powerful enough to exer-cise permanent despotism over the others, but in which many strong elements exist together, stimulating and restraining each other, will be far more rich and varied, and far longer lived—a civilization inclos-ing in itself principles and powers which, by their constant action on each other, will ever renew its youth and vigor." President White, whose recent thoughtful paper on this subject merits repeated pe-rusal by every friend of education, and every lover of his country, cites Spain, Russia, and the Spanish-American Republics as types of the immobile civilization which is developed when one principle reigns supreme. Venice sprang with unparalleled rapidity into unpar-alleled glory, and sank as rapidly into insig-nificance; while England and Germany are fair samples of the healthier growth. We behold the remarkably rapid and brilliant develop-ment of the United States, and ask what has controlled this marvelous growth? Listen to the eloquent but ominous reply of President White : " The one element which has become not merely dominant, but all-prevailing, is a combination of the industrial spirit with the trade spirit—*mercantilism*. Here is evidently the mind which moves the mass. The rail-ways, canals, telegraphs, manufactories, mines, furnaces, city after city made up of lines of shops, great hotels filled with dyspeptics, long trains of cars filled with hurrying men and jaded women—all these outward, visible signs point to one inward and spiritual grace—that of trade. Mercan-tilism in great cities and in small towns, in society and in the individual, is becoming a disease—feverish, cancerous. Of the great political questions now before the nation— the education of the freedmen and the illiterate generally, the reform of the civil service, the rectification of the electoral-college system, and tariff reform—the one question of which we hear the most, and the only one in which the nation at large seems to take any interest, is the tariff; the one question which has to do with trade and manufactures. The political spirit, the spirit of patriotism, is dominated by the mercantile interest, and the same is true of education, science, and literature. The strength of these elements in the ordinary normal development of our American civilization, compared with that of mercantilism, is weak."

What, then, is to be done? How shall mercantilism, which has thus far been in the main a great blessing, be prevented from becoming, in obedience to an inexorable law of history, a curse? The essayist answers that "the greatest work which the coming century has to do in this century is to build up an aristocracy of thought and feeling which shall hold its own against the aristocracy of mercantilism." So far as this can be done by education, it must be done—at least so far as foundation work is concerned—in the public school. And the neglect of the great opportunities for spreading enlightenment which our rapid attainment of wealth has thrust upon us—in other words, the neglect of the most thorough development of popular education—will certainly secure for us the fate of Venice or of Peru.

This thought brings us by natural transition to the last point to which I will call your attention—the imperative necessity of

V.—TRAINING THE MORAL FACULTIES OF THE YOUNG.

The criminals of to-day will soon have all passed into the grave. Who, it has been sadly asked by a thoughtful writer—who will fill our prisons and reformatories a score of years hence? who, of the next generation, will supply the daily records of burglary and arson, licentiousness and murder? Some you will find to-night where they are to be expected—loitering in the streets, or lounging on the corners, or breathing the air of some vile den, with nothing to do but to learn the language of vice, as it comes from the lips of their older companions. Manifestly, our first duty concerning these is to gather them into the schools and to teach them trades—else they will remain where they now are, in the ranks of the army of illiterates. But the best knowledge of books and of trades will never rid the world of rascals. Nay, aside from moral culture, such knowledge is even unable to perpetuate itself. It is a painful fact that many of our future criminals dwell in the best of our homes, and are trained in the best of our schools. And the whole trend of their influence is as certainly downward intellectually as it is in morals. In other words, the illiterates as a class are vicious, and will remain so until educated; while the influence of educated criminals tends directly to the increase of ignorance.

"I see but one way in which we can rid ourselves of rascals," said Dr. Holland, "and that is to stop raising them. We have imprisoned them, we have fined them, we have hanged them; we have tried to reform them by the best appointed machinery; we have blessed them and cursed them alternately, but the stock is undiminished. As one dies another takes his place, and does his best to bring a companion with him. Reforms do not reclaim and revivals do not reach them. I repeat it, I see but one way to rid ourselves of them, and that is to stop raising them."

But how can we stop raising them? Thousands of our homes are hopelessly corrupt; hundreds of thousands of our children are beyond the influence of Church and Sunday-school, and if their moral faculties are to be trained at all it must be in the public school. We have spent our time and strained our tempers in paltry quibbles about the reading of a few verses from the Bible, or the perfunctory repetition of the Lord's prayer, and have neglected the weightier matter of direct ethical culture. Meanwhile a generation has slipped past us into manhood with moral faculties largely untrained.

The claims of the illiterate, the defects of our common-school system, the duty of compulsory education, and the need of national aid, have already been emphasized, and will be reiterated, by voices more eloquent than mine. The task allotted to me has been to bring to your attention, in the briefest possible manner, elements which for the most part lie beyond the reach of State or nation, but not beyond the puissant sway of the heart and brain of the people. We look back sometimes with pride over the path-way of our country's progress, and behold a century of unexampled prosperity. It is for us to say whether that prosperity shall continue. Our hands are on the lever which sways the switch; our acting and our thinking, our voting and our prayers, are to direct the nation toward a future still more glorious, or turn it aside to moral, mental, and physical decay.

As I stand, to-night, in this beautiful sea-side resort, within sound of the billows' endless monotone, I am reminded of one of the most solemn visions that was ever evoked by the "fine frenzy" of prophet or poet. A queenly figure stands in lonely grief upon the shore of time, and thus bewails her wasted opportunities:

"I stand amid the roar
Of a surf-tormented shore,
And I hold within my hand
Grains of the golden sand.
How few!—yet how they creep
Through my fingers to the deep
While I weep!
O God! can I not clasp
Them with a tighter grasp?
O God! can I not save
One from the pitiless wave?"

Friends, half a century of negligence will turn that weird picture into a type of our country, and put into the mouths of our children that mournful lament. For unvalued advantages soon pass beyond reach, and in education, as truly as in religion, NOW is the day of salvation.

But before the imagination of the enlightened patriot no such hopeless scenes as this arise. Up through the long vistas of coming ages he hears the clock of eternity strike the hour that shall call nations, as well as individuals, to the bar of God for judgment. One by one they come, lamenting their failures and pleading, in extenuation, their virtuous achievements. To their lamentations and their pleadings let us for a moment give ear.

See the plaintive figure of Judea Capta crouching in degradation. Beside her is the harp of psalmody, whose chords shall never again be struck. At her feet lies the prophetic scroll. She weeps over her sins, but faintly pleads her unrivaled service to the world in the dissemination of the divine law and the divine message of mercy.

Listen to the Genius of old Greece, as she stands in cowering beauty—like a dethroned Venus—confessing her profligacy, her countless wasted opportunities, but pleading, "Nevertheless all art is mine, and all philosophy; my shame should be allowed to die with me, for down to the farthest ages my glory is shed."

See cruel, lecherous Rome, acknowledging a thousand abominations that even Gibbon never recorded, but pointing in sullen pride to the great structure of modern civilization as built on her foundations.

There, too, are gathered the great powers of modern times. Brilliant, sensuous, volatile France, mother of the sneering Voltaire and the murderous Robespierre, sobered at last, calls to mind the names of Calvin and Coligny, and her thought-ful and heroic sons of later days. Phlegmatic Germany claims credit for the Reformation and for the motherhood of modern philosophy. England, dignified and stately even in that climactic hour, pleads a career given, in spite of many grievous backsets, to the advancement of the race.

What shall the Genius of our own beloved country say as she stands before that august tribunal? Much of error and failure must be confessed. Listen: "I came too late upon the scene of action to give the primal impulse to any of the great movements for the elevation of mankind. My art I had to borrow from Athens, my religion from Jewry, my law from Rome. Among all my sons I can point to no Homer nor Cæsar, to no Raphael nor Mozart. But this one thing I have done. By a proper appreciation of the dignity and of the solemn responsibilities of manhood; by a lofty and discreet estimate of true womanhood; by a correct understanding of the value and of the ends of rational education; and by conscientious attention to moral culture, I have secured to each of my sons and daughters a practical, comprehensive, thorough fitness for the manifold duties of life. Thus have I not only avoided the dangers whose evils were intrinsic, but, by the help of the almighty Ruler of nations, have turned even the stumbling-blocks of illiteracy into stepping-stones toward national enlightenment."

4. THE DANGER OF DELAY.

HON. ALBION W. TOURGÉE,

Editor of "The Continent," Philadelphia, Pa.

I AM very glad that the subject assigned to me this evening is the danger of neglecting or delaying national action in regard to education. I do not use the phrase "national aid to education," which has come into vogue through its use in the platform adopted by the Republican Convention of 1880, not only because it is insensible, but also because the phrase itself is stamped with the hoof-mark of cowardly evasion. It was the danger likely to result to the nation from the ignorance of its voters that first directed my attention to the subject; it was this apprehension that led me to elaborate a plan of national action for the extinction of illiteracy; it was the apprehension of this danger that has inspired all my efforts to implant this idea in the minds of the American people; and it is to this danger, which hourly grows more serious, that I beg to call the earnest attention of this audience during the time allotted to me.

National action upon the subject of general education, for the present at least, if not forever, should be confined to the extinction of illiteracy—the promotion of primary education among illiterate masses. To be able to read and write is to have the key of all knowledge and all power. He who has the ability to read may know all that man hath wrought and taught. All that the ages have learned or that God has revealed is open to him who reads the printed page, while he who wields the pen speaks to every soul that stands between himself and the hither shore of eternity. The lack of this knowledge we call illiteracy—speaking more accurately, we might say mental blindness—and its possession we call intelligence. The man who cannot read must take all his knowledge on trust. The breath of his fellow is his only means of learning what lies beyond the scope of his own vision or the line of his own experience.

Every government, whatever its form or character, has a twofold interest in the intelligence of the citizen or subject. In the first place, intelligence increases his value as a unit of the national life. Economically considered, the wealth of the whole community depends on the productive power of its individuals. A man who can read and write is worth more as a laborer, a wealth-producer, and he is far less likely to become a burden to society, both because of the wider field of industry open before him and of the pride developed by intelligence, that makes him shrink from pauperism as the Oriental does from leprosy. In this respect the interest of our general government in the intelligence of the masses of its people is directly very much less than that of any other government in the world. It is only indirectly that our national organism is affected by any consideration of individual wealth or poverty. It does not concern itself with the citizen as an economic factor at all. Whether a man is rich or poor, pauper or millionaire, it is all the same to the nation. Its revenue is not directly affected by the one fact or the other. The nation maintains no poor-houses and levies no *ad valorem* taxes on the citizen's possessions. In this respect the several States of the Union only have any direct interest in the education of our illiterate masses. To them it is of the utmost importance that the citizen should be afforded every possible means of self-support and be withheld from pauperism by every conceivable influence. Education as an investment is purely within the purview of the State governments. The jails as well as the poor-houses are all their property, and the prisoners their charge. Within this line the general government does not seek to come. Save for its own protection and defense, or in assertion of the rights of its citizens, it cannot interfere in the administration of justice or the relief of pauperism.

It is on this alone that not only the right but the duty of the general government to secure the intelligence of the masses rests. The United States have no right to tax the rich to educate the poor simply *because they are poor*. That pertains entirely to the polity of the State, and is the basis principle of all our State systems of education. The *State* finds it sound policy to educate the children of the poor rather than support the pauperism that would accrue from their ignorance. The general government has no right to tax the people of Massachusetts to educate the children of Missouri for the sake of reducing the proportion of criminals in that State.

There is one respect, however, in which the interest of the general government is exactly co-ordinate with that of the State in the intelligence of the citizen, and that is *in*

so far as it affects his capacity for self government. Crime and pauperism are matters for the State alone to consider, but *good government is a thing of common interest to both State and nation, and it is equally the duty of the State and of the nation to see to it that the citizen is made capable of performing intelligently, honestly, and fearlessly the duties devolving on him as such. To both the intelligence of the citizen is a matter of equal and common concern.* The same law of self-preservation that makes armies and navies a necessity of all governments to resist foes from without, makes the school-house an indispensable bulwark—indispensable in a republican government to guard it against the still more dangerous encroachment of foes from *within*. This, then, is the basis of all right or authority vested in the government of the United States to take any action, appropriate funds, or exercise authority, or in any respect to interest itself in the education of the citizen, to wit: *Intelligence is necessary to the proper exercise of electoral power. By its abuse the nation is exposed to danger. It has, therefore, the right to defend itself from harm and perpetuate its own existence by the extinction of illiteracy or its reduction to an innocuous proportion.*

Our system of government, both State and national, is based upon the hypothesis of equal power in each individual voter.

It is based, too, upon the principle that the will of the majority, if not always correct, is the nearest approach to the right which it is possible to attain. If this principle is not a true one, then republican government is radically defective, and must always result in ultimate failure. To render it even approximately true, however, three things must co-exist:

1. Each individual voter—each co-ordinate king—must have a distinct and intelligent opinion in regard to the question which the collective sovereignty is called upon to decide. 2. He must be able to express that opinion by his ballot. 3. He must be honest enough and brave enough and keen enough to resist corruption, defy violence, and defeat fraud.

These things can never be true of a whole people, and in so far as either of them is lacking, so far the elective power is debased and the government ceases to be the will of a true majority—a government by the people. The first two of these essential conditions are dependent entirely upon intelligence. No illiterate man can form a reliable opinion upon a matter of public policy, or be able to know that his ballot expresses such opinion. He may be right, but he cannot *know* that he is so. His ballot *may* express his will, but he can only have another's assurance that it does. The intelligent voter may be wrong, but he is far more likely to be right than if the whole world of printed facts was excluded from his consciousness. His ballot may not accurately express his purpose, but it is infinitely more likely to do so than if he could not read the names it bears.

So, too, the third essential attribute of the voter is in a great measure dependent upon intelligence. It is very true that intelligence does not, of necessity, make a man honest, or brave, or patriotic. But it protects the honest man from fraud, increases his power to prevent imposition, makes him competent to watch over the ballot-box, and to see to it that the will of the majority is carried into effect. Intelligence enhances the moral sense also, and if it does not always baffle corruption, throws a thousand obstacles in its pathway. Intelligence may aid one man to commit fraud, but it will also arm a thousand to detect it. The printed page may lend itself to deception, but it brings also the remedy. While one demagogue hangs out thereby a false light upon a lee shore, a thousand honest lamps mark distinctly the safe and true channel. If the ignorant man is right it is by accident; the intelligent man, with equal honesty, is a thousand times more likely both to understand and to do that which ought to be right. It is this doctrine of an intelligent choice that lies at the root of republican government. There will, of course, always be men in every community who will be mistaken, weak, mercenary, and corrupt, for this is simply human nature. There will be men who neither know nor care any thing about the public weal. There will be a large class who, while entirely capable of performing this highest act of citizenship honestly and wisely, are either too careless, too selfish, or too busy to attend to their part in the work of self-government. These will be found in all communities in greater or less proportions. They are like bad rulers and corrupt legislators, in that they can never be entirely eliminated. For this reason no human government can be made perfect. For the performance of this high duty, however, every one must see that intelligence is the first prerequisite. An ignorant voter is like a blind swordsman. He may destroy his enemy, but he is quite as likely to slay his friend.

The republican idea is not based upon the calculation of chances, but upon the principle that the mass of the people are sufficiently intelligent to know what will constitute the greatest good to the greatest number; that a majority of them are honest, incorruptible, and brave enough to stand by their opinions and see that they are carried into effect.

Because the public weal is affected only by the action of majorities, however, the mere numbers of the illiterate to be found in any community afford no reasonable criterion by which to estimate the danger that may arise from a lack of intelligence on the part of the

voter. The electoral power—the individuals who make up the body politic—will always be divided more or less evenly between two great parties, or, to speak more accurately, will be divided between the affirmative and negative of some specific policy. There will always be a party who wish something to be done and a party who do not wish it to be done. There may be infinite gradations of thought among the individuals. One may think it should be done to-day or to-morrow; another that it should be delayed until next week or next year, or forever. Still the same wall separates them. To do or not to do is always the line of demarcation. There may be times when this line is difficult to trace—when, perhaps, it is only traceable at all by reference to the past. The impetus of a heated struggle may carry party organizations far beyond the point aimed at in the outset. After any specific idea has become a part of the public policy, parties may still be divided for a considerable time on the question whether it ought to have been approved or not. But in the past, the present, or the future, the fact that separates parties in a republic is the doing or not doing of some particular thing, and so single is the human mind in its action, that one idea usually dominates each party, rather than the composite declaration of faith found in party platforms. Where the intelligence of a community is fairly divided between two conflicting ideas, and party-spirit is equally intense upon both sides of the dividing line, a very considerable proportion of ignorance may be regarded as an element of little danger. Suppose a farming community at the West to be pretty evenly divided between two great parties, and to have in its midst ten, twenty, or even thirty per cent. of illiterates, who are of the same stock, of the same religious faith as the rest of the community, and pursuing the same general vocations. Suppose (if it be possible to suppose such a thing) that it were a Protestant community, of New England descent, devoted to agriculture, having twenty per cent. of illiteracy among its voters, and its intelligence thus equably divided between two parties. In such a case it is probable that even so large a percentage of illiteracy as this would not seriously affect any political result. The intelligence being so evenly divided, the two wings of like character and influence, and both equally allied by race, creed, and interest to the illiterates, these latter would in all probability be divided in about the same proportion as their intelligent neighbors upon the issues on which the parties stood opposed.

The mere statement of the number of illiterates in any State does not of itself, therefore, convey any definite idea of the danger to be apprehended from that source. If the population be homogeneous in race, religion, and occupation, it can be safely disregarded. If, however, the main body of the illiterates be distinguished from the mass of intelligence by race, creed, or occupation, or if they be aggregated in one portion of the commonwealth and not found in another, then ignorance becomes at once a source of peril that cannot be for a moment overlooked. If, for instance, the illiteracy of the State of New York were evenly spread over its entire extent, and thoroughly amalgamated in sentiment and interest with its people, they would not be found almost entirely upon one side in politics, and, as a body, they would at once become politically insignificant. That very instant the problem of municipal government in the city of New York would become one easy of solution. At present, the whole question of the government of the metropolis may be said to resolve itself into an attempt to find some method by which to neutralize the power of its massed illiteracy. Its vicious and degraded classes; its unassimilated foreign population; its almost indivisible Catholic element—which classes embrace nineteen twentieths of its illiteracy —these are the dice with which its politicians gamble. They are isolated very largely from the balance of her population, not merely by the fact of illiteracy, but by the sentiment of creed or race. The only possible method of assimilating such classes, and constituting them a safe and reliable element in self-government is to extinguish illiteracy, or reduce it to a minimum, and open the way to a clear apprehension of the general interest by the individual voters. Of course, the vicious and corrupt will always remain, but the honest, intelligent man, whatever his creed or race, will, soon or later, come to understand that the good of the whole is his own highest advantage. Intelligence is the avenue by which genuine naturalization comes—it is the menstruum by which seemingly destructive ingredients are resolved into a consistent and innocuous whole.

It is only in a few great centers of population at the North that illiteracy has as yet become a matter of serious public concern, or is at all likely to do so. Even in these this evil may safely be left to the care of the States in which these great cities are situated, because those States are abundantly able to apply the remedy, the public sentiment therein is in favor of its application, and there is no insuperable obstacle to its general adoption. In other words, the public-school system of the North, with the public sentiment that stands behind it, is quite sufficient not only to hold in check, but to reduce to insignificance, the percentage of illiteracy within its own borders. All that the people of any Northern commonwealth need to know is that illiteracy is increasing, or that it is becoming dangerous to the State, and they will stamp it out at

any cost. So far as the Northern States are concerned, there is no cause for national action, and the pittance that would come to each from any fund distributed on the basis of illiteracy would be so insignificant in comparison with its own appropriations for educational purposes as to be almost unworthy of consideration. When we come to look at the state of affairs subsisting in the Southern States, however, we find all these conditions reversed. The proportion of illiterates in those States is so great that even under the most favorable circumstances the ignorant voter must, for a generation at least, constitute a serious obstacle to prosperous and effective self-government. If there were no distinction of race, color, or previous condition, if there were no conflicting interest springing out of the general relation of employer and employed, or of landlord and tenant, still the problem of illiteracy at the South would be a serious and difficult one. What is that problem? To state it broadly, *from forty to fifty-five per cent. of the voters of those States are unable to read the ballots which they cast!* Or, to put it in another form, we may say that in the sixteen States in which the six millions of colored people are chiefly to be found. *eighty per cent.* of the colored and *thirty per cent.* of the white population are illiterate.

There are more illiterate voters in South Carolina than there are electors who are able to read their ballots.

In Kentucky there are more white than colored illiterates.

Despite all, the fact that the people of the North have given *twenty millions* of dollars to the South for educational purposes since 1865, and although those States have done what they have in that direction, there were *more illiterates in the South in 1880 than in* 1870, and there are more now than then. *Children are born there faster than they are taught to read.*

These are general statements of the same fact, to wit: A vast proportion of the governing power in those States are utterly and absolutely incapable

1. Of forming an intelligent opinion of the questions they are called upon to decide.

2. Of knowing whether their ballots express the opinions which they have; and

3. Of exercising such watch and ward over the ballot after it is cast as shall insure its due effect upon the result.

In other words, they have the power without possibility of knowledge as to its righteous, independent use as constituent rulers of the State and nation.

Does this fact mean any thing to the nation? A vote cast in Florida is just as potent for national good or ill as if cast in Maine. The sixteen States in question represent *three fourths* of a majority in the Electoral

College, *more than two thirds* of a majority in the House of Representatives, and *eight ninths* of a majority in the Senate of the United States!! The illiteracy of the South, *plus* ten per cent. of its intelligent voters, acting together and their ballots being honestly counted, would elect *seventy-four per cent.* of a President. If the illiterate vote be suppressed in whole or in part by fraud or otherwise, then it would require only a majority of the intelligent vote to choose the same proportion of electors. To place this fact in a still more striking light, we may say that *one fifth of the electoral votes of the North*, added to a South *made solid either by the suppression or by the predominance of its illiterate masses*, is sufficient to determine the character of our national government. The nation's interest in the intelligence of the voter in these States is, therefore, overwhelming and intense.

These facts, startling as they are, however, only faintly show the real interest which the people of the United States have in the extinction of illiteracy and the extension of intelligence among the people of the South. There are other facts which enhance the danger a hundred-fold, and make the instant application of the only practicable remedy a duty of the most urgent necessity.

1. Between the intelligence and illiteracy of this region there is an immense gulf. The one class comprises the land-owners and the other the land-workers. Socially, also, they represent the extremes. Poverty, degradation, and dependence mark the line between the two.

2. Perhaps two thirds of the illiteracy belongs to a race which for nearly three hundred years has occupied a servile relation, has been regarded as essentially inferior, has been rigidly excluded from all exercise or assertion of individual right or authority, and is forever distinguished from the dominant race by the fact of color.

3. This race is increasing at a rate unparalleled before, even in this land of marvelous growth,—poverty, enforced exertion, a simple and abundant diet, and a free, untrammeled life. It is not possible that it should gain in wealth so fast as in numbers. It is hardly possible that the growth in intelligence should keep pace with its gain in power. If it grows in the future as it has in the past, *within the life of the child now born the colored race will be in a majority in five States, and double the number of the whites in two of them.*

4. The intelligence of that section, instead of being evenly divided upon questions of national polity, is almost entirely to be found in one party, and that one bitterly hostile to the one in which by far the larger portion of ignorance is to be found. Because of the sentiments from which this division of parties

arose, it is likely, in effect, to outlast the present generation.

5. The proportion of white illiteracy has not materially decreased during the past decade, while the actual number of illiterates has increased.

6. The sentiment in favor of public schools in these States is not sufficiently strong to enable them to meet and surmount this tide of ignorance, even if they were financially in a condition to do so, and a large proportion of the whites are still bitterly opposed to the education of the Negro. A bright, intelligent lady. living in one of these States, who is an author of no mean powers, writing to me not many months ago, said, in all seriousness, "In my opinion the two worst things the South has to contend with to-day are fences and *free schools*. It will take more than we can raise to fence the crops and *educate the Negroes.*" She is a type, and a type of the best blood and brain too.

7. The voluntary charity of the North cannot be expected to last always. During the past eighteen years it has been an enormous force in promoting the enlightenment of the South. More than a million dollars a year have been freely given by the people and churches of the North, and thousands of devoted lives have been consecrated to the work of education at the South. Hundreds of school buildings have been erected and thousands of the colored race prepared to teach their fellows. This bounteous stream cannot be expected to flow on forever. The Negro, as an object of benevolence, is shrinking out of sight. The enthusiasm that took thousands of our brightest and best of both sexes to the new mission-field which the war opened up is now dying out. Pity for the state of the slave is changing into apathy with regard to the freedman. The momentum of the past will, no doubt, carry it somewhat farther into the future, but within a decade we may look to see this charity diminish by at least four fifths of its present volume.

This, then, is the logical conclusion from all the existing facts:

Unless the national government intervene, or a miracle be wrought, the present state of affairs at the South must grow steadily worse; the debasement of the ballotorial power continue, and the evils likely to arise therefrom grow hourly more and more imminent.

Can we afford to permit this? Dare we allow it to be so? When slavery and freedom marked the line between the sections, the whole North rallied to the cry that "the nation cannot remain half free and half slave." Yet slavery was almost innocuous beyond the borders of the States where it prevailed. In national power the slave represented only two fifths of the influence of a Northern white voter. Now, the ignorant colored man or unlettered poor white can, by his vote, blindly and ignorantly given, neutralize your influence in the government or mine. It is no longer a question of pity or philanthropy, but one of safety. Dare we, as citizens of the country, permit the elements that now mingle angrily and unwillingly in Southern life to remain as they are? The dominant sentiment of that section may be in favor of being let alone, though it is more than probable that enough of its best men and women have by this time come to realize the danger that threatens them even more seriously than it does the nation at large, to be willing to accept a remedy.

Sumner said that by giving the Negro the ballot, we had "chained him to the chariot-wheel of our national progress." He was right, though in a different sense from what he meant to be understood. The nation began the liberation of the slave to wound its enemy; it must complete it to save itself. Whatever slavery may have been as regards the individual, it was a national error. It nourished ignorance and begat poverty. The poor white of the South was its product as well as the helpless slave. We put the ballot into the hands of both and made them co-equal kings with ourselves. We must now make it possible that they should rule wisely—rule us wisely as well as themselves, for they are our rulers as we are theirs—or perish ourselves by their misrule.

This is the danger. It is one that every citizen of the North or of the South, white or black, intelligent or illiterate, Republican or Democrat, has an equal interest in averting. It is a danger that hourly grows more pressing, and demands from the people of the whole land that earnest and serious attention that Americans only give to the most imminent public peril. The means by which the remedy may be applied are not within the scope of my assignment, and if they were the time would not permit of their discussion. In a more fitting form I shall take occasion at an early day to express, in detail, my views upon that branch of a question now fairly launched upon the field of public thought.

5. OPENING REMARKS.

REV. W. F. DICKERSON, D.D.,

One of the Bishops of the African Methodist Episcopal Church.

THIS seems to be rather an auspicious day for our American civilization, for our Christian institutions—a day when such men as are gathered here can be called from their various and varied duties to discuss topics of such unselfish importance, and from day to day an audience can be held hour after hour, session after session, to listen to them. It is, indeed, auspicious for our American institutions. I think, however, that we have given illiteracy too far a start ahead of us, and we shall have to run pretty fast and make pretty good time in order to catch up. We have got to be united in this work: we have got to stand shoulder to shoulder in this work; we have got to be self-sacrificing in this work. We must, then, enlist the sympathy, the support, the heart, hand, and brain labor of every man and every woman on this continent, in order that we may wipe out that foul blot of illiteracy. Dangers are increasing daily from our home-born illiteracy and from foreign. Juvenile illiteracy is increasing with every new birth in every section of our land; adult illiteracy is increasing with every arrival of an emigrant ship from foreign ports. It is well that we have come together to consider this matter. While down in Mississippi the Episcopal Church is making an effort to see how it shall begin to do this work, it is well we should meet at Ocean Grove, not merely to tell how to do it, but to begin to do it. There are to me two United States of America; that is, two separate classes of States which I call united: One, the intellectual United States, and the other the political. If the intellectual United States shall do this work as thoroughly, shall be as earnest, shall use as many means, shall enter into its work with as much zeal and earnestness as the political United States does, then this hard lot will be easily wiped out. It will take not simply sentiments to do this, and yet we must create them. We must have these sentiments, united sentiments—the people thoroughly aroused in this matter—and yet we must make the intellectual work of our people; and you bear in mind that when I say our people, I am speaking as an American. I am, in every respect, an American, thoroughly identified with all American institutions—American by birth and by training, by every thing. I am thoroughly an American—if not absorbed I am completely identified with America. So I say we must do this work because this land is becoming, has become, the theater of action for all the peoples, of all the races, from all quarters of the globe. They are here, and still they are coming. I felt this morning, I feel now, it is a little late for us to be doing with the American Indian what was done by Cæsar with the Briton in the past. We must do this work as it comes to our hands and our hearts.

In Switzerland they take us to see what is called there the "Meeting of the Waters," where the Rhone and the Arno come together. It is a beautiful sight; there the Rhone, coming down from Lake Leman, meets at this point a mad, rushing, wild stream. Here they come together, but, seeming to dislike each other—for the one is red, while the other is blue; the one steady and still, and the other swift and maddening in its rush—apparently disliking each other,

they do not become one. I asked the guide if at any point they became one, and he said that far down, some five or six or eight miles, they became one. Drop by drop, they become included with each other. They finally become one stream, and go on into the Mediterranean. It seems to me that all races from all quarters of the globe meet here, having heard of America, having heard what a grand climate we have, what noble hearts we have, how filled with sympathy, how we take every man into our souls, how that even the Chinese come—some of them find out to the contrary. There may be some differences which may be repulsive for a time, but at last these many shall become blended into one harmonious and glorious whole.

---

6. THE POOR WHITES OF THE SOUTH : WHO THEY ARE AND WHY THEY ARE.

REV. L. B. CALDWELL, PH.D., TENNESSEE.

VIRGINIA, Maryland, and Pennsylvania furnished a large quota of the original population of the Central South. This fact is applicable to the whole South, except the coast cities and some of the adjacent lowlands. The area of the South may be divided into the lowlands or river bottoms, the low plateaus, and the mountain regions. The first of these has always, or until very recently, been held in large tracts, and worked by men of capital. The plateaus lying midway between the bottoms and the mountains really furnished homes for a middle class. But the mountain region and the piney lowlands have been the home of the poor whites. This mountain population is almost exclusively Protestant. In fact, it is difficult to find a Roman Catholic in this original stock. The religious faith of this people may be indicated by the names they have inherited. John Knox, Martin Luther, Asbury, Cook, Soule, and Bascomb are household treasures with this people. And without casting a reflection upon the political caste of any man, it is but just to say that these mountaineers were largely loyal to the United States Government. Here life may be lived—prolonged, at very little cost.

Had the best blood of Virginia divided on this line, the result to-day would have been an absolute separation of the families, the rich and poor whites. These poor whites are not a people imported from the isles of the sea, or an outgrowth of fancy, but they are of us—our brothers. No better mental metal exists anywhere than may be found in

these cheerless cabins, where real comfort has never smiled. Fifty or seventy-five years of cheerless drill are not likely to stimulate a very high ambition for home delicacies. If you inquire why they are so poor and ignorant, I can only say they have never been lifted out of the rut of their fathers. They live in a climate where something for their subsistence can be grown for nearly ten months of the year; yet they are not utilizing this fact, and are poor. This mountain country is not a cheerless, valueless region, but is simply waiting the touch incident to culture. If the *Mayflower* had touched at Mobile, and the Pilgrims had worked their way inland from the Gulf of Mexico, the North-eastern States might have been to-day to this region what Alaska is to Southern Michigan. Here is a wealth of timber, which, for variety and quality, is not equaled on the continent; and mineral wealth, from coal to native gold, is scattered almost broadcast. Perhaps a single range of these mountains contains more bituminous coal than the world has ever used, while iron is too plentiful to be of value. Gold is not uncommon in the mountains of North Carolina, Georgia, and Tennessee.

Unlike Utah, Nevada, and New Mexico, these mountains are very fertile. Yet this people is poor—poor because they do not know how to be otherwise. But we approach a more vital question: Why are they ignorant? You must not overlook the fact that prior to 1865 the public-school system of the South was a failure, and since then, though improving, is practically but little better. It was not expected that the colored man, the slave, should be taught to read. A public-school system, practically carried out, would endanger this class of chattel. Hence the planter of the South had no need of the common school. He could furnish private instruction for his children until they were prepared for college, when they could be sent from home to finish their school training. I am not here to reflect upon the man who could, or can, provide private literary advantages for his family. I would do the same to-day if it were within my possible limit. If possible, my boys should have all the pleasures of home life until fitted for the university. The planter could and did do this, so to him there was no call for the public school. This left no alternative for him who could not pay for private instruction for his family, nor send them abroad, but to grow them as he grew his mules—for manual labor. Do you begin to see the line which divided the families of the rich and poor white men of the South? It has come to be a line of money and letters. While, perhaps, you may carry in your mind the results of the lack of common schools for a few years, you must measure up to the numberless results following a dozen decades to reach the magnitude of the evils existing now. Do you blame them for this condition of things? It was not in their power to avoid them. Put yourself in their place. We have no home schools, and no money to send poor children away from home to be educated. Do you say you would have provided some way to educate your children? Perhaps you would have done so. You may say that eighteen years of peace ought to have made a great change with this people. But before you prophesy great results, please weigh the effort which has been made for them. Without an effort you recall the stroke of that pen which cast into the lap of the nation a witless ward, 4,000,000 strong. It would have been cruel to have neglected this trust. It was not in the providence of God that the American nation should shrink from such a responsibility. I need not recall to your minds how the money necessary to carry on those majestic plans flowed into the coffers of the Churches. How the care of the Freedmen became the pulse of the nation. How grandly this work has been done, and is being done, it may not be in the power of words to tell. But the result of fifteen years has more than settled the question of the possibility of making men and women of this common chattel. Whatever their future as a factor of the nation may be, this one thing is settled—they can learn and they can teach. I would not if I could divert a single dollar from the channel through which they have been flowing to build men and women from this crude ma-

terial. Yet is it not passingly strange that, during all these years of magnificent giving, the poor whites of the South have been so entirely overlooked? Just as ignorant, as helpless, and as much a factor of the nation, yet until very recently left without aid, or even sympathy, by Church or State. It must be remembered that for those four dreadful years it cost more to be an American citizen in this region, either in "Blue" or "Gray," than it did to be a slave. Life was worth but little, and property less, for it was very uncertain whether you would possess either on the morrow. Those who braved or dodged the danger and came through with a grip on life, could simply boast of the power to be. It may be easy to prophesy what might have been if certain conditions had been met fifteen years ago. But, gentlemen, we are confronted by a living ghost, which will not down. We cannot ignore the fact that we have a vast native population of white persons in our midst who cannot write. I am not here to-day to plead for all the white population of the South, nor am I giving you a sketch of dreams. Early in July I spent a little time in the mountains of Tennessee and Georgia, and, as an instance, I will give you the facts as I gathered them.

In one little district of Polk County, Tenn., I sought out one of the old citizens, who for eighteen years had been a justice of the peace. He had taken some interest in school matters. In his school district there were 102 children of school age, 12 of whom could write, and 20 of whom could read. Look at 87 per cent. in one district who cannot write, and 80 per cent. who cannot read. In this voting district there were 100 voters, 20 of whom could read the ballot they cast. In the same district there were 106 women, 15 of whom could read. And observe there was not a colored person living in this district. It is such a mistake to suppose that the illiteracy of the South is confined to the freedmen.

The social natures of the freedmen induce them to make their homes where they can meet often. You may look for them in or near the cities or towns. This town life of the freedmen has placed them where their school privileges have been far better than those of the poor white man living farther away. There are large sections of the South where the colored man is almost as rare a sight as in the rural districts of New England. And there are places where ignorance prevails to an alarming extent.

There are sections, which, for convenience, you may call the foot-hills, where the white and colored man have worked side by side. How the condition of the white man is improved by his association with the Negro!

Of the 138 electoral votes cast every four years for the President of these United States, these men have not a little to do in giving political and moral coloring to the same. Has it occurred to you that nearly three fourths of the votes required to elect the President of the United States are made up among this people? Do you realize that these unlettered men have very much to do in making up the 84 per cent. of the majority of the United States Senate, and are no inferior factor in determining the character of the House of Representatives? Charge what you will of the illiteracy among the whites of the South to the system of American slavery, yet it is a fact we must meet, that almost all over the South illiteracy is increasing. Look at Kentucky, with 106,000, and North Carolina, with 96,000 white persons, 21 years old and over, who cannot write. Tennessee gave birth and being to the first antislavery paper published on this continent. Yet beautiful, fertile, liberty-loving Tennessee has to-day nearly 72,000 white women who cannot write their names. These are the mothers of your coming statesmen, who hold, and will hold, so firm a grip upon the balance of political power in the nation. And this ratio of power cannot diminish, for this section of country will not depopulate while this climate retains so much of paradise.

The States of Tennessee, Georgia, North Carolina, South Carolina, and Arkansas return as unable to write a net increase of white boys and girls, from 10 to 15 inclusive, in 1880, of about 30,000 above the same class in 1870. They will be men and women when the next record is made. Pardon me if I still ask your attention to these figures. In 1870 Alabama returns, as unable to write, 31,001 white women and 17,429 white men, 21 and over. In 1880, in the same class, she returned 35,724 women and 24,450 men, a net increase of illiterate men and women of 11,743. In the same class, in 1880, Tennessee returned 71,786 white women and 46,948 white men as unable to write, a net increase of illiterates, in ten years, of 12,196. In the same period Georgia had gained, in the same class, 9,271. And the proud old State of Kentucky had made, in the same decade, a net gain of the same class of illiterates of 18,172.

In the presence of his foes, I would not let the wing of the American eagle touch the dust. But, in the midst of his friends, let me speak the truth. Has it occurred to you that in our proud America about 13 per cent. of our white boys and girls, 10 to 14 inclusive, cannot write?

Please change your point of outlook again, and test our strength. Now Jersey has 7.2 per cent. of white women, 21 and over, who cannot write. But put New Jersey and Alabama together, and *they* have a population, of this class, of 20.3 per cent. New York has 7.3 per cent. of white women, 21 and over,

who cannot write. But put New York and North Carolina together, and *they* have, of the same class, 22.7. Take the 4.1 per cent. of Maine, and join it with South Carolina, and *they* have 24.9 white women, 21 and over, who cannot write. Another feature rendering this question still more important to the nation is its geographical relation. This dark yet snowless belt lies in and stretches across the very heart of the continent. Commerce, leaving the smoking factories of New England, may reach the tea fields of Japan and China by a route nearly 1,000 miles less than by the Golden Gate. And, again, the abundance of water-power, and absence of frost to interfere with machinery, is a guarantee that our crude material will be manufactured at home. Unless special attention is given to this question, history will here repeat itself, and the per cent. of illiteracy will increase with our incoming manufacturing population.

In the presence of these facts, we are forced to the question: What can we do for these people? Some one has said that public roads are great civilizers in any country. These we lack. There are splendid exceptions, but in the mountain regions they are still trails about the same as when Boone and Crockett dodged or dared the Indian upon them. Settlements, ten miles apart by straight line, have no communication but by footman or rider. They could have good roads, but do not. But the great want is common schools; not a *system only*, but a great, active, live fact of making men and women out of this crude material. It is not impossible to find some walking fossils yet in the South who oppose the common schools. It tends to destroy good breeding, you know. Yet these are going out of sight—to heaven, I suppose—as fast as a well-bred corner can be fitted up for them. The demand for a reading manhood is blotting out this folly—let it go.

The college and university have their work to do in the South. But the great demand is for the improvement and invigoration of the common school. The South, or any country, must have public schools, or fail. Can you sustain the river system of any country without the mountain springs and foot-hill rivulets? Neither can a healthy, vigorous life flow through any nation, giving green banks and fresh fields, but from a healthy common-school system. In the sections for which we particularly plead, school buildings (except when church buildings are used for that purpose) are a failure, and as devoid of comfort as the moon is of heat. Perhaps a taste for better school building must follow, not precede, a higher state of culture. In this region school furniture is almost unknown, and the seating is as crude as a rail. The per capita school fund is supposed to sustain the schools for five months in each

3

section. But here there is often a difference between theory and practice.

It might not be wise to invest large sums in permanent buildings, but in the normal-school work and that of practical teaching. Too much cannot be said in favor of normal-school work for this country. Guard the disbursement of this fund carefully. It must not become the patronage of any political party, but should be most emphatically a fund for the people, with this one distinct thought in its creation and use—to aid the poor to learn to read and write. As in the North and East, the higher institutions of learning will largely be sustained by funds which flow naturally through denominational channels. But the public school cannot, must not, be denominational. But it is important that a fund be created at once, sufficient to sustain competent teachers all over this field. Take one more fact which you may gather from the United States census of 1870 and 1880. We will make our estimate from nine of the States which lie in this dark belt—Alabama, Georgia, North Carolina, South Carolina, Tennessee, Virginia, West Virginia, Kentucky, and Arkansas. By comparing the census of 1870 with that of 1880, you will find a net increase of illiterate white men and women, 21 and over, in those nine States, of a little more than 105,000. I do not, dare not, comment here further than simply raise the question: How long can this record continue with safety to the national life? You will observe that I have not taken into this count the 84.1 per cent. of colored men and the 86.5 per cent. of colored women in Alabama; the 87.2 of colored women and 76.4 colored men of Georgia; the 84.7 colored women and 78.2 colored men in North Carolina; the 85.5 colored women and 73 of colored men in South Carolina, and the 78.2 per cent. of colored women in Tennessee. But I have held my calculations closely to the conditions of the poor whites of the South. Yet the fact that North Carolina can show that 33.4 per cent. of her white women cannot write, does not give a correct view of the illiteracy of this class known as the "poor whites." If you were to count out those who do not properly belong to this class, but belong to the planters and their families, and the whites who have recently moved into this country,

it would, doubtless, raise the percentage of illiterates of this class, in the places mentioned, to from 70 to 80 per cent. of their population. Yet they are not heathen, but blood of our blood. These are almost exclusively Protestant, and largely members of Christian churches, of whom the Baptists have by far the larger enumeration. With the illiterate immigration from the Old World, and the disintegrating effect of home ignorance, even America cannot stand. Age and strength have not been the heritage of any nation which has neglected the education of her people. And America, never conquered and never to be conquered by a foreign foe, must take warning by the fate of nations, and care for her illiterates, or history must repeat itself in another national failure. New York may possibly become a little Rome, in the midst of an immense, ignorant people. Boston may become a Venice by the sea, but the glory of a nation cannot depend upon her universities alone—her masses must read.

Where is the hand—perhaps by Providence concealed—which shall remove this huge, this awful, wart from the fair brow of the Goddess of American Liberty? Were I a political party, were I looking toward the electing of the President of these United States in 1884, I would plant myself firmly on this plank—government aid for the illiterates of this nation, such aid to be distributed in proportion to the illiteracy of each State and Territory.

Has it occurred to you that, say, nine tenths of this money would be distributed where three fourths of the electoral votes are created, and that these votes cannot fail of being largely influenced in favor of the party standing on this plank? If my political party were as sure of heaven as of success under such circumstances, I think I would cut the rope, throw out the ballast, and translate at once. If retrenchment be necessary, we can bear it anywhere better than carry this body of death. Let the postage remain as it was, let the harbors and rivers wear and waste for a while, and turn, if need be, the tide of internal improvements in our midst, which time must waste away, to the eternal improvement of our boys and girls, which the friction of the ages can only brighten.

On motion of Rev. Dr. M. E. STRIEBY, of New York, the National Education Assembly of 1883 adopted the following:

Resolved, That the Constitutional duty to provide for the safety of the Republic is in full force at all times, and in the face of all dangers; and that, in urging Congress to deal immediately and adequately with the problem of illiteracy, which has assumed appalling proportions, we are only asking it to meet this obligation—the discharge of which cannot be called a charity, the neglect of which must prove a fatal crime.

III. NATIONAL AID TO COMMON SCHOOLS.

1. THE YEAR'S WORK.

REPORT BY PROF. C. C. PAINTER,

Corresponding Secretary National Education Committee.

IT is difficult to report the unreportable. An assiduous, and ardent lover may indeed present an elaborate and exact statistical exhibit of the calls, visits, and presents made during a given time, all of which may possibly bear no certain relation to a real progress in his effort to gain the hand of his shy mistress. Something of the same difficulty embarrasses your secretary in the report expected of him to-day.

To say that six thousand circular letters, more or less, were sent to leading educators throughout the country for further distribution by them, asking co-operation in this effort to secure national aid to common schools, and that several hundred letters have been received in reply, unanimous in their assurances of sympathy and help; that several thousand blank petitions have been circulated for signatures, and the names of from forty thousand to fifty thousand petitioners have been received and presented to Congress from twenty-three States and several Territories; that eight different States have, either by formal joint resolution by the Legislatures, or petitions signed by members of the Legislatures and by the executive officers, asked the national Congress to grant the aid we seek: that resolutions passed by conventions and associations of superintendents, teachers, and Boards of Education; by representative religious bodies, etc., etc., in various States; petitions by the trustees, professors, and pupils of many colleges,—that enough of these have come up during the year to lumber the pigeon-holes of the committees to whom they were referred, and call forth serious protest from some Senators against their being spread out on the pages of the Congressional Record: all this, while it shows that a sentiment is growing throughout the entire country and is uttering itself in the ears of Congress, demanding that these things shall be done, while it gives great hope, yet does not enable us to mark any certain progress toward the consummation we desire.

Certain it is that when this sentiment becomes general and outspoken, it will be respected and obeyed, but as yet the average Congressman regards it simply as the opinion of sentimental educators and philanthropists, and not of the practical politician who constructs the platforms and runs the caucuses of his party; a sentiment to which he may bow a profound reverence due to the character of those who utter it, but, as yet, one he is not bound to obey, since it has not been taken up and expressed by the "boys" of the district which he represents.

That this report is made by the Secretary of the National Education Committee—a committee created by the great assembly of last year, and of the broad constituency which it represented, of itself marks a long step in advance of the previous year, when, as a member of the faculty of Fisk University, he was detached and sent on this special duty by the American Missionary Association, aided by certain persons in Boston, Philadelphia, and New York, whose co-operation and pecuniary assistance were secured by General Armstrong, of Hampton, Virginia. The effort first made to enlist the moral and pecuniary support of the societies now represented in this committee failed, and the work done by him was done under the embarrassment of suspicions that he might be seeking some denominational end or advantage. Fortunately, through the efforts of Dr. Hartzell, the work was broadened, not in its nature, conception, or aim, but in its constituency, by the organization effected last year, and has of necessity gained immensely by it. The aim first enunciated, and the methods and purposes first adopted, have been, without modification, adhered to and urged: National aid to the common schools of the States and Territories distributed on the basis of illiteracy; help *immediate*, and not *remote*—from such sources as Congress may deem wisest, and so given as to stimulate, not supersede, local effort, and so administered as not to interfere with local systems and methods, and yet under such supervision as will secure, in the most efficient way, with equal justice to all classes of citizens, the end sought; this was the object first announced, and the one to which we have strictly adhered during the past year.

The facts showing the necessity of this aid, the appalling increase of illiteracy among the voters of the country, and the inadequacy, not alone of the schools already existing in many of the States, but the impossibility of sustaining a sufficient number, the practical limit of taxation having been reached—these facts were gathered and urged upon the attention of the public by distinguished men in all parts of the country, whose co-operation was secured in one way or another. They were urged upon the attention of the Legislatures of the various States, upon conventions and associations of influential men, wherever opportunity offered. They were spread before the public through the press, and then, in various ways, gathered up and brought to bear upon the Committees of Education and Labor in two Houses of Congress, until action was secured. Two bills were reported to the Senate supplementary of each other—one proposing a permanent fund from the sale of public lands and other sources, which will be available in the future; the other proposing immediate and adequate temporary help from moneys already in the treasury, to be distributed, on the basis of illiteracy, to the States, and expended by them under the joint supervision of an official appointed by the State and a federal officer, also a citizen of the State, appointed by the President.

In the House a bill was also reported by the Committee on Education and Labor, proposing temporary aid—$10,000,000 per annum, for five years—to be administered by the State Boards of Education of the several States, making a satisfactory report to the Secretary of the Interior as to the expenditure of each year, as a condition of receiving its apportionment for the succeeding year. These bills could not secure a place on the calendar which gave any chance of consideration by the last Congress except by a test vote under suspension of the rules—a vote which clearly foreshadowed their passage had there been time to consider them. They had the right of way on the calendar when Congress died by constitutional limitation, and but for want of time there is little doubt that some one of them, or a new one with slight modifications, would have passed.

When the committees in both Houses had favorably reported bills in favor of such aid, there was no need of urging the necessity of such legislation upon them, and so the work of the last was quite different from that of the previous year.

Then it was with and before the committees almost exclusively; during the past year it has been with the members at large; therefore more scattered and more difficult. It has been the object of your secretary to find out, by a personal interview, the attitude of the leading men of the different sections toward this measure, and, when found to be hostile, or doubtful, to secure, if possible, the co-operation of some wise and influential man in the effort to convert him; and, if that wise and influential man happened to be one of his constituents, this fact has not been found to be hurtful, for it may as well be confessed that controlling motives and influences must be sought, for the average leader of his party, not always in the beneficial results of proposed legislation to the nation at large, but in the view the voters of Podunk, and White Oaks, and other voting precincts in his district are likely to take of it.

The work of the year has been, therefore, of such character as to discover, not alone what the members of Congress think of the measure, but also what they think the voters at home are thinking about it, and the judgment formed by your secretary and other friends of this measure in position to judge is such as to give great hope that what we seek for will be done. Those who had charge of, and the responsibility for, the National Education Association last year know how difficult it was to secure any, even respectable, not to say adequate, consideration from the members of the press. A single line or paragraph of common-place mention of our meetings, where a horse-trot or walking-match commanded squares and columns. Some degree of urgency might secure the insertion of a brief article on the subject in some of the dailies if they were not too much crowded. This was about all that we were able to do up to the beginning of last year, but, during the past winter and spring, leading papers in New York, Philadelphia, Boston, Providence, Hartford, Springfield, Albany, Cleveland, Cincinnati, Chicago, Louisville, Washington, Baltimore, and in all the principal cities of the South, have, again and again, urged upon Congress the immediate and urgent necessity of national legislation in behalf of education.

The literature published on this subject, outside of the speeches made in Congress, would make quite a large volume. An immense meeting, called in Cleveland, Ohio, last October, in connection with the annual exercises of the American Association, in behalf of this object, was addressed by ex-President Hayes, Pres. A. D. White, of Cornell University, and Dr. Curry, of Richmond, Va. Their able addresses were printed, not alone in the papers of that city and widely circulated, but also by that Association, and a large number put at the disposal of your secretary for circulation.

Early in November a large gathering was held in the chapel of Fisk University, Nashville, Tenn., addressed by Prof. Northrop, of Yale College, and Pres. A. G. Haygood, of Ga., agent of the Slater Fund. Their addresses on this topic were printed and widely circulated through the South. In December an invitation was extended to Hon. John Eaton to address the Union League of New York on this subject, and this able and exhaustive address was published by the League, and circulated directly by itself and partly through your secretary among the leading men of the country. The Union League of Philadelphia, in January last, invited the Hon. Commissioner of Education to repeat the address before its members, which also ordered an edition of the address for its use and circulation, and subsequently, so great was the interest awakened, invited Dr. Mayo, of Boston, and your secretary to address it on the same subject. Dr. Hartzell and Bishop Simpson also addressed the League.

Meetings of a similar character and fully attended have been held in Washington, Richmond, and other cities, especially in the South, where the necessity for the action we seek has become so urgent that no opportunity for giving expression to it goes unimproved.

If time allowed it might with truth be said that the secretaries and managers of these great societies, represented here to-day, have become missionaries of this new crusade, and have preached it whenever opportunity has offered. Such men as Dr. Curry, Dr. Mayo, and Pres. Haygood have gone up and down the land preaching it.

The complexion of the next Congress is very greatly changed, and much of the work that has been done must be done over again, because some of the most earnest advocates of this measure are no longer members of the House; but it is not believed that the prospect is less hopeful for our measure on this account.

The conviction is gaining ground that the national government has a constitutional duty to discharge in this matter. Constitutional objections to such action are beginning to give way before the more logical and constitutional position that Congress cannot discharge its constitutional obligation to secure to each State a Republican government except as it secures to it the conditions of such a government. This cannot be done by bayonets and the armaments of war, but by the school-master, who is a more legitimate and constitutional officer in a republic than is the recruiting-sergeant.

Thought and discussion of this subject are leading many back to the ground, considered fundamental by the fathers and founders of the nation, that a republic can stand only in the intelligence and virtue of its citizens, and that the first and most imperative duty of government is to provide for its own life, by providing these prime conditions of life. Each of the several States can and must say to the parents of its future citizen: "I have an interest in the education of your child, which I cannot allow you for any reason to jeopardize by neglect; if you are too poor to educate him, I will provide the school; if you are too ignorant, or so avaricious that you will not do it, I will compel it. He must not and shall not grow up in such ignorance of his duties that he is of necessity a danger to the public safety."

If the State must take this ground—and no sane man who believes in a Republican form of government can deny that it must, it seems to many a very short and not illogical step to the conclusion that the general government may say to the several States: "I have an interest with you in the education of your voters which I cannot and will not suffer you to neglect. I cannot hand over to others absolutely, and so place beyond my power and right to control, conditions which are essential to my own existence. If you cannot qualify those whose votes are to affect my life for the duties with which they are charged, then I will help you take such measures as are necessary to my own safety. If you will not, then I must take your ignorant voters under my own supervision, and will either disfranchise them, or see that they are qualified to vote."

Whether it is wise for the general government to take the education of its citizens out of the hands of the several States, and do it by its own agents, is like the question whether it is wise for the several States to abolish the local school-boards, and attempt the work of education by State officials. The answer is obvious. Certainly the local board can do it best. But if in any locality there is no school, either because of the poverty of the people, or their unwillingness to educate their children, can any one doubt the right of the State to deal with the case as in its wisdom it sees best?

The work which we begun is by no means completed, and its urgency is not less, but greater. There is increasing evidence that the end sought will be secured by a patient continuance in well doing on our part.

The moral support given by the organization accomplished last year was great, but not all that it might have been. In many ways it can be made more efficient, and it is hoped that your attention may be directed to this end.

But it may be confidentially whispered,

in your ears, that the pecuniary support from the organization was nothing at all. The plan proposed was found impracticable; and, as a matter of fact, the effort did not receive the support it otherwise would, since those who had supported it deemed it unnecessary to do so with all of these societies represented on its executive committee. And so the support for the last year was: $500 pledged and secured by Dr. Strieby, of New York; a like sum pledged by Gen. Armstrong: and $100 more from three gentlemen in Philadelphia, New York, and New Britain, Conn., making in all $1,100 for the necessities of the year's work.

When your secretary had paid out $250 of this for necessary travel, printing, and postage, but little was left to support himself and family, and the work necessarily suffered from want of funds to do many things which must be done in all successful efforts to create, awaken, gather, and make efficient a public sentiment for the purpose of shaping national legislation.

It is evident that a decisive halt has been called in the reduction of revenue. The producing interests of the country are manifestly opposed to reducing the duties on imports, and no statesman having the fear of his political enemies before his eyes, on the eve of a presidential campaign, will dare to propose such a measure. Despite the reductions effected last winter it is safe to say the surplus of the present year will be $100,-000,000, and this will continue as long as our laws remain as now.

This surplus will pay off the only indebtedness which the government has the privilege of paying before 1891, (the sum of $336,286,950,) in three and one third years; and so during the next five years, money would accumulate at the rate of $100,000,000 per annum.

What we are to do with this is a question which is beginning to trouble our politicians, as was evident in the recent conventions of both political parties in Pennsylvania; as also to our publicists, as you may have seen from recent articles in the *Philadelphia North American.*

Let it be the work of those represented here to-day, to convince our national Legislature, that this is a work more vitally related to our national welfare than the opening of some stream for interstate commerce which is known only to the influential politician who has a mill upon it, and one demanding immediate attention, upon which some of this money may be wisely expended.

We would deprecate as utterly ruinous a reckless tossing of large sums of money into the States which would demoralize their efforts to sustain their own schools. We would deplore any and all assistance or interference which would weaken the interest of the local school-district in the support and management of its own schools, as disastrous; but, on the other hand, the reckless manner in which National and State legislation has thrust the ballot into the hands of millions of voters who have no proper qualification for the duties with which they are charged, and who have no ability to qualify themselves for them, has created an emergency of such vast and urgent proportions that no power short of that of the national government can deal with it.

We grant the difficulties and dangers of what is demanded but at the same time assert that those to be met are so much greater and more immediate, that the wisdom must be evolved which shall disarm them, or our republic will sink under them.

The danger is from the ignorance and consequent vice of the voters; this ignorance can be enlightened alone by the schoolmaster with adequate school facilities; these cannot be furnished by many of the States, and must be provided by the Nation at large. To do this wisely is the duty and task of statesmanship. It is ours, as an association seeking this, to emphasize this necessity, and to demand of our representatives that they furnish a solution for the problem or give place to those who can; for the solution must be found, and found speedily.

---

2. NATIONAL AID TO POPULAR EDUCATION IN EUROPE.

HON. J. P. WICKERSHAM, OF PENNSYLVANIA,

Ex-United States Consul to Denmark.

NO one desires the Government of the United States to undertake the control of popular education. This duty is best discharged by the several States, each for itself.

Esteeming an educated people the only safeguard of free institutions, patriotic statesmen, at different periods of our history, have advocated the policy of granting aid to popular education from the national treasury. This question has assumed special importance at the present time. It has been of late much discussed in Congress and before the people; several of our Presidents have expressed themselves strongly on the subject, and the educational necessities of a considerable portion of the Union are such that the agitation will most likely grow in intensity until the issue shall be finally settled.

Personally, I am opposed to any intermeddling on the part of the general government with the practical work of popular education. A National Bureau of Education, organized like ours at Washington, is an admirable instrumentality for disseminating information concerning education, but any enlargement of its powers that would tend to remove the management of the schools from the hands of the people would be, in my opinion, a fatal mistake. Holding these sentiments, I am still warmly in favor of aiding, in a judicious way, by appropriations from the national treasury, the struggling school systems of the South. As a Northern man, a Pennsylvanian, I am not particularly anxious for aid to our schools from the general government. As a fixed policy, I can see many objections to it. Here, at the North, we can maintain our own schools, and I am not at all sure it is not best for us to do it. But with the hope of bettering the educational condition of the States of the South and giving them something like a fair start' in the work of establishing schools, with the hope of helping them lift themselves from under a weight of ignorance that must crush them down or reduce them to a state of barbarism, for the sake of the whole Union, which is strong only in the strength of all its parts, I am ready to give my voice for the appropriation of a generous sum by Congress to aid, while the existing necessity continues, that section of the country which so badly needs such help.

Popular education is regulated, to a greater or less extent, by the central government in every nation in Europe, except Switzerland. Next to Switzerland, the people exercise most control in the management of their schools in the British Islands, but elsewhere they have about as little to say respecting schools and teachers as they have respecting armies and soldiers. This policy necessarily determines, to a great extent, the source from which the schools obtain the funds that support them. Centralized systems of public instruction must be maintained and strengthened by grants of money from the central power, and such grants are made on a liberal scale by nearly all the nations of Europe.

England has a complicated system of public instruction. Under the Act of Parliament passed in 1870, and its supplements of 1873 and 1876, there are schools in London and elsewhere throughout the kingdom called "Board Schools," organized very much like the American common schools; but elementary instruction in England, up to

the present time, remains mainly in the hands of societies established under Church auspices. The government has never attempted to make full provision for the support of schools, but the policy of aiding local effort by grants of money from the national treasury was adopted as early as 1839, at which time £30,000 were set aside for this purpose. In 1846 the grant was £100,000, and in 1859 £836,000. At present there is at the seat of government in London an Education Department, with powers of a general character, and an efficient system of school inspection is in operation, extending to the denominational as well as to the board schools. Grants of money are made to every school inspected on certain conditions concerning the school premises, the length of time the school remains in session, the attendance of the pupils and their proficiency in study, and the kind of instruction imparted. Account is also taken of the financial ability of the locality or organization supporting a school. These grants, in 1875, amounted to £1,356,746 19s. 5d., of which £1,093,378 18s. 8d. were given for instruction, £34,491 13s. 2d. for building and furnishing school-houses, and £94,376 19s. 4d. for the support of training-colleges or normal schools for teachers. In 1882 the grants from the national treasury for educational purposes in England and Wales had increased to the magnificent sum, expressed in our currency, of $13,749,315. The government does not build a single school-house or manage a single school; the money is given to aid the local authorities, to whom the practical work of education is intrusted.

The elementary schools of Scotland and Ireland are supported in much the same way as in England. In 1882 the grants of Parliament for educational purposes in Scotland amounted to $1,736,160; and in Ireland, for the national schools alone, to $2,677,080.

A Republic in name, France still retains the main features of the University of France, instituted by Napoleon in 1808, which centralized in one vast corporation all the educational institutions, from the primary school to the college, and all the teaching forces of the country. The French army is not more compactly organized, better officered, or more under the control of the central power, than the French system of public instruction. The expense of supporting this great system is met partly by the nation at large, and partly by the departments and the communes into which France is divided. Every commune, which is the smallest territorial division, must provide its own school-houses and teachers' residences, but, where most needed, aid in the discharge of this duty is generously given from the national treasury. If a commune neglects or refuses to impose a tax for school purposes, the government takes its place in the performance of this duty; but if it happens that a commune, on account of poverty, disaster to crops, depression in business, or the devastation of war, is unable to pay a school tax, the government makes up the deficiency, so that no calamity is allowed to deprive French children of the privilege of an education. As much can hardly be said of all the children in the United States. Like generosity is sometimes extended to a whole department, a territorial division corresponding to one of our States. The more fortunate sections of the country seem to approve the course of the government in helping the weak and allowing the strong to help themselves, and no one is known to have ever risen in the national councils to complain that such treatment is either unfair or unjust. Every wise father governs his household on this principle; and to this extent parental government is of universal application among the nations of the earth.

The King of Prussia was crowned Emperor of Germany at Versailles in 1871. A constitution for the Empire was adopted the same year. This constitution provides for a Minister of Public Instruction, and furnishes ground for certain general legislation on the subject of education. But there is no system of education in Germany common to the whole country, although such a system has many advocates, and would be in accord with the present centralizing tendencies of the Empire. As it is now, each Kingdom, Grand Duchy, Duchy, Principality, etc., of which the Empire is composed, is left undisturbed in the power it has long exercised of supporting and managing its own schools. Alsace and Lorraine constitute a notable exception to this imperial policy. In these conquered provinces educational affairs are directed from Berlin through the German general; and, with a view to the healing of the wounds of the past, and attaching the people to the government that now rules them, special grants of money for school purposes have been made from the treasury of the Empire. The old University at Strasburg, which had been broken up and its buildings partially destroyed during the war, received at one time a grant of a million of Prussian thalers, and, in addition, there has been voted to it an annual allowance of two hundred and twenty thousand thalers. Such an example of reconstruction deserves to be imitated in America.

In Prussia, the general policy is to support elementary schools by local taxation and by fees paid by the pupils; but aid is generously given to communities unable to maintain schools for themselves in the manner prescribed by law and to special institutions of learning of various kinds. The money thus appropriated, in 1882, amounted to $10,000,000. Bavaria votes an annual sum for the salaries of teachers, pensions to su-

perannuated teachers and the widows and orphans of teachers, and for other educational purposes. In 1882 the sum voted was $4,000,000. In Saxony, in 1882, the government expenditures for education amounted to $1,500,000; in Würtemberg, to $2,000,000; in Baden, to $488,547.

Of other European countries, according to statistics compiled by the Bureau of Education at Washington, the government of Russia expended, in 1882, for education, $9,000,000; Austria, including Hungary, $8,800,000; Italy,. $6,000,000; Belgium, $2,467,400; Denmark, $320,000; the Netherlands, $2,500,000; Sweden and Norway, $2,900,000; Portugal, $500,000. Switzerland makes annual appropriations for the support of the National Polytechnic School at Zurich, but her elementary schools are wholly supported by local taxation.

The brief statement now made shows, first, that national aid to popular education is almost universal among the nations of Europe; and, second, that in distributing the money discrimination is almost everywhere made in favor of those sections in the several countries which are the weakest financially, or which for any reason are unable to carry forward the work of education for themselves.

There is in the example of European countries, with respect to the management of their school affairs, much that is worthy of imitation in the United States; but it must be added that their centralized systems of public instruction are ill adapted to the political condition of this country. It is, without doubt, best for us to continue the policy of intrusting the control of our common schools to the several States and to the counties and townships into which they are divided. I am well convinced that with us the more fully the management of these schools is placed in the hands of the people, the stronger and the better will be our system of popular education. Cut off this root and most likely it would die. An individual succeeds in acquiring knowledge, succeeds in business, succeeds in any undertaking whatever, in proportion as he depends upon himself, relies upon his own resources. A nation is but an aggregation of individuals, and that line of conduct which gives most strength to one will give most strength to the whole. In respect to popular education, the principle of local self-government is a vital one in a republic, and should be guarded with the utmost care.

But as an exception to the general educational policy which I deem best in a government like ours, as a step pressingly demanded by the existing state of affairs in a large portion of the country, I think it would be eminently wise and just for Congress to make a contribution, or a series of contributions, in aid of the feeble educational systems of the South; and, if I could have my way, I would make them in a scale so liberal as to place a school within the reach of every child now suffering for the want of instruction. The same hand that struck down the rebellion should now be outstretched with kindliest help to supply the Southland's greatest need—the education of her people. That statesmanship is extremely narrow which votes money without stint to destroy and conquer, and has nothing to spare to repair the waste places and to heal the gaping wounds left by the storm. There is as much patriotism to-day in keeping an army of school-masters in the South for the purposes of peace, as there once was in sending thither an army of soldiers for the purposes of war.

Besides, national aid to the educational systems of the South is a matter of self-defense. A political body, like the national body, is weakened by the weakness of any of its members.

If the South could bear her own burdens, if she could, unaided, lift herself from the slough in which she struggles, it might be best to allow her to help herself; but her most courageous men see little hope of this, and work on in despair. With one accord, they declare that without help she will never be able to dissipate the dense ignorance that darkens the whole country and clogs every avenue to progress and prosperity. Says one who has been foremost among the school officers of the South, and who has had the amplest opportunities of knowing where-

of he speaks: "We must educate or surrender. We can become the Bœotia, the Ireland, the Poland, of the American government. We can die as to civilization, as many States have died before; we can hang as a body of death on the back of the great republic." And then he adds, with fearful emphasis, "Does the nation desire this?" So sad a condition of affairs in the South can be bettered in only one way: prompt, generous help from the United States government. As we have seen, Great Britain apportions her grants to schools so as to give most help to those districts whose necessities are greatest. France generously builds school-houses and pays the salaries of teachers in communes where the people are too poor to do it for themselves. Germany stretches out her broad hand to help even those who still hate her in Alsace and Lorraine. A loss of crops or the devastations of war in a province of any country in Europe brings special aid to its educational institutions from the parent government. Let the United States, with a full treasury, be equally broad in her policy and magnanimous in her appropriations. The money thus given, like seed sown in good ground, will bring forth fruit a hundred-fold, in gratitude from the beneficiaries, in millions of children rescued from ignorance worse than death, in a new Union, greater, grander, more prosperous, more deeply rooted in the affections of the people than any of which by-gone patriots ever dreamed.

3. CONDITIONS AND PROSPECTS OF TEMPORARY NATIONAL AID TO COMMON SCHOOLS.

HON. H. W. BLAIR,

United States Senator from New Hampshire.

THERE can be no doubt of the power and, consequently, whenever the need exists, of the duty, of the nation to secure the education of the people so that they may intelligently enjoy and exercise the rights of citizenship. This power is inherent in the nation, and is its chief weapon of self-defense as well as of progressive life. It has been exercised from time to time, to a limited extent, during nearly the whole period of our history, and has never failed to be proclaimed by the most eminent patriots and statesmen as the corner-stone of republican institutions. If we are ever to make any advance in this world some things must be taken as already proved to be true; and therefore I shall on this occasion assume,

first, that the sun shines; and, second, that the nation has the constitutional power to give national aid of a pecuniary nature to common schools.

I am willing to concede, for the purposes of this case, as the lawyers say, that the power should not be exercised so long as the family and the local communities in the States and Territories are able, without bearing unjust burdens, to properly educate their children, and do actually perform that duty.

The real question, then, which arises between the friends of wise measures for giving national aid to common schools, and those, if any there be, who object to such appropriations of the public money, is this: Is there such danger to national citizenship and national republican institutions, arising from the ignorance, present or prospective, of the common people, as to justify the expenditure of the common funds, for the common good, in the support of common schools ? Elsewhere I have had the honor to give to the public such facts and arguments as seemed to me to be pertinent to the subject. The debate has proceeded now for at least two years, with a constantly growing conviction in the minds of the American people that such aid is indispensable to the safety and permanence of the republic. I believe that the overwhelming sentiment of thoughtful citizens is that such assistance must be given, and given *now*; that, in no matter of vital human concern was ever delay more needless or more dangerous, and that, in fact, whenever the Congress of the United States shall be again in session, the great practical question will be found to be not *what* shall be done, but *how* shall it be done; not whether aid shall be given at all, but upon what terms and conditions, and in what way, shall the most judicious and profitable application of the public money be made to the purposes of common-school education.

Questions of practical detail are not, for the reason that the necessity that something be done is generally conceded, of any the less importance, nor are they less really obstacles to the desired result.

How to frame a bill making the desired appropriation, so as to actually get a warrant which will draw the money from the treasury, and distribute its beneficent influences throughout the land, is a matter of supreme consequence; for, if no bill whatever becomes a law, the effect is the same, or worse even, than if it failed, because there was no admitted necessity for its passage.

I believe that the expenditure of national money can only be made for national uses; that it can be justified in support of common schools only because the national good requires the education of the national child who is to become the national citizen; that the best possible way to expend the money of the nation is under the supervision of officers having a direct responsibility to the government; that, when the State and the nation expend money jointly for a common end, there should be a joint supervision thereof; that, when the States maintain school systems adequate in extent and quality for the proper education of the children who are to become citizens of the State and the nation alike, the nation should not interfere; when the State fails, from any cause whatever, so to do, then the nation, *ex necessitate*, must interfere in self-defense, and interfering thus is no trespass upon State rights whatever, for the right of the State to educate the children within her borders is not an exclusive right. It is a duty, but not a duty even which it alone can discharge. It is a national right, the duty to exercise which arises when the State fails to discharge it. It is a right and duty which both State and nation owe to the rising generation. It is their joint tribute to the high destinies of the human race, and a tribute which must be paid by them, either severally or jointly, to avoid the destruction of both, and in no other way can the nation fulfill its guaranty of a Republican form of government to the States, or secure that form to herself.

Therefore it is that while I believe the proper way to secure the best application of national money to the education of the children of the whole people is by direct supervision and control by the nation wherever, in States and Territories, no schools are provided by local authorities, and by a joint supervision of State and national officers—the functions of both being united in the same person, so as to avoid division of effort whenever it is deemed desirable, and thus the compensation of these underpaid officials, being increased by their combined salaries so as to secure to their high talents and lofty devotion something above the starvation wages for which they now, in the most needy States, wear out their invaluable lives: that I *also* believe, if it is necessary in order to secure the great end itself, to place the national money in the hands of the States, in trust for its proper expenditure for the common good of both nation and State, and of the children, who are both the nation and the State which is to be: that the nation has the right to make the appropriations and expend them directly through the authorities of the States.

This is no surrender of the right of the nation to educate her children within her utmost borders. It is, rather, the exercise of that right through local instrumentalities. It is as though the nation should see fit to exercise its powers of defense against foreign or domestic violence through State officers and armies, and by State laws and State forms. But it might be necessary to do so even under these disadvantages rather than not at all; and I am rejoiced to say that the developments of the last few years, in those portions of the country where national aid to schools is chiefly required, demonstrate, in my belief, the general, though not universal, determination of the people and of the local powers, sacredly and honestly, to apply all obtainable moneys to the removal of the great curse of illiteracy from the masses of the people.

Such is my own sense of the exceeding gravity of the situation that I am in favor of *any* reasonable bill which appropriates the money rather than that no bill be passed. It is not a case which admits of delay, nor of long deliberation as to the precise method in which the remedy is to be administered. Money is the specific for the disease, and the main thing is to get the medicine into the patient—the body politic at large. It is not so much matter whether the national doctors, or the State doctors, or men holding diplomas from both institutions, give the dose, as that it be taken, and in allopathic quantities. Fortunately, the disease is one where the patient is ready to receive this particular medicine from almost any hand. I should prefer that the institution which furnishes the medicine should have something to say in its administration, but this nation is too sick of the wounds and bruises and deadly diseases which grow out of the all-prevailing and increasing ignorance of the common people, to justify much delay or haggling over secondary questions. I will venture further to say, however, that I believe all danger of conflict in administration between State and Federal officers is purely imaginary, and is born of prejudices of the past that should have no place in this new era in which the interests, the hopes, and the destiny of the individual and the nation, of the county and of the continent, are, and should forever remain, "one and inseparable."

But, sir, this great assemblage of ability, stirred by devotion to a great cause, will be useless as a glorious sound in the air unless it stimulates the performance of practical things, which shall result in actual legislation for appropriations from the national treasury.

The prose and poetry of our theme should be just this: The common schools and an appropriation. Education, physical, industrial, intellectual, and moral, is the primal necessity; and money is the one agency which can purchase this, like every other good thing. The direct effort of every man who comprehends this great emergency in the affairs of the people is indispensable, in order to bring home to the legislators of the country the will of the masses, that these appropriations be made. I have never conversed five minutes upon the subject of national aid to common schools with a voter, who was not also a member of Congress, without listening to expressions of strong approval on his part. The people desire it, and are surprised that any one should oppose it. But this universal sentiment unvoiced is like the electric forces of all nature locked up by insulation. You must let this sentiment loose, and make the electric connection with the hands and hearts of your Senators and Congressmen. These public servants are always ready to obey the general, well defined, and unmistakable will of their constituents. The appropriation of national money directly to the support of schools has never been made. It is not strange, then, that unusual and emphatic and comprehensive manifestations of the public will should be waited for before the necessary legisla-

tion can be obtained; nor that the representatives of those sections which expect comparatively small direct benefit should be sensitive and careful as to terms and conditions and results for which their constituents will hold them strictly responsible. There should be at once a grand effort inaugurated all along the line, and throughout the whole country, to secure an expression of the public will upon the appropriation of national aid to common schools.

All the powers of the press, the pulpit, the platform, and of personal intercourse, should be called into full action. If every editor in this country who believes in it would write one strong editorial, and every clergyman would preach one powerful sermon, and every lecturer, who could appropriately, would utter one eloquent sentence for national aid for common schools within the next six months, any reasonable bill would pass Congress by a two-thirds vote at the next session, and be at once heartily approved by the President.

But the most powerful weapon of all is the right of petition. In a free country, to petition is to command. The people should exercise it. Every citizen of the country should send his memorial to the Congress which he has created, demanding national aid to common schools. This convention can initiate and conduct a movement which shall bring to every member of the House and Senate the prayer of his constituents for national aid to common schools. Let circulars be prepared, and every one of the ten million voters in the United States be given the opportunity to make his petition for national aid to common schools. Let every religious and educational organization, every association of mechanics and laborers and craftsmen of every degree; every order, society, grange, and institution, whether of learning, benevolence, or of industry, in the land, whose members believe that general education is essential to the public welfare, urgently memorialize Congress for national aid to common schools. Get through the cordon of politicians, and appeal to the hearts of the people. Deal with this, not as a partisan question, but as one of self-preservation.

Common schools and republican institutions are convertible terms. Without them, neither parties nor politicians could be; for popular rights, to subserve which these exist, cannot survive in the poisonous night of ignorance which is threatening our beloved land. Whatever thing is neglected, let not this be neglected. Let the people utter their voice. Especially let the cry come up from those who most need help. But here we must remember that the patient does not always know that he is sick. Therefore, let the physician cry out. The philanthropist and the educator who is silent commits high crime. If the missionary spirit of the country would for a single session concentrate on this great movement to procure a few millions of national aid to public schools, what an impetus would it not give to its own great work! This is the natural duty of the clergy, of educators, of the press, and of every man who loves his country or cares for the welfare of mankind.

The prospect of success depends upon the performance of the conditions of success. If proper efforts are made to bring the pressure of the public interests and of the public will to bear upon public servants, national aid to common schools will be secured. This subject can no longer be made a party issue. Opposition has been developed when it could have been least expected, and support has sprung up where only the poet could have hoped for it in his dreams. Nothing has so demonstrated to my own mind that we have in truth entered upon a higher career, and that He hath indeed made all things new. Where I had hoped for sympathy and leadership in this great movement for aid to common schools I have found the remnants of effete statesmanship and the narrowest forms of local littleness when home necessities did not exist. Where I feared that the might of generations of anti-republican and class influence would prevent, there I have found anxious and hearty co-operation. The time is not far distant when the common school will be the new peculiar institution of the South. Give her people and her statesmen a chance. Once the common school acclimated there, and her vast rural population educated and elevated by the diffusion of universal knowledge, and the great South will be the conservator of our institutions and the sheet-anchor of human liberty. I believe that no party there will oppose, but all will ardently advocate, national aid to public schools. There is more danger of inconsiderate and unfortunate opposition from the rich and powerful North. But no political party, North or South, ought to live which fails to support this measure. I believe that no public man in any party can long survive the emphatic condemnation which opposition to national aid to common schools will receive from the American people. I trust that this will not become a political issue, because I believe that no party, and least of all the Republican party, can afford by its opposition to array the national instinct of self-preservation against it. Yet, when the test vote was taken last session upon the Sherwin bill, the passage of which would have been of more benefit to this country than all the legislation since the Act of Emancipation and the amendments which secured the suffrage, the record of ayes and noes made me sick at heart.

The Republican party cannot repeat that record in the next Congress, and survive the next Presidential election. Some, however, voted adversely to the bill, not upon its merits, but because they desired opportunity for discussion and for amendment. There be those in the Republican party who must imbibe from some outside source new life and new ideas, or that party will not long survive.

We hear much about standing with our faces to the morning, but it is yesterday morning with too many men who have their official grip on the destinies of this country. It is time to learn something new and to move forward. But it is hard for one generation to rise to an appreciation of the opportunities and to the performance of the duties which belong to their successors, and it is too much, perhaps, to demand of the generation which destroyed slavery that it should fully reconstruct the foundations and edifice of our liberties. Yet the fathers wrote their perfect charter and model in the cabin of the *Mayflower*, and we are but called upon to apply the great principles of civil and religious freedom which they enunciated in the administration of the law, and to fortify them forever by the intelligence and virtue of the people. We have no excuse and cannot escape "the deep damnation of the taking off" of republican institutions, if we permit the children of American citizens to come to the control of a government, based upon the knowledge and virtue and disciplined mental powers of the people, incapable of discharging the functions of sovereignty, and the ready prey of despotic power.

Soon or later the American nation will educate its children. Now is a crucial emergency, and we are being weighed in the balances. Shall we be found wanting? What record are we making as we pass away?

The public finances may not always so easily permit the expenditure as now. A generation of children are educated by an average of five years' common-school life, and two generations thoroughly taught in the common branches of knowledge throughout the whole land; and the people in every locality having once tasted of the heavenly gift will never afterward fail to secure to their posterity the inestimable blessings of universal education. The work once done will remain forever done. To perform it is our highest duty, our God-given opportunity, and our glorious privilege.

This assembly will answer for itself. Before the snow flies success will be assured or neglect will have rendered defeat unavoidable.

Every thing will depend upon the demonstration of popular sentiment which shall be manifested to the next Congress of the United States. The work hitherto done has been great and invaluable. But the new Congress is composed largely of new men, and nothing can be taken for granted.

I believe that this assembly will perform its whole duty, and that within two years the great work will be accomplished. If we fail, miserably fail, and if those who come after us likewise miserably fail, the time will come in free America—then, alas! no longer free—when cursed shall be the night when it is said within her borders that a child is born.

4. THE VOICES OF FOUR PRESIDENTS.

GEN. GRANT, in his message, announcing the ratification of the Fifteenth Amendment, says:

I would call upon Congress to take all measures within their constitutional power to promote and encourage popular education throughout the country, and I call upon the people every-where to see to it that all who possess and exercise political rights shall have an opportunity to acquire knowledge which will make their share in the government a blessing and not a curse.

President HAYES, in 1880, repeats and enforces a former recommendation:

The means at the command of the local and State authorities are, in many cases, wholly inadequate to furnish free instruction to all who need it. This is especially true where, before emancipation, the education of the people was neglected or prevented, in the interest of slavery. Firmly convinced that the subject of popular education deserves the earnest attention of the people of the whole country, with a view to wise and comprehensive action by the Government of the United States, I respectfully recommend that Congress, by suitable legislation, and with proper safeguards, supplement the local educational funds in the several States where the grave duties and responsibilities of citizenship have been devolved on uneducated people, by devoting to the purpose grants of the public lands, and, if necessary, by appropriations from the treasury of the United States.

President GARFIELD, in his inaugural, uses these emphatic words:

All the constitutional power of the nation and of the States, and all the volunteer forces of the people, should be summoned to meet this danger by the saving influence of universal education.

President ARTHUR, in his message, adds his voice to that of his predecessors:

There is now a special reason why, by setting apart the proceeds of its sales of public lands, or by some other course, the government should aid the work of education. Many who now exercise the right of suffrage are unable to read the ballot which they cast. Upon many who had just emerged from a condition of slavery, were suddenly devolved the responsibilities of citizenship in that portion of the country most impoverished by war. I have been pleased to learn from the report of the Commissioner of Education that there has lately been a commendable increase of interest and effort for their instruction; but all that can be done by local legislation and private generosity should be supplemented by such aid as can be constitutionally afforded by the national government. I would suggest that if any fund be dedicated to this purpose it may be wisely distributed in the different States according to the ratio of illiteracy, as by this means those localities which are most in need of such assistance will reap its special benefits.

The following letters were received while the Assembly was in session:

Hon. CORNELIUS HEDGES, Superintendent of Public Instruction, Montana, says:

I am, in a moderate degree, favorable to national aid to education, but not to take the place of State responsibility, which will insure variety and healthy emulation. I think the South ought to educate the blacks as well as the whites. The chief reward would be theirs, and they, too, by all the strongest considerations of justice, should bear the burden; but rather than not see it done at all, or to have it done the sooner, would favor a moderate grant to extinguish illiteracy—would have the government found and support the best university in the world, with the best man in the world at the head of each department. The government should only aim to provide a balance-wheel and distributory reservoir in our school system.

I am a true friend to the Negro, but he must understand that elevation is to be his own work, and a hard, slow work it will be.

Hon. DANIEL L. PRATT, of Michigan, says: While I am in favor of liberal appropriations by Congress in aid of our public schools, I am in favor of the States disbursing the money appropriations. I think the work can be done more economically and efficiently by the States than by the general government. I think our country is suffering from the want of an educated conscience; and that any system of education that neglects systematic instruction in the principles of sound morality will be sadly defective, and do very little to elevate the illiterate masses.

The Hon. WILLIAM F. WELCKER, Superintendent of Public Instruction, Cal., writes: I presume no one would recommend the declining to receive such aid if the general government finds itself able and willing to extend such assistance; but in my judgment it should be given to the State authorities to dispose of without interference from Washington; and with the sole proviso that the money should be expended for the salaries of *primary and grammar-school teachers.* School-houses, apparatus, and other appliances should be furnished by the local authorities.

The Hon. G. J. ORR, Commissioner of Education, Georgia, says: My delay in writing you has been brought about by the hope that I might see my way clear to do all the work expected of me here, and still render the general cause the service which you ask at my hands. Recent developments here have satisfied me that this cannot be accomplished. I am compelled, therefore, reluctantly to decline your invitation. I send you a preamble and resolutions unanimously adopted by the General Assembly of Georgia, and approved December 13, 1882, which I feel represents the sentiment of our people in this State:

Whereas, As a result of the late war, the colored people of the South were set free and made citizens; and

Whereas, The white people themselves were greatly reduced, many of them to a state of destitution very nearly as extreme as that of the colored people; and

Whereas, The facts herein recited have rendered it impossible, for the time being, for this State to make adequate provision for the education of our youth; and

Whereas, Wide-spread illiteracy, conjoined with universal suffrage, have put the institutions of the country in peril; therefore be it

Resolved, by the General Assembly of Georgia, That we hail with pleasure the movement now being made in the Congress of the United States to raise a fund for distribution for a term of years among the States in aid of popular education, the distribution to be made upon the basis of illiteracy.

Resolved, That the proposition to have this fund applied under State laws, and by the

regularly constituted State authorities, to the support of common schools, normal schools, and other agencies, for securing an adequate corps of well-qualified common-school teachers, meets our hearty approval.

Resolved, That our Senators and Representatives in Congress are hereby requested to use their best endeavors to secure the passage of an educational bill which shall be liberal in its monetary provisions and well guarded against improper federal interference in the educational affairs of the States.

Resolved, That as our now limited fund is applied to the education of all children, without discrimination as to race, so shall any fund which may be furnished by Congress be applied with equal impartiality.

Resolved, That his Excellency, the Governor, is hereby requested to have copies of these resolutions made out and forwarded to Washington at once, to be laid before both Houses of Congress at the commencement of the approaching session.

Hon. THOMAS B. STOCKWELL, Commissioner of Education, Rhode Island, says: I desire to assure you of my deep sympathy with the purposes of the meeting, believing the question of popular education to be the *vital* question in American politics, using that word in its best sense. The life of the nation, always inseparably connected with the education given to its children, is, just at this juncture, owing to the two great currents of illiteracy which emancipation and immigration have turned in upon us, only to be preserved by the most extended and united efforts in all legitimate directions.

Hon. HUGH L. THOMPSON, Governor of South Carolina, says: I realize fully the importance to the whole country of securing prompt and liberal appropriations from the national treasury to be used in aid of public-school systems, and to be expended on the basis of illiteracy. I have given much thought to this subject, and I see no other way of averting the evils with which illiteracy threatens our free institutions.

Hon. E. H. FAY. Superintendent of Public Instruction, Louisiana, writes: I hope the action of the Assembly will be such as to impress upon the general government the necessity of doing something for education in the South. Mr. Blair's bill (Senate, 151) I like, save one or two objectionable features. Any bill proposing to aid the cause of education in the States must trust the State authorities solely, under legislative restrictions, to disburse the funds impartially, as they do their own State funds, and must not provide for an army of commissioners to act in conjunction with State authorities. If the States are unworthy to be *trusted,* they are unworthy to receive aid from the government.

5. THE NATION THE ONLY PATRON OF EDUCATION EQUAL TO THE PRESENT EMERGENCY.*

BY HON. JOHN EATON, LL.D.,

United States Commissioner of Education.

NEARLY twenty years have passed since the declarations of universal freedom; yet the slavery of ignorance remains with all its perils. Joy is increasing in all the land that man no longer has property in his fellow-man; yet we must confess that the evils threatened by African slavery are only partly averted. The millions in ignorance are not free as American liberty must make free; their ignorance invites vice, crime, and petty demagogism to become their masters, and by ruling them to assail the foundations upon which rest the very citadel of our liberties.

The colored persons, ten years of age and upward, unable to write, as returned by the late census, number 3,220,878, or a number equal to the entire population when the original thirteen States were first united under one form of government. The foreign white population, of ten years of age and upward, unable to write, number 763,620; and the number of native white persons of the same age unable to write is 2,255,460. The total number, ten years old and upward, unable to write, in all the States and Territories and the District of Columbia, is 6,239,-958, showing, as compared with similar figures from the census of 1870, relatively an advance of three per cent. in intelligence, but an actual gain in the number of illiterates of 581,814, in spite of all the educational activities of the intermediate ten years.

Notwithstanding this mass of darkness, we are among those who believe in all the possibilities of our destiny for good for our posterity and for the other nations of the earth; but we know that a house divided against itself cannot stand. Intelligence and virtue, trained in the love of freedom, are always ready for its defense against all the hosts of ignorance and evil. But here the irrepressible conflict remains, and it is the part of wisdom to consider how it may be terminated by measures of peace and moderation, and not involve future generations in a catastrophe more bloody and calamitous than our own civil war.

We offer no Utopian schemes. We do not come as destructives purposing to tear down every thing; we do not propose to arrest the growth of our institutions. On the contrary, we invoke greater activity on the part of all the agencies that enlighten, or mold, or preserve society for good.

Among the foremost of these to which we turn with assured expectation is the family; and where outside of the borders of America is there a larger proportion of families to the whole population? Where have its better aspirations equal opportunity? All the possibilities of American citizenship are before its every child. How many hallowed home influences guard the life of infancy, train its earlier activities, mold its power to high purposes and noble action! But, alas! how many homes are broken up by the death of father or mother, or by the weakness or criminality of the parent, and childhood's tender years exposed to the perils of orphanage, or thrown into the midst of vice and crime. Society, in its benevolent action, already counts these children in localities by tens of thousands. That noble effort of Brace and his coadjutors, in your city alone, has taken over sixty thousand from the perils of city streets to the safeguards of country homes. Our reform schools and orphan asylums give most appalling testimony to the aid our home-life requires, and show the disproportionate increase of neglected children. All the efforts of organized and enlightened charity are not equal to the demand. Amid vital statistics, Rachel every-where mourns her infant children. Nearly half the children die in infancy, and come not to the chances of future good or evil among men.

Near the family is the Church, that other Divine institution, established for man's enlightenment in his duties to God and his fellow-man, and for the conservation of the best interests of society. For this great institution, too, we invoke greater activity, and we believe that the American Church is not hindered, but quickened, to greater power by its separation from the State. We believe, thereby, it occupies an ideal position, toward which its wisest adherents the world over would have it move as the sphere in which it may most serve man and honor God.

Where else has the Church greater respect or more power over the consciences and lives of the people? Where else has its press or pulpit greater influence? Where, besides, in the same length of time, has it garnered a richer literature? Where are its schools on the Sabbath more effective? And yet, according to the last well-authenticated

* Delivered at opening of the National Education Assembly for 1882, at Ocean Grove, N. J., August 8.

figures, their membership numbered only about seven millions and a quarter; and yet, if none but youth attended these schools, there should be in them from fifteen millions to twenty millions. Yet in what nation under the heavens have the schools of the Church of all grades more freedom, and gained such endowments, or given promise for greater future triumphs?

Some claim for the Church such exclusive control over education, that we must look more carefully into the possibilities of provision for this great emergency by denominational agencies.

The separate schools of theology, including Catholic and Protestant, number 142, having 633 learned professors, 5,242 students, and have invested in buildings and grounds, $6,221,607. The productive funds of the Protestant schools amount to $8,537,-683, and yield an income of $576,897. All the investments in all forms for instruction in the professions of law and medicine bear no comparison to these figures.

But the Churches have achieved far greater results in the provisions of college instruction for men and women. Of these institutions announced as belonging to one or the other of the denominations of Christians, Protestant or Catholic, there are 438, with 4,543 professors, and 60,947 students. The value of their buildings, grounds, and apparatus is $31,898,510; the amount of their productive funds, $23,403,945, yields a reported income, with tuition fees, of $3,068,554. In this connection it is interesting, however unsatisfactory, to remark that the productive funds invested for the education of women is not one fiftieth of the amount similarly invested for the college education of men.

Of that other grade of institutions established for secondary instruction, such as high-schools, academies, and preparatory schools, there are reported under denominational control, 837, with 4,205 teachers, and 73,770 students, owning in buildings, grounds, and apparatus, $10,779,334, and having in productive funds, $1,684,359.

In these three classes of schools, those of theology, and those for secondary and superior instruction under denominational control, we have the grand total of 139,826 students, and an investment in property and productive funds amounting to $82,195,728.

But we must pass to another great and special work of the Churches. Rejoicing in the American Sabbath for man's rest and freedom to worship, the several religious denominations acknowledge it to be their special responsibility on that day to preach the Gospel of man's redemption. Learning and eloquence may well rejoice in the power of their pulpits. The multitudes whose attention they command in places of worship no cursory glance can number; but our purpose requires a nearer view.

We have not the data expected from the great census of 1880, but on the supposition that the ratios for that decade may be substantially the same as for the previous one, (1860-1870,) the following statistics will be sufficiently accurate for our argument.

Great as is the Sabbath worship on the first impression, allowing that there are now 28,170,000 sittings in the religious edifices of all the various denominations, there would be required 21,830,000 additional sittings to accommodate the total population of 50,000,-000, which, at an average expense of $12 per sitting, would cost $261,960,000. To supply the preachers required, at the usual average of 1 to 375 persons, there would need be an addition of 58,213 clergymen. Now, should the Churches undertake to give these men a preparation of only three years at the present rates of aid, and with present facilities, it would cost, over and above all that the young men could do for themselves, at the rate of $100 a year, $17,463,900; and their first year's salary as preachers, should they be able to live on an average of $500, would demand for its payment $29,106,500. The total of those three items for the supply of the preached Gospel to all of our fifty million people would cost $308,530,400.

Another special means of promoting religious progress is the circulation of religious books, newspapers, and especially the Holy Bible. Great and excellent as is this service as now rendered, how many hundreds of thousands of souls are unreached by either agency! It would require a circulation of 10,000,000 religious papers to furnish one to each family.

When the spirit of American civilization invites religious organizations to a work so vast, so far beyond their present means and efforts, so out of proportion to all that they are undertaking, would it not border on cruelty or absurdity to demand of our Churches, as some would do, that they should assume entire control of the education of the people in all its forms, under all conditions? But would the idea of those who advocate exclusive Church direction of education limit that great work to a few, or to the ruling classes, or to those who could pay? Could the friends of the Church consent to an idea so consistent with the illiteracy and degradation of the masses?

We believe the New England fathers wisely sought a better way. Studying profoundly in the light of the Divine word all the data in human experience that they could command, after prolonged struggles they reached their well-known principles of liberty and right of conscience, person, and property. They also became profoundly convinced that the preservation of these principles which they so dearly cherished could be assured for the future only by the training of the young to whom they were to be committed, and that this education could only be made universal and sufficient for a free people by that other institution, the State, which they cherished as divine, while announcing its total separation from the authority of the Church. They welcomed all voluntary action by the family and by the Church, and we have seen how conspicuous were the results attained; but they wisely committed to the State, in which only resided the power that could touch all the people and tax all the property within its borders, the guarantee of the education of all the children. So they expected the family to teach justice, so they expected the Church, by all its moral power, to enforce justice between man and man; but they reserved the guarantees of this justice to the civil organization. Thus they expected the family and the Church to do their utmost for the education of society; but the final assurance, the absolute guarantee, of this education, supremely necessary to the continuance of free institutions, they laid in the very foundations of the civil government. Their conceptions and practices have so commended themselves to American lovers of liberty that in every State and in every Territory that has any organization in law there are legal provisions for the public education of the children. The schools of the people, the common schools, are justly and wisely regarded with the profoundest interest. Statesmen and publicists the world over have not looked in them in vain for the sources of many of the excellences of American life. May it be always and every-where true of them, as the great Webster was able to testify to an English inquirer. After remarking that he had been familiar with the New England system of free schools for more than fifty years, and avowing his hearty applause of it, he continues:

"I owe to it my own early training. In my own recollection of these schools there exists, to this moment, a fresh feeling of the sobriety of the teachers, the good order of the school, the reverence with which the Scriptures were read, and the strictness with which all moral duties were enjoined and enforced. In these schools, or it may be partly by my mother's care, I was taught the elements of letters so early that I never have been able to remember a time when I could not read the New Testament and did not read it. Many moral tales and instructive and well-contrived fables, always so alluring to childhood, learned by heart in these schools, are still perfectly preserved in my memory. And, in my own case, I can say that, without these early means of instruction ordained by law, and brought home to the small villages and hamlets for the use of all their children equally, I do not see how I should have been able to become so far instructed in the elements of knowledge as to be fit for higher schools.

4

"In my opinion, the instruction communicated in the free schools of New England has a direct effect for good on the morals of youth. It represses vicious inclinations, it inspires love of character, and it awakens honorable aspirations. In short, I have no conception of any manner in which the popular republican institutions under which we live could possibly be preserved, if early education were not freely furnished to all, by public law, in such forms that all shall gladly avail themselves of it."

He proceeds, in language almost prophetic:

"I may be permitted to add, that, in my judgment, as the present tendency of things almost every-where is to extend popular power, the peace and well-being of society require, at the same time, a corresponding extension of popular knowledge."

The favorable side of this public-school system cannot be contemplated without gratification. In every State, by the provision of the State university or agricultural college, the ladder of learning, with one foot standing in the gutter, invites every child, step by step, by a free course to the highest instruction. The conception of the theory is an honor to the human mind. None are excluded; every one is invited to some measure of instruction, be he sound in health, or be he feeble-minded, or deaf, or dumb, or blind. What blessings are offered to the poor! Here is a family struggling for subsistence, and has no money to pay a penny for the instruction of its children, that perhaps number four; one, of a sound mind, goes to the public school, and, if he has the capacity, through the collegiate course, and is then capable of high trusts and responsibilities; the second, an idiot, is taken to the school for the feeble-minded, and becomes self-supporting; the third is blind, and the State offers the school for the blind; the fourth is deaf and dumb, and the State offers the school and the nation the college at Washington. It is a glory of American law that what is left for these unfortunates elsewhere to charity, here has the certainty of public administration.

Why should we not, glancing over the annual column of educational work, congratulate ourselves that there are 48 schools of law, with 3,134 students; 120 schools of medicine, with 14,006 students; 364 universities and colleges, with 59,594 students; that there have been given for education in the last ten years over $61,000,000 by private individuals of wealth; and that annually there are nine millions in attendance upon the public schools, and an annual expenditure for these schools of eighty million dollars from the public treasury?

But we must not pause here; we must look at the reverse side. New England, to-day, has but one college student, male and female, to every 167 families; whereas, at the end of the first 23 years of New England history, or when there were 20,000 souls in the settlements, there was one university graduate to every 40 families. May we not say that hence came such wisdom in laying the foundations of those States? When will the educated classes anywhere attain the same relation to the whole body of the people?

But against this attendance upon the public schools there is the non-attendance of 5,754,759. Allowing that these odd hundred thousands are in private schools that are not reported, there remain 5,000,000 of children of school age untaught. To furnish these sittings in buildings, at the usual average of $20 per sitting, would cost a hundred millions in money; to furnish them teachers would require an increase of 30,000 to the teaching corps, and a single year's preparation of these teachers at the average rate in New York would cost ten millions of dollars.

The pay of these 30,000 additional teachers for one year of ten months, at the rate of $32 a month, which is about the average throughout the country, would amount to $9,600,000. Add to this the items for preparation and school-house sittings necessary for these non-attending school children, and you have the grand total required for the first year of $120,000,000.

There has been an attempt to raise a laugh at the proposition of the Hon. Senator Logan to appropriate $60,000,000 in aid of education, but I give you here figures which cannot be invalidated, showing that his proposition falls $60,000,000 short of the sum which would be required to furnish, for a single year, all our school children now without school sittings and teachers. Mr. Senator Blair, in his examination of this point in his recent speech, considering that Texas has a school period of only six years, states that, if the school life were properly lengthened in that and other States, the number reported without school accommodations and without teachers would be increased by three millions.

In our cities we are accustomed to expect the best teachers, best school-houses, best methods, and best supervision; but laws making attendance obligatory are wanting in more than half of the States, and, on an average, two fifths of the children are not enrolled in the schools. Here are forced upon us the terrible problems encountered in older civilizations and more dense populations.

These deficiencies, we must note, moreover, are not equally distributed throughout the entire country, but are mainly concentrated in the Southern States, where the late war left its most disastrous effects. The white people were impoverished, and the colored people entered upon their liberty in total destitution. The setting up of the public-

school system was one of the crucial tests of the revolution that was transpiring in the affairs of the Southern people, and was most obnoxious to the whites. All their antecedent notions rose up against it, but in spite of the prevailing poverty and indifference or opposition, the public-school idea gained ground.

The fifteen States and the District of Columbia where slavery prevailed, having a legal white school population of 3,899,961, had 2,215,674 enrolled in schools, and with a colored school population of 1,803,257, had 784,709 enrolled, and expended $12,-475,044. This money, it should be remembered, is divided pro rata without distinction of color in all States excepting Kentucky and Delaware. In the former State the colored people have had for educational purposes the benefit only of the income of the tax upon their own property and polls, and specified fines and forfeitures. By an act of the last Legislature, however, provision was made for submitting to the people the question of adding a two-mills tax upon property for educational purposes, uniting this and the amount from the previous provisions for education, and distributing the whole pro rata per capita. In Delaware $2,500 are now appropriated for the colored schools. What has thus been accomplished in these States for education may be taken as a pledge of what they will do.

In considering the local necessities of the South, embarrassed by the ignorance of the colored population, it should not be forgotten that there are now conducted, for the benefit of the colored people, 44 normal schools, with 7,408 students; 36 schools for secondary instruction, with 5,237 students; 15 universities and colleges, with 1,717 students; 22 schools of theology, with 800 students; 3 schools of law, with 33 students; 2 schools of medicine, with 87 students, and 2 institutions for the deaf, dumb, and blind, with 122 students.

These institutions for higher instruction of colored youth are mainly due to the benefactions of benevolent Christians; and it is claimed by the several denominational agencies at work that they have expended in this direction some ten millions of dollars. In the same regions it is known that the nation expended through the Freedmen's Bureau, in behalf of education, $5,262,511. Here, too, the great Peabody benefaction, managed with the greatest skill in educating both blacks and whites, has expended $1,191,790, and now the Slater fund of a million is provided to give greater efficiency, especially for the education of the blacks.

In these late slave States the family, the Church, and other agencies for the enlightenment of society have been rehabilitated, and substantially restored to their normal conditions of activity; and yet the census shows that there are in these States 1,676,939 white persons, and a total of whites and blacks of 4,741,173, ten years old and over, who cannot write.

To which great agency can you assign the additional burden of educating these illiterates? To the family? How many families of the most cultured and best conditioned are unable to educate their children as in former times, or as they desire; and among those colored people the least supplied with schools, how widely is the family a minus quantity as a factor in promoting the improvement of the young? Shall we then look to the Church for the light to overcome this darkness? How inadequate are the resources of the Church in the South to supply sittings and preachers for the special function of declaring the Gospel? How generally are they in debt? What appeals are they compelled to make to their friends in other quarters? Shall we turn, then, thirdly, to the States, already impoverished and loaded with taxes and embarrassed by questions of repudiation? In reply, let me invite attention to the fact that the taxable real and personal property in those States is given in round numbers as $3,379,000,000, while the real and personal property in New York and New Jersey alone is worth nearly an equal amount, or $3,292,000,000. What would the people of these two States say to an additional assessment on their property sufficient to erect all the additional school-houses and supply all the teachers for the instruction of the millions of illiterates in the South? All are familiar with the sensitiveness in the several Northern States to the assessment of any additional tax for education or any other purpose, and there the total wealth as assessed is reported as $13,-095,000,000, or nearly ten billions more than in the South.

It should be remembered, in addition to the short period in which schools are already taught in the South, that there are 2,702,835 children of school age not enrolled for instruction. Take another comparison: Charleston, South Carolina, now levies a tax of three mills on a dollar; but to furnish the children of that State a fair approach to the instruction given those in Massachusetts would require a tax on the property of the State of nearly three cents to the dollar! This the friends of education in Massachusetts or any other State would hesitate to propose in their own case.

In view of these facts need we ask, why have the benevolent of all classes, the friends of humanity, of order, of law, of progress, been so profoundly moved by anxiety? Why have the consciences of so many been urging the provision of education for these people? One thing is clear: these earnest patriots have sought no harm to either race; they have not acted in antagonism to any of the great agencies for the reformation and blessing of society, the family, or the Church, or the cities or States of that region, but their aim has been to relieve burdens that would paralyze these agencies. They have labored to secure for the youth of the South that instruction and training which by precept and example inspire to a higher and better life. They believe profoundly that lust and avarice and anger creep in the dark jungles of man's ignorance.

In their studies of social science they read the story of "Margaret, the mother of criminals," wherein they learn that the neglect to care for that single Juke family living on the outskirts of a New York village resulted in a marvelous multiplication of criminals and paupers. Mr. Dugdale traced 1,200 descendants. Of these 280 were adult paupers, and 140 criminals and offenders, guilty of seven murders and of numerous thefts, highway robberies, and nearly every offense known in the calendar of crime; and cost society for their support or punishment $1,308,000, "without reckoning," as Mr. Dugdale observes, "the cash paid for whisky, or the entailment of these evils upon posterity, or the incurable diseases, idiocy, and insanity, growing out of their debaucheries, and reaching further than we can calculate."

Much has been said and written of the effect upon the increase of the comforts of life and the increase of wealth by that education which tends to develop a sound mind in a healthy body, and an intelligent, healthy, honest men and women. This material result of right education may be set forth in numerous ways. All political economists recognize it.

I must not pause to elaborate these points, but supposing (1) that the labor of an illiterate is increased in value 25 per cent. by teaching him to read and write, 50 per cent. by fairly educating him, and 75 per cent. by giving him a thorough training; and (2) that the average value of the labor of literates is the same as the average wages paid employes in manufactories, then the following computations give sound conclusions.

By the census of 1880 the number of persons of 21 years and upward in the Southern States who were unable to write was 2,984,387. If 75 per cent. of them should be taught to read and write, it would increase the value of the labor of 2,238,290 persons 25 per cent. The present value of their labor is, approximately, $248 a year each. The increase of value would be $62 a year per capita, a total of $138,773.980. If 15 per cent. of the illiterates should be fairly educated, it would increase the value of the labor of 447,658 persons 50 per cent. or from $248 to $372 a year each. The

total of this annual increase would be $55,-
509,592. If the remaining 10 per cent. of
illiterates should have the value of their labor increased 75 per cent. by being thoroughly trained, the industrial value of 298,-
439 persons would be raised from $248 to
$434 a year each, a total of $55,509,654.
By adding the three totals just given, it is
seen that the increase which would come to
the industrial value of illiterates in the
Southern States would be, were they educated as indicated, $241,727,220 a year.

A similar computation may be made for
the entire country. The average annual
wages paid by manufacturers is $345. The
number of persons 21 and over unable to
write is 4,204,263. By teaching 75 per
cent. of these to read and write, the labor of
3,153,272 individuals is increased in value
from $345 to $431 a year, a total gain of
$271,181,392 each year. The gain which
would come from educating 15 per cent.
(830,654) of the illiterates so that their labor
would be increased 50 per cent. in value
would be $108,787,815. The same amount
would be gained by so training the remaining 10 per cent. of illiterates that their labor
would be of 75 per cent. more value; and
the total annual profit to the country by the
conversion of illiterate into educated labor
would be, according to the premises assumed as a basis of computation, $488,757,-
022 a year.

Need I go further to indicate that education is a most profitable investment for both
labor and capital?

Amid these masses of figures you will not
expect me to give in greater detail the statistics showing the depreciating influence of
ignorance upon agriculture, upon the mechanic arts, upon commerce, upon all the
great activities by which society lives and
moves, nor will you desire me to trace in
detail the share that ignorance pure and
simple has in the degradation of the pauper
classes, in the increase of criminality and its
cost, or the propagation of disease and the
insecurity of health and life; but I cannot
dismiss this vast ignorance without a word
with reference to its possible political evils.
Omitting any reference to the influence of
illiteracy during minority or any bearing of
the illiteracy of the female adults, the late
census shows us that there is a great army
of 1,870,216 adult males or voters who cannot write, an army nearly double that ever
in the field during the late deplorable civil
war. You will certainly excuse me from
any delineation of the horrors of the devastation that might follow their united and
concentrated efforts against the peace and
order of society. I simply call your attention to what may be the injurious effect of
their silent action at the polls. The members of our respective political parties believe in the rightness of their principles and

seek to make their appeal to the reason and
consciences of the people; but the figures
disclose the alarming fact that in eleven
States these illiterate voters outnumbered
the votes cast in the last Presidential election by either of the political parties. Thus,
should they unite under any strong, impassioned, successful leader, they would have
absolute control of legislation and offices in
those States, and of the election of twenty-
two members of the United States Senate.

Again, running the column of these alarming figures, and taking into account the votes
of the two political parties in the last Presidential election, we find that in all but five
of the States in the Union there are enough
of these illiterate voters to have reversed
the result of the election in each of these
States. The press, the public mind, are occupied with questions of tariff, questions of
capital and labor, questions of corporations
and private rights. Do they sufficiently consider what material these ignorant masses
offer for the destructive revolutions that
have occurred in connection with these
questions in older civilizations and under
other forms of government? Does the
press consider that none of its information,
none of its pleadings, none of the considerations it presents can be read by 4,943,451
persons ten years old and over, and that for
them its voices of warning and instruction
fall on deaf ears?

Before passing from this class of considerations you will pardon me for reminding
you that many of our intelligent people, dis-
gusted, as they say, by the ignorance and
corruption they meet, show a disposition
not to participate in political action; and
that generally the more ignorant can be
rallied to do what their leaders desire. In
the light of this general fact I beg you to
turn to the "Tribune Almanac" for 1882,
and, after adding up the columns of votes
cast, draw out of its total the number in
each State whose votes were not cast or
were not counted in the last election: you
will find the startling result that these votes
not cast or not counted make a grand total
in all the States of 3,353,186; or more than
three fourths of the number who voted on
either side, and as a rule in each State sufficient, or two or three times enough, to have
reversed the election.

No summary of educational points from a
national view should omit the condition of
education in the Territories. Here we are
confronted with all the Indian problems,
which could be speedily solved if the 60,000
Indian children should be educated in the
conduct of life for a few school generations.
In the Territories, too, are the children of
the 30,000 Alaskans without legal provision
for their education. Here, too, is the large
Spanish and substantially foreign population of New Mexico, with little or no pro-

vision for instruction in the English language or American thought. Here, too, are the children of the 150,000 polygamists, in spite of the Edmunds Act said to be increased this year by 15,000 immigrants from foreign countries.

Another question that is springing up all over the land is, what can be done by education in the absence of apprenticeship, and the progress of society to give skill to handicraft? For this purpose essential modifications in methods and appliances must be made and will cost large sums of money. Yet they must come. This country, like the rest of the world, is moving steadily toward industrial training. Besides, in cities, in addition to the absence of millions of school age already noted, there are multitudes below that age who are so exposed to death or disease, or the formation of evil and destructive habits, that public action will be required in self defense, if for no other reason. Already this necessity has been recognized in France, and so-called maternal schools have been provided, in which there are now 600,000 children from two to six years of age.

Passing from point to point thus abruptly along these outline views, opening here and there into vast vistas that we have no time to study, allow me to ask, What are you going to do about these questions? Will you leave affairs to float on as they are, trusting that there is an overmastering power in the form of our government to prevent the evils so destructive to society in a monarchy or aristocracy? Before trusting ourselves entirely to this dangerous fallacy, it may not be amiss for us to remember that before we have passed far beyond the first century of our existence as a nation, two Presidents, two Chief Magistrates, have been removed by the hand of the assassin! And were not Abraham Lincoln and James A. Garfield, as men, as characters, rising from the humblest walks of life to the highest positions in the gift of the people, in a peculiar sense the products specially claimed for our institutions? And again, before charging the evils of Greek and Italian brigandage to a monarchical form of government, and asserting their impossibility in the midst of our free institutions and under our glorious banner, will it be amiss to recall the story of the James Brothers, and the honors bestowed upon them in this our day and in the very center of our boasted civilization? I repeat, shall we leave the cure of these evils to the agencies now operating—those that we have enumerated, and the great voluntary activities of temperance and science and reform. Have we not seen how each and finally all of the agencies are unequal to the task of universal education which, "like Spring," shall "leave no corner of the land untouched?"

Has there not been in our hearts and on our lips one great patron of education, the Nation, not yet sufficiently invoked? And is not this the only one available, equal in power and ample in means to meet the present emergency? This patron does not and need not displace or control either family, Church, or State, or voluntary activity. The nation need act only by its patronage, by its moral influence, by a reasonable disbursement of aid accompanied simply by conditions that shall make its expenditure honest and efficient. It need act only as a patron, whose aid given to the States shall lift the burden impossible for all other agencies to bear, and by suitable aid stimulate them to greater endeavor by assuring their hope of success.

Clearly this aid by the general government to education can do no violence to that constitutional provision which authorizes Congress to act for the general welfare, and under which so many millions of dollars have been so freely voted to roads, rivers, and internal improvements. The policy of this aid accords with the traditions and practices of the government from its foundation. Out of it came the great grants of land to common schools, to agricultural colleges, and to universities, amounting to nearly seventy-nine millions of acres, that have had such incalculable influence upon the destiny of the newer States.

The general government is the largest patron of science. Under it more researches are conducted than under any other agency among us.

For the enlightenment of the citizen it carries on one of the largest printing establishments in the world. Its aid in the establishment of libraries reaches millions of dollars. This sending abroad of light and knowledge to every nook and corner aids every locality to judge and act intelligently for itself. This diffusion of knowledge is not centralization of power, but the reverse.

Further, the general government aided the establishment of the first institution, that at Hartford, for the instruction of the deaf and dumb, and has crowned all the institutions of that class in the several States by that noble one, the Deaf-Mute College at Washington, the first of its rank in the world, be it said, to the honor of American statesmen.

When the blind had in vain sought aid in obtaining a literature elsewhere, the general government gave a permanent fund of a quarter million of dollars for a printing-house for the blind, and those in every Congressional district may have the benefit.

In 1836, when the national treasury was as it is now, more than full, a surplus of over twenty million dollars was disbursed among the States that received it as a loan, and in a number of instances used it to increase their school funds. Thus the national treasury promoted that revival of education which was then arousing the indifferent and overcoming the hostile, and therefore specially contributed to the preparation of the generation that saved the Union.

Only the general government can do justice to all the interests affected by that great river the "Father of Waters." Only the general government has been able to cope with that terrible plague, the yellow fever. So only can the nation meet the greatness of the present emergency by adequately aiding existing agencies, and thus enable the people to cope with the plague of ignorance more fatal to human good than any leprosy that can assail the body. Besides, we should not forget that the nation by the Constitution must guarantee to each State a republican form of government; and by later provisions we are aware that the nation has assumed to protect the citizenship of those formerly slaves. Do we not know, if the theories are sound on which rest our institutions of freedom, that in the execution of either of these trusts the nation would in vain marshal armies until they were as oppressive as those of the old world? Equally in vain it would add statute to statute, if the people themselves, the people resident in the locality in peril, do not possess or do not acquire that intelligence and virtue without which a republican form of government and the enjoyment of American citizenship are absolutely impossible.

It was the belief of the fathers, and it is a truth by which we must abide, that the free, intelligent choice of the people is our only safety. If the nation may use its navies and armies to guarantee this safety, and fail, as it must, if no other means are employed, may it not rightfully, at least as a generous patron, bestow the means to aid the States in building school houses, or in paying teachers, whereby the people may be so enlightened that they shall come of their own free will to know, cherish, achieve, and defend this result?

Are not the great patriotic thought and the increasing anxiety for the Republic strongly gravitating to this conclusion, and pointing to our national statesmen as the men on whom rest the final responsibilities' for adequate action?

The fathers of the republic, before they had gone the half of twenty years, found the defects and weaknesses of the Articles of Confederation. They achieved their greatest triumph of statesmanship in revision and in giving us the Constitution. Have not our statesmen in the great changes of the last score of years seen the imperative need of other revisions, and discovered the opportunity by giving to universal suffrage the guarantee of universal intelligence, to add new assurance of the prosperity of the country, and of the continuance of our liberties, and new glories to American citizenship?

Then shall

"Columbia, Columbia, to glory arise,
The queen of the world and the child of the skies,
Thy genius commands thee; with rapture behold
While ages on ages thy splendors unfold."

IV. THE NEGRO IN AMERICA.

1. OPENING REMARKS.

REV. R. S. RUST, D.D., OF OHIO,

Secretary Freedmen's Aid Society of the Methodist Episcopal Church.

In presiding at the fourth session Dr. RUST spoke as follows:

THE topic of discussion this morning is "The Negro in America." The Negro is here in common with the representatives of all other nationalities. Europe, Asia, and the Islands of the Sea are represented here, and why not Africa?

The Negro is here under circumstances differing from those of the representatives of any other country. The Negro is here by invitation. Other races and peoples are here by their own free will and accord. Some fled here from the persecutions of the Old World for protection; others came for gain or pleasure, but all voluntarily.

But the Negro is here on invitation, after earnest solicitation, and he is our guest, and is entitled to kind and respectful treatment. Yea, more; he came by compulsion! We fitted out vessels to bring them over, and New England is steeped to the lips in guilt by her participation in bringing Negroes to this country and selling them into perpetual bondage.

The Negro has contributed largely to the material prosperity of this country. The agricultural, manufacturing, and commercial interests of the nation have been greatly aided by the labor of the Negro, and, in the late rebellion, he contributed valuable service toward the preservation and perpetuation of the nation.

In the history of the Negro in America there are three important epochs. The first embraces the foreign slave-trade; the next item of that epoch the domestic slave-trade. You know the whole history of African slavery, beginning with the petty African princes making captives and selling them into bondage. You understand the character of the voyage from Africa to America; you are familiar with the horrors of the "middle passage." Thank God, the foreign slave-trade is broken up! Then followed the interstate slave-trade. Such a trade was a burning disgrace to the nation. I never shall forget the sight in Washington

I once saw when a boy—a coffle of slaves—men and women chained together, marching through the streets at the sound of a fife and drum, half famished, half clad, poor, miserable wretches, going down into the perpetual bondage of the South. Thank God, the interstate slave-trade is broken up! In a single year Virginia sent down into the far South forty thousand human beings, yielding a return of $25,000,000! So disgraceful was this traffic that one of the representatives in the Legislature of Virginia said: "Virginia is one grand menagerie, raising human beings, like oxen, for the shambles." Thank God, that the nation is no more disgraced with that inhuman traffic!

The next epoch is the emancipation epoch, the toils, struggles, and triumphs of which are too fresh in your minds to need repetition.

The third epoch includes the reparation of the wrongs of the slaves and the preparation of these millions of emancipated ones for Christian citizenship.

Why emancipate them? Why break up the relations of the slave-trade? Why annihilate the system of slavery, unless you mean to educate them; unless you intend to repair the wrongs you have inflicted on this people? Why strike the fetters from their limbs, and leave their minds in the bonds of ignorance and degradation?

Every argument for the overthrow of the slave-trade, both foreign and domestic—for the emancipation of the slaves—in thunder tones demands for them education and elevation. The work of this third epoch is the most important of the three. The struggles of the three center in this. Better not to have begun than not to finish up this work by education. We must recognize the manhood of the freedman. Break up the cruel system of caste, and treat the colored citizens as men and brethren. Nothing short of this will meet the demands of the age and the approval of God.

2. THE COLOR LINE: WHAT IT IS, AND WHAT IT THREATENS.

REV. B. T. TANNER, D.D.,

Editor "Christian Recorder," Philadelphia.

GEOGRAPHERS the world over—this world of Christendom, at least—understand the significance of such phrases as the "Horizontal Line" and the "Equinoctial Line;" and the common sense of enlightened humanity recognizes the legitimacy of such. And the same may be said of the "Battle Line" (Line of Battle) and the "Defense Line" among military men; the "Dip Line" among geologists, and the "Beauty Line" (Line of Beauty) among æsthetes. Even the significance of a phrase as the "Life Line" of the palmisters comes in for a very general understanding, and for an indorsement equally general. But what shall we say of the "Color Line," which the white citizens of this country have conjured up, and which the black citizens of the same have more largely accepted and nurtured than is generally thought? It is to be remarked that it is a something peculiar to the United States. While the other lines of which mention has been made are universally recognized and indorsed by the enlightened wisdom of the world, this line of color is such a novelty in its way, that outside our own Republic, especially outside the influence it exerts, it is a something entirely unknown; and, strange to say, even where pains have been taken to explain it, the greater the explanation the greater the doubt as to its possible existence. We repeat: our white fellow-countrymen have never been able to make the color line understood, much less give it respectable standing. By the influence they exert, republicanism, with a high respect for the majority, has been made popular in many lands and among many peoples; but, as we have said, they have utterly failed to give the color line a footing anywhere. It is a plant so thoroughly indigenous as to refuse to be transplanted.

The color line: What is it?

Of the color line, it is to be said that it presumes to regulate the society of our country. In this, however, it treats with contempt the recognized principle as well as the recognized regulations of the Christian world, of which it forms no inconsiderable part, and essays to lay down a new social code, if not for all nations, at least for itself. According to the principle and regulations accepted by the peoples of all lands, equals may be said to be guaranteed the right of associating with equals, irrespective of race or color. Is a man royal? Then may he

seek association among royalty, as was illustrated in the case of the son of African Theodore, the Shah of Asiatic Persia, and even Kalakaua and Cetawayo. Is a man titled? Then may his associates be among the titled. Is he rich? The rich may be his company. Or learned? Men of his rank take him by the hand. And all this, as we have said, irrespective of race or color, which are esteemed but as accidents. And yet it is to be said that no authority exists to compel an unconditional acceptance of the principles and regulations recognized. Even autocrats and despots respect personal liberty to this extent. If the Autocrat of all the Russias prefer even a questionable princess, he is still the autocrat. If the English Princess Louise prefer a mere marquis, she is allowed the liberty of choice, and, in her social standing, loses not an inch of her height. If the Baroness Burdett-Coutts prefers a plain Mr. Bartlett, and he an American, there is none to step between—no statute to imprison, no mob to hang. And so of each of the grades we have mentioned. In no single instance is association or non-association compulsory.

Ordinarily, the social regulations are accepted, but the man or the woman who elects not to accept, in no way is made to suffer for his temerity.

Fortunately, or unfortunately, without royal or titled classes among us, in the working of this code, we are spared the painful necessity of beholding one king snub another, because forsooth he was not of the same race or color; or, one prince snub another for the same reason. And so of members of titled classes, supposing us to have them. We are spared the necessity of seeing one duke scratching the name of another, in every way his equal, probably his superior, because his color was not as his own.

And yet, without having such classes among us, we are made to witness incidents as thoroughly foolish and hurtful among the unroyal and untitled of our country—unroyal and untitled only as the people themselves are unroyal and untitled—witness them to-day and will more surely witness them to-morrow, as would possibly be the case were the classes mentioned among us. We see to-day, and will see to-morrow, if this new social code is to last, not only equals snubbing and scratching equals, but downright inferiors snubbing and scratching men who are in every way their superiors; and all for the reason that the color of the people composing the nation is not one and the same. According to this new code, men equally rich, or talented, or cultured, or religious, or pious, are forbidden, on pain of public displeasure, to become associates. Our white men are taught, in the make-up of their friends, in every instance to ask, not the standard questions: Is she rich? Is she accomplished? Is she thoroughly good? questions fundamental to humanity—but, instead, are taught to ask largely in lieu of them all, certainly as deciding them all: Is she white? And as are taught the men, so are taught the women. "Let your associates," comes belching from the guns which guard the color line, "let your associates be white and of the right stamp; but let them be white anyway."

This, then, is the color line, and woe be to the man or the woman who is sufficiently "gritty" as to defy it; for though aristocratic and despotic Europe may and does tolerate personal liberty to this extent, Democratic America shakes her head and says: "No such liberty shall be allowed." If you doubt that America means what she says on this score, witness, before you go to the South to inspect its prisons, where are incarcerated those who were fortunate enough to be rescued from the mob—witness, we say, the social ostracism practiced against all such in the North—an ostracism so complete as to make men shun even their own kindred, if they dare to offend, as the ancient leper was shunned. What shall we say of this new social code?

First, It comes too late to be effective. Whether the whites and the blacks of the country shall mix is no longer an open question, being settled by the fact that the mixing has already, and to a very large extent, taken place. The black man already shares in the best blood of the land. Is he taunted us to regularity? His reply is, that among the people toward whom our white fellow-countrymen of English, and even of European, descent love to claim kindred, it has never been esteemed either honorable or sensible to despise the natural sons of great men.

Our opinion of the color line is: It is meddlesome, in that, as a third party, it essays to make its own that which is purely the business of the parties of the first and second part. It is foolish, in that it hopes to have success. It is tyrannical, in that it restricts human liberty in matters where of all liberty is to be most enjoyed.

Lastly, of the color line it is to be said that it is suggestive of immorality, if such be possible between those joined of God but kept apart of men.

Supposing such a code to become universally accepted, what does it threaten? To give any thing like a satisfactory treat-

ment to this most important portion of our paper would require more than our allotted time. It will therefore be necessary for us to simply give points. The peoples of our country—what are they now? What will they be in fifty or a hundred years hence? In round numbers we have now 43,000,000 whites, 7,000,000 blacks, and possibly 1,000,-000 reds and yellows in the persons of Iudians and Chinese. What the number of these will severally be in fifty or a hundred years hence various estimates have been made; most notably that of Professor Gilliam in the February "Popular Science Monthly." According to this reputable authority, the number of whites in the country in the year 1950 will be 168,000,000; the number of blacks ten years later, in 1960, will be 96,000,000. He takes no account of the reds and the yellows, classes destined to figure more conspicuously in our future history than most imagine.

Dr. Abel Stevens, in the July "Methodist Quarterly Review," makes the following reference to the blacks; we forego quoting his words in regard to the whites: "Our colored population is already much larger than the whole population at the beginning of the nation—hard on to double the latter. We must bear in mind that its superior rate of increase is without the aid of immigration, upon which the growth of the whites so much depends. If it should double, not its own present rate of increase, but at that of the general population, say in about every twenty-seven years, it will be greater, within the life-time of our children, in about seventy years than the present population of some of the important States of Europe; greater by millions than that of France, and advancing hard up toward the present figure of our whole population, white and black.

"In about eighty-one years it will be some two millions more than our aggregate population at the last census—but three years ago."

According to a calculation which we ourselves have made, we find the population of the blacks, in the year 1960, to be 67,654,-737, estimating the increase to be for each intervening decade what it was in the decade just past, to wit, thirty-four per cent.

Accept whichever calculation we may, this fact is apparent, that the blacks, to say nothing of the whites, are to be immensely numerous in the years to come. The blacks fifty years hence will not be the helpless and the spiritless creatures they are now; for the bow will have regained its natural bend. Educated, rich, manly, and in position, they will be as ready to give as to take. In position, we say. What says Judge Tourgée, referring to Prof. Gilliam's paper: "In view of these facts and the apparent probability that in the lives of our grandchildren, if not of our children, not less than thirteen States of the Union may be controlled by the colored race —at least if numbers are to prevail—how important does not the question of national education become."

As we gaze upon these millions of whites and millions of blacks confronting each other, and remembering that where there is no association there can be no certain amity, and where there is no amity there can be no lasting peace, we are made to ask, What will the harvest be?

As there cannot be other than one government, so there must not be ultimately more than one people. The Union, of which we so justly boast, must comprehend both. But we are not to be understood as hope-

less of the future. In the words of that historic Southerner, Dr. Atticus G. Haygood, we say: "The social spheres arrange themselves to suit themselves, and no laws promulgated by State or Church will change the social affinities and natural selections of men. Men choose the circles for which they have affinity, seek the companionships they prefer, and find the places that are suited to them. No human force or sagacity will change the social laws which bring men together or repel them."

This is law as ordained of God; and because it is law, soon or later it will dominate, all color lines to the contrary notwithstanding. Let us have peace; peace now, and peace forever.

3. THE NEGRO AND HIS ASSIMILATION IN AMERICA.

REV. J. W. HAMILTON,

People's Church, Boston, Massachusetts.

THE problems of a century puzzle the people of a generation—not unfrequently the puzzle runs on into the succeeding generation, and, it may be, generations. Few men have scope of vision far-reaching enough, and sagacity of soul adequate, to compass and comprehend the problem of a hundred years. But there is a presiding genius in every nation whose counsel and control will not permit a people to live and thwart the purpose and plan of human history. In some way and in some time the problem must be solved. That is among the decrees. He is a wise man who never attempts to withstand the determinate counsel and foreknowledge of God.

The Negro in America is the problem of a full hundred years—yes, the problem of five centuries. It has taken half the time already to state the question; we have now the other half to work at it. We spent some time in bringing him here, more time in getting him located after he was here, a great deal of time in talking about getting him away from here, and for twenty years we have been settling down to the fact that he is here to stay. The last census declares the colored population of the United States and Territories to be six millions five hundred and eighty thousand seven hundred and ninety-three. These figures do not, however, state the whole question; they only locate the part of it which has reference to the year of grace and of the census, 1880. The past and future of these figures come before us to give volume and significance to the discussion in which every citizen of the Republic must soon or later engage. It was in the same year in which the Pilgrims landed on Plymouth Rock when slavery was first introduced into the North

American colonies by a Dutch vessel which landed at Jamestown. One idea came ashore in Massachusetts, another in Virginia. Then the problem was announced; and the idea at Jamestown had two or three months the start. Massachusetts surrendered to Virginia, and in 1641 was the first colony to pass an enactment in favor of human slavery. And from Massachusetts to Mississippi the traffic in men and women and children ran on until a whole nation had sought to traduce a race of beings to merely marketable and serviceable chattels. The rights of man were exchanged for the rights of property. The war for our own rights ended with American Independence, but left seven hundred thousand persons within our territory whose rights no white man was bound to respect. The more the value of the property increased, the less the rights of the race were esteemed. The war for freedom became inevitable when "the mere value of the slave as a laborer, judged by the standard of the ox or horse, was estimated as high as two thousand millions of dollars" The rebellion over, emancipation left the Negro where slavery had driven him. Such was his degradation, when it was proposed to make him a citizen, that many who had favored his freedom turned from him in hopeless lament. The author of one of the most noted books in our political history, the favorable mention of which by one of the candidates for the office cost him the Speakership of the House of Representatives in the American Congress, so far forgot the reputation he had made for himself in the appeal to his Southern people for the abolition of slavery, as to write another book when the citizenship of the Negro was proposed, in which the delineations of the character of the black man were made to exhaust the resources of contumely and epithet. He declared him a cannibal and bloodthirsty by nature, heathenish, lying, thieving, drunken, and shameless. "How can the Negro," said he, "be a fit person to occupy in any capacity our houses or our hotels, our theaters or our churches, our schools or our colleges, our steamers or our vehicles, or any other place or places of uncommon comfort and convenience which owe their creation, their proper uses, and their perpetuity to the whites alone?" American slavery made it essentially necessary that every prerogative of manhood be denied the slave, and that his common origin and relations with other men be disputed and disproved. What, then, if there be no virtue? If every slave was a thief and debauchee, was not slavery responsible for the lost virtues? Mere property has no conscience, and upon such impersonal values the decalogue can have no claim.

But "the teachings of physiology, as well as the inspirations of Christianity, settle the question that all the tribes which inhabit the earth were originally derived from one type." "God that made the world" "hath made of one blood all nations of men for to dwell on all the face of the earth." The unity of the races settled, all questions of ethics follow for the black man as well as the white. There are no shackles forged which can bind a human soul. They may force a struggle, but triumph will somewhere and somehow crown the contest. The slave-holder must lose sight of the soul, and this he did. But the sighing and sorrowing, the hope and joy, of the Negro, thrilled him with the soul-presence, which ever and anon threatened until it finally snapped the chains of his bondage and set him free. Lorenzo Dow speaks of a master who called his slave to account for the relation of his Christian experience, and said to him, "that can't be, for you have no soul." "Well, massa," replied the slave, "if de black man hab no soul, religion make his body feel mighty happy." We have traveled too far by the days gone off to return no more even to understand the possibility of such robbery as infested the manhood of the Negro a score of years ago. We can scarcely believe that Abraham Lincoln once uttered such words as these: "I have said that I do not understand the Declaration of Independence to mean that all men are created equal in all respects. Certainly the Negro is not our equal in color—perhaps not in many other respects. I did not at any time say I was in favor of Negro suffrage. Twice—once substantially and once essentially—I declared against it. I am not in favor of Negro citizenship." But "emancipation in the United States was a growth rather than an enactment." The revelation of the whole truth seldom comes forth from any one period of the Christian Church. Christian ministers were wont to declare in

conferences and assemblies that slavery was "an institution as truly an ordinance of God as marriage or the filial relation." It was believed to be a long step in the advance when the missionary spirit for colonizing the Negro seized the Churches. "Is this country to be the ultimate home of this people?" said a minister from his pulpit. "No," he answered. "They were brought to this land for tutelage and trial." But who has thought of colonization these twenty years?

The rapid march of our civilization has led us to pass by the difficulties involved in the discussion of war problems as related to the slave people. We are in the midst of other issues—present issues—whose outcome demands the most careful consideration. It is less a question, and will continue to lessen, what we shall do with the slaves which slavery bequeathed us, than what we shall do with the children coming on since slavery was abolished. And the difficulties in the way of dealing with this new population will arise more from an attempt to apply the old methods of civilization than in conceiving and working new plans born of the present necessities. The sooner we forget slavery and all its horrors and distinctions the better for us and our work. The relations of master and slave are ended, and with them all distinctions of duty and privilege which they involved. It will not matter what you or I think of the settlement of the old disputes or difficulties. *They are settled.* This nation now can only be one people. We can have no solid South as against a solid North, and no people of the South different from the people of the North. There must be one nation, and that America.

We are not a German people, nor an Irish people, nor an African people, but an American people. No two races can live side by side in this land, one the reproach of the other. We cannot be confederated. We must be assimilated. All the social, intellectual, and constitutional elements crept into our civilization must mingle in a oneness of relation, inseparable. There can be no distinction of rights, as there must be no restriction of privileges.

The one truth, of the unity of the race, I repeat, forever settles its outcome in privileges—duty. And, when the nation is committed by its Constitution and Declaration to an equity of privileges before the law for all its citizens, its mission and ministries are pre-determined. Every restriction of right, practically imposed, is against the theory of the republic and an evidence of national hypocrisy. The nation is pledged by its very right to exist to defend the humblest citizen in all his right to life, liberty, and the pursuit of happiness.

Every good state promotes the education of its citizens. There can be no more prolific source of danger to a state than the illiteracy of its citizens. The last census gives far more than one half of the Negro population of the nation as unable to read or write. As a matter of governmental regulation, national aid must be given to the education of these unlettered masses. The very protection of the state argues for a liberal education as its best police requirement. No charity can be better bestowed than a good education. All progress of the state is dependent upon the better education of its most illiterate classes. The Negro is entitled, under his constitutional rights, to an education, to have equal facility with every other ward of the state or nation. The restriction which closes the door of any school of the nation to the Negro, because of his race or previous condition, is a thrust at his rights before the law, and an attack upon the national integrity. Thirty-five years ago, the fourth day of next December, Charles Sumner delivered his famous argument on the unconstitutionality of separate colored schools in Boston, and, in six years and thirteen days from that time, a public meeting was held in Tremont Temple of the same city to celebrate the "Triumph of Equal School Rights in Boston." That meeting was a pledge of the certainty of a similar triumph in every great city in this country. The education of a school which inhibits the presence of a scholar because he or she may be a Negro, is unsafe, and the school stands as a menace threatening the peace and welfare of the community. But in no direction is the peace of the nation more threatened than in the restriction of the religious rights of the Negro to worship. We build churches which the black man is not permitted to enter unless he may slip in unnoticed, when God is alone, or with the congregation when he is hired as a sexton. The enemy of color has commissioned the very messengers of God until they stand in their pulpits, behind the altars, under their epaulettes, to pronounce against a man because of his race and skin. There is a proneness among ministers to prefer, in the work of our ministry, the man or woman, men or women, whom we labor to save from sin and death, when that preference is based solely upon their worldly importance. Because a man has money or friends or talent or influence, or is colored white in his skin, more prayers are offered for his salvation than for the man who possesses no one of these recommendations. But "we see Jesus, who was made a little lower than the angels, for the suffering of death crowned with glory and honor, that he, by the grace of God, might taste death for every man." That he tasted more death, or death more, for one man than another the New Testament nowhere reveals.

Dr. Draper, late of the New York University, attributed the color of the skin

entirely to the action of the liver. When we find conferences—religious conferences—so organized that a man, competent to fill, and eligible to, the office of a United States Senator, would be refused membership in them, and solely upon the ground of his color, may we not relegate the whole matter to the action of the liver? In the one case the secretions of bile seem to have taken to the blood in finding the surface, in the other have they not taken to the prejudices?

But the destiny of the Negro in America will determine the outcome of our inhuman discriminations against him. Notwithstanding the millions pouring into the country during the last half of a century, the tenth census only gives 6,679,943 foreign-born persons among us. They mingle, mix races, and would disappear were it not for the flowing tides of immigration. There are 1,337,664 persons in these United States and Territories who have native mothers while they have foreign fathers. There are no races in America which have not mingled, in some degree, with other races found here. The Indian and the African have mated and mixed their families, while the Chinese and the British have married and multiplied, the Ethiopian and the Italian, the Cuban and the Mexican, the French and the Spanish, the white and the black, the yellow and the brown, have mingled in a civilization at New Orleans, until there is little unmingled blood in the creoles of three generations. As mulattos, quadroons, and octoroons measure the dissipation of race distinctions, so the second and third generations of mixed people from the ends of the earth, as found in great cities, foreshadow a homogeneous nation whose God is the Lord. Despite the laws of the States, with severe penalties against much of this miscegenation of races, the endless varieties of combination have existed and increased, until more than ten millions of the Irish and German, Scandinavian and English, and probably more than five millions of all others, not thus specified, have mixed their families in promoting the oneness of blood.

Thirty years ago the total mulatto population was one to every fifty-eight of the whole population, and one to every eighteen of the white population in the slave states. What must it be now? Among all these diverse nationalities, these "widely acting processes," are fast shaping the national type of race in the New World. In the face of law and social proscription and prejudice one third of our whole population is already a mixed people with tendencies toward still more "widely acting processes." Five generations more with a continuous immigration will mix America as thickly or thinly as the Crescent City is mixed to-day.

As the first remove from the original races staggers prejudice, and the second stunts its growth, the third will hush its voice, and the rapidity of the rate of increase in our population will multiply these removes, until we are "fused into a distinct sub-race of mankind alone peculiar to the American people." Society is not a mixing of oil and water; it will be all water, all oil, or no mixture. I know we stand aghast at the mixture of some waters, but, if they run in the same channel, they take care of themselves. Far down the Mississippi can be seen running the Missouri, water in water, but who can tell the Missouri from the Mississippi at New Orleans? Both are emptied of their colors when they reach the great Gulf. It stirs the blood of some of us to think of a colored population of nearly seven millions running out into the great white stream of people to which we belong; but that is none of our business; if we have no liking for such waters we can run along within the same banks as the great rivers do for many miles below the mouth of the Missouri, but to hinder the mingling we cannot. The great black waters have already struck the Mississippi, and there is but one outlet to the sea. Help it, we wont. Hinder it, we can't. When we made laws in the great States, as I have said, forbidding the mixture of certain races, there was *more mixture in those States than in the States where no such laws existed.* Nor is it my business to settle who another man's wife must be. I have seen trouble enough in such matters for you and me to leave the whole business alone. If he and she can't settle the matter, or they can and do, I repeat, you and I had better let the thing be. How much trouble has this nation ever had or made about the marriage of a man of Malacca, Japan, or the islands of the sea? A mandarin, who may come as a merchant among us, can settle his name in honor upon a house as yellow as the fruit of the mango tree. All this, but no Ethiopian must change his skin or look up to an equal place among the best of men. I am telling you of what will be because of what must be. Equitable relation must precede equitable privilege.

"The rank is but the guinea's stamp—
The man's the gowd for a' that,
For a' that, and a' that.
It's coming yet for a' that,
When man to man, the warld o'er,
Shall brothers be for a' that."

The nation, by law, has already eliminated every distinction of political, business, social, educational, and religious rights, which were invidiously made against the Negro after his enfranchisement. Let him be educated, intellectually and morally, and become a land-owner, and his political and social rights will take care of themselves. Put a controlling interest of Western Union and the presidency of some great trunk line

in his hands, and he will not need to be elected to have influence in Washington. Give him a few millions to carry round in his pocket, a clever education to take care of his money and position, and an election to the United States Senate from some Southern or new Western State, and prophecy will be fulfilled at once, when seven women shall take hold of one man, and they will all be white women at that.

The first man who was of the earth, earthy was not white, if the Bible has properly and significantly named him, and the last man which is from heaven will be like him. "The ideal or type man of the future will blend in himself all that is passionate and emotional in the darker races, all that is imaginative and spiritual in the Asiatic races, and all that is intellectual and perceptive in the white races. He will also be composite as regards color." "If any fact is well established in history," said a writer on this subject, "it is that the miscegenetic or mixed races are much superior mentally, physically, and morally to those pure or unmixed. Wherever on the earth's surface we find a community which has intermarried for generations, we also find evidences of decay, both in the physical and mental powers." If Harvard College were only to educate Boston boys and keep at it, and the boys never got abroad to see outside the university, but married and repeated themselves at home, eye-glasses and canes would be called into requisition much more than they are, until New England would run full and spill over a race of dudes which must mix outside or in time develop clear out. "The English people are great because they are a composite race. The French, notwithstanding that they are called Celtic, are also originally of many diverse bloods. Germany is also made up of a wide mixture of nations and races." And America holds infinite possibilities within her borders. But we shall not see her greatness at once, or justice meted out in a day. "If God," said the great German astronomer, "could wait six thousand years before he revealed to me the laws which govern the heavenly bodies, I, too, can wait until men accept them as true." The last great revelation of the Father of the race is the brotherhood of man, and if all men would only inherit the blood of the Great King, they must come to

"Shiloh's brook, which flows
Fast by the oracles of God."

When the bronze castings were being completed for the statue of Liberty on the Capitol at Washington, at the foundry of Mr. Mills, near Bladensburg, his foreman, who had superintended the work from the beginning, and who was receiving eight dollars per day, struck, and demanded ten dollars, assuring Mr. Mills that the advance must be granted him, as nobody in America except himself could complete the work. Mr. Mills felt that the demand was exorbitant, and appealed in his dilemma to the slaves who were assisting in the molding. "I can do that well," said one of them, an intelligent and ingenious servant, who had been intimately engaged in the various processes. The striker was dismissed, and the Negro, assisted occasionally by the fine skill of his master, took the striker's place as superintendent, and the work went on. The black master-builder lifted the ponderous, uncouth masses and bolted them together, joint to joint, piece by piece, till they blended into the majestic "Freedom" who to-day lifts her head in the blue clouds above Washington, invoking a benediction upon the imperiled republic. Let it be remembered that the Great Master-Builder, who presides in the council of nations, is building out of our diverse civilization a great people, whose chief glory shall be in doing his will. He is no respecter of persons, and will only take account of work done. Shall it be that the weak among us, the despised and rejected, shall come to honor, and the high and lifted up shall be cast down? "Let no man take thy crown."

4. EDUCATION AN INDISPENSABLE AGENCY IN THE REDEMPTION OF THE NEGRO RACE.

PROF. S. B. DARNELL, B.D.,

Principal Cookman Institute, Jacksonville, Florida.

WHO is the Negro? He is a man—God's noblest work in all creation was a man. From this primitive type came this race. Here is the proof. God "hath made of one blood all nations of men, for to dwell upon all the face of the earth."

Climatic changes, survival of the best adapted, the retreat, transformation, or death of the least adapted gave rise to the distinctive features of the various races; and by this method of modification, under a tropical sun, came to be the Negro race. Most scientists and biblical scholars unite in this conclusion.

Of the American Negro we speak: Where the ceaseless waves of yon ocean begin or end no mathematician can designate. Where the tints of the distant clouds begin their growth or end their shades no lover of the beautiful can point! It is equally impossible to define the metes and bounds of the Negro race. The fact is, the class of whom we speak to-day is far more American than African, and about as much Anglo-Saxon as of pure African blood. But few of those now living in the great black belts on Southern soil ever saw the African shores. They are to the manor born, and to the country chained with links forged deeper than ever slaver's shackles. They are Negro-American citizens, and prouder far of the distinction than you and I have credited them.

In eleven years' residence in Florida I have met just two that were captured on the Dark Continent. One in one thousand may have known the darkness and horror of the slaver's hold, but from the ratio of increase, the precarious conditions under which the traffic was placed, and the liable loss of vessels and imprisonment of men, the trade was well-nigh annihilated. So that the vast majorities are Americans born. And, in the unsettled condition of the civil and political affairs consequent upon the breaking up of the old and the inauguration of the new system, many more fatalities would occur than in more peaceful and law-abiding conditions, so that it would not be strange if one-half of the original four million sons of Ham, and those crossed with Japheth's erring ones who heard the trumpet tones of that Magna Charta of their liberties, have passed beyond the scenes of toil to the Elysian fields of which they sang in their quarters or sighed for the burning sun of their unrequited services; consequently one-half of the seven million freedmen have been born since slavery died.

Before another score of years shall have gone not one in twenty will be found who has tasted the bitterness of American bondage. Yes, these are Americans, colored Americans, descendants of the slaves, shaded from the softest salmon to the blackest black. I need not raise the question, Who is responsible for their presence in our midst? or that equally pertinent one, Who is responsible for the lightest shades of the colored man? but of the latter I will simply say, the quantity and quality of pigment determine as a physiological element the tints of skin from fairest blonde to deepest black, and they are, as a rule, in mathematical proportions to those residing in the parents; and what a startling fact does this bring to our notice. viz., that not one-half of these colored and freed men are of pure African blood. These shadows are passing round, and the time will come when none of these deepest shades will be found. However we may feel on this question, the stern logic of sequences will make, in the coming years, "Our Brother in Black" a misnomer, and the diverse streams of blood will so mingle that our posterity shall quote again. "God hath made of one blood all nations of men for to dwell upon all the face of the earth." Do not be alarmed at this, but strange and intricate problems are coming upon posterity, and the solution will come in the ages. To these the living must adjust themselves. A writer of no mean pretensions raises a note of alarm from North Carolina, and submits the probable relative numbers in the South for the next century. He finds the white race doubles every 30 years, and computes as follows: 12,000,000 for 1880, 24,-000,000 for 1910, 48,000,000 for 1940, 96,-000,000 for 1970.

For the Negro race, commencing at 1880 with 7,000,000, he doubles them in every 20 years, making 14,000,000 for 1900, 28,000,-000 for 1920, 56,000,000 for 1940, 112,000,-000 for 1960, or 168,000,000 against 96,000,-000 in 1970—nearly twice as many colored in 90 years. This, he declares, must culminate in an irrepressible conflict.

It will not do for posterity nor for us to say, Colonize them! Colonize whom? Expatriate them! Banish whom? They are not aliens from the commonwealth of America. The "must go" given to the poor Indian, if applied to the colored American, would raise the question, Who must go? and whose are to go? Some may wish to welcome skeptics of the Rhine, give greetings to the guzzlers of beer, and say to the poor Italians, Come, grind on your organs; but poor freedmen and mixed bloods of the South, You must go. We never will endure what you indicate as the inevitable. Well, now, dear friends, all this has a solution, the world has rolled on these few thousands of years, and the little pigmies, called men, cannot stop it; and we must not distrust the harmonizing and molding power of Christianity, especially in the light of such triumphs as crown its proud pages of the past. This class of citizens are to be the monuments of its grandest triumphs, and while removing the reproach of the past, they will be the demonstration of its vital excellence in subjugating men to its holy principles of universal brotherhood. No such severe test now remains of national importance as the American Negro, and what shall we do for and with him? Shall he drift along with the sea of humanity, surround the ship of state, check her speed until in some trough of rolling seas we all sink together, and thus allow to perish the asylum for millions? Shall he who has been the good Samaritan so often, though a slave, be turned away and perish when he has nursed our soldiers, cared for the helpless, nurtured the young, fought our battles, and defended our grand old flag?

Shall he be turned loose to grope in ignorance, sin, and the moral desolation in which freedom came to him? or shall he be lifted to plains of civilization where he may have an equal chance in the race for life?

We must stand up statesmanlike, and meet the responsibilities of this *national* question squarely, with Christian fidelity, and provide for the cultivation of this susceptible soil, and expect the gracious fruits of *Industry, Integrity,* and *Intelligence.*

In regard to their *Industry:*

Do you wonder that some felt like taking a life-long jubilee? Had I been "a slave, to fan my master's cheek and tremble when he woke," surely the trumpet-sound of freedom would have had restful tones for me more than one Sabbath in a week. But nature's necessities, some good examples and sound exhortations by others, have set the many hands at work until their taxable property in many of the Southern States ranks among the millions, and this, too, in the presence of immense embarrassments to their thrift and frugality, e.g., "the fraud of the Freedman's Bank," and those *safe* deposits in misplaced confidence never to be returned. True, we have some lazy laggards who are imitating the virtues (?) of their masters, and this is due to the natural characteristic of others about them, and the good imitative powers of the colored man. But with all this accursed indolence the pest of tramp life has not reached this class; it is unknown in the South, save a few vagrants sent down for climatic advantages in the winter.

Their integrity is often called in question. This element suffered from some causes we must explain. Conscience, which sits at once as parent and judge of the moral actions, was almost obliterated by the devastations through which they passed. Might was right, and every human hope and tie was held in the master's hand. Statutory and common law alike forbade the agency of the slave; no action of his could bind his principal. He was a *thing,* not a person, in the eyes of the law. Could not bind himself by oath, or charge aught against another. Personal responsibility *did not* inhere, *could not inhere,* in the chattel. Manhood was gone. Conscience was almost obliterated from the mental horizon of the man. All the faculties which play in moral activity had gone into winter-quarters and become so benumbed that it takes the white heat of our best civilization, and grace added thereto, to restore them to normal action; and any people so *overpowered* by the hand of such wanton oppression would have broken down; but their rebounding natures, from the wreck and ruin of this old system, have produced already many prophetic examples for the present and coming generations. Men can be found in any community upon whose broad shoulders rest the honors and responsibilities requisite for a first-class cook, eat, and sleep in one large room—a citizen—we have many such in Florida. Of would-be home, but characteristically dethe hundreds of students we have trusted, scribed by their expressive phrase, "De and the thousands of dollars entered as *place* wor I stays at." In this huddled concredits on our books, not five per cent. is dition, what of home knowledge or true charged up to loss account. What has been social life could possibly be obtained by and what may be accomplished of this moral these parents, children, men, and women resurrection is due to intelligence and the *herded* together. The wonder is that the grace of God. Of the former of these we home life and social tie survived at all. But have now to speak. Without some knowl- the great evils naturally suspected do not edge grace is impotent. Many thought that *prevail.* Married life and individual chastity conversion and reconstruction were all these are illustrated by vast majorities; and, in childlike minds needed, but, alas! while some view of the superior intelligence enjoyed by by peculiar endowments and fortuitous cir- the whiter race, not serious odds are to be set cumstances have come to an excellent estate, down against the Negro. If others shall the millions are yet under the cloud. Like draw a darker picture, then so much more the enfranchised six weeks' emigrant, he can reason is there to insist on the necessities vote only as a machine. His loyalty, how- for education. But what have been their ever, can never be questioned. intellectual opportunities. The answer is

Some improved the advantages afforded formed already in most minds. I urge you body-servants, and walked into the halls of to ponder it more carefully. Here we had a legislatiou, where once their masters stood, positive and successful prohibition. How but the vast majorities have had no oppor- vigilant these guardians were to maintain tunities to learn their duties as citizens. The the honor of the statutory and common law, positions in commercial and mercantile life lest some poor ebony-face should be enlight- are hedged about with more than a Chinese ened with one ray that might guide them to wall. Out of over two hundred qualified for the north star of deliverance. What could ordinary mercantile life, in Cookman Insti- dispel the Egyptian darkness that possessed tute, of which I am president, one is a pho- their minds? A few Christian hearts broke tographer, one a book-keeper, two are over these lines, but they were watched, cir- dealers in merchandise, and two I ave had cumvented, and prohibited, sometimes chas- valuable positions in the Departments at tized for the infraction of the law that made Washington. it a crime to teach the Negro. It was well

A white face is almost a *sine qua non* understood that education cut the cord that for a successful effort to obtain a clerkship bound the slave, and well did they reason, or merchant's position in the land where vigilantly did they guard the limitations that these people live, and our whole country is bound the giant, and firmly did they hold not free from the sin. Secretary Lincoln the prostrate mind, lest it should learn to had not the nerve to cause the papers of know its strength and assert its rights to Livingston, our graduate, to be produced at liberty.
West Point. The case was wrought up at Now that the possibilities are open to him, Washington to preclude investigation, and and freedom has been crowned with the his *alleged* failure magnified when he had perilous privileges of franchise, his igno- passed a competitive examination and out- rance—the occasion of his subjugation then stripped three white men for the cadetship, —must be counteracted now by conferring and since, by another examination, won a the interdicted agency as the only and abso- place that gives him $1,200 a year and lute condition, the only lever of power, that affords him an opportunity to graduate in will lift him to the level of ordinary and medicine in two years to come. Yes, the dutiful citizenship. This has been advocated prejudice is mountain high, but, like an ice- from rostrum, pulpit, and press, but the berg, it will thaw out under the tropical sun remedies thus far employed have been of intelligence and the heat of Gospel truth, wholly inadequate. The spasmodic effort of and these alone will accomplish it. House- Christian heroes to go South to teach spent hold servants saw what civilized life was, its force, did good; their memory should be and their ideas of domestic economy were embalmed in our hearts forever; but, worn- somewhat developed; some became experts out by care, grown old in service, circum- in cooking and general duties, consequently vented by the plots of designing men, chilled some good homes are found among them to- with the long ostracism by persons who day; but what are these among the millions? ought to have hailed them as angels of light, It must not be forgotten that they were a one by one, by death or removal, marriage, small percentage compared with the men and or retirement to their more congenial homes, women who toiled under a Southern sun, this *noble* band has scarcely a representative either on the broad savannahs, or fingered among the common schools of the entire the boles of snowy cotton, and who, never South. The next possible resource was the crossing the threshold of the mansion, results of their work, the ill-trained, imma- turned away to the dingy cabin quarters to ture minds among the freedmen themselves.

Some of these did become teachers of no mean proficiency, but the thousands required were wanting, and are to-day being only partially supplied by the efforts of our denominational schools. These are working up to their fullest capacity, but their products do not supply more than one-tenth of the demand. Not a small portion of their qualified teachers get into positions of greater emolument. Home and parentage take away a large percentage; and so, while the normal is the prevailing idea, yet the supply afforded has to be a constant flowing stream.

Nor can we look to the Christian Church, with all its vitality of moral forces, to furnish this absolute necessity for redeeming the colored race. Its preachers may preach, its prayers ascend, conversions ensue, but that does not become a substitute for education even here in the North, much less can it succeed in the South. Intelligence must precede or accompany the grace of God to elevate the man to conditions of Christian character, and character-building is the aim of all true education. Primary principles must be taught, discipline of mind must be attained, but all means employed and individual efforts put forth that *do not* aid in the establishment of character, in the strengthening of purpose, and in ennobling the nature, *are of little avail.*

Now, what is universally acknowledged to be a necessity to the *strength, protection,* and *perpetuity* of all other races, must be conceded to be essential to the welfare of this race, and the utter failure of the States to afford adequate means to inaugurate and sustain this remedial agency causes the race in whose name we plead to-day to stretch out its imploring hands, to raise the cry again, "O Lord, how long shall these blessings of freedom be denied us!" More than this,

"A poor, blind Samson is in our land,
  Bound hand and foot and prone upon his
    back,
But, who knows, that in some drunken
    revel,
He may rise and grasp the pillars
Of our temples' liberties, shake the foundations,
Till all beneath its broken columns lie in
    ruins."

Let the pleadings of the people, the dangers that threaten, and the alarms sounded by their friends or foes, the welfare of the several States, the safety of the whole body politic, the future stability of our great government, alike appeal to the strong hand of the nation's aid, to interpose and declare by the use of millions—*Let there be light.*

5. ASSIMILATION, NOT SEPARATION.

REV. JABEZ PITT CAMPBELL, D.D.,

One of the Bishops of the African Methodist Episcopal Church.

THAT the Africo-American, or colored man, commonly called the Negro, is the subject of a most cruel, wicked, and unjustifiable prejudice in America, which does not appear to exist against him in any other grand division of the earth, is a fact beyond the power of successful contradiction.

Many persons who are, as they suppose, unjustly numbered with this class of persons against whom this prejudice exists, are goaded in their feelings into little, if any thing, less than desperation, and despair, finally, in some cases. They are forever looking at the dark side, and never at the bright side, of this picture. It is commonly said, and it is said because it is commonly believed, that the American "white" people are prejudiced against the Negro in their heart on account of his color—that the American hates the Negro on account of the color of his skin.

But it is not so. They who are thus persuaded are laboring under the influence of a mistaken notion. The American people are

5

no more prejudiced against the Negro on account of the color of his skin, than the most refined people of Europe, who never dream of hatred toward the Negro on account of his color.

The American gentleman, like the European, wears black cloth, black hats, and black boots; and he drives black horses, keeps black dogs for his pleasure-taking and sporting purposes, and he deals in black things generally. The American lady, like the English and French lady, whom she follows as her fashionable guide, wears black dresses, black bonnets, and black shoes. And she has her black cats, and her black lap-dog, which she is often seen carrying in her arms or upon her hands, without the shadow of a sign of her being prejudiced against him on account of his black color. The charge that American prejudice against the Negro has its foundation in the color of his skin is not true, it is a false assumption.

But it is condition, not color, that stands

athwart the Negro's progress—it is *caste*, the curse of the earlier civilizations. To illustrate:

Some years ago I had occasion to deliver a lecture at Burlington, Vt., upon the subject of slavery, and the bad effects of it upon both races—white and colored people. Speaking concerning American prejudices, I endeavored to show that the American prejudice was against the Negro on account of his condition, and not his color.

After the conclusion of my lecture, a well known, very wealthy gentleman arose and made a statement which confirmed the truth of my position. He said that some years ago a colored young man was sent by the American Missionary Board to labor as a missionary on the coast of Africa. Before leaving America he married a wife. They went to Africa, and stayed there about twelve years before they returned.

They came home on a visit, and after their arrival in New York, the secretary of the society wrote to the above-named gentleman to get up a meeting for the missionary, and also requesting him to provide a stopping-place for the missionary, his wife, and child. The gentleman was heartily willing to obey the order, but he forgot to inform his wife, and to show her the letter of the secretary. He met them upon the arrival of the steam-boat on Lake Champlain. He took the woman by the arm, and the little girl by the hand, directed the man to take his carpet-bag, and they went up to the house of this wealthy merchant. He rang the bell of his own front door. The Irish waiting-maid came and opened it. But when she saw a colored woman having hold of the arm of the master of the house, she fell back from the door. He paid no attention beyond giving her an order to call the mistress of the house, and ask her to come into the parlor. The order was executed, and the lady of the house was immediately forthcoming. She was introduced to the Rev. Mr. Blank, and then to his wife, Mrs. Blank, to both of whom, in a very lofty and stiff, yet lady-like manner, she said, "How do you do? and I hope that you are well." She was then told that the little girl was their daughter. She then said to the child, "How do you do, little one?" This being done, our gentleman said, "My dear, these persons have come here all the way from New York, and they have had nothing to eat to-day. Can you not give them breakfast, or something to eat?"

She said, "I cannot."

With very great surprise he asked why she could not give them something to eat. She answered that there was nothing in the house. The husband again asked, "But, my dear wife, can't you give them something, if it is only a lunch?"

She said, angrily, "I cannot. I told you that I have nothing in the house to eat, and don't you believe me, sir?"

He answered, "O, yes, my dear wife, I believe. I always believe you. I only thought it to be very strange that you should have nothing in the house to eat." "But," said he, "my dear wife, let me tell you that this man and his wife are the missionaries that our Missionary Board, of which you and I are members, sent to Africa some twelve years ago, when this woman married this man, to go with him into our African Mission work. They are the persons whom you have been most faithfully laboring to sustain in that mission from that time until the present. They have only come home on a visit to see their former home and friends, with the intention, when they have accomplished their design, to return to their former field of labor. And this little girl is their only living child, which was born under the Board, of which you are a member, and which you have been laboring hard to support."

Hearing this statement, she was at once filled with wonder, amazement, and a glad heart, to see the little girl that was "born under the Board." Tiddy was immediately sent in haste to call in the children of wealthy neighboring families, to see the little girl that was "born under the Board." They came, and very soon the parlor was filled with them, all of whom were overjoyed to see a little girl that was "born under the Board."

Although his wife had nothing in the house to eat so as to enable her to give the Negro preacher, his wife, and child a breakfast, she that day gave the best dinner, out of many, which he had eaten for eighteen months, all on account of the little girl that was "born under the Board." The knowledge of that fact caused the badge of prejudice, the black color of the skin, to cease to be an object of hatred and a bar to social Christian fellowship and friendly intercourse during the time of their sojourn in "the land of the free and the home of the brave."

The color of his skin is only a badge by which the class is known to which the American Negro belongs under the laws of *caste*. It is not a badge of universal application to men of other nationalities, such as are the Indian of this country, the Chinaman, the Japanese, the Spaniard, the Portuguese, and the men of other nations who are black, or brown, or tawny colored, but who are not white men.

Assimilation, not separation from the American people, is the right of the Negro upon the American continent, and this right will be accredited to him by the people. We assume to say, without the fear of contradiction, that the heart of the American people is on the side of liberty, the existence of involuntary servitude to the contrary notwithstanding. The actual existence of slavery among them was the exception, and not the rule.

The Puritan fathers represented by the pilgrim passengers on the *Mayflower*, and who landed at Plymouth Rock in 1620, left the Old World and came to sojourn in the New in order to escape both religious and political oppression, and enjoy both religious and political liberty in the New World. Those Puritans became the right seed, the root, and branches of the American nation. They laid the foundation of liberty and freedom upon the American continent. To them may be traced the origin of that statement which amounts to little less than inspiration from the Almighty, namely, "That we hold these truths to be self-evident, that all men are created equal, and are endowed by their Creator with certain inalienable rights, among which are life, liberty, and the pursuit of happiness."

That statement is the soul—the heart—of the American people, upon which all the institutions of the land are founded, human chattel slavery excepted. And let it be forever kept in mind that the term slavery was never permitted nor allowed to appear in the original Constitution of our country. It is worthy of note that slavery never existed by national constitution. The national heart would not admit of such an anomaly in the organic law of their free institutions or the Constitution of the United States. All the indications of divine Providence in the near past, and in the present, point most unmistakably to the fact that on this continent must be developed a homogeneous people out of the heterogeneous masses who flock to this land—*the American idea* must be accepted by them, and they must be thoroughly baptized into it, or this must cease to be their dwelling-place. And, indeed, may it not be that the God of all the earth intends, from this American continent as a center, to radiate a more perfect civilization and a broader Christianity to all the ends of the earth?

The Negro, though forcibly brought and detained here, accepts, and heartily adopts, *the American idea;* he links hand and heart with his white brother, and whenever allowed, and even when not allowed, he gains his temporal and spiritual well-being with his brother of lighter hue, laboring in the field, in the shop, in the counting-room, with him, and side by side kneels with him at a common shrine.

The final result of the complete development of our American homogeneity looks toward a new era in the history of the world, called by some the millennium, or the ultimate triumph of Christianity over the whole earth.

6. THE DANGER LINE IN NEGRO EDUCATION.

REV. WILLIAM HAYES WARD, D.D.,

Editor New York "Independent."

I CONFESS I do not quite like to speak of Negro education. In some portions of our country the native has no place. We have no separate class, called Negroes, which must have a separate education. We have Negroes, large numbers of them, in our cities, but in education we do not know them from whites. They go to the same schools, recite to the same teachers in the same classes. I remember, when a boy of ten or twelve, going to the same public school with Negro children. We had no problem of Negro education. To be sure this happy state of things is not quite universal North, but it is extending so as to embrace its exceptions. New York city has lately abolished its colored schools without a word of objection being heard. We have Chinese schools yet, private Sunday and evening schools, because the Chinese are adults, and cannot talk our language; but there is no such necessity for Negro schools. Chinese children, if there were such, would be welcome to our public schools with other children.

But, in certain portions of our country, portions where it is hard work to keep up one system of public schools, public sentiment requires that two systems be maintained, one for the pure whites, and the other for the partly white and the wholly colored. Public sentiment requires this so imperatively, that it is no use to think of overcoming it. Neither logic nor Christianity can do that for years to come, and we must, meanwhile, submit to the absurd and the inevitable. Prejudice will, of course, give way in the end, but we must not delay education for that. We will do things as we can, if we cannot as we would, but with a constant protest. Leaving now the protest, however, which we do not wish to carry to an impracticable limit, we proceed to discuss the Danger Line in Negro Education.

While I think the danger line is not so

much in Negro education as it is in the lack of it, yet, in the progress of the education of a people coming out of absolute illiteracy, there comes a period when their little learning, which ought to steady them, may unsteady them. The chief of all economic virtues, on which a community is built, is patient faithfulness in labor, chiefly physical, manual labor. That virtue can be possessed by a very ignorant, illiterate people. If they possess that sole virtue they will be successful and happy. Labor, patient labor, carries with it home and family and health. It will be rude labor, hand labor, mostly agricultural labor, but such labor will be both domestic and reasonably honest. It will not cultivate vice or anarchy, though it may be a tool of it. It makes for virtue and peace. There seems to be an impression abroad now, however, that, as the Negroes are educated, they become unwilling to engage in regular labor, and that we are in danger of educating the Negro race out of their present sphere of usefulness into a condition of ambitious and mischievous idleness. We hear complaints of half-educated Negroes who are too proud and lazy to work, and who are only demoralizing those who do work. Indeed, a South Carolina statesman (not noted for his love for the Negro) has lately expressed the opinion that his State would be enriched by the emigration or deportation of two hundred thousand of its colored people. This remarkable proposition either contradicts the accepted truth of political learning, that every laborer has a definite money value, and is a part of the wealth of the state; or it asserts that the Negro laborers are not laborers in fact, but that they are unproductive drones, or, at least, that they produce no more than they consume, and that they occupy the ground so as to keep out really productive labor. I do not know that Senator Butler would assert that the two hundred thousand whom he would deport are the more educated Negroes, but those who make his complaint of the unreliable character of Negro labor, and the deteriorating condition of the Negroes, are apt to be among those who are most suspicious of Negro education, and who have the sharpest eye to see its failure. We are told that as fast as they are educated they are unwilling to work, or that they wish to get their living by their wits.

In considering this complaint one of the first things that occur in reply is that the education of the Negro is not progressing at any such rate as to inspire immediate dread. During the ten years, from 1870 to 1880, the number of voters in the South who cannot read or write increased by nearly two hundred thousand, an increase very evenly divided between white and black voters. In Georgia the illiterate white vote, during the decade, increased by eight

thousand and the colored by sixteen thousand. In Kentucky the white illiterate vote increased by seven thousand and the colored by five thousand. In Tennessee the white illiterate vote increased by nine thousand and the colored by four thousand. In Texas the white illiterate vote increased by fifteen thousand and the colored by twelve thousand. In Alabama the white illiterate vote increased by seven thousand, the colored by five thousand. In Mississippi the white by three thousand, the colored by eighteen thousand. In North Carolina the white by eleven thousand, the colored by twelve thousand. In South Carolina the white by fifteen hundred, the colored by twenty-three thousand. In Virginia the white by four thousand, the colored by two thousand. In these nine representative Southern States—Virginia, Kentucky, Tennessee, North Carolina, South Carolina, Georgia, Alabama, Mississippi, and Texas—the white illiterate vote increased by sixty-nine thousand, the colored by ninety-six thousand. If we take the whole country through, North and South, the white illiterate vote increased by one hundred and thirty-eight thousand, and the colored by one hundred and sixty thousand, the great bulk of increase, in both cases, being in the South.

It will be seen by these figures that both the whites and the blacks are holding their own in the matter of ignorance. If ignorance be the road to virtue, industry, or thrift, then those who have been frightened by the rapid education of the Negro may calm their fears. There is no immediate danger but we shall have ignorant voters enough to preserve the contentedness with which both races will sink as low in the ranks of labor as will please the most aristocratic taste.

I do not forget how much is doing for the education of the Negro. I remember that every State in the South, almost without exception, has, on paper, a passably fair system of free schools for both races, and that progress is making almost every year in the character or conduct of their schools. If the number of illiterates is increasing, so is also the number of those who can read and write. Much as I dislike the common-school system of the South, which is based on the ungodly principle of caste, declaring that whites and blacks must be educated separately; that each town must have two sets of schools, one for its white brahmins and one for its black pariahs, a system that, in this country, at least, nearly or quite doubles the expense of supporting the schools, or else greatly reduces their term of continuance and efficiency; yet this can be said for it, that it is an education better than nothing. It is a system unchristian and bad, terribly expensive, and one that perpetuates, because it is based upon, the spirit of caste. Further, it is false because it assumes to be based on the color line, which line does not exist; for there is no color line. The gradation between white and black is so nice that no human being can tell where the line runs. It even assumes to give the lie to facts, by classing as Negroes those in whom no eye can see a trace of Negro blood, and to force their children into the Negro schools. But I will not stop to dwell on the evils of a system which happens to be the best that can now be had. A society which has grown up on caste, which has for generations made one race masters and the other slaves, and which has laid down always the law of violence and cruelty that the children must follow the mother, cannot be converted in a day. The old subject-race, too, will have its ignorance as also its vices, which will be easily made the excuse for perpetuating the wrong. Separate schools will, for many years, with all their extra expense, seem to be a social necessity at the South. It is all we can expect if the colored people may have a system of free schools supported out of the common taxation, in which they shall have a share proportioned, not to their taxes and their wealth, but to the numbers of their children. But we cannot even temporarily be satisfied with a school law like that of Kentucky, in which State not only are the white schools separate from the Negro schools, and kept so separate even in a population where one race is in a large majority on penalty of losing all State aid, but a law which requires that school moneys shall not be distributed according to the numbers of those of school age, but according to the taxes paid—the school-tax of white people going to white schools, and those of colored people to colored schools. Such a school law has its reason in a desire that the Negro shall not be educated, and that the poverty and ignorance with which he came out of slavery shall be perpetuated as long as possible. Submitting, however, for the present, to the inevitable, we see with gratitude that the free education of the Negroes of the South is making progress even under a bad system, or with a vast number of utterly incompetent teachers. If the number of illiterates is increasing, so also is the number of those who can read and write. And we acknowledge with satisfaction the noble work done for Southern education by Northern charity. The South is dotted all over with normal schools and colleges, every State has them, for the education of the Negro—schools not supported by Southern money, but by Northern benevolence. In these the Congregationalists led, and still lead, the way with their long line of universities and industrial institutes and normal schools—Hampton Institute, Atlanta University, Fisk University, and

others—not that they give more to the South than others, but that they have preferred to put their money into general education rather than to establish churches of their own order. They are followed hard by Methodists, Presbyterians, Baptists, Episcopalians, United Presbyterians, Friends, and others, from all of whose institutions there is pouring out a constant stream of young men and young women fitted, after a fashion not equal generally, it must be confessed, to the fashion of the North, but yet fitted fairly, to act as teachers. Nor do I forget how, through these and other schools, the Peabody Fund, now closing up its activity, or the Slater Fund, now beginning to work under the admirable conduct of that noble man, President Haygood, are doing their part in Negro education. No man can visit those schools, year after year, without being delighted with the progress made. It is true that the Negro begins a thousand years behind the white man; but, through these various school agencies and through the religious instruction he receives, he is rapidly gaining, and making up the lost ground quite as rapidly as could be expected. If the volume of ignorance has not diminished, indeed is increasing, yet the volume of education is increasing, and that at a faster ratio. There is progress, though not such rapid progress as need greatly frighten our reactionary neighbors who fear that education will spoil the Negro as a laborer.

But let us come right down to the question, Does education spoil the laborer? If it spoils the black laborer it must equally spoil the white laborer. Does it? In communities all of whites there must be a laboring class. Is that class in England, in Germany, in Massachusetts, spoiled by being educated? Does it cease to labor? If such be the fact, the world has not yet discovered it. England, Germany, Massachusetts, are still going on sublimely ignorant of it, working harder and harder to extend and improve their system of free and universal education. Indeed, we suppose it to be a common belief or superstition—it has come to be an axiom—that the voter must be educated, whether a laborer or not. Indeed, we are every-where coming to the rule of compulsory education. We say, by law, that children *must* be educated—the children of the poor as well as of the rich. We make laws in New Jersey forbidding children to labor in factories at an age when they ought to be in school. Our reason is not that these children may not become laborers, but that labor may be educated. We must educate it, or we perish. In this matter are colored people different from white? Not at all. Ah! there is not the difficulty at all. The real root-trouble is this: those who complain that the education of the Negro will ruin him as a laborer want to keep him ignorant.

If they cannot have slavery they want serfdom. They want the Negro to be a hand-laborer and nothing else, and without ambition to be any thing else. They wish to be gentlemen and property holders themselves, and they do not want the Negroes gentlemen and property holders. They do not want to see them teachers, ministers, physicians, lawyers, merchants, manufacturers, land-holders. They want to see them day-laborers, and contented to be nothing more.

We must have day-laborers, and they will be those who, for the most part, have not sought a liberal education. The world cannot get on without day-labor. The question is, Shall our labor be serf or free? Shall it be intelligent or ignorant? Shall we try the Massachusetts system or the system of Russia? Shall our laborers know how and why they vote, or shall they be the tools of demagogues? Does uneducated labor work well in Russia? Tell us, enemies of Negro education, how has your plan worked in the South? Is an ignorant ballot such a success in the South that you wish to perpetuate it? The real fact is that those who wish all labor to be ignorant do not wish it to be free. They are as much opposed to the ballot for the Negro as to the school-house. But, whether we will have it so or not, the ballot has come to the Negro, and has come to stay. It is only a fool that can wish a voting citizen to be ignorant.

To those who tell us, then, that there is a danger line in Negro education, that if they learn too much they will be too vain or too ambitious to be laborers, we reply that they have got to risk it. It is a bigger risk to have your voters ignorant. We do not propose to build the structure of our American institutions on the rim of a volcano. An ignorant suffrage is a boiling, bubbling volcano. If you tell us that you will take the ballot from them, we tell you you shall not, you cannot. The ballot is there, so you must fit it by education for its work. The eternal facts of God and nature force you to go forward. You can't go backward. You must go forward, with all its risk. Do I say, with all its risk? Nay, with all its beneficent blessing; nay, more, with all its justice, fair justice, to a race to which we who have so long oppressed it, who are the authors of its faults, owe all and more than all that we can ever pay. The Negro of the South must, *must* be educated.

But when I am told that the educated Negro is deteriorated by his learning, that he is unfitted for work thereby, I utterly deny the assertion. Is, then, a white man spoiled by education? Who dares propose to the American people that you pull down that ladder by which the poorest snipe of the gutter may climb to the university? Intelligent white labor is worth more, is more diligent, than

ignorant white labor; so the same is true of colored labor. In this matter there is no difference between white and black. The color is only skin deep. No; the objection to colored education does not come from an honest fear that educated Negro labor will cease to be efficient, but from a desire to keep it *under*, to keep it servile.

It may be true that educated Negroes will not all wish to engage in the lowest manual labors. Do educated white men? They are fitted for higher work, that which tasks brain as well as hands. Are we unwilling to give a black man a fair chance to do the same? Are not white men workers unless they dig ditches or hoe cotton? Count up how many thousands of teachers are needed in the South for the colored people. Not less than 50,000 colored teachers are needed in the South, all well educated, and all hard workers. It will take a great while yet to secure them, with all the work which our funds and our societies can do.

But I resent the assertion that education does, in fact, make the Negro lazy and worthless. Let us look at representative facts. A year ago there were collected the statistics of the employment of the 426 graduates of the Hampton (Va.) Normal and Industrial Institute, including with them 37 *senior* undergraduates. Of these 426, (two thirds males,) more than three fourths, have made teaching their regular and constant profession, and over 90 per cent. have engaged in teaching. That means work, honorable work. Do you ask me what else they have done? I bid you remember that they are all young; that a number were pursuing their further studies elsewhere; but I will tell you what else they were doing: 37 are reported (I hope this will please those who want to see the Negro stick to his manual toil) as carpenters, waiters, common laborers, tailors, housemaids, seamstresses, servants, janitors, shoemakers, miners, etc. I believe their education has done them good. Our objector, I trust, will allow that it has not spoiled them. Then there are 30 physicians, ministers, missionaries, book-keepers, clerks, postmasters, and merchants. Those are good, honest lines of business. Then, 153 of these young men report themselves as the owners of land or other property. Seven own over 100 acres; 18 more own over 50; 4 more over 20; 14 more over 5; and 59 more less than 5. They have proved that their education makes them thrifty, not thriftless. They have already, out of their scanty wages as teachers, begun to save a competence to become property holders. They have an interest in the public welfare. They have given hostages to the state. They have set a good example to their neighbors, white and black. Such is the record of the graduates of one school, and a similar record could be given by the representatives whom I see about me—Dr.

Rust, Dr. Hartzel, Dr. Strieby, and others, of all our societies for promoting the education of the Southern Negroes.

I am willing to allow only this truth in the complaint, that education is making our Negroes worthless and shiftless. It is possible that in some States a number who can just read, but who have not enterprise enough to seek a real education, are froth and scum. Of course there are such. They are in every white community, and hang about our street-corners, and lounge in our groggeries. If Senator Butler could deport a hundred thousand of them from New York the State would be richer. But that is not a vice of color. It belongs to white and black alike. It comes from the inborn laziness which is a big part of the natural depravity of man. Men must be regenerated before they are cured of it. Education will relieve it, especially religious education, but it is a universal vice of human nature.

This further I grant: that the Negro, while being educated to be a teacher, must not learn to despise manual labor. I would have a manual-labor department in every one of our colored normal schools or colleges. I go further than that, for I say that there is no color in education. I would have all the grammar and high schools in the North and South, which are supported by the State, teach the elements of agriculture, carpenter-ing, and blacksmithing to every boy, and good manual labor in housework and sewing to every girl who does not learn it at home. To that, I think, we must come in these days when the old, silly system of apprenticeship has passed away, and nothing is taking its place. A manly character will not despise hard labor. Give us more Hamptons. Let our schools, North and South, follow more that model.

But our benevolent societies cannot do all the work. The States cannot do all the work. They are poor. But the United States can do it. The government is rich. It is paying off the debt at the rate of $100,000,000 per year. Let just a few millions be given for the education of the South, of white and black alike, and our institutions will be safe. At present they are in imminent peril. You gentlemen of the Freed-men's Aid Societies, who are so loudly appealing to the unwilling North for money to educate the South, know the danger. As you recognize that the danger is now quite as imminent for the whites as far the blacks, we, the people, demand of our representatives in Congress that they allow us, the people, to educate our own people. We will have it. We cannot consent to see our citizens growing up in increasing numbers the tools of designing knaves. Give us an educated suffrage, or we perish.

7. OPENING REMARKS.

REV. H. L. MOREHOUSE, D.D.,

Secretary American Baptist Home Missionary Society.

Dr. Morehouse presided at the fifth session, and said :

I CAME to this meeting with the purpose of saying not a word except what might be necessary in the introduction of the speakers who are to address us this afternoon. Although I am suffering from a severe cold, yet it is sometimes harder not to say something than to speak.

We were interested this morning in the discussion of questions relating to the Negro in America. I am not sure but that the thing which we are after might be put in the reversed form—America in the Negro. That is what we want. When we say the Negro in America we mean, not only the Negro on our soil, but the Negro in the midst of American civilization, American ideas; and what we mean by America in the Negro is American civilization, American ideas of citizen-ship, of Church membership, of the family life, etc., incorporated into the Negro character.

Much has been said in some quarters recently concerning the Americanization of the people who come to us from foreign shores. That among the Germans particularly, among the Irish, perhaps, as well, there is a tendency not to assimilate with American character and American customs, but to preserve their distinctiveness, to transplant, indeed, on American soil European ideas concerning the Church, concerning the Sabbath, and concerning other things; and we say in America that this separateness of one class of people from the bulk of the people is an anomaly. So we say, let the Germans cease to be Germans, let the Scandinavians cease to be Scandinavians, let the Irishmen cease to be Irishmen, and let them feel and act as though they were Americans. We want the American idea to expel the European idea, the German idea, and out of these heterogeneous elements make a homogeneous mass. The Negro is distinct from us; nevertheless, he is here, and'on the part of the colored man there came about an inclination to separate himself from the white man, which dated from the close of the war; and what we want to do is to get the American idea in the Negro—that he is an American citizen; that race counts for nothing. and manhood for every thing. We have the greatest problem on our hands in the next twenty years that we have ever had. The self-assertion of some is becoming manifest. What we want to do is to devise those means and those measures which will bring those men to feel that, in common with other American citizens, these liberties began in the war. It has cemented us as nothing else could; the Revolutionary War made a national sentiment, and so did the War of 1812; in the War of the Rebellion there was a beginning of this development of a common sentiment, because in that struggle the colored man participated with the white man. There sprang up on the part of the colored man toward the white man a sympathy, and also on the part of the white man toward the colored man. So that war resulted in a unification of feeling as nothing else could have done. In the emancipation of the slaves of the North, it was done in the first place by individual States, and when it came to the emancipation of the slaves of the South, it was the hand of the nation, and the colored man looked upon the national law as his liberator. He knew something about the nation and a national feeling, though he belonged in South Carolina or Georgia; and that he belonged to the United States. This feeling must go on until he shall realize that he is not only an American citizen, but also until he have a broad and intelligent sense of all the duties involved in that high prerogative. He must be made to feel that ho must fear nothing because he is a black man, and he is to expect no favor because he is a black man.

---

8. THE NEGRO IN AMERICA: HIS SPECIAL WORK.

REV. J. C. PRICE, A.M.,

President Zion Wesley Institute, Salisbury, N. C.

THE providential government of God is an established fact. Every individual, race, and age contributes to the well-being and happiness of mankind by the due performance of peculiar and specified work. Paul, Bacon, and Shakespeare each did his work as no other man could have done. The dispersed Jews are the chosen depositaries of God's truth, and the peculiar race trained for the religious education of the world.

The Greeks in their culture and art. the Romans in their civilization and laws, handed down distinct benefits to the nations that have succeeded them.

To say that the American Negro has a peculiar work is not startling.

The first glimpses of our history in this country make it evident that our mission here is providential and peculiar. Although every page of this history, from 1620 to 1863, is written in blood and tears, it was the carrying out of a Divine plan—the execution of a part of the great work of God. Some one may ask, Can you look at your ancestors torn from their native land, see children separated from parents and wives from husbands, and say it was God's plan? Can you bring to mind the horrors of the "middle passage," and then follow the wrongs, cruelties, and inhumanities of more than two centuries, and say it is God's way? I answer, Yes. But while I recognize an end in view, I do not commend the means to that end. But I would say to the "trader in human flesh," as Joseph said to his conscience-smitten brethren, "It was not you that sent me hither, but God." The slave-trader meant evil, but God intended it for good. In this, the wrath of men is to praise him.

In the seventeenth century it was almost universally admitted that the Negro had a "special work" in this country. It is not unreasonable to say that he has, under new developments, a special work in the nineteenth century. But how did he perform the former?

The drained marshes, cultivated highlands, fertile plantations, stately mansions, and railways of the South attest that it was *well done*.

But we would be more zealous and earnest and laborious in that which is yet to be done, than in that which is done.

The receding past, despite its unpleasantness and bitter expense, brings the consolation of a work completed through a Divine injunction.

The present, with its accompanying privileges and duties, is not without its encouragement. And, notwithstanding the solemn responsibilities that "loom up" amid the "uncertainties of the future," we feel that there is "guidance for our footsteps and inspiration for our work."

But you ask, What is the work? Whence comes its peculiarity? This question seems unnecessary, when we reflect a moment on American history, interwoven as it has been with that of the Americanized African.

The degradation arising from centuries of enslavement cannot be removed in a score of years. Very often the injury of a moment is only remedied by years of careful attention. The heavy shackles on the limbs of the slave were fit emblems of the heavier bonds of ignorance and superstition on the soul. These darkened intellects, blunted morals, and distorted characters of nearly seven millions of people, are now to be enlightened, quickened, and righted. Who are to do it? Let us try to find out. Will the Southern white people do it? We think not.

The "peculiar institution" made a line of demarkation between the white man and the black man in that section, if not in other sections. It told the white man he *must not* come in social or personal contact with the Negro. Hence the teaching and preaching among colored people in the South is not done by the white men and women of that section.

Many of them desire to see the colored people educated; and by individual donations and through legislation they contributed to this end. This has been witnessed in the work of Zion Wesley Institute, at Salisbury, N. C., and is also seen in the annual appropriation for Atlanta University in Georgia. But they do not think that they are to come into personal contact with the Negro and do this work.

Will the whites of the South do it? Northern philanthropists have contributed to the work among the freedmen with a generosity that is most commendable. They have sent their millions into the South. But they, even, feel that they are not to do this work by personal contact with the colored man.

I gratefully acknowledge that many noble, self-sacrificing men and women (too much praise cannot be given them) went into the South during and after the war to lift up the fallen. They have accomplished a glorious work. We always welcome them.

Many of them, in doing this work, were insulted, persecuted, and some had to escape for their lives. Others were ostracised. Men, their wives and daughters, were considered disreputable, were not allowed into white society, simply because they taught Negro boys and girls. Many could not stand this ostracism, and consequently they either returned home or engaged in what they considered more congenial business.

God be praised for the good men and the good women who proved equal to the emergency! But are these teachers and preachers doing the bulk of the educational and religious work in the South? With the exception of the colleges and universities conducted by white men, (and many of those are controlled by white and colored men,) the educational work in the Southern cities, towns, and rural districts is carried on by colored men and women.

Again, the Churches in the South, like the generality of those in the North, are separate—one for the white and one for the colored people. So the colored ministers are the religious instructors for the millions of their people.

The whites who are engaged in the Southern work are just helping the Negroes do it.

The four millions have grown to nearly seven millions. To uplift this people is whose special work? I only voice your sentiments when I say that this great work, in all of its increasing proportions—as far as personal contact is concerned—is to be done by the Africo-Americans whose training fits them for teachers and leaders among their people.

They are to mold the sentiment, determine the course, and shape the future of this race.

The solution of the vexing Negro problem is to come from within him rather than from without.

The Negro himself, both by inward resolution and external irrepressibility, is to solve his own problem. Our relation to the Negro and our knowledge of him argue our fitness for his reform and regeneration by the Word and Spirit of God.

We must lead on in the great work committed to our charge. Every day of added intelligence, every trained young man or woman, every school-house, every college or university, adds to our power to do this work. Under the guidance of God a prospect opens before us unequaled in attractions and not excelled in mighty possibilities.

That the Negro is to be the future educator of his race, no unbiased mind will deny. This truth comes to the present generation with great force. A score of years has brought to them advantages which were withheld from the generation preceding us, in whose footsteps we now tread. They, nor we, must no longer grovel in the sins in which they were once taught to indulge. But instructed as to the errors of the past, aroused to the duty of the present, and directed to the prospect of the future, these once debased souls will aspire to and practice what good men love and God approves.

But why attach so much importance to the education of nearly seven millions of poor, ignorant men and women, almost lost amid forty-three millions, rich in learning and independent in wealth? To what specific ends is it to be directed? Many every way.

First, These millions have souls that can be better and more readily saved through an intelligent apprehension of the way of salvation.

Secondly, It may be that an opportunity through this education will be given the *mouse* to return some favors of the ridiculing *lion*.

Thirdly, There are ends immediately affecting us as a people. Chief among these is self-duty.

Self-preservation is instinctive and preeminent as a law in man's nature. Therefore a knowledge of duty owed to ourselves is a vital constituent in the development of any people. That the freedmen should be without this knowledge is natural. They were saturated with the doctrine that all their duties and actions had reference to the well-being of their masters—so-called. What did they know of self-duty when they had no self? What did they know about the responsibility of family, or the training of children? The "peculiar institution" taught them that they had no family—no children. They did not even concern themselves about the coarse food they ate nor the ragged garments they wore.

How could they learn self-duty?

Emancipation, of course, exploded the doctrine of involuntary and unrequited servitude to another, but it did not teach them the duties they owed to themselves. But proper training will enable them to see that they owe duties to themselves as well as to the brotherhood of men.

Ignorance on this point is a great obstacle to the progress of any people. It will occasion useless clashing of ideas, a jarring, a restlessness, a cherished confusion out of which can come no order.

Education aids men in learning the true relation they bear to others; "for man is no isolated being. The love, friendship, and pity of which he is capable, kindle into a holy flame only when fired by the sparks from a kindred breast."

Again, the peace and quiet of the country —politically, I mean—the cessation of persecution, fraud, and bloodshed, especially in certain parts of this country, are to be secured through this "special work." The sudden enfranchisement of the Negro, however necessary, is considered a doubtful good by some of his friends and many of his foes. It has distracted the country, caused bitter controversies, and occasioned thousands to lose their lives.

This suffrage, however, cannot now be withdrawn. The ballot cannot be put into the hands of an ignorant man, even, and then taken away by his own vote.

But by increased intelligence we can prepare the voter for a judicious use and exercise of his great "weapon and shield of defense." For the safety of a country—especially of a republic—the perpetuity of its glory and the stability of its institutions are commensurate with the intelligence and morality of its citizens, whether they be from the "Emerald Isle" or in the "Sunny South."

"The danger," said Mr. Garfield, in his inaugural address, "which arises from ignorance in the voter cannot be denied. We have no standard by which to measure the disaster that may be brought upon us by ignorance and vice in the citizen, when joined to corruption and fraud in the suffrage."

For the present alarming ignorance we are not responsible. But it is a part of our "special work" to see that our succeeding generation does not enter the political arena "blinded by ignorance and corrupted by vice." The power that creates can destroy.

The Negro occasioned the greatest civil war of modern times; and his fidelity to the Union decided that momentous issue.

He has made a yawning chasm between the North and South, which can only be bridged as he is enlightened and made a better citizen.

His citizenship has lashed the waters of American politics into fury, and they can only be quieted as his good conduct, mellowed and softened by culture, exclaims, "Peace, be still."

But intellectual culture without heart culture may be a curse instead of a blessing.

It has been truly said that "men may be as cultivated as Robespierre, and yet become as dark-minded and desperate as he. They may be as polished as was Dr. Webster, and may be as wicked."

Slavery deadened the Negro's moral sensibility, but it could not destroy it. It lived in spite of the constant and purposed perversions to which it was subjected, because it was inbreathed by God.

But what the master—so-called—could not destroy, he turned into an opposite direction. Avarice prompted him to change the whole current of the Negro's morality, and make it take a backward course. For more than two hundred and fifty years the Negro was told by precept and by *example* to call wrong right, evil good, and immorality morality.

To correct these accumulated wrongs of centuries is a part of this "special work."

Men must now be taught a morality that is consistent, to say the least. It must not consist of formal rules that may be suspended and even violated at will. It must be such as will transform the character as well as change the outward conduct.

The Negro must have instruction in that morality which declares that every species of vice must be hated because it is vice; and virtue must be loved in all her forms because it is virtue. He must know through our example and precepts that crimes are not only liable to civil punishment, but that they are also disgraceful; that on account of a high moral sentiment in society, the condemnation of his fellows will be as much feared as grated jails or walled penitentiaries. For (to paraphrase the words of Sumner on peace and war) there is no morality that is not honorable, and there is no immorality that is not dishonorable.

But morality is only a fruit of true religion. Therefore our work as ministers of the New Testament cannot be overestimated. While our commission is as far-reaching as humanity, circumstances often limit the preaching of some to a race or country. Such is a feature of our *special work.*

Of the multitudes of our people among the mountains, in the valleys, and in the plains of South-land, each soul is worth more than worlds. Yet many are lost for want of teaching, or through incorrect teaching, as to Bible truth. And as the dark struggles with the intellectual dawn, they look through the gloom of the scarcely unbroken night of ignorance, and discern advancing that which will bring them to the light of the Gospel, and break unto them the bread of everlasting life. We cannot disappoint them, but must go to their rescue, and lead them forth unto the highway of holiness, that they, too, may join the white-robed ranks who, with the inspiring ensign of the Cross, the undented shield of faith, and the invincible sword of the Spirit, are sweeping with irresistible triumph toward the city of the living God. This is our "special work." But it is not bounded by the area of eleven Southern States, nor circumscribed by the twenty-two hundred thousand square miles of American territory.

Through the mysterious method of God's providence this work stretches across the boundless, raging sea; and connects with it a whole continent—the largest in the world.

In their land no Star of Bethlehem points to the Redeemer of men. Its inhabitants sit in the darkness unpenetrated by the light of

the Cross. But He who said "Go preach my Gospel to *every* creature," wills that these two hundred and fifty millions shall come from bondage to liberty, from the power of Satan to the power of God.

Vying nationalities may extend their territorial possessions in Africa through wars and commerce; the wicked trader in human flesh may visit her to increase his ill-gotten gain; and the explorer may tread the tangled maze of her unknown interior that he may enlarge geographical knowledge and pave the way for civilization. But it remains with us to save the immortal souls of her people through the peaceful agencies of education, the Word, and the Christian ministry made effectual by the Holy Ghost.

When "girded" and enlightened, with the torch of intelligence in one hand and that of Christianity in the other, neither the magnitude of the work nor the perils that may attend it will deter the American Negro. Men brave the treacherous deep to obtain African gold; they expose themselves to her malaria for her ivory; and for a few feet of African soil they crimson her land with the best of foreign and native blood—even that of kings and princes.

There is something more precious than the gold, more excellent than the ivory, for which to suffer—to *die*, if die we must. A continent teeming with millions is to be snatched from endless perdition. A land wronged for centuries must be righted. A country whose fertile streams are emblematic of her outpoured blood and streaming tears must be healed and consoled. Then our "special work" is grand. Whether we view it in the uplifting of the seven millions in America, or the ultimate reform and regeneration of two hundred and fifty millions in Africa, this work is grand. Grand in itself, grand in its object, grand in possibilities, grand in final results, *grand* in the crowns which shall reward it—crowns whose brightest gems shall be the sparkling "tear-drops of penitence, shed by some lone pilgrim whom we led to the Cross of Christ our Lord."

9. THE FREEDMEN PROGRESSING.

REV. J. C. HARTZELL, D.D.

THE progress of the Negroes in America since emancipation has been marvelous. They came out of slavery poor in body, mind, and soul. Their bodies were cursed with generations of degradation; not of labor—for that, if followed as it should be, is enno-

bling—but of unnatural labor, where every refinement of taste and habit was sacrificed to the demand for muscular endurance. Their minds were cursed with generations of enforced ignorance. Their souls, those inner sanctuaries of human instinct and purity, where dwells the image of God, and out of which flow the holiest and best forces of life —even these had, by generations of cruel bondage, been belittled in capacity, and warped in sentiment, and lowered in instinct, until, in not a few respects, the distinctions between right and wrong were lost sight of in practical life. To the Negro in slavery, true marriage, except at the will of the master, was unknown. Among the masses the Negro slave woman was taught that for her there was no virtue, and her mission in slavery was to propagate her species for the auction block! And this in Christian America for two hundred and fifty years!

To understand any thing of the progress of this race since emancipation, we must look into the awful depths of the moral state in which freedom found them. I do not forget the work of Christian missionaries among the slaves of the South; much good was done by them, but only a few comparatively were reached, and with even these the fundamental demands of virtue were subject to the accident of the master's whims or necessities respecting his property.

With only a few individual or family exceptions in a neighborhood, the great body of the Negroes came out of slavery absolutely penniless, and with scarcely enough rags to cover their nakedness; with every influence of the Church and State and commerce and social life opposed to their freedom, and determined that, if not slaves, their future, of right, ought to be and must be one of dependent subserviency to the white race.

They were given the ballot in the midst of their ignorance and poverty, and were expected to stand with their few "carpet-bag" and "scallawag" friends for the maintenance of the national authority in the South against the combined wisdom, wealth, and statesmanship of what was, a few years before, a mighty confederacy.

Whatever progress the freedmen have made has been chiefly because of the splendid qualities they possess, in spite of not only what slavery could do, but in spite, also, of many very great disadvantages since freedom. Whatever helps have come to them they have laid hold of with tremendous faith and tenacity. Go into the schools established by Northern benevolence all over the South. In them to-day are more than twenty thousand young Negro men and women. Nearly all of these are there by their own exertions, or by those of their parents or relatives as poor as themselves. They are climbing up into the higher realms of learning; the silver tones of their orators and the enchanting music of their songsters are heard in all that South-land; their mathematicians are communing with Newton, and their metaphysicians are mastering Hamilton. Leaving these schools, their young men are entering the pulpit, are on the rostrum, and in the school-

room; and they are there to lead. Their young women are teaching, or becoming wives of men worthy of them, and doing their part in building up Christian homes. Go into the public schools of the South. Eight hundred thousand Negro boys and girls are there. One hour in any such school sweeps to the wind all pro-slavery theories about the Negro's capacity to learn. It is a sad fact that a large proportion of the freedmen are yet but little beyond where freedom found them; but that so many should have advanced at all, and that so large a proportion of those who have advanced should have gone so far, is simply marvelous. Where the best are to-day, the great majority will be in the near future.

They are acquiring much in the fields of mechanical skill and activity, and in the self-respect and independence which these bring. In many portions of the South they are not only the field-laborers, but they are the carpenters and bricklayers and blacksmiths! They are engineers and head-men on multitudes of the smaller plantations, and on some of the larger ones. They are gaining property. They own fifteen millions of dollars in Louisiana. They pay taxes on five hundred thousand dollars of property in Atlanta, Georgia; and in that whole State they possess, probably, ten millions of dollars in real estate. That means nearly one hundred millions of dollars in property for the Negroes of the South, acquired mostly since the war. That is not much for six millions five hundred thousand people, but it is a good beginning.

The Negro is improving morally. Go to their churches all over the South, and with the eye and heart and common-sense of a friend and philanthropist, study their work in church-building, Sunday-school organization, and administering discipline. For thirteen years I have studied this people in every part of the South, and seen them in their cabins and in their best and poorest churches. I have studied their weaknesses and follies and successes, and if I know any thing of human nature or human progress I must say that vast multitudes of the Negroes of the South, to-day, are leading virtuous and Christian lives, and that these, under the lead of a fair proportion of their ministry, are powerfully leavening the whole mass.

For whatever the Negro in America is to-day, in morals or poverty or ignorance, the white people of the nation are largely responsible. Slavery is gone, with its accursed effects. Let now the whole nation do for the Negro, *as a free man*, just what ought to be done for him, in sympathy and helpfulness, if he was a white man in our midst, and as needy, and another generation or two will see the Africo-American in our nation an assimilated part of American enterprise, thought, and success.

10. A PLEA FOR PRACTICAL EDUCATION FOR THE NEGRO.

REV. C. K. MARSHALL, D.D.,

Pastor Methodist Episcopal Church, South, Vicksburg, Miss.

EDUCATION is the suggestive and prolific theme that seems just now to dominate every department of human inquiry. At this seemingly late period in the progress of the races and their education, whatever it may have been, it is a singular fact that, what to teach? how to teach? when to teach? and whom to teach? are still unsettled questions. A widening field, greater facilities, higher standards, more thorough and exact knowledge, the growth of the sciences, the thirst for the untasted, and the desire of enlarging usefulness, are, together, obvious characteristics of the times. They must, therefore, greatly tend to the entire discontinuance or great modification of the methods of the past, and suggest new measures, new or peculiar specialties, adapted to the rising demands of the world at large. Whole continents are asking the English-speaking nations for their alphabet and first readers. and for educated teachers who can and will devote their lives to their instruction. We are accustomed to think it the duty of certain persons to go abroad as messengers of the Cross and teachers of religion. But teaching the thrilling significance of the simplest elements of knowledge may,-perhaps, be found as much the obligatory calling of many gifted and cultured persons as the preaching of Christ is the duty of others. It may, also, be the solemn duty and life-work of some to teach the various branches of manual labor—farming, navigation, and mechanism. The world's greatest needs lie along those paths, and civilization marks its onward march by the triumphs of the plow, the keel, and the loom. Much has been said, written, and done for the spread of the knowledge and possession of this desirable civilization. Still, so vast is the field that nearly nothing seems as yet to have been accomplished.

If we turn our thoughts to the Africans in America and in Africa, we shall find ourselves no little perplexed to solve the questions respecting their education in the material arts and in the various and indispensable branches of the mechanic arts.

Therefore it seems to me that mechanical philosophy, and practical education in constructing, making, and the repairing of all sorts of things, from a cradle to a palace, from a fish-hook to a steam-ship, from a hobnail to a telegraph, from a sewing-machine to a reaping-machine, from a telephone to a locomotive, ought to be taught the young Negroes; and that with a direct purpose of their going to Africa to aid in working out its great destiny. But if no colored man should ever again go to Africa, his development at home must be sought in the mechanical branches of knowledge. Should he, however, in such numbers as wisdom would dictate, see fit to go as an educated mechanician, who can tell the influence he could exert as a collateral force to missionary effort? What could make a stronger impression upon an intelligent African chief, king, or ruler, than to see a youthful immigrant set to work and build a neat residence. He has planned and drawn all the parts of the house himself—the architect and builder —and shown his superior attainments in the most practical and convincing way. Or, if one were to introduce the American loom, show its movements, prove his ability to teach the native its uses; and, perhaps, the way to make looms, and repair them when out of order; would such an advent among the natives—interior tribes, and progressive inquirers—make no impression in favor of a higher life and nobler ends to be attained? In America, trade learning is no longer what it was fifty years ago. A carpenter then made with his own hands all the curious and artistically wrought materials in the construction of an edifice. A first-rate workman had a fortune in his trade. But on this continent carpentry is a lost art. A piece of timber is now run through a mysterious machine, and it comes out a door, a panel, a console, a blind, a spiral molding, a mullion, or a modillion, and the attendant and feeder is not the carpenter—but the machine. So of every other branch of the mechanic arts. Watches were once made by hand, hair-spring, main-spring, chain, and regulator—all. Now nothing of the sort is known on this continent. All watches are machine made. This renders an African watch factory a possibility, even on the loose and absurd theory that the African could not learn to make a watch as a Switzerland journeyman does. It also shows the ease with which advanced mechanic arts may be introduced into Africa, where the white man cannot survive the climate.

It matters not whether the Negro goes to Africa or not in large numbers. He should be put upon the path of his best development, and then left to choose the field of labor according to rising circumstances. The locomotive, the telegraph, the sewing-machines, and other kindred presents made by our government some years ago to Japan, did more to open the eyes and hearts of that people than a hundred missionaries might, possibly, without those forerunners, have accomplished in many years. The same will be true, has been true already, in a small way, in Africa. The Japanese were advanced in mechanism, and only needed models. The African—almost the whole continent—is yet to be inducted into the proper knowledge of those arts.

I am not now saying any thing for the general colonization of our Negroes in Africa. *That is forever to be a matter of their own unbiased choice.* But I do believe that Africa is to be civilized and Christianized by Africans. Thousands of our Negro students at academies, colleges, and universities will find their highest honors, greatest pleasures, and most gratifying usefulness in teaching the natives of the father-land: not only the glorious Gospel of the Adorable One, but, also, how to forge at the anvil, turn at the lathe, file at the vice, mold for the casting; in a word, to construct a steam-engine, to manufacture hoes, plows, shovels, scythes, or any other article in brass, wood, silver, or gold, the people may need; nor does it make any difference if we are told that all these things, and all other possible articles of merchandise, will be made in America and Europe and pushed into Africa cheaper than they can be made there. So are they now made in the Northern States of this continent and pushed southward, and yet the South needs and maintains innumerable mechanics and shops and factories all over its broad expanse.

Africa needs a host of intelligent, well-trained Negro mechanics in every branch of business known to the white artisans. That country is soon to be webbed from east to west, and from north to south, with railroads; and a call will be made for Negro engineers, conductors, clerks, book-keepers, express officers, and mail-carriers, postmasters, and responsible Negro men to take paying offices and good positions, and enjoy the opportunity of putting their acquirements where they will do the most good and bring to all concerned the largest returns.

The Negro is capable of all this work. Instances, not a few, can be cited in the South, of his excelling in law and medicine, in architectural and mechanical drawings; of his leading the business over white competitors in horseshoeing in a large city; bossing the molding floor in a large foundry; commanding equal wages with the best white carpenters; painting, shoe-making, engineering, book-binding, tailoring, etc., and all this in the teeth of organized "Trades Unions," that resisted his progress to their utmost.

Now, the momentous inquiry arises as to how the young freedmen, thirsting for knowledge and longing for fields of useful-ness, are to become fitted for these special labors—manly, reformatory, civilizing, ennobling labors—to which I have directed your attention. True, we have colleges with agricultural and mechanical appendages. But it seems to me that the Negro of the coming time demands and needs a mechanical college, with a grammar-school attachment, where one may win his parchment as an accomplished artisan, and yet learn enough of mathematic grammar and correct English composition to constitute a solid foundation for a future superstructure, if inclined to erect it, with his own industry and application.

As for agriculture, there are now hundreds of well-taught tillers of the soil, whose services could be commanded for any emergency, and yet these are passing away. If, however, we can answer the momentous inquiry as to how we are to teach the young Negro the mysteries of a machine-shop, and prepare him to teach others—and he is capable, if the opportunity be given him—then a great mountain will have been rolled from the door of the Dark Continent, and new fields of immense usefulness be opened to hundreds of brave and Christian colored men—and the welfare of that continent as well as this will be greatly advanced.

This, then, brings home the greatest question to be considered under the subject for the day, "The Negro in America." On this continent he must be qualified for every part he is to act on life's great stage, for at least one or two generations to come. I am not unmindful that, in a very moderate and inadequate way, some attempts have been made to teach a few colored boys trades, and train them in the annexes of colleges, but if they have not all proved failures I am misinformed. I would reverse that order and annex a grammar-school to a multifarious collegiate machine-shop, and graduate intelligent mechanics. One hundred such graduates will do more for the uplifting of Africa in the next century than can be accomplished by a thousand university graduates who shall have accomplished the highest curriculum in languages, sciences, and polite literature. Not that I oppose the college proper or the university. I like them all. But we may produce a lopsided generation of aspirants for more places than call for them, and so do harm. This is one of the hardest problems we have to solve in connection with the future of the Negro race, both here and elsewhere. How shall we train the Negro to be a first-rate mechanic? Whoever shall answer that question is the man the 200,000,000 of people in Africa will honor, and whose name will be held in reverence among them, as long as the morning sun shall salute her mountain peaks and her valleys resound with anthems of civilization and religion.

V. ILLITERACY, WEALTH, PAUPERISM, AND CRIME.

1. THE RELATION OF EDUCATION TO WEALTH AND MORALITY AND TO PAUPERISM AND CRIME.

DEXTER A. HAWKINS, A.M.,

Of the New York Bar.

ONE of the most interesting and important questions in social science is how to increase wealth and morality to a maximum, and to reduce pauperism and crime to a minimum.

This is a topic especially appropriate for investigation by the National Educational Assembly, a body whose chief aim is the improvement of society through a better education of the people.

One set of philosophers, led by Benjamin Franklin, proclaim that the surest road to wealth is industry and economy. But another answers that the Chinese, for two thousand years, have excelled all other races and nations in these two virtues, and yet are distinguished, not for their wealth, but rather for the poverty of the great majority of their people.

Something, then, besides mere industry and economy is required even to amass wealth.

The great religious reformers and prophets, as Buddha, Confucius, Plato, our Saviour, Mohammed, and Luther, have held up religion as the panacea for all *moral obliquity*, and yet history declares that the ages and countries most fervid with religion—as, for example, Europe from the tenth to the fifteenth century, have been pervaded with crime.

The great Christian Churches of the Roman Catholic rite and of the Greek rite declare that "Ignorance is the mother of devotion," and that devotion to these churches is the safety of humanity. Yet the seat of the Greek Church, Russia, where nine tenths of the population are illiterate, last year made the world shudder at the barbaric crimes committed in that empire upon the brethren of the Founder of Christianity, the Hebrews: the most intelligent and thriving subjects of the temporal head of the Greek Church.

Ireland, for a thousand years one of the most faithful devotees of the Church of Rome, has just completed the entire curriculum of crime, from refusal to pay debts to murder in the first degree, and made both life and property unsafe within her borders.

It is clear, then, that "ignorance and devotion" will not bring on the millennium. Evidently the problem of what will accomplish the most complete and efficient prevention of pauperism and crime, and produce the highest average increase of wealth and morality, is not yet solved. Its solution is difficult.

One of the best teachers and most scholarly gentlemen that this country has produced often encouraged his pupils in their investigations by quoting to them from Terence the lines:

"Nil tam difficile est
Quin quaerendo investigari potest."

"Nothing is so difficult but that by study it may be solved."

This is as true in social problems as in those from mathematics. The importance of this question is ever pressing upon us, for the support of paupers and criminals, and the protection of society against the latter impose a burden upon society second only to that of war.

In New York, for example, this burden, including, necessarily, police, criminal courts, reformatories, jails, penitentiaries, asylums, almshouses, and the poor outside of public institutions, amounts to over six millions of dollars a year; and that city contains only one fortieth of the population of the United States.

I propose to treat of the relation of education to wealth and pauperism, and to morality and crime; and what kind of training is the surest and best safeguard against the two great social evils, pauperism and crime: and where this training is to be obtained.

The Relation of Education to Wealth and Pauperism.

As civilization advances the apparatus and operations of every-day life are becoming more and more expensive, on account of the constantly increasing and multiplying wants of humanity. To-day even the rudest and simplest occupation—farming—is carried on chiefly by machinery. The sharpened stick for planting and the forked tree for plowing are no longer in use. A farm laborer of a hundred years ago, if suddenly dropped down upon a modern farm upon a Western prairie, could scarcely understand any thing that is going on.

Even the plows, the harrows, the cultivators, the drillers, the sowers, the hoeing machines, the mowers, the reapers, the headers, the threshers, the winnowers, the very wagons and carts and harnesses, would each and all be a mystery to him; to say nothing of the more complicated appliances and the scientific processes required to convert the raw products of the field into food, clothing, and shelter. The treatment of the soil, the rotation of crops, the method of preserving and utilizing and marketing the harvests to advantage, all require knowledge.

If this is true of farming, it is still more true of every other department of human industry.

In the days of Homer and Pericles, Virgil and Augustus, Shakespeare and Queen Elizabeth, cotton and wool, and flax and silk, were all spun and woven by hand, and sewed by hand! Now a single machine tended by one skilled workman does the spinning that formerly required hundreds of busy hands and nimble fingers; another, tended by a single person, does the weaving that once demanded three or four hundred human beings; a third will cut out forty or fifty garments at a time, and do it quicker than one could be cut by hand; a line of sewing-machines, run by steam or electricity, will each do the work of twenty sewing-girls, and do it better. The hand labor in a pair of lady's fine kid boots formerly amounted to several dollars; but now, aided by cunningly devised machines, tended by skilled workmen, it is only nine cents. This state of society makes it difficult for an ignorant laborer to find a place to work at all, and when a place is found, he can scarcely earn enough in competition with his skilled competitors to keep soul and body together. He finds himself on every hand rejected or thrown out of employment because of his ignorance, unskillfulness, incompetency, and inability to do, or even to learn to do, things in the modern way.

The net results of his rude industry compare with those of his trained rival in the same ratio that the quantity of grain transported to market by the ignorant peasant of the last century on the back of his mule, in one end of a bag, and balanced by a stone of equal weight in the other so as not to slide off, compares with the amount transported by the intelligent farmer of the present day, who puts a whole crop into a freight car and makes coal and water roll it over a railroad track hundreds of miles in a single day.

Thirty years ago I saw the Neapolitan peasants carrying their small, hand-made, bottle-shaped cheeses, in strings of two or three dozen, on their backs from the pastures of the Appenines to the market in their beautiful city by the sea.

Four years ago, while standing on the snowy crest of Pike's Peak, in the Rocky Mountains, fourteen thousand three hundred feet high, a railroad train in the valley below, but in full view, puffed across the broad acres of a cheese-ranch, the property of a son of New England. It halted at the door of his cheese factory, was soon loaded with the whole summer's product of his dairy, and then steamed away twenty-five hundred miles to New York, where in a few days it delivered in perfect condition its tons of rich yellow freight, cheaper per pound than the Italian peasant was able to produce his and carry it a hundredth part of the distance. But the selection of the herds of cows for this Colorado ranch, their care and management, the milking machines, the scientific processes of cooling and curdling the milk, and the preparation, pressing, preserving, and boxing the cheeses, and their shipment, and the location, construction, and management of the railway—all require knowledge.

Can we determine how much this knowledge adds to the value of human labor?

In 1870 the Commissioner of Education at Washington sent out a series of carefully drawn, comprehensive, and searching questions, to the great centers of labor in all parts of the United States. These centers were so selected as to represent every kind of labor, from the rudest and simplest up to the most skilled. The object of the questions was to determine the relative productiveness of literate and illiterate labor. I have tabulated, reduced, and generalized the answers so as to get at what seems to me to be the average result over the whole country. This investigation—one of the most interesting ever made—brought clearly to light the following facts:

1. That an average free common-school education, such as is provided in all the States where the free common school has become a permanent institution, adds fifty per cent. to the productive power of the laborer considered as a mere productive machine.

2. That the average academical education adds one hundred per cent.

3. That the average collegiate or university education adds from two to three hundred per cent. to his average annual productive capacity, to say nothing of the vast increase to his manliness—to his God-likeness.

By the census of 1880 we had in the United States four million two hundred and four thousand three hundred and sixty-two (4,204,362) illiterate adults — white and colored. Now, putting their labor at the minimum annual value of one hundred dollars each, (which is far below the average even for farm labor, while the wages of manufacturing operatives, including fifteen per cent. of women and children, as shown by the census of 1880, average in the whole country $345 each per year,) and the annual loss to these persons—from the lack of at least a common-school education—would be fifty dollars each. This, for the whole number of four millions two hundred and forty thousand three hundred and sixty-two, is two hundred and ten millions of dollars per year; a sum twice as large as the entire annual expenditure for public education in the whole country. This sum—two hundred and ten millions of dollars—is a clear annual loss, not only to these illiterates, but to the community, by reason of their illiteracy.

A State filled with ignorant citizens is like a farm of pine-barrens, its crop is scarcely worth harvesting. Poverty clings to the illiterate closer than a brother. Like the fabled shirt of Nessus, this kind of poverty poisons and disables whomsoever it covers. Three quarters of these four millions two hundred and four thousand three hundred and sixty-two of illiterate adults were in the late slave States, and their effect on the production and preservation of wealth there is shown by the last census. In ten of these States, notwithstanding their rich soil and mild climate, the assessed value of property in the ten years from 1870 to 1880 decreased twenty per cent.; while in the State of Maine, with its universal education, notwithstanding its thin, poor soil and cold climate, the wealth in the same period increased fifteen per cent., and in the State of New Hampshire, under like hard conditions of life, it increased eleven per cent.

The late slave States complain of their inability to pay the expenses of free common schools, and they raised for public education in 1880 only ten million eight hundred and eighty-three thousand one hundred and four dollars ($10,883,104). The amount of the annual loss in these same States, from their labor being illiterate, is at least one hundred and fifty million dollars, ($150,000,000.) The extra productiveness of their laborers over what it is now would—had they been educated, as in Maine and New Hampshire—establish and support free common schools nine months in the year for every child of the school age within their borders, and

6

leave a surplus sufficient to support a free academy in every county and a free college in every State.

Education is the key to wealth. Educated labor is not likely to be imposed upon; and is not given to strikes. It knows its reasonable and just rights, and maintains them in a legal and peaceable manner.

The relative ability to gain a livelihood of the literate and illiterate in society, on a large scale, can best be determined by analyses of the censuses of different States and countries. These, properly worked out and understood, will give us the naked facts of the relation of education and pauperism.

A careful examination of the census of England, Scotland, Ireland, and of the several countries on the continent of Europe, indicate that, other things being equal, pauperism is in the inverse ratio of the education of the mass of the people; that is, as education increases pauperism decreases, and as education decreases pauperism increases.

In the Grand Duchy of Baden they put into operation, in 1854, a rigorous system of universal, compulsory education in the elementary branches. The effect in seven years upon pauperism was to reduce it twenty-five per cent. It has been calculated by statisticians and students of social science that ninety-six per cent. of pauperism could be exterminated by universal, compulsory education in the elementary branches of knowledge and industry.

But the elements of industry should be taught in our schools as well as the elements of knowledge. This can be done without adding to the cost of the schools; while it would increase vastly the practical value to the masses of their education. The Kindergarten method of training recognizes the necessity of industrial education and the capacity and desire on the part of the very young to learn *to do* something. This capacity and desire should be cultivated, developed, and disciplined through the whole course and for all classes in the public schools. Such a system of public education rigorously enforced would confine pauperism to those without property and incapacitated for self-support by old age, or infirmity, or infancy, and having no relatives to take care of them.

The exhaustive analysis of the census of 1880 which the government is making will not be completed for some years; but that of 1870 is before us, and the facts on this question, developed by each census, all go to establish the same principle; so that either is a safe guide. In Pennsylvania, Ohio, and Illinois, three great central States, where self-support is not difficult, one in ten of the illiterates is a pauper, while of the rest of the population only one in three hundred is a pauper. In other words, in those three great central States, a given number of children suffered to grow up in ignorance produce thirty times as many paupers as when given an average common-school education.

In 1870 a special investigation was made, in fifteen States, of the inmates to the number of seven thousand three hundred and ninety-eight of almshouses and infirmaries. Of these, four thousand three hundred and twenty-seven, or nearly fifty-nine per cent., could not read and write: while in those fifteen States the average percentage of illiterates was only six per cent. of the whole population. From this six per cent. came that fifty-nine per cent. of the paupers; or, to express it in another form, a given number of children in those fifteen States, suffered to grow up in ignorance, produced twenty-two times as many paupers as the same number of children would if given a fair common-school education.

Similar results may be obtained from the census of almost every country in Europe or America.

We may safely say, then, that it is a general law of modern civilization that an illiterate person is from twenty to thirty times as liable to become a pauper and a charge upon the public as is one with an average common-school education; and that the annual loss to the community, in the United States, in the productive power of the illiterates, and in the support of paupers made such by illiteracy, is nearly if not quite equal to the amount that would be required to establish and maintain a free common school the year round in every State in the Union, amply sufficient for the whole fifteen millions of the children of the school age in the United States.

The annual expense of maintaining paupers—ninety-six per cent. of whom have become such through lack of proper training while young—is at least ten times as great as would have been the expense to the public of securing an education while young to each of these paupers sufficient to have enabled ninety-six per cent. of them to support themselves instead of being a charge upon the public.

Education leads naturally to industry, sobriety, and economy; hence it makes one conscious of the benefits resulting from these habits.

Statistics proclaim in no uncertain voice that *education is the surest preventive of pauperism;* and that the expense of providing and applying in season this preventive would not be one tenth that now brought upon society by pauperism.

The first incentive to action is self-support—gaining a livelihood. This is the very basis of personal independence of individual character, respectability, and influence. The key to self-support is education. Money and labor, invested in education, are capital invested in such a manner that the principal is absolutely safe, and the income large, sure, and promptly paid. The State should see to it that a reasonable investment of this kind is made in and for every child as it grows up.

We bring nothing into the world except possibilities. It is said we carry nothing out. I doubt that. Education once acquired inheres in the human mind and soul. It goes with them. We not only enjoy its benefits so long as this life lasts, but who can prove it separates from us at the beginning of the life to come? The natural inference is that it goes with us, and that the soul of a highly and properly cultivated man in the next world excels that of an ignoramus as much as "one star surpasses another star in glory."

SECOND.

The Relation of Education to Morality and Crime.

It is said that crime came into the world with knowledge, and that had not man partaken of the fruit of the tree of knowledge, he never would have committed crime. A more correct way of stating the true rule is perhaps this: that so long as man remained a mere animal, without knowledge of right or wrong, or power of discrimination between good and evil, he could not commit crime any more than a brute beast could do it. Crime implies, in the actor, moral responsibility. But the moment man acquired the power to discriminate between right and wrong, good and evil, and had bestowed upon him freedom of will sufficient to enable him to choose between good and evil, then for the first time it became possible for him to commit crime, or be guilty of sin. In other words, as soon as he became, in any proper sense, a rational, responsible being, and endowed with knowledge and with freedom of will sufficient to direct and control his own actions, and not before, it was proper to characterize his actions as criminal or innocent, according as they were or not infractions of law.

The optimist may say that God, the Creator —the active personification of all good—having created man in his own image, as man's knowledge expands he necessarily increases in goodness and in tendency to right action.

The pessimist may hold that God is simply the personification of might, and that whatever he orders is right because of his omnipotent might; and that man, as he increases in knowledge, simply enlarges his power to do evil, without strengthening his desire to do good. Hence the late Cardinal Antonelli, who for a generation controlled the papal power, said to me in Rome, thirty years ago, in speaking of public education, that he thought it better for a child to grow up in ignorance than to be educated in such public schools as those of Massachusetts. His theory seemed to be that his Church held a sort of exclusive patent for all right action; and unless one obtained a license and came in under this patent, every act of life would necessarily tend only to evil.

Another set of philosophers teach that mere knowledge is indifferent to right and wrong; and that man, in order to keep the track of righteousness, like a locomotive with steam up, must be guided by some superior, benevolent, distinct, and outside power.

But, theories aside, for all practical purposes the safest and surest method of investigation for us to pursue on this question is the inductive system of Lord Bacon. We must have recourse to the facts and follow their direction. These will give us the tendency of education.

The question before us is, What is the effect of education, such as is usually obtained in the schools of the community, upon morality and crime? Does it increase the one or the other? or does it diminish it? or does it have no effect at all upon it? The statistics of the census will answer this question; for however we may prove on principle things ought to turn out, facts will show how they do actually turn out. The homely old adage, "The proof of the pudding is the eating," is the safest guide.

In France, in 1868, one half of the inhabitants could not read nor write. From this half came ninety-five per cent. of the persons arrested for crime. From the other, the educated half, came only five per cent. In other words, a given number of children left to grow up illiterate, produced nineteen times as many persons arrested for crime as the same number would if educated, at least to the extent of the elementary branches.

In the Grand Duchy of Baden, from 1854 to 1861—seven years—the government, by a rigorous system of universal, compulsory, elementary education, reduced the number of prisoners actually arrested fifty-one per cent., and the number of crimes committed fifty-four per cent.

In the six New England States, in 1870, seven per cent. only of the inhabitants above ten years of age were unable to read and write; and yet this seven per cent. produced eighty per cent. of the criminals. Or, in other words, a given number of children in New England, at that time, suffered to grow up illiterate, produced fifty-three times as many criminals as the same number would if educated to the extent of the curriculum of the public schools. This fact is a complete vindication of the moral effect of the New England system of public education, Cardinal Antonelli to the contrary notwithstanding.

In the State of New York, in 1880, the illiterates produced eight times their *pro rata* proportion of the criminals in that State;

that is, a given number of children brought up illiterate, on the average produced eight times as many criminals as the same children would have produced if educated to the extent of the curriculum of the public schools.

In the city of New York, in 1870, among the illiterates, one crime was committed for every three persons; while among the literates there was only one crime to twenty-seven persons. Or, in other words, the ignorant class in that city furnishes nine times the criminals they would if educated in the public schools.

In the commonwealth of Pennsylvania, in 1870, the illiterates, according to their numbers, committed seven times as many crimes as the literate class.

In Pennsylvania, Ohio, and Illinois, taken together, the illiterates committed ten times as many crimes, according to their numbers, as the literate class.

Take the whole of the United States together, according to the census of 1870, the illiterates committed ten times their *pro rata* proportion of crimes.

In Pennsylvania, in the years 1879 and 1880, one thirtieth of the population above ten years of age could neither read nor write, and this one thirtieth committed one sixth part of the crimes, or nearly six times its proper proportion. But if we class with the illiterates the criminals who could barely read and write—but who had no education beyond bare reading and writing—it will then appear that the one thirtieth of the population of Pennsylvania that is illiterate commits one third of the crime, or more than fourteen times its legitimate proportion.

A careful examination of the statistics of twenty States shows the following average results:

First. That one sixth of all the crime in the country is committed by persons wholly illiterate.

Second. That one third of the crime in the country is committed by persons wholly or substantially illiterate.

Third. That the proportion of criminals among the illiterate class is, on the average, ten times as great as it is among those who have been instructed in the elements of a common-school education or beyond.

Fourth. That the expense imposed upon society to protect itself against a few thousand criminals, most of whom were made such through the neglect of society to take care of their education when young, is one of the heaviest of the public burdens. *In the city of New York it is fifty per cent. more than the whole cost of the public schools.*

In that city the annual appropriation for police, criminal courts, reformatories, jails, and penitentiaries is over five millions of dollars; while that for the training of the 385,000 school children in the city is only $3,500,000.

The average attendance at the schools in 1882 was 138,329. The "Compulsory School Age"—that is, the age within which *all* children are *required* by law in the State of New York to attend school—is eight to fourteen years. The number of children of this age in the city of New York, in June, 1880, was 144,474; while the average attendance on the public schools of children of all ages from five to twenty-one in that year in the city was only 133,096. As a logical consequence of this neglect of education, the city jails and almshouses are crammed, and taxes are high.

The city, in its meager provision for education and its enormous taxation for criminals, (to use an old but expressive adage,) "saves at the spigot but loses at the bung."

What is true of the metropolis of the country is equally true of every city, town, village, and neighborhood.

These facts could be multiplied almost without limit.

The examination of the statistics of criminality and illiteracy in the census of any civilized state or country will give results substantially in harmony with the above.

Carlyle says that:

"If the devil were passing through my country, and he applied to me for instruction on any truth or fact of this universe, I should wish to give it him. He is less a devil knowing that three are six, than if he didn't know it; a light spark, though of the faintest, is in this fact; if he knew facts enough, continuous light would dawn on him; he would (to his amazement) understand what this universe is, on what principles it conducts itself, and would cease to be a devil!"

God created man in his own image. It is natural to suppose, then, that man prefers right to wrong; but he requires enlightenment to enable him to discern and choose the right.

The very laws of human nature unequivocally declare that the most efficient means of eradicating crime from society is universal education.

It is not claimed that crime will thus be utterly exterminated; for some crimes, as forgery, embezzlement, conspiracy to defraud, and bank-burglary, require a certain amount of knowledge; and temptation is often greater than human nature can resist. These, however, are the exceptions to the general rule of humanity, the same as are cases of physical deformity, idiocy, and lunacy. Even those criminals could be reformed by teaching them that if they would devote the same labor and skill to honest industry that they do to criminality, they would, beyond any doubt, have much greater financial success; besides escaping the misery that is inseparable from wrong-doing and its attendant privations and punishment.

The rule as deduced from the facts is that *crime is in the inverse ratio of the education of the people.*

THIRD.

What kind of education is the surest guaranty of wealth and morality, and the best preventive of pauperism and crime? and where is it to be obtained?

Education is not a training of the intellect alone; it deals also equally with the physical organs and the moral faculties.

Mens sana in corpore sano, "A sound, healthful, well-developed mind in a sound, strong, vigorous body."

The true system of education develops each faculty of the human organism in well-balanced harmony from earliest infancy to the end of life. This development is obtained in the first instance, say from the fifth to the twentieth year, chiefly in school.

There are in general two kinds of schools in enlightened countries: (1) Church Schools. These came in with Christian Churches, and for centuries were almost the only schools which the common people could enter. (2) The Free Public Schools, provided and supported at public expense.

The parochial schools, working in harmony with the Churches, wrought in time in Christian countries a change in public sentiment on the question of education, and led the way to the establishment of the *free public school.* Under the influence of the free public school it has come to be held as a fundamental principle of well-organized society that "*It is the duty of the property within the State to provide elementary education for all children within the State, sufficient to fit them to perform intelligently and honestly the duties required of them as citizens.*"

The child, however poor, has upon the property holder a clear claim for an education at public expense, sufficient to make him a useful member of society. This claim is the logical outcome from the second commandment: "Love thy neighbor as thyself."

As these two kinds of schools began to move on together, it naturally and properly resulted, in course of time, that the parochial school confined itself more and more to religious instruction; to making a convert of the child to its particular shade of religious belief; and it gave less and less attention to imparting mere secular knowledge; while the free public school gave more and more attention to fitting the child to take care of himself in this world, and to perform his duty here as a member of the body politic. It left religious instruction to the parents, to the Sunday-schools, and to the Churches, unless the government maintained a State religion; then instruction in that was included in the curriculum of the public school. But in this country we have no State religion. Church and State, by the organic law, are separate. The Church—religion of all kinds—is within the State, but is simply protected, not supported, by the State.

The relative effect to-day of the parochial school and of the public school upon wealth and morality and pauperism and crime, is evident to the observer in traveling through two neighboring countries where the respective systems have each for a long period been in exclusive control of education.

The line of demarkation between the two systems is as plain as between cloud and sunshine. Switzerland, thirty years ago, was a good illustration. In the Cantons that depended on parochial schools, material and intellectual life was stagnant. The buildings, except the churches, were dilapidated; industry was rude; the faces of the people were dull; and the highways infested with beggars. Dickens describes them as characterized by "dirt, disease, ignorance, squalor, and misery."

But the Cantons that supported free public schools were filled with a bright, active, ingenious, intelligent, industrious, and independent people; or, as Dickens puts it, by a population noted for "neatness, cheerfulness, industry, education, continued aspiration."

Italy was then another striking illustration. The Papal and Neapolitan States had the parochial system alone; while Tuscany had, to a certain extent, the free public school. A general dilapidation, dirt, vermin, criminals, beggars, vagabonds, and monks proclaimed the sway of the parochial school; while neatness, order, and thrift announced the presence of the free public schools. Ireland and Spain, with parochial schools, swarmed with beggars and criminals. Germany, with her rigorous system of free public education, has become a hive of study, thought, and industry.

In France, previous to 1870, the religious orders, led by the Jesuits, controlled primary education, and half the population could not even read; and manly virtue, as was demonstrated in the conflict with Germany, was wanting.

So marked were these distinctive results of the two systems, that Switzerland, Italy, and France, in the interest of society, have now made elementary education free, secular, universal, and compulsory.

The fruits of the two systems up to 1870 existed side by side in our country. The census of that year shows a foreign-born population of five and a half millions; most of whom came from Ireland and England, countries up to that time dependent upon parochial schools, though England has now adopted and put in operation the free public school with compulsory attendance. Hence, at that date, though not now, our foreign population may be justly taken, intellectually and morally, as the fair average product of that parochial mode of education.

Of these five and a half millions, those above the age of ten who could not read or write were fourteen per cent. of the whole. The paupers were four and one tenth per cent., and the criminals one and one tenth per cent.

While, on the other hand, it appears by the same census that in twenty-one of our States having the American system of non-sectarian free public schools, there was a native population of twenty millions. This native population had been educated in this system of schools, and in like manner may be justly taken, intellectually and morally, as the fair average product of this method of education.

Of these, the illiterates, above the age of ten, were only three and one half per cent., (·035) of the whole number; the paupers, only one and seven tenths per cent., (·017;) and the criminals, only three fourths of one per cent., (·0075.) In other words, from every ten thousand inhabitants the parochial school method on the average turned out fourteen hundred illiterates, four hundred and ten paupers, and one hundred and sixty criminals; while the non-sectarian free public school method turned out from every ten thousand inhabitants only three hundred and fifty illiterates, one hundred and seventy paupers, and seventy-five criminals.

Or, if we take Massachusetts by itself, whose system is the type or model of our free public schools, with its 1,104,032 native inhabitants, in 1870, the number is still less, namely, seventy-one illiterates, forty-nine paupers, and eleven criminals to the ten thousand.

Tabulating the foregoing figures for comparison, we obtain the following result:

	Illiterates.	Paupers.
Parochial system	1,400	410
Public-school system in 21 States	350	170
Public-school system in Mass.	71	49

	Criminals.		Inhabitants.
Parochial system	160	to	10,000
Public school system in 21 States	75	to	10,000
Public-school system in Mass.	11	to	10,000

Society under the parochial school produces four times as many illiterates, two and a half times as many paupers, and more than twice as many criminals as under the average public school; or, if we take the Massachusetts type of public school, society under the parochial school produces twenty times as many illiterates, eight times as many paupers, and fourteen times as many criminals, as under the public school.

We have also for five years and eight months, from 1871 to 1875, inclusive, the data in the city of New York for this comparison of the effect on pauperism and crime of the two systems of education.

The Department of Charities and Correc-
tions during that period cared for

Irish paupers............ 98,787
German paupers.......... 24,273
American paupers........ 63,178
Of all other nationalities... 17,563

In addition to these there were each year
several thousand of the Irish race assisted
by the numerous charitable institutions of
their Church, of which for that period we
have no reliable data, though the city contributed from the public money half a million
dollars a year to these Church institutions.

The above table, reduced to a comparative
ratio, based on the census of 1870, of each
race, in that city—and taking the American
as the unit of the ratio—gives the following
result:

American paupers .... 1·00
Irish paupers .... 3·50
German paupers............ 1·33
All others .... 1·50

The Irish were, substantially, all educated
in the parochial school; the Germans nearly
all in the public schools; the other foreign
nationalities partly in the parochial and partly
in the public schools.

From this table it appears that a child educated in a parochial school is so much more
poorly fitted and furnished for supporting
himself in the city of New York than he
would be if trained up in the public schools,
that he is three and a half times as likely to
become a pauper as he would if he attended
the free public schools in the city.

During the same time, in that city the
number of

Irish arrested was 571,497
Germans 119,659
Americans 387,154
All other nationalities.... 92,934

while the names of those arrested show
that a large percentage of the class denomi-
nated Americans in the above table are of
Irish parentage; and hence, to a large extent,
were educated in the parochial schools.

But taking the table just as it stands, and
reducing the figures to a comparative ratio,
based on the number of each race in the city,
as fixed by the census of 1870—and taking
the American as the unit—gives the following:

American criminals .... 1·00
Irish   "   .... 3·28
German   "   .... 1·07
All other races........ .... 1·27

In other words, a child trained in the parochial school is during life more than three
and a quarter times as likely to get into jail
as the child trained in the free public school.
The above tables are the result of so large
a generalization, running through so many

years, that they are safe and sure indications
of the comparative outcome of the two systems of education.

Many of our philanthropists are so well
satisfied that the most efficient instrument
for the prevention of crime in society is the
Church, that they give their whole heart and
surplus money to the multiplication and development of churches; instead of increasing
the appropriation for public schools, multiplying school-houses and academies, and their
endowment, and securing the regular attendance of all school children.

There is little danger in this country of
too much attention being given to churches;
the more we have of them the better; but
one must not forget that the school deals with
the mind and heart when young, plastic, and
easily molded, while the Church is adapted
more especially for adults, and has to do
chiefly with those whose habits are to a certain extent formed and crystallized; hence it
is reasonable to expect that the school will
be a more effective preventive of crime than
the Church; besides, the penalties held up
to the mind by the Church are, necessarily to
a certain extent, so remote and avoidable as
to lose much of their reformatory virtue.

The relative efficiency of the Church and
the school in preventing crime was investi-
gated by the Kingdom of Bavaria in 1870.
The churches in that kingdom were almost
exclusively Roman Catholic; hence the results are strictly true only of that Church;
but in principle they apply to all Churches.
The difference on this point is merely one of
degree.

In Upper Bavaria there were 16 churches
and 5¼ school-houses to each 1,000 buildings,
and 667 crimes to each 100,000 inhabitants.
In Upper Franconia the ratio was 5 churches,
7 school-houses, and 444 crimes. In Lower
Bavaria the ratio was 10 churches, 4½ school-
houses, and 879 crimes. In the Palatinate
the ratio was 4 churches, 11 school-houses,
and only 425 crimes, or less than one half.
In the Lower Palatinate the ratio was 11
churches, 6 school-houses, and 690 crimes,
while in Lower Franconia the ratio was 5
churches, 10 school-houses, and only 384
crimes. Tabulated for clearness of comparison, it is as follows:

	Churches.	Per 1,000 buildings. School-houses.	Crimes per 1,000 souls.
Upper Bavaria....	15	5½	667
Upper Franconia..	5	7	444
Lower Bavaria....	10	4½	870
The Palatinate	4	11	425
Lower Palatinate..	11	6	690
Lower Franconia..	5	10	884

In short, it seems that crime decreases almost in the same ratio that the schools increase; while more or less churches, at least
of the class of those of Bavaria referred to in
the above table, produce comparatively little
effect upon it.

The Church supplements the work of the public school, and is a very necessary, important, and efficient supplement; but it cannot till the place of the public school, even as a preventive of crime. The chief aim of the one, as at present conducted, is to prepare us for the *future* life; that of the other, to fit us for the *present* life; and crimes are of the present life.

Those unerring guides to the statesman—statistics—demonstrate that the most economical, effective, and powerful preventive of crime is the free common school, supplemented by the academy, the college, and the Church.

Universal education tends to universal morality.

The training of the public schools in this country, though a far surer preventive of pauperism and crime than that of the parochial schools and churches, is yet very far below what it ought to be, and may easily be made to be. The instruction deals too much with the abstract, and too little with the concrete; too much with words and names, and too little with ideas and things. The child should be taught to memorize less and to think more. The elements of industrial education could be taught with great advantage, and should be taught, in our public schools, as they are and have been for years in the public schools of Germany. This would enable the children to do something as well as merely to know something, and would tend directly to prevent and reduce pauperism, by qualifying them on leaving school at once to begin earning a livelihood. Instruction and training in the universal laws of right and wrong and moral responsibility are now, through fear of trenching on sectarian religion, too much neglected in the public school. These laws are common to all sects and churches; they are, so to speak, the foundation upon which not only all sects build, but upon which civilized society rests. If they were made more prominent in the public-school curriculum it would not offend the religious denominations, and would add still more to the efficiency of these schools in preventing crime and fitting the pupils for citizenship.

Our country, with its free democratic republican government, based on universal suffrage, should, as a matter of political safety alone, be sprinkled all over with free common schools within easy reach of every child of the school age. Attendance upon these schools of every child between the ages of eight and fifteen years should be required by law, and enforced, unless the child is obtaining an equivalent education elsewhere; and the public-school authorities of each district, town, and county should be charged with the enforcement of this beneficent law.

These schools, like the stars in the heavens, will perpetually illuminate the whole Republic with rays of intelligence, industry, and morality. Their benign influence should be aided, strengthened, and intensified by the academy, the college, the university, and the Church.

In this way pauperism and crime, and the burdens imposed by them upon society, would be reduced to a minimum; and order, prosperity, and wealth increased to a maximum.

2. RELATION OF EDUCATION TO MORAL CHARACTER.

REV. C. W. CUSHING, D.D.,
Pastor First Methodist Episcopal Church, Rochester, N. Y.

THE aim of education is to make useful—valuable to society. It contemplates, therefore, the development of all there is in a man. But to make the most of a man his balance must be preserved, or if he lack this it must be secured.

No one is efficient only as he is well poised. So that this question of poise underlies the whole question of education. And education, that education at which the State aims, or should aim, is the development, the building of the man; for only such education can make the best citizens. To educate one part of a man to the neglect of other parts is to destroy the poise.

Intellectual development elevates a man on one side, makes him keener, and in that degree more influential. Physical development makes him more enduring, capable of greater exertion. But moral development only will make him corrector, purer, and hence more useful.

To make a man who shall be keen and far-reaching in his plans, there must be intellectual education; to make him honest and upright in his purposes there must be moral education; to make him able to push his plans to success there must be physical education. These combined will fit a man for responsibility and successful work, and nothing less will. This, therefore, is the education at which the State should aim. Nothing short of this can compass the end of citizenship.

Now let us inquire what is the relation of such education to moral character. What is character? Is it not the true representation of the inward man? Literally, character means to engrave. Then it is that which the thoughts, purposes, and plans of a man have engraved upon him—or better, that which they have hewn him into, for character is the man—not what men think he is, but what he really is. This may be either better or worse than men think him to be—it is about as liable to be one as the other—but it is his character. The child is born without character. He may have proclivities, strong biases; but these are not character. Nothing which inheres in the child at the outset can, strictly speaking, be called character. It is only an endowment; while character is an outgrowth, a development; something to be cut out and built. Moral character is this same attainment in moral subjection—under the control of moral impulses and principles.

It has been a question whether a purely intellectual education will make a man any better morally.

Moreover, if we turn to history, we shall find that intellectual culture has been no guaranty of this. There was a time when Egypt was famous in letters—when science was pursued as nowhere else; when her great and justly renowned university drew to its halls many of the great men of the world, not excepting the great philosophers of Greece. But all this did not elevate her morally. The same will be found true of Athens, Rome, and other nations. What, then, is the source of morality? It is sometimes said, it is religious teaching. This may or may not be true. It depends upon the character of the religious teaching. Egypt, Assyria, Babylon, Greece, and Rome, abounded in priests and priestesses, and had religious teaching ad nauseam. The same is true in many Roman Catholic countries. But the very religion of Egypt and of other countries named was, of itself, demoralizing. How could it be otherwise when the priests and priestesses at the altars were debauchees and recreant to all the claims of virtue. And this recreance was a part of their religion, too. We find, also, that in many Roman Catholic countries much of the religious teaching is such as tends to lessen the bonds of morality. Nay, more. Not only in those countries, but in our own as well, the largest proportion of criminals is often found among the adherents of Rome.

But all this aside, it is doubtless true that the highest type of morality is the fruit of religious teaching. But it is the religion of the New Testament.

Some of the prodigies of this age of wisdom claim to have made the marvelous discovery that the Bible is an immoral book. How comes it, then, that no man or woman was ever yet made immoral by the honest study of it? How comes it that the most strictly moral persons have been those who have studied the Bible the most carefully and obeyed its teachings the most implicitly? These are facts which cannot be gainsaid.

Perhaps the old Aryan race, the early inhabitants of the most ancient India, came as near the true standard as any pagan nation which has had existence. Their system of philosophy and morals puts to blush many of the more pretentious systems of later days. And yet, under these, the race steadily degenerated in every thing essential to national beauty and grandeur. Now, then, we come to ask, What is the aim of the State in her educational work? Is it not to make men? To make the most reliable, the most trustful and efficient citizens? What, then, is the real character of such? Are they ever immoral? True, immoral men have, in some instances, done valuable work for the State. But are they the men to be relied on for such work? Would not men with the same abilities, and with strong moral characters, be more trustworthy and more efficient even? Is the government ever safe except in the hands of such? Suppose the bulk of the people under a government like ours should become immoral. What must be the character of the laws and of the government itself? Does the stream ever rise higher than the fountain? Does a pure stream ever flow from an impure fountain? No more can good and wholesome laws proceed from an immoral people. A correct sense of justice is indispensable to the creation or proper administration of law.

And now, granting what has been said, that the highest type of morality is the outgrowth of Christian teaching, that a strong and symmetrical morality has seldom, if ever, been produced except under the influence of Christian education, or something tantamount to it, and that wherever such a *régime* has been established and consistently worked, this has been the legitimate and uniform fruit, it cannot long remain a question in regard to the duty of the State in this matter.

Let me not be misunderstood here. When I speak of the importance, and necessity even, of a Christian education, I do not mean the teaching of creed or catechism in any form or in any sense. I mean simply the implanting of the principles of integrity and virtue, which underlie all the teachings of Christ and his apostles, and may be said to grow out of them. Let me say with emphasis that I do not mean what is meant by the Romish Church or any other when it makes a demand for the privilege of teaching its own creed and dogmas. Nay, but this is subversive of the aim to secure a Christian education; and I affirm without hesitation that the education given in the Roman Catholic schools of this country is in no proper sense a Christian education. The children are taught the catechism and the incredible fables of that Church, instead of the broad principles which underlie virtue and integrity. This is not random talk. Facts go to show that the teaching does not secure the end which should be sought, viz.: morality in its subjects. For, while the entire constituency of this sect is more thoroughly indoctrinated than any other class—more uniformly receives what they call a Christian education—still, statistics show that a larger proportion of our criminals come from that class than from any other. This fact forces us to the logical conclusion that the teaching is not Christian, but purely sectarian.

I should deeply deplore as a great public calamity the establishment of public schools which would teach the peculiar doctrines and usages of my own Church, much as I believe in these doctrines and usages. It would be a narrowing down of the great work to such a scale as could but be harmful, and result in clogging the wheels of progress in the great work of educating the nation. The State can never safely recognize the establishment of schools by any sect for the work of public education.

With this hedging, we are now prepared to say that it is the duty of the State to provide and insist upon a true Christian education for all of her children. Chief-Justice Story, than whom higher authority need not be sought, says: "It is impossible for those who believe in Christianity to doubt that it is the special duty of the government to foster and cherish it among all its citizens and subjects." I know that this view alarms many, lest it should in some sense involve the idea of a union of Church and State. But what possible harm could come from such a union as this contemplates. The experiment has never yet been tried, unless it were in the Jewish republic. England, France, Italy, Spain, and many other countries have given us examples of the effect of the union of sect and State, but never an instance of Church, or of Christianity, and State. The Church is immeasurably broader than any sect, covering and embracing all sects. In no sense would we recognize or advocate any connection in the direction of secular or pecuniary interests; but such a connection, and such only, as relates to the work of the State in protecting itself. We would have the State make use of those agencies which are within its legitimate sphere, for the purpose of building up and protecting her own interests. If the government finds that stanch moral integrity is indispensable to her prosperity and to her perpetuity, if she finds that such moral integrity is only secured, or even *best* secured by a Christian education, there remains no room for doubt as to her duty. If she ignores or neglects

this demand, she is recreant to her highest trust—for self-preservation is among the first duties.

No one doubts that it is a leading duty of the government to prevent crime. But it would be axiomatic to say that, as a rule, crime will be in proportion to the lack of moral character. There are instances, to be sure, where crime is greatly lessened by police regulations. A man may have murder in his heart, but be prevented from committing it in the place where he is, while, in another place, no such barrier would have been interposed. For instance, by statistics gathered in France and Prussia, in 1854, it was found that crime was as fifteen as common in Prussia as in France. But, aside from this, there was no evidence that the people of France were any more moral than the people of Prussia. It is also declared by many travelers that drunkenness is almost unknown in Paris; and the inference, triumphantly announced, is, that the habit of wine-drinking, to which all Paris is given, is a sure preventive against drunkenness. How often we have heard this. But any careful investigator, who talks with policemen and examines the police records, will find that this is due largely to the admirable police regulations of Paris. Any man who shows the first symptoms of drunkenness is hurried away and shut up until fully recovered. And the number of such arrests is very large.

All this does not invalidate the self-evident truth that crime will be measured by the moral character of a people.

In the report of the Commissioner of Education for 1872-3, the late Dr. Edward D. Mansfield says: "One of the great facts revealed by statistics is that, in the same moral condition of society, the same proportion of crimes will be brought out." "This was proved by Quetelet in his statistics; was observed by Madame De Staël; and is made much of by Buckle in his 'History of Civilization.'" "If the moral condition of society changes, then this apparently uniform proportion will change also."

The Commissioner of Statistics for the State of Ohio for 1861 says: "The great mass of crimes, however, keeps an exact proportion to the population, and, *unless the moral condition of society is changed*, will continue to do so." "So long as society presents the same moral conditions, so long it will present the same proportion of crime; but society has the moral power of self-reform. Shall it be said that society refuses to exercise this power?"

It may be said that a large proportion of criminals are destitute of education altogether. But statistics do not quite agree in regard to this. Statistics gathered in France, between 1866 and 1869, show that, out of the one half of the population who could neither read nor write, the arrests were one in forty-one, while from the one half commonly educated the arrests were only one in ninety-two hundred and ninety-one. Showing that the criminals from the uneducated classes were two hundred and twenty-six times as many proportionally as from the educated classes. This is an extraordinary showing and really exceptional.

A summary of statistics gathered from different countries shows that one third of all criminals are totally uneducated, and that four fifths have but slight education.

We may now consider the final question, the question of greatest importance in its bearings upon this whole subject: What is the real source of that moral character without which men are unfitted for the duties of citizenship? How is it to be secured? The advocates for a secular education virtually admit the importance of this moral character by the very tenacity with which they insist that a secular education will secure it.

It would be folly to parade argument for the purpose of showing that, in a country where every man has equal voice in making law, and where the laws must be what the majority declare they shall be, whatever the character of that majority, moral character is indispensable. It would be equal folly to attempt to show that, in proportion as a people become corrupt, in that proportion they sink. The history of the past is eloquent with the concentrated testimony of nations upon this point. Then, if the state will live, she must guard well the moral character of her citizens and subjects. To do this most effectually she must aim, in all her work, but specially in her educational work, at the creation of moral character. In this work it should never be forgotten that "Whatsoever a man soweth, that shall he also reap." It has already appeared that such moral character as we are in search of is never found in its perfection only where the Bible and its doctrines hold sway. Hon. Josiah Quincy said: "There can be no freedom without morality, no morality without religion, and no religion without the Bible."

We claim to be seeking the highest type of civilization, and the laws which will be most effectual in securing it. Edward Everett says: "Grotius was the founder of the science of international law, and that he laid the foundation of his treatise in the Scriptures of the Old and New Testament." The learned Fisher Ames says: "No man need hope to be a sound lawyer unless well read in the law of Moses." Everett says again: "The Bible is the foundation of the most characteristic portion of our modern European and American civilization."

Why, then, I ask, in the name of the rights of our civilization and the rights of our children, why this clamor against the Bible in our public schools? Is it said there are some who do not accept its teaching? It may be said with equal pertinency that there are those who do not believe in the political economy and the Constitution of the United States. Will the state, therefore, exclude our political economy and Constitution from the schools?

It is said, again, there are religious sects which do not desire to have it there. Do they object on the ground of its moral teaching? Do they offer any thing as a substitute whose record and teaching is better? Would they object to having their own catechism taught? I suspect these objections are merely specious. Are not these sects planted upon this Bible? If not, let it be known. Are they afraid of its influence? Would they put the traditions and incredible fables of the "Fathers" before it? Are they afraid of its interpretation except by hooded monks? If so, let it be acknowledged openly. It is time this issue was squarely met. The Bible is not a sectarian book, and it is possible this is just what is the matter. At any rate it is out of the schools in many places, and that in the interest of sectarianism. It ought to be in the schools in the interest of morality and the rights of the state. Let the whole aim of our educational work be to make broad, intelligent, and independent citizens, with a moral character which shall make them thoroughly reliable. Then may we continue to boast of our public schools as the hope of the nation. Then, too, will our nation maintain her true position as the vanguard in the onward march of nations.

VI. THE AMERICAN INDIAN PROBLEM.

1. INTRODUCTORY REMARKS.

GEN. T. J. MORGAN,

Principal State Normal School, Potsdam, N. Y.

As presiding officer of the morning session, Gen. MORGAN spoke as follows :

IT is not my purpose this morning to make any speech myself, but simply to preside over the deliberations of those who are called upon to make addresses. But I want to congratulate those of you who are here to-day on the privilege of taking part in these meetings. It is often said that the aspiring and ambitious young American thinks that the great thing for him to accomplish is to go to Congress. You cannot all go to Congress, but here we have really the Congress of the American people, where American citizens come together to discuss great American problems, and it is from meetings like this that go forth the instructions that shape the deliberations of Congress, and give them direction.

The solution of the questions, What shall be done with the Negro? what shall be done with the Indian? what shall be done with the Mormon? and other great problems, must come from the American citizen —from the American Christian public; and, I say, I congratulate you on your privilege in taking part in this meeting, and, by your presence and your counsel and your aid, helping to shape the thought and legislation and destiny of this Republic.

2. AN IMPORTANT LETTER.

HON. H. M. TELLER,

Secretary of the Interior, Washington.

DEPARTMENT OF THE INTERIOR, WASHINGTON, *July* 14, 1883.

J. C. HARTZELL, D.D., Ocean Grove, N. J.

Dear Sir : I regret that I am not able to accept your kind invitation to attend the meeting of the "National Education Assembly " to be held at Ocean Grove, in August. You especially invite my attention to what you designate as "Our Indian Day." By this I infer you have devoted one day to the consideration of the "Indian Question," and you will, doubtless, consider the subject of Indian education, as well as that of making them citizens, securing for them homes, etc.

I think it may be assumed that it has been fully demonstrated that the Indian can be educated. I do not think this can be seri-

ously questioned by any one who has given this subject the attention that its importance demands. With the education of the Indian, in a great degree, our responsibility with reference to him is at an end. An educated Indian is a civilized man, and as capable of taking care of himself as the great majority of the civilized people of the world. I do not intend by the term education to be confined to mere book knowledge. That education is the best for man that enables him to take the best care of himself, and to provide the most liberally for his mental, moral, and physical wants. The Indian has much to learn: he must be taught many things his civilized neighbor acquires in his infancy by his associations, if he does not inherit them from his civilized and enlightened parents. If the Indian mind is largely a blank, it readily takes the impressions sought to be stamped on it, whether the lessons are intellectual or physical. His moral perceptions are not as sensitive as his mental. The number of successful Indian schools now under the control of the Interior Department, the almost universal demand that comes up from Indians all over the country for such school facilities, is most encouraging to the friends of Indian education, to those who see through the means of manual labor schools the solution of the Indian problem that has so vexed the philanthropic during the last two hundred years. If a sufficient number of manual labor schools can be established to give to each youth the advantages of from three to five years of schooling. the next generation will hear nothing of this difficult problem, and we may leave the Indian to care for himself as his white neighbors do. During the last year, schools have been established at Lawrence, Kansas; Genoa, Nebraska; and Chilocco, Indian Territory; all to be conducted on the same plan as those of Carlisle, Hampton, and Forest Grove. It is expected that these schools will provide for the education of about six or seven hundred children. About four hundred and fifty will be placed in manual labor schools in various States, to become the associates of white children of their own age. There will be in all the manual labor schools about 2,464 children, and at the agency schools about 1,820, and at boarding schools about 1,971, making a total in school of 6,255 out of a school population of nearly forty thousand. The agency schools are not regularly attended, and the children derive but little benefit therefrom. The number of children that may be put in manual labor schools is limited only by the provision made for their support. If Congress will increase the appropriation for that purpose the department will find no difficulty in securing the attendance of the children. But with the present appropriation it is impossible to materially increase the number of children in schools. I desire to call your attention to a portion of my report for the fiscal year 1882:

"With liberal appropriations it is quite possible to provide for the education of ten thousand Indian youths in manual labor schools during the fiscal year 1884, and at least twice that number during the fiscal year 1885.

"The care, support, and education of 10,000 Indian youths during the fiscal year 1884 ought not to exceed $2,500,000, and with the increased number of children there ought to be a reduction in the cost, and the expense of 20,000 children ought not to exceed $4,000,000 per annum. To the 20,000 costing annually $4,000,000 ought each year to be added not less than one fourth that number, which, at the same expense per

capita, will necessitate an additional appropriation of $1,000,000, and the account will stand thus:

10,000 children, fiscal year 1884,
  computing the cost at $250
  each...................... $2,500,000
20,000 children, fiscal year 1885,
  at $200 each............... 4,000,000
25,000 children, fiscal year 1886,
  at $200 each............... 5,000,000
30,000 children, fiscal year 1887,
  at $200 each............... 6,000,000
25,000 children, fiscal year 1888,
  at $200 each............... 5,000,000

"The per capita allowance is greater than the cost at the agency boarding schools, but these schools are not kept up more than nine or ten months, while this estimate is for attendance for the full calendar year.

"At the close of the fiscal year 1887, 10,000 children, having completed their school course, can be discharged, leaving, with the 5,000 to be added for the fiscal year 1888, 25,000. Ten thousand of these may be discharged at the end of the fiscal year 1888, leaving, with the addition of 5,000, 20,000 for the fiscal year 1889; and every year thereafter one fourth of the whole number may be discharged, and the like number added. Thus, at the end of the fiscal year 1888, there will have been discharged 20,000 children, who will be able to care for and support themselves; and the total expense of the education of this number, with those remaining in school, will not exceed $22,-500,000, or about two thirds of the amount of money expended for the suppression of Indian hostilities during the years 1864 and 1865.

"Since 1872, a period of only ten years, the cost of Indian hostilities and military protection against the Indian is estimated by the military authorities at $223,891,264 50, or an annual expense of $22,389,126 45. To this must be added the yearly appropriation for subsistence, which averages about five millions a year. To this must also be added the loss of life and the horrors of an Indian war, only to be understood by those who have had the misfortune to be participants in or witnesses of them. This cannot be computed in dollars, but ought to be considered in determining the policy of the government in its dealing with the Indians.

"It is useless to attempt the civilization of the Indian through the agency of schools unless a large number of children, certainly not less than one half the total number, can have the benefit of such schools, and even then it is not wise to depend wholly on that agency. The children on returning to their homes should have some encouragement and support."

To meet this demand, not made without careful consideration, Congress appropriated about seven hundred thousand dollars. It is apparent, then, that the last Congress did not intend to accept the suggestions in the report just cited, and that unless the friends of Indian education make a determined effort, the government will go on in the future as in the past, partially educating a small number of children, to be returned to their parents to be surrounded by ignorance and vice, against which they will be unable to stand, and they will soon return to their original state of savagery. If we put five per cent. of the Indian youths in school, and return them at the end of three or four years to the tribe, they will be unable to withstand the evil influences that surround them, and they will make no impression on their heathenish associates. But if, on the other hand, the government will educate thirty or forty per cent. of the children, the minority with their superior knowledge, having enough associates to form their own society, will conquer and subdue the greater number of ignorant youths. The time has come when this work can be well and cheaply done. The Indian is ready and willing to receive civilization at our hands, in the only way he ever will, that is, through labor and education. He cannot and ought not to be supported as a pauper. He must accept civilization and become a producer among men, or disappear as a race.

Should the government withdraw its protection and aid from the Indian he would soon disappear. This protection and aid costs many millions of dollars each year, and if we continue in the way we have for many years past the civilization of the Indian is in the very distant future. Economy as well as humanity require that an effort should be made by all good citizens to secure a liberal appropriation for their education.

May I hope to secure the active co-operation of the "National Education Assembly" in this great work? I do not believe the Assembly can engage in a work that will be of more lasting benefit to the human race than this. I would not, however, have you think I am so much interested in the cause of Indian education, which has been specially intrusted to my care, that I have lost sight of the necessity for greater facilities for the education of other than Indian children. I can but repeat in substance what I have said before in the Senate, as well as in my annual report, that "the nation has duties to perform in this regard as well as powers to exercise;" and I trust the day is not far distant when the national government will extend to the States unable or unwilling to provide suitable school facilities such generous aid as shall encourage and strengthen the State governments to greater exertion in the cause of general education. In all your efforts in this direction you have my hearty sympathy and support. Very respectfully,

H. M. TELLER.

3. THE LEGAL STATUS OF THE INDIAN.

HENRY S. PANCOAST, ESQ., OF PHILADELPHIA.

NO less an authority than Sir Henry Sumner Maine has declared that progress is not a general characteristic, a normal condition, of the human race. It is in the nature of man, he says, to stand still. The races that advance are the exception, and not the rule. However this may be, it is certainly a curious fact, that the progress of humanity seems to have depended on the progress of one great branch of the human family—the Aryan branch. From the mysterious rise of this Aryan people in the dim beginning of history until now, it has been the moving factor in the development of mankind. From its rise until now it has had a mission to civilize, to startle the lethargy and stagnation of the other races, to bring progress and life, though they came by the sword and by destruction. From its starting-point, north-west of the Caucasian mountains, the Aryan people pushed to the south-east across the Indies, and, spreading over India, founded one of the most splendid and venerable of the civilizations of the world; and, on the other hand, sweeping to the north-west, it laid in the mighty forests and untilled spaces of a remote wilderness the foundation of the Europe of to-day.

Nor is its mission ended. Humanly speaking, the future of the race upon earth demands that the Aryan civilization shall go on. But how? In its progress this highest development ever reached by man is brought face to face with the most primitive races of mankind. The Aryan civilization must do one of two things; it must exterminate or it must civilize. Advance it must, but in that advance it must come either to destroy or to fulfil. Now, the peculiar difficulty it finds *to-day* in being true to its mission to civilize, lies in the vast intellectual and moral difference between it and the other races. This enormous difference in the scale renders assimilation more difficult than it was in the ruder times, when men were more nearly on a level; while a purer standard does not permit the use of the more violent methods of subjugation or forcible extermination. No longer do we seek to propagate Christianity by sword and rack; the conquest must be not merely the conquest of force, but of mind. This assimilation can be effected only by an enormous and almost instantaneous stride on the part of the lower races. It is expected that the lower race will either suffer itself to be immediately translated to that higher life which the higher race has been able to attain only through centuries of struggle, or will give place to a progress in which it can have no part. While we may hope that, eventually, time will soften or obliterate many ethnological distinctions which we have been accustomed to consider fundamental, the primary effect of thus bringing together elements so incongruous is to give rise to many curious questions of great difficulty. In our own country, we have before us not only the task of assimilating large and incessant additions to our population from many sources, but the problem of dealing with three races differing widely from each other and from the rest of our people, and apparently destined to be a permanent element in our population—the Negroes, the Chinese, and the Indians. In our relations with each of these three races the question presented is individual and distinct, yet in each case the end to be attained is the same. When a foreign race is an organic part of a nation, it must be compelled to surrender or abandon those race peculiarities which materially conflict with or retard the progress of the community; just as, by the doctrine of political economists, the individual is bound to yield so much of his natural liberty as is necessary for the preservation and good government of society. The nation, on the other hand, is bound to give to the foreign race the political and legal protection it grants to the rest of the community. It is for the nation to consider how it can best compel or effect a surrender of such race peculiarities as it may deem hurtful, and safely and wisely extend to a distinct people its system of law, and invest them with the political privileges of its citizens.

The necessity of thus politically incorporating the Indian tribes is becoming more and more painfully apparent. It is seen that to continue much longer their curious and unjust legal status is impolitic and well-nigh impossible; yet the difficulties in the way of bringing under our laws and investing with our rights a race so radically diverse seem almost insuperable.

There are, I suppose, comparatively few who believe that any such amalgamation can be effected simply by the easy path of

legislative enactment. An act of Congress is not an incantation or a charm that will change a savage into a citizen by declaring him one. What is needed is an organic change in the nature of the man himself, and it is worse than idle to thrust on him responsibilities he is incapable of appreciating, rights he is incapable of exercising intelligently, or to subject him to laws he is utterly unable to comprehend.

Yet we should not overlook the fact that a cautious and gradual change in his *legal status* may be one of the most important agencies in effecting this *radical, organic* change; that proper legal changes should work side by side with the more direct influences of religion and education toward one and the same end.

Let us examine the legal position of the Indians as tribes and as individuals, that we may consider what changes should be made in that position.

What is their relation, as tribes, to the general government? What rights have they, if any, as separate, organized bodies of men?

By what tenure do they, as tribes or as individuals, hold their land? Can they become citizens? What standing have they, collectively or individually, in our courts? Such are some of the questions which naturally suggest themselves. Let us glance, first, at the legal position of the Indians, as tribes or nations, and examine first the tribal tenure of land.

To understand this we must look at the early colonization of the country.

Although America, at its discovery, was an inhabited country, almost the first act in the history of European occupation was an utter disregard of those inhabitants. Pope Alexander II. solemnly divided the whole of the unknown world between Spain and Portugal. The validity of this grant being naturally questioned by the Protestant nations, it soon became evident that difficulties were likely to ensue between the different European powers almost simultaneously touching the shores of the great continent at many points. " To avoid bloody conflicts, which might terminate disadvantageously to all, it was necessary for the nations of Europe to establish some principle which all would acknowledge, and which should decide their respective rights as between themselves. This principle, suggested by the actual state of things, was: ' That discovery gave title to the government by whose subject or by whose authority it was made, against all other European governments, which title might be *consummated* by possession.' " [1]

But, although it was declared by our Supreme Court that the European nations

[1] Worcester v. the State of Georgia, 6 Pet., 543-544, (6 Wheat. 579.)

did acquire an absolute title by discovery, a title which, after the Revolution, vested in the United States, yet the court held that this *ultimate* title was subject to a right in the Indian tribes to *possess* or *occupy* the land. It was thought that wild, nomadic bands could acquire no permanent interest in or right to the soil; it was theirs but while they used it. While they chose to remain on it, it could not lawfully be taken from them; but when they left it their right was gone. The tribes have, our Supreme Court has declared, no higher title than this right of occupancy, and they can sell or surrender that only to the holder of the absolute ultimate title, *i. e.,* to the United States. But the court, at the same time, declared this right of occupancy a sacred right, a title which could not lawfully be taken from a tribe without its consent.

The political relations between the tribes and our government were settled in the early days of the Republic, in the well-known case of the Cherokee Nation v. the State of Georgia. Without stopping to inquire into the facts of the case, it is sufficient for our purpose to state the point on which the decision turned: "Had an Indian tribe, recognized by the United States as a nation, in repeated treaties, a right to sue in the national Supreme Court?" It was contended by the counsel for the Cherokees that they came within the constitutional provision giving to foreign nations a right to sue in our Supreme Court. The Cherokees were, it was urged, not citizens, but foreigners; they possessed the organized government and right to regulate their internal affairs characteristic of nationality; they had, moreover, been recognized by our government as a nation in treaty after treaty. A nation composed of foreigners must of necessity be a foreign nation. The decision of the court rested on the ground of jurisdiction. It was admitted that the Cherokees were a foreign nation, recognized as such by the United States in the several treaties, but denied that they were within the constitutional clause giving to foreign nations a right to sue. An examination of the Constitution showed, it was asserted, that it was not its intention to include the Indian tribes in that class. The Cherokees had, therefore, no standing in court.

It would be both presumptuous and useless to criticise the decision in this case; but whatever may have been the legal correctness of the position taken by the court, the anomalous standing in which it left the Indian tribes is, to say the least, unfortunate and inconsistent.

The Executive had, by treaties with many of the tribes, placed them in the position of foreign nations; they were, by its deliberate act and will, included in the very class for whose protection the clause in the Constitu-

tion was framed. The *Executive*, one branch of the supreme power, solemnly gave them an "unquestionable right;" the *Judiciary*, another branch of the same supreme power, as solemnly denies them a remedy. They were foreign nations, inasmuch as they could make treaties with us on equal terms, but they had not the right of foreign nations to legally enforce them. They were nations when we wished them to grant *us* land, but not nations that could call on us to protect them in the possession of the land we had left them forever. Surely, wherever the fault lay, there was a fault somewhere.

But, right or wrong, the tribal position of the Indian was determined. Henceforth there was among us a class of men, recognized as nations, to whom, as a class and as nations, we denied the equal protection of the law; nations in which we magnanimously recognized rights which we refused to enforce; nations with whom we were free to make treaties since we were also free to break them; nations to whom we could at our pleasure give land forever one year and take it back again the next; nations for whom there was but one law, the law that the strong may oppress the weak; nations to whom in their despair we left but one remedy, the remedy of war.

In 1825 the plan of removing the tribes beyond the Mississippi, to what was then the remote West, was inaugurated by President Monroe, with the assistance of his Secretary of War, Mr. Calhoun. It was hoped that in the yet untenanted depths of the vast continent these hunted and scattered bands might find a breathing-place; a brief time to learn from our teaching those arts of civilization which alone could prevent their utter ruin. The policy of the government was then, as now, the policy of isolation; a policy which has been one of the most effectual checks on the advancement of the Indian. This deliberate excluding of the race from the refining influence of contact with civilization has been largely rendered necessary by the simple fact that there is no proper law to protect the Indian in his relations with the whites. While the Indian is at a legal disadvantage, while he has no personal standing in the court to enforce his rights, he must be penned up in reservations from a contact which would make him the lawful prey of the community.

But even this policy of quiet seclusion has not been carried out. It is not necessary to more than allude to the fact that the various tribes have been given no opportunity to settle on the land and learn agriculture and the arts of peace. The course of the government has been a weak yielding to the local pressure for Indian lands, a shiftless, hand-to-mouth way of providing for the present at the expense of the future, with an utter indifference to the Indians' legal right of occupancy and the rights solemnly given by treaty.

This long line of broken treaties, this endless making and breaking of promises, this complaisant ignoring of justice and even of common honesty, is but the natural consequence of a decision which denied a feeble and broken race the protection of the law. Gradually the legal position of the tribes became what it is to-day. From the honorable position of nations, self-supporting, self-governing, and capable of treating with the United States on equal terms, the tribes have sunk to a position of humiliating dependence. Practically they have lost the right, theoretically theirs, of regulating their own internal affairs. As the agent has usurped greater and greater authority the power of the chiefs has decreased, until we have before us to-day the isolation, the hopelessness, and the despotism of the "Reservation System." We see to-day the great walls of civilization—or what we are pleased to term civilization—pressing closer and closer, like the four blank walls that slowly closed upon the wretched prisoner, with a mechanical, stifling, crushing pressure, as cold, as pitiless, and as inexorable.

In 1871, after the tribes had been recognized as nations by the United States in nearly four hundred treaties, they were summarily deprived of their nationality by an act of Congress, which took away their rights of making treaties with our government "as separate nations, tribes, or powers." [2]

"This act," says one writer, "destroys the nationality, and leaves the agent in the anomalous position of finding no authority within the tribe to which he can address himself, yet having in himself no legal authority over the tribe or over the members of it." [3]

It is not easy to determine the precise legal position of the tribes since the passage of this act. The United States has continued to make agreements, contracts, or whatever we may call them, with the tribes. It still considers them as organized bodies of men, as corporations, capable of contracting through their recognized officers, the chiefs or head men. Yet these organized tribes have been deprived of all but a miserable remnant of their right of self-government.

They have been deprived of it, so far as I am aware, by no authorized means, by no act of Congress, by no judicial decision, simply by the gradual and constant assumption of power by the Indian Agent. The power of the chiefs has become a shadow, and the agent, from the position of an embassador at the court of a foreign nation, has drawn to himself the absolute

authority of an Eastern despot. Now, the point I wish to call your attention to in this connection is this: This irregular assumption of power is not the fault of the agent, it is a necessity, a necessity for arbitrary power arising from the absence of law. Power there must be, of some kind. So long as we neglect to protect and control these Indians in their individual relations, by the moderate, restrained, and consistent power of the Law, just so long will the necessity exist for the exercise of a despotic and irresponsive power by the agents. The agents themselves are in many cases the first to acknowledge the necessity for law. The fault is in the system. We have deprived the tribes of the internal dependence of "domestic dependent nations," yet we neglect to give them the benefit of our law.

Such, then, is the legal position of the Indians as tribes.

By a legal decision they have been denied the rights of foreign nations to sue in our Supreme Court.

By statute their nationality has been destroyed, by depriving them of their right to treat with us as nations. [4]

By the circumstances and necessities of the case their very right of self-government has been supplanted by the rule of an agent with great and indefinite powers.

What are the main points in the position of the Indian as an individual?

While the members of the Indian tribes are more absolutely under the control of our government than any other part of our population, not only are they not citizens, but they are not within our naturalization laws. An Indian can acquire no title to land, except in some tribes under the provisions of particular treaties. It is true that, under one statute, if an Indian separate himself from his tribe, renounce his tribal relations, he can take a claim among the whites. The natural shrinking on the part of the Indian to go out from among his people, and settle among a race of widely different habits and speaking an unknown tongue, a race that he has good cause to regard with fear and aversion, makes this statute of no practical importance. But, besides this statute, if he leave his tribe and merges in the community, he becomes entitled to the personal and judicial rights of an alien; and his children, being born out of the tribal allegiance, are citizens by birth, under the fourteenth amendment. [5]

It is difficult to define the cases in which our Federal courts possess jurisdiction over the reservation Indians, especially as that jurisdiction is subject to local modification under particular treaties. The jurisdiction of the courts over the Indians may be given in two ways. It may arise under the power of the United States over the person—that

[2] Rev. Statutes U. S., p. 366, sec. 2079.
[3] Indian Citizenship, International Rev., May-June, 1874.
[4] Opinion Atty.-Gen., 746.
[5] Exp. Reynolds 18 Alb. Law, J. 8.

is, over the Indian apart from the place he may be in—or from the power of the United States over the *place;* that is, because the courts can punish offenses committed within the exclusive jurisdiction of the United States.

First, as to the power of the United States over the person.

This arises under the clause in the Constitution by which the United States is "given power to regulate commerce with the Indian tribes." [6]

Under this clause numerous acts regulating commerce, known as "Intercourse Acts" have been passed.

"This power," it has been judicially said, "includes not only traffic in commodities, but intercourse with such tribes, the personal conduct of the whites and other races to and with such tribes and the members thereof, and *vice versa.* This intercourse is a subject of Federal jurisdiction, the same as the naturalization of aliens, the subject of bankruptcy, or the establishment of post-offices."

But besides this power of the United States over the person of the Indian, there is the power of place, because the Indians are on land over which the United States has exclusive jurisdiction, an Indian reservation being on the same footing in this particular as United States forts, arsenals, dock-yards, etc. This power of locality is under the general power of the United States over the Territories and the following sections of the Act of 1834:

"Except as to crimes, the punishment of which is expressly provided for in this section, the general laws of the United States as to the punishment of crimes committed in any place within the sole and exclusive jurisdiction of the United States, except the District of Columbia, shall extend to the Indian country."

"The preceding section shall not be construed to extend to crimes committed by one Indian against the person and property of another, nor to any Indian committing any offense in the Indian country who has been punished by the local law of the tribe, or to any case where, by treaty stipulations, exclusive jurisdiction over such offenses is or may be secured to the Indian tribes respectively."

It will be seen that, so far as the Indians themselves are concerned, neither the locality of the offense nor the power over the person, gives the Federal courts any jurisdiction. In all *internal* questions the Indians are left by the law absolutely to themselves; it is but in their relations with the rest of the population, where our intercourse with them is in question, that the Federal courts are able to relieve and punish.

Thus, according to some local decisions, the Federal courts have jurisdiction when a white man steals from an Indian, and *vice versa,* [7] or in the murder on the reservation of an Indian by a white man, [8] and this whether the reservation be on a Territory or within the limits of a State. [9]

And as the power of the United States is not merely of *locality,* but of *subject,* it extends to offenses committed by Indians *off* the reservation, over which the Federal courts would have jurisdiction had they been committed upon it. [10]

Yet, in saying this we have probably given too liberal an idea of the power of our courts. It must not be forgotten that in these cases, while the Indian may be brought into court as a defendant, as a plaintiff he has in his own person no standing. He can bring no suit in his own name. He is not, in the eyes of the law, a reasonable, responsible being, a *person;* he is a ward of the government, and suit can only be brought for him by his guardian, the United States. From the testimony of those who have practical knowledge of Indian affairs, I have good reason to believe that in the great majority of cases this is equivalent to the Indian having no legal means of redress at all.

Such, then, is an outline of the position of the Indians as tribes and as individuals in their relations with the whites.

As tribes, they have absolutely no means of legal redress; as individuals, they possess in some cases a very inadequate and precarious one.

Nor is their internal condition one whit better. Were any one to be questioned as to the best and most obvious way of preserving order and good morals, of settling disputes and preventing crimes, in a community, he could have but one answer—by the efficient administration of a proper system of law. Were he to be told that among one class of men in *this* community—the class we are most anxious to educate in the ways of order and quiet living, the class from whom we are in constant dread of an outbreak—there is no provision made for any administration of law whatever, that the government expressly disclaims any judicial authority over the members of this class in their relations with each other, yet permits its agents (often ignorant and unscrupulous men) to exercise a power often as irritating as it is unconstitutional, would he not exclaim at the utter fatuity and criminal indifference of such a course?

It is conceivable that at first, when the nationality of the tribes was—for such purposes as suited us—conceded, the right of

[6] Cons. U. S., art. 1, sec. 8.
[7] U. S. v. Brindleman, *supra.*
[8] U. S. v. Martin, (Dist. Ct. D. Oregon,) 14 Fed. Rept., 817.
[9] *Ibid.*
[10] U. S. v. Holliday, 3 Wall., 407.

the Indians to regulate their internal affairs would be allowed; but now that nationality (except in the case of the five civilized nations) is practically destroyed, with what possible consistency can we permit the agent to exercise a control as unlimited as it is irregular, and yet assert that the introduction of law is an invasion of national privileges?

I have left myself too little time to speak of the crying necessity for law, of the enormous advantages it would bring with it, and of the manner in which it should be introduced.

Concerning the need for it, all those entitled to be heard speak with one voice. Think of it yourselves. The power of the chiefs to enforce the rude tribal laws is fast departing, or entirely gone, and were they ever so rigidly enforced, they are utterly inadequate to the growing needs. They are of necessity no higher than the moral standard of the tribe, and that is often pitifully far from a civilized standard. Many acts which we believe to be terrible, degrading violations of right and morality, are in no way recognized as crimes or punished by these tribal laws. What is the natural consequence of leaving communities of eight, ten, or twenty thousand people to the arbitrary and inconsistent decisions of agents or to an utter absence of law?

It is not merely by telling the Indians in our schools and churches that such things are right and such things are wrong, and that they must do the right; it is by actually and consistently *punishing* the wrong and supporting the right, that they will best learn the meaning of the distinction. If the active, forcible power, unceasingly *compelling* men to deal justly with their fellow-men, which we call Law, is essential for the welfare, the very life, of a *civilized* community, how absolutely vital is it to the regulation and development of semi-barbarous tribes. " Wish well to the Indians as we may," says Bishop Hare, " and do for them what we will, the efforts of civil agents, teachers, and missionaries are like the struggles of drowning men weighted with lead, as long as, by the absence of law, Indian society is left without a base."

But how is this law to be introduced? The ultimate object in all changes relating to the Indians should be to level all distinctions between us and them, to make them politically and socially, as far as possible, like other people. Yet, while we should never waver in our adherence to this central principle, we should be careful neither to overlook nor underestimate the many and great differences that separate their race from ours. However firmly we may hold to the doctrine of the unity of the human race, to the fact that all men are, by virtue of their manhood, in some wonderful and

far-off way in the image of God, faltering and broken though the image may be—however we may hold to all this, we are bound to recognize the terrible foundation differences that centuries of diverse influence have built between their race and ours.

It has been proposed to bring the Indians under the law by extending over the reservation the laws of the State or Territory in which that reservation is situated—to give them a right to sue and be sued in the local courts; to put them, in other words, in the same position as unnaturalized inhabitants so far as their rights in the courts. While this suggestion has the great merit of simplicity, while it seems the most obvious and easy way out of the difficulty, there are objections to it which, to my mind, are conclusive. It does not, for one thing, allow for the stubborn fact of race difference. How is it right or desirable for a sweep of the legislative wand to subject a savage to our highly artificial and intricate system of law? Such laws, in the first place, would inevitably come in conflict with certain tribal customs which it would be highly dangerous and inexpedient to thus rudely and instantaneously interfere with. Take the single example of the Indian custom of plural marriages: how monstrous would it be to punish them according to the State law against bigamy.

Again, State statutes imposing large fines on certain acts could not, with any justice, be immediately enforced against Indians.

More than this, there would be the danger from the local prejudice against the Indians. We should be, in many cases, placing them in the power of their bitterest enemies. Even if the Legislature should refrain from passing acts intended to bear more hardly on the Indians than on the whites, how many proofs have we that the verdict of a Western white jury, in cases where an Indian was concerned, would be an insult to justice.

What is needed is, first, a proper provision for the enforcement of law on the reservations by special reservation magistrates. These magistrates would, in effect, be educators as well as judges, and gradually accustom the tribe to a higher standard of justice and morality. While they should not hastily nor roughly interfere with the tribal customs, they would, in all cases when it was possible, introduce white man's law, and thus prepare the way for its eventual adoption by the tribe. It is probable that there would have to be a simple code of laws prepared (as nearly as practicable in accordance with the United States law, yet allowing for difference of conditions) for the guidance of the judges. Upon the details of this plan I have not time to enter. I will not stop to consider whether the magistrate should be the agent, or a person learned in the law; but some such way, I believe, is the best to fit them for the full rights and responsibilities of citizenship. Second, to protect the Indian in his relations with the whites he should be given the right to sue in his own person in the Federal or State courts.

It has been impossible in so short a time to take more than a superficial view of a question so intricate as the legal standing of the Indian, or to do justice to the difficult problem of how that standing should be changed.

I can but hope that these hints may lead some of you to examine and reflect on this question for yourselves, that they may awaken something more than a passing pity for the wrongs and struggles of a race who, not being under the law, have been forced to their undoing and to our shame, to be "a law unto themselves."

4. CHRISTIANITY IN ITS RELATIONS TO INDIAN CIVILIZATION.

HERBERT WELSH, ESQ.,
Germantown, Philadelphia, Pa.

THE dignity and fame of a great nation may be maintained only by her power to bear her burdens, to meet her responsibilities, and to rid herself of whatever evils, springing out of the richness of her increase, threaten to enfeeble her energies or to imperil her existence. It is now nearly twenty-five years since the question of Negro slavery and the right of secession, ultimately put to the arbitration of civil war, was the paramount thought which confronted every citizen of the United States. The bitter divisions which rent us in those days are passed, let us trust, for ever. The storms which darkened above the nation in 1861 have to-day sunk below the horizon, leaving a sky from which the sunshine of prosperity freely falls. Is there, then, no burden to which we of to-day must bend the back and nerve the arm, or is further effort unnecessary to the welfare and honor of our country? Three great questions challenge us now, and demand an answer: First, the reform of the civil service. Second, the elevation of the Negro in the South. Third, the elevation and protection of the Indian in the West.

To this latter question I would call your attention this morning. First let us ask ourselves, Is it possible to accomplish this result? Then how can it be accomplished? That it is possible to accomplish this result I am myself profoundly convinced, simply by the evidence of what has already been done in this direction which has come within my personal observation. This result can only be attained completely by bringing the actual condition and capability of the Indian clearly and constantly before the earnest Christian people of the United States. It cannot be attained by any spasmodic burst of indignation at wrongs which the Indian has suffered in past times, or of which he may still be the victim. Patient wisdom, increasing self-sacrifice, unfailing energy, advancing through the most varied channels and attacking the most diverse difficulties, as gons to such as must be encountered in any great reform, these alone can win a final and complete success. I can, perhaps, present to your minds this morning most readily a picture of the Indian's present condition and needs, and the work which must be done in his behalf, by giving to you some details of a visit which I have just made to the Great Sioux Reservation of Dakota, rather than by attempting to discuss the theoretical solution of the Indian problem.

Let me state briefly, by way of preface, that it has been my privilege during the past winter, as the Corresponding Secretary of the Indian Rights Association, to visit many of the large cities of the East, from Portland to Washington, and to speak to them in behalf of a just and wise treatment of the Indians. The interest every-where manifested in this question seemed so strong and deep that the Executive Committee of our Association in Philadelphia commissioned me to visit the Sioux Reservation, during the past spring and early summer, in order to ascertain the condition and needs of the Indians resident upon it. In obedience to this request, I reached the town of Pierre, in Dakota Territory, on the east bank of the Missouri River, on the evening of May 18. Pierre is a typical Western town, of some 2,000 inhabitants, and is flushed with the enjoyment of present and the prospect of future success. It lies opposite the Great Sioux Reserve, which stretches northward and southward for over two hundred miles, eastward and westward for one hundred and eighty miles, and at present acts as a serious hinderance to the spread of civilization. In consequence of this fact its people are deeply interested, as are the citizens of Chamberlain and other Western towns, in the opening of the reservation, by which the Chicago and North-western Railroad, which at present finds its terminus at Pierre, and the Chicago, Milwaukee, and St. Paul, with its terminus at Chamberlain, may press onward until they reach Deadwood in the Black Hills.

It has, therefore, been proposed, and a commission has visited the various tribes of the Sioux nation during the past winter to obtain their consent to the proposition, to take from the center of the reservation a section of territory measuring eighty miles from north to south, and about one hundred and eighty from east to west, and comprising about eleven million acres of land. This would give to the United States a valuable tract of country for settlement by whites, permit free access of civilization from east to west of the reservation, and bring valuable advantages to the Indian by a closer contact with skilled farmers and mechanics. The friends of the Indian would do nothing to check this opening of the reservation were the terms of the agreement by which that object is to be accomplished in all respects wise and just. But what does this agreement propose: First, To pay the Indians for the land ceded in cattle, the value of which, by the most liberal computation, is trifling compared to the value of the land which is to be given up. As nearly as can be computed, lands worth $6,875,000 are to be resigned for $970,000. or at the highest possible estimate, $2,470,000. Second, Many who have, at the urgent request of the government, engaged in farming and other civilized pursuits, will be removed from their lands, which heretofore they have been urged to occupy and cultivate. Third, No provision has been made by which religious bodies are to be protected in the possession of lands and buildings which they now occupy for missionary and educational purposes, or compensated for losses sustained through enforced removals. These religious bodies have undertaken to Christianize and civilize the Indians at the urgent request of the government, and have spent large sums in the prosecution of this work, and yet, as the agreement now stands, their land and property is liable to be taken from them at any moment by any citizen of the United States who may choose to file a claim upon them when these lands are open for settlement.

I would state, in addition, regarding this agreement, that an important provision of the Treaty of 1868 was disregarded by the commissioners who framed it, and by whom the commissioners who framed it, and who were authorized to procure the consent of the Sioux Indians to its adoption. The clause to which I refer provided that no further cession of land should be made by the Indians unless agreed to by three fourths of the male adults, and the same expressed in writing with their signatures attached. This clause was completely ignored by the com-

missioners, who were content to receive only the signatures of the chiefs and head men. These objections to the agreement, as it now stands, were sufficient to prevent its passage during the last session of Congress, owing to the vigorous efforts of the friends of the Indians to defend these almost defenseless people from the infliction of so great an injustice, which, notwithstanding, barely failed of consummation. I have ventured to dwell thus long upon these details, as I regard a knowledge of them an absolute necessity to any who would gain a clear idea of the present position in which this—the largest and most important of the Indian tribes in the country—now finds itself placed, and of those dangers which constantly threaten the Indian from the supreme legislative body of the United States—dangers which can only be averted by the strenuous exertions of right-minded and well-informed citizens.

But now permit me to present to you a brief sketch of my journey. On Saturday morning, May 18, I made my way by stage over the bleak, and at that time barren, hills, which lie between Pierre and Cheyenne River Agency. After having traveled from the town some six miles, we reached Peoria Bottom, a fertile strip of country bordering the Missouri, where the Rev. Thomas Riggs is carrying on a work of marked success among a settlement of Indians numbering about one hundred families. For years this earnest Christian man has labored as a missionary of the Congregationalist Church for the benefit of these people. Well has he succeeded! But only after encountering many trials and discouragements. With the personage and mission church as a center, he has gathered about him a colony of people, once wild and warlike, but now transformed into industrious and peaceable farmers; men who own individually one hundred and sixty acres of land, who live in log cabins, some of which they have themselves erected, who care for their crops and their cattle, and who, I am told, exercise the right of voting like white citizens. We arrived at Cheyenne River Agency on Saturday evening, and were there met by Mr. J. C. Kinney, the principal of St. John's School, an institution of the Episcopal Church, under the supervision of Bishop Hare. In company with Mr. Kinney we arrived at this place about sundown, having passed Fort Bennett and the agency buildings on our way. Here we met Bishop Hare, who had just returned from a visit to the mission on the Moreau, some seventy miles from the agency. This gentleman accompanied me during the greater part of my journey through the Indian country, and to him I am indebted for much useful information and many facilities afforded me during my visit. St. John's School accommodates over thirty Indian girls, all of whom come from Cheyenne River

Agency, and most of whom are of full Indian blood. Its efficiency is remarkable. The most perfect order and cleanliness reigned every-where, although all household work is performed by teachers and scholars only, without the aid of hired servants. The progress which has been made by the children in the class-room and in speaking English is very satisfactory, and would, I think, convince one of the important work which a reservation boarding-school may perform. The agency day-school, a government institution, which accommodates between twenty-five and thirty children, most of whom are half-breeds, is doing an excellent work, with the hearty encouragement of Agent Swan. This work of schools upon the reservation seems to me a most valuable one in relation to the more elaborate course of instruction given at Hampton and Carlisle, institutions to which the cause of Indian civilization is so deeply indebted for the interest which they have awakened in this question among the people of the Eastern States. Schools on the reservations should form the complement and support of those at Hampton and Carlisle.

At Lower Brulé Agency the work of the Episcopal Mission, under the care of a native clergyman, the Rev. Luke Walker, and the appointment of Rev. Mr. Gasman as agent, form encouraging features in the history of these people. At this place the Sioux Commission seem to have been altogether unsuccessful in their efforts to obtain signatures to the agreement, and the object of their visit was productive of excitement and alarm among the Indians. The cause of this is apparent, since the agreement provides for their removal from their present reservation, and the consequent abandonment of their farms and homes. This seems to me an unnecessary hardship, and one which tends to destroy newly-formed habits of industry, and leaves the Indian in painful doubt as to whether his home in the future will prove more permanent than in the past. Constant removals of location, in violation of national promises, nourish doubt in the mind of the Indian as to the sincerity of the government, until that condition has at last assumed a chronic form, and to him the terms "white man" and "liar" have become synonymous.

From Lower Brulé we went to Crow Creek Agency, where about nine hundred of the Sioux Indians are located along the arable bottom lands, well supplied with timber which skirts the stream. Their progress in modes of living, a knowledge of agriculture and carpentry, and industry in their pursuit, we found most encouraging. Their well-ordered farms, cleanly and comfortable homes, some of which they have themselves erected, and their civilized dress and demeanor, give them rank among some of the most

advanced Indians whom I have visited. I believe great credit for this favorable condition of affairs is due to one of their former agents, Captain Dougherty, who rendered them valuable assistance in house building, and to the Rev. H. Burt, who has labored among them as a faithful missionary.

Leaving this agency, we continued our journey to Springfield, a small town of several hundred inhabitants, which lies on the Missouri, one hundred miles below Lower Brulé. Here we found Hope School. Here some twenty-five to thirty Indian boys and girls are being educated by the Episcopal Church.

Santee Reservation was the next point visited, where the Congregationalists and Episcopalians have established churches and schools, and have secured valuable results. These people, who are among the most civilized of the Sioux tribes, have been living quietly upon their present reservation for nineteen years. If protected in its possession their future seems secure. Under a provision of the Treaty of 1868, fifty of them have recently taken out permanent patents for one hundred and sixty acres of land individually, and are thus trying to gain a settled hold upon their territory.

And now let me draw your attention, before closing, by a very brief account, to one of the most important, and, hitherto, one of the wildest, agencies in the country, that of Pine Ridge, which lies about one hundred miles further in the wilderness than Rosebud, and is under the able management of Dr. V. T. M'Gillycuddy. When this gentleman first assumed the position of agent, some four years ago, the eight thousand Indians placed under his care were huddled together in one immense camp about the agency, living in idleness, and fed upon the bounty of the government. Dr. M'Gillycuddy was led to suspect that, although he was issuing no more than the due allowance of rations, the Indians were receiving more than they had any need for. By personal examination he discovered supplies of flour, sugar, bacon, and other provisions, hidden in the lodges, and actually spoiling for want of use. He found, also, that white men were gaining an easy living from the Indian superfluity. White men, in some cases, bought from the Indians sacks of flour worth $4 50 for 50 cents. He then began a gradual but steady diminution in the issue of rations, until within the last four years $200,000 have been saved to the department. Most unfortunately, Dr. M'Gillycuddy was unable to use this money in a way in which it is sorely needed, namely, for an increase of skilled employes and farmers who would be invaluable for the purposes of directing these Indians in the arts of industry. The crowded camp about the agency now no longer exists, as the people have been scattered out upon the arable bottom lands, bordering the creeks and streams, to a distance of twenty, thirty, or even fifty miles. In each of the half dozen villages into which the Ogallalas have formed themselves, the agent has planted a day-school provided either with a white or a native teacher. These schools I can testify are doing an admirable work. At the agency a large boarding-school has been built, and is ready to begin work in the coming autumn. Dr. M'Gilly-cuddy has also organized an efficient Indian police force, the members of which are responsible for the good order of all the reservation. This force is composed of some of the best men upon the reservation, and is under admirable discipline. Indian teamsters transport all the freight which is used at the agency from the railroad station at Valentine, in Nebraska, a distance of one hundred and nineteen miles. This work is honestly and faithfully performed. As much progress has been made in farming and house building, considering the absolute ignorance of such arts which has hitherto existed among these people, as could be expected. Many hundreds of Indians are engaged in farming, and I saw houses which would compare quite favorably with frontier dwellings, which were the result of Indian industry. Time forbids a more detailed statement of the excellent condition of affairs at Pine Ridge, and I may close by the remark that, were men of Dr. M'Gillycuddy's executive ability and hearty interest in the advancement of this people generally employed as Indian agents, the solution of the Indian problem would be near at hand.

From this hasty and necessarily incomplete picture of the condition of those Indians whom I have visited, some estimate may be formed of the character of the work which must be done before they shall be educated and absorbed into the mass of our population. In this education and absorption lies their only hope. To retain them on their present reservations for any long period of time as a separate and distinct people from ourselves is neither desirable nor possible. Thus their

ignorance, helplessness, and consequent degradation would be preserved and fostered indefinitely. It is impossible so to retain them because the pressure of our own population upon them is irresistible so long as the Indian remains a barbarian. As savage tribes they must inevitably disappear before the advance of civilization. But while they must die as nationalities, the individual man may be saved by a new birth into a better and nobler life. Of the truth of this statement there can be no doubt, since on each of the reservations which I have visited there are many whose lives bear witness to its correctness. The question, then, before us is, how render the agent and reservation system the efficient nursery and school-room by which the Indian shall be ushered into independent manhood speedily and safely. Then, and only then, can the agent and reservation system, by virtue of its own effectiveness, be prepared for dissolution, and the Indian be transformed into a citizen of the United States. The motive power by which this object can be obtained I believe to be none other than an effort, wise, patient, unremitting, upon the part of the Christian people of this land, which shall exert its influence through regularly organized channels, such as the National Indian Association, and the Indian Rights Association, of Philadelphia, upon the public sentiment of the country at large, and upon both the executive and legislative departments of the government. Congress must, by every just means, be influenced so as to grant far larger appropriations for education, to enact wise measures looking toward the elevation and protection of Indians, and must also be restrained from such legislation as will permit them to be unjustly dealt with. Such reforms as I have endeavored faintly to outline as necessary to the solution of the Indian problem demand for their accomplishment the united effort of Christian people throughout the land. Only through them can the tide of selfishness and oppression be stayed, and the Indian be saved from impending ruin.

---

5. WOMAN'S WORK IN SOLVING THE INDIAN PROBLEM.

MRS. AMELIA S. QUINTON,

Gen. Sec. National Indian Association, Philadelphia, Pa.

THAT the present calls for woman's work in all the great moral movements of the day no one doubts. Since she is a soul, having also intellectual activities and heart, or emotional governance, God, in daily life and in revelation, makes woman as responsible as man for all she can do worthily for the

wide world's need; and as the mother consciously or unconsciously leads in, and is, equally with man, responsible for the home, so in the State, consciously or unconsciously, is woman, equally with man, responsible for whatever her thought, effort, and influence can do for its welfare, or to correct wrongs and abolish abuses within it. The State is but the nation at home, indeed, and its righteousness or unrighteousness will be largely according to woman's wisdom or ignorance, to her duty done or avoided. The leadings in national history have been according to the loves of the leaders' hearts; according to ambition or patriotism, avarice or benevolence. What is needed, then, is heart, much heart, and right heart, to sway the nation's will in its great questions, and especially in that before us to-day. For the solution of the Indian problem woman's heart and heart are needed, and *because* these are *needed, God* has already employed both.

WHAT HAS WOMAN DONE ON THIS BEHALF?

Much in way of mission work in connection with the various religious denominations; much in way of school work in government and other schools. Much has been done by individuals with pen and tongue. All deeply interested in Indian welfare know of the great service of "H. H.," Mrs. William Jackson, of Colorado, in the press, and by her book, "A Century of Dishonor," and of scientific work done by Miss Alice C. Fletcher, of Boston; work which has also recently interested the people in Indians, and of the service of both these, under Government, in dividing Indian lands in severalty, to the Mission Indians of California by the former, and to the Omahas of the North-west by the latter. Not of these, however, am I to speak to-day, but of that union of the women of ten denominations known as THE NATIONAL INDIAN ASSOCIATION. This society has now helpers and auxiliaries in twenty States, and during its four years of effort has circulated a million of pages of appeal and information from official sources upon the Indian question; has circulated and presented a petition to Congress annually; has secured the indorsement and co-operation of hundreds of churches, of the entire ministry of various denominations in various leading cities, and of great denominational benevolent societies. It has published hundreds of articles in the press in different sections of the country, especially in religious papers, and has held many popular meetings in different States, and thus has awakened a wide and deep sentiment in influential centers in favor of a new Indian policy which shall result in the civilization and Christianization of Indians.

The first impulse in this work was sympathy with Indian women and children, and the first effort was to help create a strong, *united Christian sentiment,* which should achieve just Congressional action on behalf of Indians. The four lines of work just alluded to have been pursued to that end, and with marked and growing success. During the winter of 1882 and 1883, the mass-meetings in New York, Philadelphia, Brooklyn,

Boston, Hartford, Portsmouth, and other leading cities, brought to the subject much new interest, and women of national reputation became helpers and officers of the various auxiliaries of the association. Among these are Mrs. Harriet Beecher Stowe, Mrs. President Porter, of New Haven, Mrs. ex-Governor Claflin, Mrs. Joseph Cook, Mrs. Augustus Hemenway, Mrs. Julia Ward Howe; the wives of Bishops Paddock, Simpson, Andrews, and Nicholson; of Senators Hawley and Hoar; of Rev. Drs. John Hall and Ormiston; Mrs. William E. Dodge, and others well known in benevolent and literary work. Of the influence and effect of work undertaken by such women none can doubt. The making of public sentiment, however, is not the chief aim of the association, important as this is, but is to be soon.

EDUCATION AND MISSION WORK *among the wild tribes where none now no religious society is laboring for Indians.*

Here the association hopes to organize mission schools whose aim shall be to teach Indian children and young parents how to speak English, to become *self-supporting,* to *make* homes, and keep them in civilized and Christian fashion; thus supplying knowledge and self-support to Indians who cannot go East to our grandly successful government schools, but who, without this proposed mission-school work, must grow up in barbarism still. Nor will this work interfere with or duplicate the labors of denominational societies, for it is proposed, as soon as a school is in good working order, to give it over to the care of the evangelical mission nearest it. Thus the association will do pioneer work for all the evangelical denominations in turn, and, it is hoped, secure thus new financial help for all.

To this great work of civilizing and Christianizing the now uncared-for wild Indian tribes of our land all American Christian women are most earnestly summoned; and they can do this work while mere politicians are objecting that, with the sure success of such labor, their political gains from the barbarisms of the past Indian policy will be gone. Some Indian agents may object to such schools upon the reserves, but this will only be where the plan is not understood, or where the agent is himself not fit to be master, as now, of hundreds or thousands of human beings. Where the barbarism, squalor, vice, suffering, and dense ignorance are, there should the Christian teacher be with the remedies of "light." One agent said, "These Indians are savages, and any lady would shrink from coming here; she would shrink with loathing and disgust." Not if she had a really Christian spirit. What is ladyhood for, but for the elevation and illumination of the degraded and ignorant? The Christian lady is solemnly covenanted to such work, and the history of missions assures the success of it. In proof of this we have but to point to the story of the evangelization of the Sandwich Islands, and to the successes of our Indian Missions in the Indian Territory, and in the North-west. This lowly work in lowly homes, or where human beings live without homes, must be a success, or the Gospel, God's remedy for sin and want and anguish, is a failure.

If any thoughtful woman needs inspiration for this work let her read the statements of the last reports of Secretary Teller, of Commissioner Price, and of the Board of Indian Commissioners. Let her reflect that there are still 68 tribes without missionaries; and let her note the dire helplessness, poverty, suffering, and defenseless state of whole tribes of human beings in this Christian land. Let her look into the condition of the Apaches, the Hualipis, the Papagoes, and other tribes in the South-west, for whom officers of the army plead, and for whom the wives of officers plead, with tears, that women teachers may be sent among them with a *practical* as well as heart-healing and enlightening Gospel. Another call for woman's work in the Indian problem is for a united and enthusiastic

PETITION TO GOVERNMENT FOR MONEY APPROPRIATIONS

Adequate to the industrial education of all Indian children, as already promised in various treaties, and as due, for value received, from the government. Let all good women unite in such a plea, and repeat it until the plea is granted; and let all such efforts come to members of Congress from their own districts, as well as before Congressional committees. Let women ask, too, that salaries adequate for securing men of ability and integrity as agents upon the reservations be paid, while reserves are needed, temporarily, pending the disappearance of the agency system before the desired distribution of lands in severalty, and citizenship voluntarily embraced, by Indians.

There is much, also, that women can do by conversations, leaflets, addresses, and articles in the press, to remove obstacles to the full solution of the Indian problem in

CORRECTING POPULAR ERRORS

Concerning Indian characteristics; as, for example, that Indians are naturally more revengeful and cruel than are other races. With the records of the Inquisition, the deeds of Alva, the massacre of St. Bartholomew, and other such facts against our own race, and, to come to our own time, with the accounts of Chivington's massacre of Indians at Sand Creek, of the massacre of Piegans by Baker, under Sheridan, and of the scenes on the occasion of the return and slaughter of the Cheyennes in 1878—with all

these before us, we cannot rail at savages as being more cruel than ourselves. In like manner, with the multitude of facts in official reports to draw from, it is as easy to prove that Indians are not wanting in aspiration, willingness to work, faithfulness, domestic affections, and mental, spiritual, and political capability. It is easy to prove that they are simply, like ourselves, human, and, therefore, reachable by ordinary human motives and interests, and that being human they are salvable, and can be of value as a fresh element in our varied population, while that to citizenize them will be also to avoid the enormous expensiveness of Indian wars, Indian agencies, and Indian appropriations. That the Indian is a man of force and character is overwhelmingly proved by the fact that he has survived our treatment of him. What has he not endured of robbery. war, and persecution at our hands. and yet has held his own against us all! What heroisms of barbarous defense of barbarous homes and principles has he shown again and again, and what noble defense of noble principles also! There has been many a Chief Joseph among the race. And what has the Indian wife and mother not suffered from our race! Recall the case of those Northern Cheyenne women who, when offered food for themselves and children, after weeks of pursuit by United States soldiers, and five foodless days in a freezing prison, and all for the crime of returning to their own home, refused to come out and leave their husbands and brothers to the rifle and bayonet. Not a woman of them stirred. Not a child left a starving parent to live in response to that call. Have such not human hearts and souls? Are such not worth saving? Will not womanly women and knightly men champion such as these? And shall not Christians secure all these human affections, this self-control and intrepidity, devotion and loyalty to God. and for righteousness? The Indian can do and bear any thing for his real principles. Not even death can daunt him. Let Christians, then, teach him that to be forbearing where anger would be applauded, to be loyal to right where treason would be compensated, and to be loving where murder would be humanly justified, is what God calls brave, is the pattern he reveals, the task he gives, and the Indian may yet lead us all in national righteousness.

WOMEN CAN HELP, IN THE SPHERE OF LAW,

To secure righteous laws on behalf of Indians. This aid can be given in various ways; as, for example, by circulating information about our past unjust and imbecile Indian policy; by pointing out its blunders and crimes, its untold cost and inhumanity; and by calling attention to the reforms recommended by the present administration, to the economical educational schemes of Secretary Teller, and to the earnest plea for Christian work by Commissioner Price.

Ten thousand Christian women should at once send for the leaflets of THE NATIONAL INDIAN ASSOCIATION, become members of it, and share in the evangelization and civilization of the 262,000 native Americans within our national area. Would not such a rally secure the power of the moral tides for human help? And would not such effort appeal to the strongest human motive, namely, gratitude to God, and be thus the strongest leverage for the elevation of the Indian?

Pastors, editors, philanthropists, statesmen, and all thoughtful people recognize and indorse this movement, and it only waits the co-operation of the women of the Churches to make it a complete success, to give a fair opportunity to the helpless Indian to rise into manhood, citizenship, and Christian character.

6. A NEW PHASE OF THE QUESTION.

REV. C. H. KIDDER,

Rector of St. Clement's Protestant Episcopal Church, Wilkesbarre, Pa.

DISRAELI once said of Bishop Colenso that "he went to convert the Zulu Kaffirs, and the Zulus converted him." In a better sense this may be said of sincere efforts to Christianize the Indians. Four years ago I was requested by Bishop Hare to take charge for a time of two converted Indians, in order to give them an opportunity to study the civilization of the East on the spot. I had them in my family for three months, and I must say that the little benefit that I was to them bore but a small proportion to the great benefit which they were to me. One of them was in deacon's orders in the Protestant Episcopal Church, the other a teacher in St. Paul's School, Yankton, D. T., where both had been educated. Both had been genuine savages. The clergyman, at one time in his life, shot buffaloes with arrows. Neither could tell the day of his birth, their rude Indian chronology having preserved only the month. Far from perceiving any difficulty in their adapting themselves to the customs of civilization, we found that the instruction which they had received at boarding-school had left us nothing to teach. Their behavior at table, their courtesy, their constant demeanor, was such that they could rather have been examples to many brought up under the so-called "influences of civilization." I remember distinctly their horror when, coming home from church, our path lay near a hotel which was a resort for Sunday excursions, and the sound of music and dancing was heard. They looked at me inquiringly, and I saw mingled in their looks horror and surprise that civilized people could engage in or permit any thing of the kind on God's holy day.

The clergyman, David Tatiyopa, although he knew but few words of our language, was, by the loveliness and earnestness of his Christian life, a lesson to all with whom he came in contact. There was some difficulty in communicating with them, for, though the teacher was better acquainted with English, he was very bashful about using it. When a more skillful interpreter was obtained, inquiry was made as to what had most pleased them during their recent visits to factories, churches, and other places of interest. David spoke of a trip across the Delaware to see shad-fishing in progress, and, when asked the cause of his preference for this, he replied (something to cause shame to the many who pay so little attention to the Scriptures) that it reminded him of the disciples drawing their nets when our Saviour called them to his service. So it was at all times. He was quick to see every such analogy with the teachings or history of the Bible. Upon one occasion we were walking some distance by the light of a lantern. David, pointing to the lantern, said a few words in Dakota to his companion, and, on inquiry, I learned that he was quoting the text, "Thy word is a lamp unto my feet and a light unto my path." And then I thought of the many who in the midst of light are walking in darkness, caring nothing for the enlightenment so highly prized by this convert from heathenism. In thinking over all this, forcibly it brought to mind the anecdote so frequently told, but never told too often, of the traveler in the Alps who, when in danger of yielding to the cold, saw another traveler lying prostrate in the snow. Unselfishly using his best efforts to awaken life in that poor fallen one, he found that those very efforts, successful in the end, were the means of his own preservation, and thus two were saved. So it is with our attempts to Christianize and elevate the Indians. As we meet with success, and see how highly they prize what we so often despise or lightly esteem, we shall find that, as we convert them, they in turn will convert us to a higher appreciation of the blessings of our holy religion.

7. WHAT SHALL BE DONE WITH OUR SAVAGES?

H. K. CARROLL, ESQ.,

Assistant Editor of "The Independent," New York.

WHAT shall be done with our savages? is a question which is as old as our country, and yet men are not done asking it. All the answers which have been attempted can be summed up in one word—extermination. Practically, this is what all parties desire. They differ only in the methods by which they propose to reach this end. But this difference is as wide as the difference between right and wrong, between humanity and inhumanity, between civilization and barbarism, between the Christ spirit and the spirit of Moloch. What basis is there for this demand of extermination of savagery?

Our society is the organization of the highest civilization. It not only seeks for continued development in the direction of the ideal, but it sets itself sternly against all that tends to dwarf or thwart its progress. What it cannot assimilate it crushes remorselessly. Indian savagery opposes this progress, and the forces of society combine against it. They drive it farther and farther into the wilderness; they isolate it; they surround it with danger-signals; they must finally drive it from its last hiding-place. It is doomed, and we cannot save it if we would. The simple question—but it is a question of the greatest concern—is, what process of extermination shall prevail? One method is personal extermination by force of arms. Another proposes simply to allow the forces of civilization to work their will. If the Indian can comply with the terms they impose, without aid or encouragement, well and good. If not, the extinction of the race will free us from a burden. A third method aims to exterminate the savagery and thus save the race, to rescue the man from a mode of life which society cannot tolerate.

The first two methods may be classed together as repugnant to our faith, our humanity, and our spirit of brotherhood. Their supporters deny, either positively or practically, that the Indian is reformable. They say that there is no good Indian but a dead Indian, and if they do not all agree that all Indians ought to be made good in this way, they do not believe in wasting time and money and patience on any other process of trying to make them good. They deny or ignore two basal facts in the constitution of man, which can no more be doubted than the existence of God, in whose image he was made. *First*, No race is so low mentally and morally as not to possess the germs of nobility and intelligence. *Secondly*, These germs are educable.

It is simple faith in these facts and in the Gospel which has inspired missionary work among the lowest tribes known to the world, the Hottentots, the Australians, and the Patagonians. Darwin, many years ago, scouted the idea of sending teachers among the natives of Terra del Fuego. They had, he thought, no more mental power than a bird. But before he died he frankly acknowledged that the faith of the missionaries had not been misplaced, that if the Fuegians were animals they were reasoning animals, and that the line separating man from the brute creation must be drawn below and not above them. Now, the argument which establishes the teachableness of any race of mankind settles conclusively the duty of teaching, upon the performance of which depends the final universal triumph of Christian civilization. If it is our duty to cross seas to carry light to benighted tribes, what do we owe to the natives of our own land? If we can lift in fifty years a people like the Sandwich Islanders from their depths of moral, physical, and mental wretchedness to the dignity and usefulness of an enlightened Christian manhood, what excuse have we to give for the existence of hordes of savages in our own territory after the lapse of at least a century of opportunity? I stand here to-day to say that, while our duty to the Indian remains unfulfilled, we are consenting to an extermination which morally fixes on us blood-guiltiness. "His blood will I require at thine hand," because thou hast not warned him.

It is not that our Indians are not teachable; it is not that they are unwilling to be taught; it is not that we are unable to teach them—it is because, with culpable indifference, we have neglected them; it is because *we* have failed that so many of them are still savages. I have sometimes thought that it was a misfortune to the Indians that they were not all born on an island somewhere in the broad Pacific. If they had been, they might all have been Christianized long ago. Is it because they are too near home that our missionary societies do not work more extensively and energetically among them? Some of the societies say that their missions in India and China and Japan pay better. Our force of missionaries abroad is being constantly increased, and it is to our glory; but our missionaries among the Indians are not being increased, and *this* is to our shame. Some of our denominations deem it their duty to send missionaries to England, and yet England does more missionary work on the American continent than *we* do, outside of our strictly domestic missions. It is working among the Indians of British America under difficulties and at sacrifices of which we know nothing. Bishop Bompas has a diocese three thousand miles long, stretching north to the Arctic Circle, and very sparsely populated. Other great missionary dioceses divide up much of the remaining territory, which has little to attract civilization. Bishop Ridley, west of the Rocky Mountains, finds the sunsets the most glorious pictures of nature in those lovely regions; but, after all, he says, "the Sun of Righteousness has produced a far more beautiful transformation in the character of the Indians. The church-bells ring, and from both wings of the village (of Metlahkatlah) well-dressed men, their wives, and children, pour out from the cottages, and the two currents meet at the steps of the noble sanctuary their own hands have made, to the honor of God, our Saviour." The Bishop of Saskatchewan says: "I do not believe that in all the wide world there has been so large a proportion of a heathen population converted to Christianity as among our red Indians, in so short a time."

Such triumphs are not rare among our own Indian missions. We have so much to show for our outlay that there ought to be no room either for discouragement or in-difference. I want to lay great stress upon Christian instruction as an element in our problem of exterminating savagery. The Commissioner of Indian Affairs speaks very emphatically on this point: "In no other manner," he says, "by no other means, in my own judgment, can our Indian population be so speedily and permanently reclaimed from barbarism, idolatry, and savage life, as by the educational and missionary operations of the Christian people of our country." While the government is devoting increased appropriations to school and industrial training, it well knows that it can neither exterminate savagery nor secure a sound and lasting civilization without the help of the Churches.

This places a heavy responsibility on the Churches. If the Indians are not saved to civilization it will be the fault of the Churches. If they continue to be pests to society, if they fail to become Christians, the guilt will rest upon the Churches. It is not an impossible task. Our pagans compare favorably with the idolaters of Asia and Africa. The poor Indian's

"Untutored mind
Sees God in the clouds,
Or hears him in the wind."

He believes in immortality, in the land of spirits, and in the Great Spirit.

"Think ye he prays not when on high
He hears the thunders roll?
What bade him look beyond the sky?
The savage has a soul."

8. PRACTICAL RESULTS OF INDIAN EDUCATION.

J. M. HAWORTH, ESQ.,
Superintendent of United States Indian Schools.

FOR more than a hundred years our government has been wrestling with the question of Indian affairs, intrusting its management first to one arm of its service, now then to the other, with unsatisfactory results in both. Now treating with them for large districts of country, and designating others where they may settle and remain in undisputed ownership as long as grass grows and water runs. How parched and barren would our green earth have grown, and how thirsty for drink its rippling brooks, had nature been as fickle and changing as our treaty-making. But few seasons' growth of grass would witness the red man in his new home, until his white brother would discover that that very country was needed for the rapidly-increasing white population, and again the decree would be made, "The Indians must go." If necessary to accomplish it, an Indian outbreak was brought about; and he who was responsible for it, causing all the train of terrible consequences incident to an Indian war on the frontier, went with bloody hands unpunished, and perhaps applauded, while the Indian, who had been goaded into war, and acting in accordance with his education—"an eye for an eye and a tooth for a tooth"—was made to bear all the blame and all the punishment.

A new treaty becoming necessary, a new home for the Indian followed; a new farewell to the graves of his fathers; and with face again turned to the setting sun, his march would be taken up, and his course seem emblematic of his race. And so it has ever been, back and still back, nearer and still nearer the setting sun, he has been compelled to move, until to-day he stands upon the last hill; there is left for him no wilder country than the one he occupies to which he can go. Civilization almost encircles him. Look whichever way he may, the smoke from the white man's chimney meets his eye. His original way of procuring a living is rapidly being cut off by the advance of the white man's lines.

Where he shall go, or what he shall do, are momentous questions to him. He sees the change. He begins to realize that something must be done. Never in his existence has he felt more need of friends, or needed them more, than now; and, may I not add, never has there been a time when friends were more ready to respond to his wants, and help him in his needs, than now.

Congress two years ago gave one hundred and fifty thousand dollars more for educational purposes than the Indian Bureau asked for, and at its last session added largely to the amounts of previous years' appropriations. The doors of the treasury begin to loosen in his favor, indicating a disposition to atone in the future for the bad treatment of the past. Year after year treaties have been made, and in many cases broken. Many of them were wise in provision, and would have presented the Indian question in a very different light to-day if they had been carried out in good faith. As has already been said, for many years unsuccessful or unsatisfactory methods had been adopted in the treatment of the Indians and management of Indian affairs. Thousands of lives and millions of money have been sacrificed and wasted to no purpose.

The massacre of a camp of friendly Indians, most of whom were unarmed and encamped in a locality selected for them by the commandant of a post near by, in the late fall of 1864, caused a war resulting in the death of hundreds of the frontier people, and the expenditure of over $30,000,000. This unnecessary war invited the attention of the country, demanding that peaceful agencies should be resorted to, and Congress appointed a joint committee to examine into Indian affairs, whose report shed great light upon the subject; and a commission, consisting partly of military officers, was appointed to visit the plains and make treaties with the Indians, whose labors were attended with success.

The Society of Friends (Quakers) had become interested in the matter, and a conference of members from several of the yearly meetings, from different parts of the country, on December, 1868, met in Chicago, and again in January, 1869, in Baltimore, and prepared a memorial setting forth the abuses and frauds of the system then in operation, and urging the necessity of some more humane and just way of dealing with the Indians. This memorial they carried to Washington, and laid before a joint session of the Indian Committees of Congress, where the matter was very fully discussed. General Harney, who had had large experience as a military officer with Indians, was present, and fully confirmed the opinion expressed, that it is easier, better, and cheaper to conquer Indians by kindness and justice than by unscrupulous war. The conference also visited General Grant, president-elect, who gave them a pleasant audience, and replied to them in substance that he was familiar with the past management of Indian affairs, and sensible of the injustice that had been done them, and that he was desirous, so far as he might have the power, to remedy the abuses of the Indian system, and to harmonize their best interests with those of the country at large.

At his inauguration he stated that the proper treatment of the Indians deserved careful study, and that he would favor any course toward them which tends to their civilization, Christianization, and ultimate citizenship. Soon after the visit to President-elect General Grant, he caused letters to be written to certain Friends in Philadelphia, setting forth his desire of inaugurating some policy to protect the Indians in their just rights, and to enforce integrity in the administration of their affairs, as well as to improve their general condition. He also asked for a list of names of Friends who could be indorsed as suitable persons for Indian agents. This brought the matter before the society for action, which, after a conference of representatives of the various yearly meetings, resulted in a list of names being forwarded to the President for his consideration and action. The Agencies of the Central Superintendency and the office of Superintendent were assigned to the Orthodox Friends, and the Northern Superintendency and Agencies, situated in Nebraska, to the Hicksite Friends, while all the other agencies were placed in charge of army officers.

The instructions to these officers may be interesting as additionally confirmatory of his desire to have the wards of the nation justly and fairly dealt with. They were:

"You will endeavor to keep constantly before the minds of the Indians the pacific intentions of the government, and obtain their confidence by acts of kindness and honesty and just dealing with them, thereby securing that peace which it is the wish of all good citizens to establish and maintain. Your success in the accomplishment of these objects will depend greatly upon the efficiency, discretion, and care to be exercised by you in the economical expenditure of the means placed at your disposal for the purpose, and it is confidently hoped that the result will prove the wisdom and expediency of your appointment for this responsible duty."

It is, perhaps, due to the truthfulness of history, as well as to the Society of Friends, to explain here that their memorial to Congress and conferences with President-elect General Grant did not express, either in words or by inference, their desire to have the management of Indian affairs turned over to them. Only an earnest desire that some better way might be found, more merciful and just to a people who had from time to time been provoked into war, and then cruelly punished, while he who provoked it went unwhipped of justice. Their desire to see the further shedding of blood cease, and that leniency which becomes a powerful nation be extended to the children of the forest, who had been struggling for their right to live upon the soil of their ancestors.

In his first message to Congress President Grant alluded at length to Indian affairs, and Congress in 1870 enacted a law practically preventing army officers from holding positions in the Indian service. Whereupon, President Grant caused letters to be written to other denominations, mooting their co-operation, if coinciding with their views, and asking them to forward the names of suitable persons for agents, to which most of them responded favorably; and thus the peace policy, which had commenced in 1869 with but few agencies, spread out to include all the tribes, and most of the Churches enlisted in the work.

For much of the foregoing information regarding the origin and commencement of the peace policy, I am indebted to an unpublished document of extracts taken from the Minutes of Conferences of the Committee on Indian Affairs of the Society of Friends.

Up to the time of the introduction of the peace policy but little attention had been given to the educational and industrial interests of the Indians, aside from those who were regarded as civilized tribes.'

With the great mass of the people the Indian was simply an animal of curiosity, thought of only when the papers announced some terrible massacre, and when seen regarded with fear, hatred, and contempt. But few p ople besides the noble-hearted missionaries had any just conception of his abilities for good as well as for learning, and the missionary had cultivated the field with very little help or sympathy from the government or people.

Most of the treaties made with the Indians have had some educational provisions, and in some instances these provisions have been carried out, but in many cases almost wholly disregarded.

Referring to this matter, the Commissioner of Indian Affairs, in his last published report, says: "In general, it may be said that when the treaty stipulated the payment of a certain annual sum for education, the promise has been kept; but when the support of certain schools was pledged, without specifying the annual expenditure to be made therefor, the promise has been only partially kept."

He does not present a calculation of the cost to have made good the promises from the time they should have commenced, but presents a table showing the deficit between the promise and the performance in the years 1877 to 1881 inclusive, as follows:

Total cost of buildings required to accommodate the school population of these tribes, less such buildings as have been erected between the dates of the treaties and the year 1881......	$334,000
Appropriations required to support the schools called for by those treaties:	
1877....................... $486,000	
1878....................... 488,000	
1879.. 486,000	
1880....................... 484,000	
1881.. 371,250	
	2,315,250
	$2,649,250
Amount specifically appropriated for the support of the above schools:	
1877....................... $44,880	
1878....................... 48,080	
1879....................... 46,580	
1880....................... 46,280	
1881....................... 34,080	
	219,900
Balance due said tribes for five years...	$2,429,350

There are now 75 boarding-schools and 72 day-schools at agencies, the former with capacity for about 5,000 pupils, and the latter about 4,600, making a total agency capacity of 9,600. Carlisle and Forest Grove and Hampton Institute will accommodate about 650 more, making the present capacity equal to about 10,250 pupils.

One hundred children have been put in industrial schools in several different States during the past year, and more are arranged for this year, and we hope to increase the number to 400.

Besides these government arrangements there are some missionary schools, which may have 350 more children provided for, making a grand total of 10,950 Indian children provided with school privileges, out of a school population of over 40,000.

Additional facilities will be added this fall and winter by the completion of a building in the Indian Territory near Arkansas City, Kansas, with capacity for 150 children; one at Lawrence, Kansas, for 300 children, and one at Genoa, Nebraska, for 150 more, to which we hope during the coming year to add accommodations for several hundred additional pupils. Most of this is the work, or rather the result of the work, of the last twelve years, under the embarrassing circumstances of small appropriations and, generally speaking, less sympathy. One of the greatest obstacles to our cause has been the opposition of the wild tribes. This had to be overcome before they would surrender their children for school.

It was my privilege, as agent, to open the first school among the Kiowas and Comanche tribes for their children. It required a great deal of patient toil and labor to get them to consent to send their children. It was a new departure, in violation of all the traditions, and in conflict with their superstitious ideas; and when the day came for the opening it was a very solemn occasion for them. Like giving up their children, parting from them forever: they were to become changed beings, to submit to new ways, abandon the Indian world, and enter the new one made, as they supposed, especially for the white people. Some of the chiefs came to me to intercede for the long hair of their boys: they did not want it cut off; if done, either the boy or some of his very near relatives would die. The hair is cut with them only as an emblem of mourning, and they trembled at the idea of a departure from that custom. It was cut, however, with some care and uncertainty as to consequences at first; but the matter soon changed with the boys, and the last of them came voluntarily and asked to have it done. At the close of the session I invited all the families represented in the school, and gave them a feast in celebration of the fact that we were providentially permitted to return to them all their children without the loss of one. Although some had been sick, none had died, and our heavenly Father had indeed been good to us.

When the vacation had passed, and the doors of the school-house were again thrown open for the school year of 1876–77, the children returned willingly, and the building was soon full. It was the same way with all wild Indians; it required great persuasion, and sometimes force, to get them to put their children in school. But the evidence of passing years is teaching them that good and not bad results have followed their actions in this matter. A new world is opening out before their children, which is reflecting its light upon their benighted homes; and realizing that their children cannot live as they have done, by the chase, many of them rejoice that a better way is being found for them, and are glad that they surrendered their children for school.

With most of the wild tribes the feeling of opposition to schools has passed away, and they willingly give up their children, not only to the agency schools, but to go to the more important ones, situated entirely outside their own country.

The Southern Utes, who have been regarded as the most obstinate in school matters, recently gave up twenty-seven children, who were taken to the boarding-school at Albuquerque, New Mexico.

The interest of the Indians having become aroused, and with it a willingness to allow

their children to attend school, makes the educational the important matter in Indian affairs of to-day, and the duty of the government to provide the ways and means for them.

Our system of settling up the country is rapidly cutting off the Indians' opportunities to live as Indians do. Frontier lines can hardly be said to exist; or, if they do, it is between two advancing columns of civilization. which must soon meet. And then our country's flag will float over a whole country dedicated to civilized industry and human elevation. The Indian cannot be educated and remain an Indian, and he cannot longer resist some kind of education. The once almost impassable reservation line is found to be of that imaginary character which by many is easily passed, and especially is this true of many whose influence is for evil; and, while they are not teaching from books, they are educating with that kind of tutorage which comes from association and example, and intuitively enters into one's being.

If it is true, as said, that an Indian cannot be educated and remain an Indian still, then he must become a part of our body politic. If this is to be the case, we are all interested in his proper preparation for it, and he is not an exception to the rule or idea "that he who casts a ballot should be able to read it, and, if need be, to affix his signature." The cost of accomplishing this would be insignificant compared with the vast sum annually expended in supporting an army in watching and guarding the exposed parts of the country against depredations by both whites and Indians.

The Hon. Secretary of the Interior, in his last report to Congress, makes this statement: "Since 1872, a period of only ten years, the cost of Indian hostilities and military protection against the Indians is estimated by the military authorities at $223,891,264 50, or an annual expense of $22,389,126 45; to which must be added the yearly appropriations for subsistence, which average about $5,000,000 a year. To this must also be added the loss of life and the horrors of an Indian war, only to be understood by those who have had the misfortune to be participants in or witnesses of them; this cannot be computed in dollars, but ought to be considered in determining the policy of the government in its dealings with the Indians."

This immense outlay of money would rapidly diminish were but one tenth of its annual amount diverted to the channel of educating the people who are claimed to cause its expenditure; enough would soon become educated to exert an influence for peace and safety, and good order and industry would reign where the saber only now holds sway.

An Indian is as ambitious for fame and

glory as his pale-faced brother; a chief, however humble, is always flattered and proud to have his speech written down, and enjoys as much having his name in the papers.

This ambition exerts over him a wonderfully controlling interest. In his natural state the profession of arms holds out to him the only road to the temple of fame. To show himself worthy as a leader in this, he endures the severest tortures without exhibiting any emotion of pain. Death has no terrors for him, and cowardice is despised.

The Sioux young man, baring his breast, cuts two gashes and, lifting the flesh between them, passes a lariat through it, which he makes fast to a post or two, and then, with his weight thrown against it, dances until the flesh is broken loose and he is free to become a leading warrior. It is said of Little Big Man, a Sioux war chief, that when he was thus dedicating himself—being, as his name indicates, a small man—his weight was not sufficient to tear loose the flesh, and, moving the post to which his lariat was attached, he made a bound, and, turning a somersault, freed himself, much to his own satisfaction and the admiration of the spectators.

The Kiowa young man shows his agility by dancing three days and nights without food, with his eyes at all times fixed steadily upon the sun, while it shines, and not ceasing the dance when night hides the light from his view.

The per cent. who are able to successfully endure this severe test is said to be quite small. All wild tribes have some ceremony or test to which the young and ambitious are subjected, all requiring great will power, which only needs to be directed in the proper channel to show itself capable of good ends. Education opens new avenues to fame, and does away with these barbaric customs.

But the education and civilization of the Indian is no new problem; it has been successfully carried out already as respects a portion of the six nations and many of the five civilized tribes of the Indian Territory.

And daily evidence is added to the testimony in the results, not only at Carlisle, Hampton, and Forest Grove, but at some of the agency schools. If any one has doubts on this point let him visit either of the leading institutions: a day there will dispel his doubts. The testimony of the manufactured articles in the shops speaks louder and more emphatically than any man's tongue or pen can do. The evidence of the ability of the wild Indian child to become of highly intellectual culture, as well as a skilled artisan, is there found incontrovertible, and so demonstrated by many individuals from various tribes.

Hampton and Carlisle furnish most of the shoes, harness, tinware, and part of the wagons, used at many of the agencies. It is interesting to remember that these are made by boys who but a few years ago were as wild as the chickens on the prairie. Indian teachers generally agree that Indian children are much like white children in their learning and school days. The boys soon learn to amuse themselves with marbles, tops, and hoops, as well as bows and arrows, while the girls as naturally take to the jumping-rope, play house, and doll-baby.

In school hours, when the teacher's back is turned, paper wads fly at random, and the ceiling shows the effects of good marksmanship; a change of position of the teacher finds each one intently interested in his lesson. Pillow battles often furnish amusement for the night, and rarely is a teacher able to find them not all asleep. Teachers whose hearts are in the work enjoy it and rejoice in being able to see the fruits of their labors growing up; but their labors are necessarily more arduous than if in a white school, from the fact that they must not only start an idea, but cultivate it, too, as the Indian child cannot, as the white one, go home and have that idea developed, as his people know even less than he does; hence an Indian teacher's work is not done when the school hours close; he must be instant in season and out of season. It may truthfully be said that the Indian child comes to his teacher with a mind as susceptible of molding as potter's clay. How important and responsible, then, the position of that teacher. I call to mind a circumstance bearing upon this point.

A little Caddo boy, who for two years and a half attended school at the Kiowa Agency, after leaving school was taken sick and died. His teachers had not only taught him how to read in his week-day lesson books, but, also in the Bible, and in some degree understand its beautiful precepts and promises, and had given him a Testament to take home. While confined to his sick bed he talked to his family of what he had learned of that beautiful world beyond, and what the Good Book said about it. His own eyes had grown too dim to read it, and none of the family to which he belonged could read it for him, and his mother placed it gently on his breast; and there it laid when the curtain of life was lifted, revealing to him the better world. His mother brought me the message to send to his teachers—that the lessons they had taught him had not been forgotten, and he had gone to live forever.

Joe Easan, a Pawnee, now a man grown, gives an interesting circumstance in his history, an illustration of the influence of education as well as the power of faith. He had been a school-boy long enough to learn how to read and write, and receive some ideas of a better life and way of living.

After he became a married man, and the head of a family, money was scarce with him and the larder was empty, his family were hungry and suffering for food.

His faithful gun was called into requisition and, at early dawn, he started out to find and kill something to eat. All day long he hunted, until the sun was getting low; fruitless had been his search. He remembered that when a school-boy he had been taught that God's ear is ever open to the cry of those in distress, and surely that was his condition; getting down upon his knees he lifted his heart in prayer and told his condition to the needy one's Friend, and asked for help. Opening his eyes and looking ahead, only a few rods from him stood a fine fat deer, which he without difficulty killed. In relating it he said, I believe God heard me and "sent that deer." And who will venture to say otherwise?

A few years ago I traveled over the State of Nevada—in the winter, when the mercury would not tell the whole truth of coldness—hunting up the Pah Utes, to find out their wants and needs, and got many of them together in council, in the Court-House in Minnemucca. My interpreting was done by Princess Sarah Minnemucca, now Mrs. Hopkins, who performed the duty so well and satisfactorily that I was impressed with the opportunity of talking to them of the great advantages there are in education. Taking Sarah's interpreting for the foundation of my remarks, warming up with my subject I said: Look at what a noble woman Sarah is, listen to her talk, how beautiful her language, how elegant her style. Now, what has done all this? What has given her all these advantages over the other women of your tribe? There are, no doubt, others there as intellectual, as smart as she was, but— "Stop! hold on," said one of the full-blood men, in good English, "that will never do. I am a married man. My wife is a smarter woman naturally than Sarah; if she had half her education I could do nothing with her. That must do." The laugh of the houseful of spectators was at my expense, and my eloquent talk was lost in its roar.

A beautiful example of the results of Indian education is before us to-day, in the persons of the Carlisle Indian Band. Only a few years ago most of these young men were numbered with the wild children of the far West: clothed with the blanket, leggings, and moccasins; with long, and in some instances, unkempt, hair; with no idea of the English language, or of their own powers to cause such sweet strains of music from the dumb metallic horn. Their appearance and actions are the strongest possible evidence of the practicable results of Indian education.

It is impossible for those of you who have not visited the homes of the blanket Indians

to fully realize the wonderful transformation a few years of education has made in these young men, and can make in the Indian child.

These may not be classed as exceptions, but representatives of their tribes.

The Modocs were brought as prisoners of war, only a few years ago, from the lava beds of Oregon to the Indian Territory. I need not stop to describe or more than refer to the terrible scenes enacted by them, in which two of the commissioners, General Canby and Dr. Thomas, appointed to treat with them, were killed, and the life of the other member, Col. Meacham, miraculously saved. They believed they were doing as they had been done by. It is impossible to imagine a more uninviting appearing mass of human beings than they were when they reached the Indian Territory.

Christian hearts opened for them and Christian hands took hold of them, with day-schools for the children and night-schools, part of the time, for all. They have been wonderfully changed to an industrious, well-clothed community of farmers, living in good, comfortable houses of their own building; their children averaging as well as farmers' children usually do in learning. Of only about one hundred souls in the tribe, over fifty of them are professed Christians, with Steamboat Frank a minister and Scar-faced Charley an elder in the Society of Friends.

In 1877, Joseph's band of Nez Perces were upon the war-path, and made one of the most wonderful fighting marches of which history gives us any account—successfully crossing over almost fifteen hundred miles of country, with an army in the front and rear, with but a small loss of either people or property, finally voluntarily surrendering at Bear Paw Mountain, Montana, from where they were brought, as prisoners of war, to the Indian Territory, in 1878. In 1879, two young men of the same tribe, who had been educated by Miss M'Beth at their Idaho home, came to work with them as teacher and missionary. One of them, Archie Lawyer, after a few months' faithful service, was taken sick and returned home, remaining there over two years; the other, James Reuben, remained and, fitting up a carpenter-shop for a school-house, commenced a school for their children through the week, and preached to them all on Sundays. Out of a school population of sixty-five the average attendance was sixty-two. The influence of the school was felt, and exercised a strong control over the entire band, until all have cast aside the Indian customs, and dress as white people. One hundred and seventy-two have been admitted as members of the Presbyterian Church, of which they have an organization, and of which Archie Lawyer is now the pastor, and the officers are chosen from their own number. The service is conducted in the Nez Perce language and entered into heartily by all those attending.

Another very notable example of the civilizing effects of education is found in the Flandnau Colony of Sioux, in Moody County, Dakota. Under the provisions of their treaty of 1868, the Sioux can absolve themselves from the tribal relationship, enter upon government land, just as white people do, and become citizens of the United States. Taking advantage of this provision a number of Santees gave up agency rations and annuities, and, selecting homesteads in the valley of the Sioux River, in Dakota, have made themselves homes. When I visited them they numbered over four hundred souls, and were getting along as well as their white neighbors. Most of them had good, comfortable houses, and well-selected farms; their crops were good. I found them threshing wheat with two eight-horse-power machines, managing the machinery and business themselves.

They had two churches, Presbyterian and Episcopal, a good school, taught by one of their own people, a graduate of the training-school under the care of the Rev. A. L. Riggs, at Santee, and the general testimony was favorable. They had paid their taxes and kept their credits good in bank and store. Another similar neighborhood is located in the Peoria bottom in middle Dakota. These are both the results of the missionary and educational labors of two noble and devoted families—the Riggses and Williamsons—the younger generations of whom were missionaries by birthright and have grown up in the work, the good fruits of whose labors are found in all the branches of the large tribe of Sioux.

The results of education are very noticeable at agencies where boarding-schools have been well conducted; the influence is reflected upon the adults in many ways. If the school is industrious, as all should be, the opposition to labor, on account of its being ignoble, is overcome; in fact, it may be said that the advance in civilization at agencies of equal possible opportunities is much greater at the one where a good boarding-school is conducted; it educates those outside the building as well as those in, and demonstrates the fact that education is the greatest civilizing agent we can employ in lifting up the old as well as the young from barbarism. While the well-conducted agency schools have been educating those in and near them, and overcoming the superstitious opposition to schools, and making possible the more important ones away from the agencies, such as Carlisle, Hampton, Forest Grove, and, I may add, that of Albuquerque, N. M., they too have been doing a grand work, not only in educating the Indian youths sent to them, and through them the Indians at the agencies, but the country in general. They

8

have more effectually advertised to the world that the Indian is a man, susceptible and capable of intellectual and heart culture, as well as the mechanical arts; that beneath the paint which in his wild state spoils his face there is true manhood and a heart which may be made a fit temple for the Most High. Carlisle and Hampton in the East, and Forest Grove in the West, and Albuquerque in the South-west, have all done a good work in creating public opinion in favor of Indian education. While the first three named are national in reputation, the last is cherished with as much local pride; and among the first suggestions by the citizens to the visitor to Albuquerque is, You must see our Indian school!

The grand work of these institutions in favor of Indian education, and through it the civilization of the tribes, cannot be estimated, and will only be fully appreciated in the years to come, when great praise will be awarded their founders and conductors, whose business to-day is to kill only to make alive again. By their help a demand is created for additional similar institutions, some of which are already being provided; and we believe Congress will give even more liberally, and that others can be started; and we hope more such men as we now have may be found to conduct them.

But some are discouraged because a few who return home from these institutions go back again to Indian ways. This is to be expected, and, until a larger number are educated, and a stronger sentiment created in the tribes against it, it will continue; but even now the per cent. is very small, and when the number of those educated is increased, as it will be very materially in a few years, the number going back to Indian ways will grow less and less.

The influence of the Indian girl educated and trained at any of these schools is not lost, even if upon returning home she has to submit to the laws of the tribe and be sold as a wife by her uncivilized father to some wild or uncivilized young man for a few ponies, and for a time bury her light under a bushel; her own home, if only a tent or a tepie, will soon begin to bear evidence of knowledge received elsewhere than from her own people. And when a number from the same tribe get together, it cannot be otherwise than an influence for good upon the whole tribe. Many of the boys go out and find work, and this will increase as the number increases, until, the tribes becoming educated, new avenues for business will naturally present themselves.

The Indians, as well as their friends, have cause to rejoice that at the head of the department, and of the bureau having this matter in charge, are men deeply interested in promoting the best interests and welfare of the Indians. Many years' residence in the far West has given them a thorough knowledge of Indian character, as well as an appreciation of their wants and needs, their capabilities for good or evil. This knowledge, guided with an honesty of purpose, enables them to do much for the benefit of the Indian. With minds unprejudiced either by sympathy or dislike, they endeavor to do, and have done, for the Indian that which will the soonest and most effectually make him a self-reliant man, as well as relieving the government from his care and support, which they believe is to be done by industrial as well as intellectual education.

A few years hence the educational influence will be much greater than now, as the numbers returning home from outside institutions are increased; but a great deal of hard, patient labor, and many years of time will pass, as well as much suffering among the Indians be experienced, before the full fruition of the educational efforts is seen.

Indian education means a great deal. It means broken up tribal relationship, individual ownership of property, severally, in lands, farms, and settled homes. In a word, the acceptance of the white man's civilization, to become an integral and homogeneous part of this great nation—not simply a receiver of its bounties, but a sharer of its responsibilities and a supporter of its laws.

9. INDIAN CIVILIZATION A SUCCESS.

CAPT. H. R. PRATT,

Principal of Carlisle Training-School, Carlisle, Pa.

" INDIAN Civilization a Success " is the theme given to me by the director of this assembly. I am not instructed to argue for or against. Following my own inclinations, based upon experience in Indian work, I shall say that Indian civilization is not a success. The Negro race occupied our attention yesterday. Comparing their condition, their rights and privileges, their numbers, and the position to which many of them have attained in the country, with their condition before they came to this land, two hundred and fifty years ago, it is evident we have an example to guide us in forming a conclusion in regard to our Indians.

The Negroes are in the country seven millions strong. Their ancestors came from the other side of the globe, and from a condition as purely savage as that of our Indians, either present or past. They are to-day politically a part of us, our equals. And, in the short space since their freedom began, they have produced senators and representatives, governors, professional men, lawyers, educators, clergymen, etc., worthy to stand upon the platform with those of the same professions of our own race. We have in the country two hundred and sixty thousand Indians, or about one twenty-seventh as many people as there are of the colored race. We find among us but few advanced examples of the red race at all equal to them, and they have no like disposition to claim citizenship or equality in the country. The Indians, in fact, have not become in any considerable numbers educated, industrious, self-supporting, or Christian. There must be strong reasons for the condition of advancement of these seven millions of blacks, and for the lack of advancement of these two hundred and sixty thousand Indians. I find these reasons in the greed of the white man. Greed made the Negro property and brought him into the country as an article of commerce, scattered him over the land, and placed him under individual civilizing influences. Because he was property it was policy to increase his industrial capacity, multiply his numbers, to make him forget his own tongue and learn that of the country; and so, having many teachers, he speedily learned to meet the demands of his new situation and extended his value rapidly.

On the contrary, the Indian had nothing of this value in him. He would not submit to slavery—he gave up his life first. Finding enslavement impracticable, the white man sought after that which the Indian had which was valuable, and found in the broad acres he possessed all the commercial value to be derived from him. To get these acres it was necessary to drive out and destroy the owner, to resort to the cunning arts and cheats of trade. And by the many devices the white man possessed, because of his education, he did wrest from him the lands he possessed, until to-day he has temporary right only to much less than the one hundredth part of his former possessions. That which the white man has gained is the rich, valuable part; while that which remains in the hands of the Indian is mainly of the poorest.

No association with our higher and better

life has been in any considerable degree allowed to the Indian. He has been driven back upon himself, and by all our course of treatment forced to compact against us. It is a very strange condition that, of all the nations and tribes upon this great earth, all are invited to enter into and become a part of the people of this country, except the original inhabitant. The Chinaman, the Japanese, and even the Hottentot, is welcome, and finds a home wherever he will. But the Indian is corraled and imprisoned upon his reservations, and forcibly held aloof from the association which alone would elevate and civilize him. He meets with no welcome, no invitation, to stay outside of this prison life. The Negro is welcome everywhere. He finds in most of our public schools abundant opportunity for his higher development. He is at rest, at peace, in the land.

I am to-day introduced to you by a black man whom we are all glad to welcome among us, to listen to, because of his evident culture and refinement. There is no reservation for him. He is not told he must go back and live with his people. But my Indian boys, sitting here, are told by every sentiment—governmental, individual, Christian, or other—that they must go back to their reservations, to their people. This is the curse; this is the oppression that bars the way of Indian progress in civilization, and so hard does it bear down upon them, that I say to my boys at Carlisle, When you have enough English to understand us, when you have sufficient knowledge of some industry to enable you to stand among us, my advice to you is to take ship, go to sea, and come into the country by the way of Castle Garden. Then you can go and bide where you will. None will hinder. Then you may be men among men. Then you may feel that the country is yours—that the whole world is yours. I say to them, If you cannot get in this way, then, when you start for home, go by way of sunrise, and you will see much people and many nations, and you may find a better freedom. If you do not, when you arrive at your own homes, after having passed around the earth, you will have gained much knowledge and more courage to claim the rights of men, even in America.

I tell you, my friends, that unless we can come to this point, and accept in this country of these our Indian brothers upon just these terms, and with this fullest liberty, we shall continue to fail in our work and duty, and the Indian will remain a savage among us— a curse and a blot upon our history.

We have tried the reservation principle from the beginning. We have tried the processes of building up and developing our Indians as a separate and peculiar people. And what is the result? We have in this,

our own free and Christian America, to-day, in almost all of our large tribes, a condition of ignorance and savagery pitiful, disgraceful, and shameful to look upon. Only a few days ago the public mind was tortured by statements in the public press of the degrading practices of the Sioux Indians at their medicine dance, and of other barbarous and heathenish customs of the Cheyennes, the Zunis, and other tribes.

We have tried the system of reservation education, of mission education, at the agencies and in the tribes. We have even tried a system of creating a written language for different tribes, and the results prove only failures.

Where is Eliot's Bible to-day? What good is it doing? It is simply a literary curiosity, with only one man in the whole world who claims the distinguished honor of being able to read it.

We do not try to continue our German brothers, our Irish brothers, our French brothers, our Italian brothers, as Germans, Irish, French, or Italians, in this country. O no! If we did we should have in our free America a German empire or a French republic.

We have established systems of schools which make all these foreign tongues English-speaking peoples—which Americanizes them. We do not compel the Germans to locate in one particular place in our country; nor any other tribe or nationality. When they reach the great door-way at New York they have only to express their desire to go here or there, and they are speedily forwarded to their destination. By every means possible we endeavor to make their interest one with ours. We teach them to revere and respect the old flag, and they do it, and fight for it. But these Indian peoples are held off, are told, by every influence we bring to bear upon them, that they are not of us. They must remain as Sioux, as Cheyennes, as Comanches, etc. And so all their ambitions, all their desires, are bounded by tribal interests. Educated in their tribal schools, upon their reservations, those of them who reach the highest development desire nothing more than to remain as Indians of their own tribes. Our Choctaws, Chickasaws, Creeks, and Cherokees, whom we call civilized, have no desire to be any thing else but Choctaws, Chickasaws, Creeks, and Cherokees. The same course of treatment shows like results with the Senecas, Tuscaroras, and other tribes of the great Empire State. Their education is so managed that to be an American and a citizen of the whole country does not come within the limit of their inclinations or aspirations.

What is the cure for this condition of the Indian? In my judgment it is to be found in the establishment of a general system of education, reaching every Indian child of school age, and so arranged as to bring the subject as quickly and for the longest time possible into personal contact with the masses of our own children.

Over in Pennsylvania, years ago, they had German schools and English schools, and the public-school fund of the State was distributed with reference to these different kinds of schools. It was apparent, after years of this system, that they were educating a mass of people inimical to the best interests of the other masses. On all political and social schemes of advancement the Germans went in a body. There was no expression of individual preference or judgment, because very often there was no knowledge of other than one side of the question. Thad. Stevens and other statesmen looked upon this dangerous course and changed it, and the public-school funds have since been disbursed to the schools of the State, without reference to language. And so these language lines have about disappeared, and there is a better state of things, because individuals know better and understand better the questions upon which they are called to express opinions.

Now, in our Indian work, if we want to be completely successful, we must go forward somehow to a system that will bring our Indian children into the common-school systems of the country. I believe in Indian schools at the agencies. I believe in mission schools at the agencies. But I believe in them only as the merest stepping-stones, the small beginnings that will start to a reaching after better things.

We must have schools away from the Indians—plenty of them. But these should be only tentative—additional stepping-stones, higher in the scale than the agency schools, but still far below the top. Our Indian children must be educated into the capacity and the courage to go out from these schools, *from all these schools*, into our schools and into our life. Then shall they have many teachers. Then will they learn, by comparing their own strength, physical, mental, and moral with our race, just what they lack. Then will they become ambitious to be of us —to succeed as well as we do. Then will they learn that the world is theirs, and that all of the good of it their trained capacity is able to grasp is theirs as well as ours.

Ethnologists may tell us that it is impossible to change a people, except through generations and centuries of gradual development, when all around was darkness, but it is not true in the light and under the powerful influences of our civilization in this nineteenth century. I know nothing of their theories and abstractions. My experience is wholly practical, and enough has transpired within it to show to me that all our Indians need is just this broad and en-

larged liberty of opportunity and training to make them, within the short space of a few years, a perfectly acceptable part of our population, and to remove them from a condition of dependence, pauperism, and crime, to a truly civilized condition.

We are made to cry out and blush with shame when many of the wrongs we have, as a nation, committed against the Indians are recited. Many of these wrongs could never have been committed but for the ignorance of the Indians. To continue him in a state of ignorance invites further wrong. I say to you what I do know, that two years, under proper training, is enough to give to a young Indian a sufficient knowledge of the English language, sufficient intelligence, and sufficient industrial capacity to enable him to make himself acceptable, and even self-supporting, as a part of our agricultural population—ay, and he will have the desire to do it! With this two years' start he may go into a farmer's family, may earn enough to pay for his own clothing and food, and secure to himself the advantages of our public-school system. I have tried it in hundreds of cases, and in nineteen twentieths of them have found it a success. The Indian is capable of acquiring a knowledge of any ordinary civilized industry. With the same advantages he may be as good a carpenter, blacksmith, farmer, or what not, as his white brother; but he need not stop with these; he may occupy an honorable place in any professional life. We are very careful in our civilization to bring to bear upon all our growing youth industrial and educational influences; why not the same for the Indian?

The government has charge of our Indians. It is great, powerful, and rich, and it parades before us, as it has here to day, figures to show what it is doing for the Indians committed to its care. They are so stated as to make us believe that all is being done that can be or ought to be done. Mr. Haworth, who has charge of the schools, tells us that ten thousand children are to be provided with schools next year. But he says little or nothing about the forty thousand who are left out of schools. Fifty thousand Indian children is about all we have—fifty thousand Indian children in schools, growing forward from agency and mission schools at the agencies to schools in the midst of our better civilization, and from them into our public and other schools, with as much of industrial training and contact with our industrial systems as possible, will speedily accomplish the civilization of our Indians. We must not stop content with any number short of the whole.

In working forward to this end there need be no further robbery of the Indian, of his land, or other rights. Whatever he has of land that we need for any purposes of our own we are now rich enough to pay a fair price for, and if we do pay a fair price for it, it will give all the means needed for the education of all Indian children, and still leave to every individual Indian as many acres as he may need to begin life with.

We have no hesitation in breaking up the tribes of Europe, inviting them to become American; why should we hesitate at the breaking up of our Indian tribes? If we can fairly and honestly show to the Indian that his greatest advantage lies in losing his identity as a Sioux, a Ute, or a Creek, and becoming an American citizen, and he is sensible enough to do it, that is the end.

And now, in closing, I want to say to you all here gathered to-day, in the interests of the education of the illiterate masses of the country, and to you Christian people, that it seems to me no grander opportunity was ever offered to a civilized, Christian people to do good—to raise the fallen—than is offered in the work of redeeming our Indian brothers from their savage condition. Individual Christians may work for individual Indians; may give of their means, of their personal labor and influence, and so share the responsibility of this great work with the government itself, and accomplish it far more speedily than the government would be able to do with the most liberal appropriations. Indeed, I believe that it will only be through the large and hearty co-operation of Christian people that this can be accomplished at all.

10. OUR INDIAN NEIGHBORS.

The following table from the Census Report of 1880 presents the statistics of the civilized Indian population in the United States :

STATES AND TERRITORIES.	Total.	Male.	Female.	NATIVE.			FOREIGN-BORN.		
				Total.	Male.	Female.	Total.	Male.	Female.
Alabama	213	107	106	212	106	106	1	1	....
Arizona	3,493	1,941	1,552	3,437	1,910	1,527	56	31	25
Arkansas	195	111	84	194	.10	84	1	1	...
California	16,277	8,328	7,949	15,968	8,088	7,880	303	240	69
Colorado	154	64	90	151	63	88	3	1	2
Connecticut	255	128	127	250	126	124	5	2	36
Dakota	1,391	675	716	1,229	594	635	162	81	81
Delaware	5	3	2	5	3	2	....	....	....
District of Columbia	5	5	...	5	5	....	....	....	....
Florida	180	96	84	178	94	84	2	2	....
Georgia	124	63	61	123	63	60	1	....	1
Idaho	165	83	82	163	82	81	2	1	1
Illinois	140	82	58	114	70	44	26	12	14
Indiana	246	112	134	245	111	134	1	1	..
Iowa	466	218	248	464	217	247	2	1	1
Kansas	815	413	402	806	411	305	9	2	7
Kentucky	50	26	24	49	25	24	1	1	....
Louisiana	848	441	407	840	437	403	8	4	4
Maine	625	312	313	576	290	286	49	22	27
Maryland	15	7	8	14	7	7	1	....	1
Massachusetts	369	185	184	338	166	172	31	19	12
Michigan	7,249	3,696	3,553	6,960	3,542	3,418	289	154	135
Minnesota	2,300	1,144	1,156	2,227	1,101	1,126	73	43	30
Mississippi	1,857	941	916	1,857	941	916	....	....	....
Missouri	113	64	40	112	63	40	1	1	....
Montana	1,663	779	884	1,395	638	757	208	141	127
Nebraska	235	112	123	235	112	123	....	....	....
Nevada	2,803	1,546	1,257	2,789	1,535	1,254	14	11	3
New Hampshire	63	34	29	36	20	16	27	14	13
New Jersey	74	38	36	68	35	33	6	3	3
New Mexico	9,772	5,149	4,623	9,742	5,131	4,611	30	18	12
New York	819	435	384	739	397	342	80	38	42
North Carolina	1,230	600	630	1,230	600	630	....	....	....
Ohio	130	73	57	129	72	57	1	1	....
Oregon	1,694	828	866	1,683	821	859	11	4	7
Pennsylvania	184	101	83	181	99	82	3	2	1
Rhode Island	77	37	40	71	33	38	6	4	2
South Carolina	131	68	63	131	68	63	....	....	....
Tennessee	352	183	169	352	183	169	....	....	....
Texas	992	521	471	892	452	440	100	69	31
Utah	807	428	379	795	422	373	12	6	6
Vermont	11	9	2	8	7	1	3	2	1

STATES AND TERRITO-RIES.	Total.	Male.	Female.	NATIVE.			FOREIGN-BORN.		
				Total.	Male.	Female.	Total.	Male.	Female.
Virginia	85	37	48	85	37	48	....	....	....
Washington.............	4,405	2,090	2,315	4,204	2,036	2,168	201	54	147
West Virginia...........	29	16	13	24	12	12	5	4	1
Wisconsin...............	3,161	1,585	1,576	3,141	1,574	1,567	20	11	9
Wyoming................	140	71	69	140	71	69	....	....	....
Total................	66,407	33,985	32,422	64,587	32,983	31,604	1,820	1,002	818

11. THE NATIVE TRIBES OF ALASKA.

REV. SHELDON JACKSON, D.D.,

Superintendent Presbyterian Missions in Alaska.

THE native population of Alaska is about 34,019,* including 1,683 creoles or half-breeds. Of these, 19,698 are classed as Orarians and 12,698 as Indians.

The Orarians are composed of 17,484 Innuit or Eskimo, and 3,897 creoles and Aleuts. The Indians are divided into 5,913 Tinneh, 5,937 Thlinkets, and 788 Hydah. These are again subdivided into smaller tribes and families.

The Orarians occupy almost the entire coast line of Alaska, with the outlying islands from the boundary line westward along the Arctic coast to Behring Straits, thence southward to the Aliaska peninsula, over the peninsula and the Aleutian islands, and eastward and northward along the coast to Mt. St. Elias, with the exception of a small territory on Cook's Inlet and at the mouth of Copper River, where the Indians from the interior have forced their way to the coast. Occupying the coast line, they are bold navigators and skilled fishermen and sea hunters.

The Indians occupy the vast interior, only reaching the coast at Cook's Inlet, Copper River, and the Alexandrian Archipelago from Mt. St. Elias southward. They are hardy hunters and successful trappers.

The term Innuit is the native word for "people," and is the name used by themselves, signifying "our people." The term Eskimo is one of reproach given them by their neighbors, meaning "raw-fish eaters."

The Innuits of Alaska are a much finer race physically than their brethren of Greenland and Labrador.

They are tall and muscular, many of them being six feet and over in height. They have small black eyes, high cheek-bones, large mouths, thick lips, coarse brown hair, and fresh yellow complexion.

In many instances the men have full beards and moustaches. In some families the men wear a labret under each corner of the mouth in a hole cut through the lower lip for the purpose.

They are a good-natured people, always smiling when spoken to. They are fond of dancing, running, jumping, and all athletic sports. While they speak a common language from the Arctic to the Pacific, each locality has its different dialect.

Their usual dress is the parkas, made of the skins of animals, and sometimes of the breasts of birds. However, where they have access to the stores of traders, they buy ready-made clothing.

Their residences have the outward appearances of a circular mound of earth covered with grass, with a small opening at the top for the escape of smoke. The entrance is a small door and narrow hallway to the main room, which is from twelve to twenty feet in diameter, and is without light or ventilation.

Their diet consists of the wild meat of the moose, reindeer, bear, and smaller fur-bearing animals; also of fish, the white whale, the walrus, seal, and various water-fowl. In the northern section they have a great aversion to salt.

While they will eat with great relish decayed fish or putrid oil, they will spit out with a wry face a mouthful of choice corned beef.

Men, women, and children are alike inveterate smokers. While they travel continually in the summer, they have permanent winter homes. Their religious belief is quite indefinite. In a general way, they believe in a Power that rewards the good and punishes the bad, by sending them to different places after death. They are savages, and with the exception of those in southern Alaska, have not had civilizing, educational, or religious advantages.

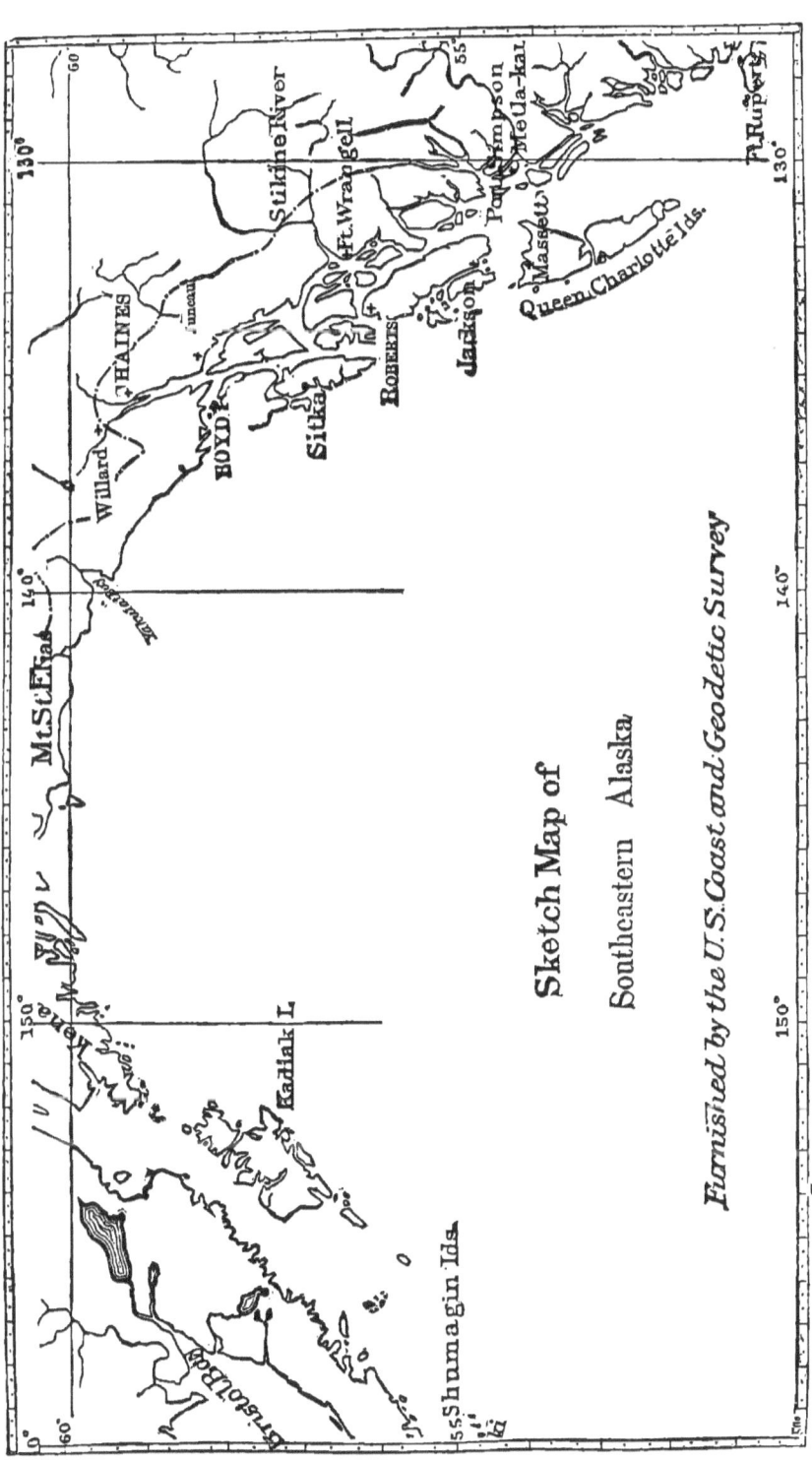

Sketch Map of

Southeastern Alaska

Furnished by the U.S. Coast and Geodetic Survey

From the boundary line to Behring Straits along the bleak Arctic coast, villages are placed here and there, wherever there is a sheltered harbor with good hunting or fishing. The population of these aggregates 3,000.

At the mouth of the Colville River they hold an annual fair, to which they come from hundreds of miles.

At Point Barrow, the extreme northern point of land in the United States, and within twenty-five miles of being the northernmost land on the continent, there is a village of thirty tupees or houses and two hundred people. Like the other houses of that whole section, they are built partly under-ground for warmth. The upper portion is roofed over with dirt, supported by rafters of whale jaws and ribs.

Around Kotzebue Sound is a number of villages. Some of the hills surrounding this sound rise to the height of a thousand feet, and are covered with a species of wild cotton that, in its season, gives the appearance of snow.

Into this sound empties the Noyatäg River. It is not put down in the charts of the country, and yet it is a broad, deep river, taking the natives thirty days to ascend to their villages. This is one of the places where the people come in July, from all sections of the country, for the purpose of trade and barter. The Innuits of the coast bring their oil, walrus-hides, and seal-skins; the Indians from the interior their furs, and from Asia come reindeer skins, fire-arms and whisky.

It is to these gatherings that the traders come in schooners fitted out at San Francisco or Sandwich Islands, with cargoes of whisky labeled "Florida water," "Bay rum," "Pain-killer," "Jamaica ginger," etc. The finest furs of Alaska are obtained at these fairs.

Kotzebue Sound is the northern limit to which the salmon come.

Another center of villages is at Cape Prince of Wales. This is a rocky point, rising in its highest peak to an elevation of 2,500 feet above the sea. At the extremity of this cape is a village of four hundred people, the westernmost village on the mainland in America. These people are great travelers and traders, skilled in hunting the whale on the seas or the reindeer on the land. They are insolent and overbearing toward the surrounding tribes, and, traveling in large companies, compel trade at their own terms. They are reported the worst natives on the coast.

In the narrow straits separating Asia from America is a small group of islands called the Diomede. On these islands are three hundred Innuits.

These, with those at Cape Prince of Wales, are the great smugglers of the North.

Launching their walrus-skin boats, (baidars,) they boldly cross to and fro from Siberia, trading the deer skins, sinew, and wooden ware of Alaska for the walrus ivory, tame reindeer skins, and whale blubber of Siberia, also fire-arms and whisky.

On King's Island, south of Cape Prince of Wales, are the cave-dwellers of the present. The island is a great mass of basalt rock, with almost perpendicular sides rising out of the ocean to the height of seven hundred feet. On one side, where the rock rises at an angle of forty-five degrees, the Innuit have excavated homes in the rock. Some of these rock houses are two hundred feet above the ocean. There are forty of these cliff dwellings.

When the surf is wildly breaking on the rocks, if it becomes necessary for any one to put out to sea, he gets as near the surf as possible, takes his seat in his boat, (kyack,) and at the opportune moment two companions toss him and his boat over and clear of the surf. They are noted for the manufacture of water-proof seal throat and skin boots, that are lighter, more enduring, and greatly preferred to rubber.

Directly south of Behring Straits is the large island of St. Lawrence. Formerly it had a population of eight hundred. They were the largest and finest-formed people of the Innuit race—but slaves to whisky. In the summer of 1878 they bartered their furs, ivory, and whale-bone to the traders for rum. And as long as the rum lasted, they spent their summer in idleness and drunkenness, instead of preparing for winter. The result was that over four hundred of them starved to death the next winter. In some villages not a single man, woman, or child was left to tell the horrible tale.

From Behring Straits around the shores of Norton Sound are a number of villages, aggregating a population of six hundred and thirty-three.

In this district is St. Michael, a trading post originally founded by the Russians in 1835. The place consists of a few log houses, enclosed by a stockade, the property of the Alaska Commercial Company, and a chapel of the Russo-Greek Church, with an occasional service by a priest from Ikogmute. Across the bay is the trading-post of the "Western Fur and Trading Company." This is the point where the ocean-going steamers transfer freight with the small steamers that ply on the Yukon River. To this point the furs collected at the trading-posts in the interior, some of them two thousand miles distant, are brought for reshipment to San Francisco.

This is also the dividing line between the Innuits of the Arctic and the Pacific. Half a mile from the trading-post is an Indian village of thirty houses, and one dance-house, or town hall.

We come now to the region of the densest population in Alaska, attracted and sustained by the abundance of fish that ascend the mighty Yukon and Muskoquim Rivers, and the many smaller streams. Their fish diet is supplemented by the wonderful bird life of the country. The variety and numbers of wild geese and ducks is said to be greater than in any other section of the known world. To fish and fowl is added the flesh of the moose and reindeer.

On the delta of the Yukon, and southward to the mouth of the Muskoquim River, are from forty to fifty villages, with a population of two thousand. From the mouth of the Yukon to Anvik are fifteen or sixteen villages, with thirteen hundred and forty-five people; while on the Muskoquim River are some forty villages, aggregating a population of thirty-six hundred and fifty-four.

On the lower banks of this river the high land free from tidal overflow is so fully occupied with houses that it is difficult for the traveler to find space to pitch a tent.

In the adjacent Bristol Bay region are thirty-four villages and four thousand three hundred and forty people. Somewhere in this general region an industrial boarding-school should be established for the children of these eleven thousand three hundred and thirty-nine Innuits.

A short portage across the Aliaska peninsula brings us to the settlements of the civilized Innuits.

In 1792 Gregory Shelikoff formed a settlement on Kadiak Island, and commenced the subjugation and civilization of the people. Soon after he organized a school, which was the first in Alaska.

Also the first church building in Alaska was erected on that island.

For a long time it was the Russian capital, the chief seat of their power and operations. The present village of Kadiak numbers two hundred and seventy people, living in one hundred and one frame houses. They have a few cattle, and cultivate small gardens. They have a large church and a resident priest, also stores of the Alaska Commercial Company and the Western Fur and Trading Company, a deputy collector of customs, and a signal weather office.

A small school is kept at the expense of the Alaska Commercial Company.

Opposite Kadiak is Wood Island, with one hundred and fifty-six people. They have four horses and twenty cattle, a saw-mill, large ice houses, which are annually filled for a San Francisco company, but never used. The village also possesses a small ship-yard, and a road around the island twelve or fourteen miles long. This and a road one and one half miles long at Sitka are the only roads in that vast territory. The place possesses the usual Russo-Greek Church, but no school.

Near by is Spruce Island, where a Russian monk kept a small school for thirty consecutive years, giving instruction in the rudimental arts and agricultural industries. The school is now discontinued for want of a teacher.

Near by is the village of Afognak, with a population of three hundred and thirty. These reside in thirty-two good frame and log buildings, and cultivate one hundred acres in potatoes and turnips. They have a large church and ought to have a school.

On the western side of Kadiak is Karluck, with three hundred and thirty-nine people. A church, but no school.

On the south-eastern coast is Three Saints Bay, with two hundred and nineteen; Orlovsk, with two hundred and seventy-eight; and Katmai, with two hundred and eighteen people. Each of these villages possesses a church, but no school.

In the Kadiak district are two thousand six hundred and six civilized Innuits, or Eskimo and creoles.

They are a well-to-do, industrious population, living in frame houses, provided with the simpler furnishings of civilization, and on Sabbath and festal occasions the men dressing in broadcloth suits and calf-skin boots, the women in calico and silk dresses modeled after the fashion plates received from San Francisco. They are an orderly, law-abiding people, and yet are denied educational advantages for themselves and children.

ALEUTS.

From the Innuits we pass to the consideration of the second great class of Orarians—namely, the Aleuts. The origin of the word Aleut is not known. The designation of themselves by themselves is Unŭng'-un, the native word for "our people."

They occupy the chain of islands and portions of the Aliaska peninsula, from the Shumagin Islands, sixteen hundred and fifty miles westward to Attoo.

The average height of the men is about five feet six inches. They have coarse black hair, small black eyes, high cheek-bones, flat noses, thick lips, large mouths, broad faces, and light yellowish brown complexions, with a strong resemblance to the Japanese.

The marriage relation is respected, and, as a rule, each family have their own house, with from two to three rooms. They use in their houses a small cast-iron cook-stove, or neat wrought-iron cooking-range, granite-ware kettles, white crockeryware dishes, pewter or plated silverware, and feather-beds covered with colored spreads. Their walls are adorned with colored pictures, and their houses lighted with kerosene in glass lamps. Nearly every home possesses an accordeon, a hand-organ, or music-box, some of the latter costing as high as $200. They dress in American garments, and their women with great interest study the fashion-plates and try to imitate the latest styles.

Large numbers of them can read; an Aleutian alphabet and grammar having been provided for them by Veniaminoff.

They are all members of the Russo-Greek Church, and outwardly very religious. They ask a blessing at their meals, greet strangers and friends with a blessing for their health, and bid them adieu with a benediction.

The Hon. Wm. S. Dodge, ex-mayor of Sitka, says of them: "Many among them are highly educated, even in the classics. The administrator of the fur company reposed great confidence in them. One of their best physicians was an Aleutian; one of their best navigators was an Aleutian; their best traders and accountants were Aleutians. Will it be said that such a people are to be deprived of the rights of American citizenship?"

This, of course, was more particularly true of the past, when the Russian Government gave them educational advantages. Now they are compelled to see their children grow up under the United States Government without an education. Surely, it is neither sound policy nor justice to leave them outside of the educational advantages of the country.

The great industry of the country is the hunting of the sea otter. From this source some of the villagers derive a revenue that, if economically used, would make them wealthy, averaging from $600 to $1,200 a family. But their extra income is spent for kvass, (quass,) a home-made intoxicating beer.

Commencing at the westward on the Island of Attoo, is one white man and one hundred and six Aleuts and creoles. They are very poor. The village consists of eighteen houses (barrabaras) and one frame chapel with thatched roof. A church, but no school.

This is the most westernmost settlement in the United States, and is as far west of San Francisco as the State of Maine is east.

The next settlement eastward is on Atkha Island, with a population of two white men and two hundred and thirty four Aleuts and creoles. They have forty-two houses and a church, but no school. They are wealthy, using freely at their tables the groceries and canned fruits of civilization.

They excel in the manufacture of baskets, mats, etc., out of grass.

On Oomnak Island are two white men and one hundred and twenty-five Aleuts and creoles. They are well-to-do financially, having sixteen houses and a church, but no school.

The next settled island is Oonalashka, with a rocky, rugged, jagged coast. In the small bays are a number of villages, the principal one being Oonalashka (Illiuluk).

This village has a population of fourteen white men and three hundred and ninety-two Aleuts and creoles. They have a church, priest's residence, the stores, residences, warehouses and wharfs of the Alaska Commercial Company and Western Fur and Trading Company, eighteen frame residences and fifty barrabaras. One-half the population can read the Aleutian language. It is the most important settlement in western Alaska, and the commercial center of all the trade now in that region, or that shall develop in the future. It is the natural outfitting station for vessels passing between the Pacific and Arctic Oceans.

From a cave at the southern end of this island were taken eleven mummies for the Smithsonian Institute.

One hundred and ninety miles west of Oonalashka are the celebrated Prybyloff, or as they are popularly called, Seal Islands.

The village of St. Paul, on an island of the same name, is laid out in regular streets like an American village, and has a sixty-four houses, together with a large church, a school-house, and priest's residence.

The population is thirteen white men, two white women, and two hundred and eighty-four Aleuts.

Twenty-seven miles to the south-east is the' companion island of St. George, with four white men and eighty-eight Aleuts. They have a church and school.

These islands are leased by the United States Government to the Alaska Commercial Company at an annual rental of $55,000. By the terms of the lease, the company is allowed to take one hundred thousand seal-skins each year, upon which they pay the government a royalty of $262,500. The revenue of these islands since 1870 has returned to the government more than half the sum paid to Russia for the whole country.

From these two islands come nearly all the seal-skins of commerce. There is a small school on each island, supported at the expense of the company.

The native population are encouraged to deposit their surplus earnings in a savings-bank.

In the immediate vicinity of Oonalashka, on the island of Spirkin, is Borka, with one white man and one hundred and thirty-nine Aleuts and creoles.

This village is noted for its cleanliness. With their white-scrubbed and neatly-sanded floors, their clear, clean windows, neat bedding, tidy rooms, and abundance of wild flower bouquets on tables and window-sills, they may properly be called the Hollanders of Alaska.

But with all these evidences of civilization and thrift, they are deprived of the advantages of a school for their children.

To the eastward near the southern end of the Aliaska peninsula is Belkofsky, with a population of nine white men, two white women, and two hundred and fifty-seven Aleuts and creoles. In addition to the buildings of the great trading firms, the village has thirty frame houses and twenty-seven barrabaras.

In 1880, they raised among themselves $7,000 for the erection of a new church. One-half of them can read and write in the Aleutian language, and they support a small school. Their revenue from the sale of sea-otter skins amounts to about $100,000 a year, or $373 for every man, woman, and child in the village.

On the island of Ounga, one of the Shumagin group, is a settlement of fifteen white men and one hundred and seventy natives. As, by a regulation of the United States Treasury Department, only natives are allowed to hunt the sea-otter, these white men have married native women, and thereby become natives in the eyes of the law. The revenue of the sea-otter trade in this village averages about $600 a year to each family.

Off the south coast of the Shumagin Islands are the famous cod banks of Alaska, from which are taken from 500,000 to 600,-000 fish annually.

In the Aleutian district are 1,890 Aleuts and 479 creoles.

Adding to these the civilized Innuits of the Kadiak district and the civilized Indians of the Kenai district, and we have the strange sight in this land of schools of six thousand civilized people in one section of our country for whom no public provision has been made for education.

Surely it is high time that the American people should demand that Congress provide at once for that distant portion of our common country. The case is the more urgent as only one in one hundred can speak our language, and one in five hundred read it. It is a matter of national importance that that large civilized population should have English schools, so that their children should grow up acquainted with the language and in sympathy with the institutions of the country of which they are citizens.

From the consideration of the Orarian family, savage and civilized, we pass to the second great family stock of Alaska—the Indian.

TINNEH.

The first large subdivision of these people is the Tinneh.

This family extends from the Arctic Ocean to old Mexico, and includes a great many tribes; among them being the Apache and Navajo of Arizona.

Tinneh is the native word for "people." The Tinneh of Alaska are tall, well formed, strong and courageous, with great powers of endurance.

They are great hunters and fishers. They consider it a disgrace—an unfair advantage over a black bear—to shoot him, but boldly attack him with a knife in a square open fight. Polygamy prevails among them, frequently having more than one, but seldom more than three, wives. Wives are taken and discarded at pleasure. Among some of them female infanticide is prevalent. The bodies of the dead are buried in boxes above ground. Shamanism and witchcraft, with all their attendant barbarities, prevail. They also believe in a multitude of spirits good and bad.

On the lower course of the Yukon and Muskoquim Rivers, and in the great range of country north and south bordering on the Innuit tribes of the coast, are the western Tinneh, the Ingaliks of the Russians, numbering in three bands about eighteen hundred.

From the junction of the Yukon and Tananah Rivers westward to the British line, from the Innuit on the Arctic shore almost to Lynn Channel on the south, is the home of the Kûtchin tribes. They number, with the Ah-tena tribe on Copper River, about three thousand three hundred.

Into their country the American miners are now pressing for gold, and if we would improve on the experience of the past, and save future bloody, cruel, and costly wars—if we would do justly and conserve the cause of humanity and promote the highest interests of the State, we will hasten to send Christian teachers into that region before the native population becomes embittered against the American people. "An ounce of prevention," etc.

Around the shores of Cook's Inlet is the Kenai tribe, numbering eight hundred and thirteen souls. They have largely been brought under the influence of the Russo-Greek Church and become civilized. They dwell in substantial and well-built log houses with spruce-bark roofs. They have churches, but no schools.

THLINKET.

The second large subdivision of the Indians is the Thlinket family, composed of ten tribes occupying the islands of the Alexander Archipelago and coasts adjacent. They number six thousand.

Intimately associated with these are seven hundred and eighty-eight Hydahs, occupying the southern end of Prince of Wales Island.

The Thlinkets are a hardy, self-reliant, industrious, self-supporting, well-to-do, warlike, superstitious race, whose very name is a terror to the civilized Aleuts to the west, as well as to the savage Tinneh to the north, of them.

Occupying the extreme northern section of Lynn Channel and the valleys of the Chilcat and Chilcoot rivers is the Chilcat tribe, num-boring 988. They are great traders, being the "middlemen" of their region, carrying the goods of commerce to the interior and exchanging them for furs, which are brought to the coast, and in turn exchanged for more merchandise. Their country is on the highway of the gold-seekers to the interior. This summer two salmon canneries have been established among them.

In the summer of 1880 I established a school among them, with Mrs. Sarah Dickinson, a Christian Tongas Indian woman, as teacher. In 1881 the station was enlarged by the arrival of Rev. Eugene S. Willard and family from Illinois, and the erection of a teacher's residence. In 1882 Miss Bessie M. Mathews, of Monmouth, Ill., was sent out to take charge of a boarding department, which was opened in 1883.

The station is called Haines, and has a post-office. Thirty miles up the Chilcat River, in the village of Willard, is a branch school, in charge of Mr. and Mrs. Louie Paul, native teachers.

One hundred miles southward is the Hoonyah tribe, occupying both sides of Cross Sound, and numbering 908. In 1881 I erected a school-house and teachers' residence at their principal village on Chichagoff Island, and placed Mr. and Mrs. Walter B. Styles, of New York city, in charge. The station has been named Boyd.

A few miles to the eastward, on Admiralty Island, is the Auk tribe, numbering 340. In their region valuable gold mines have been opened, and an American mining village established at Juneau. A summer-school is furnished them by Mrs. W. H. R. Corlies.

A few miles to the south, on the main-land, is the Takoo tribe, numbering 269. A summer-school was held among them in 1880 by Rev. and Mrs. W. H. R. Corlies, of Philadelphia. In 1882, pressed by the importunities of the leading men of the tribe, he took up his abode among them, and erected school and residence buildings at Tsĕk'-nŭk-sänk'-y.

On the south-western side of Admiralty Island is the Hootzenoo tribe, numbering 666. This tribe has for several years been asking for a teacher, and probably next season one will be sent.

Last fall a United States revenue cutter found it necessary to shell one of their villages. The necessity for such action would have been averted if they could have been under the influence of a judicious Christian teacher. The North-west Trading Company has established large fish-oil works and a trading-post among them.

To the south, on Kou and Kupriánof Islands, is the Kake tribe, numbering 568. These will probably be furnished next season with school facilities at Roberts, on the north end of Prince of Wales Island.

Eastward, around the mouth and lower course of the Stickeen River, is the Stickeen

tribe. They number 317. Their principal village is at Fort Wrangell, on an island of the same name.

At this point, in the fall of 1877, I located Mrs. A. R. M'Farland, the first white teacher in South-eastern Alaska after the transfer. In 1878 Rev. S. Hall Young, of West Virginia, was sent out, and a boarding department for girls established by Mrs. A. R. M'Farland. In 1879 Miss Maggie A. Dunbar, of Steubenville, was sent out, and the erection of a suitable building commenced, which was finished and occupied the following year.

The same year Rev. W. H. R. Corlies and family arrived. Mrs. Corlies opened a school on the beach for visiting Indians, and her husband a night-school for adults. He also served as missionary physician to the place.

In 1882 Rev. John W. M'Farland was added to the teaching force, and Mrs. S. Hall Young commenced a small industrial school for boys.

Two hundred miles south of Fort Wrangell is the Tongass tribe, numbering 273. Some of them cross over to British Columbia, and find school privileges at Fort Simpson, a station of the Wesleyan Methodist Church of Canada.

West of the Tongass, on the southern half of Prince of Wales Island, is the Hydah tribe, numbering 788. They are a large, well-formed, and handsome race, with light complexion, and have long been noted for their bravery and ferocity in war. Terrorizing all the neighboring tribes, they were known as the "bulldogs" of the North Pacific. They have not even hesitated to attack and plunder English and American vessels. In 1854 they held the captain and crew of an American vessel in captivity until ransomed by the Hudson Bay Fur Company. Their villages are remarkable for the number of totem sticks. These are carved logs from one to two feet in diameter, and from twenty to sixty feet high. Some of them contain hollow cavities, in which are placed the ashes of cremated dead chiefs; others are heraldic, and represent the family totem or orders. In some cases a large oval opening through one of these sticks forms the entrance to the house; in others the pole is at one side of the entrance. The house is a large, low, plank building, from forty to fifty feet square, with a fireplace in the center of the floor, and a large opening in the roof for the escape of the smoke. Some of them have inserted windows and doors into their buildings, and procured bedsteads, tables, stoves, dishes, and other appliances of civilized life. Their food consists largely of fish, dried or fresh, according to the season. Their country also abounds with wild berries and deer. The berries are preserved in fish-oil for winter use. Their coast also abounds with good clams. They raise large quantities of potatoes. The Hydahs are noted for their skill in carving wood, bone, gold, silver, and stone. The finest of the great cedar canoes of the North-west coast are manufactured by them. They practice polygamy and hold slaves. The husband buys his wife, frequently while a mere girl, from her parents. If she does not suit she can be returned and the price refunded. Chastity is uncommon. They are inveterate gamblers.

Like the other heathen tribes on that coast they live in perpetual fear of evil spirits, and give large sums to the conjurers and medicine-men, who by their incantations are supposed to secure immunity from the evil influences of the spirits. In sickness their main reliance is upon the incantations of their medicine-men, and death is ascribed to the evil influence of an enemy, or witchcraft; and whoever is suspected of exerting that influence is killed. The dead are usually burned, and the ashes placed in a small box and deposited in a house or a totem stick. An election to chieftainship is purchased by a "pot-latch," or giving away of presents of goods and money. These are common to the native tribes on the Pacific coast from Puget Sound to Alaska.

An ambitious young man will work hard for years, and save his earnings that he may make a pot-latch. If unable to accumulate a sufficient sum of himself, his relatives will add to his collection. When the time arrives the Indians are invited for hundreds of miles around. It is a season of dancing and other festivities, during which the entire accumulation of years is given away, and the giver impoverished.

He, however, secures position and renown, and soon recovers in the gifts of others more than he gave away.

The customs of the Hydahs are largely the customs of all the Thlinket tribes.

On the 22d of August, 1881, I established a mission among them at the village of Howcan, placing Mr. James E. Chapman in charge as teacher. In the spring of 1882, Rev. J. Loomis Gould and family, of West Virginia, were sent to the Hydahs at Jackson. The same year some ladies in Brooklyn, N. Y., provided a saw-mill for the station. And in the fall of that year Miss Clara A. Gould was added to the teaching-force at that station.

In the northern portion of Prince of Wales Island is the Hanigah tribe, numbering 587. The establishment of a school among them at Roberts is under consideration.

To the north of Roberts, on the western coast of Baranoff, is the Sitka tribe numbering seven hundred and twenty-one. Their chief village is at Sitka, the old capital of the Russian possessions in America. It was their political, commercial, religious, and educational center. As early as 1805 a school was opened at Sitka. It held a very precarious existence, however, until 1820,

when it came under the charge of a naval bone, who kept a good school for thirteen years. In 1833 this school came under the direction of Etolin, who still further increased its efficiency. Etolin was a creole who, by force of ability and merit, raised himself to the highest position in the country, that of chief director of the Fur Company and governor of the colony. He was a Lutheran, the patron of schools and churches. While governor he erected a Protestant church at Sitka, and presented it with a small pipe-organ, which is still in use.

In 1840, besides the colonial school at Sitka, was one for orphan boys and sons of workmen and subaltern *employés* of the Fur Company, in which were taught reading, writing, arithmetic, grammar, mechanical trades, and religion. The most proficient of the pupils, at the age of seventeen, were advanced to the colonial school and prepared for the navy or priesthood. The number of boarders was limited to fifty. The school was in charge of Lieutenant-Commander Prince Maxutoff, assistant governor of the colony. In 1847 the attendance was fifty-two; in 1849, thirty-nine; and in 1861, twenty-seven.

In 1839 a girls' school of a similar character was established and the number of boarders limited to forty. The course of study comprised the Russian language, reading, writing, arithmetic, household work, sewing, and religion. In 1848 the school numbered thirty-two; in 1849, thirty-nine; and in 1861, twenty-six.

In 1841 a theological school was established at Sitka, which, in 1849, was advanced to the grade of a seminary. In 1848 it reported thirty pupils, twelve day pupils, and twelve creoles being educated in Russia. Of those in Russia, two were in training for pilots, one as merchant, one gunsmith, one fur dealer, one tailor, and one cobbler. In 1849 the attendance was reported twenty-eight, with eleven others in Russia.

In 1859 and 1860 the common schools at Sitka were remodeled in order to secure greater efficiency. The course of study consisted of Russian, Slavonian, and English languages, arithmetic, history, geography, book-keeping, geometry, trigonometry, navigation, astronomy, and religion. A knowledge of Russian, reading, writing, and the four rules of arithmetic, was required for admission. A pupil failing to pass examination two years in succession was dropped. The course extended over five years. Extra compensation was allowed teachers who secured the best results. The faculty consisted of a principal, who was a graduate of the School of Commercial Navigation; a free pilot, who taught navigation; an *employé* of the company who taught book-keeping and commercial branches; one priest and two licentiates, graduates of the University of St. Petersburg.

The corresponding school for girls was in charge of a lady graduate of one of the highest female schools in Russia, with two male teachers.

This made five schools at Sitka: two for the children of the lower class, two for the higher class, and one seminary.

About the time of the transfer the teachers were recalled to Russia and the schools suspended. This condition of things lasted until the winter of 1877 and '78, when I secured the appointment of Rev. John G. Brady for Sitka, and in April, 1878, a school was opened by Mr. Brady and Miss Fannie E. Kellogg. In December, through a combination of circumstances, it was discontinued. In the spring of 1880 Miss Olinda Austin was sent out from New York city, and reopened the school April 5 in one of the rooms of the guard-house with one hundred and three children present. This number increased to one hundred and thirty. Then some of the parents applied for admission, but could not be received, as the room would not hold any more. Miss Austin received the support and substantial assistance of Captain Beardslee, then in command of the United States ship Jamestown, who proved himself a warm friend of the enterprise. In July the school was moved to the old hospital building. In November some of the boys applied to the teacher for permission to live at the school-house. At home there was so much drinking, talking, and carousing that they could not study. The teacher said she had no accommodations, bedding, or food for them. But they were so much in earnest that they said they would provide for themselves. Upon receiving permission, seven Indian boys, thirteen and fourteen years of age, bringing a blanket each and a piece of tin for a looking-glass, voluntarily left their homes and took up their abode in a vacant room of one of the Government buildings. Thus commenced the boarding department of the Sitka school. Soon other boys joined them. One was a boy who had been taken out and shot as a witch, but was rescued by the officers of the Jamestown and placed in the school. Capt. Henry Glass, who succeeded Captain Beardslee in command of the Jamestown, from the first, with his officers, took a deep interest in the school. As he had opportunity he secured boys from distant tribes and placed them in the school, until there are twenty-seven boys in the boarding department.

In February, 1881, Captain Glass established a rule compelling the attendance of the Indian children upon the day-school, which was a move in the right direction and has worked admirably. He first caused

the Indian village to be cleaned up, ditches dug around each house for drainage, and the houses whitewashed. These sanitary regulations have already greatly lessened the sickness and death-rate among them. He then caused the houses to be numbered, and an accurate census taken of the inmates, adults and children. He then caused a label to be made of tin for each child, which was tied around the neck of the child, with his or her number and the number of the house on it, so that, if a child was found on the street during school hours, the Indian policeman was under orders to take the numbers on the labels and report them, or the teacher each day would report that such numbers from such houses were absent that day. The following morning the head Indian of the house to which the absentee belonged was summoned to appear and answer for the child. If the child was willfully absent, the head man was fined or imprisoned. A few cases of fine were sufficient. As soon as they found the captain in earnest, the children were all in school. This ran the average attendance up to two hundred and thirty and two hundred and fifty, one day reaching, with adults, two hundred and seventy-one. In April Mr. Alonzo E. Austin was associated with his daughter in the school, and Mrs. Austin was appointed matron.

With the increase of public attention to Alaska, and the growing interest of the country in the education of Indian children in industrial schools, the time has come to add an industrial department to the school at Sitka.

The nearest school of the kind to Alaska is at Forest Grove, Oregon. But Forest Grove is one thousand five hundred miles distant from South-eastern Alaska, and two thousand five hundred miles away, by present routes of travel, from South-western Alaska. Then the resources and character of the two countries are different. Oregon is largely agricultural, while Alaska has very little agricultural interests.

As the object of an industrial training is to enable the boy, upon arriving at manhood, to earn a support that will sustain his family in a civilized way, it is important to train him to utilize the resources of his own country. The resources of Alaska, in addition to her fur-bearing animals, are her vast supply of fish and great forests.

Therefore the training school of her children should be on the coast, where they can be taught navigation and seamanship; the handling of boats and sails; improved methods of fishing and handling fish-nets; improved methods of salting, canning, and preparing fish for market; a saw-mill; a carpenter shop, cooper shop, boot and shoe shop, etc. A school where they can be taught both the theory and practice under conditions similar to those they will meet when they undertake to support themselves. The need of such a school is urgent. A new era is opening for Alaska. Two years ago gold mines were opened about one hundred and sixty miles north-east of Sitka, and the mining village of Juneau was established. From these mines $150,000 worth of gold dust was taken last season. Rich discoveries were also reported in the valley of the Upper Yukon River. These reports have considerable interest in the mining regions of Arizona and the Pacific coast, and hundreds have, within the past few months, gone to Alaska.

As a mining excitement first opened California, Colorado, and Montana to settlement, so the present movement may be the commencement of the development of Alaska. That development has already commenced. In addition to the quartz-mills and mining interests, trading-posts have been established at a number of native villages. The Northwest Trading Company has established extensive works at Killisnoo for the manufacture of fish-oil. Four salmon canneries have been established at different points, and several fisheries at others. Extensive codfisheries are in operation at the banks, off of the Shumagin Islands, and saw-mills are

running at Sitka, Roberts, Klawack, and Jackson.

These changes again bring up the question of education. Shall the native population be left, as in the past, to produce, under the encroachments of the incoming whites, a new crop of costly, bloody, and cruel Indian wars, or shall they be so educated that they will become useful factors in the new development? The native races are partially civilized, industrious, anxious for an education, readily adopt the ways of the whites, and, with the advantages of schools, will quickly, to all intents and purposes, become citizens. To accomplish this, requires the sympathy and co-operation of the friends of education throughout the country.

As they feel ashamed that any large section of their land should be left without educational privileges—that Alaska should be worse off than when under Russia, the United States having failed to continue the schools that for many years were sustained by the Russian Government—let them show their interest in a substantial way by writing to the member of Congress from their district, asking him to use his influence in procuring an appropriation for the establishment of common schools in various sections of Alaska and an industrial training-school at Sitka.

On motion of Gen. T. J. Morgan, of Potsdam, N. Y., the National Education Assembly in 1883 adopted the following :

Resolved, That we recognize with profound gratitude to God the cheering progress that marks the efforts to civilize the American Indians ; that we see in this an unanswerable argument in favor of the continuance on the part of the government of the so-called peace policy; that we urge upon Congress the enlargement of the work already in progress, until adequate provision shall be made for the systematic education of all Indians of proper school age; that we specially urge the importance of appro- priation of money for general education in Alaska and for the establishment of an industrial and normal school at Sitka; that we pledge ourselves, and call upon all philanthropists, not only to aid the government in this great work, but to do all that can be done, privately and publicly, to carry forward this great enterprise, until the American Indians become American citizens, with individual rights of property and suffrage and individual responsibilities and duties.

The following letters were received at the Assembly :

Hon. HIRAM PRICE, Commissioner of Indian Affairs, Washington, in a letter of regret, addressed to Dr. HARTZELL, that he could not attend, says:

I hope you may be able to set in motion waves of influence, mighty and resistless as the waves of old ocean, on whose margin you stand, that shall reach the hearts of the people and the Churches, until a public sen- timent shall be created that will result in such action as will benefit, not only the Indian, but the nation.

Hon. WM. F. WELCKER, Superintendent Public Instruction, Cal., says:

It seems to me that all Indians, not now civilized, should be broken up as tribes and dispersed by families throughout the United States. We should abandon the fiction of their being *quasi* nations, and the folly of treating with them as such. We should not sever household ties; but should take families consisting of parents and minor children and settle them among the whites. They should receive for a temporary period, not longer than absolutely necessary, whatever assistance shall be found indispensable to their education and to *assist* in their support. After that period they should be left to take care of themselves like other American citizens. Being Americans, they are entitled to all the privileges of citizens, and should assume all the responsibilities and be required to perform all the duties of such.

Hon. CORNELIUS HEDGES, Superintendent Public Instruction, Montana, writes:

As to the Indians, we have seen much of them. There has been little honest, intelligent effort made yet to improve the Indian. There seems most promise in the direction of educating the children. But, when educated, they are lost if sent back among the savage remnant.

Work must be done along the whole line.

Something must be done among the old ones. Those of fighting age I would have taken into the military service, and each one paid the same as white soldiers, who could mostly be returned to useful life. For all frontier service I would use only Indians. Those not thus employed should be given land in severalty, and taught how to make their own living out of it. The moneys allowed us consideration for their land title should be funded, and only the interest allowed for education. Indians should be taught and made to work. Feeding them at agencies, in idleness and vice, is foolish and cruel kindness. We should like to see such an Indian fighter as Gen. Crook made Indian Commissioner. He has succeeded better than any one I know of in controlling and gaining the respect and confidence of the Indians. Promiscuous kindness is as demoralizing as promiscuous cruelty. It needs a strong, brave, steady, honest, open, and firm nature to deal with the Indian. If, in addition to his present military powers, he could have all the civil powers of Indian Commissioner, and Congress would support him in what he would recommend, I believe in ten years he would accomplish more than has been done in the past hundred years.

VII. THE AMERICAN MORMON PROBLEM.

1. THE UTAH PROBLEM.

REV. A. J. KYNETT, D.D., PHILADELPHIA.

AMONG the burning questions demanding the imperative attention of this Educational Convention is

THE UTAH PROBLEM.

It is one of the marvels of our history that such a question should, in so short a time, grow to such proportions.

Born of folly and fraud, nurtured by ignorance and superstition, clothed in the guise of religion, yet ever ministering to lawlessness and lust, Mormonism has, within the lifetime of young men, fastened itself upon the fairest of our central Territories, diffused its poison among those around it, and challenges, to-day, the united efforts of all our educational and missionary agencies, and the wisdom and skill of our best statesmen, and defies the power of the Federal government.

At its birth, in 1830, it seemed only an innocent and sickly superstition, and was gently carried, a year later, upon the little tide of emigration from Western New York into Northern Ohio. Here, in seven years, it grew to such a bad childhood, that it was driven, as with a scourge, into Far West Missouri. Refused a resting-place there, it returned, in 1838, to the east bank of the Mississippi, in Illinois, where, at the head of the lower rapids, upon a beautiful plain, it built for itself the city of Nauvoo.

Any system of religion that was not also a system of crime might have found here a safe and congenial home, but Mormonism, in the course of another seven years, had so nurtured and practiced crimes against society, that its neighbors rose up against it, and its chief prophet, Joseph Smith, was imprisoned and slain, and under the guidance of his famous and *infamous* successor, Brigham Young, it sought a more congenial home within the territory of our sister republic, Mexico, beyond the reach of the civilization and laws which had every-where refused it protection. But Divine Providence did not propose to leave the solution of this problem to another and a weaker people, and so, the year following the migration to Utah that Territory, included with others of the South-west, was ceded, in 1848, to the United States, and Brigham Young and his followers found themselves again under the government from which they had fled and against which they had never ceased to rebel.

So the problem still confronts us. So far from being solved it has grown in magnitude, increased in complexity, and stands ready, with new expedients, to come as new revelations, to meet any possible emergency. At the first recognizing and preserving the family, which lies at the foundation of our Christian civilization, in 1843, a new revelation to its prophet, Joseph Smith, gave it *polygamy*. If the people of the United States wish to know what this means let them study the results of polygamy in the genealogies of olden time—amy in the genealogies of olden time— of Esau, with his three wives, for instance—and then speculate, in a mathematical way, upon the results to follow in Utah, as in our centenary year, thirty years after his migration, Brigham Young might be seen with his seventeen wives, fifty-six children, and two million dollars' property.

This system sends out its emissaries by the hundreds, and by fraud and false pretense gathers its thousands of deluded votaries from among the ignorant and superstitious of this country and of Europe, and in its distant mountain home lays upon their persons and property the iron hand of its priestly despotism, multiplies them by polygamous marriages, scatters them through Utah and adjoining territories, until the handful that found their path to the wilderness, less than twoscore years ago, have become a multitude of nearly two hundred thousand, whose deceivers and oppressors snap their fingers in the faces of civilization and law, and insultingly inquire, "*What are you going to do about it?*"

Ay! That's the question to be considered by the fifty millions of free people whose moral sense is outraged and whose expressed will is defied by this modern abomination.

What are you going to do about it?
I suggest:

1. *Let the recruiting business be stopped.* Let the policy of President Hayes be revived and earnestly applied at the sources of supply in Europe. He directed our representatives in foreign countries to notify the governments abroad of the character of this system, and of its unfriendliness toward the government and laws of the United States, and that the suppression of such emigration was to be desired.

I do not know why President Hayes's policy has not been followed, but I do know that Mormon emissaries go abroad by hundreds, and that Mormon emigrants arrive by shiploads, and are sent by rail to Utah.

Our several State governments at home might profitably consider what could be done to protect their own citizens against a system the character of which is so well defined.

2. *Let the laws against polygamy be enforced,*

and amended and enforced, until every device for escape is closed, and violators of law are made to suffer the consequences.

3. *Let missionary agents be strengthened and multiplied,* not only in our own English language, but in the mother-tongue of the thousands there from the Old World.

Of a total male population over twenty-one years old, in 1882, of 32,773, 18,283—much more than half—were of foreign birth.

4. *Let the children of Utah be gathered into schools*—into our free mission schools—as rapidly as possible, and into non-Mormon government schools as rapidly as they can be provided under a system of enforced education by the authority of the government of the United States. And I should hope that with the application of suggestions like these, and others that have been made by other gentlemen to-night, the Utah problem might be solved in the next half century.

---

2. MORMONISM: EFFORTS OF CHRISTIAN CHURCHES.

REV. HENRY KENDALL, D.D.,

Secretary of Board of Home Missions of the Presbyterian Church.

THAT Mormonism, or, as the Mormons themselves call it, "The Church of the Latter-Day Saints," with its 150,000 or 200,000 adherents in Utah and the neighboring States and Territories, should exist in this nineteenth century, and in the heart of the territory of the United States, is one of the wonders of the age.

When we look at it in the character or in the abilities of its founders, in the light of its doctrines and its practices, the wonder does not grow less but rather greater. That so-called Church has no respectable defender, outside of itself, in all the world. It has not the sympathy of a single nominal Church in Christendom, and yet it continues and prospers in spite of all predictions to the contrary, and was never stronger nor more hopeful than to-day.

In the town of Manchester, Ontario County, New York, in the year 1830, this Church was formed. Its founder, Joseph Smith, an idle, vicious, and hardly reputable young man, who was accustomed to associate with fortune-tellers, and who laid claim to the power of second-sight, by means of the crotched witch-hazel and a stone, supposed to have like magical power, came at length to claim superhuman and prophetic powers. He claimed to have had it revealed to him that, buried in the earth, near at hand, was a record, inscribed upon gold plates, which

he only could read and interpret, and that he had transcribed the same, and hence a book was printed in Palmyra, New York, entitled "The Book of Mormon, an account written by the hand of Moroni, upon plates taken from the plates of Naphi. By Joseph Smith, Jr., author and proprietor."

There is the best historical evidence that the substance of this book was written, as a kind of pastime, by a Congregational clergyman, in Pennsylvania, by the name of Spaulding, without any thought on the part of the author to palm it off upon the world as a divine revelation; but, after his death, others, as unscrupulous as Smith himself, joined him, and the manuscript was obtained and with we know not how many modifications it became "The Book of Mormon," which is accepted by the Mormons as a new revelation from heaven. The Church of Jesus Christ of Latter-Day Saints was organized in April, 1830. But, in the neighborhood of its organization, it was esteemed nothing more than a nine days' wonder. A few curious people used to visit the place, to see the "prophet," the new bible, and to hear what its advocates would say. But it made no sensible impression on the intelligent Christian people of Western New York.

Hence, perhaps in 1831, it was revealed to them to move their head-quarters to Kirtland, Ohio. Here they remained for nearly or quite seven years. Then came a collapse in the financial affairs of the concern. A bank, which Smith had organized, and of which he had become president, failed in such a way that he was obliged to flee to escape being arrested for fraud. The community considered itself outraged, and rose up against the Mormons, not with armed resistance, but with such outspoken disgust and abhorrence that most of the Mormons followed their prophet and gathered next in the State of Missouri. But here they were so poor and lawless that they were accused of thefts and larcenies till the people rose up in armed resistance and drove them out of the State. They then gathered in Illinois and established the city of Nauvoo. Here, again, they became obnoxious to the surrounding community and came in conflict with them. The State militia was called out to enforce the law. The Mormons armed themselves for resistance. Joseph Smith and his brother, Hiram at length surrendered to the civil authorities, and were lodged in jail. But on the same evening, the 27th of May, 1844, the mob surrounded the jail and made an assault on it, and both Joseph and Hiram Smith were killed.

It became impossible for the Mormons, with their peculiar practices and doctrines, to live peaceably in any settled community at the West, and another movement became necessary. Brigham Young was chosen to fill the place of Joseph Smith, and with characteristic skill organized the scattered Mormons, to the number of about 16,000, and began the pilgrimage to the Salt Lake Valley, which was a journey of several months. The Territory of Utah was organized in 1850, and Brigham Young was appointed its first governor. And as governor, or as head of the Church, he was substantially governor of the Territory as long as he lived, as John Taylor is now.

From that time to this Mormonism in Utah has prospered and grown strong.

What has been the secret of its prosperity and power?

1. *The Consummate Ability of Brigham Young.*

Success often depends on good beginnings. Many good projects promise well, but never succeed, because they seem never to have had a good start. Brigham Young saved Mormonism from utter defeat and early extinction. Mormonism failed in New York, the State of its birth. It failed in Ohio. It failed in Missouri. It failed in Illinois. Then Joseph Smith was slain, and then his followers were dispersed and scattered abroad. It always failed under the leadership of Smith. It could not have survived another failure. At this juncture Brigham Young came to the presidency, and he brought to the administration of its affairs indomitable courage and great practical good

sense. The resolution to gather up these poor people and go to Salt Lake Valley, the ability to silence all opposition to so wild a scheme, to inspire the requisite courage for so long and perilous a journey across well-known deserts, through hosts of hostile savages, with small supplies to start with and no supplies on the way, and then through many weary months to successfully conduct the campaign, with women and children and old people, through winter and summer, is a wonderful fact in history, and shows the pluck and capacity of a master mind. Practically, Brigham Young made few mistakes, and when he did, no one saw them sooner than himself, and none could change his attitude more adroitly and successfully than he. He never started a fraudulent bank, as Smith did, at Kirtland, Ohio. He did not pull down a printer's office and destroy his press, as Smith did, at Nauvoo; and if he did bring his people almost into collision with the United States government and its troops, as he did at an early day in Utah, he was skillful enough to avoid the collision and yet retain the respect of his followers; and as to collision with the *people*, as Smith had in Missouri and Illinois, Brigham Young was very wise to remove his forces to a place where there could be no surrounding people to collide with.

When, nineteen years ago, I asked Brigham Young, in his own office in Salt Lake City, if he would have any objection to our Board sending a missionary to Salt Lake City, he mildly replied that he should have no objection whatever, but should rather like it, for, he said, he should like to have his young people know what the *other* denominations believed. I regarded his reply as signifying that he was so strong that he had nothing to fear from any Missionary Boards; but the two United States Judges in the Territory at the time thought that it was rather because he felt *weak*, for General Conner's guns at Fort Douglas, a mile away, were trained on his houses. And when, not a week later, a provost-marshal's office was opened in the City of the Saints, greatly to the disgust of the Mormons, and their military forces were called out, and General Conner sent word to him that at the first drop of blood shed by them he would blow Brigham Young's head-quarters into dust, his soldiers melted away and disappeared like dew before the rising sun. Brave as he was to advance, he was not less skillful to beat a retreat when policy demanded it.

Brigham Young was a born leader of men. While he had only an ordinary or common-school education, he was gifted with a species of rough oratory that was fitted to be very successful with such a people as he was chosen to lead. Read his published sermons, and you will find he leaves questions of theology mostly to others. He grapples with practical matters, he discourses of cattle, of crops, of fences, of irrigation. and gives the wisest of counsels as to the physical comfort and welfare of the people. His exhortations are most forcible, and clothed in his language they had the force of command. In those discourses it is apparent, too, that his ears were not closed against the murmurings of discontent, and on such occasions he would lash his hearers with the bitterest invective and most biting sarcasm, and overwhelm the malcontents with vituperation at one time, and at another with ridicule; vulgar even to indecency, he gave his hearers no peace till he was already master of the field.

2. *Another Source of their Strength and Prosperity is their Thorough Organization.*

We cannot but admit that John Wesley was a great organizer. His plans for work for all, and a place for all to work, and his system of class-meetings for the careful oversight of all the members in his churches, and their development of Christian character, were most admirable. We are apt to give great credit to the remarkable oversight which the Roman Catholic Church exercises over all its members. It is very thorough. Every man, woman, and child is watched over, all their benevolent contributions are watched over, and the grace of giving is pressed with great thoroughness and persistence, and poor as many of their people are—day-laborers and servant-girls—put to shame any of our Protestant Churches in the aggregate of their gifts. But neither the Methodists nor the Roman Catholics can compare with the Mormons in the completeness of their oversight of their members. As a writer has recently said: "The Mormon population reaches only 125,000. But over this number, to discipline and direct them in all things both temporal and spiritual, are set more than 22,000 church officials, such as a president, 2 counselors, 12 apostles, 60 patriarchs, whose business it is to bless at $2 a head; 25 presidents of 'Stakes of Zion,' 'or fields or districts;' 275 bishops, 3,045 high-priests, 11,545 elders, of whom every one can preach, baptize, lay on hands for the reception of the Holy Ghost, and anoint for the healing of the sick; 1,286 priests, 1,576 teachers, and 4,100 deacons. Here is the strength of Mormonism, in the number of office-holders for which it provides in the rigid system of subordination from top to bottom."

As Joseph Cook says: "Every *fifth* man is an officer, and from the highest to the lowest every one is liable to promotion if his superior falls out, and so much the more sure of promotion as he is faithful to the tenets, traditions, and practices of the Mormon Church. Not a Mormon can step into one of our chapels on the Sabbath or send

his child to one of our week-day schools or Sunday-schools without being liable to reproof from a Mormon official; and if he perseveres, he falls under suspicion, and is watched more carefully; and if he finally ventures, under the stress of his convictions, to abandon the Mormons, he knows he does it at the risk of losing caste or social position, as surely as he would in India, and suffers the withdrawal of all business from him so far as lies in the power of the Mormon Church."

One of the marvels of this feature of the case is how a few men, without experience in public affairs, without any extensive reading, should have been able to originate a system of oversight or espionage, a system so admirable in all its practical details for growth and development, and almost at the first draft. But in this, as in all the initial facts of Mormon history, the hand of Brigham Young is conspicuous. His consummate organizing capacity, exercising itself with the masterly outline of a great movement, and in all the minor details, shows how fortunate it was for the Mormons when he came to the front. The compacted unity of the whole scheme, and the harmony of all the parts. the ecclesiastical and secular religion, trade, and commerce all combined, are an illustration of his wisdom and the perfection of the organization of the system.

3. *Another Element of the Strength and Prosperity of the System is the Exclusion of its Adherents from the Society of the Rest of the World.*

They separated themselves from the rest of the world when they went to Salt Lake City, or Salt Lake Valley. Hundreds of miles intervened between themselves and any other people, except wild savages. In all their bounds there were no churches but Mormon churches, no people but Mormon people. Whatever might be said about other people, about their beliefs or practices, there were none of them there to say it was not true, or give the lie to Mormon utterances by word of mouth or by their deeds. Is it any wonder, then, that the children of Mormons should grow up believing that other Christian people are idolaters, as some children of Mormons are said to do at the present time? This separation was a great element of strength in the formative period of the Mormon system. There was no dissent because there were no dissenters, and, with the exception of two or three merchants in Salt Lake City, there were none to call in question the absolute certainty of their faith for the first twenty years of their residence in Utah. The children grew up in absolute ignorance of any other professing Christian people. In that time the system had become an accepted one, if there ever had been any doubters they were silent, and whatever seemed essential to compactness had been adopted. But some of their religious opinions and practices have contributed greatly to the compactness, unity, and strength of the people, notably

POLYGAMY.

It has been remarked that no great system of false religion has ever had any extensive prevalence that has not, at last, in some way, administered to the lusts of men. Nothing could more effectually do this than the adoption of polygamy; so Mohammed saw, so the leaders in the Mormon faith saw, and they saw it early. And after what our Lord had said about it, and its positive condemnation by him, it is most surprising that in this age of the world any people, especially claiming to be the people of God, could adopt or accept it. But polygamy has been of great service to the Mormons in keeping them distinct from all other people. When a governor or a merchant of non-Mormon faith took a wife to Utah, she had no social intercourse with the Mormon women or the Mormon women with her. Brigham Young was never known to take his seventeen wives and call to pay his respects to the Governor of the Territory and his wife. The Mormons have socially ostracized themselves from all the respectable society of the civilized world. It is not to be supposed that they thought of this as a point to be reached, but nothing could more completely segregate the Mormons from the rest of the world than polygamy.

In like manner, though not to the same extent, is another feature of their faith, which has in it all the elements of ancient Phariseeism. Mormonism claims that its adherents are the special favorites of heaven. They are the *Latter-Day* Saints. To them, in distinction from all other people, has a revelation from heaven been made; to them alone has the ancient spirit of prophecy and the power of working miracles been restored. It *offers its adherents all the best things of this world and the world to come.*

The Christian religion offers the glories of heaven to those that believe in Christ, but only as they leave all for Christ. Persecutions, and losses of all things earthly, and death itself, have been the lot of those who follow Christ. Even Paul could count all things but loss for the excellency of the knowledge of Christ, and the only serious trouble with men in accepting the offers of salvation has been the necessary abandonment of the world for Christ. If men could pursue their cherished pleasures, if the denial of darling sins were not essential to the attainment of heavenly glory, it would not be hard to persuade men to become Christians. But Mormonism promised to its followers the best things of earth and the highest seats in glory. The Latter-Day

Saints are to fill all the earth. All the earthly governments are to crumble to pieces. The nations are corrupt, and must disappear, and the Mormons are to take possession of all the earth; and the old tradition, which has not been abandoned, is that the center and imperial city is to be set up in the State of Missouri! But the idea that the Mormons are to have all the best positions, wealth, and honors, and pleasures, and dominate all the earth, is a prominent article of their faith. Herein is their similarity to Mohammedanism, which is now said to have 180,000,000 adherents. Like the Mohammedans, they may have a plurality of wives on the earth, the more the better; and the more wives they have on earth the higher their place in heaven. If the lust of the flesh—abounding sensuality—and the lust of the eye, and the pride of life, are not provided for in the system of Mormonism, with everlasting life, we do not see how they could be incorporated into any scheme. The Mormons are a praying people, above all others; they are a very religious people in their way. But if a close examination does not reveal them as profane, and vulgar, and worldly, and licentious in the forms of polygamy, then those who have the best opportunity to study their conduct have done them great injustice.

Such a theory naturally engenders self-righteousness; for if we can flatter ourselves that " we are not as other men," that we are superior to all other of God's professed children — the undoubted inheritors of all that is good in this world and the world to come, nothing more is necessary to make them righteous in their own eyes and to despise all other men.

4. The Book of Mormon is an element of Power.

The long-lived religions have their sacred books. What would have become of the Christian religion but for the Bible? What would have become of Mohammedanism but for the Koran, or the old religions and superstitious and idolatries of the Hindus but for their sacred books? I do not put these books and the Koran on the same plane or to be compared with the Bible, but to affirm that a book which is claimed as divine—a book that can be seen and handled and read, that has laws and precepts, no matter how absurd—will outlive the forms of faith that have no such basis. And such religions are all more tenacious of life because we, as Christians, hold on to our Bible with so much tenacity. As we cling to it, so the Mohammedan clings to his book and the Hindu to his. If we have a book of laws, precepts which we claim to be a revelation from God, so the Mormons claim to have had another subsequent revelation from God. If we of the Church of God have had prophets and priests and apostles, who could work miracles, why should not they have the same? It is in vain that you show such people how absurd are their revelations, how contrary to history, how irreconcilable with facts; they may not be able to meet you in the argument, but they have a *book*, a book from God, and that tangible, visible symbol of their faith is a great power with them, as our Bible is with us.

This is the system of Mormonism as it exists in Utah.

Perhaps it was never more vigorous or prosperous than to-day. Perhaps never more missionaries went out through the civilized world to win and bring in converts than the present year. Perhaps the tithes were never paid more promptly than now. Perhaps there was never greater unity and compactness in the system than now; a hardy, thrifty people congregated in the cities and large towns and spread over the valleys and out upon the foot-hills of the mountains that surround the valleys of Utah, and even extending into New Mexico, Arizona, and Idaho, are these misguided people.

We used to say polygamy is the strength of the system; let Congress legislate against polygamy and it will be a death-blow to the system. Twenty years has the legal condemnation against polygamy stood on the records of Congress, one polygamist has been convicted and imprisoned; but the practice of polygamy has never been checked a single instant. We used to say let the railroad pass through the Territory, let it be safe for the wives of polygamous husbands to speak out, and they will lift up their voices against the unclean system; and yet when some Gentile women organized an effort against it, a mass-meeting of Mormon women, 2,000 strong, declared that "polygamy is as essential to woman's happiness as her salvation;" and one of the speakers said: "I would not abandon polygamy to exchange with Queen Victoria and all her dependencies."

But we must understand that in such utterances polygamous wives are speaking for themselves and their children, for if polygamy has not the divine sanction (it has not the legal human sanction) they are but concubines and their children illegitimate. So it has been said, "Let Brigham Young die and the system will fall to pieces; no other man in Utah has his capacity to command and control men;" and yet when he died his successor was chosen with scarcely a ripple of commotion, and things continue as they were. It was said, too, that "if we would send in missionaries and preach the truth, the imprisoned and priest-ridden slaves of the spiritual tyranny would break their shackles and accept the truth as it is in Jesus." Men have sickened of the tyranny, and have broken away from the thraldom of the priests, but instead of thronging to our

Mission Churches, they, mostly, repudiate all Churches; having become convinced of the hollowness of the Mormon system, they also repudiate all faiths and all Churches, and become open infidels. At length the government arose in its majesty and might and passed the Edmunds Bill, and we expected to see Mormonism shattered as when a shell falls on the deck of a merchantman, and the Mormons have gone on marrying and giving in marriage, only *more abundantly.*

An anachronism, a colossal development of religious fanaticism, a mixture of Judaism, Mohammedanism, and Heathenism, defying the government of the United States and all the forces of Christianity, Mormonism still stands, in the heart and center of the territory of the United States, apparently as safely environed and shut out from all outward attack as if the hills that surround the valleys of Utah were impassable mountains.

What of it? Settled in their own homes, pursuing peaceful pursuits, what concern is it to the Christian Church? Mainly this: If they, teachers and taught are deceivers and being deceived; if, claiming to be saints, they are the dupes of Satan; if they are going, and are leading their children, down to everlasting perdition, 125,000 or 150,000 in the midst of this Christian land, then it is the greatest possible concern to the Christian people of this land to know what to do about it.

We will not wholly despair of the influences that have been mentioned. Railroads—the introduction of a Gentile population, so-called—may not have accomplished all we hoped for, but they have not been in vain; a bold front and noisy defiance and vigorous defense of positions long held, are quite as much the devices of weakness as they are the evidences of strength. Let us not despair. The United States government may do something yet if it tries. *It has never tried!* But let us not despair. Growing defiance may, at length, call out counter efforts that will avail.

But one thing is certain. The Gospel will prevail against Mormonism. It is the power of God, to the pulling down of strongholds. All other things may fail. The preaching of the Gospel will not fail.

But as we begin among the children in heathen lands, and reach through them to their parents, so must we do among the Mormons; and especially since it may be true, as many believe, that even the most ignorant and besotted heathens are more accessible to religious influences than those who have known the words of life and perverted them to their own destruction, so all the religious denominations that have undertaken Christian work in Utah and among the Mormons have attempted to reach the people by means of missionary teachers and Christian schools.

The Protestant Episcopal Church began operations in Utah in 1867, and its first practical work was the establishment of schools. Bishop Tuttle and his helpers saw at once that the chief instrumentality for gaining a permanent Christian influence must be the education of the children, and the absence of any free school system, or the hope of one, rendered it an imperative necessity to make every available contribution for the supply of that want.

The Episcopalians have 7 clergymen, 5 churches, 395 communicants, 5 Sunday-schools, with 730 scholars, 5 schools, 25 teachers, 770 pupils, (4,400 from the beginning,) and a hospital which within ten years has received 3,000 patients.

May 8, 1870, Rev. G. M. Peirce, the first Methodist preacher in Utah, arrived with his family at Salt Lake City, and began the work of planting Methodism on Mormon soil. One week later he began his labors in Independence Hall.

The Methodist Church opened its first mission school in Salt Lake City September 26, 1870, with an enrollment of 28 pupils. Now the Methodists have 10 ministers, 6 churches, with 189 members, 5 schools, 6 teachers. 450 scholars.

The churches and mission stations under care of the Presbytery of Utah extend from Malad, Idaho, to St. George, in Southern Utah, a continuous line 450 miles long. There are 12 organized churches and 33 mission schools, under charge of 19 ministers and 53 teachers. These churches and schools are so grouped geographically as to furnish each minister with a *circuit*.

In the winter of 1873-4 Prof. John M. Coyner, of Indianapolis, Indiana, spent a few days in Salt Lake City, on his way to the Pacific coast. While in the city he made the acquaintance of Rev. Josiah Welch, pastor of the Presbyterian Church, and from him learned the religious and educational status of the Territory. They both agreed that Utah furnished a remarkable field for future educational enterprise, and that the Presbyterian Church should be engaged in this important work; and when they parted, as Prof. Coyner left for San Francisco, he said to Mr. Welch:

"When you get ready to inaugurate your educational work, let me know, and, God willing, I will aid you."

But neither one expected events to develop so rapidly. At that time only a lot was purchased, but not paid for. But in less than twelve months a large church was erected, with basement rooms; and, true to previous agreement, Prof. Coyner had been invited to, and had accepted, the superintendency of

the Salt Lake Collegiate Institute, which was opened in the basement on April 12, 1875. The Presbyterians have 310 members, 12 churches, 34 schools with 2,000 scholars, and 1,800 in Sunday-schools. Real estate is owned in 23 towns, worth $97,000, and the annual cost of churches and schools is $36,000.

THE NEW WEST EDUCATION COMMISSION.

This society of Christian philanthropists was organized in Chicago about two years ago. It looks to the Congregational Churches of the country for its constituency.

The Congregationalists have two churches, with 180 members; 7 ministers occupying 11 points; 11 Sunday-schools, with upward of 500 scholars; an academy, and 15 free schools, with 23 teachers and 530 scholars; church and school property, costing some $75,000. and all maintained at an annual expense of $18,000.

The Baptists have a good beginning in Ogden, and are now building a fine church edifice in Salt Lake City.

In the past fifteen years, and mainly within half that period, including only what relates to the five Protestant denominations, we have 27 churches, 41 ministers, 1,100 communicants, 50 Sunday-schools, 3,430 scholars. All this is scattered over 50 of the principal towns. The total cost of church and school property is not less than $425,000, and the yearly expense of carrying on these Christian institutions, $140,000.

These schools are all in reality, though not obtrusively, Christian schools. All their teachers are really missionaries, and they do much in the way of personal missionary labor, not in the schools only, but in Sunday-schools and from house to house. Moreover, the schools are located as to be in reach of some one of the missionaries, and usually constitute one of his mission stations where regularly, at stated intervals, he preaches the Gospel. Thus the preachers and the teachers constitute one consecrated and harmonious band engaged in undermining the whole system of Mormonism. Looking at its elements of strength we must expect a long, hard struggle; but looking at the weapons of our warfare and the great Captain of our salvation, who is God over all, blessed for evermore, we will not despair. Victory is certain at last, and when the last result is put on final record, those who have contributed to it by prayer, by pecuniary benefactions, by personal labors, will have abundant occasion to rejoice and to thank God that they were counted worthy to share in such a glorious triumph of the truth, to the glory of our common Lord.

3. DISLOYALTY OF MORMONS, AND EDUCATION IN UTAH.

PROF. J. M. COYNER, PH.D.,
Salt Lake Collegiate Institute, Utah.

HE who, through ignorance, carelessness, or prejudice, misleads mankind in regard to any subject that involves obligation and consequent duty, must be held, to a greater or less degree, responsible for the evil influence thus exerted. He who intentionally does the same commits a crime both against the laws of God and the laws of society. The writer of this paper realizes the truth of these propositions, and while he holds himself responsible for the statements he makes, he professes to be well guarded in these statements.

Every citizen of Utah who writes or speaks upon the Mormon question should weigh carefully every argument presented and examine well every expression used, lest he appear to be influenced by prejudice or prompted by selfish motive.

He should remember that he is dealing with a national subject of great moral importance, and if his position enables him to have any influence in molding public opinion he should see to it that the impressions made are on the side of individual rights and public virtue.

Mormonism is no longer a local question. It has assumed great national importance, and must enter largely into the future politics of our country.

Some of us remember the expression of former days, "There is a negro in the national wood-pile," and we also remember what it cost to get that negro out.

There is now most assuredly a Mormon in the mountain canyon, and it requires more than "human ken" to say what it will cost to get him out; for there can no more be harmony between Utah Mormonism and American Republicanism than there could be in former days harmony between slavery and liberty.

One or the other *must* go to the wall. And there must be a continued strife while the two exist in our commonwealth.

The most dangerous element of the Mormon power is not its polygamy; is not the fact that it destroys the unified home and ignores individual manhood; is not that it reduces woman to the level of the slave, and robs her of all that makes her man's co-equal; is not that it turns the hands of the clock of the world's morality back on the dial of time for four thousand years, and would engraft on the nineteenth century the barbarism of the Dark Ages. But the element that is the tap-root of this upas-tree, and that

gives life to every branch and leaf of the system, is its *disloyalty.*

Let it be distinctly understood that the Mormon power is not a Church in any true sense of the term. It is a political association; an organized government, a kingdom with a crowned king, and its subjects are so bound by oaths of allegiance to that king that no man that is a faithful Mormon can be loyal to the government of the United States.

The fundamental idea of the Mormon doctrine is that God revealed to Joseph Smith that through him Christ's temporal kingdom was to be established on earth; that to the Latter-Day Saints was to be given the power to finally rule all the nations of the world; that the Mormon power is the stone cut out of the mountain that will finally crush all other principalities and powers. And history shows that, from the first organization of the Mormons in Ohio, they have endeavored to carry out the idea that they are the Lord's people, and every thing they could appropriate to their use belonged to them, for "The earth is the Lord's and the fullness thereof," and what belongs to the Lord belongs also to his saints.

With this fundamental idea always in mind the Mormon hierarchy has established one of the most thoroughly organized systems of government that has ever existed. In fact, Europe to-day presents no example of a despotism more complete, of an absolute monarchy more thoroughly organized, than that of the so-called Latter-Day Saints.

It is true that most of this organization lies deep hidden in the secret mysteries of the Endowment-house, and is not revealed even to the masses of the rank and file; they being taught that " obedience is better than knowledge." But this very secresy lends a binding influence, and makes the despotism the more complete. The American people should quickly comprehend the fact that the Mormon power is not a Church in any sense of the term. It is a political organization that, under the cloak of religion, is endeavoring to conceal its true character until, vampyre-like, it can suck the life-blood of the nation.

As a citizen of Utah, the writer has for nearly ten years watched the course of events. He has listened to scores of their speakers in Tabernacle, Assemby Hall, and ward meeting-house. He has mingled with the masses, and learned from various untold sources much that has surprised him, and has convinced him that there is a power, a purpose, a vitality, and a national danger connected with the Mormon hierarchy that the people in general do not comprehend.

This is not said in the spirit of persecution. No rightly disposed person wishes to persecute the Latter-Day Saints for their religious views.

They have equal rights to worship God according to the impulses of their own consciences. But religious liberty is not political license, and when they, under the cloak of religious belief, organize a political association whose purpose is to overthrow our national polity—when, in carrying out their so-called religious belief, they violate law both human and divine, and trample upon constitutional enactments as well as the recognized rights of civilized society—it is not only the privilege, but the duty, of every American citizen to earnestly oppose them.

While Utah remains a Territory, its control is largely in the hands of the general government; for while States are much the same as children who have come to a legal age and can vote and act for themselves, Territories are minors, political wards to be cared for by the general government. The Mormon hierarchy feel their relation in this respect, and chafe under it. The control of the United States is a bitter medicine that they are compelled to take; though they are always willing to bribe the nurse not to administer the dose that the physician has prescribed.

In view of this fact an important part of their plan is to have Utah admitted as a State. This done, a grand step would be taken to secure the fulfillment of their designs. Then the capital of the Mormon Kingdom would be practically free from the control of the United States. Then we would have no loyal governor to absolutely veto bad bills, no loyal secretary of this Territory or United States marshal to protect us from wrong, or loyal judges to see that we have justice done. All would then be under the control of the despotic rule of a despotic so-called priesthood. Then would come the time referred to by Brigham Young, Jr., when speaking in the great tabernacle, he said: "If I had my own way I would say to every Gentile in this territory, you get out of here or take the consequences," and it is coming to this.

It is the opinion of the loyal citizens of Utah, that if she is ever admitted as a State under Mormon control, such admission will so fasten the political and moral cancer upon the body politic that it can only be removed as was its twin sister—Slavery. We, therefore, earnestly appeal to the educated, thinking, loyal minds of our country to see to it that by no trick of party demagogism shall there ever be admitted into the sisterhood of States one controlled by the Mormon power. For if one such State should be admitted, and the precedent be thus established, they would,

by their system of organization, in a few years capture at least half a dozen of the future States of these mountain regions, and thus have the balance of power in our government. It is true that the system of morality as taught and practiced by the Latter-Day Saints is a dangerous one, and one that will sap the foundation of any government founded as ours is.

Yet it is not the province of the nation to legislate on purely moral questions. But we emphasize the position already taken, that Mormonism must be regarded as a political, and not a religious, institution.

But it may be asked, is not the legislation already enacted sufficient to control the evil? We answer No. Indeed, every step taken thus far by the government has strengthened the Mormon power. Even the Edmunds Bill is not an exception. For while the polygamists are disfranchised, they, through their organization, have such control over the masses that they can secure the election by large majority, and every one thus disfranchised holds himself up in his community as an example of persecution for righteousness' sake. What, then, should be done?

1. Take from the Mormon hierarchy every vestige of power, both territorial and municipal. Place them in a position that they cannot wield their despotic lash over their subjects. Give in this way the rising generation an opportunity to become American freemen; for there are many thousands who would gladly assert their freedom if it was not for fear of the terrible lash of the priesthood. And if such were placed in a position where there would be a good hope of success, they would arise in their might and either overthrow this system or compel it to take its proper place as a Church of religious belief.

Congress has the power to control the Territories as she thinks best. Let her then assume the responsibility. Let her make such laws in regard to marriage as will break up that moral pest-house of disloyalty, the Endowment-house.

Let her appoint a legislative commission with such constitutional powers as will compel in this Territory the same obedience to laws as elsewhere, and that will give an opportunity for the loyal element of the people to be the controlling power.

2. Let the government step forward, and assume the education of "Utah's best crop." Utah is the only part of the United States, except Alaska, that has not a public-school system. There are two classes of schools in Utah—those connected with the five religious churches, Episcopal, Catholic, Methodist, Presbyterian, and Congregational, and the Mormon schools. The former are called mission schools, and are supported partly by tuition and partly by funds from the Mission Societies in the East. The number of these

schools is about 65, with an enrollment of over five thousand children. These schools are doing a good work, but are not aided by any territorial money or government patronage.

The Mormons have a school-house in every ward. In Salt Lake City there are 21 such houses, and several hundred through the Territory. These buildings are erected and kept up by a general tax levied alike on the Mormon and non-Mormon. The teachers for those schools are selected in most cases by the Mormon bishops of the wards, and are paid partly by a general tax levied on the entire property of the Territory and partly by tuition. It is a rare thing for any one to be appointed a teacher unless he or she is a baptized Mormon, and is willing to teach the Mormon doctrines, and use every influence to strengthen the power of the priesthood. These school-houses are also used as assembly-rooms for their so-called religious gatherings, and the writer has heard from the speakers in their meetings the most treasonable utterances.

It will thus be seen that the educational system of Utah, instead of being the bulwark of national patriotism, is made to subserve the purpose of a designing priesthood in fastening the chains of bigotry and disloyalty upon the minds of the rising generation.

The Mormons bring thousands and tens of thousands of children from the Old World, but give them no opportunity to become Americanized.

How long is this state of things to continue? Must our government see this constant stream of disloyal emigration filling all these mountain regions, and make no effort to secure the rising generation from the ignorance, superstitions, and disloyalty of their fathers?

No, there is a moral power back of party spirit, deeper than political excitement, that will in the near future let demagogues know that it is better to educate citizens than to fight criminals.

We believe it is the duty of the government to take the entire control of the education of the children in Utah; to organize a territorial school board of loyal citizens, and through this board establish a public-school system that will be, both in theory and practice, entirely under the control of loyal citizens.

In brief, let Congress enact such laws as will take all political and municipal power from the leaders of the Mormon Church, and also compel them to send their children to good schools, where they will be under influences that will tend to make them worthy citizens of the United States.

It may be said these are radical measures. Admitted; but they are constitutional, and are on the side of right. Nothing but radical measures will cure this disease.

The patient has gangrene in the foot. The surgeon advises amputation. The patient demurs. The disease spreads to the ankle. The surgeon again urges radical measures. The patient hesitates. The leg is diseased. It is now prompt action or death. The limb is removed near the body to save the life. The nation has three paths before it. Prompt radical measures; the knife near the body; or the death of the patient.

4. SOURCES OF MORMON STRENGTH.

REV. ROBERT G. M'NIECE,

Pastor Presbyterian Church, Salt Lake City.

Rev. J. C. HARTZELL, D.D.

Dear Brother: In your letter of the 12th, in reference to the National Education Assembly at Ocean Grove, in August, you ask me to give you a statement of what I regard as "the most dangerous facts in Mormonism, and the chief duty of the government in the premises." I deem it my duty to comply with this request, for I know no better way to hasten the uprooting of Mormonism, as a great social evil and political conspiracy against civil liberty, than to give the American people definite information concerning its tremendous strength, and its deliberate use of that strength for the most pernicious and dangerous purposes conceivable in the heart of a free republic.

Let me begin by saying that my knowledge of Mormonism has been derived from a six years' residence at its head-quarters, in the Mormon capital of Salt Lake City, together with a diligent study of its entire history, and personal observation of its results in various communities in the northern half of Utah. Hence, in saying that, in proportion to its numbers, there is not another organization on the face of the earth that equals Mormonism in *resources and inclination* for all sorts of social, civil, and moral mischief, I am not speaking at random; and it is only because the great mass of the American people are in the dark in regard to the strength of this diabolical system, and the danger connected with that strength, that they are doing so little for its overthrow. Let it be the aim of the first part of this letter, therefore, to bring out, as far as conciseness will allow, the facts on these two points: I. The Strength of Mormonism. II. Its Dangerous Use of that Strength. This will prepare the way for looking at the other point you ask my opinion about, namely: The duty of the government concerning the matter.

Five things go to make up, in the main, the greatly under-estimated strength of Mormonism.

1. *Thoroughness of Organization.* The Territory is first divided into some twenty "stakes," or districts, each having its spiritual presiding bishop and his subordinates. These twenty districts are again subdivided into some two hundred and fifty wards, each with its secular presiding bishop and his subordinates, and all under the iron rule of President Taylor, his two counselors, and the twelve apostles, who constitute one of the most despotic tribunals on the globe.

I ought also to add that the Mormons continue to colonize Idaho and Arizona, and virtually hold the balance of power in these future States of the Union.

Another cunning thing about this organization is the *number of offices with which to bribe the dissatisfied into acquiescence.* In 1880 the total number of Mormons in Utah and Idaho was reported by themselves at 109,-000. Leaving out 33,000 children under eight years of age, there were 76,000 members. Of this number *over 23,000 were office-holders.*

2. Another element of strength in Mormonism is its *financial system.* This is based on the tithing plan. A tenth of all that is raised or earned is required to be paid over to the priesthood. I was present in the great tabernacle, three years ago, when the annual reports were given. The proceeds of the tithing for that year were stated to be $458,000! The total receipts of the priesthood from all sources for that year were stated to be the enormous sum of $1,097,000! Think of this sum annually pouring into the lap of the most unscrupulous priesthood on earth!

3. A third element of strength in Mormonism is its *missionary policy.* Some three hundred missionaries are kept scattered through the various countries of the globe, encouraged to activity by the hope of some higher office as the reward of their success. Nor do they spread their drag-net of deception over the earth in vain, since every year, when their net is hauled up upon the shores of Utah, it is found to contain from 2,200 to 3,000 converts. Last year, from April to

December, there were landed in Salt Lake City alone 2,280 of these converts, to say nothing about other parts of the Territory and of adjoining Territories. Thus far, nearly 1,800 have arrived the present season. The Scandinavian countries and Great Britain furnish the greater part of these proselytes. Just contrast this with the fact that the aggregate of all the accessions to all the Protestant Churches in Utah, during the same length of time, does not reach one hundred and fifty.

4. A fourth element of strength, which need be only mentioned, is the fact that the disloyal priesthood who are carrying on this dangerous conspiracy against the Republic and its most sacred institutions are clothed with the privileges and powers of American citizenship.

5. But the crowning element of strength lies in the fact that *these vast resources are in the hands of a priesthood whom the people are taught to obey with the most implicit submission, as possessing Divine authority.*

So much for the elements of Mormon strength. Now let me speak, in the second place, of the *dangerous use which is made of this strength* by the Mormon priesthood.

1. The compact organization is used as a most terrible engine of oppression toward the deluded people. No freedom of opinion or action is allowed—not even in regard to the newspaper one wishes to read, the store he wishes to trade at, the school he wishes to patronize; not even in regard to the control of his own property. And if a Gentile can be deterred from settling in a community, whether as farmer, merchant, teacher, or minister, by all sorts of annoyances, such as shutting off his irrigating water, pulling down his fences, besmearing his doors, breaking out his windows, hooting and yelling about his premises at midnight, or by putting in his way all sorts of obstacles to the purchasing of property, even from those who wish to sell—if any or all these things combined can deter an upright and loyal American citizen from settling in one of these Mormon communities, over which the American flag pretends to wave, it is considered a great and honorable victory by the Mormon priesthood. Did space permit I could illustrate every one of these particulars with actual occurrences, most of them coming within my own personal knowledge. Of course, such priestly tyranny and outrages are confined mainly to the rural communities, and can no longer interfere with Americans in towns like Salt Lake City and Ogden. But the crowning part of such outrages is, when some priestly Mephistopheles, like Geo. Q. Cannon, or President John Taylor, stands up in the great tabernacle on Sunday, before a goodly collection of Gentile tourists, and with angelic smiles, which Satan himself could not surpass, and patriotic

tones, which Benedict Arnold could not equal, dilates upon the superior friendship of the priesthood for the sacred principles of American liberty, and the heartiness with which they welcome Americans of all parties and creeds to Utah as permanent residents! Seldom does a Sunday pass in Salt Lake City, from May to October, when this lying farce is not enacted by some assumed Melchizedec or Aaronic priest, while Satan and his attendant imps chuckle in their sleeves under the protecting shadow of the galleries.

2. No pen can describe the dangerous use which the Mormon priesthood make of the enormous financial income of over a million dollars. If some doubtful Congressman, visiting Salt Lake City, is to be captured by having his hotel bill paid at the Walker House; or by free carriages for himself and party about the city; or by free liquors at some Mormon residence, or on a special train to the Lake; or if other Congressmen, in Washington, are to be conciliated by elegant champagne suppers at the delegate's residence; or by choice presents of various kinds; or if daily papers, like one in Omaha and one in New York, are to be subsidized into defense of Mormonism, the tithing-fund, and half-a-dozen other funds, are ample for such and other purposes.

Within a month, a prominent American who held a Cabinet position under President Grant, and was also Minister to England, (Edwards Pierrepont,) was captured by the notorious Cannon, and was hobnobbing with the nasty criminal here in Salt Lake City, to the shame and indignation of every patriotic American who witnessed or knew of the humiliating spectacle.

3. *The dangerous use that is made of the missionary policy of the Mormons.* The three hundred or more missionaries who are kept abroad are trained to take advantage of every conceivable form of deception and misrepresentation, in order to entice into the terrible Mormon net the honest but uneducated peasantry of Great Britain and the Scandinavian countries. Keeping the Book of Mormon and the odious and peculiar doctrines of Mormonism in the background, the Bible and the general truths of Christianity are put in the foreground. Then, taking advantage of our free-land system, the cunning missionary paints before the dazzled eyes of the landless peasants attractive and resistless pictures of the free homes which the Mormon priesthood can give them in the saints' paradise in Utah, where the Lord's people have assembled out of wicked Babylon for his pure worship and service. Out of the immigration fund a loan bearing ten per cent. interest is granted to the moneyless converts to pay their passage. Once in Utah, there is little opportunity for the poor to escape. And, in fact, their little ten, fifteen, or twenty acres of ground, which they never

could have secured in the old country, reconciles them to the unpleasant things in Mormonism which, for the sake of their homes, they are ready to shut their eyes and gulp down. Placed under American influences, they would become a worthy class of citizens; but, placed under the terrible instruction of this deceiving, anti-American priesthood, deceived into thinking that the American Government is trying to rob them of their civil and religious rights, and that the enforcement of the laws is persecution because of their religion, the terrible result is that there is being built up here in Utah a commonwealth that is permeated through and through with bitter disloyalty and hatred, not only toward the government, but toward American ideas and institutions. Yet, on public occasions, there is a cunning and plausible assumption of great friendship for the government, and great loyalty to the Constitution and the laws, on the part of prominent Mormons. But it deceives no true American.

4. *The dangerous use that is made of their political privileges.* The priesthood train their people to vote in solid mass, and to regard the claims of the priesthood superior in every way to the claims of the government. The result is that no American has ever been allowed to take his seat in the Legislature. I say American in distinction from Mormon. Americans have been elected two or three times, but have not been allowed to take their seat, although Americans pay nearly one half the Territorial taxes. In Salt Lake City, although the non-Mormons are two fifths of the population, they are not allowed a single representative in the city government. To prevent this the twenty-one wards of the city are consolidated on the election-ticket. The political privileges possessed by the Mormons are used for no other purpose than to build up the interests of the priesthood which are in bitter hostility to the interests of the American people and their government. Indeed, a true and concise definition of Mormonism is simply this: An organized conspiracy against free government and good morals, carried on in the interest of a score of unscrupulous men calling themselves "the holy priesthood." Is it not time for the American people to say: *Down with such a conspiracy!*

5. Then the crowning danger of all is this assumption of supreme authority, here in the heart of the Republic, by a cunning and audacious priesthood which assumes to have power to open and shut the gates of heaven and hell. The people are required to consider this priesthood supreme over American government and law. They are made to swear the most terrible oaths of allegiance to this priesthood in the unclean Endowment-house. This is the essence of Mormonism. Not only a union of Church and State, but

such a union as merges the State into the Church. The Mormon priesthood is supreme in all civil and religious affairs. Polygamy is simply a little sprout on this poisonous tree. Defiance of the government is another sprout. Why should the American people fool away their time in trimming off these sprouts—sure to grow again? I say, in the name of patriotism and Christianity, *let them uproot the tree!* But how is this to be done?

Evidently, the first duty of the government is to take away the privileges of citizenship from every person who holds office under this hierarchy, on the ground that these privileges have been forfeited by their perversion to the upholding of a conspiracy against the government. A good beginning has been made in the Edmunds Bill, by disfranchising the polygamists. But every solid reason which can be assigned for such disfranchisement applies with far greater force to the disfranchisement of every one of the 23,000 members of this disloyal priesthood. A band of rattlesnakes in the Rocky Mountains, obstructing the path-way of American citizens, seems to me to have just as much right to the privileges of American citizenship as this band of priestly conspirators against American law and liberty here in Utah.

The most effectual way of depriving this priesthood of their forfeited privileges of citizenship, that I know of, is Governor Murray's plan of abolishing the Territorial Legislature, and substituting a Legislative Commission of about seven men, appointed by the President. Instead of filling this commission with adventurous politicians from the East, on a fat salary, I would have them taken from the intelligent and patriotic American residents of Utah, who are thoroughly familiar with the peculiar situation. And I would give them only a nominal salary, say of a thousand dollars a year. As a government measure this would be no more radical in principle than the present commission under the Edmunds Bill. And the present commission is a failure, both from their lack, as strangers, of a clear understanding of the peculiar state of affairs here, and because the fat salary of $5,000 for a few weeks' work tends to make them

indifferent as to how long this unsettled state of things shall continue. But with the legislative power in the hands of a commission of loyal Americans, with no election of Territorial officers at all, the Governors, the Judges, and the U. S. officials remaining as now, the government would then be in a condition to establish here the American free-school system, by means of the Legislative Commission, and could appropriate funds for that purpose.

But on such assemblies as yours at Ocean Grove we, who are contending for free government and Christian education in Utah, must depend for so informing and arousing public opinion that our legislators at Washington shall feel compelled to embody the intelligent and earnest opinions of the people in clear and vigorous Congressional enactment, which will uproot from the land this powerful and dangerous conspiracy.

Let me add to the foregoing the following encouraging statistics of the present condition of Christian work in Utah, for which I must tax my memory, the documents containing them being all in the city:

Five Protestant denominations are represented—the Episcopalian, Methodist, Presbyterian, Congregational, and Baptist, the last having come in only within the past eighteen months. There are about 42 ministers, 28 organized churches, and 1,100 communicants. They possess church and school property worth about $325,000. The school work is confined to the first four denominations mentioned. They have 58 schools in about 55 different towns, employing about 91 teachers, and educating upward of 4,000 pupils, three fourths of which pupils are from Mormon families.

There are about the same number of Sabbath-schools and Sabbath-school pupils. This entire Church and school work is carried on at an annual expense of about $120,000, about equally divided between the two departments. This is *what Christianity is doing for the redemption of Utah.* It is a suggestive question to ask: What is Rationalism or Infidelity doing?

Yours in behalf of Christian education and American liberty, ROBT. G. M'NIECE.

---

5. POLYGAMY WOMAN'S CREED OF MORMONISM.

MRS. ANGIE F. NEWMAN, LINCOLN, NEB.

PENDING the test of the constitutionality and efficiency of the Edmunds Bill comes the protest against infraction of the higher law of religious liberty.

Mormonism and polygamy are not identical.

Polygamy, not Mormonism, is the political problem. In this era of universal thinking, private opinion, injected into public thought, rapidly crystallizes into sentiment. Sentiment is the pivot upon which issues balance. To arrest sentiment touching the insidious recognition of the vile system which this protest implies, we shall attempt to show that polygamy is not only the Woman's Creed of Mormonism, but that it is the hostile flag run up to the American people. To cut it down, the Mormon hierarchy, in whose hands it is held, must be dethroned.

In the early creed of the Church of Latter-Day Saints it is true no polygamous tenet is recorded. The Mormons, at the inception of their order, were a simple, religious people, at variance with the Christian Church in form of worship rather than spirit. Britain was the scene of their greatest activity. At their General Conference Session, held in London in June, 1857, the conference statistics registered in Europe 50 conferences, 700 organized branches, and 6,000 men ordained to the priesthood. Not until nine years after Joseph Smith had promulgated his " Revelations " on " Celestial Marriage," and the apostles were living in its fruition, was the infamous document known in England. It was first published in the *Millennial Star*, a Liverpool Mormon paper, thence communicated to the missions by mail.

Once introduced, polygamy was the virus which corroded their spiritual life and became the disturbing element which threatened disintegration, so much so, that in Europe, in six months after its promulgation, from a membership of 31,000, 1,776 had apostatized. Woman being foremost in the revolt, the leaders got themselves to devise a revelation declaring polygamy essential to woman's salvation. How well they succeeded is shown in the fact that to-day polygamy is the key-stone in this whole structure of Mormonism. The difficulties which confront the Utah Commission in the execution of their work proves they have invaded a thoroughly-organized ecclesiastical system, such as the world has seldom seen.

The *very existence* and *perpetuity* of *this* system is made possible by enfranchised plural wives.

The Mormons teach paradise is an immediate or lower realm, where dwell angels and cherubim and the spirits of those who have died in other faiths. Here, there is no marrying nor giving in marriage. The *celestial kingdom* is the highest and polytheistic realm of the eternities. Polygamy is basal to the celestial kingdom. Here the holy priesthood of the Church of Latter-Day Saints sit upon thrones and are not angels, but are gods, as are Isaac and Jacob and Solomon. The family each possessed on earth shall be the nucleus of the kingdom which he rules, and the favored wife the queen who sits with him on the throne. Here, also, shall be marrying and giving in marriage, and they shall expand their dominions thereby throughout infinite ages. The saints and angels of heaven are subject to these, and shall per-

form for them the most menial offices because " they did not abide my law," that is, enter into polygamy on earth.

The *soul*, according to the Mormon theory, has three stages of existence.

1. The ante-natal.
2. The human.
3. The post-mortem.

To the perfection of a soul, the second state is necessary. Even the spirit of Christ himself was unfitted for celestial relations until he had passed the crucible of human life. So each pre-existing spirit is floating through space, waiting earthly tenement. Refusing to enter into polygamy, woman denies her Heavenly Father the opportunity to perfect a soul. This is the unpardonable sin for which she shall be damned.

She denies the waiting spirit earthly tabernacle—deprives it of eternal happiness by shutting it out of the celestial kingdom. For this, the loss of a soul, she shall be damned. She limits the radius of her husband's celestial kingship, for which she shall be damned. A more subtle device to enthrone man's lowest passions upon the altar of woman's religious life could not have been arranged elsewhere than in Satan's realm, or have been communicated by other than himself. It is a standing demonstration of the personality of his Satanic majesty. It involves every motive of the Moslem harem, the Hindoo suttee, the African slave jungles, or the American brothel. It is at once woman's subjugation, her high privilege, her political capital, her celestial exaltation.

" To provide for all contingencies, the proxy " and " spiritual " wife *régime* is adjusted. The proxy wife is the widow, who marries another Mormon for *time*, to be given over to the first husband in eternity. The proxy wife must be, at least, in part, self-supporting, and expect little attention from the husband unless he choose to give it. It is enough that he consents to raise up children to his *friend.* If no one is found willing to stand proxy to the widow, she forfeits the relation in heaven. Again, no marriage can be eternal except the ceremony has been performed in the Endowment House. Hence, if a widow has buried her husband before she reaches Salt Lake, and wishes to be his in eternity, she may first secure his transfer, from paradise to the celestial kingdom, by proxy baptism, (of which sacrament hereafter,) and then she enters the proxy marriage relation, which act insures to her dead husband the marriage relation in the kingdom, and the opportunity to build up a family of his own among the celestials, to which shall be added the children she has borne him on earth in the proxy relation. And thus a man may, by proxy marriage, secure the release and transfer of a deceased friend, or of the distinguished dead whom he would honor.

Spiritual wives are of two classes. The one is on the affinity theory. If the husband and wife are not kindred spirits, the wife, finding her affinity, may be secretly sealed to him for *all eternity*. Or, if the affinity does not last, they may be divorced and try again. Instances are recorded of "sealing" from three to nine husbands to true souls met. Sometimes a man is sealed to his first wife for eternity to gain her consent to take a second wife. If so, the first wife becomes the female head of his eternal kingdom.

The second class consists of old ladies of wealth, whose property needs protection, and "generous elders marry them and look after that same property." She will be his *real* wife when she is "rejuvenated" in eternity, "which prospect," says an authority, "is very fascinating, for I have known very youthful elders display their self-sacrifice by marrying very old but very wealthy ladies."

Eliza Snow is the most notable woman in the Mormon Church. She was a plural wife of Joseph Smith and a proxy wife of Brigham Young. She personates *Eve* in the marriage ceremony of the Endowment House, is on the editorial staff of the *Woman's Exponent*; a poetess of merit, she has written many of the sacred hymns of the Church, has been to Palestine to establish Mormonism within its sacred boundaries, and has written a history of her travels. In manner she is gentle, persuasive, dignified. In a close conversation with the writer upon the sanctity of polygamy, she said: "The holy men of old entered into polygamy to build up an earthly kingdom, and *we* to build up a heavenly. Nowhere are words of censure written against Rachel for becoming the second wife—or against her *sister* Leah for the strategy she used in securing a husband, nor against either for giving their handmaids to Jacob; nor yet against Jacob for receiving them. Rachel's children were the boys, Joseph and Benjamin, whom God honored; but he first blessed Leah with sons because she was hated of Rachel. The sons of the handmaids, moreover, were not illegitimate —they were counted among the twelve." "Yes," said I, "but Christ instituted the better system of monogamy." "You believe in Christ?" There was an earnestness in her dark eyes that was incomprehensible, as she answered: "How have *you* read the gospels, that you do not know Christ himself was a polygamist, Bethany his earthly home, the *sisters* Martha and Mary his plural wives, Mary Magdalen another, and the favorite, for she was with him at the cross and the sepulcher?" Eliza Snow *believes*, and hence she draws many a faltering young girl into the fearful maelstrom by the magic of her resistless touch.

The sophistry of the Mormon theory of an improved race under the polygamic *régime* has proof in their offspring, without collat-

eral evidence. It may be read, without an interpreter, in the distorted figure, the blank, soulless eye, the inelastic steps, of the Mormon youth; in whom there is an entire absence of character.

A Saturday afternoon in Zion's Co-operative Mercantile Institution, where they did, last year, a business of $4,500,000, will convince any doubter of the low grade of the common people. These country women, looking themselves as though they had been exhumed from some charnel-house of the Middle Ages, its mold still hanging upon them and hiding in their frayed garments, come, dragging troops of half-clad, wretched children, who hide in each tattered fold, and shrink if one speaks softly to them. They are as untutored as the coyotes of the sage brush. The only thing which saves the Mormon people from race annihilation or imbecility is the constant influx of other nationalities. These are mainly from the vigorous laboring classes who, *per se*, must survive a generation or two. No Hindu or Moslem harem, no hut of savage or camp of debauchee, furnishes such a type of polygamy. The marriage of two sisters in a single day to one husband is no novelty, nor yet the marriage of the mother to the husband of her daughter. Where longevity permits, the Mormon patriarch may have the grandmother, mother, and the daughter as wives at the same time. The Greek tragedy repeats itself. The son marries the mother, not by accident, but design, and neither Œdipus puts out his own eyes, nor Jocasta hangs herself for shame. All this is done in the name of religion. "All souls are begotten of the gods before they come to the earth for tabernacles or bodies." Hence any union is justifiable so the souls, weary of floating through space, be furnished tabernacles.

There is an abundance of testimony bearing on this phase of Mormonism, but it is too gross to be reproduced—sworn affidavits which have been circulated in current literature in Salt Lake without protest or denial by the Mormon Church; and yet, such is the loyalty to the order of this system, that in these very homes, if death stand at the bedside of the first-born, the mother must meet her agony alone. If the father be spending the week with another wife, though only a board partition separate him from the scene, he must not be disturbed. So of the wife. She may come to the verge of the valley *alone*, even though her husband be so high in virtue as to sit in the halls of Congress and frame laws for the less enlightened.

That there are women who, through all this, stand inimical to the laxity of morals engendered by the system, and to death keep the sanctity of marriage, only proves the intensity of their religious life. These may be recognized when met by the compressed lips, the pallid cheeks, the wild, averted eyes, which seem to stand as sentinels at the bolted doors of the soul, to give no sign of the conflict within. These women have, as martyrs, laid upon the altar of the Church that one indivisible treasure which God intended should be hers in its entirety—the love of one strong, manly heart. To be sheltered thus is to be beyond the swoop of the angry storm, where the spent thunder may be heard, but cannot break. To open this defense to another, and another, and another, is to invite the lightning's flash and the black line of its fatal trail. Many a trembling hand has lifted the latch which has withered in the effort, and the palsied heart has given no tale to the bloodless lips. Dumb before that shrine on which the fires are now kindled by stranger and unwelcome hands, she watches the lurid blaze with hollow eyes which "murder sleep" and wonder if the thorns which, in her side do prick and sting her, are the only materials which compose a crown. Then passes before her wandering eyes a dim vision of that other crown, the spear, the blood, the agony. This is her Gethsemane. The disciple is not above his Lord; she falls upon her knees by the deserted altar on which these strange fires are still burning, and mutters, in broken syllables, "Not my will, but thine, be done." O, strange infatuation! a curse on those blind guides who ensnare innocence for lust and teach immortal honors; who decoy young lambs into this jungle to enfold them to bosoms filled with barbed arrows. The shepherds of this flock are abroad in the land. There's not a green pasture on God's footstool these marauders have not traced. That they have gleaned faster than we know we shall presently show.

The Mormon apology, that polygamy disposes of the social evil, is equally fallacious. Eminent jurists and Christian writers, resident in Salt Lake, assert there is "more private prostitution and illegitimacy in Utah than in any other place in the civilized world." Further than this, almost every home is an "establishment." There is no need of closed doors and darkened windows to designate its character, for the Church has set its seal of approval, and all things are legitimate. "Some two years ago an investigation of the subject of plural marriages was made by a committee, at the request of a society in the East, and, from the facts obtained, the conclusion was reached that about eighty per cent. of the plural marriages were necessitated by previous immorality." Two classes of men enter into polygamy—the ambitious and the gross. Every office in the Church or Territory is held by a polygamist. Thus the lust of the flesh and the lust of office are co-partners.

Two classes of women, also, are attracted to the system: 1. The illiterate peasantry, upon whom great honor is conferred in being chosen as wives to God's—elect. 2. The highly sensitive, over-wrought, religious enthusiast. The number of women proselytes is, by far, the greater. This is due to woman's credulity and the dominance of religious sentiment.

Empire is the colossal dream of the Mormon hierarchy. To insure its fulfillment, they have built an iron-clad, ecclesiastical system, vulnerable at no point from within, and capable of great resistance to outward attack. It is a theocracy of president and councilors, of bishop and apostles, of prophets, priests, and elders, organized of God and serving in accordance with *special revelation.* Nevertheless, these inspired autocrats resort to intrigue impossible to men less holy. They devise plausible schemes to build up and perpetuate their temporal power, in the execution of which individual liberty is a lost atom. They excommunicate and anathematize, they "blood atone" or send to the nethermost hell the violators of their decrees. The absolutism of man-power is nowhere in the civilized world so complete, or its sway so despotic. The inauguration of any civil measure which promises enlarged liberty to the people is sure to involve the conservation of priestly tyranny. For such a purpose and to such end was *the elective franchise extended to woman!* The practical sagacity of Brigham Young enabled him to foresee the loss of civil power to the Church by the influx of Gentile population, following the completion of the U. P. R. R. and the development of mining interests.

The ballot was put in the hands of Mormon women to avert this disaster. Its very exercise is tyranny. The Territorial law was amended to read, "every male citizen and his wife." If a man marry a girl of twelve to-day, to-morrow she is qualified to vote. The religious services of the Mormon Church are held in the Tabernacle (which has a seating capacity of 12,000) on Sunday morning, and in the ward meeting-houses in the evening. On Sunday eve before election, *at these meetings,* the printed ballot is put into the hands of the voter; and no one *dares* vote other than the Church ticket. Salt Lake has twenty-one wards. The election is general. Should any one ward have a Gentile majority, it is lost in the general aggregate. If a Mormon have seven or twenty wives who, for reasons, cannot go to the polls, he votes the seven or twenty tickets, *plus* his own. There is standard and multiplied Mormon authority for the statement that *babes* are entered in the voting list. Ann Eliza Young says: "Every person of the female sex, from the babe in the arms to the oldest bedridden imbecile crone, have the elective franchise." "The most hateful part of it is, they are helping to tighten their own bonds, and are doing it, too, under compulsion." Mrs. Stenhouse adds testimony: "Brother

Brigham, instead of having his own single vote, would have nineteen for his nineteen wives, to say nothing of his daughters and his whole army of spiritual wives which he might produce." "I have seen one solitary man driving into the city a whole wagon-load of women of all ages and sizes—they were going to the polls, and their votes would be *one.*" It must be borne in mind these ladies have spoken and written of their experience, and no Mormon has dared assail their statements.

A writer in the February number of the *Anti-Polygamy Standard,* published in Salt Lake, says: "The masses of the people cast a ballot or *cut* a throat from precisely the same motive—the duty of obedience to Church superiors—and, consequently, not one in ten thousand, male or female, understand the responsibility attached to the free exercise of the ballot."

But, it is asked, if polygamy involves mental as well as physical courage, why did the Mormon women flood Congress with petitions against its suppression? For precisely the same reason, it is the behest of the Church sovereigns. During the Grant administration, a monster petition was sent Mrs. Grant by the Female Relief Society, of Salt Lake, asking her influence with the President in favor of polygamy. Eliza Snow inaugurated the plan. "Hundreds of names were copied from the books of the society without any permission being obtained, or even asked, of their owners—and the names of those who had been *dead* many years were added." The same coercion was exercised in the petition sent to Congress after the introduction of the Edmunds Bill. The Salt Lake *Tribune* published the following concerning the method of obtaining these signatures:

"In every village and hamlet in Utah last night men were tramping about with the petitions. Telegraphic dispatches went forth from the Church to complete the work in a single night, and there was not a Mormon house or cabin in the Territory that was not visited by vile-minded curs asking little children to indorse their own shame and their parents'. These signatures will be all collected in Salt Lake, and a monster petition, several hundred feet long, will be sent to Congress, calling upon it to forbear to strike the blow. While the petition is going, thousands of mothers who compelled their children to sign because they *dare not do any thing else* will be on their knees praying for a happy deliverance from polygamy and better days for Utah. Each school was canvassed, and every little boy and girl old enough to hold a pen was required to sign. If they could not make a legible scrawl, the teachers or bishops would get permission to write the names for them. The children looked upon the thing as a sort of diversion which broke the monotony of the regular

10

routine of school life, and had the petition memorialized Congress to give them all the small-pox the signing would have gone on just the same."

Again, the inquiry is put, "Why, if polygamy has no redeeming element, do notable women of Mormonism lecture in its behalf in a crisis like the present?" One of the missionaries, who is now on a lecturing tour, is Mrs. Zina D. Young, wife of the deceased President. She has spoken in Washington and been "presented" to many members of Congress. A "Mother" gives in the February number of the *Anti-Polygamy Standard* Sister Zina's private views on the subject. A friend, whose husband had taken a second wife, went to Mrs. Young for counsel: "Tell me, Sister Zina," said she, "tell me honestly, for you are so much wiser and holier than I am, does the fault lie in myself that I am so miserable ; or is the system to blame for it? I have prayed long and earnestly for submission, and if the trouble arises from the wickedness of my own heart I am ready to die, if necessary, to expiate that sin, for I cannot live in this agony any longer." Zina replied :

"Sister, you are not to blame, neither are you the only woman who is suffering torments on account of polygamy. There are women in this very house (Brigham Young's) *whose hearts are full of hell,* and in that room yonder," pointing to a door, "is a woman who has been a perfect fury ever since Brother Young married Sister Amelia Folsom. *Brigham Young dare not enter that room, or she would tear his eyes out.* It is the system that is to blame for it, but we must try and be as patient as we can." And yet Sister Zina, who has seen a house full of women with hell in their hearts on account of polygamy, goes now around the country preaching the doctrine. Mothers of America, for God's sake, shield your innocent lambs from these decoying wolves !

And this is from the pen of one who drinks to the dregs of this poisoned chalice which is held to her lips by *other* hands, because in it is the elixir of life eternal.

It is evident from the foregoing that the political status which polygamic relations have given woman has neither broadened her sphere nor dignified the State. The ballot in Utah is no synonym for liberty. Its use has brought about a condition of things of which American slavery furnished no parallel, the serfdom of no despotic countries can equal.

It is a condition which calls less for sentiment and more for action ; less for the divine, and more for the human, effort. Let the woman heart which clamors, the woman hand which frames petitions for civil rights to her sex, beware lest, is so doing, she inflict civil wrongs which may awaken in her own soul Macbeth's despairing cry,

" Will all great Neptune's ocean wash this blood Clean from my hand ?"

For, be it remembered, many a noble-hearted woman, in playing her part in this travesty of freedom, bends her neck to the stroke in the same spirit as did that dauntless woman of the French republic, Madame Roland. The scaffold had been erected at the foot of the Statue of Liberty. Madame Roland had ascended. Her head was about to be laid upon the guillotine. A wild protest was surging through her brain. She called for pencil and paper, and, with the last pulse-beat of her impassioned soul, she hurled upon her persecutors that startling anathema which still rings in the ear of the oppressor, " O Liberty! what deeds are done in thy name."

The following are some of the letters received during the session of the Assembly.

Rev. T. C. ILIFF, D.D., Superintendent Methodist Missions in Utah, says :
Rev. J. C. HARTZELL, D.D.
Dear Brother: In reply to your favor of the 12th, I am forced to plead want of time as the excuse for not complying with your request to furnish a paper setting forth what I may regard as the most dangerous facts in Mormonism, and the chief duty of the government in the premises. I am just now, and will be, very busy till the annual meeting of Utah Mission, Aug. 2, preparing full reports of this charge and of the entire work.

I heartily approve of your giving a day to a question that not only deeply concerns this Territory, but which, soon or later, must interest the whole country, and, unless speedily adjusted, must affect the honor, if not the security, of the national government.

Of one thing be assured: this Utah problem is not only unsolved, but its solution is becoming more and more difficult each year. The Edmunds Bill is powerless to correct the evil of polygamy. And, so far as it may have any political significance, it can do but little toward changing the situation. The people will continue to vote as instructed by their bishops and teachers, and the offices filled according to priestly dictation. I have no hope of any satisfactory settlement of the Mormon question until the general government "means business." In the meantime, the Christian Church must plant a line of sentinels up and down these rich valleys, keeping the tryst of a glowing evangelism.

Hon. WM. F. WELCKER, Superintendent Public Instruction, California, says:
No persons have a right to set up a system of religion the observance of which involves a constant and deliberate violation of the laws of the land. Still less have others the right to come from abroad into that land to aid in such a purpose. It was the duty many years ago, of the federal government to have suppressed all those practices of the Mormons which were unlawful. Every day of delay but augments the difficulty of the task, prolongs crime and demoralization, and increases the amount of human suffering when the suppression shall come, as come it must.

Hon. CORNELIUS HEDGES, Superintendent Public Instruction, Montana, writes:
As to the Mormons, I feel profoundly the danger and humiliation to which we are exposed from this direction. I should not consider the introduction of cannibalism as one half as dangerous as the degradation that attends upon polygamy. National legislation thus far has been only trifling. We should repeal the Organic Act of Utah and place all the Mormons under martial law, quarantine against them as we would those who had leprosy, small-pox, or yellow fever.

On motion of Rev. J. C. HARTZELL, D.D., the National Education Assembly of 1883 adopted the following :

Resolved, That it is the duty of the American nation to wipe out as speedily as possible that damning spot which curses Utah and adjacent Territories known as polygamous Mormonism, and that we call upon the government to renew the policy of President Hayes by which the importation of emigrants from Europe for polygamous purposes be prohibited.

Resolved, That we look with horror upon the fact that scores of Mormon agents are at work among the ignorant and superstitious whites of the Southern States, and are annually shipping to Utah hundreds whom they deceive.

6. THE DOCTRINES OF MORMONISM.

REV. THEOPHILUS B. HILTON, A.M., B.D.,

Late Principal of Salt Lake Seminary.

THE principal books whence the theology and doctrines of the "Church of Jesus Christ of Latter-Day Saints" are derived are the following:

(1) The Bible. (2) "The Book of Mormon." (3) "Doctrines and Covenants." (4) "Materialism." (5) "Celestial Marriage." (6) "Key to Theology." (7) "Spencer's Letters." (8) "The Voice of Warning." (9) "Mormon Doctrine; or, Leaves from the Tree of Life." (10) "Catechism for Children." (11) "The Women of the Bible," and (12) "The Pearl of Great Price."

Mormonism teaches that:

1. God is a person, with the form of a man clothed with flesh and blood.

2. Jesus Christ is the first-born Son of God; a perfect and sinless man, but not equal with the Father.

3. The Holy Ghost is a person possessed with the Spirit of the Father.

4. All men born into this world are spirits from another sphere sent into this world as probationers for a higher state of existence after death.

5. Man is not naturally depraved, is not born in sin, and is not responsible for any sin but his own.

6. Man is a free agent, and is fully responsible, and will be held accountable for his sins.

7. There are four orders of beings: (a) Gods, who are immortal spirits, perfect in organization of soul and body. This will be the final state of *men* who have lived on the earth in a perfect state of obedience to law. (b) Angels, who are immortal beings who have lived on the earth in a state of imperfect obedience to law. (c) Men, who are immortal beings in whom a living soul is united to a living body. (d) Spirits, who are immortal beings, and fill the air, waiting to be supplied with bodies. The millions that fill the air around our globe compose only one of the many colonies of spirits.

The immortal part, or spirit, of all who die in this world goes into prison, or an intermediate state. The gospel (of Mormonism) is and will be proclaimed by angels to all the spirits in prison. All who receive that gospel will be saved; all who reject it will be damned to all eternity.

Mormonism teaches the doctrine of the witness of the Spirit and the gift of the Holy Ghost. God reveals his will not only by Scripture revelation, but by the word of his mouth or by the voice of an angel. God comes in contact with all true believers, revealing his will by his Spirit, or by an angel, or in his own person in dreams, visions, and impressions. God comes to his people just as he came to the ancient saints, talking face to face with his children. The Bible is God's revealed Word, but is not a complete and full revelation of God's will concerning his children. Hence the necessity of supplemental revelation. God spoke in a special manner to Joseph Smith; he speaks to his successors and his followers, guiding them in all the concerns of life. The Holy Ghost is bestowed by baptism, the rite being administered by a Mormon priest of the Order of Melchizedek.

The gift of the Holy Ghost bestows miraculous power, power to speak in tongues, foretell the future, heal the sick, cast out devils, cure the maimed, give sight to the blind; in a word, to perform miracles of every kind.

In cases of healing, the afflicted is restored by anointing with consecrated olive oil, and by laying on of hands, accompanied with prayer.

This rite, or ceremony, is quite similar, if not identical, with that performed by Dr. Cullis, of Boston, for similar purposes.

Mormonism teaches that, at the end of time, this earth will be purified and made a new earth. That Jesus Christ will appear to judge the world and reign in righteousness.

There are two orders of the priesthood—the Aaronic and Melchizedek. The latter is eternal. The Mormon priests maintain that they hold the keys of heaven. That their organization is the only true Church of God. That John Taylor, the successor of Joseph Smith and Brigham Young, is God's vice-gerent on earth, and the head of the true Church and only authoritative priesthood on the earth. Whatsoever is loosed on earth by this priesthood is loosed in heaven, and whatsoever is bound on earth is bound in heaven.

The following are the "Articles of Faith," as drawn up by "Joseph the Seer," published in "Times and Seasons," (vol. iii, p. 709:)

"We believe in God the Eternal Father, and in his son Jesus Christ, and in the Holy Ghost. We believe that men will be punished for their own sins, and not for Adam's transgression. We believe that, through the atonement of Christ, all mankind may be saved by obedience to the laws and ordinances of the Gospel. We believe that these ordinances are: First, Faith in the Lord Jesus Christ; second, Repentance; third, Baptism by immersion for the remission of sins; fourth, Laying on of hands for the gift of the Holy Ghost. We believe that a man must be called of God by prophecy, and by laying on of hands by those who are in authority, to preach the Gospel and administer in the ordinances thereof. We believe in the same organization that existed in the primitive Church, namely: Apostles, prophets, pastors, teachers, evangelists, etc. We believe in the gift of tongues, prophecy, revelation, visions, healing, interpretation of tongues, etc. We believe the Bible to be the word of God, as far as it is translated correctly; we also believe the Book of Mormon to be the word of God. We believe all that God has revealed, all that he does now reveal, and we believe that he will yet reveal many great and important things pertaining to the kingdom of God. We believe in the literal gathering of Israel, and in the restoration of the Ten Tribes; that Zion will be built upon this continent; that Christ will reign personally upon the earth, and that the earth will be renewed and receive its paradisaic glory. We claim the privilege of worshiping Almighty God according to the dictates of our conscience, and allow all men the same privilege, let them worship how, where, or what they may. We believe in being subject to kings, presidents, rulers, and magistrates, in obeying, honoring, and sustaining the law. We believe in being honest, true, chaste, benevolent, virtuous, and in doing good to all men; indeed, we may say that we follow the admonition of Paul: We believe all things, we hope all things, we have endured many things, and hope to be able to endure all things. If there is any thing virtuous, lovely, or of good report, or praiseworthy, we seek after these things.

"JOSEPH SMITH."

THEFT AND ROBBERY.

Mormonism teaches theft and robbery. I do not say every Mormon is a thief and a robber, for some men are better than their creeds. But I do affirm that Mormonism teaches that to rob and steal for Christ's sake is well pleasing to God.

The 'robber-bands of Nauvoo and the plundering expeditions of the Mormons while in Missouri, and their extensive pillaging of emigrants since they have been in Utah, are the practical results of Mormon doctrine.

John D. Lee, a bishop of the Mormon Church, who was convicted and shot for participation in the Mountain Meadow massacre, an atrocious murder ordered by the Mormon Church, says, in his confessions, page 72:

"The Mormons made an attack on Gallatin one night, and carried off much plunder. I was not there with them, but I

talked often with those that were, and learned all the facts about it. The town was burned down, and every thing of value, including the goods in two stores, was carried off by the Mormons. I often escaped being present with the troops on their thieving expeditions by loaning my horses and arms to others who liked that kind of work better than I did. . . . Men stole simply for the love of stealing. Such inexcusable acts of lawlessness had the effect to arouse every Gentile in the three counties of Caldwell, Carroll, and Daviess, as well as to bring swarms of armed Gentiles from other localities."

Lee is loud in his lamentations over the evil deeds of the Mormons. On pp. 157-160 he gives an account of several murders committed in and near Nauvoo by order and sanction of the authorities of the Mormon Church. He clearly shows that murder was a Mormon method of getting rid of those who were in any way offensive to the Mormon saints, or whose property was needed for Church purposes and could not be obtained as an offering.

BLOOD ATONEMENT.

Mormonism teaches the doctrine of Blood Atonement. This doctrine may be briefly stated as follows: There are sins so offensive to God that the transgressor cannot receive forgiveness unless his life is taken and his blood poured upon the ground as an offering to appease the wrath of God. If a Mormon becomes an apostate, or even weak in the faith, that one, in order to be saved, must have his throat cut and his blood spilled upon the ground.

This doctrine is taught and believed by all good Mormons. It has been enforced in the past in Utah, and would be practiced to-day were it not for Gentile influence.

Did the Mormon leaders ever teach the doctrine of Blood Atonement?

George Q. Cannon said to the Washington correspondent of the Inter-Ocean: "There has been a great deal of talk about the doctrine of blood atonement. This talk originates in the fact that we do not believe in hanging. We think that if a man sheds blood, his blood should be shed by execution. In Utah Territory a criminal who has been sentenced to death can elect whether he shall be shot or hung. This fact has furnished a basis for all the talk about blood atonement. It does not follow that because we believe a man who kills another should have his blood shed each Mormon is going to be the executioner. It is a process of law, and has no reference to any Church ordinance."

The following is taken from a discourse delivered by Brigham Young in the Tabernacle, Salt Lake City, February 8, 1857:

"Brother Cummins told you the truth this

morning with regard to the sins of his people. And I will say that the time will come, and is now nigh at hand, when those who profess our faith, if they are guilty of what some of this people are guilty of, will find the ax laid at the root of the tree, and they will be hewn down. What has been must be again, for the Lord is coming to restore all things. The time has been in Israel under the law of God, the celestial law, for it is one of the laws of that kingdom where our Father dwells that is near at hand. But now I say, in the name of the Lord, that, if this people will sin no more, but faithfully live their religion, their sins will be forgiven them without taking life. You are aware that when Brother Cummins came to the point of loving our neighbors as ourselves, he could say yes or no as the case might be; that is true. But I want you to connect it with the doctrine you read in the Bible. When will we love our neighbor as ourselves? In the first place, Jesus said that no man hateth his own flesh. It is admitted by all that every person loves himself. Now, if we do rightly love ourselves, we want to be saved and continue to exist; we want to go into the kingdom where we can enjoy eternity and see no more sorrow nor death. This is the desire of every person who believes in God. Now take a person in this congregation who has knowledge with regard to being saved in the kingdom of God and our Father, and, being exalted, one who knows and understands the principles of eternal life, and sees the beauty and the excellency of the eternities before him compared with the vain and foolish things of the world, and suppose that he is overtaken in a gross fault, that he has committed a sin that he knows will deprive him of that exaltation which he desires, and that he cannot attain to it without the shedding of his blood, and also knows that by having his blood shed he will atone for that sin, and be saved and exalted with the gods, is there a man or woman in this house but what would say, ' Shed my blood that I may be saved and exalted with the gods?' All mankind love themselves; and let these principles be known to an individual, and he would be glad to have his blood shed. That would be loving themselves even unto an eternal exaltation. Will you love your brothers or sisters likewise when they have committed a sin that cannot be atoned for without the shedding of their blood? That is what Jesus Christ meant. . . . I have seen scores and hundreds of people for whom there would have been a chance (in the last resurrection there will be) if their lives had been taken and their blood spilled on the ground as a smoking incense to the Almighty, but who are now angels to the devil, until our elder brother Jesus Christ raises them up—conquers death, hell, and the grave. I have known a great many men

who have left this Church for whom there is no chance whatever for exaltation; but if their blood had been spilled it would have been better for them. The wickedness and ignorance of the nations forbid this principle being in full force, but the time will come when the laws of God will be in full force. This is loving our neighbor as ourselves; if he needs help, help him; and if he wants salvation, and it is necessary to spill his blood on the earth in order that he may be saved, spill it. Any of you who understand the principles of eternity, if you have sinned a sin requiring the shedding of blood, except the sin unto death, would not be satisfied nor rest until your blood should be spilled, that you might gain that salvation you desire. That is the way to love mankind."

Remarks by President Heber C. Kimball, delivered in the Bowery, Salt Lake City, August 16, 1857:

" I do not feel vain, but I feel to say, brethren and sisters, lay aside your vanity and your feelings to exult; there will be a time when you can exult and do it in righteousness and mercy. There will also be a day when you will be brought to the test— when your very hearts and your inmost souls will melt within you because of the scenes that many of you will witness. Yes, you will be brought to that test, when you will feel as if every thing within you would dissolve. Then will be the time you will be tried whether you will stand the test or fall away. I have not a doubt but there will be hundreds who will leave us and go away to our enemies. I wish they would go this fall: it might relieve us from much trouble; for if men turn traitors to God and his servants, their blood will surely be shed, or else they will be damned, and that, too, according to the covenants."

The Mormon leaders assert that " the word of Brigham Young or the priesthood is the word of the Lord."

To prove the prevarication and dishonesty of George Q. Cannon in his interview with an *Inter-Ocean* correspondent, we cited several paragraphs from the sermons of Brigham Young and Heber C. Kimball, as published in the standard or authorized works of the "Church." We proved conclusively that such doctrine of blood atonement is a fundamental principle of salvation in the Mormon "Church," as well as showed the duplicity, cunning, and false statements of George Q. Cannon, First Vice-President of the Church of Jesus Christ of Latter-Day Saints. No Mormon of intelligence dare deny the publication of such teachings by the "Church," for they have been published to the world. No doubt Cannon and others could heartily wish they had not been published, for they stand a lasting disgrace, and a horrible feature in the system pretended to be molded according to the teachings of the meek and lowly Jesus. But the words can never be erased. The facts cannot be annihilated. "What is written is written." The great wonder is that George Q. Cannon—that any man—can unblushingly deny that this horrible doctrine was taught and is still believed, for the masses of the Mormon people believe in it fully, but are restrained from practicing it by public opinion, the Christian influences that surround them, and fear of the national laws.

Ashamed of their teaching, as they may be, as their denial seems to indicate, it is nevertheless true that blood atonement was a doctrine taught and practiced by them, is believed by them now, and would be practiced and rigorously enforced, if only circumstances of isolation and ability permitted. The few selections that we made, taken from the so-called sermons of Brigham Young and Heber C. Kimball—many more can be produced—seem harsh, severe, cruel, and horrible to Christian, or even moral, minds; they cause a shudder of horror to all who read them. But we know, from positive and direct information which admits of no denial, that the discourses, as delivered on the stand in the Bowery and Tabernacle by Young and Kimball and others, were much more cruel, wicked, and bloodthirsty than they appear in the printed works. Many testify that it was blood-curdling to hear them when spoken. The Mormon leaders taught the people that God was a great Moloch, greedy for human flesh, and thirsting for human blood.

The "sermons" were reported by G. D. Watt and J. V. Long, in phonographic shorthand, and they, when transcribing for the printer, left out many blasphemous and bloody expressions, unfit for the public eye. Then these reporters placed the corrected manuscripts in the hands of Albert Carrington, who was then Brigham Young's confidential clerk or private secretary, and who was also the editor of the *Deseret News*. He pruned the manuscripts thoroughly, cutting out many severe and bloodthirsty passages, so that the "sermons" might appear less disgusting and less distasteful to the public eye—Brigham Young asserting that it was "not well to give too strong meat to the world." This cutting down and pruning by the reporters and the editor of the *Deseret News*, "for wise purposes," offended Heber C. Kimball very much, and he publicly and privately complained that "they have taken the music out of my speeches."

Thus we learn that the "sermons" by the triumvirate — Young, Kimball, and Jeddy Grant —were unfit for moral ears or even worldly eyes, and in fact were really diabolical. They are bad, very bad, as now published, but what must they have been when blurted out without let or hinderance by those ungodly fanatics! Let not the Mormons forget this pruning process; this cutting down

and patching up to make "sermons" appear decent; and let them henceforth never deny, but own with blushing, that direct blood atoning was and *is* one of the cardinal doctrines of salvation in the "Church" of Jesus Christ of Latter-Day Saints.

TREASON.

A belief that the government of the United States ought to be overthrown is one of the leading doctrines of the Mormon Church. Treason against the government of the United States is preached in every tabernacle and meeting-house in Utah.

A multitude of quotations like the following might be given. Brigham Young said, in a discourse in 1856:

"It is not the prerogative of the President of the United States to meddle with this matter, and Congress is not allowed, according to the Constitution, to legislate upon it. If we introduce the practice of polygamy, it is not their prerogative to meddle.... I say, as the Lord lives, we are bound to become a sovereign State in the Union, or an independent nation by ourselves; and let them drive us from this place if they can. If they get rid of polygamy, they will have to expend three hundred million dollars for a prison, and roof it over from the Rocky Mountains to the Sierra Nevadas. The sound of polygamy is a terror to the pretended republican governments. Why? Because this work is destined to revolutionize the world, and bring all under subjection."

Orson Pratt has said:

"There is another reason why this plurality should exist among the Latter-Day Saints: We believe that the nations of the earth are doomed to destruction; we believe that, according to Mormon revelation, given in the Book of Doctrines and Covenants, that the sword of the vengeance of the Almighty is already unsheathed and stretched out, and will no more be put back into the scabbard until it falls upon the head of nations, until they are destroyed. We believe that the Saints are being gathered to Zion from among the nations, to become the instruments in the Lord's hand of accomplishing his will."

Mormonism is hostile to our institutions and disloyal to our government, declaring, by President Brigham Young, that the politico-ecclesiastical government of the Mormon Church "circumscribes the government of this world."

And again declaring, by the chief of its twelve apostles, "that all governments, save the government of the Mormon Church, are *unauthorized* and *illegal*, while any people attempting to govern themselves by laws of their own making and officers of their own appointing are in direct rebellion against the kingdom of God."

The following will illustrate their attitude toward our officers: The Sunday following the reception of the news in Utah that President Garfield was shot and mortally wounded, when every loyal heart was aching, and every loyal head was bowed in sorrow, Hugh S. Gowans, a leading Mormon, said to a large congregation in Tooele: "President Garfield will soon be dead; this is what we have been praying for. Our prayers are being answered. Garfield raised his hand against polygamy; therefore God Almighty struck him down." Hundreds in the congregation shouted, Amen! Amen!

OBEDIENCE TO THE PRIESTHOOD.

The inspiration of, and obedience to, the priesthood is one of the essential doctrines of Mormonism.

Obedience to their leaders is an absolute requirement, and extends to all the acts of life. A member of the Mormon Church has no right to leave the Territory of Utah without first obtaining *permission* of President Taylor.

The members of the Mormon Church are under oath not only to pray, not only to vote, as the priesthood may dictate, but they have sworn to obey absolutely all commands, even to the taking of life. The blind dupes of Mormonism yield implicit obedience. To refuse to obey even counsel is almost unthinkable to the mind of the zealous Mormon. A few leaders govern with great rigor, I might say with tyranny, the souls and bodies, the energies and earnings, of their superstitious followers. The hierarchy hold the people in a grip from which nothing has been able to release them.

POLYGAMY.

The doctrine of polygamy is *not* an *essential* principle of Mormonism, but is certainly one of the leading doctrines of the Mormon Church. And to the *men* who are zealous Mormons it is one of the most precious revelations of their great prophet.

And the doctrine grows more precious in proportion to the growth of the animal nature. In fact, polygamy was born of inspired animalism.

The theory of polygamy is that the atmosphere around our globe is full of spirits, forming one of the many colonies of spiritual beings. These spirits are vehemently clamoring for bodies, and if we had microscopic ears we could hear the piercing wail of these spirits pleading for bodies. It is the duty of men and women to exert themselves to the utmost to supply these spirits with bodies.

Polygamy, or plurality of wives, is ordained of God and given to Joseph Smith by revelation. Mormonism teaches that "it is the duty of a woman to give other wives to her husband, even as Sarah gave Hagar to Abraham. But if she refuse, then it shall be lawful for the husband to take other wives without her consent, and she shall be destroyed for her disobedience."

Mormonism teaches that "no woman can secure exaltation in heaven unless united in marriage to a Latter-Day Saint of the Mormon Church."

Mormonism teaches that God is not only a man, but a married man; that he was married cycles of ages ago, and all beings in the universe are his natural offspring by his numerous wives. Men are a race of gods in embryo, and are eligible to celestial thrones. The greater the number of wives and children a man has in this world, the greater will be his kingdom in the future world.

Some Mormons are married for time and eternity, and their union will never cease. Others are married for time only, and death separates them, and in eternity they will live with other parties.

It has often occurred in Utah that those married for time only have been sealed to other married persons for eternity. This has been the cause of much immorality. One case will serve to illustrate thousands. A young couple were married for time only, and living but a short distance from my house in Salt Lake City. The young man was an industrious mechanic. His wife was young and quite attractive. A Mormon bishop cast lustful eyes upon her, and they were "sealed" for eternity. The bishop was only human, and it was human to *anticipate* the joys of eternity, and the young wife was induced, partially by promises of the Mormon bishop, whom she supposed a man of God, and partially by threats, to allow him to become her husband in practice, if not in name. When these relations were discovered by the young husband, by an accident, of course he was heart-broken, and found relief by being sent on a mission to England. This is only one case out of a multitude of similar ones.

Mormonism teaches that God has many wives, and that Jesus Christ is his first-born son by his first wife, and in a special sense is God's heir, and the eldest brother of the human family.

Mormonism teaches that Jesus Christ was married to the sisters Mary and Martha, and to Mary Magdalene, and is now living with them in the celestial world.

Mormons believe not only in the fatherhood of God, but also in the motherhood of God.

In regard to some of these relations, Mormonism teaches such strange and horrible doctrines I dare not even repeat them—I tread on the verge of blasphemy against the Holy Ghost.

In Utah marriage between brother and sister has taken place, and men have treated their own daughters as if they were their wives.

These things, as far as I know, are *not* common. But it is a thing of frequent occurrence for a man to marry his nieces, not only one at a time, but all of them. It is a common thing for a man to marry a whole family of sisters. Many a man in Utah has married his mother-in-law. I know of a number of cases where a mother, daughter, and granddaughter are all married to the same man, and all living with him as wives and bearing children. Disraeli used to say, " It is the unexpected that happens." In Utah it is the incredible, the unthinkable, that happens daily.

The following quotations are taken from published sermons which were preached in Utah some years ago, and are now referred to more or less every Sunday by Mormons as final authority on the question of polygamy.

Heber Kimball said :

" How long do you suppose it will be before my posterity increases to over a million ? A hundred years will not pass before I will become millions myself. Brother Brigham and I are becoming like Abraham and Isaac and Jacob. We have taken a course of exaltation and put our lives and strength to usury, and we shall inherit the blessings of the faithful to whom the promise is given."

Brigham Young said, in a discourse in 1856 :

" The principle of increase is the grand moving principle and cause of the actions of men. The Latter-Day Saints are bound to put in practice those principles that are calculated to endure and tend to a continual increase in the world to come."

Orson Hyde, in a sermon preached in the Tabernacle, October 6, 1854, said :

" Polygamy is the cord that shall revolutionize the whole world, and it will make the United States tremble from head to foot. There is such a tide of irresistible argument in it that, like the grand Mississippi, it bears on its bold current every thing that dares oppose its course. The revelation of the Almighty from God to a man who holds the priesthood and is enlightened by the Holy Spirit, whom God designs to make a ruler and a governor in his eternal kingdom, is that he may have many wives, that when he goes to another sphere he may still continue to perpetuate his species, and of his kingdom there shall be no end. . . . In yonder world, those who have the priesthood and by their faith and obedience obtain the sanction of the Almighty, they are sealed on earth and in heaven, and will be exalted to rule and govern forever, while those who would not listen to the holy commandments, and died without having a wife sealed to them, are angels—lower spirits and servants to them that rule. . . . When the servants of God go to heaven there is an eternal union, and they will multiply and replenish the world to which they are going."

President Wilford Woodruff, in the priesthood meeting of the last conference, boasted of the fact that he had three wives and twenty or thirty children. In a sermon

preached in the Tabernacle, in referring to this part of their doctrine, he said :

" There is one principle I would impress with power on the mind of every saint of God, upon the rulers of our nation, and upon all the inhabitants of the land, namely : that the Gospel of Jesus Christ, with all the ordinances thereof, with the priesthood, which holds power both in the heavens and on the earth, and the principles instituted for the salvation and 'exaltation' of men—these principles cannot be annihilated. No combinations of men can destroy them; prisons cannot confine them, nor grave entomb them, because they are eternal. Men might be put to prison who professed them, as was Brother Reynolds, but the principles are as firm and independent as the pillars of heaven. Rulers and the inhabitants of the earth have tried to destroy them, but it mattered not; these eternal principles could never be destroyed."

How do polygamous Mormon husbands support their large families ?

In the vast majority of cases they do not support them. There are exceptions, but this is the rule. Even Orson Pratt's wives and children were compelled to earn their own living.

If a Mormon husband furnishes a " house, flour, and fuel," he is considered a " good provider." I could fill a volume with facts which demonstrate that polygamous Mormon wives support themselves.

ARE POLYGAMOUS WIVES HAPPY ?

I answer, No. From the time of the first attempt to introduce polygamy into the house and transform it into a harem, there never was a woman who desired to share her husband with another woman.

No man can please or make happy more than one wife. Abraham tried it, and, failing, was compelled to drive Hagar and his child into the desert.

Sarah consented to admit Hagar into her tented home, but the presence of another woman sustaining this unnatural relation to her husband, was torture to the soul of Sarah, and she could not rest until Hagar was cast out.

Some of the women of Utah, who have been taken out of the lowest grade of society in the old world, and transferred to the harem of the New West, may not have much intelligence or refinement, and hence be incapable of great suffering ; but, on the other hand, there are many women in Utah who have been living martyrs to their religion. They have submitted and received the revelation on polygamy because they believed it to be their duty ; because, their lecherous priests told them God demanded it, and unless they yielded, damnation would be their reward.

Mrs. Mary Ann Angel Young, the first wife of Brigham Young, said to me, in a conversation held about a year before she died :

"I have never rebelled against my Church, and while a woman's nature may rebel against polygamy, and she may feel herself a martyr to this cause, yet a woman can afford to be a martyr for a few years for the sake of eternal reward."

Mrs. Young, who at this time was quite aged, said many things proving that all her life she had endured her religion because she deemed it her duty to crucify woman's nature for the sake of the "eternal reward."

It seems strange that any intelligent woman can believe that "a revelation fro a Jesus Christ" could contain such a disgusting doctrine as polygamy, but Mormonism is not the only superstition in the world.

If there is any thing that will degrade and *degrade* and *degrade* a woman until she forgots her divine origin, it is the practical effects of polygamy.

Some of the more ignorant women of Utah may have received the doctrine of plurality without being capable of realizing fully what they were doing, but there are multitudes who have been tortured almost to the point of agony for years, and then finally submitted to this infamous decree of lust by crucifying their noblest feelings. There is also a third class who would not accept the doctrine of polygamy, and who have protested with all the might of helplessness against this horrible doctrine, all to no purpose; the weak have been overpowered by the strong. Yet, so revolting is polygamy to some, that the high-priests of Mormonism have resorted in vain to the most fearful threats, threats of damnation and blood atonement, in order to compel their wives to subject and joyfully and willingly receive the revelation on polygamy.

The following are some of the exhortations to induce women "to live their religion:"

J. M. Grant, one of the first presidency, in a sermon delivered September 21, 1856, and published in the *Deseret News*, said: "And we have women here who like any thing but the celestial law of God; and, if they could, would break asunder the cable of the Church of Christ; there is scarcely a mother in Israel but would do it this day. And they talk it to their husbands, to their daughters, and to their neighbors, and say they have not seen a week's happiness since they became acquainted with that law, or since their husband took a second wife. They want to break up the Church of God, and to break it from their husbands and from their family connections."

Brigham Young, in a sermon delivered the same day, said:

"Now for my proposition: it is more particularly for my sisters, as it is frequently happening that women say that they are unhappy. Men will say, 'My wife, though a most excellent woman, has not seen a happy day since I took my second wife; no, not a happy day for a year.' It is said that women are tied down and abused; that they are misused, and have not the liberty they ought to have; that many of them are wading through a perfect flood of tears, because of the conduct of some men, together with their own folly. I wish my women to understand that what I am going to say is for them, as well as all others, and I want those who are here to tell their sisters, yes, all the women of this community, and then write it back to the States, and do as you please with it. I am going to give you from this time to the 6th day of October next for reflection, that you may determine whether you wish to stay with your husbands or not, and then to say with your husbands or not, and then I am going to set every woman at liberty, and say to them, Now go your way—my women with the rest—go your way. And my wives have got to do one of two things: either round up their shoulders to endure the afflictions of this world and live their religion, or they may leave, for I will not have them about me. I will go into heaven alone, rather than have scratching and fighting around me. I will set all at liberty. 'What I first wife, too?' Yes, I will liberate you all. I know what my women will say—'You can have as many women as you please, Brigham.' But I want you to go somewhere, and do something with the whiners. I do not want them to receive part of the truth and spurn the rest out of doors. . . . Let every man thus treat his wives, keeping raiment enough to clothe his body; and say to your wives, 'Take all that I have and be set at liberty; but if you stay with me you shall comply with the law of God in every respect, and round up your shoulders to walk up to the mark without any grunting.' Now, recollect, that two weeks from to-morrow I am going to set you all at liberty. But the first wife will say, 'It is hard, for I have lived with my husband twenty years or thirty, and have raised a family of children for him, and it is a great trial to me for him to have more women that will bear children.' If my wife had borne me all the children that she ever would bear, the celestial law would teach me to take young women that would have children. . . . Sisters, I am not joking; I do not throw out my proposition to banter your feelings, to see whether you will leave your husbands, all or any of you. But I do know that there is no cessation to the everlasting whinings of many of the women of this Territory. And if women will turn from the commandments of God and continue to despise the order of heaven, I will pray that the curse of the Almighty may be close to their heels, and that it may be following them all the day long. And those that enter into it and are faithful, I will promise them that they shall be queens in heaven and rulers for all eternity."

President Heber C. Kimball, in a discourse delivered in the Tabernacle, November 9, 1856, spoke as follows:

"I have no wife or child that has any right to rebel against me. If they violate my laws and rebel against me, they will get into trouble just as quickly as though they transgressed the counsels and teachings of Brother Brigham. Does it give a woman a right to sin against me because she is my wife? No; but it is her duty to do my will as I do the will of my Father and my God. It is the duty of a woman to be obedient to her husband; and unless she is, I would not give a damn for all her queenly right and authority, nor for her either, if she will quarrel and lie about the work of God and the principles of plurality. A disregard of plain and correct teachings is the reason why so many are dead and damned, and twice plucked up by the roots, and I would as soon baptize the devil as some of you."

In a sermon delivered October 6, 1855, Heber C. Kimball said:

"If you oppose any of the works of God you will oppose what is called the spiritual-wife doctrines, the patriarchal order, which is of God. That course will corrode you into apostasy, and you will go overboard. Still a great many do so, and try to justify themselves in it; but they are not justified in God. ... The principle of plurality of wives never will be done away, although some sisters have had revelations that when this time passes away, and they go through the vale, every woman will have a husband to herself. I wish more of our young men would take to themselves wives of the daughters of Zion, and not wait for us old men to take them all. Go ahead upon the right principle, young gentlemen, and God bless you for ever and ever, and make you fruitful, that we may fill the mountains, and then the earth, with righteous inhabitants."

President Heber C. Kimball said in a discourse instructing a band of missionaries about to start on their mission:

"I say to those who are elected to go on missions, Go, if you never return—and commit what you have into the hands of God—your wives, your children, your brethren, and your property. Let truth and righteousness be your motto, and don't go into the world for any thing else but to preach the Gospel, build up the kingdom of God, and gather the sheep into the fold. You are sent out as shepherds to gather the sheep together; and, remember, that they are not your sheep; they belong to them that sent you. Then don't make a choice of any of those sheep; don't make selections before they are brought home and put into the fold. You understand that, Amen."

The Mormon leaders will maintain polygamy at all hazards. The high-priests of Utah have again and again hurled their defiance at

the national government. They publicly scoff and deride such puny measures as the Edmunds Bill. When I was in Logan City, Utah, I heard Mr. Anderson, the President of the Young Men's Mutual Improvement Society, eloquently exhort his young friends, at a great meeting in the Logan Tabernacle, to ignore all legislation and go into polygamy. Among other things, he said: "The Edmunds Bill ought to be trampled under foot by every true Latter-Day Saint."

Mr. Preston, President of Cache Stake, also declared that the Mormons would " ignore all legislation in regard to polygamy." Apostle Snow, a great Mormon leader, said in the Tabernacle in Salt Lake City: " Let Congress persecute us, let Congress disfranchise us and be damned; we shall stand by polygamy." In Provo, in the presence of a large mixed audience, this same apostle of Mormonism, while discussing the Edmunds Bill and its relation to polygamy, used language so profane and obscene that it cannot be repeated here. The Mormons propose to maintain polygamy despite all legislation.

THE EDMUNDS BILL.

The following are the provisions of the Edmunds Bill as passed by Congress and approved by the President:

Be it enacted by the Senate and House of Representatives of the United States of America in Congress assembled:

That Section 352 of the Revised Statutes of the United States be, and the same is hereby amended so as to read as follows, namely:

Every person who has a husband or wife living, who, in a Territory or other place over which the United States have exclusive jurisdiction, hereafter marries another, whether married or single, and any man who hereafter simultaneously, or on the same day, marries more than one woman, in a Territory or other place over which the United States have exclusive jurisdiction, is guilty of polygamy, and shall be punished by a fine of not more than five hundred dollars, and be imprisoned for a term of not more than five years; but this section shall not extend to any person by reason of any former marriage whose husband or wife by such marriage shall have been absent for five successive years, and is not known to such person to be living, and is believed by such person to be dead; nor to any person by reason of any former marriage which shall have been dissolved by a valid decree of a competent court, nor to any person by reason of any former marriage which shall have been pronounced void by a valid decree of a competent court on the ground of nullity of the marriage contract.

SEC. 2. That if any male person, in a Territory or other place over which the United States have exclusive jurisdiction, hereafter cohabits with more than one woman, he shall be deemed guilty of a misdemeanor, and on conviction thereof, shall be punished by a fine of not more than three hundred dollars, or by imprisonment for not more than six months, or by both said punishments, in the discretion of the court.

SEC. 3. That counts for any or all of the offenses named in sections one and two of this act may be joined in the same information or indictment.

SEC. 4. That in any prosecution for bigamy, polygamy, or unlawful cohabitation, under any statute of the United States, it shall be sufficient cause of challenge to any person drawn or summoned as a juryman or talesman, first, if he lives or has been living in the practice of bigamy, polygamy, or unlawful cohabitation with more than one woman, or that he has been guilty of an offense punishable by either of the foregoing sections, or by Section 5352 of the Revised Statutes of the United States, or the act of July 1, 1862, entitled, " An act to punish and prevent the practice of polygamy in the Territories of the United States and other places, and disapproving and annulling certain acts of the Legislative Assembly of the Territory of Utah;" or, second, that he believes it right for a man to have more than one living and undivorced wife at the same time, or to live in the practice of cohabiting with more than one woman ; and any person appearing or offering as a juryman or talesman, and challenged on either of the foregoing grounds, may be questioned on his oath as to the existence of any such cause of challenge, and other evidence may be introduced bearing upon the question raised by such challenge; and this question shall be tried by the court. But, as to the first ground of challenge before mentioned, the person challenged shall not be bound to answer if he shall say upon his oath that he declines on the ground that his answer may tend to criminate himself; and if he shall answer as to said first ground, his answer shall not be given in evidence in any criminal prosecution against him for any offense named in sections 1 and 2 of this act; but if he declines to answer on any ground, he shall be rejected as incompetent.

SEC. 5. That the President is hereby authorized to grant amnesty to such classes of offenders, guilty before the passage of this act of bigamy, polygamy, or unlawful cohabitation, on such conditions and under such limitations as he shall think proper; but no such amnesty shall have effect unless the conditions thereof shall be complied with.

SEC. 6. That the issue of bigamous marriages, known as Mormon marriages, in cases in which such marriages have been solemnized according to the ceremonies of the Mormon sect, in any Territory of the United States, and such issue shall have been born before the first day of January, A. D. 1883, are hereby legitimatized.

SEC. 7. That no polygamist, bigamist, or any person cohabiting with more than one woman, and no woman cohabiting with any of the persons described as aforesaid in this section, in any Territory or other place over which the United States have exclusive jurisdiction, shall be entitled to vote at any election held in any such Territory or other place, or be eligible for election or appointment to, or be entitled to hold any office or place of public trust, honor, or emolument in, under, or for any such Territory or place, or under the United States.

SEC. 8. That all the registration and election officers of every description in the Territory of Utah are hereby declared vacant, and each and every duty relating to the registration of voters, the conduct of elections, the receiving or rejection of votes, and the canvassing and returning of the same, and the issuing of certificates or other evidence of election in said Territory, shall, until other provision be made by the Legislative Assembly of said Territory as is hereinafter by this section provided, be performed under the existing laws of the United States and of said Territory by proper persons, who shall be appointed to execute such offices and perform such duties by a board of five persons, to be appointed by the President, by and with the advice and consent of the Senate, all of whom shall not be members of one political party, a majority of whom shall constitute a quorum. The members of said board, so appointed by the President, shall receive a salary at the rate of $3,000 per annum, and shall continue in office until the Legislative Assembly of the Territory shall make provision for filling said offices as herein authorized. The Secretary of the Territory shall be secretary of the board, and keep a journal of its proceedings, and attest the action of said board under this section. The canvass and return of all the votes at elections in said Territory for members of the Legislative Assembly thereof shall also be returned to said board, which shall canvass all such returns and issue certificates of election to those persons who, being eligible for such election, shall appear to have been lawfully elected, which certificates shall be the only evidence of the right of such persons to sit in such Assembly; but each house of such Assembly, after its organization, shall have power to decide upon the election and qualifications of its members. And at or after the first meeting of said Legislative Assembly whose members shall have been elected and returned according to the provisions of this act, said Legislative Assembly may make such laws, conformable to the Organic Act of said Territory, and not inconsistent with other laws of the United States, as it shall deem proper, concerning the filling of the offices in said Territory declared vacant by this act.

The Mormons boast that, although two decades have passed, polygamy has not been prohibited nor polygamists punished. Many asserted that the completion of the great continental railroad, in 1869, would soon effect the destruction of polygamy; but polygamy was not destroyed by contact with non-Mormon influences.

Again, it was affirmed that the death of Brigham Young, in 1876, would cause the death of polygamy. Brigham died, but polygamy lived.

Once more: it was said that polygamy was dying a natural death. But so tenacious of life has polygamy proven itself to be, that it has steadily increased during the past few years, and, at present, is spreading with alarming rapidity. The plague-spot is enlarging.

Notwithstanding these facts, many comfort themselves with the thought that the Edmunds Bill will not only check, but, in time, utterly extirpate, polygamy. I hope so, but do not believe it will accomplish what it proposes. I judge the future by the past. This bill has some points that recommend it. Its passage shows a *great advance in public opinion*. It is an advance in the right direction, but it falls short of what Utah needs.

In an editorial in the March number of the Utah *Review*, I asserted that this enactment will fail to solve the Utah problem.

There has been great rejoicing among the Gentiles over the passage of this bill. The sentiment of many found expression in sentences like the following: "Glory to God;" "The first victory in twenty years;" "The morning dawns;" "Light breaks at last;" "Praise the Lord." At a prayer-meeting in one of our churches in Salt Lake City, some asked the Lord to restrain their emotions lest they become too joyful over the passage of the Edmunds Bill.

Congress has declared by law that polygamy is a crime, and the Supreme Court of the United States has pronounced the enactment constitutional. We have had enough vaporing about Mormonism. We want no more fruitless talk or impotent bills.

Polygamy is a crime; a very great crime; a crime against civilization; a crime against nature; a crime against posterity; a crime against womanhood. To compromise with such an evil is simply infamous.

Polygamy must be stamped out by the iron heel of a rigid law.

There ought to be an immediate, unconditional, and absolute abandonment of the system called celestial marriage.

The leaders who have lived in defiance of the anti-polygamy enactment ought to be punished to the full extent of the law, just as we punish other felons.

It is not enough to simply *disfranchise* polygamists. Polygamy must be destroyed. How can this be done? We answer: Abolish the Territorial Legislature of Utah, and vest the government in a legislative commission, appointed by the President, with the approval of the Senate. Give Utah such a commission as the Willetts Bill provides for, and then we may hope to accomplish something. Let us cease to legislate, or pass a law that will prove effectual, that will be adequate to the end proposed.

We believe that this is an irrepressible conflict. The Mormons propose to stand by polygamy, and namby-pamby legislation will produce nothing but Mormon contempt. Religious fanatics who practice the greatest crimes for Jesus' sake cannot be reformed by telling them "it is naughty." They must be coerced. We have toyed and tampered with Mormon polygamy for twenty-three years. Congress has pursued a weak and contemptible policy, and this has only made the law-breakers bolder. Polygamists have declared that God has thus far rescued and saved them, whereas they have gone unpunished, and Mormon murderers, who, from Sunday to Sunday, in the Tabernacle, lift their red hands in prayer, have gone unhung because of the impotence of Congress. We sent an army, in 1857, under General Albert Sidney Johnson, to Utah, but the result was humiliation to every American to the last degree. The imbecile course of that officer furnished a text to Mormon elders by which they convinced their superstitious slaves that God had interposed and laid bare his arm to save Mormonism. Let us trifle no longer. Utah needs a commission. When President Hayes was visiting Zion, several persons wisely suggested to him the propriety and justice of appointing a commission to govern Utah, such as controlled Louisiana after that territory had been purchased from the old Napoleon. President Hayes, acting on this suggestion, recommended a commission for Utah. This is what we need. This will cut out the Gordian knot called the Utah Problem. By this means Utah could, in time, be redeemed and Americanized.

If law-abiding citizens, East and West, would now unite in urgently pressing upon Congress the necessity of a commission, the Willetts Bill, or an equivalent measure, might be passed. Again, I say, polygamy must be stamped out. You cannot reason with rottenness. Polygamy is a crime, and no revelation can change its nature. Though an angel from heaven should preach polygamy, we proclaim, Let him be accursed.

VIII. EDUCATION IN THE SOUTH SINCE THE WAR.

1. THE SOUTH, THE NORTH, AND THE NATION KEEPING SCHOOL.

REV. A. D. MAYO, BOSTON, MASS.

I SUPPOSE myself invited to address this assembly of eminent school men and friends of education, because of some unusual opportunities for observation of Southern affairs, as related to the rising school life of this portion of our country during the past three years. Without enlarging on the details of this interesting experience, or even quoting authorities for my conclusions, I will confine myself to a plain statement of some opinions that have been forced upon me through the entire period of my investigations, and which have now assumed, in my mind, the form of established convictions.

I shall speak of what has been done in the sixteen States, which include our former slave territory, since 1860; endeavor to show how this marvelous work has been accomplished, in the only way it could have been, by the combined effort of the South, the North, and the nation keeping school for the children; and, from this estimate of these several educational forces, and the prodigious work that still remains to be done, I shall try to outline the true method of success in the future.

If I were required to present to a European audience the most forcible illustration of the workings of republican institutions in our country, I should certainly select the history of the development of what we may call the new education in our Southern States, from the breaking out of the civil war in 1861 to the present date.

I speak of the *new education* in this connection. Up to 1860 the slave States had a system of education well adapted to perpetuate the dominant form of Southern society. It consisted of a reasonably thorough and extended system of collegiate, academical, and military schools for the sons of the superior class and such recruits from the lower orders of the white people as gave promise of unusual ability, with a large

development of the ordinary female seminary of a generation ago for the corresponding class of girls. A considerable number of the sons and daughters of wealthy people were also expensively educated by private tuition at home, attendance on Northern schools, or at institutions abroad. There was also a good deal of the sort of family and church instruction in political, religious, and social ideas that is always going on in a concentrated and aristocratic order of society. The result, as we all know, was the training of, perhaps, the most intelligent and forcible aristocratic class in Christendom, which displayed an energy in revolutionary politics and on the battle-field which, for four years, held the fate of the Union in suspense, and arrested the attention of the civilized world.

But, of course, in this scheme of education, all but two or three of the twelve millions of the Southern people were left with no systematic or persistent attempt at schooling.

The four millions of slaves were almost completely shut out from every sort of school; although American slavery, itself, was perhaps the most effective university through which any race of savages was ever introduced to civilization. In that severe training-school the African Negro learned to work, acquired the language of a civilized people, and took on at least some apprehension of the only religion that ever proposed to break every yoke and proclaim all men the children of God.

The several millions of non-slaveholding white people were not left entirely destitute. Many of the better sort were partially educated with their superiors. Almost every Southern State had a periodical experience of waking up to the importance of a system of common schooling for all white children. And especially in Virginia, the Carolinas, Kentucky, Alabama, and Louisiann, this was attempted, though, outside a few cities, always with imperfect success. But the Southern non-slaveholding white people, outside the rim of "poor white trash," corresponding to our Northern tramp, had the schooling which comes from discipline implied by the settlement of a new country and the enjoyment of citizenship in a republican state. It was a training that brought the Southern masses up to the point of that astonishing military efficiency which, along a line of battle of a thousand miles, held this mighty Union at arm's length through four terrible years.

I linger over this picture of the old Southern education because ignorance of it has created many false notions of the educational problem among our Northern people. In 1861 the South was not that abode of mental imbecility and dismal ignorance which many an enthusiastic teacher going down there has imagined. On the contrary, it was a country where, perhaps, one fourth the people were thoroughly trained for leadership in the aristocratic form of society, and where the Negro and the poor white man had received a discipline in the university of American life which was the best possible preparation for the new era of education, through schools, teachers, and books, upon which the South entered the very year of the outbreak of the civil war.

History will record that never before was such a spectacle witnessed as the sudden waking up of Christian and patriotic zeal for the education of a people in a state of revolt against national power. It is true that the missionary of religion has often followed an army of subjugation to change the faith of nations of savages and barbarians. But, in our case, the Northern people displayed at once their immovable faith in the Union for which they were fighting, and their confidence and radical respect for their Southern brethren in revolt, by taking the school-house as the most prominent article in the baggage-train, and leaving the teacher to build up the waste places in the track of desolating war. The most thoughtful of our Northern people, from the first, believed that a good system of popular education of the Southern masses would have prevented the war and opened a way for the peaceful abolition of slavery. But, since that was not permitted, they believed that the only security for the restored Union would be that general enlightenment of both races which would bring the vast majority of the Southern people to a condition of intelligent citizenship. And, having no doubt of the success of the war, the same class "took time by the forelock," and within a year from the firing on Sumter had established the school for the "Contraband" along the Atlantic coast, from Washington to Beaufort, down the Mississippi, through the inland south-

west, and at the city of New Orleans. In short, the school master and mistress followed the army during the progress of the war; instructing thousands of the Negroes of every age: expending large sums contributed by the benevolence of the Christian people of the North; every-where supported by the military power and, to a considerable extent, aided indirectly by the government.

In 1862 the national government voted a munificent donation of public lands for the establishment of agricultural and mechanical education in all the States. Anticipating the immense value of this donation to the South, the lands of these revolting States were religiously held in reserve against the time when they should be claimed in a restored Union. It is impossible to estimate the present and prospective value of this gift to the Southern people at their present crisis of agricultural, manufacturing, and mining industry.

In 1865 Congress took up this educational work, which had already outgrown the resources of private benevolence, and, through annual appropriations continued for six years, the gift of national property, and the diversion of confiscated lands, under the direction of the Freedmen's Bureau, gave an impetus to the work of Southern education, especially among the freedmen, which it has never lost. In the ten years, from 1860 to 1870, it is probable that not less than twenty millions of dollars were thus expended by the North and the nation for education in the South. Meanwhile, the Peabody Educational Fund of two millions of dollars had been devoted to the building up of the public school through the entire South. And this magnificent benefaction has been followed by many large contributions, like those of the Vanderbilt family, Mr. Corcoran, Seney, and Slater, Mrs. Stone, and Mrs. Hemenway, with great numbers of others, which have poured a constant stream of helpful aid southward for the past fifteen years. Neither should it be forgotten that the great majority of Northern teachers who have wrought in this field have virtually made their work a "labor of love;" the compensation, even of presidents of colleges, being less than the wages of Northern mercantile book-keepers, and of the majority of subordinate teachers not above that of reliable servants in Northern cities.

For the last ten years, outside a few prominent institutions for the education of white people, the great effort of the North has been made, through the mission organizations of the several Churches, toward the establishment of all grades of schools for the freedmen. When the history of the educational work in the South by the Christian people of the North is fairly written, it will be, in itself, the most conclusive answer to the whole impeachment of our modern

Christianity by its enemies of every grade. The history of the world cannot produce a more affecting spectacle than the growth of this mighty Christian philanthropy which, beginning amid the din of battle, has steadily marched on, through all sorts of misunderstanding, neglect, opposition, and disparagement, with amazing patience, forbearance, and wisdom, to its present state. To-day, there are probably not less than a hundred important schools, twenty of them bearing the title of college, with ample buildings and excellent facilities for religious, mental, and industrial education, established for the Southern colored people, chiefly taught by Northern men and women; a body of instructors not inferior to any similar class in the country in general capacity for such a difficult work. In these schools not less than fifteen thousand of the superior young colored people are being prepared, not only as teachers and professional characters, but, what is more significant, trained for leadership of the six millions of American colored citizens. The whole problem of Negro citizenship is involved in the formation of a genuine leading class—an aristocracy of character, skilled industry, and intelligence that shall, at once, give direction to the millions of these people, and become their true representative in all dealings with the white people of the Republic.

And it is not too much to say that the colored people, the South, and the nation, will be indebted to the Christian schooling in these institutions for the beginning of this prodigious undertaking. Perhaps the most gratifying feature in this work is the fact that, at the end of fifteen years, it has conquered all vital opposition among the leading classes of the South. Half a dozen States now make annual appropriations to these collegiate schools. Southern gentlemen are included in their boards of management. The State of South Carolina, first in secession, has been the first to include a colored college in the organization of its State University. Many of the schools of lower grade are now being included in the new system of public schools. The graduates of the higher seminaries are in constant demand as teachers. In short, it seems as if, within a generation, all these great seminaries will become virtually Southern universities, largely controlled by the Southern people of both races, endowed by Northern munificence, the most splendid offering in behalf of "peace on earth and good-will to men" ever made, under similar circumstances, by the Christian Church, in any age and land.

Thus, within the past twenty years, the people of the North, in connection with the government of the United States, has shown its confidence, respect, and affection for the Southern people by a mighty work of educational beneficence, conducted on lines of operation where it was hardly possible that the South could help itself, involving an outlay, probably, all things considered, of not less than fifty millions of dollars. And the point we wish to press is, that this has been done in the characteristic American republican way. The nation has not gone into these States to establish schools, antagonizing their people and paralyzing home effort, but has simply given twenty-five millions of property to aid in a good work, and established, in the Bureau of Education, one of the most potent agencies for inspiration, encouragement, and instruction possible under our form of government. The Northern Churches and people have not gone down South to build fortresses of propagandism. They have wisely adjusted their educational work to the condition of the freedman; trained him to pay money and labor for good schooling, and sent him forth, a superior person, for all the uses and duties of Southern citizenship. And, although I have no right to speak for any Church engaged in this great work, I believe, after careful observation, that nothing would be more satisfactory to the Northern Christian people than to see this splendid cluster of schools, with their investment of perhaps $20,-000,000, past and present, lapse gradually into the hands of the Southern people as a permanent gift to their new educational life.

But we shall greatly mistake if we suppose the most important work in Southern education, during the past fifteen years, has been this friendly demonstration from the North and the nation. No people can be educated permanently by another people. As far as concerns its educational life, every State of this Union is practically a separate people. Although much can be done, at certain critical periods, as in our new States of the West, by material aid and the inspiration of superior teachers and advanced methods introduced from abroad, yet each of those great States to-day has built up its own system of education, in some respects better than corresponding systems in older commonwealths. So must it be with the South in the building up of the vast enterprise of the new education. If these sixteen States, or those of them which were involved in the experiment of the Confederacy, had lain dormant through these fifteen years just outlined, or if they had wrought in an obstinate spirit of opposition to education, the prospect now would indeed be hopeless. For there is not power enough, under our system of government, in the nation, the Church, or the people of the North to force the American type of education even into Delaware against its will, to say nothing of the gigantic folly of attempting to school a region larger than Europe, with eighteen millions of people, at arm's length, across a hostile border-land, in the face of political, social, and ecclesiastical disagreement, intensitied by a race problem more complex than was ever presented to any civilized land. Thus we can only understand the real significance, and predict the outcome of what has already been done by the North and the nation in Southern education when we understand what has been going on through these sixteen States during the time already described.

How should we expect the home educational movement to begin in a country so prostrated, demoralized, and socially turned upside down as the South in 1865? And here I record my opinion that the Northern people have never realized and cannot understand the wide-spread ruin of every vital interest that fell upon the revolting States in 1865.

The Confederate resistance to the overwhelming power of the Union was like the heroic, almost preternatural, attempt of the inhabitants of a new Michigan village to fight off an all-consuming fire that is steadily advancing its awful circuit, only to close in with more fatal destruction at the end. No people in modern history had been left so thoroughly prostrate as every class in these revolting States at the close of the war. And in such wholesale overturn the school always goes first. In 1865 there were probably not a score of the old academies and colleges in these States in actual session. Many of their buildings were destroyed and all dilapidated; their endowments had vanished; their teachers were dead or scattered, and their patrons were at work driving the wolf from the home door, with no ability to send their growing children to any school, or to establish any thing to take the place of their former system. The effort of the provisional government to place the Northern scheme of free elementary education on the ground, continued in some States for ten years, deserved far more respect than it received and more success than it attained. The radical weakness of this movement was the attempt to establish an expensive system of popular education among a people who had never tried it, had not come to believe in it, were not able to pay for it, and, naturally, looked upon it as a hostile movement of the victorious party in the civil war. Yet the South to-day will agree with us that even this experiment had its uses, and left on the ground a large number of school-houses and a growing desire for popular education among the masses of both races which has been a powerful stimulant to the home effort of the past ten years.

But only an educational enthusiast will believe that a permanent educational movement can be inaugurated until the educated and responsible class is convinced of its importance, and prepared to take it up in a practical way.

And, just here the leading class of the Southern States displayed that wonderful common sense and "gumption" which is the rarest outcome of our republican order of human affairs. It is possible that a French populace of a century ago might have been fired up with a prodigious enthusiasm to undertake the schooling of the ignorant masses while the whole upper story of educational life was a hopeless wreck. Fortunately for our country, the superior class of Southern people began their new educational work in the plain common-sense way of first rebuilding the school by which their own children could alone be saved from a lapse into the barbarism of ignorance. The most pitiful spectacle on earth is the reverting of an educated people to ignorance; and that was the most imminent peril that faced the Southern school man in 1865. The three or four millions of superior and variously educated white people of the South in that year found themselves in hopeless poverty, scattered over an area as large as Europe, outside Russia; the vast majority sparsely distributed through an open country; their homes swarming with children and youth, and no established system of schools to give them that mental training which would be their only outfit in the struggle for success.

In this emergency it would have been unnatural if the people had proceeded in any other way than they did: to get on the ground, at least, a temporary arrangement for the education of their own children and those of their white neighbors more destitute than themselves. To this work they bent themselves with a singleness of purpose and a pertinacity thoroughly American and deserving of all praise. Whatever they may have thought of the great effort of the North and the nation in behalf of the Negro, they knew that it would be a questionable gain to give the crude elements of knowledge to the children of the freedmen if the offspring of the only educated class in the country was permitted to lapse into barbarism. I have studied carefully the progress of this prodigious effort of the upper strata of the Southern people, within the past fifteen years, to re-establish the upper side of education. We must remember that, in States where the vast majority of respectable people live in the open country, the establishment of even the secondary public school must be the work of years, and the first generation will be fortunate if it gets an effective elementary education fairly on the ground. For fifty years yet the academy in the country town and the college, as we now find it, will be the chief opportunity of all classes of white people for any thing beyond the mere elements of schooling, through at least a dozen of these great States. So, for the past fifteen years, these people have toiled, as nobody can know but themselves, through sacrifices almost incomprehensible to our wealthy Northern communities, to rehabilitate their little colleges and academies, and to furnish the small amount necessary to give their children such education as they might in these schools. I undertake to say that this effort alone entitles the South to the profound interest, even admiration, of all thoughtful school men every-where. The effort has been a most gratifying success. Leaving out the great drift of worthless and indifferent private schools that have sprung up with a mushroom growth, thirty-five of them, as I found, in one little city of five or six thousand white people, the academies and colleges that have been actually organized, newly founded, or put in working order, are now, perhaps, sufficiently numerous, if well endowed, to meet the present wants of the people. But to do this it has been necessary that the most eminent teachers should be overwhelmed with work and live on starvation wages; that great numbers of women of the highest social position, and the daughters of the leading families, should give their lives to the work of instruction; that families strangely impoverished should contrive to pinch themselves for the schooling of their young people; and that great numbers should still be dependent on the benevolence of neighbors and school corporations for what they obtained. It is impossible, of course, to say how much this great rehabilitation has cost the Southern people in money. Outside an occasional gift from the North, and two or three munificent endowments—like Vanderbilt, Tileston, and Emery—this money has been a home contribution, by a people just struggling up to comfortable living, in behalf of the secondary and higher education, always under Christian influences, and every-where reasonably progressive. To understand what this effort means, even to-day, is to suppose a State like Connecticut suddenly reduced to poverty; school funds and endowments swept away; with the ability, at best, to keep afloat a three or four months' district school for the masses; with an occasional graded school in the cities; and the upper third of its youth gathered in schools where the widows of its governors and judges and the daughters of its proudest old families are teaching, in overcrowded classes, at wages ranging from three to five hundred a year, with an occasional prize of a $1,000 salary at the top; and the vast majority of its enterprising boys compelled to leave school at fourteen to "keep the pot boiling" at home. I know well enough the characteristic defects of this, the upper side of the New Education in the South, and appreciate the great advance that has been possible in Baltimore, Washington, and St. Louis, and now in New Orleans, through the gift

11

of several millions of dollars by Southern men like Hopkins, Pratt, Tulane, Corcoran, and the noble group of men who have founded the Washington University of St. Louis. But until I see how a Northern State would do better things for the children under similar circumstances, I must be pardoned for my unaffected admiration of this prodigious undertaking of the leading Southern people since the close of the great war.

But the Southern people have not paused with this attempt at the reconstruction of the secondary and higher education for the white race. Beyond this, of their own notion, in every State, within the past ten years, the people's elementary common school for white and colored children has been placed on the ground, defended through the dangers of its infancy, made better every year, until it has become a vital institution of Southern civilization. And when we consider that even England waited until within twenty years before she seriously undertook to be responsible for the education of the masses; and that all Europe, outside Germany and Switzerland, has been ev n more tardy in this respect; that the free public schooling even of white children was practically unknown in the South, on the large scale, previous to 1860, while all instruction was forbidden to the Negro; that the whole education and entire political, religious, and social training of the leading classes was opposed to the common school; that, in most instances, all public-school funds were sunk in the war, and all the money, save a few hundred thousand dollars yearly from the Peabody and other funds, must be taken from communities where there is every thing to be done and so little to do with; that in several States more than half the amount is given to the freedmen, while little comes back from their taxation; also the almost insurmountable difficulties of climate, and the condition of the open Southern country during half the year; this effort assumes a magnitude worthy of all respect. In every Southern State the establishment of the public school has been fought through in the face of every enemy that threatens its existence at the North. Wide-spread poverty has been the standing argument against taxation. Sectarian narrowness and clerical zeal, Catholic and Protestant, has raised the cry: "Godless," "secular," "immoral," "communistic." Social exclusiveness has turned the cold shoulder and, as Gen. Grant said to me at the White House, "there is too much reading and writing already to suit a good many statesmen in the Capitol." In certain districts, and perhaps in the State of Louisiana, to-day, this bitter conflict between the people and their adversaries still goes on. Yet it can be said that in every one of these sixteen States the battle for the people's common school, in its whole range of development, from the country district to the State university, has been won. Every Southern State, this year, is doing a little better for its children than last year. Say every thing that can truly be said in disparagement of the new public schools of the South: their establishment and support, to this date, is the most notable educational fact in Christendom within the past ten years. We must understand just how far this is a home work in its magnitude. The two or three hundred thousand dollars of annual appropriation, and the labors of the agents of the Peabody Fund, have been a great help. The training of colored teachers in the mission colleges, supported by the North, has been even a greater assistance, although partially kept up by the tuition paid by the colored people themselves. The influence of the Bureau of Education and its apostolic secretary, John Eaton, has been good and only good through all these years. The support of a superior system of public schools in Washington, partly at the expense of the general government, has furnished an excellent model for the whole South. But all these influences, together with the friendly encouragement of Northern teachers, have been but a small element in this vast undertaking of the organization of the Southern common school, which is even more truly the work of the Southern people, unaided from abroad, than the establishment of the Western public school has been the work of the people of the West.

For three years past my own time has been engrossed by travels, studies, and labors, largely bearing on the present condition of the public school in the Southern States. I have done a good deal of work in twelve of these States, and think I understand pretty well what is going on in all of them. Their schools range from two or three months, in Louisiana, to five months, in the country in Virginia, and in many localities the school goes on for a longer time by private contribution. In all the larger cities, and in many smaller towns, the graded school is established for both races, and, in many cases, handled with great ability, by the best methods, for eight or nine months of the year. In every State the County Institute for the training of teachers; in several the Summer Normal Institute of several weeks' duration, and in some the proper State Normal School for white and colored pupils are established. Outside a certain class of fossil and antiquated pedagogues, and the usual drift of incompetent youth working for pay, these schools are taught by the choice young people of both races. A better class of people, more earnest, more determined to improve, more self-denying, working on wages painfully and sometimes pitifully inadequate, cannot be found in any Christian land than the ma-

jority of the public-school teachers of the South. The State Superintendents of Education, and many of the city and county supervisors, are the same sort of people as our leading educators in the North. With occasional exceptions, I believe school funds are honestly and economically applied, and, in all but two States, divided with reasonable fairness among all the children. It is not possible to give the average colored child as good a school as the white child; because he cannot take it; but the colored public schools are every-where improving, and are hindered as much by the ignorance and jealousies of their own people as by any other cause. The charge that the Southern public schools, except in very occasional individual instances, are schools of disloyalty, I know to be untrue. The attempt to publish series of sectional or even Southern school-books has broken down, and the Northern educational "drummer" is on the heels of every school trustee and superior teacher from Delaware to Texas. Our Northern summer schools are crowded with these teachers, and thousands more would come if they had the money.

In short, the Southern common school is the American common school in all respects, save its bitter need of more money, longer sessions, and more thoroughly-trained teachers. It has already saved thousands of the children of respectable white people from ignorance and, for the first time, brought the lighted candle of knowledge to other thousands of homes where mental darkness brooded before. Its graduates are not the lazy and shiftless, but the superior, skilled working class in all their communities. And if any man, however eminent, honest, or Christian, declares that these schools are godless, immoral, or even unmoral, I must be pardoned for telling him that he does not know what he is talking about. If any body can look at the colored children and youth of Washington, graduates of the public schools, and contrast them with the awful crowd of untaught Negro humanity that swarmed the streets of any Southern city before the school-mistress came in; or will compare the white school-children of Atlanta, Richmond, and Savannah with communities where ignorance still prevails; and will then deliberately prefer this charge, I can only say his make-up is so different from my own that there is no common basis for an argument in the premises. And I would remind my objector, on this ground, of the fact that there is one plot of "holy ground" in every Southern community, where the whisky bottle, the smutch of tobacco, the pistol and knife, profane and obscene speech cannot enter, by common consent; and that spot is the school-house and lot, public even more than private and collegiate, established by the Southern people within the last fifteen years. Besides this, the whole subject of the superior and industrial education of the colored people is being debated in every Southern community. The State and the Church are both beginning to move on lines of advance. And in all Southern cities there is a hopeful movement for the æsthetic and the higher industrial training prophetic of valuable results in the near future.

Thus, while the North and the nation have been at work, chiefly on the lower side of this vast educational South ro problem, during the past twenty years, spending perhaps $50,-000,000, a large part of it for the elementary training of the colored people, and testifying their confidence, respect, and faith that the South will appreciate their work; this confidence, respect, and faith has not been misplaced. The Southern people have responded to this magnificent demonstration, not by flinging up the hat in applause so much as by taking off the coat and working, at the other end of the problem, as no other people ever wrought before. The result is that, during these memorable years, the Southern people have not only restored their secondary and higher education to a condition, in some respects better than before 1860, but have also established in every State the American system of public instruction, and committed themselves to its support, according to their ability, in every grade. It is impossible to estimate the money investment in this enterprise during all these years. Last year the South paid not less than $15,000,000 for education, and this year the sum will be increased. At least as much money and far more labor has been given by the South, out of its poverty, than by the North and the nation, out of their abundance, for Southern education since the war. More than $50,000,000, meaning to that people many hundred millions, judged by Northern standards, has thus been laid upon the altar of the children's hope.

And now the traveler through the Southland finds himself every-where in the presence of an educational revival as marked as in New England in the days of Horace Mann. And the blessedness of this revival is that it is bringing together the children and youth, their teachers, the younger parents, and the more thoughtful people of North and South, as no movement in the political, the ecclesiastical, or even the industrial sphere of national life can possibly succeed in doing. It is easy enough for stalwarts, sectarians, sectionalists, and soreheads of all descriptions to find food for denunciation and gloomy foreboding in Southern society; and our Northern municipal life, to say nothing of certain ugly tendencies in other regions of society, will still provoke the return fire of the diminishing Southern "old guard" that holds the fort against the North and the nation. But the time has come when, in behalf of the children, all Christian men and women should call a halt in such recriminations, and hold counsel together in the interest of that education of the head, the heart, and the hand which can alone make us one. For twenty momentous years the American people, in sixteen Southern States, have been laying the foundations and raising the opposite walls of the massive temple of the New Education. While the North and the nation have been toiling, on the one side, "all orders and conditions" of Southern men and women have worked, according to their light, each on his own angle, but all on some section of the mighty building where the children shall be gathered in. That these workmen have sometimes mistaken the beat of rival hammers and the clink of rival chisels around the corner for a new tramp of hostile forces, is not surprising. But one thing will be not only surprising but disgraceful and disheartening beyond compare; if, when these rival workmen have really built up the walls and met each other around the dome that crowns their common work, they should fall out, fling their tools at each other, and fight over the miserable wrangle of precedence to the bitter end; while they should be clasping each other's hands and running up the old flag with prayers and songs of dedication and ringing shouts of joy as of a people whose most devious ways have been along providential paths; all ascending to the summit of a nation's hope and a new triumph for the human race.

But all that has been done, on the whole so well done, is only the overture to the mighty wo k of educating the whole people, to which the South is now waking up. Our Southern friends are fortunately gifted with a boundless faculty of hopefulness in all matters pertaining to their own future. It will be fortunate if a laudable satisfaction at their present achievements does not blind them to the fact that, after all, this prodigious co-operative effort of the past twenty years has barely placed on the ground the machinery for educating the coming generation, while the work to be done is so vast as to be almost appalling. Massachusetts began to educate her people two hundred and fifty years ago, and has stuck to it more persistently than any civilized people. Yet, to-day, there are nearly a hundred thousand people in Massachusetts unable to read and write. Only a practiced school man can estimate the terrible obstinacy of chronic ignorance; how it fights and runs away, and skulks and shirks to escape detection; and, when "brought to the book," goes through another dodge of masquerading through all the phases of sham knowledge; and how short a time is required for a generation to lose its grip and begin to revert to its old estate! The South will do well to turn a deaf ear to all educational flatterers and optimists for the next half century, and pay good heed to what its own wisest men and women are all the time telling it: that the enormous work of instructing its whole people, even in elementary knowledge and mental discipline, is only begun, and that it needs a redoubled effort at home, with all legitimate help from the North and the nation for a generation to come, to do the work which patriotism, Christianity, and a wise self-interest demand.

The first point to be aimed at is to get the children actually into school and extend the term of instruction, in the country districts, to at least six months in the year; while the city and village graded school should be sustained at least eight months. The Superintendent of Instruction for Kentucky reports that one third the children of that State are in no school, and great numbers of the public schools are thoroughly inefficient. It is doubtful if one half the children of North Carolina are receiving even three months of reliable schooling. Louisiana, Florida, and Arkansas are even worse off, and all the Gulf States but little better. Thousands of ignorant people are keeping their children out of school for the pittance obtained for their work, and vagrancy and absenteeism from the school-house in the open country greatly impair the value of the schools. Too many unbelievers are filling the country with the absurd cry that schooling makes the Negro lazy, and that the ignorant workman is only reliable. But the fact is, that, out of certain favored localities, chiefly in towns, the experiment of thorough, continuous, intelligent schooling has never yet been fairly tried on these dense masses of white and colored ignorance. A poor school, poorly attended, badly taught, neglected by the superior people of a community, is a hot-bed of many vices. When the South succeeds in getting her illiterate millions actually in range of the educational forces that make up the American system of education, it will realize that such training will treble its industrial power and lift up the whole basement story of its life into the life and warmth of modern times.

But two conditions are necessary for this achievement. The first is a resolute determination, in every Southern State, to strain every nerve to increase the amount of money appropriated for public schools. And especially to establish the habit of local taxation for education. At the most, $100,000,-000 may have been expended for every sort of education in these sixteen States since 1860. But the State of Massachusetts has expended nearly that sum during the same period. New York State spends $100,000,-000 in ten years. Cincinnati pays as much every year as the State of Georgia, and Boston more than any Southern State, with

perhaps two or three exceptions. Our new North-west, besides its vast landed endowment, imposes the State tax, and then often shoulders a local assessment beyond any portion of the country.

Second. If any thing has been proved in educational matters at home and abroad it is, first, that the Church never succeeded in educating a people; second, that the family has always failed more decidedly than the Church; third, that private enterprise never did more than educate a favored class; fourth, that in our country the common school, to be respectable, must be free to all; fifth, that neither the nation nor the State can be relied upon for any thing more than the most general supervision, encouragement, and partial support of the people's school; sixth, that no community succeeds in educating its children until it faces the hard fact of local taxation, and trains itself to the persistent and generous assessment of all its property for the common good. The most dangerous weakness of education through vast regions of the open Southern country is the fact that the people of both races do not understand this, and are looking to the State or to private benevolence and various other expedients to keep their schools alive. Another valuable result of this habit will be the training of the Southern people in that local self-government which has been so effective in the history of New England. Already this result has been marked in many localities. The present year, North Carolina has passed a valuable law, empowering school precincts to tax themselves, and the people of Texas have indorsed a constitutional amendment proposing the same thing.

Third. There must be a concerted effort at the training of teachers suitable to handle the common school by improved methods. A great deal of the school keeping of all sorts in these States is inefficient and almost useless from the lack of teaching skill. Just now the South has the best material in the world for good teaching; for the superior class, of both sexes, among the colored people, and the superior young women of the white people, are thronging this profession. But even this will not save the school unless these young people can have, not only academical, but professional training. So far, the word normal school in the South is little more than a name for an academical grade of any sort. Even our universities and colleges for colored youth, with a few exceptions, have given no effective training in the art of teaching to their pupils. The Southern people need skill in the school-room, especially on account of the absence of many outside helps to the average child. The Peabody Fund has struck the key-note in giving nearly all its income for the training of teachers in its own school at Nashville, in Sumner Institute, and paying the salaries of sk lled superintendents. The Slater Fund should give no money to any institution, for training teachers, except on condition of a thorough normal department under an export, with a practice school annex. Every Southern State should make haste in some effective way to push on the training of teachers, and every Southern academy and college should establish a department for the same purpose. It is in the schooling of such masses of children as are now brought into their classes that skill is especially required, and it is not a moment too soon to begin the gigantic work which half our Northern States have not yet compassed, but which every wise school man everywhere knows to be a prime condition of success.

Fourth. There is a great field for industrial education in the South, while there is danger that, in handling this complex matter, great and fatal mistakes may be made. There are two specious un-American notions now masquerading under the taking phrase " Industrial Education. First, that it is possible or desirable to train large bodies of youth to superior industrial skill without a basis of sound elementary education. You cannot polish a brickbat, and you cannot make a good workman of a plantation Negro or a white ignoramus until you first wake up his mind and give him the mental discipline and knowledge which comes from a good school. The first thing that the illiterate classes need every-where in our country for their permanent industrial elevation is six months of thorough elementary training in schools handled by good teachers, for five or six years of their life, and only a generation so taught can ever learn to work in connection with the labor-saving agencies which are revolutionizing every sphere of human industry. Second, that it is possible or desirable to train masses of American children on the European idea that the child will follow the calling of his father. Class education has no place in our order of society, and the American people will never accept it in any form. The industrial training needed in the South must be obtained by the establishment of special schools of improved housekeeping and the various styles of artisan work that its new manufactures w ll open for girls, with mechanical training for such boys as desire it, and a general improvement of agriculture through local associations of farmers and their wives. This will open into larger provisions for the higher form of technical schools. And this training should be given impartially to both races, without regard to the thousand and one theories of what the colored man cannot do. But any attempt to recast the public school into a semi-industrial institution, in my opinion, will fail of both the ends pro-

posed in the present state of Southern education.

Fifth. The time has come to call a halt in the establishment of new academies and colleges for both races until those on the ground are better endowed and made more effective. The educational scourge of these States now is the great army of broken-down people who are forcing themselves on the public as teachers or private and semi-parochial schools, with no real qualification for the office of instructor. In more communities than is known this wasteful practice deprives the people of any thing like thorough education, and fills the community with children and youth wretchedly prepared for the duties of life. There are now good secondary and collegiate schools in the South, enough to educate the people, if the people will give them fair support, and their communities will work persistently for their endowment. And with this should go on a general movement for the establishment of free libraries in every community. It will be a questionable advantage to teach a million Southern children to read if they turn to the dime-novel, the lower side of the press, or the horrible trash with which every railroad is flooding the country. Every school-house and church should have its children's libra y, and every community its collection of books suitable for general reading open to all.

Sixth. The Southern people will do well to give every child the great American chance of a fair elementary education, and see how he will turn out. That is the only national, scientific, practical, or Christian way to educate a people. The opposite way is to predict, in advance, what any set of children cannot do, and then see to it that they have no chance given them to do it. And, just here, if my words could reach every school district in the South-land, I would say : Give no heed to this noisy crowd of Northern educational cranks who are now filling the press with their preposterous, false, and silly denunciations of the American system of public schools The American public school has great defects, like every thing else, public or private, in the country. But its defects are only those common to every American institution, and it is to be judged, like the American family, business, politics, society, literature, and the Church, by understanding its better features, marking its direction, and observing its spirit of progress. Judged in this way, our American education, of all grades, in the North, is fully abreast of any thing in the country, and is, perhaps, on the whole, more thoroughly alive to its own defects, and more earnestly striving for improvement than any other region of our national life. So I would say to our Southern friends—when Richard Grant White and Gail Hamilton denounce the common school as a failure all round; when ultra scientific experts ridicule it as superficial and misleading; when Bishop McQuaid declares it godless, immoral, and communistic; when Dr. Nathan Allen tells you that New England manhood and womanhood are physically going "out the little end of the horn;" when Zachary Montgomery and the crowd of journalistic scribblers declare that the schools are the nursery of laziness; when international novelists and literary lights sneer at our popular education as a nursery of vulgarity; when venerable college presidents and academical principals publish the high school and the normal school a failure—it will be perfectly safe to turn a deaf ear, and to go on building up every sort of good school in the South that now exists in the North; for, while cranks die and go to their own places, good schools abide.

And out of this review of the educational outlook in the South comes to my mind the unanswerable argument for a wise, generous, and immediate policy of national aid for the people especially of a dozen of these States, against the appalling illiteracy which is the one great bar to their prosperity. In my view, this aid should be immediate and generous; graduated with the sole view to stimulate the energies of the people; kept sharply outside sectarian, religious, and partisan politics; left to the State authorities for administration—of course, under all proper safeguards; and supplemented by judicious continuation of private and Christian beneficence from the North, with a universal effort to make it the occasion of a great revival of kindly feeling through all sections. I believe the time has come when all this can be achieved; but better wait longer than have any imperfect, partisan, or partial attempt that will fail and leave misunderstanding and new jealousy in its wake.

Several results of such an act of eminent statesmanship I am confident would be assured.

First. The obstructive class in every community whose greatest leverage now is in the acknowledged defects of the schools, would become a feeble minority as soon as public education took on the form of respectability and efficiency, which such aid would assure.

Second. It would enable thousands of bright young people to obtain the elementary education at home which would fit them for a successful term in the secondary or collegiate school, and lay the foundation of professional success. Now the Southern academies and colleges are clogged with multitudes of students who have grown up with no elementary education, and are, therefore, unable even to use the opportunities obtained by so much sacrifice and toil. A considerable per cent. of national aid should be given for the training of

teachers by the most practical methods that can be devised by the school authorities of these States.

Third. It will be a mighty encouragement and stimulant to local effort. Hang up a sum of money, to be obtained by any community on the sole condition that it strains every nerve of home resource, and every public-spirited man, every anxious mother, and every aspiring and eager youth besets that community to do its best. There are thousands of neighborhoods in the open Southern country, and hundreds of little villages and settlements, where such an offer would stimulate the people and, for the first time, bring them together in a hearty movement for the common education of their children.

Such aid, continued for a reasonable time, would root the people's common school in all except peculiar communities, and educate their inhabitants to its permanent support. I have never heard of a community which has enjoyed a good common school for a term of years giving it up for any cause but such as would destroy every public institution. The reason is, that a good public school is the most potent stimulus to every other good institution. While, in itself, it is a a powerful agency for mental growth and intelligence, a potent disciplinarian in the common moralities, a nursery of industry and patriotism, it is, all the time, stirring up the family and the Church to new efforts, and, in a variety of open and secret ways, refreshing the social, industrial, and civic life of the people. The American people know a good thing when they have it, and the Southern people can be trusted to take good care of the school thus rooted and confirmed by national aid.

I leave to others the large and important sphere of argumentation that enforces this imperative duty on the ground of justice, political policy, Christian philanthropy, or defense against impending national calamities, more threatening, even, than any peril of the past. And I must be excused for taking but little stock in the gloomy predictions and dismal apprehensions of many good people in all sections of the country in regard to Southern and national affairs. I do not think I have been deceived in my widely extended observations of the Southern educational situation, or have been blinded by the uniform kindness of these people to the difficulties still to be overcome. I can understand that even wise men, viewing Southern life from a local and limited angle of observation, can differ widely from me in their estimate; or, again, that eminent educators and social philosophers may be oppressed by anxious doubts concerning the outcome of American society as a whole. But, looking at this Republic along the line of historical perspective, it seems to me that, for the past hundred years, our new country has been maneuvering for position among the nations of the earth, and that now it stands before the world in an attitude more hopeful, with greater possibilities for a Christian nationality, than any people in Christendom. I cannot discover any defect or danger in any section which will not yield to a true education of the head, the heart, and the hand, continued through a few decades, supported by the abundant means, pushed by the united executive capacity, and sanctified by the Christian spirit of our people. And, because I believe in this; believe in the pos-

sibilities of human nature; believe in the outcome of our American way of dealing with man; believe that the Southern people, even in its most illiterate regions, is at heart thoroughly American; believe that all foreign, obstructive, and un-American classes will either be finally absorbed or cast out from American society; believe that the vision of the fathers will be realized in the glory of the children, I have given my life to this glorious "ministry of education," and have come here to bear my own humble testimony in the great enterprise in which you are embarked to-day.

2. ADDRESS OF WELCOME TO NORTHERN TEACHERS AND MISSIONARIES IN THE SOUTH.

REV. CHARLES H. FOWLER, D.D., LL.D.,

Secretary of the Missionary Society of the Methodist Episcopal Church.

MR. CHAIRMAN, Teachers, and Missionaries who have been laboring in the South, Fellow-workers in the bonds of supreme loyalty: It is my privilege to bid you welcome on account of your noble work and heroic spirit—welcome from the hot season of your sweltering fields, welcome to this great Christian gathering, to this distinguished center of religious influence, to this time of spiritual insight, to this healthful retreat by the loud-resounding sea.

I am expected not only to proffer you a welcome that shall invoke upon you blessings as numerous as the sands of the sea, and as wide as the bosom of the sea itself, but also to make brief reference to the great moral and religious principles that underlie your work, the environments where you are applying those principles, and the results, actual and possible, that follow the application of those principles.

I am not here merely to say pleasant words and deliver commendatory sentences. This would be a pleasant task, in which the impulse of my heart would be sanctioned by the approval of my conscience. It has so often been my task to stand for the minority, as advocate for needy causes, so often my duty to befriend "the under dog in the fight," that it would seem a strange experience to utter only words of commendation.

I must limit myself in such a luxury, and handle rather the weightier matters of this work. As I look into your faces I am thrilled as in the presence of a divine demonstration of the truth and power of the Gospel. Jostling so constantly against men who measure every thing by how it will

advantage them, hiding when the sky threatens, and whining out to the passing storm, "We did not do it," never daring to utter one manly word for an imperiled cause or a wronged brother man, it is refreshing, it is inspiring, it is transfiguring, to look into the faces of men who, turning away from the turmoil of the mart and shutting out the glare of the world, have gone down into the secret depths of their own nature, and there, watching their own convictions as they bubble up from the deep fountain of their being, have listened to the still, small voice within, and have gone forth unostentatiously into the heroism of obscurity, into the solitude of ostracism, and into the anguish of desertion, for the sole purpose of teaching the ignorant, of guiding the wayward, of improving the imbruted, and of saving the lost. To meet such a company is to stand on the threshold of heaven, and feel the powers of the world to come.

We cannot but admire the soldier who, hearing the first tap of the war-drum, springs from the couch of his ease and the home of his comfort, takes a hurried farewell of wife and babes, and, arming amid the gathering gloom of the coming conflict, goes forth into the darkness to defend an imperiled cause, or die amid the ruins he is not willing to survive. For him history records his deeds; poets sing his praise; sculpture chisels his statue; patriotism emulates his examples: posterity piles his monument, and mankind cherishes his memory. It is in the deepest and best of our rich human nature to enrich ourselves by praising and emulating him. For we feel, with Lowell:

"Then to side with Truth is noble when we
share her wretched crust,
Ere her cause bring fame and profit, and
'tis prosperous to be just;
Then it is the brave man chooses, while
the coward stands aside,
Doubting in his abject spirit, till his Lord
is crucified,
And the multitude make virtue of the faith
they had denied."

We are living in the golden age of martyrs.
For the last twenty-five years the blood of
the race has run richer and thicker and
stronger than ever before. Men in former
ages have died for liberty, as at Thermopylæ
and on the many fields of the Roman republic, But Athens was little more than an
interior country-seat, and free Rome a
modern city. Both combined could not resist some single States we could select. And
the gulf between their soldiers and the citizens makes comparison with this time almost
impossible. Men have died for the truth
under the persecution of tyrants. But, with
exceptional and fanatical cases, death sought
them in dens and caves and deserts; and
they died because there was no room on
the earth where they might live with the
truth. Men have perished for an idea, as in
the Crusades. But as a law they wandered
like tribes, finding but little difference between their successive camping-grounds.
Leaving few comforts, they hardly perceived
additional discomforts. Men have died for
gold, as in the expeditions into India, to the
New World, and to California in the early
days. Every style of martyrdom has been
produced in history, and often with great
profuseness. But for their number, for their
ability, for their intelligence, for the comforts
they left, for the peace and quietness out of
which they marched, for the elevated character of their motives taken as a mass, all
things considered, the heroism and spirit of
this quarter of a century is not equaled in all
the ages. There were single regiments that
could man and brain all the governments of
the earth, and all the civilizations of the
world, from guiding the ships of State to
creating a newspaper; from changing the
color of lilies by chemical baths to improving
the breed of fish in their changing baths;
from building a locomotive in the desert to
operating a telegraph-office in a hollow tree;
from the engineering that could span almost
any gulf, as Roebling hung a mile and a
fourth of Broadway above the masts of the
sea, to the skill that can polish the pivots
of a chronometer till it can track the comets
within two seconds to the century. These
men, pregnant with all the possibilities of
the race, went forth by the thousand, by the
ten thousand, by the hundred thousand, by
the million, to die for an idea, for liberty, for
justice, for fair play, for equal rights—wont

forth to take the bonds off and let a race up
into light and liberty and manhood and ac-
countability. We live in the golden age of
martyrs.

We are just where we can properly
estimate their quality and fiber. The notes
of martial music have faded from our ears.
The canvas cities of the soldier have vanished from our plains. The smoke of burning cities no longer darkens the horizon.
Rich harvests of cotton and sugar-cane grow
on the fields that were plowed by shot and
shell, and billowed by the graves of the dead,
with nothing to excite or alarm or enrage, as
we can to-day coolly estimate the spirit and
glory of this age.

It is pre-eminently an age of ideas. All
the passage-ways up into modern life are
doored by the daily paper and the New Testament. No man who has not a free use of the
key, the alphabet, can find his way up into
the real forces that mold and fashion the
races. The government stood that is now
expected to carry, not trample, the people,
has a curb-bit in his mouth. That bit is the
press. A rein runs from that bit to almost
every hand in the land. If this noble steed
prances or frisks too much, he is sure to feel
the weight of some vigorous hand. This is
a reign of ideas. The printing-press has set
up a new monarch over all governments and
over all kings, who puts up rulers and casts
them down; before whose steadfast eye all
shields dissolve and all helmets melt. That
supreme ruler is Public Opinion, and his
decisions are law. Absolutely nothing can
stand against him. When Public Opinion
pronounces an institution like slavery right,
there is no power on earth to enforce enactments against it; when Public Opinion pronounces a law like the fugitive slave law
wrong, there are not armies enough in the
land to enforce it. This is an age of ideas.
The great conflicts are conflicts of ideas.
Beasts fight with claw and fang, but men
fight with ideas. Armageddon is the Anglo-
Saxon skull. Dominion is to be determined
by the back-hold and hip-lock of logic. The
work of to-day is to *mold* public opinion. It
cannot be resisted. It cannot be overcome.
It must be created anew. It must be guided.
This is the strong work. This is the delicate work. This is the highest field for
heroes and martyrs. To go down among the
lowly, to sit by the stool of the untutored,
and there, by patience and tenderness and
all-loving ministrations, put a new light in
the lusterless eye of ignorance, a new fire
in the dull brain of stupidity, a new hope in
the leaden heart of stolidity; to pick up this
new creation, set its face toward the future,
lift up its brow toward the heavens, put steel
into its sinews and a holy ambition into its
blood, and thus to open a new future with
new convictions, is to create a new king.
To do this quietly and patiently, while prej-

udice clubs you over the head, and malice stabs you in the back, and cowardice opens pitfalls beneath your feet, is unwittingly to enter into the first rank of heroes, and into the copartnership of redemption, by which we are permitted to make up a part of the afflictions of the Redeemer which are behind. Teachers and missionaries—such workers are the ripest products of sixty centuries of Divine instruction and nearly nineteen centuries of Gospel preaching.

Bishop Ames was invited to share the carriage of a German baron on the occasion of the great military review in Washington at the close of the war. They had a favorable position for viewing the procession. Hour after hour the soldiers marched by. There rumbled the field artillery; there crowded by, with dripping sides and champing mouths, the cavalry, and there tramped the unwearying infantry. At one time there passed a brigade newly clothed for the day —every uniform clean and beautiful, every bayonet and sword polished and gleaming. The drill was perfect. The men were at the top of their condition. Every motion and look bespoke the soldier. As they marched by the baron turned around to Bishop Ames and said, " Pishop, those men can whip the world." Presently there followed by in the procession some old veterans, just as they came from their long campaigns in the South. They were soiled and ragged. One man had one leg of his pants patched out by strange cloth; another had no coat; another had a tea-kettle strung on his gun over his shoulder, another had part of a ham on his bayonet. So they represented the breaking up and utilities of the camp. They rolled along with an easy, swinging gait, chatting, laughing, occasionally imitating some animal, giving a bark, or a howl, or a screech, yet keeping step and in line. As these men, with their tattered uniforms and tattered flags, went by, the baron sprang up and, throwing his arms around Bishop Ames said, " My Gott! Pishop, these men could whip the devil!"

So it seems to me to-day, as I look into these faces that have been trying to illuminate the way for the lowly and the benighted, till they shine like the face of the old Hebrew deliverer, that nothing is impossible to these men.

Brothers, as I look at you and see the winters of New England in your blue and steel-gray eyes, and find the vigor and freedom of New York and the great North-west in your architecture, and still discover the hot kiss of the Southern sun upon your cheeks, I am convinced that there is no longer any sectional South. That South is a factor of history. It is our South. It belongs to the whole Republic. It belongs to Freedom. Liberty says: " *My Maryland,*" " *My South.*"

This is an age of miracles as well as of martyrs. Changes in population surpass the changes by Alladin's lamp. New England, the real New England, that thinks, and lights, and trades, and wriggles, and conquers—this immortal, invincible New England—has gone west of the Hudson and stretches away over the Alleghanies. It has seized the great valley beyond the mountains. It has gone into the sunny South, and the South has come up the great river and pushed out on to the great plains. The South is in Kansas in force. It is on Fifth Avenue in elegance. It is in Wall Street in power. It is enthroned and ruling in Massachusetts; New Orleans reigns in Boston. There is no sectional South. It is ours. We bought it. We paid for it with ten billions of treasure. We baptized it in blood—no mere sprinkling, but a genuine immersion. We have seeded it down with $30,000,000 worth of school-houses and ideas. It is vitalized by the throbbings of the national heart and warmed by the common life-current. In God's good order it belongs to those who can make its soil produce the largest liberties and the most cotton.

Happy are we that it is ours; we may need it in the near future. Since the surrender of Massachusetts and the threatened transformation of New England and Manhattan Island into papal provinces, it is impossible to forecast how great our needs may yet be. Protestant and native South may yet bring to us the chalice of life for the olive-branch of peace. Let us rejoice in the new South, the non-sectional South.

We have great hope for the South. True, many of its old ideas and old convictions still remain, but the almanac and the tide of emigration into the West will soon neutralize their power for harm. The Anglo-Saxon will rule. Enlightened, he must rule in righteousness. The North, the nation, by schools and the Gospel, must put upon the throne the 8,000,000 of poor whites, and teach them to love liberty and fair play. Then the colored man can have his rights secure, and be allowed to make his own future.

Brothers, you went into the South to teach. There was much need of it there, as in many other parts of the country. You have had many branches of knowledge to impart. You have taught *Geography* until everybody now knows that the United States is bounded on the south, not by the Ohio River, but by the Gulf of Mexico. You have taught *Mathematics.* It is now accepted that the whole is greater than any of its parts. The lad who enlisted in Louisville, Ky., and marched south-west for ten days, and still camped in Kentucky, and wrote home to his father, saying, " If the United States is bigger than Kentucky it must be awful big," has learned some geography and some mathematics. You have also taught *Orthography*. There are whole communities now able to spell war without an *h*, and pronounce it with an *r*. Last winter I saw a bright New Hampshire girl in a school in New Orleans teaching a class to pronounce "*r*." It is something to rescue a lost "*r*." An old German professor, on his death-bed, handed his glory down to his son, saying, "I have given my life to rescue a lost dative." We are rescuing a lost "*r*." On that awful day, when word came of the assassination of President Lincoln, a friend of mine, a D.D., was on the train nearing St. Louis. Every body was excited and spoiling for a fight. It was before the great bridge was built over the Mississippi River. The passengers got out of the ferry into the 'buses. This D.D. sat near the end of the 'bus, next to an old lady. A stranger swung into the 'bus, and swaggered a little, till the umbrella under his arm struck the old lady in the face. This D.D. pushed it down with a jerk, knocking some packages from the stranger's arm. He turned round and said, "Whoh dahd to touch my pehson." The D.D. responded, "I did, and I can whip any man. to-day, who cannot pronounce 'r.'" A sailor at the other end of the 'bus said, "That is right; go in, my laddie, and if you need any help I'll sail down." It is quite worth while to teach this American people how to pronounce "r."

You are also teaching Sociology, which in its last analysis reduces to two principles: First, the value of the longest pole in its relation to the persimmons; second, that the strong must help the weak. Natural science insists upon the fundamental law of "the survival of the fittest," but you have taught the obligations of the fittest. You have also taught Ethnology, that of one blood God hath made all the nations to dwell upon the face of the earth. You have crowned this magnificent round of sciences with the great Theology, that "by the grace of God Jesus Christ tasted death for every man," including Negroes and poor whites. These great ideas are well planted in that Southern soil, and soon all the people can rejoice in their healing shade.

The growth of the South is marvelous. In considering this growth we must not forget the prejudices and hatreds and bitter feuds and wounded pride that the war inevitably left in its track. The people did not have a fair chance to exercise their sense. It would be more philosophical to wave a red blanket at a bull, and ask him to be judicial in his judgments, than to take a Southern people, just out of the last ditch, with their old slaves exercising authority over them, and ask them to strike the best and wisest policy at once. It is not in human nature. The nerves will leap and sting after the searing iron. The flesh will crawl after the knife. The marvel

is not that the South were vengeful, but that they are cooling and righting so rapidly.

At the close of the war hardly a percepti- ble per cent. of the colored people of the South could read. To-day over thirty-five per cent. can read the Bible. However bit- ter the pill, the South has allowed so much to be done. And to-day you can hardly find a leading man in the South that does not want the colored people educated. Not anx- ious to do it themselves, they are willing we should do it. They are not much nearer mixed schools than many of the people of the North, but they are willing they should have their own schools. This is a mighty advance.

In large sections of the South the colored man can work and secure fair compensation for his labor. This is not universal. But the South is marching to the front on these great questions of labor. Rocked, as we are, on the stormy bosom of labor strikes, it may not be a favorable time to compare the condition of labor in the two sections.

The colored man is having the best time with his religious nature ever known in the history of the country. In the decade from 1870 to 1880 the population of the whole country increased 30 per cent., while the colored population increased 35 per cent. The communicants of evangelical Protestant Churches increased 50 per cent., which is 20 per cent. more than the increase of the popu- lation. But the colored communicants in- creased 137 per cent. Surely we can hardly ask for clearer demonstration that the col- ored people have at least had a fair chance religiously. This growth in religious life indicates a quickening of the intellect, and means that new forces are working in the South. With these increased liberties and activities there comes also increased pros- perity. In the old days, with slave labor, the South produced 3,000,000 bales of cot- ton per year. Last year, with free labor, she produced about 7,000,000. No rational observer of events can doubt that the South will soon rise to be a great, free, rich. and powerful people. Traveling through the South one is impressed with the vast stretches between the cities, school-houses, and church- es, but these stretches are being broken up by the power of the new life.

One of the principal native educators in North Carolina, teaching in the same school where his father and grandfather taught be- fore him—a school where a large per cent. of the children of the leading families of the State have been educated ever since the days of the Revolutionary War—has planted him- self squarely in favor of colored education, and encourages his pupils to enter this work. In the three great educational conventions of North Carolina last year he presented his views, and spoke as one having authority. He said to the assembled teachers: "I would join with you in putting any stranger into the nearest horse-pond who would venture to tell us the truths I intend to utter. But we cannot afford to suppress the truth. You may call me Yankee if you will, but I have seen such environments in Boston that the leading public-school teachers receive as high as $5,000 a year, and women as high as $2,500 a year. Now, call it what you please. If we can create such a state of the public opinion that teachers can be so paid, we shall be on the highway to prosperity. I have seen whole States where the majority of the population are within five miles of a railroad depot, and hardly a family can be found ten miles away. If we are to become great and rich and powerful, we must use the means; if we can imitate Massachusetts in prosperity, I am in favor of imitating her in the use of the means." The growth of the South in ideas is something marvelous. In the future, when she has cleared her atmosphere, and is prepared to do well by new-comers, the tide of immigration will turn into her genial climate rather than into the colder regions to the North. She has postponed the day of her power, but it will come. The South of to-day is a babe—a small, puling babe—compared with the South of the future; and blessed is the man who has a hand in molding her institutions and convictions.

In a land like this, where there are no dominant sectional interests, where each part belongs to all the other parts, one cannot look toward the future without being awed by the magnificence of that future. This country is to be as the theater for Anglo-Saxon activities and for the Protestant religion. As I look over the arc of the future the ages are rolled together, and I see the untold millions of freemen, by the grandeur of their life, drawing all nations up to them. We are in at the beginning of things. We ought to act like the fathers and founders of history. It is a great thing to be in at the founding of great empires. We venerate the memory of the Signers of the Declaration of Independence. They had the opportunity for greatness, and seized it. We are also blessed with the chance to nurse great events and forces. It seems but yesterday when George Washington made his way through the wilderness to Pittsburg. Only 130 summers have passed, yet how wonderful the changes, with forests cleared and homes built to the far-off Pacific. The two and a half millions have grown into 50,000,000. How great it was to have a chance to move these millions! Now, turn that short measure toward the future, and what have you? One hundred and thirty years hence, and the stars and stripes will float over a thousand million citizens, almost as many as the entire population of the earth to-day. What a privilege to have a hand in forming and de-

veloping the institutions of to-day! The 6,000,000 colored people will be grown to 150,000,000, with great universities and renowned scholars, with statesmen and rulers, with honors second to none known to the race. It cannot be a vain thing to purify the fountain out of which such a vast stream shall flow. Brothers, be patient. With 150,000,000 back of you, nothing shall be impossible to you.

The resources of this country are beyond computation. Take the population of India as a standard. While in England a population of 200 to the square mile means a town or a mine or a factory, in India some agricultural districts rise to 985 to the square mile. That would give us 3,500,000,000, about three times the present population of the globe. Swing into the future as far as the landing of the Pilgrims is in the past, and this continent will hold and feed thrice the present human race.

We are in at the beginning of things. War must soon yield to the spirit in the *treaty of Washington*, by which the *Alabama* claims were settled. Intemperance must shortly fall beneath the awakened conscience of the people. Service from inventions will multiply. As England to-day has machinery working for her people equal to 19 men to serve and wait upon each man and each woman and each child in all the kingdom, so, soon, each American shall be served by machinery equal to fifty servants. Brothers, it has been a long process to build up this Anglo-Saxon race, but it is well built, and has a future.

Go back yonder to Britain. Away back in the dim traditional ages we find the Gaels occupying England. By and by the Leogrians came over from the eastern extremities of the continent, and drove the Gaels back into the mountains of Scotland and over into green Erin. About 500 years later the Cambrians made a landing in the south of the island, and drove back the Leogrians. About 500 years later the Britons crowded in, and subdued the Cambrians and Leogrians, and made for themselves a home and a future. About 500 years later the Romans, under Cæsar, established themselves on the island. About 500 years later came the Saxons, and conquered the land. Then about 500 years later came the Normans, under William the Conqueror, and subdued all that preceded them. Thus one nation and then another, one layer after another, fighting, struggling, sweeping over the island with sword and fagot, till they almost paved the whole land with their fallen heroes, uniting, mingling their blood in their veins and in their streams, rising by every conflict and by every new re-enforcement, they have succeeded in building up the mightiest civilization known to history.

By these weary and bloody processes this English-speaking people have been created;

but they are created and ready for use. Still we are in at the beginning of things. The centuries are at our feet. The millions are in our hands. We can fashion them for righteousness if our faith fail not.

Yonder, in India, on the banks of the Jumna, stands the most beautiful and wonderful structure ever erected by man. It is most finely described in "The Land of the Veda." It was ordered by the great ruler of Delhi, Shah Jehan, and it was created by a French architect, Austin de Bordean, in the second quarter of the seventeenth century. It hovers over the center of a spacious park. It is approached through a gate-way of red sandstone, inlaid with mosaic and inscriptions from the Koran in white marble. The avenue from the gate to the tomb contains eighty-four fountains, and a large marble reservoir bordered by rows of cypress trees. The songs of birds mingle with the rippling of the fountains, and the air is burdened with the fragrance of the rose and the orange. The Taj stands on a marble terrace thirty feet high. It is built of white marble. The dome, shining like a globe of silver, is seventy feet in diameter, and the golden crescent at the top is two hundred and seventy-five feet from the terrace. The whole of the Koran is inlaid in black marble on the outside, and in precious stones within.

It is difficult to apprehend its richness and the vast outlay for its erection. Among the treasures of the wealthy you will find opals and rubies of a few grains' weight. But wrought into this wonderful structure are 3,870 pounds of opals and 4,644 pounds of rubies. Woven about in the marvelous designs are 8,342 pounds of emeralds, and shining every-where are the 12,470 pounds of sapphires. Add to this nearly 39 tons (77,400 pounds) of carnelian, and 20,640 pounds of turquoise, and 37,840 pounds of lapis lazuli, with 22 1-2 tons of agate and onyx, and the mind is lost in the immense values. These vast figures help our thought up toward the $16,000,000 paid for the materials, and the 140,000,000 of days' labor put forth in its erection. These vast figures dwindle into obscurity when one contemplates its delicate finish and its breathing, *spiritual* beauty. The walls of the cenotaph are of white marble, inlaid with flowers that look like embroidery on white satin. Thirty-five different kinds of carnelian are used in a single leaf of a carnation, and in one blossom, not larger than a dollar. twenty-three gems are seen. A single flower contains three hundred different stones. Surely, this was "planned by Titans and built by jewelers." It stands to-day the wonder of India, that land of vast empires and ancient dynasties. The soft music of the flute echoing up through the hundred arched alcoves, and returning from the dome to the floor seems the finest and sweetest of any complicated

music ever heard on earth. One says, "It is to the ear what the building itself is to the eye." It is a worthy human ambition to work one's life into such a structure, even though it is only a tomb.

Brothers, as I look, another building rises before me. Its park is this continent. It is terraced up by the ancient mountain ranges. Its borders are washed by the tides of the oceans. Its fountains and reservoirs are rivers and lakes, inland seas. The materials for this edifice are gathered out of all lands. The great body of its walls and dome are of white Anglo-Saxon marble, first found on the North Sea. This is richly inlaid with the black marble from Africa. Then come treasures from every country and city under the stars. The large-brained German, with his industry; the long-headed, open-faced, silent Scot, with his broad plans and enduring purposes; the sprightly, artistic Frenchman, with his treasures of acute science and his love of glory; the stolid, enduring Slav from awakening Russia; the witty, hopeful sons of the heart from green Erin; the free-born, hardy, liberty-loving men from Scandinavia; the aspiring Japanese, the uncomplaining Chinaman, the reflecting, philosophical Hindu, with the stoical sons of the wilderness and the desert; from all lands and from all isles of the sea they come, and are wrought into this temple of liberty. Up and down all its sides, and over all its wide arches, inwrought by the faith and the patience of the saints of to-day, you can read the full Gospel of the Son of God. While standing beneath its vast dome 3,000,000,000 freemen sing "Liberty and righteousness. The Lord God omnipotent reigneth."

Brothers, it is an ambition worthy of the immortals to build our lives into such a structure, which is not a tomb for the dead, but a temple for the living. Let us emulate the patience of God, and do our work at our best —bring to perfection whatever we have in our pattern, whether it be the broad name of the King himself emblazoned over the great dome, or only some hidden lily of the valley in some obscure corner, and we shall be rewarded by Him who guides not only the leaping lightning to its mark, but also the timid dove to her nest.

Sometimes it seems so long to wait. We cannot see results as we wish. We forget that they are certainly coming. We seem to be toiling in the midst of hopeless confusion. In 1641 Evelyn visited Amsterdam, and went up into the tower of St. Nicholas's Church to note the playing of the marvelous chimes. He found a man away below the bells, with a sort of wooden shoes on his hands, pounding away on a key-board. The proximity of the bells, the clanging of the keys when struck by the wooden gloves, the clatter of the wires, made it impossible to hear the music. Yet there floated out over the sea and over the city the most exquisite music. Many men paused in their work, and listened to the chiming, and were glad. It may happen that in your watchtowers, where you are wearily pouring the music out of your life into the empty lives of the lowly, that the rattling of the keys and the heavy hammers, the twanging of the wires, the very nearness of the work, may all conspire to prevent your catching even one strain of the music you are creating, that far out over the populous city, full of weary souls, and far out on the eternal sea, the rare melody of your work blends with the songs of angels, and is ringing through the corridors of the skies. It may gladden some burdened souls here, and sweeten even the rapturous music of heaven.

3. RESPONSIVE ADDRESS.

PROF. SAULSBURY,

Educational Superintendent American Missionary Association.

I CAN think of no valid reason why I should have been called to respond for the veteran workers of the American Missionary Association, except that I am *not* a veteran.

The veterans of any warfare are modest. It is a matter of comment that the survivors of Stone River and Chickamauga, of Chancellorsville and Gettysburg, seldom speak of their exploits except it be to each other.

And so, none of the heroes or heroines, who have carried the flag of the American Missionary Association for the last score of years, could stand here and sound their own praise. But I, a new-comer, a recruit, albeit honored with an officer's commission, may speak of that which I have seen.

The great moving fact in Christian history, the great principle which has given both force and guidance to the Christian world, the idea of duty, an abstraction, an ideality, but never barren, always fruitful and efficient. It has not moved all men—thousands seem never to have felt its sovereign touch. It has moved some, through lack of wisdom, to excesses and follies. It sent the hermits into the desert and the friars to their cells, and kindled the fagots of the Inquisition.

It has done its great work in and through a small minority of mankind, a chosen few; but, through the elect few, it has uplifted the world and brought forth all the greatest glories of the human race.

It has sustained martyrs at the stake, has nerved the Savonarolas and the Luthers, as well as the Gustavuses and Cromwells.

And yet its greatest work has been in the silent, unobtrusive ways and walks of men. In Christian homes, in the burden-bearing of Christian parents and children; in the sacrifices of Christian givers and philanthropists, but, most deeply of all, in the patient missionaries of the Christian Church, has this ideal of duty, of loyalty to God and his law of love stiffened the sinews and strengthened the heart of the world.

Renan, the famous Orientalist and skeptic, in his last little book, pays a beautiful tribute to the French priests who were the teachers of his youth. He says: "My tutors taught me something which was infinitely more valuable than criticism or philosophic wisdom: they taught me to love truth, to respect reason, and to see the serious side of life. This is the only part in me which has never changed. . . . I have never departed from the sound and wholesome programme which my masters sketched out for me. I no longer believe Christianity to be the supernatural summary of all that men can know; but I still believe that life is the most frivolous of things unless it is regarded as one great and constant duty." But this ideal as it now lies in the skeptic's mind and heart, beautiful as it is, is but a dim and diffused reflection of that fire which glows in the heart of the Christian missionary.

Perhaps you have thought that the heroes were all dead and the patterns lost, that the Rolands and the Sidneys, and even the Judsons and the Martyns, were now only historic examples of a lost and no longer visible type. I tell you nay. There are men in our Southern land who, for a score of years, have shown a courage and a devotion equaled only by the martyrs of the Church, indefatigable as Jesuits, unyielding as the Puritans they are.

There are gifted women there who have spent their young womanhood and come to middle age in labors as self-denying as any that history records, sacrificing youth, health, society, marriage, every thing but duty, for the helping of lowly humanity and the service of the lowly Christ.

I could name to you a score of these whom it is my pleasure to know, and before whose moral heroism I take my hat in hand and walk humbly. Meeting from the outset with the bitterest prejudice and opposition from those, even, who professed the same name, braving obloquy and ostracism and personal violence, bitten sometimes by dogs, and threatened oft with the torch and the shot-gun, the missionaries of our and kindred organizations have gone unflinchingly forward to prove and publish the capacities of the downcast race, and show to the Negro himself and all the world that mind is mind and man is man.

And these men loved not simply the poor, defenseless freedman, but the whole people. And, as the Saviour of the world came to all men, and was received by only a few Galileans, so these men and women, going in His name, have been held, like the Christians in imperial Rome, as outcasts and enemies of society.

But they have lived to see a brighter day. It surely *is* a brighter day when a Southern man, "to the manor born," can stand before a Southern audience and speak, as Dr. Haygood did at Monteagle the other day. Said he: "In all truth and common sense there is no reason for discounting, in any respect, a white man or woman simply for teaching Negroes. It is utterly absurd. I believe it to be also sinful. . . .

"Will some master in such fine knowledge explain just wherein it is very nice to sell goods to a Negro, or buy from him, or to practice law for him, or to give him medicine, but a thing abhorrent to teach him whatever he can learn that we can teach? Of what shams we are guilty."

This is not the slogan of fifteen years ago, nor of five years ago. Verily, to modify the language of the Rev. Jasper, "The world *do* move."

But these just ideas have not yet thoroughly permeated Southern sentiment. It is only now and then that a man, standing forth like a herald on the mountain top, can speak thus.

The veteran corps of the American Missionary Association enlisted for life, and during the war, and the war is but half over. True, we have captured the outposts in our front. We have advanced our lines and thrown up heavy fortifications. Fisk and Atlanta, Hampton and Berea, Straight and Talladega, Tongaloo and Tillotson, Avery and Le Moyne, Emerson and Beach, Wilmington, are our strong forts and heavy batteries, laid in solid masonry and manned with skilled artillerists. Earth-works and rifle-pits are not wanting, with thousands of newly-trained cadets out on the skirmish line. Our allied armies, whose war secretaries have graced this platform to-day and yesterday, have their great lines and fortresses. It is only the warfare against ignorance and sin, waged under the banners of the Lord, bright with their inscription, "In hoc signo vinces." It is a winning fight, from which its warriors may some day rest and boast as he that putteth off the armor.

But the end is not yet, and our forces, now in summer quarters by Northern lake and stream, with the coming of October will swiftly rally and again man the works. And they will return with stronger hearts from the contact with sympathizing friends and from offerings like this which have been made to us to-night. In the name of my associates, I thank you all for this expression of your great good-will.

It is not all Northern people, even, who are willing to give us the hand of fellowship. Many, at least of those who have lately made their home in the South, have no word of recognition for us. They have their own business interests to further, their own social status to secure; they cannot afford to compromise themselves by affiliation with those who have the effrontery to sit at table with colored youth.

But do not think that these missionaries are given to repining. Those who have labored longest and suffered most repine the least. In the gratitude and the progress of those they teach, and in the consciousness of the Master's smile, they find their satisfaction and reward. But to you, our friends, we make the appeal that you slacken not the giving hand. The millennium has *not* yet come to the South-land, only a glimmering dawn. The need is dire. The situation is still desperate. We have gone to the front; but you must stand behind us.

4. HISTORY OF THE EDUCATIONAL WORK OF THE AMERICAN MISSIONARY ASSOCIATION.*

BY REV. M. E. STRIEBY, D.D.,

Corresponding Secretary.

THE honor of founding the first school for the Freedmen belongs to the American Missionary Association. That school was opened at Hampton, Va., where, under shelter of the guns of Fortress Monroe, the escaping slaves first found protection as contrabands of war. There these people, though safe from the grasp of their old masters, were without money or work, and were in danger of starving. The Association sent a minister of the Gospel to see what could be done for them. He reached Hampton in the evening, and found a large number of colored people assembled in a long, low, old building, praying that God would send deliverance to them out of their present distresses. The minister, after listening to their prayers for a while, arose and told them that he had come from their friends at the North to bring them help. If the roof of that building had been open and an angel from heaven had descended before their eyes they could scarcely have been more overjoyed or more fully persuaded that God had heard their prayers. Provision was made, so far as might be, for their immediate wants; a Sunday-school was soon opened in the house of ex-Pres. Tyler, and a few days later, Sept. 17, 1861, only five months after the first gun at Fort Sumter, that first day-school was begun. Its first teacher was Mrs. Mary S. Peake, a very intelligent Christian woman, who represented the white and the colored races, and who had, in some way, obtained an education before the war. That spot on the Hampton Roads, where that school was located, had witnessed (two hundred and forty-one years before) the entrance of the first slave-ship into the line of the American continent. That ship brought to our land slavery and all its woes—the curse that cast its baleful blight over the South, that stirred up enmity between the two sections of the country, which it aggravated into direful civil war, amid whose thunderings and lightnings and earthquakes it was itself overwhelmed. That school on the Hampton Roads, the harbinger of all the freedmen's schools that followed, was the morning-star that heralded the dawn of knowledge and of a pure Gospel for the colored race in America, and that is destined to shed its effulgence over benighted Africa.

The beginning thus made was followed early next year by schools opened by the Association in the old Court-house at Hampton, and also at Norfolk, Newport News, the Port Royal Island, Washington, D. C., and Cairo, Ill. The next year, 1863, was inaugurated by Pres. Lincoln's immortal Proclamation of Emancipation. The Association followed this great act by an enlargement of its work. Its day-school at Norfolk numbered twelve hundred day and eight hundred night scholars. In the vicinity of Norfolk were the mansions and plantations of some of the aristocratic families of Virginia, but when our army occupied Norfolk these families found it convenient not to be at home. As the plantations were abandoned, the government permitted the Association to open schools in a number of these mansions—that of Gov. Wise being one. As the Governor had declared before the war that the way to

meet abolitionists was with "Dupont's best and cold steel," as he had hanged John Brown and promptly joined in the rebellion, he must have experienced a vigorous degree of surprise, at least, when he learned that Yankee abolitionists were teaching a Negro school in his own house.

The 4th of July, 1863, greeted the nation with the surrender of Vicksburg, and opened up the Mississippi River and the country adjacent. The colored people, following in the wake of the army, were congregated in vast camps, and thither the Association sent its teachers, starting schools at Columbus, Ky., Memphis, President's Island, and Camps Fiske and Shiloh. Thus, as the guns of the army liberated the slaves, the Association came to enlighten—the rainbow following the storm.

At the end of the war, in 1865, the Association had enlisted the sympathies of the people on both sides of the ocean, and had greatly enlarged its work, so that its receipts, which were only $65,000 for the year before the war, reached $250,000 for the year after the war, and its teachers sent to the freedmen in 1866 numbered 320. These teachers deserve special mention. Most of them were ladies, and were from the best Christian families of the North; many of them had won distinction in the best schools there, and, in the spirit of the highest Christian self-sacrifice, they left honored social positions, the comforts and embellishments of refined homes, and gave themselves, sometimes without compensation, and always with very meager salaries, to the privations, ostracism, and danger of their new position. All honor to these heroic, consecrated Christian workers!

Without following the details of the work of the Association in the line of common-school instruction, it may suffice to say, that it sent forth its greatest number of teachers (532) in 1868, in the gloomy days when Andrew Johnson ruled in Washington and the Kuklux ruled in the South. The teachers were often threatened, mobs sometimes surrounded their dwellings, and one of their number was at length deliberately murdered. But their faith and courage never failed, and they pursued their work heroically and successfully.

But the progress of the pupils in the schools, and the provision made in the States for popular education—though this latter was more in the promise than in the fulfillment—made it plainly the duty of the Association to establish schools of higher grade, and of a more permanent character. The plan for this purpose, largely now realized, has been to plant in all the principal Southern States schools of high grade, introducing into them normal teaching, and as rapidly as needed college and theological instruction, the object being especially to prepare teachers of schools and preachers of the Gospel. Such higher institutions have been established at Berea, Ky., Hampton, Va., Nashville, Tenn., Atlanta, Ga., Talledoga, Ala., Tongaloo, Miss., New Orleans, La., Austin, Texas, and, to complete the list, land has been purchased for one at Little Rock, Ark. Interspersed among these, and in greater number, are normal and graded schools, located at Wilmington, Charleston, Savannah, Macon, Memphis, etc.,—into one of these we intend to introduce kindergarten instruction. Besides these we sustain in whole or in part many primary schools. These institutions and schools may thus be summarized: Chartered institutions, 8; graded or normal schools, 11; other schools, 35; total, 54. Whole number of teachers among the Freedmen for the current year, 319; students, 8,884. I said the object of the higher and normal schools was for the training of teachers and preachers, but we do not forget the needs of preparation for the callings and duties of practical life. Hampton Institute and Tulladega and Tongaloo Colleges have industrial departments; all our boarding-schools give the girls training in domestic work—washing, ironing, cooking, sewing; many others afford instruction in sewing and household duties, and one adds training in nursing; a kindergarten is to be established in Atlanta, and we intend to try the experiment thoroughly.

Perhaps I cannot give a better view of the aim and spirit of the Association than by a brief sketch of the planting and growth of a few of these higher schools.

I introduce Berea College, Ky., first, because it had a history, as an abolitionist institution in a slave State before the war, which has some bearing on its future course as a school where the two races study together. That earlier school was established in 1857 by the intrepid John G. Fee, the son of a Kentucky slave-holder, educated at the North for the Gospel ministry, converted to antislavery views, which he unflinchingly proclaimed, and for which he was disinherited by his father. Returning to the scenes of his youth as a missionary of this Association, in 1848, he organized two white churches and the school at Berea on an antislavery basis. As might have been anticipated, he encountered severe opposition, and was repeatedly assailed by mobs. On one of these occasions he and a brother minister were dragged to the woods, where his companion was severely whipped on the naked back with heavy sycamore rods, and was so much injured that he could not walk the next day. Mr. Fee was then assured that he should receive five times as many unless he would promise to leave the country. He firmly declined and knelt to receive the blows, but at that moment some one in the crowd said, "Don't strike," and the mob dispersed leav-

ing Mr. Fee unharmed. The teachers and colonists at Berea were at length expelled from the State. But at the close of the war, in 1866, they returned, and the school was re-opened and black pupils admitted. This created great excitement, and all the scholars left except thirteen. But the teachers were firm. Slavery had been conquered, but its chief ally and supporter, caste—the curse of society here and the foe of Christianity in India, China, and other mission fields—was still in arms. These teachers believed that in America the battle must be fought against the one as well as the other, and they had the triumphant distinction of having dashed across the color-line, and of having won a marked victory over caste. The pupils in Berea College are now nearly equally divided between both races, and the school enjoys the favor of both blacks and whites throughout the whole region; the very people who once persecuted now applaud.

Fisk University, Nashville, Tenn., was founded in 1866, was located in some old hospital buildings, and remained there until their rotting walls and timbers admonished the inmates that more permanent quarters must be obtained. In this emergency God raised up George L. White and his company of Jubilee Singers. These slave children, with their sweet voices and the touching rendering of the old plantation songs, melted the hearts of men and women in this country, and kings and queens in the Old World applauded and shed tears of generous sympathy. Architecture is said to be frozen music, and the songs of these ex-slaves have been solidified into the tasteful and commodious Jubilee Hall, where the children of the slaves may find a Christian education.

The school at Hampton, Va., is the outgrowth of that first freedmen's school. The first purchase of land for the Industrial Department was made in 1867. The institution was incorporated in 1870, and under the energetic and wise management of Gen. Armstrong it has become one of the most successful schools in the land. Its industrial department embraced both agriculture and the mechanic arts. The agricultural rests on the basis of seven hundred acres of land which is used for farming, gardening, fruit and stock raising, and the making of brick. Its cattle are in part sheltered in a barn costing $6,000. The mechanical operations are accommodated to some extent in the building styled the "Huntington Industrial Works," costing $20,000, run by a Corliss engine worth $4,000, and within that building are a saw-mill and other related industries; while elsewhere there is in part enumerated shoemaking, tailoring, knitting, cooking, baking, and the printing and publishing of a newspaper. The teaching and boarding departments find accommodation in Virginia Hall, (one of the finest school edifices in the State,) in Academic Hall, Stone Hall, Marquand Cottage—but why attempt to enumerate the village of buildings which is constantly growing! Indeed, so rapidly have they multiplied, that last year when we were called down there to lay the foundations in one day of two large buildings, Dr. Potter, of Grace Church, N. Y., who was to lay the stone of the second building, and who at the time of beginning the service was asked to delay for a few moments on account of a passing shower, promptly answered: "No, if we wait, Gen. Armstrong will have another corner-stone ready to lay before we are done with this."

Atlanta University early won a victory for the colored people by proving their capacity to succeed in the higher studies—mathematics and languages. In 1871 the Legislature made an appropriation of $8,000 to the University, and the Governor appointed a Committee of ten persons to examine the school. The Committee were mainly of the former slave-holding class, Hon. Jos. E. Brown, a former Governor of the State, and now one of its Senators, and confessedly a leading man of the South, being its chairman. The Governor, in accepting the appointment on the Committee, frankly stated his reasons: "We held these people as slaves," said he, "because we believed they were an inferior race. They can acquire the primary studies, but will fail in the higher, and I am going to this examination to prove that we are right." The examination lasted three days—the first being in the elementary studies and quite satisfactory, the Governor remarked that this was just what he had anticipated. But as the classes appeared in the Latin and Greek, the attention of the Committee was thoroughly aroused, and their wonder as well; and the climax of astonishment and conviction was reached when the examinations extended into the mathematics. At the close of the examinations the Governor addressed the crowded audience, stating candidly the motives which had induced him to come, but with the magnanimity of a true gentleman he added: "I have been all wrong in my views. I am converted;" and the conclusion reached unanimously by the Committee was embodied in their report to the Legislature, and from which I extract these words: "The rigid tests to which these classes in algebra and geometry, and in Latin and Greek, were subjected, unequivocally demonstrated that, under judicious training and with persevering study, there are many members of the African race who can attain a high grade of intellectual culture. They prove that they can master intricate problems in mathematics, and fully comprehend the construction of difficult passages in the classics. Many of the pupils exhibited a degree of mental culture which, considering the

length of time their minds have been in training, would do credit to members of any race."

Talladega College, Ala., was started in 1868, in a building completed not long before the war for a white school. A planter, who subscribed $900 toward its erection, set one of his slaves, a good carpenter, to work out the subscription. This slave, as he toiled in the hot sun, often said to himself, "This school is for the white children; but, O! when shall our children have an education?" When the war ended, the building had a debt upon it, and had to be sold. We bought it and used it for a school and for the chapel of a church. That slave lived to become a deacon in the church, and to see his four children educated in the school—all of whom, I believe, have become either teachers or ministers of the Gospel. That old man expressed his appreciation of the boon given to his people by saying: "I expect no greater change to come over me when I pass from earth to heaven than I felt when our children were allowed to get an education."

I must be permitted a few words in regard to the sources of income of the American Missionary Association. In addition to its ordinary and liberal receipts from churches and individuals in this country, it has received from Great Britain in various forms $286,000. The Freedmen's Bureau gave it $203,469. Of large individual donors, Rev. Charles Avery, a Protestant Methodist minister, gave it in the early days of its history $190,000; and in later days, Mrs. Valena G. Stone has given it $150,000, which have gone into large and commodious school buildings, mainly for girls, at Atlanta, Nashville, Talladega, and New Orleans; besides $30,000 for Hampton and Berea. All honor to the Christian minister who had the brains to acquire honestly so much property and a heart to give it away so generously; and all honor to the quiet and unassuming Christian lady who has planned so wisely and given so abundantly for the poorest and most needy of her sex. May her days be long in the land, and the blessing of God perpetually shine upon her!

As for the future, we are engaged in telegraphing, and mean to keep at it. A strange electric wire once connected America with Africa. The battery at the African end was charged with the electricity that came from the groans of dying men, the burning of villages, and the capture of slaves; the noise that swept along the wire was the wail of the "middle passage;" and the deliverance in America was the toil, the tears, and the blood of the slave plantation. Thank God! that wire is broken, and the American batteries are all exploded. But a new sort of telegraphing has been started in America, with an entirely new set of batteries. These batteries are schools and colleges and churches, and they are charged with the

12

electricity of learning and Gospel truth; the wires are run into every city and hamlet in the South; and last of all, a line has been stretched again over the seas to Africa. The hum of the message along that line is the song of the returning sons of Africa, and the deliverance there is the preaching of the Gospel to the benighted and degraded. The American Missionary Association is in that business. Its batteries and wires are numerous, well-appointed, and in good running order; and it proposes, in connection with all other well-organized companies, to push the work till the electric spark of light and love shall reach every heart in America and Africa.

5. EDUCATIONAL WORK AMONG THE FREEDMEN BY THE METHODIST EPISCOPAL CHURCH.

REV. JOHN BRADEN, D.D.,

President Central Tennessee College, Nashville, Tenn.

THE Methodist Episcopal Church was among the first to enter the work for the benefit of the freedmen. Her members were patriotic, and entered heartily into the measures which were taken to suppress the rebellion, and to save the nation's life. They were among the first to contribute to the relief of the contrabands. They would have proved false to the teachings of Methodism had they done otherwise. The Church that was first to recognize officially the existence of the government, and its authority, could not see the nation strangled without an effort to save her from the destroyers. Hence, if the Church furnished her full quota for the battle-field, let her voice be heard in favor of law and order—stood firm for the Union, she was only acting consistently with her antecedents. This same Church had always recognized the wrong of slavery, and had been inquiring for more than half a century, "What shall be done for the extirpation of the great evil of slavery?" It would have been an everlasting dishonor to such a Church to be slow in reaching the class of people for whom prayers had ascended, churches had been rent in sunder, families had been estranged, and for whose delivery from bondage hundreds of thousands of lives had been sacrificed, and thousands of millions of dollars expended.

The Methodist Episcopal Church was early represented in the Christian Commission work among the colored soldiers, and in the camp schools of the freedmen. Her pulpits were open to the agents of the Freedmen's Aid Commission, and the contributions were most liberal. Her members and ministers were active workers and agents for these general commissions. They were engaged as teachers in the work of instruction in the camps and school-houses which were extemporized for the purpose. This Church has had her representatives, both of the ministry and laity, heartily engaged in this work since it was possible to do so. When, in August, 1866, the Freedmen's Aid Society of the Methodist Episcopal Church was formed, it was not from any special desire to get out of the undenominational work of the commissions, but to meet the growing demand for more specific work by the Church. Other Churches had found this need, and had organized special Church work. The Friends were first in this field, the United Presbyterians in Ohio organized in 1863, and in the same year the Reformed Presbyterians, United Brethren, and one branch of the Baptists. In 1864 the Old School Presbyterians undertook this work for missionary purposes. In 1865 the Congregationalists, through the National Convention, working through the American Missionary Association, began their specific Church work, and the Church (Congregational) was urged to raise a quarter of a million per annum for this purpose. In October, 1865, the Protestant Episcopal Church, at its Convention in Philadelphia, organized a Freedmen's Aid Society. In the same year the Baptists appealed to their churches to raise one hundred thousand dollars, to begin their denominational freedmen's work.

The Methodist Episcopal Church entered upon its denominational work among the freedmen in the autumn of 1866. No mission field was ever more needy, none ever appealed to the Church with such cogent reasons. Four millions of ignorant people, having the shackles thrown off with one violent convulsion, costing nearly the national life, and having all the responsibilities of citizenship thrust upon them, which seemed to many to threaten the destruction of the nation, were stimulants to this work, which had never been so potent in any other mission work, in the history of the nation. Those more closely allied to the Negro were not prepared to undertake his training for citizenship and for freedom. They lacked, at that time, the disposition and the financial ability to do this work. It was needful for the preservation of the nation that the utmost that the churches in the North could be persuaded to do be done for the enlightenment of this people, and preparing them to take an intelligent part in the sovereignty of this great nation. That some did not want the Methodist Episcopal Church, as such, in the South, was quite to be expected. That her workers would meet with special discourtesy was natural. Old difficulties are hard to settle. Duty, however, does not always permit the workers to choose the pleasantest fields of labor.

The report of the first year gives the following places where schools were organized: Manchester, Va.; Lewisburg, West Va.; Smithland, Ky.; Nashville, Murfreesboro', Spring Hill, Lebanon, Alexandria, Franklin, and National Cemetery, Tenn.; La Grange, Newman, Griffin, Oxford, Jonesboro, Palmetto, Grantville, and Hogansville, Ga.; Huntsville, Ala.; Vicksburg, Miss.; New Orleans, Baton Rouge, Thibodeaux. Franklin, and Jefferson City, La. The second year's report, in addition to the above, gives schools at Hermitage, Edgefield, McMinnville, Elizabeth, Hickory Creek, Goodlettsville, Mt. Pleasant, Buena Vista, Waynesboro', and Hendersonville, Tenn.; Covington and Rome, Ga.; Decatur and Montgomery, Ala.; Bond River and Edminton, Ky.; Evergreen, Washington, St. Martinsville, Natchitoche, La.; Weldon, N. C.; Little Rock, Ark.; Lancaster County, Va.; Charleston, Sumter, Darlington, John's Island, Camden, St. Stephen's, and Guardine Station, S. C.

In these eighteen months, for that is the length of the time the report covers, 59 schools were organized. The first year 52, and the second year 72, teachers were employed. The first year 5,010 scholars in school, and the second, 7,000. The fourth and fifth years' reports contrast quite greatly. The policy becomes one of centralizing instead of expansion. The fourth year the number of schools sustained was (in Tennessee, 17; Georgia, 19; Alabama, 3; Kentucky, 6; Louisiana, 6; Virginia, 2; Mississippi, 3; South Carolina, 6) 58, and 110 teachers. The fifth annual report shows a reduction in the number of schools to 35, showing, not a decrease of interest, but a necessary change in the form of the Society's work. In the beginning, the whole work of organizing and supporting schools for primary work was a necessity, but seven or eight years of this kind of work witnessed a change of two kinds: 1st, The States themselves undertook to do some of this primary work. 2d, Some of the colored students were able to do much of the work in the primary schools, and the people able to pay these teachers. Hence, the number of schools sustained by the Society decreased in two years from 59 to 35, and afterward still more. The necessity for helping the freedmen to help themselves was early manifest. The young people who were more advanced were put to work in the primary schools as teachers, and the white teachers, Northern teachers—"foreigners," as they were sometimes called, were gradually superseded in the primary and country schools by the better educated among the freedmen.

As the Church was released from the care of providing white teachers for the common schools, the work of providing colored teachers became imperative. The primary schools in some of the central points were gradually transformed into normal schools, then into academies; then came the high-sounding names of theological schools, colleges, and universities. But these changes were not so much of choice as necessity. In the prosecution of this work, students with black skins finished, in due season, the arithmetic, and, what was perfectly natural, went to work on algebra, then geometry, trigonometry, conic sections, calculus. They studied Latin, and read Nepos. Cæsar, Virgil; they studied Greek, and read Homer and Demosthenes; then mastered the elements of natural science, and *Belles-lettres*, and did all these just as if their bodies had been covered with a white skin; and having demonstrated that they had the ability, the Church went with them through the course, and said to them, Well done! The Church had said, at first, they must learn to read the Bible. The Negro did this, and then said, We must read Virgil. The Church said, They must know arithmetic; the Negro said, We must know how to measure and weigh cotton and corn, but we must measure the stars also. The Church was slow to say college and university, but the voice of intellect under the dark skin, and the voice of God, said, Let them go free; free to roam the fields of science, of professional and general literature; let them into the halls of science; let them scan the heavens with your telescopes, and the diatoms with your microscopes; let them search in the crucibles for hidden mysteries; let them peer into the musty tomes of the past; let them know the living present; let them know the laws of their own being and destiny, from Mount Sinai and Calvary; let them know the grandeur of the human mind, its capabilities and its destinies, and start them in the race to develop capacity, and to win the highest destiny—eternal life.

The call came for workers in this field, and the responses were equal to the demand. Four years of conflict, with their revealings of the nature of slavery, and its influence on the material, social, and moral interests of the nation, had prepared the Church to sympathize with the freedmen, and also to esteem more highly than ever the fair fabric of our national existence. Christians saw how nearly this black Samson, grinding in our prison-house, had pulled down the pillars of our temple of liberty; and that, instead of being an enemy to national progress, he might be made a friend. Multitudes leaped forward to aid in this transformation. They left homes of comfort, and sometimes of elegance and luxury, for the cabin, windowless and comfortless; churches, where worship was conducted intelligently and spiritually, for sheds and floorless houses of worship, where the great object of the preacher often seemed to be to rouse the emotions, and of the worshipers to shout, sing, jump, and have what they called "a good time." These laborers left the society of intelligent friends for that of the plantation hand, who had but little more culture than the mule he drove. They were exiled from the society of the educated whites around them, as if they had been fresh from a lazar-house; as if the work which was so highly commended by the Lord Jesus as the crowning glory of his own blessed mission, "The poor have the Gospel preached unto them," was an unpardonable offense, worthy of all the indignities, insults, persecutions, and deaths which they could, or dared to, inflict. There was apostolic heroism in some of these workers, and, when threatened with the maledictions of their enemies, they remained at their posts, saying, with one of old, "None of these things move me." And when one fell others were ready to endure hardness as good soldiers. The prejudices of the white people made it necessary, in most cases, for these teachers to live among the colored people, and then they were most heartily cursed for being socially on an equality with the Negro. This subjected them to numerous hardships in this style of living, to which they were unaccustomed, in houses that had few comforts, in society that had no other attraction than its willingness to learn something to make home more comfortable—to improve in their manner of living in the family, to have better housekeeping, better government of children, more respect for marriage and its obligations, and more intelligent views of house piety and family religion. Many of these teachers found a sweet solace in the fact that, thus isolated, they had better opportunities to learn the inner life of the freedmen, and increased power to do them good. No doubt, many humble homes of freedmen to-day are the better for having had the presence and instruction of these self-denying Christian workers. In the future, when the smoke of battle clears away, and the noise of strife ceases, these men

and women, mostly the latter, will be recognized among those who have exhibited the best traits of humanity in their efforts to bless mankind, and the history of the mission work of the Church will not be perfect without mention of these true, self-sacrificing Christian workers.

The people upon whom these teachers were to expend their efforts were exceedingly interesting. They had been for centuries in a Christian land, with a contradiction of the teachings of that Christianity ever before them. They had heard of "Our Father who art in heaven," and had been taught that God was as much their Father as he was the master's. They wondered why one brother could own and use as chattels the others. They had seen the advantages of education through the bars of their prison-house, and were forbidden to acquire it. They had been pointed to the Cross as the place of cleansing for the sinner, as the source of comfort for the sorrowing, patience for the suffering, strength for the weak; and multitudes of them rejoiced in this as their own experience. But this only increased their desire to know more of God, of Christ, of salvation. A people more hungry for knowledge was never known. True, it was limited, in most cases, to reading the Bible and hymn book, and to a little penmanship and arithmetic. Many of the older people would be satisfied with ability to read, in a stumbling way, a few chapters of God's word. They had heard from their preachers something of the word of life, and they desired more. In addition to this desire to know, the freedmen were teachable. They had but little to boast of, and they knew it. They listened to their teachers as little children, ready to hear, and generally to profit by practicing what they learned. If the education of the freedmen had been simply intellectual, it would have been something of a task; but it had to do with their morals also. They had but little correct knowledge of right and wrong, and found themselves addicted to the practice of the wrong, because it was more in harmony with their feelings. They were infants in morals, the physical dominating the spiritual. They had heard, "Thou shalt not bear false witness," but their practice was never to tell the truth if a falsehood would shield themselves or their fellows from trouble. A slave girl was brought from Nashville to Kentucky. Her mistress had taught her to read the Bible. Her new home was to be different from the old. She was sent to her room alone. She took her Bible and began to read its promises, and drew comfort and strength from its hallowed pages. Soon an old servant came in and saw her, and said: "Missus sent me to ax you whether you can read o' no?" "Yes," replied the new-comer. "Missus says if you can read she will sell you Sonf; what shall I tell her?" queried the old servant. "Tell her I dunno a letter in the book," replied the girl, thoroughly frightened at the idea of going farther South. The girl was not sold, and the old servant who told me herself the story was considered among the pillars of the Methodist society to which she belonged. "Thou shalt not steal!" had been thundered from Mount Sinai by the Almighty, and in their ears by their masters. and impressed, in many cases, on their backs, if not on their memories. "Didn't we raise the corn?" said one of them to me; "didn't enough of the corn in the crib, and of the meat in the smoke-house, to supply our wants, belong rightfully to us? If we failed to get enough rations to supply our appetites, could we not help ourselves to that which our labor had made?" This easiness of conscience in this case could easily be transferred to other cases, and the "Meum" and "Tuum" become very much clouded in the ordinary transactions of life. The Seventh Commandment they had heard of, perhaps, but its observance was rather the exception than the rule. There was no special guard thrown around marriage, no sanctity attached to the ceremony. It was simply a "taking up" with each other in most cases, sometimes by choice, and sometimes a choice with the force of the master's will behind it. As a slave, his volitions were hedged in by a force which he feared and often hated. The self-control needful for a high state of morality is not easily acquired, and it is not wonderful that the freedmen did not possess it. To remedy this defect in them was, of necessity, slow work. The freedmen were poor. Their homes were without attractions. Their cabins often not good stables. The furniture of the poorest, and but little of that. They had no tools or stock to begin work with. They had no capital, and but few friends who really stood ready to advise and aid them. They had opposition to their advancement. Men were base enough to swear by the "Eternal" that no Negro should ever go to school in their neighborhood. Children have been met on their way to school and driven home by owners of the plantations on which their parents worked, school-houses burned, and teachers murdered or driven from the field.

When we consider all the circumstances of the colored people as they came of slavery, their physical, mental, and moral debasement, and the difficulties in themselves in the way of their development, the opposition on the part of many whites, and the persistent effort to prevent the Negro from occupying positions he is entitled to as a freeman and citizen of a great nation, and the few openings in business circles for him, without capital and experience, are the results not wonderful?

The faithful teachers have done noble work. The primary scholars of sixteen years ago are the farmers, mechanics, storekeepers, teachers, preachers, lawyers, and physicians of to-day. The thousands of children then in the freedmen's schools are reading, writing, transacting business with facility and intelligence. Thousands of teachers have gone out from our schools, and hundreds of thousands of children have been taught by them.

The Freedmen's Aid Society is now supporting the following chartered schools: Claflin University, at Orangeburg, S. C.; Clark University, at Atlanta, Ga.; New Orleans University, at New Orleans, La.; Rust University, at Holly Springs, Miss.; Wiley University, at Marshall, Tex., and the Central Tennessee College, at Nashville, Tenn.; a theological school at Baltimore, Md.; the Philander C. Smith College, Little Rock, Ark.; and the Meharry Medical School at Nashville Tenn., a department of the Central Tennessee College, which has graduated thirty-six young men with the degree of Doctor in Medicine. Besides these chartered schools, there are twelve seminaries and academies which are doing excellent work for their hundreds of students. There are now over one hundred teachers in these schools, and about 3,500 students.

The Methodist Episcopal Church has expended in her educational work among the freedmen alone nearly two millions of dollars; has nearly half a million of school property among them, and the students expend in the necessary expenses of board, incidental fees, books, and stationery. with traveling expenses, not less than from fifty to seventy-five thousand dollars a year. The beginning of our Church work in the South after the war was in the cabin, the church-house, the brush arbor. Now we have college buildings, with equipments not unworthy older colleges for whites; we have professional schools of theology, law, medicine; and students who were lately slaves have graduated in all these schools with credit to themselves, and have entered upon courses of usefulness full of promise.

During the sixteen years our society has had its history, there have been taught between sixty-five and seventy thousand students, and the teachers which have been educated by these schools of the Church have taught not less than half a million of their people.

What has come of this work? First. Physically. Enter one of our congregations to-day; what a contrast with the one assembled sixteen years ago. Neatness, cleanliness, intelligence, instead of carelessness, filth, stolidity. In many of the homes of our people there has been a corresponding improvement. It may be but a cabin, but there is an air of neatness, that shows a competent head of the household. The flowers in the yard, the clean floor, the snowy spread on the bed, the whitewashed walls, speak of home and comfort. Then there are those whose homes are elegant. They have been successful in business, and have accumulated some property, and are providing for the home-life in a way that shows that they can enjoy the beautiful as well as any of the human race. Look round you, and you find many owning their farmhouses, teams, shops, with money in the bank. Second. Intellectually the growth has been steady, and, under the circumstances, rapid. Multitudes of the colored men in business do their own writing, make out their own business papers, make their own estimates. Periodicals and books are circulated extensively among them. Their intelligence is shown in their increased estimate of education. The colored people were inclined that way once, and some of the more ignorant still are; but the great mass of our colored people are heartily in favor of a good education. This is evidenced by the change in their selection of preachers. They want one that can read and write. On one of our circuits an old-time preacher had been for three years. He was the honored of all, and when he left the work the people felt that they should never see his like again. A young man followed him, with a fair English education. After serving the church two years, he was sent elsewhere. I asked one of the stewards if they wanted Brother H. back again. He answered very firmly, "No! We thought him an excellent preacher, and so he was. But we have had a young man who can read and write, and we do not want to go back to the old-time work."

There are in the Methodist Episcopal Church, among the freedmen in the South, not far from 2,500 Sunday-schools, with over 10,000 officers and teachers, and 140,000 scholars. These are very largely the result of the work of the teachers sent South by the Freedmen's Aid Society and the students educated in our schools. These schools, under the entire control of the colored people, in their management, exercises, work done, will compare favorably with the average Sunday-school of the country. Still further evidence of improvement is seen in their ministry. Our schools have set at work for the Conferences, and not a colored preacher in our Church in the South but has been more or less affected by them. Scores of the members of our Southern Conferences have attended these schools, have learned something of the common English branches, or, perhaps, having previously taken a more extensive course of study, have entered the Conferences, and by their intelligence have put new ideas into the minds of older brethren, and have stimulated them to increased activity in Church work. These young men

have been called to occupy some of the best appointments in their Conferences, and the older members have been incited to increased study in order that they might not be left entirely out of sight in Conference appointments. Of this Freedmen's Aid Society it may be truly said that its influence in waking up mind and developing thought has not only reached to the sixty or seventy thousand students who have been instructed in its schools, and the half million of children taught by these students, but, through the ministry, every one of them having been more or less influenced by this educational work, it has been a benediction to the 200,-000 of our Church members among the Negroes of the South, and five times that number who, at different times, form the congregations of the Methodist Episcopal Church among this people of the South. Then, as the Methodist Episcopal Church is the only branch of Methodism that has had any schools among the Negroes in the South until recently, and as other branches of Methodism have had their Sunday-school teachers and preachers in our schools very largely, we may say that not a Conference of colored Methodist preachers have been without one or more representatives from our schools, and in this wonderful machinery of Methodism it may be that not a colored Methodist family in the whole South but has not been benefited by our schools. Third. Morally there has been growth. On this there is difference of opinion. It is said there is more crime now than formerly by the freedmen. Suppose there is; does that prove that he is morally worse than then? There's a man confined in prison; he does not steal now. Does that prove him honest? The freedmen were slaves. As such they had but comparatively little chance to violate civil law; and when they did, it was generally settled with the lash or by selling the culprit South. Since his emancipation the freedman has had special difficulties to overcome. They were poor. Some of them had toiled long and hard. Their masters had lived off their not-well-requited labors. They saw others enjoying the fruit of their labors. Is it strange that they were tempted when their own families were suffering for bread? That they have yielded so little to the temptation is greatly to their credit. They were inexperienced in self-control. During slavery they were under such control that they did not need much self-government. The whipping-post, the chain-gang, the going South, the threatened death, were government enough. Immediately after emancipation they were aided by the government and by the commissions, and their wants were supplied. Then followed the era of the Kukluxes, during which terror reigned in many parts of the South, and the colored people were not free to act, only under a bondage of fear. Then they were ignorant. It is asserted that since they have had schools they have grown worse. It is implied that the schools have been the cause of the increase of crime. There is no greater proportion of colored prisoners in the penitentiaries that have a passable English education than white ones. And when we consider the case with which the black man is sent to prison, as compared with the white, and the frivolous crimes that at times are followed by heavy penalties, we must consider prison statistics as not altogether a satisfactory showing of the increasing immorality of the colored people. On the contrary, the educated ones of these schools have, almost without exception, been true to the teachings of moral law. Most of them have been professed Christians, and have proved true to their profession; and, to the extent of my observation, I call it a slander on the black race, as well as a contradiction of the experience and history of all the past, that Christian education tends to an increase of crime in the educated.

There is a class of people in the world whose past prophecy has been that the Negro is a lazy, worthless specimen of humanity, only made to keep his place, and that place is to be at the footstool of every other division of the human family. When a black man does a wrong, or commits a crime, the "I told you so" is the ready and joyful utterance of what seems to be the wish of these poor little specimens of the superior race—namely, that the Negro will be kept down, or keep himself degraded, by his own act. The general improvement of the colored people in finance, in intellect, in social life, in their regard for the sanctity of marriage, their higher estimate of virtue their more intelligent worship, their increased interest in the advancement of the Redeemer's kingdom—all are evidences of improved moral character. Those of us who have been on the field, and have seen the results of years of patient toil, and compare the present with the past, can say, "Ebenezer," "Hitherto the Lord hath helped us." Before us there is the outlook of a glorious future to the colored people of our land. The bright future for them is in its dawning, when God's children in ebony shall stand side by side with God's children in ivory, side by side in financial strength, in intellectual development, and in moral purity. The black arm shall handle the plow, the hammer, the plane, with a skill and strength equal to the white. The brains under the curly locks will be equally productive of grand conceptions as those under the straighter ones. The tongue, that is hidden behind thicker walls, will be as eloquent in those behind thinner ones. In the school-room, in halls of legislation, on the rostrum, at the bar, by the bedside of the sick, on the bench, in the pulpit, Ham and Japheth shall stand side by side; and not only Africa, but the millions of the other dark races of the earth, shall hear the Gospel from the dark race of our own land. When this grand consummation shall be reached, not least among the agencies God shall have used to bring it about will be the Freedmen's Aid Society of the Methodist Episcopal Church.

6. THE METHODIST EPISCOPAL CHURCH IN THE SOUTH SINCE THE WAR.

REV. J. C. HARTZELL, D.D.,[*]

Assistant Corresponding Secretary of the Freedmen's Aid Society of the Methodist Episcopal Church.

THE full significance of the educational work of the Methodist Episcopal Church in the South, since the war, cannot be understood without a survey of the whole work of that Church in that region during the time named.

In two respects this Church took a different course, in entering the South after the war, from that taken by other Northern Churches. It went into the South *as a whole Church*, to do the threefold work of establishing churches, circulating literature through her Book Concern, and of founding and supporting institutions of learning.

The pulpit, the press, and the school were her methods there as elsewhere. Other Northern Churches have been confined almost wholly from the outset to educational work. The Congregationalists, who, next to our Church, have done most in the South, report less than two hundred church edifices in the whole South. The great work of that Church had been educational. The Presbyterians and Baptists of the North are also doing excellent educational work in the South, but have built even fewer churches than the Congregationalists. On the other hand, with the Methodist Episcopal Church

[*] Substance of address at National Education Assembly, 1882.

in every Southern State, as elsewhere, the first and chief work has been to organize congregations and erect houses of worship. She has erected 3,385 church edifices in the South since 1864, and every one of these churches represents about one hundred new communicants added to the Church since that time. In 1878 and 1879 an average of over four churches were built each week.

Then, again, the Methodist Episcopal Church has gone to all classes of people in the South, as no other Church whose chief centers are in the North has done, or attempted to do. Other Churches have been and still are confined chiefly, not only to educational work, but also to work among the colored people. I doubt if all the Churches from the North, outside of our own, have built over a hundred churches among the whites in the South since the war. This Church has built, among the whites alone in that territory, 1,540 church edifices since 1864. It has also developed a vigorous Conference among the Germans in the South-west.

This going into the South as a whole Church, and going to all classes of people in every State as God opened the way, is the key to the spirit and policy of the Methodist Episcopal Church in the South since the war. No other spirit and policy would have been worthy of Methodism.

There are several questions often asked about this Southern work which ought to have definite answers. I will mention the most important of these, and try, without going into statistical details, to give satisfactory replies. My data at hand do not include statistics later than 1880. The showing would be better if the increase of 1881 and 1882 was included. For brevity's sake only Church communicants and property are mentioned; Sunday-school and other Church work would make an equally favorable showing.

1. *What is the actual strength of the Methodist Episcopal Church in the Southern States?*

The membership, including traveling and local preachers, is 410,899. The Church and parsonage property amounted, in 1880, to $8,563,416. The institutions of learning, all founded since the war, now number 43; with students in attendance, mostly advanced pupils, numbering about 6,500. The property of these institutions in land, buildings, etc., all acquired since the war and owned by the Church, is valued at nearly $500,000. There are also the weekly *Advocates* at New Orleans, Chattanooga, and Fort Worth, Texas.

2. *How much of the present strength of the Church in the South has been actual increase?*

(1) Forty-three institutions of learning, with fully $500,000 of school property, and about 6,500 young men and women in attendance each year. This is all clear gain.

Dr. Braden's paper gives the history of the development of the educational work among the freedmen. Beyond this, among the white membership of the Church in the South, eighteen seminaries and colleges have been developed, making thus forty-three institutions mentioned. At the General Conference of 1880 action was taken looking to the superintendence and development of the entire educational work of the Church in the South under one society. For the year ending June 30, 1883, the Freedmen's Aid Society expended $178,600. In other ways fully enough was expended in educational work to increase this amount to $225,-000. This was spent in educational work alone in one year. The Missionary, Church Extension, and other societies of the Church expended in the same territory and same year fully as much more in supporting pastors, erecting houses of worship, aiding Sunday-schools, etc. This work, it will be understood, has no relation to that of the Methodist Episcopal Church, South, or the African or African Zion Methodist Churches.

(2) The statistics of membership and Church property stand as follows:

1880, Membership.410,899	Ch. Property.$8,563,416	
1866, " . 87,804	" " . 2,580.693	

Increase in 14 years,

Membership 328,095   "   "   .$5,982,723

This is an average increase of more than 22,000 members each year. This gain in fourteen years in the South alone is nearly as much as that of all Methodism in America up to 1827, or during the first sixty years of its existence in this country. In 1879 40,606 persons, mostly adults, were baptized by our ministers in the South. This increase includes the erection of 3,385 *new church edifices on what was slave territory.* Every one of these churches means a fixed center of evangelistic power where probably none would have existed had not our Church entered the field. Every church also means a Sunday-school, and a great number of the church buildings are used during the week for public and private secular schools.

3. *But what of Church life, especially among the colored people?*

To the shame of America it must be said that, for two hundred years, the Negro has been the victim of systematic misrepresentation. Doomed to slavery, it being made a crime to educate him, the women taught to know no virtue; reduced physically, intellectually, and morally, as a rule, to the level of the brute as nearly as he could be by the cruel ingenuity of the Anglo-Saxon; pray, who is to blame if the Church life of the Negro is not what it ought to be? As a rule the men in the South who have the most to say of the Negro's immorality are those who have the least sympathy with any work to help educate and save him. Multitudes of good people of all classes and in every part of the South know and rejoice in the fact, that in all the essential elements of Church and religious life our Negroes are making rapid progress. In giving money out of their poverty to help care for their own poor, to support their pastors, to erect houses of worship, and to aid the benevolent causes of the Church, they do marvelous things. It is not unfrequently the case that our colored people raise for Church purposes more than do our white members on the same territory. The late Tennessee Conference (colored) raised last year $1 08 per member for support of pastors, and 14 cents per member for benevolence; while the Central Tennessee Conference (white) raised, on the same territory, for Church support only 39 cents per member, and eight cents per member for benevolence.

In the administration of discipline against every form of vice the Negro churches of the South are also improving rapidly. Wherever the minister is fairly intelligent, pure, and faithful, there is always a company of faithful men and women to rally round and help him. I know many of the churches in the South where the Discipline is as well enforced as it is in the average white churches anywhere. An eminent worker in this field forcibly says:

" There is no estimating the power of the Discipline of the Methodist Episcopal Church for the good of this people. Aside from the spiritual influence of the pure Gospel, there is no such beneficent power at work among the Negro race in the South to-day as the Methodist Episcopal Discipline. I have the best opportunities here to witness the contrast between the Methodist Episcopal and other Churches. The Methodist Episcopal Church is a militant body contending for the ten commandments and the glory of a pure people."

4. *What has been the increase of the Methodist Episcopal Church in the border States, that is, where it was organized at the close of the war?*

This border territory is included in the States of Maryland, Delaware, District of Columbia, West Virginia, Kentucky, Missouri. By subtracting the strength of the Church in that region in 1866 from what it was in 1880 we have the answer. The following is approximately true:

In 1880, Membership.221.797   Property.$6,693,846
In 1866,   " .   87,804   "   . 2,590,693

Increase in 14 years,
Membership 133,993   "   .$4,113,153

This border increase is one of the most remarkable facts in connection with our Southern work. The terrific struggles of our Church to maintain even an organization

in this territory, before and during the war, are matters of history. Over 20,000 seceded from us in Maryland in 1861. It is estimated that we lost 60,000 members on the border during the years 1861–63. If the Church had hesitated to re-enter the South —for had she hesitated at first the work would never have been prosecuted vigorously—who does not see that the intensity of opposition and conflict would, of necessity, have continued on the borders? As to what the result would have been, we can only speculate; but no one can for a moment suppose that such an increase as is above exhibited on this disputed territory would have been possible.

5. *What proportion of our Church strength in the South is among the white people, and what among the colored?*

As nearly as the facts could be gathered, up to 1880, the proportion was as follows:

Members in White Con-
ferences...............212,776 Property.$6,560,287
Members in Colored Con-
ferences.. 197,123   "   . 2,008,120

Several of our Southern Conferences are "mixed;" that is, have not divided on the "color line;" so that it is difficult to reach exact results, but the above is practically correct.

6. *What proportion of the increase in the whole South has been among the white people, and what among the colored?*

It will be remembered that the net increase in the whole South was 323,095 up to 1880. This increase is divided between the white and colored people about as follows:

White members, 1880...212,776 Property.$6,560,287
   "   "   1866... 68,000   "   . 2,330,693

Increase in 14 years..144,776   "   .$4,229,594
Colored members, 1880.197,123 Property.$2,008,120
   "   "   1866. 20,000   "   .   250,000

Increase in 14 years.. 177,123   "   .$1,753,120

The very large increase among the white people of the South is a most encouraging fact; and, as before stated, forms one of the great points of difference between our Southern work and that of any other Church whose chief centers are in the North. All other Churches from the North have as yet done but little in Church work among the white people of the South.

Dr. Stevenson, of Kentucky, has lately, in *The Christian Advocate*, developed this fact with elaborate painstaking He says:

"The *increase* of white members of our Church in the South in sixteen years is about equal to the whole number of Methodists in the world at the time of Mr. Wesley's death, after fifty years of labor from the time of building the first Methodist chapel in Bristol. It is equal to the whole number of Methodists in the United States in 1806, after forty years of effort. It is equal to the number in the Valley of the Mississippi in the year 1827, at the end of forty-one years from the time when the first missionaries entered Kentucky. It is equal to three fourths of all the Methodists in Canada. It exceeds the whole number of members of our Church in all New England at this day, at the end of a little less than a century from the time of the Rev. Jesse Lee's first entrance into that field. Let it be remembered that these comparisons are with our *white increase only*, and not with our entire white membership."

The Methodist Episcopal Church has one fourth as many white members on what was slave territory as has the Methodist Episcopal Church, South. The latter Church has increased in white membership in the South since 1864 not more than 53 per cent., while the former has increased 179 per cent. in white membership in the same territory.

A few months before his death I spent a very pleasant hour with Dr. T. O. Summers, of the Church South, in his office at Nashville. The whole question of the presence of our Church and its work in the South was discussed. On leaving he said: "Well, God bless you in educating the Negroes. After a while you must help us put them all into a big Negro Methodist Church by themselves. After that all you white men from the North must go home, and then we will have peace." Dr. Summers spoke the sentiments of nine tenths of his Church. Our work among the colored people is now acknowledged to be a great success, and hence the desire to have us, at least organically, abandon it. Our Southern brethren want still to maintain the exclusive right Methodistically to Evangelize the white millions of the South. They do not seem to realize the absurdity of that claim in the light of the above facts. There is, however, some excuse for their mistake; but what shall be said of some north of the Ohio who insist every few months in asking through some one of our *Advocates* whether or not our work among the whites of the South is a success.

7. *What has been the net increase of the Church on new Southern territory where, at close of the war, we were not organized?*

The answer is secured with approximate correctness by subtracting the increase in the whole South from the increase on the border:

Whole increase of members to 1880..........323,095   Property .$6,282,723
Border increase of members to 1880.........185,993   "   . 4,113,153
Increase, new Conferences...............180,102   "   .$2,169,570

8. *What has been the proportion of increase between the white and colored people, both on the border territory and in the new Conferences?*

The Delaware, Lexington, and Washington Conferences include the work among the

colored people on the border; and the Baltimore, Wilmington, West Virginia, Kentucky, and Missouri Conferences among the white people in the same region. A careful calculation gives the following approximate results up to 1880:

INCREASE ON BORDER.

White members......85,000   Property....$3,416,000
Colored   " 88,000   "   ...   635,000

INCREASE IN NEW CONFERENCES.

White members...... 56,000   Property... $675,000
Colored   " 153,000   "   1,033,000

The reply to this question gives an interesting view of the whole field. Our chief growth among the whites has been on the border. That is but natural. There the Church was organized from the first, and the territory was in immediate business and social relations with the great body of the Church in the North. But is it not a most remarkable fact, that fifty-six thousand white members should have been gathered in the New South in so short a time, and these, too, almost entirely from the world, and on territory where we were regarded by all the other Churches as intruders and aliens? Could the blessing of God be more truly manifest upon any work?

The chief growth of the colored people has been in the new South. This, too, is natural. There the great bulk of the colored people are, and there the Church has from the first put forth her most earnest efforts to develop her work among them.

The full significance of education in relation to Christian evangelization, among the ignorant and poor millions of the South, has not yet been sufficiently impressed upon the American Christian public. The author of "Our Brother in Black," referring to the educational work of the Churches from the North in the South among the colored people, says, that unless the North had taken hold of this work the South would now be "well nigh *uninhabitable;*" and, appealing to the North in behalf of Negro education in the South, he said, "Unless you continue to help, and help mightily, it cannot be done." And the same writer, after giving a picture of an ignorant white family in his State, and stating that there were multitudes of such in the South, says, "If you can help them, in Christ's name do it."

The work of the Methodist Episcopal Church in the South has only fairly begun. Who shall express in words the full meaning of a Church work which includes the duty of that Church to 18,500,000 of American citizens? This work includes the duty of the Church to 12,000,000 of the white people in the South. Of these many were and are in Christian churches, and yet need the inspiration of new convictions, and the transforming power of a better civilization. And of these same white millions, vast multitudes were and yet are out of the Church, and have never been touched by even the blessings of common schools, to say nothing of Church and Sunday-school privileges.

Add together all the members of Protestant Churches in the South, and multiply that number by four, to include those under the direct influence of the Churches, and you will have only about 12,000,000 out of 18,500,000. Who can estimate the duty of the Methodist Episcopal Church to that other 6,500,000? And, then, nearly all of the 7,000,000 of Negroes in America are and will be in the South. What Wesley or Whitefield or Simpson has logic or eloquence enough to demonstrate or portray the magnitude of the work God requires of the Church in behalf of these needy multitudes?

7. RESPONSIVE ADDRESS.

GEN. S. C. ARMSTRONG,

President of Hampton Institute, Hampton, Va.

In 1862 a few teachers went with the boys in blue into the field and occupied what places they could get, as the Federal lines moved on and the Confederate army moved back, pushing as they had a chance, building up their schools, gathering in their children. Up to the surrender in 1865 there had been a good many more than a thousand of these Northern teachers scattered through the Southern States, and from 1866 until 1870 planned a work for so long as the race should last. The four years from 1862 was pre-eminently a time of seed-sowing; later, from 1870 to now, they have been pushing forward the plans they laid so well then. From 1866 to 1870 came in the Freedmen's Bureau under Gen. Howard, with an appropriation of three and a half millions devoted to the cause of education.

Some five or six thousand apiece of these millions were put into the schools in the various States of the South. There is something worth looking into in regard to this: The nation appropriated three and a half millons of dollars at that time, just as the work was organizing. Most opportunely came this organization, the Freedmen's Bureau, and by wise, generous measures met the most vital point in this progress. So that by 1870 there were nearly 5,000 of selected young colored men and women who received advanced education and went out to labor among the people. That aid from the government was, I believe, the best money ever spent in connection with the whole Southern question. Look at the amount that is wasted in supporting troops, all of which will amount to nothing in the case of a great political change. While the government was fussing those ten years from 1870 to now, these teachers were doing a mighty work.

This meeting is to give them a welcome. They did a vital work—far more than any others. The soldiers have wrought great destruction—that was needed, and the waste places are being slowly built up. It was a grand, stimulating work of seed-sowing and spreading broadcast general ideas. Now, right in connection with this came that government aid of three and a half millions, which I claim is not known us it ought to be, nor appreciated, and shows that the government can help.

From 1875 to 1880 the Southern States built up their systems of free schools, supported by taxes. This was work more and more in harmony with Northern workers. To-day those of us on whom may have seemed to fall the mantle of the old abolitionists are trying to do the work, and we are in more complete harmony with the people of the South than any other class of men. These men have won the respect of all the people whose respect is worth having. In my own experience in Virginia for the last sixteen years, there has been not a single outrage upon teachers, who have gone out five or six hundred strong into the neighboring States.

This harmony of feeling unites all parties. There is a grand and growing work done. So great is the increase of the blacks that we cannot educate even this increase. Private aid has furnished many millions. We do not want the government to aid our higher schools. Political support is political control. We must not have government aid because government aid means government supervision. The Indian has been well nigh ruined by too much government aid. Political support is ruinous to any work of any kind—the system of appointments is so vicious. Now it is time for the people to take up the Indian cause, and time for the government to take up the Negro cause.

The Negroes furnish us with a great national problem. We stand or fall with them and they with us. The illiterates have the balance of power in this land. They can make and unmake the President, and almost the nation itself. On the other side the Negro, physically, has wonderful capacity, not only to increase but to labor. They furnish the raw material of the cotton mills of the civilized world. Morally, it comes to this: that the Negro is susceptible to Christian teaching. There is no mission field in the world where there is a greater return for Christian work than there is among the Negroes in the South. If they do not come up they will go down. That is the Negro question. With the Indian it is civilization or extermination. If we fight them three

white men will fall for one Indian, and that wont pay. It might be interesting, if time permitted, to refer to that other race—the Chinese. They are a strong race—the strongest of the Asiatic people.

Out West they say that the Indian can do no more than a buffalo or a wild pony. As they tried them they have known them. As the Chinese have been tried by the Christian men and women of this country—tried in New York and Boston and San Francisco—the testimony of all is that they are as easily brought in contact with civilization as any other race. There is a grand work before us, and the future is all gleaming with hope.

8. THE NEGRO IN SLAVERY AND IN FREEDOM—SUMMARY OF WORK BY PRESBYTERIANS.

REV. R. H. ALLEN, D.D.,

Corresponding Secretary of the Presbyterian Board of Missions for Freedmen.

THAT we shall reap what we have sown is a truth, not only taught in the Book of the Great Teacher, but one that is exemplified in every human experience, and is equally true in regard to families, nations, and government. "Whatsoever a man soweth that shall he also reap." We are now reaping the harvest of the seed-sowing of our fathers; and in regard to African slavery we may say with the prophet: "The fathers have eaten sour grapes and the children's teeth are set on edge."

The moral degradation and deterioration of the Negroes has, of late, been brought prominently before the Church and the country, and that we may form a just and intelligent idea of this subject, and rightly understand the relation we bear to a people who have just come out of a long bondage, we should consider the effect of slavery as it has impressed itself upon their character and condition.

Slavery no longer exists in the land, but its results are here; they are here in active operating forces both among the whites and the blacks. No institution like that of American slavery could exist in any land for two hundred and thirty years without leaving its impress on the whole nation, and especially on the character and condition of those who were enslaved. And now since they are free, and have become American citizens, if we would know and do our duty toward them, we should understand clearly the relations we have borne to them in the past, and do bear to them at the present time. If we would help the freedmen; if

we would elevate and Christianize them, we must take them just where slavery left them, which was in a very low and degraded condition.

True, God, who over-rules all things for his glory, and makes even the wrath of man to praise him, in his merciful providence has brought a measure of good out of the evil of slavery.

1. In slavery the Negroes learned the English language, which was of immense importance to them. It gave them new ideas, new channels of thought, and new means of moral and intellectual improvement, which paved the way for civilizing and Christian influences, especially when all barriers were removed, and the gate thrown wide open by their emancipation.

It brought them as heathens within the sound of the Gospel, which to many of them proved an unspeakable good.

In slavery the Negroes were taught habits of industry. They learned how to work; they learned the use of tools, so that many of them became expert builders, carpenters, blacksmiths, and cabinet-makers, cooks, milliners, dressmakers, hostlers, porters, waiters, and shopmen. *But it was slavery;* a slavery which, while with one hand it brought these Africans into a land of civilization, and into contact with elevating influences, with the other hand stood ready to smite them down if any of them under these influences attempted to rise from the childhood of slavery into the manhood of freedom. Admitting any good that may have come indirectly out of slavery, it kept the Negroes in a state of childhood, morally and intellectually. Its very object was to keep them so, in order to make them more abject slaves. True, it clothed, housed, and fed them, but only to make them more valuable property. The slave was told what he was or was not to do, his daily task was planned and laid out for him, and he was put to it just as a machine is wound up and started on its work, thus removing from him all necessity for thought or thrift or self-control. Whatever would make him a better, more contented, and even happier slave was given him, but whatever would appeal to his manhood or lead him to aspire to any condition better than that of a slave was carefully denied him. He must not be taught to read or write under a penalty of fines and imprisonments for the white man who did it and lashes to the black man who sought it. Slavery was written on every thing he saw and on every thing he touched; it was heard in the language spoken to him and in that which he must use to others. His manhood was stunted and dwarfed from the beginning, so as to keep him in a state of helpless and dependent childhood. It is said that in ancient times, among the arts of Eastern sorcerers was that of making dwarfs, playthings in human forms, who by means of inhuman tortures were kept children in size for the amusement of the courts of kings and princes.

In one of Eber's books occurs a passage describing a conversation between one of these monstrosities and the wretched woman who had made him what he was.

Said the dwarf: "If you had sent me to school, and I were not a dwarf, I would play with men as they have played with me; for 1 am as clever as they, and a hundred roads lie before me, but you deprived me of my growth and made me a cripple."

"But you are treated kindly," answered the cruel woman. "No one is better off than you dwarfs."

The dwarf pressed his hand to his heart, and in a sad but determined tone replied: "You have spoiled my life; you have crippled, not my body only, but my soul; and you have condemned me to sufferings that are nameless and unutterable. You made me what I am by your arts; you sold me for a plaything to a boy of my own age; I was dressed with ribbons and feathers, and harnessed to his chariot, and flogged when I did not go fast enough. I grew to be in mind a youth like any other, passionate, restless, and fiery I was treated like a child, a toy, while love and hatred and great projects were strong within me. If I tried to resist, they beat me with rods. Once when I forgot myself and struck the boy who maltreated me, I was hung up by my girdle and left to swing there; the rats fell upon me. See, here are the scars!—they may some day

wear out, but the wounds my spirit received have never ceased to bleed."

See you not, in this touching scene, the poor freedman of to-day, still suffering the effect of slavery, and more justly reproaching those who have dwarfed his manhood while he says: "God intended me to be a man, but you kept me a child; He gave me the powers and aspirations of a man, but you crushed them out and dwarfed them. The Bible you taught me to believe says 'A man shall leave father and mother and cleave to his wife,' and that he shall bring up his children 'in the nurture and admonition of the Lord;' but you tore my wife and children from me and from each other; you fettered my intellect and carefully closed up by laws and penalties every avenue of improvement, and then look down upon me as of an inferior race, incapable of rising above the condition of a dwarfed childhood and hopeless immorality. When, sometimes, yielding to the natural impulses of manhood, I resisted the hand that oppressed me, I sought by flight the freedom I yearned for, you flogged me into passive submission of a master's will. The scars which my body bears may wear out, but the wounds my spirit received have not yet ceased to bleed."

We have heard much lately of a "fearful indictment of the Negro race," but when weighed in the scales of truth and justice, there is a much more fearful indictment here of the white race. The moral degradation resulting from such a state of things was indeed deplorable, and it is this which makes the condition of the emancipated race so full of peril and difficulty to-day. It hangs as a mill-stone about their necks. Coming as they did from heathenism, they brought with them a low state of morality, and there was nothing in slavery to elevate their standard—there was nothing to impress upon them the sacredness of those conjugal and filial relations, on which the elevation of any race so much depend, but much to destroy what little respect they may have had for these relations in their native heathenism. In Africa they could own their wives and children, but here they had no legal right to either.

The master could and often did separate and sell them, the husband to one person, the wife to another, and the children to a third. Some of the most touching scenes 1 have witnessed in the South since the emancipation were parents among the poor freedmen searching for children and children for parents. Many of our papers were filled with advertisements for the loved and the lost who had been separated by the cruel system.

A few weeks since I was in the home of a colored family in Nashville, Tenn., and enjoyed their hospitality, whose singular history illustrates this point.

A slave in Tennessee earned and saved

money to purchase himself for $1,800. He endeavored to purchase his wife and little daughter, but their owner moved to Mississippi and took them with him. News came to the sorrowing father after a while that the child, through sickness and neglect, was at the point of death. By great exertion he raised money and bought the dying child for $350, and nursed her back to life. Years went by, and his wife being lost to him by the usages of slavery, he married again, and bought his second wife for $1,300, paying in all $3,450 for himself and family. In doing this, however, he had become embarrassed in the livery business in which he was engaged, and had to mortgage all his property. Having neglected to secure free papers for his wife and child, he learned that his creditors were about to take them and sell them again into slavery. Abandoning all his property, he took his little family and fled to Cincinnati, where he commenced life again without a penny. Here, by the help of friends, the daughter obtained an education, and about this time, by the sudden death of her father, she and her step-mother were thrown on their own resources; but, by perseverance and self-denial, this girl not only assisted her mother, but bought a little home in Nashville;—in which, after emancipation, having found her own long-lost mother and only sister, she placed them. Thus, by the strange usages of slavery, that girl occupies the anomalous position of having two living mothers. It is interesting to know that this noble girl was the accomplished pianist of the celebrated Jubilee Singers, and, now the wife of a Presbyterian minister, is with her husband about to enter on the work among the freedmen. In this incident, and it is only one among thousands, we see how the affections of the hearts of the poor slaves were estranged, with nothing left to compensate them for their loss. Mere outward circumstances of animal comfort could not do it, nor any special acts of kindness on the part of their owners.

"Kind!" cried an excited Negro, during the talk with some colored men after a prayer-meeting, when reference was made to a planter, his former master, in the neighborhood. "Kind!" he cried, with quivering lip and flashing eye, "I was dat man's slave, and he sell my wife; he sell my two poor little chil'en; yes, brudders, if dar's a God in heaven he did. Kind! yes, he give me corn enough, he give me pork enough, and he never give me a lick wid de whip—but whar's my wife?—whar's my poor chil-'en? Take away de pork, I say; take away de corn; I can work and raise dese for myself, but give me back my poor chil'en as was sold away from me."

Is it to be wondered at that there was no sacredness of the marriage tie among them— that there was no sense of shame in habitual immorality. They were practically taught that there was no distinction between virtue and vice. This continual crushing out of all that was manly and womanly in them led them to feel an utter helplessness, which made them yield more readily to what was wrong and degrading, and banished from their minds any sense of responsibility which otherwise they might have felt. Under slavery there was no social position to gain or lose. The slave who was dishonest or untruthful or unchaste felt no sense of shame, and lost nothing in the estimation of others. As has been well said by a Southern bishop: "You will find that the pressure of social standing is the control which keeps nine tenths of non-Christian people in the path of morality; and, I am afraid, a large proportion of professors also. The slave had no social position to lose, and the Negro has scarcely any more to-day."

These are the people who have been liberated from two hundred and thirty years of bondage, and this is the condition in which slavery left them, and in which freedom found them. Sad reaping of an unwise sowing.

Twenty years ago another seed was cast into this unlikely soil—*Emancipation;* five years later another—*Citizenship;* two years after another—*the Ballot.* What has the reaping been? Are there any first-fruits of a more joyful harvest? Is there any improvement in the freed race, any progress in moral and mental development, and any advance toward enlightened citizenship? Has emancipation been of any benefit to them, and have missionary enterprises and educational efforts proved a success among them? We hear it said sometimes that they were "better off" and happier while slaves than they are now—that they cared nothing for freedom. Let a single incident answer that assertion. A fine-looking old grandmother, nearly seventy, but erect as a pine tree, had two sons in the first enlisted colored regiment in South Carolina, but she and most of her family were slaves. She determined to escape, and make her way to the regiment where her sons were. Gathering her children and grandchildren, to the number of twenty-two, in a neighboring marsh, they concealed themselves till night-fall, when they started for freedom. Finding an old flat-boat on the river, they boarded it and floated down the stream for forty miles. Colonel Trowbridge was on the gun-boat when they were picked up, and he said when the "flat" touched the side of the vessel, the old grandmother rose to her full height, with her youngest grandchild in her arms, and said only, "*My God! are we free?*" In the earnest expression of this old woman you have what four millions of slaves thought of freedom. And what has emancipation done for them, and how have they borne themselves under it?

1. Emancipation gave them a country—a country which they could call their own. This they had never enjoyed before. They were a countryless race. That was a touching scene, twenty years ago last January, when a colored regiment of freed slaves, the first enlisted in the Union army, was called out to hear the Emancipation Proclamation read. Just as the speaker closed, a beautiful new flag, sent to the regiment from New York, was unfurled and waved, which now for the first time meant any thing to those poor people, and suddenly and all unexpectedly, close beside the platform, a strong male voice arose, which was instantly joined by others, while they sang:

"My country, 'tis of thee,
Sweet land of liberty,
Of thee I sing."

People looked around and at each other to see where the interruption came from; but, firmly and irrepressibly, the quavering voices sang on, verse after verse. Said their colonel: "I never saw any thing so electric; it made all the other words cheap. It seemed the choked voice of a race at last unloosed. 'Twas so wonderfully unconscious, so quaint, so innocent. The old men and women sang. and a little slave boy sitting near the foot of the platform, even he must join in." What a touching and beautiful tribute to the Day of Jubilee. Nor was it strange, when the song ceased, to see tears every-where. Just think of it!—the first day they had ever had a country; the first flag they had ever seen which promised any thing to their people. No wonder their simple souls, so full of song, burst out in their unconscious lay. From that hour the flag and the country it represented became theirs. 'Twas not long after this that one of this regiment closed an appeal for the American flag: "Our mas'rs dey hab lib under de flag, dey got rich under it and ebory ting beautiful fur de chil'en. Under it dey hab grind us up and put us in dere pocket fur money. But de fust minit dey tink dat de ole flag mean freedom fur us colored folks, dey pull it right down and run up de rag ob dere own. But we'll neber desert de ole flag, boys; we hab lib under it fur *eighteen hundred and sixty-two years,* and we'll die fur it now." Though his chronology was discharged at long range, it was an effective speech. The poor fellow did not think, perhaps, how soon thousands of them would be bleeding and dying beneath the flag.

2. Emancipation gave them a government as well as a country. Heretofore they were without any rights in courts of justice or halls of legislation. And they soon learned to know the worth of these privileges and the power of government. A colored sergeant of the guard, to a white man who had been arrested and who questioned his author-ity, made an answer that could hardly be improved. Pointing to the chevrons on his sleeve, he said: "Know what dat mean? Dat mean gov'ment." The right of citizenship and the ballot at once appealed to their manhood, and they proved that manhood on the battle-field. I know very well that men both North and South smiled at the idea of Negro soldiers. The brand of slavery was upon them, and it was concluded at once that they had neither the intelligence to learn the drill nor courage to stand before the fire of the enemy. But did they fail on either of these points? Before the end of two years after the enlistment of the first South Carolina regiment, there were one hundred thousand well-disciplined colored troops, whose courage and their knowledge of the drill had been tested on many a bloody field. That was a noble tribute to their vigilance and faithfulness as soldiers, when the white officers, returning to camp after an evening party, were eager and careful to get the countersign, saying: "The darkeys are on guard to-night, and we must look out for our lives." More than a hundred battle-fields tested the freedmen as soldiers and men, and proved them worthy of a country and a government. One single incident among many occurs to me here. Fort Wagner was about to be stormed, and a colored regiment was to lead the charge. When the line was formed, General Strong said to them: "*Is there a man here who thinks himself unable to sleep in that fort to-night?*" The earth rang with the thunder of their "No." Turning to the colored standard-bearer, he said: "Is there any man here to take his place if this brave color-bearer falls?" With uplifted hands the whole regiment shouted in one voice "Yes," "Yes." The charge was made, young Carney, the black color-bearer, was the second man on the parapet, where he at once received three wounds and fell on his knees, but still holding up his flag; and when the regiment was ordered to retire, streaming with blood, he limped along with the troops to the hospital, where he fell almost lifeless, saying, with a proud smile: "*The old flag never touched the ground once, boys.*"

Let it be remembered that the government for which these men so fought, while it paid the white soldier $13 per month, paid the colored soldier only $7—the color being the only difference between them.

3. Emancipation kindled within the Negroes a most unexpected desire for an education. Wherever the proclamation prevailed, the extraordinary spectacle was beheld of an ignorant and enslaved race springing to its feet, after a bondage of two hundred and thirty years, and with its first free breath crying for means for an education. Could such a cry come from a hopelessly degraded and inferior race? Mr. Carl Schurz, on his trip through the South at the close of the

war, said: "The first hopeful sign for the South which I saw was a Negro soldier standing guard with a blue-back spelling-book in his hand." It may not have been very soldierly, but it *was* hopeful. Said Col. Higginson, the commander of the first colored regiment: "I was encouraged and touched, on going the rounds of the camp at night, to find most of the men lying flat on the ground before a blazing fire, with spelling-books in front of them." The same was witnessed every-where. The black cook in the kitchen, the waitress in the dining-room, the hostler in the stable, and the colored hack-driver on his box, had their spelling-books beside them. These scenes repeatedly came under my own eyes in the South. Such a spectacle was never seen in any land among any people under similar circumstances.

But are the Negroes capable of receiving an education and a high civilization? This question is often asked. Now, there are two stand-points from which civilization and the people to be civilized may be looked at. A Southern gentleman spent an hour in trying to show me that a Negro had no soul, and consequently needed no education. That was one side. Simon, a shrewd old colored soldier, as he was jogging behind his colonel on the shell road leading out of Beaufort, S. C., said in a very serious tone: "I'se going to leave de Souf, cunnel, when de war is over. I'se made up my mind dat dese here Secesh will nebber be cibilized in my time." That was the other side. But, seriously, if an answer is wanted to this question, go to the schools and colleges which have been established among the freedmen—go to Biddle, Lincoln, and Fisk Universities—go to our parochial schools, where thousands have learned to read and write—look into the intelligent faces of some dusky brothers on this floor, and you will get an answer as true and convincing as it will be eloquent and touching. They are naturally a quick-witted race, and this, coupled with their earnest desire for education, has made them remarkably apt to learn.

4. Emancipation gave these people names. Heretofore they had been a nameless race. They were named very often according to the whim or fancy of the master or mistress, these names serving simply as labels by which a man's property was designated, as Gen. Johnson's *Bill*, Capt. Martin's *Tom*, or the Widow Patterson's *Dinah*. They could have no family names, as they were liable at any time to change their owners. When left to choose names for their children, the parents, unable to bestow a family name, often gave them a number of names, as if they wished to make up in quantity what they lacked in quality. You would sometimes see a little ebony form rolling in the dirt before "Mammy's" cabin, who bore the cogno-

men of "Festus-Edwin-Leander-Garrett," and not far off "Cornelia-Felicia-Thursday-McArthur." In the next cabin you would meet with "President Abraham Lincoln," and by his side a "Queen Victoria." If a child was named for any celebrated person, he took titles and all. I met a colored hack-driver in Nashville a short time ago who introduced himself as "Major-General Andrew Jackson." The most remarkable name I met was a brawny black fellow who came before the Freedmen's Bureau as George-Washington-Sophy-Ann—Sophia-Harper-Fox, having added the names of each successive master and mistress. When citizenship was given them, they, of course, had to choose family names; and it was amusing, though sad, to see them selecting their names and birthdays, for few knew how old they were. I noticed, of those who had had a number of owners, they almost invariably chose the name of the master or mistress who had been kindest to them. It was a new experience to them to find that the father, mother, and children could bear the same name, but it had its influence upon them. And right here they began for the first time to realize, in its true sense, the sacredness of the marriage relation when they found their marriages legalized, and their names recorded in the register of marriages. The first recorded marriage of the poor freedmen in the South may have been of little moment to the man who made the record, but it was a tremendous event as it stood related to the future condition of that people. I wish I knew the names of the lowly pair that form the first marriage record of the liberated slaves; for it seems to me that, though all unconscious of it, a thrill of new life must have started through the veins of the whole race.

5. The right to hold property in their own names, which emancipation brought, had an elevating and energizing influence on the Negroes. Slavery had made them thriftless and improvident, which is still characteristic of the race. Yet I found more activity and more desire for work among the poor Negroes of the South than among the poor whites. Planters and employers who pay their hands promptly and justly find no difficulty in getting Negroes to work; and among the better class of them I found provident habits rapidly forming. Ten years after their freedom they had deposited in their savings-banks over $12,000,000. In the State of Georgia they own 583,000 acres of land, and pay taxes on $9,000,000 worth of property. The last census shows us that the colored people are assessed for over $91,000,000 worth of taxable property. Does this look like an incurably thriftless race? especially when it is remembered that as a race they are really only twenty years old, after coming out of a helpless and dwarfed childhood of two hundred years, and had to make their way through these

twenty years with the brand of slavery upon them, and in the face of a wretched color-prejudice which has threatened to crush them at every step.

Since their emancipation it is very evident that great changes have come over the colored race and great improvements. They have been lifted higher. But it is said, while all is true, there is no change in their morals. If it is meant by this that *as a race* they have not been lifted up to a higher plane of morality, just as it may be said the Chinese have not, after all that missions have done for them, it is true; but if it is meant that there has been no improvement in the morals of families, communities, and whole neighborhoods, where intelligent missionary work has been carried on among them, then it is utterly false. As a race, they have only been partially reached by missionary and moralizing influences, and consequently the mass of them are still just where slavery left them; but where they have been reached, a man is willfully blind who cannot see a decided improvement in their morals. The morals which these people learned under slavery, if any, had first to be unlearned, and a foundation laid for a true morality. This has been done with encouraging success where our missions have been planted. Of this, there is abundant testimony. Take, for example, your colored Synod of Atlantic, which has in it seventy-one colored ministers and over two hundred ruling elders. Look at their character and morals. I have taken special pains to learn, from white and colored people, how these men stand in the communities in which they live for purity of life and consistent Christian conduct; and, with only three exceptions, I find they have the confidence of both white and colored citizens, and will compare favorably, in these respects, with the same number of men in any Christian body. There are thirteen thousand members in the churches under the care of this Synod, and among them many men and women of deep and earnest piety. An intelligent elder in the white church on Edisto Island, once a large slave-holder, said to me: "To know what you have done among these people, you should have seen them eighteen years ago, when your Board commenced its work here. Why, they live better, they talk better, and they work better. Many of those cabins you see, once the abodes of ignorance and vice, are now Christian homes, in which you will get as good a meal and as clean a bed as you would wish, and where you will see the household gather reverently around the family altar."

Said another Southern gentleman in a town in South Carolina, where we have a large mission: "Your missionary is doing the best work of any man in this country, white or black. You can trust the colored

people who come from his mission." I draw these facts from our own work because I know whereof I speak; but similar facts can be given from the missionary work of other denominations substantiating the same truth. Think of it!—there are in the fifteen Southern States and the District of Columbia 16,659 colored schools, 44 normal schools, 36 colored institutions of secondary instruction, 15 colored universities and colleges, 22 colored schools of theology, 3 colored law schools, 2 medical schools, and 2 deaf and dumb and blind asylums. When it is remembered that all this work is the outgrowth of earnest Christian principle, and carried on in faith and prayer by earnest Christian people, is it credible that the morals of those under such influences should remain the same as under slavery? Men prejudiced against the Negroes, and opposed to the work of Northern Christians among them, may think so; but candid and impartial observers of facts cannot.

But, after all that has been said for and against the Negro, after all the volumes which have been written and spoken about his condition and characteristics of the Negro, he is simply a man—nothing more and nothing less. General Saxton, examining with some impatience a long list of questions from some philanthropic commission from the North respecting the traits and habits of the freedmen, bade some staff officers answer them all in two words—"Intensely human." The Negro is no abnormal creation, requiring a different mode of treatment from other men. He is a man, possessing the instincts, passions, and powers of a man, and all he needs and all he asks is a man's chance. This we ought to give him. Laying aside all color-prejudice on the one hand, and all sentimentalism on the other, let him be treated simply as a man. Give him the rights, privileges, and opportunities of a man, and he will take care of himself. We hear constantly of the Negro problem. Why should there be a Negro problem any more than a white man problem? There is a class of white men who need missionary and other civilizing influences as much as the Negro.

Now, what is needed for all such people, both white and black, is the preacher and the teacher, the privileges of the Church and the school. Our own ancestors, a few centuries back, dressed in skins and offered human sacrifices to heathen gods, and were sold in the slave-marts of Rome; but under the benign influences of the Christian religion and Christian schools they emerged from the darkness of barbarism, and we are to-day what we are by the self-sacrifice, toil, and blood of the men and women who bore the Gospel to them. And the obligation rests upon us to send the same precious light to those who are in darkness, which, in regard to the Negroes, grows a thousand-fold

13

stronger on account of the relation we bear to them.

The Negroes are simply a race a century or two behind us in Christian privileges and the rights of men. Let us give them these privileges now, and they will work out the problem for themselves as our ancestors worked out theirs. The white man must learn that the Negro is also a man, and treat him as such. In his training we must go lower than his ignorance, even to the depths of his crushed manhood, and begin there to lift him up. Said an educated young colored man the other day, one who was born a slave: "It is not book-learning that we so much need as strong appeals to our manhood, and how to use it well. Deliver us from cant; give us a solid Christian basis upon which to build up this story in the temple of our republic." We must take the colored man by the hand and recognize his worth as a man. There is a strong race prejudice in us all, much stronger than we can realize until it is tested. Born and raised in the South, I had this prejudice, and it took a mighty force to wrench the wretched thing from my heart, so that I could enter the humble dwelling of the Negro, sit at his table, and accept his hospitality as I would that of any other man. And until this principle is recognized the work done for the freedmen will fail to yield its richest and best results. No white man, be he from the North or South, can ever teach the colored man successfully until he recognizes his manhood. As we look on Benjamin Bannucker, the Negro astronomer; Thomas Fuller, the Negro calculator; James Derham, the Negro physician; Frederick Douglass, the Negro orator; and Dr. Blyden, the Negro president, we behold men. Yes, and in the six and a half millions of freed slaves we see men and women—men and women who have been crushed and dwarfed by our hands, and we are bound to help them up. Jesus, who was anointed to preach the Gospel to the poor, and to set at liberty those that were bound, has laid the obligation upon us.

The freedmen have solemn claims upon the white race in this land. Here they have been enslaved, and have toiled for and enriched the white man. Here they have been emancipated, and here they are to remain as citizens and voters, and to share alike with us the weal or woe of a common country. We made them slaves and treated them as such; and now that they are free American citizens, we are bound to treat them as such. Our interests, as well as theirs, demand this at our hands.

In regard to evangelistic work, the emancipation of four millions of slaves was the opportunity of the age; and I fear the Church has failed to come up to her duty, and to take advantage of the opportunity as she should.

The harvest is perishing for the lack of the Lord's reapers, and the Lord will hold us responsible.

SUMMARY OF THE WORK OF THE PRESBYTERIAN BOARD OF MISSIONS FOR FREEDMEN.

The field occupied by the Board lies largely in the Carolinas, Georgia, Tennessee, Virginia, with a few missions in Kentucky Florida, and the Indian Territory.

MISSIONARIES.

These are preachers, catechists, and teachers; and in the work under care of the Board the present year—including assistants in schools—the number is as follows:

Ordained ministers, of whom 71 are colored..84			} 88
Licentiates,	8 "	" ..4	
Catechists,	14, all	" 14	
*Teachers, males, of whom 33 are	" ..40		} 95
" females, "	" 87 "	" ..55	
	158.		197

CHURCHES.

Organized during the year	4
Whole number under care of the Board...........	178
Communicants added on examination....969 }	1,138
" " certificate,......169 }	
Average, on examination, to each church, nearly	6
" " " minister, "	12
Whole number of communicants............	12,828
Baptized—adults.....................471 }	1,359
" infants..................588 }	
Marriages reported.......................	295
Whole number of Sabbath-schools...........	156
" " scholars in Sabbath-schools..	10,771

SCHOOLS.

Whole number of schools....................	60
" " pupils in these...........	6,095
" " teachers.................	124

Our schools continue to be strictly parochial; and statistical reports from the field show that, besides the large amount of "good seed" sown in the hearts of the young by our missionary teachers, their work still tells encouragingly in the way of TRAINING INSTRUCTORS FOR THEIR OWN RACE.

The Board has also under its care, and supported by its funds,

THREE CHARTERED INSTITUTIONS:

Biddle University, Charlotte, N. C.; Scotia Seminary, Concord, N. C.; Wallingford Academy, Charleston, S. C.

TWO NORMAL SCHOOLS:

Brainerd Institute, Chester, S. C.. Fairfield Institute, Winnsboro, S. C.

---

* Besides these, 26 others of our ministers and licentiates, and 8 catechists, have also been engaged in teaching, making in all 124 engaged in teaching.

The foregoing five institutions report as follows:

Whole number of students enrolled	1,856
Number of these professors of religion	733
Number of these in the Presbyterian Church	214
Whole No. studying for the Gospel ministry	60
Number of these that are Presbyterians	70
Number who have acted as catechists	21
Taught school part of the year	154
Whole No. of months taught this year, over.	498
Whole No. of pupils in all their schools, about	8,450
Amount of pay received, in cash and board, by all, about	$9,000

Number who superintended Sabbath-schools while teaching	88
Whole No. of scholars in these Sabbath-schools	5,050

In considering the figures of these tables, it should be remembered that those pertaining to students for the Gospel ministry, catechists, and superintendents of Sabbath-schools, came from but four of the five institutions named, as Scotia Seminary is for girls only.

9. WORK OF THE NORTHERN BAPTISTS AMONG THE FREEDMEN SINCE THE WAR.

REV. H. L. MOREHOUSE, D.D.,

Secretary American Baptist Home Mission Society.

THE American Baptist Home Mission Society, organized in 1832, was the general society for the whole Baptist denomination, until the separation between Northern and Southern Baptists in 1845, (on account of the controversies concerning slavery,) prosecuting its missionary operations in the Southern States alike among whites and blacks. When the doors, barred for sixteen years, were opened by shot and shell in 1861, the Society prepared to re-enter the field. January 30, 1862, the first man was commissioned by the Board of the Society to visit Fortress Monroe and vicinity to investigate and report concerning the condition of the blacks there congregated. Preliminary work having thus been done by the Board, the Society, obedient to the sentiment of the denomination, at its annual meeting in May, 1862, formally and energetically entered upon the great undertaking which has been unremittingly prosecuted these twenty-one years.

As illustrating the spirit in which the work was begun we quote the resolution adopted on that occasion:

" *Whereas,* We recognize in the recent abolition of slavery in the District of Columbia, and in the setting free of thousands of bondsmen by the advancement of our national armies into the insurgent States, a moral, impressive indication that Divine Providence is about to break the chains of the enslaved millions in our land, and thus furnish an unobstructed entrance for the Gospel among vast multitudes who have hitherto been shut out from its pure teachings; and,

" *Whereas,* We see in the entire reorganization of the social and religious state of the South, which must inevitably follow the successful overthrow of the rebellion, the Divine hand most distinctly and most imperatively beckoning us on to the occupancy of a field broader, more important, more promising, than has ever yet invited our toils; therefore,

" *Resolved,* That the Society take immediate steps to supply with Christian instruction, by means of missionaries and teachers, the emancipated slaves—whether in the District of Columbia, or in other places held by our forces —and also to inaugurate a system of operations for carrying the Gospel alike to free and bond throughout the whole Southern section of our country, so fast and so far as the progress of our armies and the restoration of order and law shall open the way."

Active operations were soon begun at St. Helena and Beaufort, S. C., where hundreds of the colored people were converted and added to the churches. It should be said that in many of the Southern States, Baptists had devoted much attention to the spiritual interests of the slaves, so that there were large numbers connected and meeting with the white churches, or sometimes worshiping as branch churches by themselves. It is estimated that among 4,000,000 freedmen at the close of the war there were nearly 400,000 connected, by formal profession, with the Baptist churches.

In 1863 assistants to missionaries in the South were sent out " to engage in such instruction of the colored people as will enable them to read the Bible and to become self-supporting churches." This work awakened profound interest in the North, particularly throughout New England. Contributions began to pour into the treasury of the Society, and enlargement, as fast as circumstances would permit, followed. In 1864 several missionaries and fourteen assistants were laboring for the freedmen in the District of Columbia, in several places in Virginia, in North Carolina, South Carolina, Mississippi, Tennessee, and Louisiana. At the close of the war additional emphasis was laid upon this department of missionary and educational work. President Anderson, of Rochester, also President of the Society, voiced the sentiments of Baptists in the North when, in his address at the annual meeting that year, he said: "It has been asked, ' What will we do with the Negro?' God does not require of us an answer to this. Our question is, What will we do *for* the Negro? God will tell us when it pleaseth him what to do *with* the Negro. Let us do our work and leave the rest with God. Let us organize them into churches and Sunday-schools; teach them to labor and to make of themselves men in every sense. God will do the rest."

In 1865 there were sixty-eight laborers in twelve Southern States. Twelve teachers in Washington, D. C., reported 812 pupils in attendance that year. The Society took strong grounds in reference to the rights of the freedmen, formally affirming as its opinion that "Both the undeniable right of the class referred to, and the indispensable condition of an assured peace and of the highest prosperity of the country, demand that they be invested with the elective franchise, and with all the privileges of whatever kind that belong to American citizenship."

It was also declared that this work must be prosecuted by men "emphatically loyal to good government and to God, and who feel the strongest and tenderest sympathy with down-trodden humanity," and concerning whom "there is the most abundant and undoubted proof that they are opposed to every form of oppression."

The methods of the Society included three kinds of work, all, however, so clearly related to each other that marked lines of separation were impossible. The first was the evangelization of the freedmen through the labors of devoted missionaries. The next was the instruction in Scriptural truth of the colored and utterly illiterate preachers. The third was the education of all classes, young and old, sufficiently at least to read the Bible for themselves. Some of the best men in the denomination were appointed to hold "Ministers' and Deacons' Institutes." Every missionary was expected to be a teacher. In 1867 fifty-nine teachers in day-schools reported 6,136 pupils in attendance. Fifty ordained ministers, thirty of them colored, were also under appointment.

Until 1867 there had been some difference of opinion in the denomination concerning the agency or agencies through which this work should be done. From this time onward the American Baptist Home Mission Society was designated as the single organization for this purpose, in connection with its general missionary operations ; no distinct Society. with the one specific object of looking after the educational and religious interests of the freedmen, being thought advisable. Immediately steps were taken to establish schools of a higher grade at several central points where instruction had been imparted to the freedmen, and to occupy other

points as rapidly as practicable. At the same time elementary or day schools were maintained by missionaries and their assistants, who reported from 4,000 to 6,000 in attendance annually until 1872, when the Society's efforts were concentrated chiefly on the higher and permanent institutions.

The names, locations, and dates of the establishment of the institutions founded or fostered by the Society, and which at present are doing a royal work, are as follows: Wayland Seminary, Washington, D. C., where work was begun in 1864, established 1867; Richmond Institute, Va., where work was begun in 1865, established 1867; Shaw University, Raleigh, N. C., where work was begun in 1865, established in 1867; Roger Williams University, Nashville, Tenn., where work was begun in 1864, established in 1866; Leland University, New Orleans, La., where work was begun in 1863, established in 1870; the Atlanta Seminary, Atlanta, Ga., (transferred from Augusta, where work was begun and carried on from 1867 to 1879,) established 1879; Benedict Institute, Columbia, S. C., established in 1870; Natchez Seminary, Natchez, Miss., established in 1876, removed to Jackson, Miss., in 1883; the Alabama Normal and Theological School, at Selma, Ala., started by the colored people in 1873, and adopted by the Society in 1880; the Florida Institute, Live Oak, Fla., started by the colored people in 1868, and adopted by the Society in 1880; the Kentucky Normal and Theological Institute, Louisville, Ky., started by the colored people in 1869, and adopted by the Society in 1881; Bishop College, Marshall, Tex., established in 1881. In 1882 a new site was purchased at Atlanta, and a prosperous school for young women has been conducted under the auspices of the Society. This may become a distinct school for girls. Likewise a school for girls is projected, and will be opened in the fall of 1883, at Richmond, Va. In these twelve schools last year there were 78 teachers and 2,713 pupils. The annual running expenses of the schools are about $50,000.

The actual cost of these school properties has been about $400,000. The amount paid by the Society for all its missionary and educational work among the colored people is about $900,000. If to this be added what has gone through individual channels, the aggregate amount contributed by Northern Baptists for these purposes will exceed $1,000,000. The bulk of this has been for Christian education. For several years, also, through government aid, day-schools have been maintained among the freedmen of the Choctaw and Chickasaw Nations in the Indian Territory.

The Woman's Baptist Home Mission Society of Chicago, and the Woman's American Baptist Home Mission Society of Boston have also done much, since their organization in

1877, in sending missionaries and supporting teachers in the institutions mentioned. A full summary of what Northern Baptists have done would also include the Sunday-school and colporteur work of the American Baptist Publication Society, which has supported annually several laborers in the South, and has distributed Bibles and other religious literature among the destitute.

All the schools have normal courses of study, most of them an academic course; several a collegiate course; while a specialty is made of biblical instruction, and a theological course, adapted to the wants of the attendants, is provided in all. In several schools attention is given to industrial education.

An excellent medical school with suitable buildings was opened at Shaw University, Raleigh N. C., in 1882. From the first, as accommodations would allow, both sexes have been taught together in these institutions. It is estimated that about 6,000 different persons have enjoyed instruction therein; about 1,200 of whom have had the ministry in view, while others in large numbers have gone forth to teach; some of them as professors in the institutions. Others have become editors, legislators, or occupied other positions of influence and honor.

The chartered institutions with their own Boards of Trustees are Richmond Institute, Shaw University, Atlanta Seminary, Roger Williams University, Leland University, Kentucky Normal and Theological Institute, Alabama Normal and Theological Institute, and the Florida Institute. The most valuable properties and largest buildings are at Shaw University, valued at $125,000; Roger Williams University, valued at $85,000; and Leland University, valued at $85,000. Endowment funds for scholarships or for general purposes, held either by the Society or by the Boards of these institutions, amount to a little over $65,000.

In many States the colored people have co-operated liberally, according to their ability, in building up these institutions. On the Boards of Trustees colored men serve with their white brethren, some of whom are Southern men. Generally speaking, Southern Baptists have had little to do with these educational enterprises begun and carried forward by their brethren at the North. Yet there have been not a few noble exceptions to this rule; and there are growing indications of their disposition to have a part in this work which sustains so vital a relation to the intelligence and general welfare of their own section, where the colored people are and are to remain.

The results of the efforts of which we have spoken are most encouraging. The number of Baptists among the colored people has nearly doubled in the last twenty years, being computed now at 800,000. In nearly every Southern State they have well-organized and well-conducted annual associations and general conventions for the consideration of missionary, Sunday-school, and educational matters; while several weekly or monthly religious papers are published and sustained by an increasingly intelligent constituency.

In view of these things the Baptists of the North rejoice that they have been able to do something for the uplifting of the colored people, though conscious that their work is not yet done; and, with thankfulness to God for the past, they propose to press on with courage for the completion of what has been so well begun, thus endeavoring in this respect to discharge in some measure their duty as patriots, philanthropists, and followers of Him who came not to be ministered unto but to minister, and give himself for the uplifting of the lowly, the enlightenment of darkened minds, and the redemption of the lost.

10. SOME SPECIAL RESULTS OF NORTHERN EDUCATIONAL WORK IN THE SOUTH—IT MUST BE CONTINUED.

Rev. R. S. Rust, D.D., Corresponding Secretary of the Freedmen's Aid Society of the Methodist Episcopal Church, in an address at Cleveland, O., Oct. 26, 1882, in reviewing the work of that Society, mentioned important results outside of simply educational work. The following extracts are given :

OUR work has aided in the introduction of the free school in the South, and acted as pioneer in the general educational movement southward. Our teachers have taught on the original free-school plan, embracing all modern improvements, so successfully as to impress the leading citizens and the Legislatures of several Southern States with the excellence of these schools and their necessity in securing the elevation and prosperity of the people. We must continue this movement until this whole section of country shall be dotted with these temples of science. This movement in behalf of popular education may meet with temporary obstructions; in some localities it may be imperiled and even temporarily defeated; but it will ultimately triumph, and reward the people with priceless blessings. Amid the ebb and flow of the tide of public sentiment, the well-tried system of our American free schools will rise higher and higher in the appreciation of the Southern people, and ere long will be anchored among them as firmly as in any other part of our country.

Our schools have done much in preventing the freedmen from becoming Romanists. The Papists, under the auspices of the Pope and Archbishop Manning, have sent a large number of missionaries to labor among this people, carefully selecting those who recognized their manhood and were free from prejudice on account of color. They have vast resources at their disposal, and expend them freely in the accomplishment of this object. The freedmen are so anxious to learn, that they will attend poor schools taught by Papists if Protestants do not furnish good ones; but the instruction of Romanists disqualifies them from becoming loyal citizens or intelligent Christians. There has been no agency in the world so well adapted to confront this foe as the Freedmen's Aid Society. Wherever a priest or a sister of charity went to proselyte the people and organize a church, there they found a Methodist to resist the attack. Our teachers, with large experience, were in the field, our schools were judiciously located, and our teachers efficient, enthusiastic, and pious.

Methodism, with its spiritual worship, meets a great want of the Negro, whose heart is so susceptible to religious impressions. Class, prayer, and camp meetings, fervent preaching and exhortation, singing our songs, and relating Christian experience, have proved more than a match for all the ceremony and display of the Romish Church, and have kept multitudes of freedmen from being drawn into the meshes of Romanism.

Our schools have awakened an interest for improvement among the white people. Colored children attend school, acquire knowledge and ability to lead useful lives, and this fact is a stimulant to arouse white children also to go to school and secure an education. It is not a pleasant thing for white parents to see their children growing up in ignorance and vice, while the children of colored people attend school, become intelligent, and secure places of trust and profit. Wherever a good school is located, a great change for the better takes place,

The appearance, manners, and conduct of the people change, and the whites catch the spirit that prevails and join in the effort for improvement, not being willing to be distanced in the race for knowledge by those so long looked upon by them as an inferior people.

Our schools have greatly improved the character of the piety of the freedmen. While we condemn the defective piety, boisterous worship, and inconsistent life found among the freedmen, we must remember that inconsistencies in Christian character and life are not peculiar to this people; it is possible that some of these blemishes might be found in Christians of a lighter hue, and we should not, on this account, withdraw our confidence from these brethren, and class them among the unbelievers. We must recognize the genuineness of their religion, that emotion as well as thought is essential to piety, that religious development is scarcely less dependent upon feeling than thinking, and that thought only ripens into golden fruit when quickened by the inspiration of emotion. Even truth itself in the intellect lies cold and dormant till it enters into the affections, inflames the soul, and quickens its possessor to a sublime faith and heroic life. The poor, ignorant freedman, worshiping God with all the light he has, struggling to perform the stern duties of life with a trustful heart, as well as the scholar and the philosopher, is precious in God's sight, and shall share in the joys of his kingdom.

An emotional religion, then, must not be indiscriminately condemned, for it is the only religion that can meet the wants of this poor people. We must take care, in educating the freedmen, that we do not substitute cold formality and an intellectual appreciation of the truth for an enthusiastic religious experience and a warm heart. Many of the freedmen are, without doubt, Christians, and, though they may indulge in a mode of life and worship repulsive to intelligent and refined Christians, and in striking contrast with the strict requirements of God's law, yet great allowance should be made in view of their history, ignorance, and neglect; for, in spite of their inconsistencies of life, they often exhibit a faith in God and confidence in his protection and love that is truly sublime, and entitles them to recognition as the sons of God and the heirs of eternal life.

This work in the South is only begun, the masses have scarcely been reached, and those who have so wisely commenced it cannot yet safely intrust it to inexperienced hands. It is not so firmly established and secure that its friends may retire and leave it to the tender mercies of those who lacked the interest and the means to commence it. Some ask, Why do you not commit the care and support of these schools to the people in the South ? Why not let them manage these institutions instead of controlling them from the North?

The following considerations indicate the embarrassments in the way of the proper education of the freedmen by the South:

The illiteracy of the Southern population, as shown by the United States census, is fearful, and those who are incapable of appreciating the necessity of an education for themselves can have no true conception of its importance to others.

The bad feeling engendered by the loss of property, and the failure of the cause for which they staked their all, led the whites to treat with distrust and contempt any plan for the education of the blacks. And, on the other hand, there was a lack of confidence on the part of the freedmen toward the whites that prevented their well-meant endeavors from being appreciated.

The people of this section had been educated in the idea that the race was an inferior one, incapable of culture and refinement, and with such views they could not recognize its manhood, nor educate it for any condition of life but one of servility. They had no objection to the Negro as a slave, but they could not endure him as a freeman, claiming the prerogatives of freedom.

And such were the ravages of war and the consequent impoverishment of the South, that it had not the means to establish these schools, neither has it the ability to sustain them now.

The opposition first experienced has well-nigh passed away. Our motives in organizing schools are better understood, and our efforts to train the children in science and morality are more highly appreciated, and the marked improvement of our pupils in conduct and character has attracted attention, conquered prejudice, and won general approval.

If our Southern friends can aid in this great work of the age a hearty welcome awaits them. The field is vast, the opportunities great, and the harvest promising. While a generous welcome is extended to any who can be induced to aid in this hopeful field, we cannot allow those to retire who have consecrated to this enterprise so much suffering, sacrifice, prayer, labor, and money. Let this good work be carried forward, in the same spirit and with the same enthusiasm in which it originated, and by similar agencies, and the grandest results will be secured, the people educated, harmony restored, the Church enlarged, and the nation saved.

---

11. WORK OF THE PROTESTANT EPISCOPAL CHURCH, THE UNITARIANS, AND THE FRIENDS AMONG THE NEGROES SINCE THE WAR.

THE Forty-seventh Annual Report of the Committee on Domestic Missions of the Protestant Episcopal Church, for 1881–82, shows that the receipts for missions among the colored people that year were $35,115 58. $26,821 79 of this was from legacies.

The amounts spent in those missions that year were as follows:

Florida..................	$50 00
Georgia...............	500 00
Louisiana............	500 00
Maryland	1,437 50
Mississippi	287 50
Missouri.............	550 00
North Carolina......	4,044 00
South Carolina......	1,433 33
Tennessee...........	1,100 00
Virginia.............	3,765 00
Total	$13,667 33

Fifty-five missionaries are supported among the colored people, as follows: white clergy-

men, 13; colored clergymen, 15; lay readers, 5; teachers, 4; women helpers, 18.

Missionary teachers and laborers are supported in the Southern States also among the white people.

UNITARIANS.

Rev. A. D. MAYO, of Boston, says:

In proportion to their numbers and wealth, Unitarians, as individuals, Christians, and friends of education, have contributed large amounts of money in the South since the war. Washington University, in St. Louis, has been established by Dr. W. G. Elliot, and largely endowed. Dr. Elliot himself established the first free school west of the Mississippi.

In Baltimore Mr. Pratt has just given a million dollars for a free public library. The first public schools in Richmond, Va., for whites, were established by the Soldiers' Memorial Society of Boston, of which Dr. E. E. Hale was the moving spirit. Mrs. Augustus Hemenway, of Boston, has expended large sums at Hampton, at Miss Bradley's school for poor whites in Wilmington, N. C., and at Norfolk, Va.

The wealthy people and churches of the denomination have been large and constant contributors for student aid, and probably twenty to fifty colored schools are supported thereby. Our wealthy people are apt to give as readily to orthodox schools and colleges, as elsewhere, if convinced that the work is worthy of support.

There are but half a dozen Unitarian churches in the Southern States; and, with the exception of Wilmington, Del., and a mission at Atlanta, nothing new, save in church building and paying church debts, has been accomplished in that region since the war.

THE FRIENDS.

ELKANAH BEARD, of Indiana, furnishes the following:

Long before the great political change that elevated the Negro race from slavery to the full rights of citizenship the Society of Friends had not only freed their slaves, but had been giving attention to the education of the colored people living in their limits. From year to year our committees located in different parts of nearly all the Northern States reported schools under their auspices for the education of the people of color. How many were thus taught, or how much money was expended prior to the war, I have no means of ascertaining. While we deplored the war, with all its wide-spread desolation, we were ready to embrace every opportunity to relieve suffering, and some of our members were among the first in the Mississippi Valley to render assistance to such as were seeking refuge within the Union lines.

The proclamation of freedom to the enfeebled and unlettered slave added immensely to our moral responsibilities, and in 1863 we opened three schools in Louisiana, in which over five hundred children were taught to read and write. The said schools were continued for years, and over one thousand persons received instruction in them. In 1864 we opened schools in Arkansas, Mississippi, and Tennessee, and at the beginning of the year 1865 over 1,100 were in our schools. During 1866 the number was swelled to 2,700, besides 250 deserted children gathered into orphan asylums. During the years 1867,

1868, and 1869 our schools were well sustained, and we were highly gratified with the literary, moral, and religious advancement of those under our care. Since then our work has centered upon a normal school near Helena, Ark., which is now known as Southland College, and is one of the permanent educational institutions of the South. The enrollment for the past year was 277; boarders inside the college, 52; a normal class of 32. Most of this normal class are now teaching in several different States, with not less than 1,000 pupils in charge. Add to these 150 older teachers, who have gone out from this institution, and we have an army in training several thousand strong.

The people of the North, having carried the war for the Union and equal and universal freedom to a victorious issue, cannot safely relax their educational efforts for the freed people until the lessons of self-knowledge, self-reverence, and self-control become embodied in the enduring forms of individual and national life. We regard the thorough education of such as will make practical teachers the very best safeguard against danger, and in Southland College special pains is taken to impress all the students that education and industry must not be divorced, and the highest results can be reached only when science guides the hand of labor.

From 1863 to 1878 there passed through the hands of Indiana Yearly Meeting's shipping agent two hundred tons of clothing in various forms, nearly one-half of which was new goods. During the same time our treasurer's books show about $300,000 in money expended in relieving and educating the freed people, upon which no per cent. was deducted for salaries of officers.

Since 1877 we have received and expended, mostly for educational purposes, $15,500. Last year we had a munificent gift of $25,000 as an endowment fund. This places Southland College on a basis for more permanent usefulness. We have no work that gives us greater satisfaction, or that is more productive of real good, intellectually, morally, and religiously. Our scholars have nearly all professed conversion, and have attached themselves to some Christian Church, and all discard the use of tobacco and are total abstainers from all intoxicants, and many are active workers in the much-needed temperance reform among their own people.

12. INDIVIDUAL NORTHERN BENEVOLENCE TO THE SOUTH FOR EDUCATION SINCE THE WAR.

THE North has given to the South for educational and Church work, among its poor and needy masses, fully $25,000,000 since Appomattox. This has gone chiefly to the Negroes, and has been administered mostly by the benevolent societies of the various Northern Churches. Up to this time the normal and higher instruction received by the Negroes of the South has been the work of Northern benevolence. The Southern States are now beginning to have schools of higher grades for colored people.

There have been several large individual gifts to the South for education.

The Vanderbilts of New York have given near $1,125,000 for the establishment and endowment of Vanderbilt University at Nashville, Tenn. This institution is under the control of the Methodist Episcopal Church, South.

Mr. George I. Seney, of New York, has given $200.000 for institutions controlled by the same Church in Georgia.

Other individual gifts for smaller amounts have been numerous.

PEABODY EDUCATIONAL FUND.

The Southern States have received large help from the Peabody Educational Fund, the first donation being made in 1868. The purpose of Mr. Peabody's gift, amounting to two millions, the interest of which only can be used, is to aid in the establishment of a permanent system of public schools in the South "free for the whole people." Its gifts are not confined to any race.

The fund is held and administered by a Board of Trustees, of which Rev. J. L. M. Curry, D.D., of Richmond, Va., is the general agent. The Board, through its general agent, not only bestows benefactions, but also, in many ways, through aiding in publication of educational journals, holding teachers' institutes, conventions, etc., has helped largely in awakening and directing the educational reforms now advancing in the South.

The gifts of this fund to twelve Southern States have been as follows:

1868	$35,400
1869	90,000
1870	90,600
1871	100,000
1872	130,000
1873	137,150
1874	134,600

1875	$101,000
1876	76,300
1877	89,400
1878	77,250
1879	74,850
1880	55,150
1881	80,335

Total	$1,272,035

JOHN F. SLATER FUND.

March 2, 1882, John F. Slater, of Norwich, Conn., gave $1,000,000 in trust to a corporate board, of which ex-President Hayes is chairman. The income of this gift is to apply "to the uplifting of the lately emancipated people of the Southern States and their posterity by conferring on them the blessings of a Christian education, so as to make them good men and good citizens." Rev. Atticus G. Haygood, D.D., of Georgia, is general agent of this fund. No distributions have yet been made, but the policy of the Trustees is to train teachers from among those to be taught, and to encourage such institutions as most effectually promote this work. After thirty-three years the Trustees may, if they deem it best, "apply the capital of the fund to the establishment of foundations subsidiary to those already-existing institutions of higher education in such wise as to make the educational advantages of such institutions more freely accessible to poor students of the colored race."

PAUL TULANE'S GIFT.

Mr. Paul Tulane, of Princeton, N. J., in June, 1882, gave property estimated as worth $1,000,000 "for the promotion and encouragement of intellectual, moral, and industrial education among the white young persons in the city of New Orleans, and for the advancement of letters, the arts, and the sciences therein."

SOUTHERN CHURCHES AND EDUCATION SINCE THE WAR.

The sentiment of all Southern Churches is gradually becoming favorable to common-school systems supported by the States, and which will give educational facilities to all the youth. These Churches formerly believed in parochial or select schools, which practically limited education to the few.

In the matter of denominational schools, advance is being made, and many heroic men and women are found in all these Churches who are leading in the work of building and endowing seminaries and colleges. Many institutions were wiped out by the war. Many others are yet struggling with poverty. Only the few can be said to prosper. As the commercial prosperity of the South increases, these schools will grow.

As to education among the Negroes, the Southern Churches have begun to do something, but the great mass of Southern Christians who think at all on this subject are studying two questions: "Can the Negro be educated?" and "What kind and quantity of education is best for the Negro if he has any at all?"

In each Church a few splendid men are taking hold of this work, and seeking to awaken their respective denominations. The Methodist Episcopal Church, South, by General Conference action, is committed to Negro education. It is proposed to establish an educational institute at Augusta, Ga., immediately.

The Southern Presbyterians have an institute for Negro preachers at Tuscaloosa, Ala., where, up to this time, a small class has been taught each year.

The Southern Baptists have as yet done very little except to partake of the growing sentiment that the Negro must be educated, and to co-operate in kind words with Northern Baptists who have engaged heartily in the work.

13. ROMAN CATHOLICISM AND THE NEGRO.

It is difficult to secure exact data upon the work of Roman Catholics among the Negroes since the war. Something is being done by them, but as yet but little comparatively has been accomplished, and in the presence of an aggressive Protestantism, the Negroes cannot be won to Catholicism. The showy worship of that Church may for a time attract the thoughtless and simple among them, but the Negro is Protestant by instinct.

14. EDUCATION IN THE SOUTH.

REV. J. G. VAUGHAN, B.D.,

Pastor Ames Methodist Episcopal Church, New Orleans, La.

I WILL use the word "South" as applying to that section of our country formerly known as slave territory. Differences resulting from the late war in part, but having their origin long before, have existed between this section and the North. The interests of the Southern producer and of the Northern manufacturer are not and never have been identical. There are other, and prominent, causes that have led to a difference between the two sections. Previous to the war the laborers in the North were citizens and freemen; in the South they were boudmen, slaves, and property. Some had previously been such in the North. The

North, having the greater voice in government, began to legislate against slavery, admitting certain Territories as States on the condition that they were not to become slave States. This policy was naturally resented by the South. The people of the two sections became estranged from a lack of acquaintance. Early in our country's history the West began to develop and promise rich returns for capital and labor, so the lines of travel, emigration, and the routes of commerce turned westward, leaving but little communication between the North and the South. For more than twenty years preceding the late war sectional books appeared, in both the North and the South, magnifying the interests, institutions, and advantages of their own section, by comparing them with similar interests in the opposite section, which comparisons were often odious and produced unpleasant feelings. Finally, the civilization in the North and the South are not the same.

The lines of caste are now and always have been closely drawn in the South. The caste system could be carried out very easily under the old slavery *régime*. It was done so successfully that a semi-feudal civilization pervaded the entire South, and still rules with an iron hand all social and local interests. These things have all had their influence on the moral and intellectual condition of the Southern people. Arbitrary human slavery has never been productive of high moral principles. Take any country or any section of country where it has existed for any considerable time, and its tendency has been to loosen the morals, lessen the energy, and increase the ignorance of the people. What shall I say of the South? the land I love, the land of my own nativity, the land beneath whose soil the ashes of my forefathers lie? Honesty compels me to say it is no exception to the rule. The war did not lessen the differences between the North and the South. Terminating as it did, we have no right to expect that it would have done so. The South fought for what she believed to be right, and held out against great odds with the desperation of death. Finally she was whipped, overcome, subdued, but not conquered. Unpleasant conditions were forced upon her. Has she not accepted these conditions as gracefully as we could reasonably expect?

More than four millions of slaves, whom the people had always looked upon as their property, were emancipated and made citizens of the United States, with all the privileges pertaining to citizenship.

A greater question never arose in American history than the one thrust upon the people at that time. The question was: Can the master and the slave be reconciled, recognize each other as citizens, and live in peace and prosperity under the same laws?

At first there was wild speculation on both sides. The Northern people, viewing the question with their characteristic coolness and common-sense, saw that the solution of the problem lay in the education of both races. I say both races, because the colored people were almost wholly destitute of education, and the lower class of whites was in a like pitiable condition. The Northern people were interested because they knew how dangerous a thing the right of franchise was in the hands of people who could not read their ballots. The South had not sufficient means at the close of the war to educate these people; furthermore, those in

power were not favorable to the education of the masses. Principally because the prejudice against the colored people was so strong as to preclude them very largely from the public schools, the Northern people began one of the grandest enterprises that ever originated in man's brain and found expression through philanthropists' pockets.

The country had been engaged in a bloody war, but, when it ended, ere the roar of the cannon had fully ceased, and the smoke of battle fairly cleared away, and before the grass had grown green over the graves of the dead heroes, the Northern patriots began to "beat their swords into plowshares and their spears into pruning-hooks," and reach forth a helping hand to the defeated and fallen. Missionaries and teachers were sent into the South and supported by Northern money. Thus in the past eighteen years the North has sent into the South the magnificent sum of twenty-five millions of dollars for educational and evangelical purposes. Nothing has so touched and mollified the hearts of the Southern people as this magnificent charity. At first the work was not favorably received in many parts of the South. The people naturally asked, What is the object of this work in the South? Many of them believed it was a "Yankee trick" to get the votes of the colored people. After observing the progress of the work for years, and noting the courage and devotion of the leaders, Drs. Hartzell, Rust, and the sainted Bishop Haven, and many others whom I might mention, they are beginning to exclaim, "Why, these men are not politicians!" Thousands of colored people have learned more than this, and are exclaiming, "No, they are not politicians; they are the advance-guard of the armies of the Lord that are on their way to the South to lift from our people the clouds of superstition and ignorance."

Notwithstanding the great work done in the South during the past sixteen years in education and evangelization, this section is yet in a pitiable condition. There are six millions of children of school age in the Southern States, and only one half of this number were enrolled in the public schools last year. In some of the States the per cent. of the children enrolled in the schools is becoming smaller each year, and the schools are becoming less efficient each year. This has long been the case, and the result is plainly visible. In all the Gulf States south of Virginia more than one half the entire population that is over ten years of age cannot read. In some States the per cent. of illiteracy is much larger than I have stated, but the average, taking all together, is a fraction over one half.

This illiteracy is about proportionately divided between the two races. Formerly the larger per cent. was among the colored people, but not so now. Any person who will investigate the matter honestly must admit that education is making more rapid progress among the colored than among the ignorant white people of the South. This fact is explained when we remember that the colored people have much better opportunities in many places than have the whites. The various religious denominations have taken their education in hand, and are pushing it forward independently of public schools. This was a necessity, for in many of the country districts the public money will not run the schools two months during the year. It is evident, if education makes much progress in the South, it must be done for some time through other channels than the present public-school system. From these causes and to this end the Methodist Episcopal Church is in the South. There is no mission field in the Church whe e the time, labor, and money given yield so rich a return as in this Southern field, and yet there are no causes to which some of our people contribute so reluctantly. Some have explained this by claiming that our leaders have been recreant to the trust given them by recognizing the color line. Sixteen years of labor in the South have demonstrated the fact that each race prefers a separation from the other in schools and churches. No bars are put between the two races—they divide naturally. The time will doubtless come when it will not be so, but now it is a fact, not only in the South, but from Maine to Mexico and from New York to San Francisco.

The Methodist Church is not in the South as an experiment, for it is now a demonstrated reality that it is a grand success. In

the past sixteen years she has built on what was slave territory three thousand three hundred and eighty-five churches, (3,385.) She has forty-three colleges and seminaries, with an enrollment of nearly twenty thousand students (20,000.) The increase of white members during the past sixteen years has been 133,640, which exceeds by 20,000 the entire membership of our Church in the six New England Conferences. The increase of the colored-members during the same period has been 159,000.

Our total gain during the past sixteen years has been 292,640 on what was once slave territory.

If figures and facts do not lie, let me ask you what these figures mean? To my mind they say that the Methodist Episcopal Church in the Southern States is making a grand record in the work of saving the masses.

Do not get the idea that the people are depending wholly on the North for aid; they are helping themselves as fast as they can. At the last session of the Louisiana Annual Conference the contributions to benevolent purposes amounted to nearly four thousand dollars. This is a grand showing when we remember this contribution represents the offering of only twelve thousand members, and most of them only a few years out of slavery. The idea is prevalent that the golden age of the South has passed; but not so, it is yet to come. Barriers to Southern progress are rapidly passing away. A new and brighter period than has yet dawned upon the South is in the near future. God hasten the day when the land of perpetual flowers and balmy breezes shall be redeemed from the thralldom of ignorance, when peace shall be her song, and prosperity her joy!

---

15. ILLITERACY AND POVERTY IN THE SOUTH.

Rev. J. L. M. CURRY, D.D., of Richmond, Va., General Agent of the Peabody Educational Fund, in an address on "The National Problem of Southern Education," says :

THE South, at heavy pecuniary cost, is maturing and perfecting school systems for free and universal education. I make bold to affirm that the Southern States, by any rate of taxation likely to be sustained at the ballot-box, cannot give free education to all youth between the ages of eight and eighteen. The condition of the South is little understood. In twenty years there have been signs of improvement, but lectures and arti-

cles on "The New South" often give rose-colored and exaggerated ideas of the progress. In mining, manufacturing, stock-raising, trucking, railway communication, there has been marked growth, but in general agriculture bold generalizations are needed to establish the theory of prosperity. Unintelligent and unskilled labor is a serious drawback to any country. A comparison of the assessed valuation of personal property and real estate for 1860, 1870, and 1880, drawn from census reports, will show most conclusively the paralysis of the South, and the slowness and difficulty of recovery:

STATES.	1860.	1870.	1880.
Ala.....	$432,198,762	$155,582,505	$122,867,228
Ark.....	180,211,330	94,528,843	86,406,364
Fla......	68,929,085,	32,480,843	30,938,309
Ga.......	618,232,387	227,219,519	239,472,509
Ky.......	528,212,693	400,254,204	350,563,971
La.......	437,757,205	253,371,890	160,162,439
Miss.....	500,472,912,	177,278,890	110,624,120
N. C. ..	292,297,002	130,878,000	156,100,202
S. C.....	489,319,124	183,912,337	133,560,135
Tenn....	382,495,200	253,782,164	211,778,538
Tex.....	267,792,835	149,732,929	320,364,315
Va......	657,021,336	365,439,017	308,455,135
W. Va..	....	140,558.273	139,622,705
Total..	$4,863,970,635	$2,573,792,113	$2,370,923,209

During the decade from 1870 to 1880 there has been a decrease in valuation in all these States, except Georgia, North Carolina, and Texas. In Texas the causes are obvious. While the population in these States has steadily increased, the ability to pay taxes has diminished. The Negroes are scarcely to be counted as a tax-paying element. Their taxable property is insignificant in comparison with their numbers. If one contemplates the just conclusions from these sad statistics, he will be prepared to indorse the vigorous saying of General Sherman, more condensed and expressive than the French proverb, that " War is hell."

General reflections on the evils of illiterate suffrage are of painfully practical interest when applied to the South. A few non-tax-paying illiterate voters of the same race might be comparatively harmless, as the importance of the votes would be proportionately little. The following table furnishes food for profitable reflection :

STATES.	Voting population.	Votes cast in 1880.	Illiterate voters.
Alabama..........	259,884	151,507	132,526
Arkansas.........	182,977	106,229	59,340
Florida	61,697	51,618	25,319
Georgia..........	321,438	155,651	159,306
Kentucky.........	370,221	261,304	107,730
Louisiana.........	216,787	97,201	106,801
Mississippi	336,589	117,078	127,935
North Carolina.....	294,753	241,218	145,204
South Carolina.....	205,780	170,056	117,193
Tennessee.........	330,305	247,827	122,836
Texas............	380,376	241,478	93,472
Virginia..........	334,505	212,135	142,622

In Alabama, Louisiana, Mississippi, North Carolina, and South Carolina one half of the voting population cannot read the ballots they cast. In Arkansas, Florida, Tennessee, and Virginia the number of illiterates equals or exceeds half the number of those who vot-

ed at the presidential election in 1880. In Georgia, Louisiana, and Mississippi there are more illiterate voters than there were votes cast in the election of 1880! In every Southern State, and in many Northern and Western States, the illiterate adults hold the balance of power! These revelations of the census "ought to overwhelm with shame and stimulate every power of the national intellect, and command every dollar within reach of the taxing power to provide a remedy equal to the terrible disease." What a travesty is such illiteracy upon the elective franchise! what a contemptible farce is a formal election! The most fervid imagination cannot over color.

Before the war educational facilities were liberally and adequately provided at the South for a portion of the white population. There were academies and colleges of a high order for the training of both sexes. For the education of a large number of white children the provision made was meager and inadequate. No State had a system of free schools. To those who seek causes for rebuke and censure, this failure to furnish means of even rudimentary education for the whole white population is a far more serious and plausible ground of attack than many which ignorance and prejudice have greedily seized upon.

If even half of what has been affirmed be true, then the exigency is perilous, summoning the united and gigantic efforts of every patriot and Christian. Illiteracy is a national peril. Its removal is a national problem. The school population of the United States is 18,000,000. Seven and one half millions, or five twelfths of the whole, are growing up in absolute ignorance of the English alphabet. The free-school system is the cornerstone of our republic, and popular education is the only safe and stable basis for popular liberty. Wisely the New England States and their descendants interwove public schools into the "very thread and texture of their civil institutions." The cause of free government, and the cause of universal education, are one. Men cannot be educated to be slaves. " No instruction imparted can so pervert the human faculties as to make men believe that their normal or rightful condition is servitude." If education had been universal African slavery had been impossible, and that problem would not have perplexed American statesmanship, or wrought sectional alienation.

Ignorance is the hand-maid of despotism, the implacable foe of freedom. General Garfield, in his letter accepting the nomination for the Presidency, said : " Next in importance to freedom and justice is popular education, without which neither freedom nor justice can be permanently maintained."

On motion of Rev. LEMUEL Moss, D.D., of Indiana, the National Educational Assembly for 1883 adopted the following :

Resolved, That the Christian men and women who in the past twenty years have labored as teachers and missionaries from the North in the South, healing the wounds of war and laying the foundations of all social order in intelligence and virtue, deserve and have our heartiest thanks, our highest honor, our profoundest gratitude. Their praise is in all the Churches, and their record is on high. While the American Union stands, while Christian cizilization lasts, these workers and their work will abide in growing influence, luster, and power.

———————

A telegram was received during the Assembly from the Shreveport District Conference, then in session, as follows:

SHREVEPORT, La., Aug. 9, 1883.

Rev. Dr. J. C. HARTZELL, Conductor National Education Assembly :

The Shreveport District Conference, now in annual session in this city, sends greeting and bid you Godspeed. The supreme need of our people is the Bible and spelling-book. God bless the efforts of the National Education Assembly! His South-land and this nation must be flooded with the blessings of Christian education.

STEPHEN DUNCAN, *President.*
M. E. V. CHAPMAN, *Secretary.*

IX. CHRIST IN AMERICAN EDUCATION.

1. SERMON: THE CHRISTIAN ELEMENT IN EDUCATION.

R.EV. LEMUEL MOSS, D.D.,

President Indiana University.

I WILL take as the subject of my discourse this morning the Gospel according to Matthew, the 24th chapter and 25th verse, "Heaven and earth shall pass away, but my word shall not pass away."

I desire to bring this morning a message of encouragement and strength. I remember that just twenty years ago, within a few weeks, it was my privilege to address a large gathering of soldiers at the front. On the morning after our service the Army of the Potomac was to break camp and start out on an uncertain march. I found them gathered about their camp-fires, and, as they made a little pathway for me to pass into the midst of the gathering where I might speak to them, one tall and stalwart soldier whispered in my ear, as I passed him, "Say something to encourage us, wont you?" He was thinking of the march, of the peril, of the enemy, and his heart yearned for some word in all these circumstances of trial that should give to him comfort and strength. We are gathered here to-day as soldiers of Jesus Christ; we belong, I trust, to the Lord's hosts. We are confronted constantly with the trials and with the perils of battle; we are, if true to our Leader and our Lord, ever on the march or ever in the engagement. And often and again when these terrible trials are upon us, and these perils are before us, and the earnest longing of the heart is toward the battle-field, and the yearning of the soul is for victory in God's name, there comes to us the desire for encouragement, that encouragement that can come to us only from the abiding and strengthening word of God. "Heaven and earth shall pass away;" all this magnificent universe that we see, and hear, and rejoice in, shall pass away as a scroll; the mighty sea shall cease its rolling and its roar; but the word of God, the word of Jesus Christ who is God, shall never pass away.

We have been gathered here, and are gathered now, to look great difficulties in the face, to study the problems that vex our hearts and try our minds, to see if there be any way out of this wilderness of difficulty and awe, of peril and distress. We have been looking at these great questions of illiteracy, of pauperism, of crime, and we have been asking, Is there any solution? Do not the problems multiply with every step of our advancement? Do not the questions seem, under every solution, more difficult, more perplexing, than those which we have partially understood and settled? I wish to ask you to consider the great comforting fact that so many, in the providence of God, have been settled; that by the power of Divine grace and the ever-present energy of the Holy Spirit, there have been introduced into our civilization and our life some great forces that are ruling and are to rule the world; that these great energies of God's truth that never sleep, that never relax, that never weaken, are to work out their own inherent power, to renew, to uplift, to prove, to sanctify, to save, the race. In behalf of our interests we are gathered to think, and deliberate, and plan. And so, as I speak to you of the Christian element in education, I wish to ask especial attention to what Christianity has done, what forces it has introduced, what great principles it has established, by the inner working of which many of these great questions are to be answered, many of these great difficulties are to be alleviated and removed.

What do we mean by education? What is it that, first of all, Christianity emphasizes with reference to this mighty work? What is the point of view it gives us? What the standing ground? Christianity emphasizes the worth of him for whom this educating work is done. Christianity emphasizes the worth of man, and it was not until the coming of Christ, the God-man, the Son of man, the Saviour of man—it was not until Jesus

Christ came and lived and taught and wrought and died and rose again that this great truth of man's individuality and worth was understood. We understand now, by the influence of Christianity, that all things on earth stand in direct relationship to the perfecting of the individual soul; the manhood of man is a truth of substantive value standing by itself, and all the institutions of society are contributing, and are intended to be tributary, to his upbuilding and perfecting. Man does not exist for the State, but the State for man; man does not exist for the Church, but the Church for man; man does not exist for society, but society for man. All these institutions of Divine origin, of Divine sanction, of Divine efficiency, are institutions intended for the training, for the discipline, for the upbuilding, for the perfecting of him who is made in the likeness of God and renewed after the likeness of Jesus Christ. And this truth is working to-day. Slowly we are coming to appreciate it, to believe it, to act upon it, to allow it to live in us as a perpetuating and quickening power. Man, of different race, of different color, of different clime, of different condition, wherever he may be found, whatever may be his religion, whatever may be his pursuit, man stands before God and before his fellows as a being of infinite worth, having in him the capacities of limitless development, having in him the value of an endless life. And this whole question of education, how it becomes lifted, how it becomes enlarged, how it becomes lustrous with the Divine glory, when we state that by education we mean the lifting of man out of his feebleness, setting him on that career whose goal is absolute perfectness. Do you ask for testimonies of man's worth? You find them every-where. All nature ministers to him. He is permitted to stand at the center of these mighty forces that permeate and pervade the universe of God; they carry his messages, they give to him the luxuries of life, they feed him with the dainties of the earth, and bring to him angel food and Divine service. Do you ask for testimonies to the worth of the individual man? I hear a voice from heaven, "God so loved the world, that he gave his only begotten Son, that whosoever believeth in him should not perish, but have everlasting life." And as I trace the footsteps of the Son of God to Bethlehem, to Gethsemane, to Calvary, from Calvary to Bethany and to heaven, I hear in every word of his, I see in all his life, a testimony to the value of man, whose redemption he undertook, whose redemption he achieved, whose Lord and Sovereign he is, who shall be recognized as the Saviour of the life that is to be conformed to his own, and perfected into the likeness of his own Divine image.

Now, we may be discouraged, we may be discomfited, we may find ourselves in peril, confronted by difficulties when we look at these great questions that are confronting us to-day, and we ask, How is this profligacy, how is this ignorance, how is this terrible stupidity, how is all this squalor and crime to be reached? How? By the persistent, by the incessant, activity that comes from the belief that God made man in his own image and redeemed him by the blood of Jesus Christ, that his word shall abide forever and accomplish its Divine purpose. If he shall never fail nor be discouraged until he has established his law, surely we, taking hold upon the work that he has accomplished, may follow in his footsteps with patience and confidence and assurance.

But Christianity has not only emphasized the individual value of him for whom we labor, it has emphasized also the instrumentality by which we seek to accomplish our end. What is the great instrumentality in education? In a word, it is the truth. We hope to reach these inherent and limitless capacities of man, we hope to develop them into symmetry and perfectness by the impartation of the truth, all truth, all kinds of truth, the truth of science, the truth of art, the truth of literature, the truth of religion. We hope to bring man to a recognition of his fundamental and permanent relations, relations to the world around him, relations to the brethren close about him, relations to the God who made him and the universe that he inhabits. And you recognize the very significant truth that it was not until the apprehension of the value, of the efficacy, of truth as truth that these great modern movements of science and literature and art in aid of education became a possibility. It is not until men recognize the supreme importance of a fact that they will labor to ascertain what the fact is. You sometimes wonder why men will devote themselves for a life-time, year after year, in the patient investigation of some very limited domain of science, or art, or literature, or theology, or whatever it may be. How is it that a man can fix his attention on some minute part of this existence, and hold his gaze there until, by the intense and incessant looking, he shall come to the understanding of some law, of some force, of some energy, that is at work in human history, that is at work in nature, animate or inanimate, and perhaps be able to announce on a single page the results of a life-time of endeavor and persistent toil? Why does he do it? Because there has been borne in upon him through this Christian emphasizing of the value of the truth the supreme importance of finding a single fact. He wishes to know what is, and why it is, and how it is, understanding very well that if he reaches the significance of a single truth, then other truths will become emphasized, and by and by, each laboring in his own way, in his own place, following his own line of inquiry, the result will be some apprehension of the meaning of this mighty life that pulsates through us, and of this mighty world, in the midst of which we stand, and through which we are permitted to look.

Now we have come to this recognition of the value of the truth through Him who said, "I am the way, and the truth, and the life. No man cometh unto the Father"— an apprehension of God, an acquaintance with God, and a communion with God— "but by me." So I say to-day, it is a matter of great comfort, of great encouragement, to the Christian teacher and to the worker, wherever he may be, to know that Christianity has lodged in the heart of our modern life this conception of the infinite value of the truth. And men will not rest. There may be delay; there may be hinderances; there may be obstacles; there may be many eddies in the current; there may be many windings in the path; but men will not rest since this truth has been brought to them and illustrated as it has been until they know all that can be known, mastering by their knowledge and forces the energies that are waiting to wait upon them, mastering also some conception of themselves and of their relation to this world in which we live, this world of finite proportions now and growing into infinite proportions in the ages to come.

Here is the third great truth that Christianity imparts to this mighty movement we call by the comprehensive name of education. It has to do with the method by which the result is reached. It is a very curious fact that man is the most helpless of all the beings that are born on the earth when he is born; more completely dependent, and not only dependent, but absolute in his ignorance. How helpless he is, and for how long a time he remains helpless! You try sometimes to measure the distance between the infant Newton lying helpless in his nurse's arms and Newton, the Christian philosopher, passing from world to world throughout these limitless regions of space, measuring their distance, and weighing their masses, and binding the universe of God into the order of law; and when you try to measure the distance between the one and the other, you see it is a matter of development, of unfolding the enlargement of capacities, and as you think upon it, and ponder it, and try to understand this mystery that is ever going on before your eyes, in your own household and in your own school, you see that this mastery of himself by man is through the mastery of the world that is around him, and all at once the pursuits and activities of men take on new significance.

You ask why is it that the earth must be cultivated? Why is it that our seas must be turned into highways of commerce? Why is it that men, generation after generation, must tax themselves to learn how to live and how to master the forces of nature that are about them? Why is it that they must toil as for their very lives that our mountains may be tunneled, that our rivers may be bridged, that all hinderances to growth may be removed? Why is it? Man finds nowhere just that which he wants. Here are the forests, here are the mines; but if he is to build himself a shelter, or defend himself against the cold, he must go out and master these things, and mold them to his uses. He must conquer the world and compel it to serve him, or it will be his death; for in his helplessness, without these aids and resources he must perish; and so it is a hand-to-hand fight. He must overcome the world or be overcome by it, and so every city that he builds, and every bridge that he constructs, and every ship that he sets afloat, is but a monument that he rears to the mastery of the world. He says by it, "I have overcome and made that which would have been my death my life."

Now, why all this? Certainly not for the bridge's sake; certainly not for the sea's sake; certainly not for the sake of these magnificent minerals and marbles that are hidden in the earth. All this toil and invention and activity and industry are for man's sake. Man must conquer this world in order that he may conquer himself. He must subdue these energies in order that he may subdue himself, and in becoming God's servant he becomes the master of the world. We see at once how all the pursuits and vocations of life become lifted into a new significance. They are not for themselves; they are for us. They are the means of our discipline; they are the avenues of our influence; they are the ways along which the virtue comes that passes from us to others, that stimulates and strengthens and quickens and lifts them up; and the entire universe becomes for us a school-house. And so I say, the great truth that this is God's universe, that this is God's world, and, as his world, is the training-place for men, is brought to us by the Gospel of Jesus Christ, by him who made all things and for whom all things are and by whom all things consist, showing to us that this great work thus begun and carried on shall never go back. This mighty truth is working in the hearts and thoughts and lives of men, and shall work until it becomes a universal and everywhere accepted truth. This universe is not orphaned. It has not been abandoned by Him who made it, if it ever was made; but it is God's universe; it is the great method of communication to the mind of him who was made in His image, and all the words of heaven become vocal as different voices

14

speaking to him; and this universe, instead of shutting him out, is but the telephone between the ear of the Infinite Father and the obedient child. This great truth is working in the hearts and minds of men, and when we are perplexed, when we are discouraged, when infidelity comes and seems to deny this truth, and when these evil influences wait upon us and dishearten us, let us comfort ourselves with the thought that the truth is mightier than all these opposing energies, that this world shall never go back again into this domain of darkness and sin; and with the luminous truth that shines brighter than the sun in heaven that this is God's world and is intended and adjusted to be a training-place of his creatures, and we shall have songs in the night and glad voices in the day to know that we are in God's training-school.

I have spoken of the being who has to be trained, and of the great instrumentality and of the method through the knowledge of the universe and of the Divine Providence that is moving through it. I wish to speak a moment of the end, of the goal, the outcome, that leads on in this mighty work that we call by this wondrous name, education. What is it we are seeking? What is the ideal of education in every true and worthy conception of the mighty process? It is nothing more than likeness to Almighty God. God's likeness is hidden in the heart of man. Sin has defiled it; sin has obscured it; sin has defaced it; sin has almost erased it; but Jesus Christ, the great teacher and exemplar of all life, the exemplar of all living, has come to restore it, and Jesus Christ, allow me to say it, is at the very heart of all worthy movements in the great work of education, whatever they may be.

Now we come to the apprehension of the nature of Him who originated all things and who upholds all things, and who guides and governs all things, and we see that the end and goal of this great process of ours is to bring man into the perfect likeness of God, so that he may be a worthy son of the Infinite and All-holy Father. You notice this: if you go into a gathering of savages, you find what seems to be great uniformity; and when you go down the scale of human life less and less does individuality manifest itself. All seem to be alike. When you go into a community of intelligent, educated, cultivated, refined people, nothing strikes you so much as the individuality of the persons whom you meet. No two are alike. The very process of elevation has been the development of personality; and while there has been a development of co-operation—the readiness and the ability to aid each other and supplement each other and assist each other in all ways till the person stands there in his own substantive significance—nevertheless, as this process of culture

and elevation and refinement goes on, the process of individualization accompanies it. Did you ever think of it? This is simply the lifting of this mass of humanity by the Almighty God toward himself as the moon lifts the water of the sea; and so this great work of ours in the family, in the school, in the Church, in the State, in society, by all methods and means, this great work of ours that we call education is the lifting of man toward likeness to Him who is infinite and eternal, and whom we may all resemble in our distinct individualities. What a mighty work this becomes, and what great encouragement it brings to us when we understand that this work of ours is, after all, God's great work through us in bringing many sons into glory that they may be possessed of his likeness. There oftentimes comes to the obscure teacher, hidden away from the gaze of men in her own room, with a handful or a larger number of children about her, perplexed, worried, wearied, distressed, tried, almost ready to give up— there comes sometimes in such an hour, in such circumstances, the encouraging thought, "Well, after all, I am God's missionary, intrusted in molding these spirits for him. The work is slow, but it is God's work, and if I can have the patience of Christ and the love of Christ and the quickening energy of Christ this work, so like drudgery as it is, becomes uplifted, for I am in sympathy and companionship with him who reached out and rescued and redeemed my heart."

I remember one day passing through the streets of Cincinnati at an early hour in the morning, and I saw an old, faded, and degraded-looking woman in rags with a coarse sack over her shoulder and a little iron hook in her hand; and I noticed that as she passed along she would examine the ash-barrels and the gutter, and with her little hook she would bring out some rag, some bit of paper, whatever it might be, that she could put into the sack upon her back; and I stood and looked at her, and watched, and by and by I saw that she brought out a patch of silk. O, how filthy and ragged it looked, and as she put it into the sack I began to think about it, and I said it requires no great imagination to follow this fragment of silk from this degraded woman's hand to the paper-mill; I can see it cleansed and transformed and made into the most delicate and beautiful paper; and I can follow it in thought until it reaches the banker's hand and receives from him the signature of power that changes it into wealth, and it goes out among men transfigured as the symbol of affluence and of power; and I said, What hinders the imagination to follow this degraded woman herself, and see her brought into the current of Christian sympathy and Divine love and of saving influences, seeing her transformed by the chemistry of Christ's blood and the renewing of the Divine Spirit until she is lifted up and up and up, beyond the ranks of angels and archangels, until she is seated by the throne of power beside Jesus Christ himself?

Now, brother, wherever you may be, whatever your pursuit is, you also have a commission to engage in this great work, to teach the ignorant, to strengthen the helpless, to encourage the disconsolate, and by your sympathy and your life do something for the encouragement of these great truths of Christ's coming to lift the world, the lowest of it, toward holiness and happiness and God, until the earth shall revolve in its golden orbit about the throne of Him who made it and loved it and redeemed it.

2. REMARKS.

GEN. CYRUS BUSSEY, NEW ORLEANS.

On introducing Dr. NEWMAN, the Chairman, Gen. BUSSEY, spoke as follows :

THE meetings that have been held in this tabernacle during the last four days are of as great importance as any that have ever come before the American people. The subject of education ever has and ever will occupy the minds of all good citizens. There have been two civilizations in this country: one which began soon after the landing of the Pilgrim fathers, based upon the idea of education, and the other a civilization of aristocracy, which began in the South, based on the idea of human slavery. In the South no provision was made to educate the masses. The poor whites grew up, like the Negro slave, without knowing how to read or write. It has been said that knowledge is power, and that the pen is mightier than the sword ; but it is a truth in this country, to-day, that ignorance is more powerful than all the knowledge that has come down to the American people since the days of Plymouth Rock. It is a fact, which could be established if time would permit, that a large number of the States of this Union are, to-day, politically controlled by ignorance, because the men in them have the power to give the ballot, but have not the power to have their ballot counted ; and it is possible that in a few years the whole political power in this country may pass into the hands of such men in consequence of the ignorance which prevails over a large portion of the States of this Union—where had men of intelligence control the vote of the ignorant masses. One of the highest duties of the citizen is sanitation. There is no city or village in the land that does not look out for the health of its people, by the adoption of wise sanitary measures to protect health. The great question of sanitation, as a nation, to-day, is to quarantine against the ignorance that has enthroned itself on nearly one half of this nation. For the past twenty-two years I have traveled extensively through and lived in Southern States, beginning at the time of the war and during all the dark days of reconstruction, and I say to you that I believe firmly that there never would have been a rebellion if the people of the Southern States had been as well informed as the people of the North. I believe the war grew out of the fact that a few men imposed upon the credulity of the people of the South as to the resources, ability, and power of the people of the North, until they accomplished that crime of all crimes—disloyalty to this Union and to this government.

I have had an opportunity, as a business man, of witnessing the extensive effects of this ignorance upon the people who have attempted to rise from the terrible position in which they found themselves at the close of the war ; and when I tell you that eight thousand millions of money has been dug out of the South, in cotton, sugar, rice, grain, etc., during the past twenty years, you would think that the people of that country would be rolling in the luxury of wealth. If the laboring people had been as well informed as the people of Iowa, where a school-house is never out of sight, they would be, to-day, independent. But where there are riches and wealth there a certain class of people will congregate as the buzzards congregate about a carcass. These men, supplied with bad whisky and inferior goods, which they sell to the laboring people of the South at ruinous prices, absorb their earnings and keep them poor. To-day the South stands lowest in wealth and education.

If I were to give you some of the methods by which the black man is kept poor, you would find that it costs more to be ignorant than it would to give every child a college education. It was the practice with a certain class of merchants to make out their bills dated, say 1883, and in settling with the ignorant Negroes to carry these figures into the money column and deduct them from the amount due to them. These are some of the methods that I know have been borne by the laboring people of the South, and that are borne to-day. There are many honorable merchants in the South, and the same business integrity which prevails in the North, while many of the disreputable have come from the North, and from foreign lands, to take advantage of the ignorant, dependent laborer.

Among the prominent public actors who found a place in the South at the close of the war or before the close of war, was the distinguished gentleman who is to address you to-day. Rev. Dr. Newman was sent to New Orleans in 1864, to re-establish the Methodist Episcopal Church, and its educational work, in the States of the Mississippi Valley. Under his supervision a Conference was organized, which has been subdivided and now has a large representation in Texas, Louisiana, Mississippi, and Arkansas. He not only performed the duties of a pastor of one of the largest churches in the city of New Orleans, but he served at the same time as presiding elder of a large district, was the spiritual adviser of more than a score of ministers sent out to carry on the work organized under his direction. He established a Church paper at his own expense, which he edited and distributed largely free to educate the people of his Church in the various States tributary to New Orleans. He built several churches, costing in the aggregate more than a hundred thousand dollars.

He aided largely in the establishment of what is now the New Orleans University, and also in planting an Orphans' Home and an educational institution on Bayou Teche, Louisiana. It is safe to say that, to-day, more than one hundred persons are ministers of the Gospel or teachers in schools, whose entire education was obtained in the institutions organized by him. The time came when the Bishops of the Church desired a man to fill one of the first pulpits in the land, and Dr. Newman was selected for that position.

Fifteen years ago I was in Chicago with Dr. Newman, where we met Rev. Dr. Hartzell, who has so successfully planned this National Education Assembly. He was then a young man, just out of college. I was the first man in New Orleans to extend a hand of welcome to Dr. Hartzell when he came, full of energy and enthusiasm, to assume his responsible work there. The duties of a pastor, presiding elder of a district, editor of the *South-western Advocate*, and the care of the New Orleans University and Orphans' Home were performed in a manner reflecting the highest credit upon him. When the yellow fever spread the mantle of death over that great city, claiming its victims by the hundred, both Newman and Hartzell remained at their posts and safely passed through the terrible sickness which brought them nigh unto death.

I have detailed these events in the history of these two faithful ministers, from an intimate acquaintance with their labors during the past seventeen years, believing that the work performed by them in the South has been of great service to the cause of the Church and of education.

I now have the pleasure of introducing Rev. Dr. Newman, who will address you.

3. SERMON: RELIGIOUS EDUCATION THE SAFEGUARD OF THE NATION.

REV. JOHN P. NEWMAN, D.D., LL.D., NEW YORK.

I HOPE that my friend, General Bussey, who has seen fit to identify my name and the name of Brother Hartzell with our missionary work in the South, may be happy e· ough to find that the future of that work shall justify his kind words spoken here to-day.

I understand that the character of this meeting has been somewhat changed. According to the published programme it was to have been a platform meeting; General

Bussey—a gentleman competent to the task —was to preside, and Dr. Buttz, one of our first scholars, was to speak on American scholarship, and I was to follow with the subject announced. But I understand that the spiritual authority of Ocean Grove has decided that we are to have a sermon. So it is necessary for me to choose a text, which you will find in Proverbs xiv, 34: "Righteousness exalteth a nation."

Under the light of these words, I am to

speak of the religious element in secular education, and its sanctification as a safeguard of the American republic.

Religion is naturally divided into two parts, the devotional and the ethical. In yonder tabernacle you have had the devotional.

We propose this afternoon to have the ethical; for what is the devotional without the ethical? Show me a perfect man, and I will show you a man whose morality corresponds with his devotions. We should have more ethical force in the heart and life of the Church, to give potency and glory to its devotion. So, to-day, guided by these inspired words, this formulated principle, this grand old truth that has come down baptized with the venerableness of antiquity, still fragrant with a plenary inspiration, and like its Au'hor true in the past, 'rue in the present, and to be true in the future of all nations, whether aristocratic or democratic or autocratic or republican or paternal, or whatever the form the nation may assume, let us consider the weighty question assigned us.

A nation is a community of people. Whatever may be its ancestry, or its organization, or its jurisprudence, or its culture, a nation is a congregation or community of people. Righteousness is one of those inspired, comprehensive terms which includes the devotional and the ethical, especially the ethical referring to private virtue and to public morality. Out of the private virtues issue the public morality, out of the public morality issue the national preponderance and perpetuity and prosperity. You can therefore see the depth of the meaning, the profound significance, of this venerable proverb that has come from the past, "Righteousness exalteth a nation." Because it is ever true, and because the greatest nations ignoring its truth have passed away, hence it is wise for us, on this Christian Sabbath, to consider the relations of this subject to the welfare of our national life.

There is a deep significance, my brethren, in these words, when we remember how apt we are to fancy that because this is a republic, therefore it is immortal. But there have been other republics which have passed from the vision of the world. On the shores of Africa there was one, in whose splendid harbors floated the flags of all nations, whose merchants were princes, whose cities were centers of power, and who caused the mistress of the world to tremble when that power was in its glory.

There was a republic by the waters of the Ægean Sea, a confederation of States, where the questions, not only of the state itself, but also of vassal States, were settled in the grave assembly of the people—a republic which reached the highest degree of glory in literature and in art, whose poets to-day sing for us, whose orators to-day are our models,

whose esoteric philosophies are to-day imitated by the great thinkers.

There was a republic on the banks of the Tiber, three hundred years before the Babe of Bethlehem was born, in whose citizenship was one hundred and twenty millions of people.

Yet these republics have passed away and are among the things that were. For my own part, my brethren, I can see no hope for the future if our perpetuity depends merely upon our being a republic, with its free constitution, with its right of suffrage, with its halls of justice, with its schools of learning. I must look for that hope elsewhere. I must penetrate below the surface, I must grapple with those sterner truths that lie at the very base of our individualized moral existence.

What are the safeguards of this republic? After a hundred years of national life, growth, and prosperity, we may infer the future from the past. To what should we ascribe the greatness and preservation of our country? The statesman attributes this grand result to the genius of our government, our inherent power to enforce law, our profound respect for civil obligations. But historical facts are in proof that all that is wise in law, mighty in war, rich in commerce, magnificent in architecture, and splendid in discovery, belonged to the republics of Sparta, Venice, and Genoa. Yet their glory is as a tale that is told. History has furnished no exceptions to the rule that national safety inheres in national virtue, in the correctness of the moral sentiments of the people, in the rectitude of the private life of the citizen. In all the ages moral corruption has preceded political ruin. That which undermines the commonwealth is that which civil law is inadequate to reach. It is the province of constitutions and of laws to restrain the evil and conserve the good—to protect the virtuous, but not to reform the vicious. All civil law, whether constitutional or statutory, lacks the power to purify. Law may dictate, may guide, may conserve, but it cannot reform. "For what the law could not do, in that it was weak through the flesh, God sending his own Son in the likeness of sinful flesh, and for sin, condemned sin in the flesh." The power to purify does not inhere in the penalties of law, whether human or divine. There is nothing reformatory in punishment, else every criminal would become a virtuous citizen, and every lost soul would become a saint. Something must be added to suppress sin and develop virtue. Vice and virtue lie beyond the reach and scope of law. Law can reach actions, but it cannot reach those principles whence actions spring. It is a great fact that, back of constitutions, back of laws, back of administrations, there must be a moral sentiment, which is the energy of law and the glory of all human governments. Our splendid government, the growth of a century, the ripened wisdom of the past, the purest and most beneficent on all the earth, would fall to pieces like a rope of sand unsupported by the moral sentiment of the people, who demand that crime shall be punished and virtue rewarded. That moral sentiment comes from Christianity, accepted and practiced in every-day life. It is the product of religious education, the safeguard of civil liberty.

Some statesmen assume that the government itself is the competent and all-sufficient safeguard of our rights as citizens; that from it, and of necessity, will issue public justice, competency, and happiness, and that the recognized right to command and duty to obey are the essential factors of national life. Doubtless one form of government is better than another, but it is a matter of record that all forms of government, from the paternal to the autocratic, have failed to secure the happiness of the people independent of a force which resides in the individual citizen. All history attests two great facts: that under the best civil rule known to man vice has prevailed, treason has triumphed, and the worst men have lived; while, on the other hand, under the worst of governments some men have attained the highest virtues, as the apostles under the Neros, the Waldenses under the Popes, the Puritans under the Stuarts.

The true statesman, sound in his political philosophy and strong in his religious convictions, will recognize the power of individuality in the perpetuity of our free institutions. He will feel and proclaim the imperative necessity of a political conscience, which will respond to every voice of duty and of justice. In this free country each citizen should have a clear perception of his political duties; a realization of his personal responsibility in the issues of every election; a manifested interest in the moral character of all public officials, not unlike the interest he feels in the character of the minister of his church, the teacher of his children, the agent of his business.

How to create, develop, and conserve such a conscience, is the great question of the hour. The scholar assumes that the end will be attained by high mental culture and the diffusion of knowledge among the masses. He would exalt the intellect above the conscience. Doubtless an intelligent citizenship is of greater importance in a republic than any other form of government. An aristocracy of learning may answer the purposes of the governing classes under an autocracy or a monarchy, but in a republic the common mind must be taught to think, the citizen must be educated in the principles of a free government, the true sphere and responsibility of the elective franchise, and to grapple *with* and triumph *over* the schemes of

corrupt leaders. When the government is by the people and for the people, the masses must be intelligent. The chief object of our common-school education is to train the individual mind to *think*. If we have soldiers their bayonets should *think*, if we have sailors their guns should *think*, and if we have voters their ballots should *think*.

The Christian patriot is in full accord with the scholar in the necessity of mental culture for the preservation of our civil liberty, and to mental culture he adds a religious education. What is there in mere knowledge that can purify the heart and restrain the craving passions thereof? Chemistry admits us into the very secrets of nature, into her marvelous combinations; but can a knowledge of gases, of liquids, of solids, change the vicious into the virtuous? Who knew more of chemistry than Prof. Webster, who, in his laboratory, committed the highest crime know to the law? What is there in the mere knowledge of the stars, of the rocks, of the flowers, of the winds, of the distance and proportion, of anatomy and physiology, of law and medicine, of languages living and dead, of the laws of trade and the science of statesmanship, that can change and purify human nature, which is depraved in principle and sinful in practice? It is Lord Bacon who said: "In knowledge without love there is somewhat of malignity." It is Coleridge who said: "All the mere products of the understanding tend to death." It is Paul who said: "Knowledge puffeth up, but charity edifieth." Where shall we find such history, such poetry, such theology, as among the Jews, who are now exiles in every land? Where shall we find such philosophy, such oratory, such art, as in the land which gave to the world a Homer, a Pericles, an Aristotle? Where shall we find such jurisprudence, such statesmanship, such eloquence, as in an empire which could boast of a Cæsar and a Tully? Yet, behold the ruins of the one and the desolation of the other! Listen to Lord Macaulay's description of the learning of the cultured people of ancient Greece:

"In general intelligence the Athenian populace far surpassed the lower orders of any community that has ever existed. It must be considered that to be a citizen was to be a legislator, a soldier, a judge, one upon whose voice might depend the fate of the wealthiest tributary State, or of the most eminent man. The lowest offices, both of agriculture and of trade, were in common performed by States. The commonwealth supplied its meanest members with the support of life, the opportunity of leisure, and the means of amusement. Books were, indeed, few, but they were excellent, and they were accurately known. It is not by turning over libraries, but by repeatedly perusing and intensely contemplating a few great models that the mind is best disciplined. Books, however, were the least part of the education of an Athenian citizen. Let us for a moment transfer ourselves in thought to that glorious city. Let us imagine that we are entering its gates in the time of its greatest power and glory. A crowd is assembled around a portico. All are gazing with delight at the entablature, for Phidias is putting up the frieze. We turn into another street. A rhapsodist is reciting there; men, women, and children are thronging around him; the tears are running down their cheeks, their eyes are fixed, their very breath is still, for he is telling how Priam fell at the feet of Achilles, and kissed those hands—the terrible, the murderous—which had slain so many of his sons.

"We enter the public place; there is a ring of youths all leaning forward, with sparkling eyes and gestures of expectation. Socrates is pitted against the famous atheist from Iona, and has just brought him to a contradiction in terms.

"But we are interrupted. The herald is crying, 'Room for the Prytanis.' The general assembly is to meet. The people are swarming in on every side. Proclamation is made: 'Who wishes to speak?' Pericles is mounting the stage. Then for a play of Sophocles, and away to sup with Aspasia.

"I know of no modern university that has so excellent a system of education."

Need I ask scholars where Greece is to-day?

Here are the marvelous sayings of some Frenchmen that are worthy of our consideration. Victor Cousin, the great philosopher, said to the Chamber of Peers:

"Any system of school training which sharpens and strengthens the intellectual powers, without at the same time affording a source of restraint and countercheck to their tendency to evil, is a curse rather than a blessing."

De Tocqueville says: "Despotism may govern without religious faith, but liberty cannot." Here is Herbert Spencer. One would hardly think that he would come so far on the other side, and yet he utters this truth: "The belief in the moralizing effects of intellectual culture, flatly contradicted by facts, is absurd."

And Huxley; one would hardly suppose that he would have uttered a word in favor of that good old Book: "There must be a moral substratum to a child's education to make it valuable, and there is no other source from which this can be obtained at all comparable with the Bible."

Webster said: "In what age, by what sect, where, when, by whom, has religious education been excluded from the education of the youth? Nowhere! never! Everywhere and at all times it has been regarded as essential."

And what is the great saying of the Father of his Country, that obsolete statesman, now, in the estimation of the mushroom statesmen of this day—these political statesmen who know nothing beyond party zeal and party spoils, who never visit the grave of Washington to pray that his mantle may come upon them? What does Washington say with reference to this?—"Let us with caution indulge the supposition that morality can be maintained without religion. Reason and experience both forbid us to expect that national morality can prevail in exclusion of religious principles."

And then, rising above all these in glory, the Divine Nazarene said: "Suffer little children, and forbid them not, to come unto me; for of such is the kingdom of heaven." Let me touch their young hearts; let me change their beautiful spirits into higher beauty as citizens of a national life that will be a conserving force not known to civil law, not known in science, not known in literature.

There is a striking fact in connection with the flourish to-day for fine arts among the American people. I would not depreciate the taste of my countrymen for the marble or the canvas. But there are certain professed connoisseurs who have made millions of money, and cannot tell exactly how they have made them. When they say the fine arts have a place in morality, and that we are by them to alleviate the ills of life, it is time for us to enter our voice of protest.

Hear Ruskin, he who has a right to speak of art. I confess to you, my brethren, that I stood appalled when I read these three propositions:

I. "Nations renowned for their excellence in the fine arts have been subdued by barbarians; instance the Lydians and Medes, the Athenians and Spartans, the Greeks and Romans, the Romans and Goths.

II. "The period of perfect art is the period of decline. At the moment when a perfect picture appeared in Venice, a perfect statue in Florence, a perfect fresco in Rome, from that hour forward probity, industry, and courage were exiled from their walls.

III. "Art has displayed its most energetic manifestations in the domain of superstition, of falsehood, and vice. Behold Egypt, Babylon, Greece, Italy. And art has not only been most active in the service of luxury and idolatry, but in the exaltation of cruelty. A peaceful, pastoral people, living in sobriety and innocence, never decorate the shepherd's staff and the plow-handle; but races who live by depredation and slaughter exquisitely ornament the quiver, the spear, and the helmet, and have the grandest temples wherein are the trophies of war. Out of the cottage come faith, courage, self-sacrifice, purity, and piety; out of the palace come treachery, cruelty, cowardice, idolatry, bestiality."

It is a trite and familiar saying that "knowledge is power." It is, however, a power for good or for evil, as it is controlled by a religious education which fills the mind with the noblest ideas of God, of personal responsibility, of a future state. The battle-field of the republic is the cradle of American childhood. On one side of that cradle stand the infidel, bold, brazen, impious, and the Jesuit, cunning, greedy, ambitious; and on the other side stands the Christian patriot, reverent, upright, earnest, holding in his hand the Bible without note or comment.

The great contest between the Christian and the infidel is whether education shall be secular or religious, and between the Protestant and the Papist, whether it shall be in the interest of Romanism or of Protestantism. The pregnant question therefore is: Which of these contestants shall control the education of American childhood? If the infidel, how appalling the prospect! He demands a purely secular education, from which all religious instruction shall be eliminated. He would have a nation of educated atheists. He would annihilate all belief in the existence of a personal God—respect for his character and reverence for his law. He would destroy the restraining power of that belief.

A reverential belief in the existence of God is the *supreme* reason of virtue. Virtue must be under the dominion of law, and that law should be the expressed legislative will of the Creator, whose right it is to command, and whose power is equal to execute. To deny his existence, or that we have a knowledge of his character and will, or that he has the power to enforce his will, is to banish from the mind that wholesome "fear which is the beginning of wisdom." The impression left on the young mind from a purely secular education is that there is no power in the universe to punish vice. This lessens the moral force of the child to resist evil. It creates contempt for law, order, and decorum. It is destructive of all restraint. By what power are the dangerous classes in New York held in check? It is the conviction that there is here somewhere a force adequate to maintain law and order. Destroy that conviction, and New York would be in the hands of the mob. By what power would you deter our youth from crime? By the dread of impending evil? But that dread is the sole offspring of a religious education. Modern infidelity subverts the foundations of morals and elevates expediency to the dignity of law. Morality without God as its authoritative reason is but a social compact, a human stipulation, to be broken at will or enforced against will. This, in effect, is to place virtue under the dominion of the passions, so that men will be good or bad as their passions incline. Are we willing and ready to accept this alternative?

It is a great fact that the stability of our government is in the moral convictions of the citizen. Force is necessary for the maintenance of authority. That force must be either moral or physical. There must be faith in God or trust in bayonets. Our defense is in Bibles, not in Gatling guns. Our standing army, of less than 25,000 men, in a nation of fifty millions of people, is a high compliment for the religious education of our citizenship, whose convictions of moral obligations are clear, deep, and abiding. In such an education the citizen is taught to revere God as the author of civil government, who has "ordained the powers that be," that the administration of the law is to be committed to men who fear God and work righteousness; that obedience to the laws of the land is a Christian virtue; that public morality is the sum of private morals, and that as is the individual, so is the nation. Such conserving truths are taught in the Sunday-school to the youth of our land.

Standing side by side with the infidel is the Papist, whose assaults on civil liberty are the more dangerous because made in the name of religion. He solemnly protests against the secularization of education; but his protest is in the interest of error, superstition, and spiritual slavery.

Now, I do not misrepresent the Roman Catholics. Take, for instance, the sayings of the late Pontiff:

"The Romish Church has the right to interfere in the discipline of the public schools, and in the arrangement of the studies of the public schools."

"Public schools, open to all children for the education of the young, should be under the control of the Romish Church, and should not be subject to the civil power, nor made to conform to the opinions of the age."

"While teaching, primarily, the knowledge of natural things, the public schools must not be separated from the faith and power of the Romish Church."

"The civil power is inferior and subordinate to the ecclesiastical power, and, in litigated questions of jurisdiction, should yield to it."

"The Church and State should be united."

"The Roman Catholic religion should be the only religion of the state, and all other modes of worship should be excluded."

March 25, 1879, Pope Leo XIII. addressed a letter to the Cardinal Vicar, in which he said:

That if he possessed the liberty he claims, he would employ it to close all Protestant schools and places of worship in Rome. (*London Times*, April 11, 1879.)

Cardinal Antonelli said:

That he thought it better that the children

grow up in ignorance than be educated in such a system of schools as the State of Massachusetts supports. (*Hawkins*, page 2, and *John Jay*, page 293.)

Bishop Gilman, in his Lenten address, at Cleveland, Ohio, March, 1873, said:

" We solemnly charge and most positively require every Catholic in the diocese to support and send his children to a Catholic school. If parents, either through contempt for the priest or disregard for the Church, or for trifling and insufficient reasons, refuse to send their children to a Catholic school, then in such cases only, we authorize confessors to refuse the sacraments to such parents as thus despise the laws of the Church, and disobey the commands of both priest and bishop."

In his pastoral letter, Bishop Gibbons, of Richmond, Va., said:

"The education of the youth is the engrossing topic of our times. It may be safely asserted, that the status of Catholicity in the United States is to be determined by the success or failure of our day-schools, and that the ratio of our Catholic population in the coming generation will be in mathematical proportion to the number and patronage of our parochial institutions of learning. In every parish of three hundred souls, within a distance of three miles, a Catholic school must be built. Pecuniary difficulties must not be dreaded or regarded. We never fail in our efforts to build churches, neither shall we fail in building schools for our youth."

Cardinal McCloskey said:

" Stand by the Catholic schools. We must take part in elections."

I now give you extracts from the Catholic press. The *Freeman's Journal*, of September 23, 1873, said:

" The pope, in a document set forth for the teaching of the whole Church, and, therefore, an instruction which every Catholic must receive as *infallibly true*, says that Catholics ' *cannot, in conscience, use such schools !*' No one in a responsible position dares to say that this is even a question of doubt. It is a *ruled case*—a settled law of the Catholic Church. * * * Those godless public schools are condemned by the Church of God, as bad in themselves ! They are wrong to frequent, because the Lord Jesus Christ, by His vicar, the pope, speaking infallibly, has *forbidden* to frequent them. * * * These godless schools are not simply bad because forbidden, but they *are forbidden because bad in themselves and in the use of them.* * * * There is no priest in America—there is no prelate in America, nor in the world, that has the faculty of permitting a Catholic parent to send one of his children to a school from which

the control of the ' teaching Church '—the reverend clergy—are excluded, so that they cannot enter such schools, and examine both pupils and teachers as to their faith."

" Let the public-school system go where it came from—the devil. What we Roman Catholics must do now is to get our children out of the devouring fire. At any cost and any sacrifice we must deliver the children over whom we have control from these pits of destruction, which lie inviting in their way, under the name of public or district schools."

" This subject (of the public schools) contains in it the whole question of the progress and triumphs of the Catholic Church in the next generation of this country. Catholics, let us all act together ! Let us all read and listen to the same sentiments that we may know how to act together !'

" This country has no other hope, politically or morally, except in the vast and controlling extension of the Roman Catholic religion."

From the *Western* (Chicago) *Tablet* I take the following:

" If your son or daughter is attending a State school, you may be as certain that you are violating your duty as a Catholic parent, and conducting to the everlasting anguish and deep despair of your child, as if you could take your oath to it ! Take him away. Let him, rather, never know how to write his name, than become the bond and chained slave of Satan—than to rise up at the last dread day of account to curse you in all the unavailing repentance and bitterness of final despair. Take him away, if you do not want your bed of death to be tormented with the specter of a soul which God has given you as a sacred trust surrendered to the great enemy of mankind ! Take him away, rather than incur the anger of his God, and the loss of his soul !"

From the *Freeman's Journal* again :

"Certainly it seems to us as if the devil were let loose upon the godless schools to render them abhorrent to even pagan nature !" Again: "Out of every one hundred Catholic children that are educated in the public schools of the United States, the reviewer may set down ninety-eight as a clear and certain gain to the devil."

Again I quote from the *Tablet* :

" If the *Tablet* declared sometime ago that it was better for a child to run in the streets, in which occupation he became a thief, but stood at least some chance of saving his soul, than attend a godless school whose teaching resulted in making him a rogue and an unbeliever, we see no reason to withdraw from such a sentence."

These theories are directly opposed to every right understanding of the American idea of education. I will quote from two of America's illustrious sons. Webster said:

"The power over education is one of the powers of public police, belonging essentially to the government. It is one of the powers, the exercise of which is indispensable to the preservation of society, with integrity and healthy action; it is the duty of self-preservation."

At Burlington, Iowa, on November 4, 1879, Gen. Grant said to the children:

"I believe that if there ever is another war in this country it will be one of ignorance *versus* intelligence, and in that conflict the State of Iowa will achieve a great victory. Furthermore, I think that war will be one of ignorance and superstition combined against education and intelligence, and I am satisfied that the children here will enroll in the army of intelligence, and wipe out the common enemy—ignorance."

I accord to them the right to have parochial schools, as we Methodists have our denominational schools. The only point is this: As I would not take a dollar from the State for the Methodist schools, so the Catholics shall not have a dollar for their parochial schools.

But let us see what has been the fruit of these parochial schools in other lands. Let us, for instance, turn our attention to Spain. Spain, that had fifteen governments in eighty-seven years! Spain, always under the control of the Holy Father! Three hundred years ago she had the lead of all other nations. She had the advantage of the Roman and the Saracenic civilizations. She had the glory of a new world. But all is lost. Of her fifteen millions, twelve millions do not know their letters, and only two millions can write their names! There was an election held in Medonia, where there were five hundred votes cast, and the ministerial candidate was declared elected by five thousand majority!

Take France — France, the beautiful; France, where the marble speaks and the canvas glows! Rome has had her parochial schools there. In 1869, among thirty-six millions of people only one-half of them could read and write. Out of 444,000 criminals, 442,000 were illiterate. Eight hundred French communities were totally without schools. There were 444,000 criminals, and 1,600,000 paupers. Out of 900,000 births, 74,000 were illegitimate. There were 4,500 suicides. (*See Mansfield On the Relations of Crime and Illiteracy.*) But now the record is turned, and there are in school 4,500,000 children. There are 72,000 schools of all kinds; 111,000 teachers—half of them females. The total number of pupils of all ages is 4,717,000, equally divided between the sexes. Of these, 3,878,151, from six to

thirteen, are in school. In December and January the attendance was ninety per cent. of the enrollment. In Paris there were 210,000 of school age, 170,000 of whom were in school.

Let us now review the record of Italy, the home of the Popes. There the supreme pontiff held sway for more than a thousand years, persecuting such men as Dante, Galileo, Columbus, and Cavour. As a result of this system, only 32 out of every 100 men, and only 19 out of every 100 women, could read and write, and out of 83,000 soldiers born in 1848, only 3,000 could read and write. But behold Italy now : 54,000 schools and two and a half millions of scholars, supported at $5,000,000 a year in outlay by the government.

In Austria the concordat was abolished in 1870. They now report 2,600,000 school children, with 1,691,349 of them in school. Education is compulsory, and their course comprehensive. They expend upon their schools $8,000,000 a year.

Ireland, dear old Ireland! The best country on the globe from which to emigrate! Here is the home of so many American citizens! The British census of 1871 shows that in County Connaught, where Romanism dominates, 51 per cent. of the Catholics were illiterate, while of the Protestants only 11 per cent. were illiterate. The criminals were in the ratio of six Catholics to one Protestant.

Mexico has had 56 revolutions in 60 years. With nine millions of people she supports only 8,000 schools—one to each 1,141 inhabitants. The attendance is 349,000, or less than one-fifth of all the children between six and thirteen. Her expenditure yearly is $1,632,436.

Underlying all his houses of mercy, schools of learning, temples of worship, is the love of conquest. His is a dream of the political subjugation of all nations to imperial individualism. His bold pretension is, " that, while the State has rights, she has them only in virtue and by permission of a superior authority; and that authority can only be expressed through the Church. This extraordinary assertion is based on the pope's vicegerent's claim to dictate all human affairs, to define the faith and morals of all men, and to change the form of civil government and disgrace rulers at will. The pontiff condemns free speech, a free press, a free literature, the study of the sciences independent of priestly dictation; all marriages not sacramentally confirmed—a free school, a free church, a free conscience; and claims for the Church the authority to define its own civil rights and the privilege to apply military force to secure the same.

To counterwork the impiety of infidel education and the political designs of the papist the Christian patriot offers to his country the Sunday-school. This is the great source of that moral power which will render secular learning beneficent alike to its possessor and to the nation at large. It is the appropriate supplement to our public schools. As a Christian people we may and should insist that the Bible shall be read in our common schools, as it is the great source of all true moral philosophy; yet the selections read and the manner of reading are left to the taste and spirit of the teacher, and may be a formality or a power. But it cannot be taught, expounded, or enforced. This is the office and work of the Sunday-school teacher, who can illustrate its precepts, unfold its promises, and enlarge upon its awful threatenings till the young mind is imbued with its spirit, and the youthful heart is brought under its divine influence. The time may come when majorities may vote the Bible from our public schools, and the teachings therein be altogether secular. But the morals of the children will be safe if they are trained for the Lord in the Sabbath-school, and the nation will be safe from those moral evils which issue in national ruin, when the childhood of its citizenship is reared in the nurture and admonition of the Lord.

And the Sunday-school also supplements the instructions of home. In this intense life of ours but few parents give sufficient time to family devotion. Home is the school of childhood for weal or for woe. There we are taught to think, to feel, to speak, and to act; there our characters receive their first impressions; there we die of the future is often cast. Throughout eternity we will have cause to thank God for Christian homes —their hallowed associations and blessed memories. Yet, even such homes are strengthened and beautified by the lessons, the examples, and godly influences of the Sunday-school. Blessed be the man whom the Lord raised up to be the founder of this institution of immeasurable power. It is the nursery of the Church, the fountain of the ministry, the hope of the republic. If Columbus discovered a new world for our republic, and Watt invented the steam-engine which to-day strides all continents, and Morse produced the telegraph which has transformed the earth into a neighborhood, and Gutenburg gave to mankind the art of printing which has made the Bible a universal book — to Robert Raikes belongs the honor of the organization of the Sunday-school, which has peopled this continent with Christians who are the promise that our nation shall endure forever.

4. CHRISTIAN EDUCATION AS A FACTOR IN OUR NATIONAL LIFE.

GEN. T. J. MORGAN,

Principal State Normal School, Potsdam, N. Y.

AS I passed along the beach to-night I noticed a large number of people—several hundred, I should think—standing in groups of two, or five, or ten, or twenty, some with glasses in their hands, some shading their eyes, all looking eagerly forward and asking "What is it? Is it a man?" And as their eyes looked out to the sea they saw that which seemed like the face of a man, now appearing, then disappearing. How many of your hearts were stirred to-night as that question went along the shore. "Who is it?" With what eager interest would you listen to me now if I could tell you that it was a man, that he was lost; if I should tell you his name, and his history! I am glad to tell you that it was not a human being that was in peril; but your interest was awakened because there was even a possibility that it was a human being. If you are so interested in one man, or one supposed man, in peril, what would be your interest if you stood with me to-night amid the ruins of Rome, casting your eye over the Campagna, looking at the Colosseum lifting its head to the heavens, into which the multitudes that would dwarf this vast audience went to look upon those bloody scenes enacted there? If you stood within the ruins of the Forum, if you went with me into those little temples, with what interest would you listen as I sketched for you that people's character, as I told you their history, as I told you of their great works of art. How gladly would you listen if I told you why that nation sank to do its work no more!

A great orator once said that he supposed that the sailor-boy, swinging in his hammock on the sea in the night-time, as he thought of the great depth of water beneath him, of that sea reaching out beyond him for thousands of miles, of that infinite heaven that extended way beyond the reach of the imagination over him, there would come to his soul the thought of sublimity. As I have for the last four days been sitting on this platform listening to men discussing the great questions that have occupied our thoughts here, as they have talked of education, of Christianity, of the growth of this people, of the perils that confront us, of the possibilities that stretch out before us, as they have talked of the Negro and the Indian, as they have sketched for us the vast Territory of Alaska with its people, as they have pictured what is possible for us as a nation, I have felt that the greatness, the grandeur, the power, the dignity, of this people of ours far surpasses any thought of more material greatness that may come to the sleeping sailor swinging in his hammock.

There remains in this list of topics to be discussed one which it is my privilege now for a little time to outline before you, and that is "Christian education as a factor in our national life." I say Christian education; I do not like to separate the terms Christianity and education. We sometimes hear "Christianity and culture," "Christianity and education"—but I like to think of them as combined, one incomplete without the other. We may as a matter of thought separate them; we may think of the one as apart from the other; but I like to think of them as standing together in intimate and inseparable relationship. When they laid the foundation for that bridge between New York and Brooklyn they went deep in the earth on the Brooklyn side, and they laid broad the foundations of that pier. Slowly it came out of the water until it had gained the requisite height and the requisite strength; and on the other side of the river they laid the foundation for the other pier until it had reached a height corresponding to the other; then wires were stretched across. Then the great bridge became a fact, and thousands cross it from side to side, and millions of men and women will cross it through the centuries to come; and we think, not of the Brooklyn pier, nor of the New York pier, but of the great bridge that spans them both. So I like to think of Christianity and education, and of Christian culture that binds them inseparably together.

What, then, is Christian education? It is education based upon Christ; it is an education that regards Christ as the maker of the universe, an education that regards science simply as a study of those laws according to which Christ has made the universe. Every flower in that bouquet that stands before me to-night was thought out by Christ before the world was. The stars in their courses do but obey the laws of Christ. Science, in all its forms, is but the formulation of the laws of Christ's universe; mathematics is but a statement of his laws. Christian education is an education that takes Christ as its starting-point, Christ as its goal, an education that regards every man a brother,

that seeks to strike down all caste and distinction of classes, that respects the rights of man as man; an education that seeks for men and women the highest possible development, so that they may become and may achieve all that God intended that they should achieve; an education that is Christian in its principles, Christian in its origin, accepting the Bible as the only infallible revelation of destiny.

Now what place has that education as a factor in national life? I can perhaps best bring that before you by the statement of a few propositions. First. The nation is a personality. We too often think of the nation as a congregation of people. We say we number fifty millions; but I like to think of the nation, not simply as a congregation of people, but as a moral power. You would not be contented if I said to you that the sea is simply a collection of drops. The drops are there, but they take on something of the majesty of the ocean of which they become a part. The drops are all alike, but the ocean takes on its own individuality; it has its currents and its counter-currents; it has its storms: there float upon it the navies of the world; there is borne upon it the commerce of one nation to another. So I like to think of the nation not simply as a gathering together of men and women; it is more than the record of the census; it is a great and mighty person. And the nation has its great moral problems. We are not here simply to till the soil, and to explore the mines, and to level the forests, and to build houses, and to carry on commerce, and to carry out wars; we are here for the settlement of great moral questions, and God will hold us responsible as a people for the solution that we give to them. We are to ask until these questions are settled, What shall we do with immigration? What shall we do with the Indian? What shall we do with illiteracy? What shall we do with the Mormon question? What with pauperism? What shall we do with all those great questions? We must answer them as men, as men that are responsible to God for the manner in which they answer them, and the future of this nation will be determined by the answer that is given.

Down yonder on the beach, stranded, there lies to-night a ship, sound, stanch, sea-worthy; but she sails not. The hold is empty; the sails are furled; the crew is gone; the captain sits in his little cabin looking out upon the sea as the vessels go by, longing for the day when the tide shall lift him once again upon the highway of the sea. Long and weary hours does he spend, lamenting doubtless that when the air was black and the sky was full of snow he did not turn his vessel out into the sea that it might not strand upon the beach. There are nations to-day lying idly, taking no part in the great work of humanity. In the National Gallery of England, in London, one of the great master paintings that is there, painted by Turner, whom Ruskin delights to honor, is a picture of a great ship of war, a ship that had borne a proud record in the English navy; but her days are numbered, her warfare is over, there is no longer any place for her in the modern navy of that proud nation, and, as the artist conceives of her, she is being towed away from the fleets back to the stocks that she may be dismantled and destroyed. So I have no doubt that we would like, when the record is written for this nation, that it may be the record of the old ship *Temeraire*, whose work was ended and whose career was closed. We hope that we shall not see this grand nation for centuries to come stopping in its proud career.

"Thou, too, sail on, O ship of State!
Sail on, O Union, strong and great!
Humanity with all its fears,
With all the hopes of future years,
Is hanging breathless on thy fate."

Second. That personality, that national life, that character that shall constitute us what we are to be, is determined by moral forces working from within and not by physical forces working from without. Taine says that we may know what of necessity must be produced by nations if we know the surroundings, just as a man ascending a mountain, if he knows the temperature and height, may know the tropical flowers or the stunted oak he shall meet, and at last find nothing but sterile barrenness. We are what we are, not because of the soil, of the climate, of the surroundings, but of the moral forces that are working from within; though undoubtedly we are influenced by the sea and by the mountain. As we look back over the history of nations we find that people living side by side have not borne the same character. We have in epitome here at Ocean Grove an illustration of what I mean. There goes out from this one center as from a heart that pulsates through all this village a call to prayer and to the worship of God. Tell me that it is the product of the sea. Nay! Nay! It is the product of great brains and great hearts working under God and for God. Do you say that the Jews were what they were because of the mountains of Palestine and the great Mediterranean? Nay, because of the great brains that planned and worked for them. They became what they were because of Abraham, because of the wide-reaching plans of Samuel, because of the songs of David, of the sublime poetry of Isaiah, and of the prophecies of her divine prophets. Greece became a land of culture because of the influence of Plato, and Homer, and Aristotle, and Demosthenes, and other great moral forces that

wrought so grandly for that mighty people. And we are to become what we are to be, not because of the vastness of our territory, but because of the moral forces that are brought to bear in shaping and molding, in directing and controlling, the development of our national life.

Third. The great agency for the development of national character is education. I use the term education in its broadest sense; I include in it every thing that helps to make man different from man; and I say that if we know the moral forces at work, the prevalent ideas, the hopes and the fears in the hearts of men, that we could tell the character that the nation will bear. Education does for men four things: it imparts instruction; it evolves power; it implants principles; it develops character. The instruction given to men may be the instruction of the parent, teacher, or preacher; it may be knowledge in reference to science or history or philosophy, or facts that are handed down and communicated from one to another. The evolution of power is the calling into action all the latent forces of man. The implanting of principles is putting within the hearts all those motives, those considerations that control the actions in all circumstances and on all occasions; and the development of character is the unfolding of justice, of right, of truth, of honor, of manliness, and of whatever else there is best and deepest in the man; or there is the stifling of the good and the unfolding of the evil. Now, under this comprehensive definition of education, I say that education has the power to make a nation that which it is to become. If you lay your hand upon the child in its infancy and train it, you can make it well nigh what you will. The mass of children in the country are to determine the character that this mighty people shall bear a generation hence. Men understand this when, instead of trying to exterminate the Indians, they gather them in the school-house and lay before them the great ideals of moral excellence of civilized life, and so mold from within the character of that people.

Fourth. No education is complete which is not Christian. That education that seeks to train simply the body, falls far short of doing for the man that which ought to be done. What have you done for the man when you have trained his body? You have made him simply a splendid animal, and for what purpose? Ask those two men that stood the other night, to the disgrace of our civilization be it said, and to the shame of New York be it uttered—those two men that stood the other night protected by the police of that city, encouraged by the presence of legislators and of judges. They had been trained in their physical natures, and for what? That they might in the presence of that great throng of men pound each other to pieces. A man that is trained simply as to his physical nature has not developed that which is grandest and best within him. I like to think of this body as I think of a scaffolding of a mighty building, only of value until the building itself is completed. I like to think of this body as I do of this tabernacle where we are to-night; the artist has done his work; he has made it attractive for you, these columns, these arches, this wide-reaching roof, these seats; all these surroundings have made it an attractive place. Do you come to enjoy those seats? Do you come simply to take part in the physical enjoyment that comes from this shelter? No! It is that you may listen to the truth that comes from the word of God, that you may unite your hearts and your voices in hymns of praise to him, and when the sermon has been uttered, when the speech has been delivered, when the song has been sung, when the prayer has ascended, when the doxology has rung out and the benediction been given, you cease to care, except as a precious memory, for this tabernacle. So I say that that education that trains the mind or the body alone is defective. Knowledge, if it is understood properly, ends in Christ. You look on that sea stretching far away for thousands of miles, and a child might say it is illimitable. Ask that sailor: he will tell you that he has crossed its bosom and found cities on the other side, that on every side it is bounded by the land. So the knowledge that comes to us of chemistry, of botany, of physiology, and astronomy is bounded on all sides by the knowledge of God. The study of any branch of knowledge is incomplete that does not lead the learner to a knowledge of God. Christ said "I am the truth." I have said that education is an evolving of power. That which is deepest and most Godlike in man is not the intellect or the reason or the imagination or the memory, but it is that power by which he lays hold on God. Man is a spiritual being, and a spirit by which he loves, by which he exercises faith and hope, that brings him into communication with his Maker, that which fits him for fellowship with the saints,—that is the grandest thing in him, and any education that fails to reach that, any education that fails to evolve that power, fails of its great work.

I have said that education was the implanting of principles, but there are no principles of action that will stand the test of

life except the principles that come from the word of God. The golden rule, the great law of self-abnegation, the chief law of love, regard for the immutable justice and truth unshakable as the foundations of God's throne,—these are the guiding principles that alone can direct you or a nation on the safe journey of life.

I have said that education is the development of character. The one great model of human character was Jesus Christ, the manliest of men. The one that more nearly meets our ideal was Christ; and the ideal of human character to-day is not the soldier, nor the philosopher; it is not the statesman, it is not the man of great wealth, but it is the Christian man and the Christian woman. These are the ideals of human character, and men may talk as they will of the glories of Shakespeare, or the grandeurs of Alexander, of the magnificence of the great orators; but that which is greatest, that which is grandest, that which is most glorious, that which alone redeems man in his individual capacity, or as a nation, is the development within of the power of God and the likeness of Jesus Christ.

And now, lastly. I have said that the nation is a moral personality; I have said that this personality is determined by moral forces; I have said that the great moral force is education; I have shown you that the only complete education is a Christian education; and now I say, as we look upon the problem, what shall be our institutions, what shall our people be, that just in proportion as Christian education becomes a ruling factor in our national life, just in that proportion will our life become rich and deep and broad and glorious and permanent. The nation lives for the sake of its people; we are not here at all for the sake of the wealth that we can make, of the railroads we may build, of the ships we may set afloat; we are here for the sake of the men and women that may be grown here. A man from the fertile prairies of the West, when visiting a friend in New England, looking out upon the rocks and stony field before him, said "My friend, what do you grow here?" "Well," he replied, "we grow men." And in the future that man that comes to study the records of this people, that we call American, if he be a thoughtful man, will not ask so much for the great bridge or the network of railroads, or the princely palaces, or the records of our commerce, as he will ask for the character of the men, and the character of the women, and the character of the families, and the character of the institutions that you and I have left behind us; he will not ask so much with reference to the battle of Gettysburg or of Nashville, as he will ask, "What became of those millions that were freed by the pen of Lincoln?"

Our national life will be rich and glorious

In the future and will satisfy the inquisitive student of history just in proportion as Christian education has laid its hand upon the nation, and has fashioned and molded and controlled the development of the individual, and the family, and the State, and the nation.

I have been thinking, as I draw to the close of what few things I have said, of the dignity that attaches to every one of you, whether man or woman, that takes part in this great work, whether it be in expounding the word of God from the pulpit, or teaching in some obscure school in the South, or gathering about you some of the dark faces in Alaska, or instructing the little child that comes to you. O, the dignity that attaches to helping to shape even one mind that shall fit it to take its place in this great nation of ours.

One illustration, and then I am done. Centuries ago, men, guided by the thought of great architects, planned for a mighty building; they laid broad and deep the foundations. Slowly as the years went by these walls rose to their places, but centuries passed away; governments were overturned; dynasties, generations, passed away; but again and again they returned to the work, and the mighty pile went on until, as I stood in the presence of it, I saw them laying the capstone, and that mighty Cathedral of Cologne stands as one of the marvels of the ages. Would you not like to have painted one of those windows? Would you not like to have laid that crowning stone on that tower? No, I tell you that if you have trained one child aright, if you have educated one boy or one girl aright, you have helped in the building of this mighty nation that shall become grander in its thought, grander in its results, more glorious in its records, than the records of a thousand cathedrals such as that.

5. THE BALLOT AND THE BIBLE.

BY REV. J. M. WALDEN, LL.D., CINCINNATI, OHIO.

OUR republican institutions are what they have been made through the ballot; their character in the future will be molded and their destiny determined by the ballot. Our nation has been, and still is, controlled by Christian principles, because the voter has been under the influence of the Bible; the domination of Christian principles in our national and State affairs will continue so long as the voter is influenced by the Bible, and to the extent of that influence. The obvious and possible relation of the Bible to the ballot, through the voter, furnishes a theme in harmony with the purpose and spirit of this assembly. Educational and cognate questions have been discussed chiefly in their relation to the problem of self-government—or, more properly, in their relation to the voter, who is at once the sovereign and a subject in our republic. I shall speak of the ballot and the Bible, because the ballot is the means by which the voter, educated or non-educated, of virtuous or vicious life, works his will into government, and because the Bible has been, and must continue to be, the most potent among the agencies by which the voter is prepared for his highest duty as an American citizen.

And first I name several facts that well may be borne in mind in every discussion of the ballot in its relation to our political system:

1. The ballot is in the hands of a comparatively small proportion of our population, namely, the male citizens over twenty-one years of age. In the thirty-eight States there were, according to the census of 1880, including all nationalities, only 12,571,437 males of voting age—about *one fourth* of the entire population of these States—and, from this number, must be deducted foreigners who have not been naturalized, and Chinese and Indians who are not enfranchised.

While our public schemes of education provide for our girls the same means of improvement as for our boys, the question naturally comes up betimes, Why is the ballot confined to less than one half of those who are trained in public schools at public expense? a question that may demand more thought in the near future than it now receives.

2. Four races meet on our soil—live under our flag—each of which has its place in the problem of self-government, though all, as yet, have not the ballot. I mention them in the order of their coming, namely, the Indians, the Whites, the Negroes, and the Asiatics. You have discussed educational and civil questions in relation to three of these races—the White, the Negro, and the Indian. The Chinese question has elements of interest that entitle it to careful consideration. In 1880 there were 105,465 Chinese in our country, or 39,058 more than the number of Indians reported in the national census, and about equal to one half the entire Indian population, including nomadic tribes not enumerated in the census. It is not my purpose to say more now in regard

to the Asiatic population, save that, their citizenship being a possibility, they constitute a factor in the race problem before us that schoolmen and other patriots will soon be compelled to consider.

3. Of the 12,571,437 males of voting age in 1880, 64.75 per cent. (8,129,877) were native whites; 23.75 per cent. (2,984,309) were foreign-born whites; and 11.50 per cent. (1,457,251) were colored, including Indians and Chinese, perhaps one hundred thousand in number. Excluding foreigners not naturalized and natives not enfranchised, there were about 12,000,000 voters, *two thirds* of them native whites, about *one fifth* of them foreign whites, and about *one eighth* of them colored.

4. Of the native and foreign white voters *one tenth* (1,134,300) cannot read and *one eighth* (1,418,000) cannot write; of the colored voters from *sixty* to *seventy-five* per cent. cannot read or write, making in all above *two million* legal voters who cannot read or write.

5. The body of voters is affected by the annual accession of young men who reach the voting age and of foreigners who are naturalized, and also by annual diminution through those who fall from the ranks by death. In all civil and social movements that may be retarded by ignorance and prejudice death is a factor of reform, for its effects may hasten success. Through these changes, before the century closes, the field-hands of the South, who cannot read their ballots, may be succeeded by those who are beginning to have access to schools and other means of mental and moral growth; and in every State the illiterate father may be succeeded by sons trained in our public schools.

6. A fraction more than one half of the male population has reached the voting age, hence there are twelve million boys, ranging from infancy to the verge of manhood, from whom the ranks of voters are annually recruited. Their character, when they reach manhood and become voters, depends upon what they are made during their school age. The character of those who are the voters of to-day may not be changed; but the character of these boys, who are the heirs-apparent to the crown of American citizenship, the voters of to-morrow, depends upon the mental and moral training which they receive in the homes and schools of to-day.

This brings us face to face with the duty of the States and of the nation in regard to the education of these candidates for the ballot. It is not my purpose to discuss this duty at length, at this late hour of the evening, but to submit some points which will aid in determining its character, scope, and importance.

1. As every boy, whether colored or white, born on our soil or brought under our flag by the tide of immigration, is to reach the ballot when he attains to his majority, every boy should receive such measure of education as, properly used, will enable him to readily acquire an intelligent view of all public questions which come before the voters for their verdict at the polls. One conclusion from this self-evident statement is that schools for the instruction of these youth should be provided at public expense, and that their education cannot be safely left to either the wish or the convenience of the parent; in short, if attendance at schools be not voluntary, it must be secured by compulsory means.

2. The fathers of the republic recognized the interest of the nation in education, and indicated that they regarded it a subject for governmental action, by their measures to endow our educational system. Mark, that three years before the national Constitution was adopted, (1785,) the Congress of the colonies set apart one section of land in each township in the North-west Territory to support schools; and two years later (1787) it made large grants for university education. Behold the spectacle—the smoke had scarcely cleared away from the battle-fields of the Revolution when these grants were made; questions growing out of the protracted but successful war were pending; the grave problem of a permanent form of government was unsettled; but, in the midst of all the engrossing subjects claiming their thought, the fathers, with their characteristic patriotism and a keen prescience of the future, laid aside colonial jealousies and planned for the welfare of the inchoate States and the unborn generations that should people them, embalming their convictions and purposes in the Ordinance of 1787—a state paper second only to the Declaration of Independence—a civil covenant that consecrated to freedom a territory containing 244,550 square miles, or two fifths of the entire domain of the new republic, and declared the interest and duty of the government in the immortal provision:

"Religion, morality, and knowledge being necessary to good government and the happiness of mankind, schools and the means of education shall forever be encouraged."— *Art. 3.*

3. The authority of the general government to make direct appropriations to aid the States in the endowment of an educational system can hardly be questioned in view of what has already been done. Study the magnitude of the land grants in this behalf:

To common schools....... 67,893,919 acres.
To universities........... 1,165,520   "
To agricultural and mechan-
      ical colleges........... 9,600,000   "

Total........... 78,659,439 acres.

This equals 122,905 square miles; nearly double the area of the New England States, (62,005 square miles;) larger than New England, New York, and New Jersey, (117,-030 square miles;) larger than Virginia, North and South Carolina, (118,875 square miles;) one fifth as large as all the territory south of Mason and Dixon's line, excluding Texas. With the average population of the Southern States these grants would contain 2,580,900 people; with the average of Ohio they would contain 9,643,126 people. In the case of a single State, Ohio, the school fund derived from its grants, carried in the form of an irreducible debt, is $4,289,718 52.

4. The purpose of this policy, inaugurated by the fathers, was to encourage education, and to encourage education because of its relation to good government. It must have been as obvious then as now that the end in view could only be secured by universal education—that every one who grew up in ignorance would, to that extent, defeat the objects of these grants—that is, the logical sequence of these grants for public schools is *universal education*, and that means compulsory education. For the want of this it is plain that the high purpose of the fathers has failed its fullest realization.

5. Some consider a compulsory educational system impracticable; others contend that it is not American in fact and spirit; but I assume that any thing required by the public weal must be right, and will be found practicable when a sentiment in its favor is created. The discussions of this Convention are preparing public thought to accept and then demand a system that will make common-school education universal. I barely mention two objections to a coercive system, namely:

(*a*) The rights of parents to the time and service of the child; but the State has an interest—yea, rights—in the child that is to be a citizen, and may properly demand a part of the child's time for its preparation for citizenship; and the child has an inherent right to the fair start in the race of life that a common-school education gives—a sacred right whose benefits should be secured to the child by its sovereign guardian, the State, if neglected by the parent.

(*b*) The rights of conscience involved in the parent's wish that the child receive a religious school training. Our Constitution is careful of all rights of conscience, and it is the prerogative of the parent to choose between a parochial and a public school. The case may be met by three just provisions:

(1) That the State shall protect, but not support, denominational or parochial schools.

(2) That every child shall have a given measure of school advantages—attend either a public or private school a given time.

(3) That every teacher, in private as well as in public schools, shall bear a certificate of qualification from the State.

15

6. Passing for the moment from the recognized means of the future voter's education, I direct your thought for the moment to the educational effect of the ballot on the voter. Suffrage gives rise to political parties, and parties cannot exist without organization, which means leadership, discussion, and co-operation. These have a place in any method that may be used to put candidates in nomination, and in some degree affect all who participate. The political campaign, often involving censurable measures, and attended with much that is farcical and ludicrous, is a means of political education. Under the excitement of the struggle even the sluggish mind is quickened into a receptive frame, and thousands who never study a public question by the aid of newspaper or book, listen with interest to their discussion on the rostrum. We may properly deprecate some of the incidents of partisan struggles, but in view of the customary indifference of some in regard to important questions of State and the negligence of others because of their intense devotion to business or professional demands, it is certain that these State and national campaigns awaken an interest that conserves the welfare of the country. Although partisan in their purpose they are means of a needful political education.

7. The effectiveness of this political system founded upon the ballot is seen in its results, among which are these:

(*a*) During the century great questions of State—questions growing out of three foreign wars, monetary questions affecting labor and capital in every field of industry, questions connected with and subsequent to the great civil war—all have been met and so settled as to insure peace and general prosperity.

(*b*) Many men have risen to honorable leadership; many have become distinguished statesmen. The ballot called from private to public life Webster, Clay, Lincoln, Garfield, and all that host of talented men who have honored and do honor our country by their service in the legislative, judicial, and executive departments of the State and national governments.

What of the future? Will the secular education of our public schools and the political education incident to our civil system prepare the voter to carry the government successfully forward? I shall answer this question by showing that the Bible must continue to have a part in preparing the voter for the ballot.

I mention, and only mention, some of the gravest facts which are affecting the results of the ballot now, and are likely to be more potent in the near future:

(*a*) The influence of the foreign population. The trend of this influence is already seen in its effect upon the American Sabbath as well as in the liquor question. 23.74 per cent. of males of voting age are foreigners, and we may assume that one fifth of the citizens are naturalized voters. I do not state these facts in any spirit of antagonism. So long as we revere the Declaration of Independence we ought to welcome those who really emigrate (not those who are transported) to our shores. We do bid the people welcome, but not those notions and customs that begin to mar our American civilization.

(b) The influence of our cities. Municipal government is already the most defective, Cities increase most rapidly, and gather into themselves the largest ratio of the pauper and vicious classes. One hundred cities of 20,000 population and upward in 1880 contained 9,100,863 people, or 18.45 per cent. of the people of the thirty-eight States, and 29.94 per cent. of this population is composed of foreigners. Without trying to locate the causes I cite the fact that the government of cities is becoming more difficult as they grow older and larger. How shall they affect the whole problem of government in the near future?

(c) The status of the primary meeting. This is the point of control in American politics. The larger conventions, and even the elections, seldom do more than to ratify what has been settled in the primaries. And yet their neglect by the better classes of citizens has made that tyranny of an unscrupulous minority known as "bossism" a possibility and an ominous fact.

I hasten to the question, Can the training of the *intellect*, the aim and end of our secular education, prepare voters for such problems as are thus at hand? I answer, the *conscience* must be educated as well—educated to discriminate quickly and sharply between the right and the wrong in politics—to discern and enforce duty. The only proof of this I will now offer are two or three illustrations from the past:

(a) Although there were slaves in the colonies when the national Constitution was formed, yet the word slavery is not even found in that instrument. In its elimination the fathers were not guided by intellect so much as impelled by conscience.

(b) At the same time they provided for the abolition of the slave trade, although it was then carried on under the flag of every nation that had a maritime service. Was this the behest of the intellect or conscience?

(c) The slavery question had its place in American politics for half a century. There was opposition to the system of slavery *per se*; and opposition to its extension into new

fields. Its ultimate overthrow was a war measure, but why was the result approved by the people? Not solely because it seemed to be a necessity—a matter of which they could not judge—but because their consciences recognized that it was right.

Thus illustrations of the force and province of conscience in determining the course of our public affairs can be drawn from every period of our history. As we turn from the study of the grave problems of state which have been solved to those which open before us now and lie in the near future, who can resist the conviction that the right—the absolute right—is the only safe guide; but conscience, quickened and trained, is the discerner of the right.

The Centenary of the close of the Revolutionary War has been celebrated at Yorktown; but the American Revolution, of which that war was the opening episode, still sweeps on. The fathers realized the magnitude of the work, and did their part of it well. Thomas Jefferson, who "poured the soul of the continent into the monumental act of Independence," revealed the controlling force when he said: "Can the liberties of a nation be thought secure when we have removed their only firm basis, a conviction in the minds of the people that these liberties are the gifts of God? that they are not to be violated except with his wrath? Indeed, I tremble for my country when I reflect that God is just, and that his justice cannot sleep forever."

The discernments of conscience are voiced in these words, and they indicate how constantly and completely this potent sense cooperated with the intellect in inspiring and controlling the people and their leaders in their public deeds.

So the conscience must be potential in its sway over the voters in order to the perpetuity of our republican institutions. Secular education alone cannot educate the conscience. Benjamin Franklin said: "A Bible and a newspaper in every house—a good school in every district—all studied and appreciated as they merit, are the principal supports of virtue, morality, and civil liberty."

[The address was here interrupted by the chairman's call of time under the rules, and the speaker closed with the following sentence:]

The Bible is the text-book of the conscience, and it must have its place in the education of the American voter.

6. SPECIAL SERVICES ON SUNDAY.

In addition to the three public services at which sermons and addresses were delivered, two others of special character were held. The first came at nine o'clock in the morning, and was called

AN EDUCATIONAL LOVE-FEAST.

THIS interesting service was in charge of Rev. I. W. Joyce, D.D., of Cincinnati, Ohio, and Mr. Thornley, of Ocean Grove. In opening the exercises, Dr. Joyce said:

The object of the meeting this morning is the relation of Christian experience in the work of education. There is the spiritual as well as the intellectual side in all discipline involved in this question of education.

Up to this time, during this assembly, our attention has been almost wholly called to the intellectual phases of this great work; and this was right. But we are now entering upon the hours and duties of the holy Sabbath, and it is right that now and during the day our attention should be turned to the exclusively religious side of this question; and it has been thought best to occupy this early morning hour in statements of religious experience on the part of those who are engaged in the special work of teaching. A majority of the teachers in all our schools are Christians, believers in the doctrines and work of our Lord and Saviour Jesus Christ. They therefore believe that education, to be complete, must include both the intellectual and spiritual discipline of the pupil. Consequently they are as zealous in their endeavors to have their pupils become Christians as they are to have them well disciplined in the curriculum of the college.

It is well, therefore, that this hour has been set apart for the relation of experience in this line of Christian work.

The efforts you have put forth; the success of those efforts; the abiding character of the work and its influence, are the subjects for conversation this morning.

In short, what has been your success in bringing the pupils of your several schools to Christ as their Saviour?

The presence of a large number of ministers and teachers who, during the past few years, have been doing missionary work among the poor and needy of the Southern States, and among the Indians, added much to the interest of the occasion.

The following extracts from a letter were read. It was from a lady who has given thirteen years to missionary labor in the South with her husband. She has for two years been an invalid, suffering greatly from effects of her Southern work. Her words, so full of prayer and faith, found a response in a multitude of hearts who heard them:

How I pray that the Assembly may be a holy thing—owned and blessed and wholly directed of God—not a mere sensational affair. Life is too short, too serious, with too much depending upon it, to have even a day spent in vanity.

I pray that every speaker may be peculiarly influenced by the Holy Spirit—to see and feel the great opportunity before him of impressing upon a good, intelligent, and patriotic, yes, a devout, people, the pressing needs of our beloved country, and the terrible peril and disaster which awaits her if her children of means do not at once come to her aid. Surely ours is a country-loving people, and if they can but feel in their hearts that they have a work to do it will be done. God alone by his Spirit speaking through your men can rouse the heart of the hearers, and lead them to immediate action. O that every man might be a Moses to whom the Lord would speak and send forth before your audiences at Ocean Grove to proclaim his words!

How I wish that there might be a band of holy people gathered in prayer every morning before your services begin, to pray for a special and glorious blessing upon every service!

May the Lord bless Dr. Joyce gloriously in his love-feast service Sunday morning. I will be praying for a rich, yea, a wonderful, baptism upon all present, and I pray that the Spirit may go out to every part of the ground, and hearts be touched as with a *live coal* from off the altar. "Then shall ye see great things." And let every heart give all the GLORY to God—never for one little moment asking to take any unto himself.

What an honor to be suffered to wait upon the Lord, to be used by him!

ON THE BEACH.

At five P.M. Rev. E. H. Stokes, D.D., conducted a Beach Meeting Service. Many thousands were present, and with the murmuring of old ocean there mingled the songs of praise and words of wisdom and exhortation.

Addresses were made by Captain Pratt, Dr. C. H. Fowler, Bishop Campbell, Rev. Mr. Gould, and Rev. J. C. Price.

The following service, prepared by Dr. Stokes, was united in by the vast throng, in reading and singing. Prof. Kirkpatrick led the singing, bringing to his aid cornets and trained voices. The service was entitled

WISDOM.

Leader. Wisdom crieth without; she uttereth her voice in the streets:

Cong. She crieth in the chief place of concourse, in the city she uttereth her words.

SINGING.

"Happy the man who finds the grace,
The blessing of God's chosen race,
The wisdom coming from above,
The faith that sweetly works by love.

"Wisdom divine! who tells the price
Of wisdom's costly merchandise?
Wisdom to silver we prefer,
And gold is dross compared to her."

L. How long, ye simple ones, will ye love simplicity?

C. And the scorners delight in their scornings, and fools hate knowledge?

L. My son, hear the instruction of thy father, and forsake not the law of thy mother:

C. For they shall be an ornament of grace unto thy head, and chains about thy neck.

SINGING.

"Her hands are filled with length of days,
True riches, and immortal praise;
Her ways are ways of pleasantness,
And all her flowery paths are peace.

"Happy the man who wisdom gains;
Thrice happy, who his guest retains;
He owns, and shall forever own,
Wisdom, and Christ, and heaven, are one."

PRAYER.

L. The fear of the Lord is the beginning of wisdom.

C. A good understanding have all they that do his commandments.

L. Behold the fear of the Lord, that is wisdom—

C. And to depart from evil is understanding.

SINGING.

" Workman of God ! O lose not heart,
But learn what God is like ;
And in the darkest battle-field
Thou shalt know where to strike.

" Thrice blest is he to whom is given
The instinct that can tell
That God is on the field, when he
Is most invisible."

L. For the Lord giveth wisdom: out of his mouth cometh knowledge and understanding.

C. He layeth up sound wisdom for the righteous; he is a buckler to them that walk uprightly.

L. He keepeth the paths of judgment, and preserveth the way of his saints.

C. Then shalt thou understand righteousness, and judgment, and equity, yea, every good path.

L. When wisdom entereth into thine heart, and knowledge is pleasant unto thy soul ;

C. Discretion shall preserve thee, understanding shall keep thee.

SINGING.

" How blest is he who can divine,
Where real right doth lie ;
And dares to take the side that seems
Wrong to man's blindfold eye.

" Then learn to scorn the praise of men,
And learn to lose with God ;
For Jesus won the world through shame,
And beckons thee his road."

L. My son, forget not my law ; but let thy heart keep my commandments:

C. For I give you good doctrine, forsake ye not my law.

L. Get wisdom, get understanding; forget it not.

C. Neither decline from the words of my mouth.

L. Wisdom is the principal thing; therefore get wisdom:

C. And with all thy getting get understanding.

L. Exalt her, and she shall promote thee :

C. She shall bring thee to honor, when thou dost embrace her.

L. She shall give to thine head an ornament of grace;

C. A crown of glory shall she deliver to thee.

SINGING.

" Down at the cross where the Saviour died,
Down where for cleansing from sin I cried,
There to my heart was the blood applied,
Glory to his name.

REF.—" Glory to his name ;
Glory to his name;
There to my heart was the blood applied,
Glory to his name."

L. Happy is the man that findeth wisdom, and the man that getteth understanding ;

C. For the merchandise of it is better than the merchandise of silver, and the gain thereof than fine gold.

L. She is more precious than rubies; and all the things thou canst desire are not to be compared unto her.

C. Length of days is in her right hand; and in her left hand riches and honor.

All. Her ways are ways of pleasantness, and all her paths are peace.

SINGING.

" For the love of God is broader
Than the measure of man's mind ;
And the heart of the Eternal
Is most wonderfully kind.

" If our love were but more simple,
We should take him at his word ;
And our lives would be all sunshine
In the sweetness of our Lord."

L. If thou seekest her as silver, and searchest for her as for hid treasure ;

C. Then shalt thou understand the fear of the Lord, and find the knowledge of God.

L. If any of you lack wisdom, let him ask of God, that giveth to all men liberally, and upbraideth not; and it shall be given him.

C. But let him ask in faith, nothing wavering; for he that wavereth is like a wave of the sea driven with the wind and tossed.

L. Who is a wise man and endued with knowledge among you ?

C. Let him show out of a good conversation his works with meekness of wisdom.

L. But the wisdom that is from above is first pure, then peaceable, gentle, and easy to be entreated.

C. Full of mercy and good fruits, without partiality, and without hypocrisy.

SINGING.

" He leadeth me ! O blessed thought !
O words with heavenly comfort fraught !
Whate'er I do, where'er I be,
Still 'tis God's hand that leadeth me.

" He leadeth me, he leadeth me,
By his own hand he leadeth me;
His faithful follower I would be,
For by his hand he leadeth me."

L. For the preaching of the cross is to them that perish foolishness;

C. But unto us which are saved, it is the power of God.

L. For it is written, I will destroy the wisdom of the wise,

C. And will bring to nothing the understanding of the prudent.

L. Where is the wise? where is the scribe? where is the disputer of this world?

C. Hath not God made foolish the wisdom of this world?

L. For after that in the wisdom of God the world by wisdom knew not God,

C. It pleased God by the foolishness of preaching to save them that believe.

SINGING.

" By faith we know thee strong to save;
     Save us, a present Saviour thou;
     Whate'er we hope, by faith we have;
     Future and past subsisting now.

" Faith lends its realizing light;
     The clouds disperse, the shadows fly;
The invisible appears in sight,
     And God is seen by mortal eye."

L. For the Jews require a sign,

C. And the Greeks seek after wisdom.

L. But we preach Christ crucified,

C. Unto the Jews a stumbling-block, and unto the Greeks foolishness.

L. But unto them which are called, both Jews and Greeks,

C. Christ the power of God, and the wisdom of God.

L. If thou be wise, thou shalt be wise for thyself;

C. But if thou scornest, thou alone shalt bear it.

SINGING.

" Still let thy wisdom be my guide,
     Nor take thy flight from me away;
Still with me let thy grace abide,
     That I from thee may never stray:
Let thy word richly in me dwell,
     Thy peace and love my portion be;
My joy to endure and do thy will,
     Till perfect I am found in thee."

L. Riches and honor are with me; yea, durable riches and righteousness.

C. My fruit is better than gold, yea, than fine gold; my revenue than choice silver.

DOXOLOGY.   BENEDICTION.

X. LAST WORDS.

1. SUMMARY OF THE WORK, AND SIGNIFICANCE OF THE ASSEMBLY.

REV. A. J. KYNETT, D.D., OF PHILADELPHIA.

I HAVE been asked to summarize this convention in the space of ten or fifteen minutes. To do justice to this task I should have an hour, and I should have had notice from the beginning so that I might have studied it carefully from the first. But such thoughts as I have, in the brief compass of time allotted me, I will give those of you who will stay, and, of course, I cannot give them to those of you who go away.

The representative character of this convention is one of its most striking characteristics. Territorially, there have been representatives on this platform from Massachusetts to Louisiana, from Florida to Alaska. Sixteen different States and Territories, including with them the District of Columbia, have been represented from the platform and on the programme. I suppose all the States and Territories have been represented in the congregation.

In the *personnel* of the convention, and those who have taken part in its proceedings, we have a corresponding variety of the ministry and the laity. Next, there have been educators—the Commissioner of Education of the United States, college presidents, principals of academies, and teachers in all grades of schools. Ecclesiastically, six or seven of the Christian denominations of the country have been represented; the Methodists have been here in force—three different branches of the Methodist family; the Presbyterians, the Baptists, the Congregationalists, the Episcopalians, and I know not what other branches of the Christian family; the Quakers have been represented on this platform during these four days, and the Unitarians—and they are all catholics, so that the Catholic Church of Christ has been truly represented from this platform.

There has been great variety in the aspect of those who have been present. The races —most of them—have been represented on the platform—I was going to say the Ameri-can races, but I will not—so that this Educational Convention has been quite cosmopolitan in its character.

And we have been here for one grand purpose, with unanimity of opinion, and came to this peerless Christian sea-side resort that in fourteen years has grown from nothing to be the greatest Christian resort upon which the sun shines to-day, and this educational work has joined most harmoniously with the grand purpose for which Ocean Grove was instituted and established; so that we may come together and unite in reading the words with which you have ornamented these walls: "We are come to Mount Zion, the city of the Living God."

It is a grand convention. We are here for a great purpose, an educational purpose, for Christian education, to study, analyze, understand, and promote Christian education upon Christian foundations. We are here because we believe it is possible to know something; we are not agnostics; I had half a mind to say that this convention was about as conspicuous for the absence as for the presence of certain things I have alluded to. Imagine yourselves, if you can, conducting to the front and introducing to the audience the President of the Liquor Dealers' Association of the United States, or the President of the Brewers' Congress of the United States; or imagine a representative here of that meeting a year ago, at Watkins Glen, of the infidelity of the country! We are here to promote Christian education upon the foundation of things that are knowable, and is a study of such subjects as shall educate the whole man, and so it is Christian education. Why, I have heard how friends have done in celebrating their college occasions, until I have been reminded of a possible convention of the manufacturers of head-lights for railroad locomotives getting together and telling the world what marvelous things they have accomplished in the railroad interests of the country. Why, just see how the light shines out upon the track and enables the engineer to avoid the danger. There is a good deal more than head-light.

Now, I suppose I ought to indicate some conception of this meeting's probable result. It imparts enthusiasm; I am talking six times as loud as I need to, simply because of the enthusiasm I feel. You have been filled to overflowing with it during the last four days. You have heard addresses that have started new lines of thought, and have put in action elements of power that will remain in force during the year to come. Public opinion is to be cultivated and fashioned and strengthened on the lines of right action, not only through the influence of those who have been here, but through the instrumentality of the published proceedings,

as we shall have them, and I do not want one of you to forget them. Things have been said that I desire to sit down and study by the hour. Information has been given that I desire to store away so that I can use it in the years to come. We hope that we shall stop killing the Indians, and put all their children in the schools; and if the African is in America to stay, we will bestir ourselves a little more for the uplifting of the American races. We hope the utterances of this convention will stir anew the Executive at Washington in regard to the Mormon question. I believe it to be a greater peril than the American people have apprehended. We hope the influences of this convention will last a year, and then we will come together and hold another that will be as much better than this as this is better than the convention of a year ago.

2. CLOSING REMARKS.

REV. J. C. HARTZELL, D.D.

After Dr. KYNETT's remarks, the Chairman of the closing session, Gen. EATON, said, that in spite of Dr. HARTZELL's dislike to do so, he would insist upon that gentleman saying a few parting words. Dr. HARTZELL said:

MY prayer has been answered in the establishment of this platform, here at Ocean Grove, where once a year the best Christian thought of the nation can meet and study, from a Christian stand-point, the great questions of education and practical reform, relating to our illiterate and despised masses. To the splendid men who, without regard to section, Church, or party, at my request, have contributed their valuable time, and carefully wrought out papers or addresses, I return hearty thanks, not only on behalf of myself, but also on behalf of the thousands who have been present during the Assembly. Great credit is due Hon. JOHN EATON, our

honored United States Commissioner of Education, without whose kindly aid during the year, and his presence here, such a success as we have had would have been impossible. Whatever I have had to do in making the Assembly a success has been done under a profound conviction of duty; and the success of the two Assemblies held, assures me that my conviction was of the Lord. In saying good-bye, I call upon all lovers of our common Saviour, who have enjoyed these meetings, to unite in a prayer that Christian patriots may rule our land, and that Christian thought may permeate and direct every phase of education in this nation. Amen, and Amen.

XI. HISTORICAL NOTES.

THE NATIONAL EDUCATION ASSEMBLY FOR 1882.

The annual series of popular Educational Assemblies at Ocean Grove began in 1882. To preserve the record, and as a matter of interest, a few notes are given on the origin and work of the first Assembly.

The proceedings were not published in pamphlet form, but many prominent secular and religious newspapers gave extended accounts of the Assembly and its work.

Speaking of the Assembly of 1882, the *New England Journal of Education*, in referring to its relation to national aid to common schools, said: "The meeting at Ocean Grove may be regarded as the beginning of a great national campaign, which will not cease till victory is inscribed on our banners."

The following is the programme as it was carried out:

NATIONAL EDUCATION ASSEMBLY,

Ocean Grove, N. J.,

AUGUST 8 and 9, 1882.

CONDUCTED BY

Rev. J. C. HARTZELL, D.D.

"Education is the Cheap Defense of Nations."

FIRST DAY—Tuesday, August 8.

Morning Session—10 to 12 o'clock.

BISHOP COXE, of New York, presided, and made introductory remarks.

1. INTRODUCTORY RELIGIOUS EXERCISES, conducted by Rev. E. H. STOKES, D.D., President of Ocean Grove Association.
Dr. STOKES delivered an address of welcome.
2. OPENING ADDRESS, by Hon. JOHN EATON, United States Commissioner of Education, Washington, D. C.

Afternoon Session—3 to 5 o'clock.

Dr. H. R. WAITE, Special Educational and Religious Statistician, United States Census, presided.

EDUCATIONAL CONFERENCE.—Subject: "Our Illiterate Masses."
ILLITERACY OF UNITED STATES was illustrated by maps, by Dr. HARTZELL.
SHORT ADDRESSES, by Gen. RUSLING, of New Jersey; Rev. Dr. L. R. FISKE, of Michigan, and Prof. CALDWELL, of Tennessee.

Evening Session—7:45 to 9:45 P. M.

GEN. EATON presided.

1. EDUCATION AMONG THE INDIANS, by Capt. PRATT, of Carlisle Training-School.
2. EDUCATION IN ALASKA, by Rev. SHELDON JACKSON, D.D., Superintendent of the Presbyterian Missions in Rocky Mountains and Alaska.
3. ADDRESS, by Hon. B. PETERS, Editor of the *Daily Times*, Brooklyn, N. Y.

SECOND DAY—Wednesday, August 9.

Morning Session—10 to 12 o'clock.

PROF. G. S. W. CRAWFORD, State Superintendent of Education in Tennessee, presided.

SUBJECT: "Education in the Southern States since the War, accomplished by Christian Benevolence of the North."

ADDRESSES by the following: Rev. M. E. STRIEBY, D.D., New York, of the Congregational Church; Hon. J. M. GREGORY, LL.D., Illinois, of the Baptist Church; Rev. R. H. ALLEN, D.D., Pennsylvania, of the Presbyterian Church; Rev. J. C. HARTZELL, D.D., Louisiana, of the Methodist Episcopal Church.

Afternoon Session—3 to 4:30 o'clock.

BISHOP SIMPSON presided.

SUBJECT: "The Church and Education."

ADDRESSES, by Bishop M. SIMPSON, LL.D., of Philadelphia; Rev. HENRY A. BUTTZ, of New Jersey, and Rev. J. F. SPENCE, D.D., of Tennessee.

Evening Session—7:45 to 8:45 o'clock.

SUBJECT: "Measures proposing National Aid to Public Schools now before Congress."

ADDRESS, by Hon. H. W. BLAIR, United States Senator from New Hampshire.
CLOSING REMARKS. Speeches limited to five minutes.

Prof. J. R. SWENEY, of Philadelphia, was in charge of the music during the Assembly.

Memorial to Congress.—One practical result of this Assembly was the adoption of a memorial to Congress.

The *Congressional Globe* of December 14, 1882, contains the following:

Congressional Record, United States—Senate proceedings, December 12, 1882.

Mr. BLAIR.—During the vacation there was held at Ocean Grove, New Jersey, a very important Assembly of the different religious denominations of the country, represented by their leading clergymen, upon the subject of national aid to education. This memorial is signed by Bishop A. C. Coxe, of the Protestant Episcopal Church; Bishop M. Simpson, of the Methodist Episcopal Church; Rev. M. E. Strieby, D.D., of the Congregational Church; Rev. J. M. Gregory, D.D., representing the Baptist Church; Rev. R. H. Allen, D.D, of the Presbyterian Church; Rev. J. C. Hartzell, D.D., of the Methodist Episcopal Church, and Prof. G. S. W. Crawford, State Superintendent of Public Instruction in Tennessee.

There was a very large gathering of clergymen and other influential men connected with the religious organizations of the country. They gave a very emphatic and earnest expression of their sentiment upon this subject, and have sent here their memorial, which I should be very glad to have read; but as it would, perhaps, take a little too much of the time of the Senate, I ask that it be printed in the *Record*, and along with it the letter of transmission by the Sec-

retary of the association, Dr. C. C. Painter; and I ask the attention of the Senate to this matter, as it will appear in the *Record* to-morrow morning.

The PRESIDENT *pro tempore.*—The memorial will be referred to the Committee——

Mr. BLAIR.—It should lie on the table. The bills in reference to which this memorial is presented have been reported and have been made a special order for the 9th of January, and, therefore, I move that the memorial lie on the table.

The PRESIDENT *pro tempore.*—It will lie on the table and be printed in the *Record* if there be no objection.

The papers are as follows:

NATIONAL EDUCATION COMMITTEE.

(Object—National Aid to Common Schools.)

Washington, D. C., December 13, 1882.

MY DEAR SIR: As Secretary of the National Education Committee, I have been intrusted with the inclosed memorial to Congress, which I beg leave to introduce through you.

In the Assembly which organized this Committee at Ocean Grove, New Jersey, on the 8th and 9th of last August, was largely represented the earnest religious and educational forces of the country, its culture, philanthropy, and statesmanship, so that it was truly a national assembly. And in this memorial it has voiced the deepest convictions and desires of the people in regard to the subject-matter of this memorial. I am, sir, in behalf of the Committee,

Very truly yours, etc.,

C. C. PAINTER,
Sec. Nat. Ed. Com.

Hon. H. W. BLAIR, *United States Senate.*

MEMORIAL
OF THE
NATIONAL EDUCATION ASSEMBLY.

To the Honorable the Senate and House of Representatives of the Congress of the United States :

The National Education Assembly, convened at Ocean Grove, New Jersey, August 8 and 9, 1882, representing the leading Christian denominations of the United States, and prominent friends of education from a majority of the States, respectfully relate—

1. That these great bodies of Christian citizens have been engaged during all the years since the war, through their agents and teachers, in teaching the Freedmen of the South, the Indians in the Territories, and the Illiterates of Utah, and other sections; that they have expended in this work millions of dollars, contributed by Christian and philanthropic citizens; that they have thus given education to many thousands of the young, and have trained thousands of teachers for the public schools of the destitute sections of our country, and they have organized and are now sustaining a large number of schools and institutions of learning in those sections.

2. They have thus become acquainted with the deplorable character of that vast mass of ignorance and illiteracy which the census shows to exist in those sections of our common country, and can of their own knowledge testify to the urgent need of education, a need much beyond the present power of the people, though aided by Christian philanthropy, to meet.

3. Holding with the ablest and best of the Presidents of the Republic, from Washington to Arthur, that it is the right and duty of the Government to promote the education of the people, and believing that no power short of that of the general government is able and prepared to meet the present pressing, if not dangerous, emergency growing out of the enormous extent of illiteracy, we unite with great numbers of eminent citizens, from all parts of the Union, in petitioning Congress to make speedy and adequate provision for the removal of this illiteracy by securing to all the children of the country the means for such education as is necessary to good and worthy citizenship.

4. Pressed by the magnitude and urgency of this great work, the need of which many of us have seen with our own eyes, we urge upon the representatives in Congress not to allow another session to close without appropriating from the national treasury such a sum of money as, added to the local funds and taxes, shall maintain the needful schools for all sections, and thus relieve our beloved land from a shadow so dark and an evil so full of menace to national peace and safety.

Bishop A. C. COXE,
Protestant Episcopal Church,
Bishop M. SIMPSON,
Methodist Episcopal Church,
Rev. M. E. STRIEBY, D.D.,
Congregational Church,
Rev. J. M. GREGORY, D.D.,
Baptist Church,
Rev. R. H. ALLEN, D.D.,
Presbyterian Church,
Rev. J. C. HARTZELL, D.D.,
Methodist Episcopal Church,
Prof. G. S. W. CRAWFORD,
State Sup. Pub. Ins. Tenn.,
Committee.

A true copy:

C. C. PAINTER,
Sec. of Nat. Ed. Committee.

Another, and perhaps the chief, practical result of the Assembly of 1882 was the appointment of this National Education Committee, having for its object the awakening and direction, by correspondence, petitioning, and otherwise, of public sentiment in favor of national aid to common schools; the objective point being to influence Congress to take immediate action upon this burning question.

NATIONAL EDUCATION COMMITTEE FOR 1882-3.

Bishop MATTHEW SIMPSON, LL.D., Pennsylvania, President.
Rev. M. E. STRIEBY, D.D., New York, Chairman Executive Committee.
Hon. J. V. WILSON, D.D., Washington, D. C., Treasurer.
Prof. C. C. PAINTER, Tennessee, Corresponding Secretary.
Rev. J. C. HARTZELL, D.D., Louisiana.

Hon. J. M. GREGORY, Illinois.
Hon. J. L. M. CURRY, Virginia.
Gen. S. C. ARMSTRONG, Virginia.
Rev. R. H. ALLEN, D.D., Pennsylvania.
Rev. A. D. MAYO, Massachusetts.
Rev. A. G. HAYGOOD, D.D., Georgia.
Hon. BENJAMIN TATUM, New York.
Rev. C. K. BLISS, Illinois.
Rev. SHELDON JACKSON, D.D., New York.

XII. JOURNAL OF PROCEEDINGS

OF THE

SECOND NATIONAL EDUCATION ASSEMBLY,

Held at Ocean Grove, N. J., August 9, 10, 11, and 12, 1883.

Conducted by Rev. J. C. HARTZELL, D.D.

First Day, Thursday, August 9.

MORNING SESSION, 10 A.M.

The opening religious exercises were conducted by Rev. E. H. STOKES, D.D., President Ocean Grove Camp-meeting Association. Rev. E. COOKE, D.D., President of Claflin University, South Carolina, made the opening prayer.

In welcoming the Assembly, Dr. STOKES said:

A few years ago, I stood on the Canada side of the Niagara River. I found that a few days before M. Blondin had been there and arranged for crossing that dangerous stream, which, as those of you who have been there know, flows between banks 140 feet high. This crossing was to be done upon a cord. He adjusted his rope, took a wheelbarrow, cooking-stove, cooking utensils, and went out to the center of the river, stopped his wheelbarrow, cooked an omelette, ate it, and passed over to the other side.

Why did he not fall off? How in the world could a man cross over on a rope with a wheelbarrow, cooking-stove, cooking utensils, prepare his food and eat it, over the boiling river below, on a rope, and pass to the other side in safety? I never saw such a performance, and never want to. I do not think my nerves would endure the strain.

I understand, however, that the simple method by which he maintained his equilibrium, was a long balancing-pole, with heavy weights on either end. When he found himself inclining one way he bore the other, and thus poised, passed over the chasm and landed safely on the other side. Religion and education, with their massive weights on either end, constitute the balancing-pole, by which we pass from one bank to the other, over the swirling waters of human life.

When you separate the one from the other, it is almost absolutely certain that you will fall into the chasm beneath.

Heaven grant that this separation may never take place!

I am honored to-day, and you, composing this large congregation, are also honored in having representatives among us, from the various denominations of Christians and from lofty positions in the state, men high in ecclesiastical and political preferment, from different parts of the land; and we are all highly honored, I say, in having these representatives of the great cause of education among us, and doubly honored because they will continue with us for a number of days. I am also happy to believe that all these gentlemen, standing so high in their representative capacities in the cause of education, stand equally high in their advocacy of the claims of our holy religion. So that religion and education, and education and religion, clasp hands among us to-day and kiss each other.

I simply here and now take time, in the name and on behalf of the Ocean Grove Camp-meeting Association, and in the name of our common Lord, to welcome you to these grounds.

Gentlemen, representatives of religion and education, you are welcome here.

Rev. M. E. STRIEBY, D.D., Secretary American Missionary Association, presided in the absence of Governor PATTISON, of Pennsylvania.

First Words, by Rev. J. C. HARTZELL, D.D. (See page 6.)

Opening Address, "Education and Man's Improvement," by Hon. JOHN EATON, LL.D., United States Commissioner of Education. (See page 7.)

Benediction by Rev. R. S. RUST, D.D., of Cincinnati.

AFTERNOON SESSION, 3 P.M.

Subject: "National Aid to Common Schools."

Rev. M. E. STRIEBY, D.D., Secretary American Missionary Association, presided.

Opening Prayer by Rev. B. T. TANNER, Editor *Christian Recorder*, Philadelphia.

Report of Year's Work of National Education Committee, by Prof. C. C. PAINTER, of Tennessee, Cor. Sec. (See page 35.)

On motion of Hon. JOHN EATON, seconded by Dr. R. S. RUST, the report was accepted, and a hearty vote of thanks was returned to Prof. PAINTER for his faithful work.

A Paper, "National Aid to Popular Education in Europe," by Hon. J. P. WICKERSHAM, of Pennsylvania. (See page 38.)

Address, "Conditions and Prospects of Temporary National Aid to Common Schools," by Hon. H. W. BLAIR, United States Senator from New Hampshire. (See page 41.)

Benediction by Gen. T. J. MORGAN, of Potsdam, N. Y.

EVENING SESSION, 7.45 P.M.

Subject: "Our Illiterate Masses."

Rev. HERRICK JOHNSON, D.D., of Chicago, presided. (His address will be found on page 17.)

The Opening Prayer was made by Rev. Mr. VAN METER, of Rome, Italy.

A Paper, by Hon. B. PETERS, Editor *Times*, Brooklyn, N. Y., entitled "Illiteracy in our Great Cities." (See page 18.)

Address, "Stumbling-Blocks, or Stepping-Stones?" by ROBERT R. DOHERTY, Esq., Assistant Editor *The Christian Advocate*, New York. (See page 21.)

Address, "The Danger of Delay," by Hon. ALBION W. TOURGEE, Editor *The Continent*. (See page 25.)

Second Day, Friday, August 10.

MORNING SESSION, 10 A.M.

Subject : "The Negro in America."

Rev. R. S. Rust, D.D., of Ohio, Secretary Freedmen's Aid Society of the M. E. Church, presided, and spoke. (See page 55.)

Opening Prayer was made by Bishop William F. Dickerson, D.D., of the African Methodist Episcopal Church.

Dr. Hartzell announced a telegram from Shreveport, La., District Conference, (see page 206,) and read extracts from a paper by Rev. C. K. Marshall, D.D., of Mississippi. (See page 77.)

A Paper, "The Danger Line in Negro Education," by Rev. W. H. Ward, D.D., Editor *Independent*, New York. (See page 67.)

Address by Rev. J. C. Price, A.M., of Salisbury, N. C., "The Negro in America : His Special Work." (See page 72.)

A Paper, "The Color Line : What it Is, and What it Threatens," by Rev. B. T. Tanner, D.D., Editor *Christian Recorder*, Philadelphia. (See page 56.)

A Paper, "The Negro and his Assimilation in America," by Rev. J. W. Hamilton, Pastor People's Church, Boston. (See page 58.)

Address, by Bishop J. P. Campbell, of the African Methodist Episcopal Church, "Assimilation, Not Separation." (See page 65.)

Benediction by Rev. C. H. Fowler, LL.D., of New York.

AFTERNOON SESSION, 3 P.M.

Rev. H. L. Morehouse, D.D., Secretary American Baptist Home Mission Society, presided and spoke.

Opening Prayer by Gen. T. J. Morgan, of Potsdam, N. Y.

A Paper, "Education an Indispensable Agency in the Redemption of the Negro Race," by Prof. S. B. Darnell, B.D., of Florida. (See page 62.)

A Paper, "The Relation of Education to Wealth and Morality and to Pauperism and Crime," by Hon. Dexter A. Hawkins, A.M., of New York. (See page 79.)

Address, "Relation of Education to Moral Character," by Rev. C. W. Cushing, D.D., of Rochester, N. Y. (See page 87.)

Address, "The South, the North, and the Nation Keeping School," by Rev. A. D. Mayo, of Boston. (See page 157.)

Benediction by Rev. J. A. Dean, D.D., President New Orleans University.

EVENING SESSION, 7.45 P.M.

Public reception of Missionary Teachers and Preachers who have labored in the South from the North since the war.

Hon. John Eaton, LL.D., of Washington, D. C., presided.

Opening Prayer by Rev. Dr. King, President Iowa Wesleyan University.

Address of Welcome by Rev. C. H. Fowler, D.D., LL.D., of New York. (See page 167.)

Responsive Addresses :

On behalf of Congregationalists, Prof. Saulsbury, Educational Superintendent American Missionary Association. (See page 173.)

On behalf of Methodist Episcopal Church, President John Braden, D.D., of Tennessee. (See page 178.)

Note.—Addresses were also expected by representatives of the Baptist and Presbyterian Churches, outlining the work of these bodies in the South. Although not presented at the Assembly these addresses will be found at pages 188 and 195; also addresses bearing on the same subject by Drs. Strieby and Hartzell at Assembly of 1882.

Address, by Gen. S. C. Armstrong, of Hampton Institute, Virginia. (See page 187.)

Address, "Education in the South," by Rev. J. G. Vaughan, B.D., of New Orleans. (See page 202.)

On motion of Rev. Lemuel Moss, D.D., of Indiana, a resolution was adopted expressive of the sentiment of the Assembly toward the ministers and teachers who have labored in the South from the North since the war. (See page 206.)

On motion of Dr. Strieby, a resolution was adopted on National Aid to Common Schools. (See page 34.)

Benediction by Rev. T. B. Neely, A.M., of Reading, Pa.

Third Day, Saturday, August 11.

MORNING SESSION, 10 A.M.

Subject: "The American Indian Problem."

Gen. Clinton B. Fisk, President United States Indian Commission, was to have presided, but by letter stated that he was called West on official business. Gen. T. J. Morgan, Principal State Normal School, Potsdam, N. Y., presided, and spoke. (See page 91.)

Rev. Sheldon Jackson, D.D., of New York, offered prayer.

Dr. Hartzell read an important letter from Hon. H. M. Teller, Secretary of the Interior. (See page 91.)

A Paper, "The Legal Status of the Indian," by Henry S. Pancoast, Esq., Philadelphia. (See page 93.)

A Paper, "Practical Results of Indian Education," by J. M. Haworth, Esq., Supt. U. S. Indian Schools. (See page 107.)

Address, "Woman's Work in Solving the Indian Problem," by Mrs. A. S. Quinton, General Secretary National Indian Association. (See page 102.)

Address, by Herbert Welsh, Esq., of Philadelphia, "Christianity in its Relations to Indian Civilization." (See page 99.)

A **Paper,** by II. K. CARROLL, Esq., Assistant Editor New York *Independent,* " What Shall be Done with our Savages ?" (See page 106.)

Benediction by Rev. E. H. STOKES, D.D.

AFTERNOON SESSION, 3 P.M.

Bishop DICKERSON, of the African M. E. Church, presided.

Opening Prayer by Rev. D. P. KIDDER, D.D., of New York.

A **Paper,** "Indian Civilization a Success," by Capt. II. R. PRATT, Principal of Carlisle Training-School. (See page 114.)

Address, "A New Phase of the Question," by Rev. C. II. KIDDER, of Wilkesbarre, Pa. (See page 105.)

Address, "The Native Tribes of Alaska," by Rev. SHELDON JACKSON, D.D., Superintendent of Presbyterian Missions in Alaska. (See page 118.)

Dr. HARTZELL announced letters of regret from Hon. HIRAM PRICE, of Washington, and others. (See page 127.)

The several members of the Indian Band were introduced to the audience, and a brief sketch of the life of each was given by Capt. PRATT.

EVENING SESSION, 7.45 P.M.

Rev. A. J. KYNETT, of Philadelphia, presided.

Opening Prayer by Rev. A. K. BELTING.

Dr. HARTZELL gave extracts from several letters from various parts of the country. (See pages 138, 146.)

Address by Rev. L. B. CALDWELL, Ph.D., of Tennessee, on " The Poor Whites of the South : Who they are and Why they are." (See page 31.)

Gen. T. J. MORGAN offered a resolution on the American Indian Problem. It was adopted. (See page 127.)

Rev. A. J. KYNETT, D.D., spoke on " The Utah Problem." (See page 129.)

Address, " Mormonism : Efforts of Christian Churches," by Rev. H. KENDALL, D.D., Secretary of Board of Presbyterian Home Missions. (See page 130.)

NOTE.—Two valuable papers bearing on the Mormon Problem, namely, "Polygamy Woman's Creed of Mormonism," by Mrs. ANGIE F. NEWMAN, (see page 141,) and "The Doctrines of Mormonism," by Prof. THEOPHILUS B. HILTON, A.M., B.D., (see page 147,) are inserted in the body of the work because of their importance and timeliness.

Address, "The Ballot and the Bible," by Rev. J. M. WALDEN, LL.D., of Ohio. (See page 223.)

On motion of Dr. COOKE, of South Carolina, the following resolutions were adopted:

Resolved, That this Education Assembly tender its thanks to the Ocean Grove Association for the use of its grounds and auditorium and many conveniences for the holding of these meetings, as well as for their hearty welcome.

16

Resolved, That this Assembly heartily thanks the representatives of the press who have so faithfully and correctly reported the proceedings.

On motion of Rev. Dr. KING, of Iowa, the following resolution of thanks to Gen. EATON was adopted:

Resolved, That this Education Assembly heartily expresses its high appreciation of the presence and assistance of Hon. JOHN EATON, United States Commissioner of Education, in our work. We thank him for his comprehensive and scholarly address. We desire also to record our judgment that the Educational Bureau, over which he presides, and which has been chiefly developed under him, during the past 13 years, is essential to the progress of education in this country.

Rev. E. H. STOKES, D.D., President of the Ocean Grove Association, presented the following:

In the name and on behalf of the Ocean Grove Camp-meeting Association of the Methodist Episcopal Church, I feel profound satisfaction in returning thanks to this National Education Assembly for honoring us this second time with its presence. Men of honorable positions in Church and State, of great learning, broad views, and catholic spirit, have spoken to us on high themes, involving the welfare of millions living and of millions yet unborn. To these men, who have addressed us in words of such burning eloquence as have enthused the vast multitudes which have attended these services, including Dr. HART-ZELL, who has worked out the details of this great programme, we return sincerest thanks.

To the ladies who have spoken, labored, or sympathized with the cause of education for the illiterate masses, and to all ministers, teachers, and others, whether white or colored, who have worked, prayed, or contributed to this Christ-like cause, we return our thanks; and to our brethren of the forest, sons of the red man, whom we have too long wronged, but are now laboring to bless, who have given us inspiring music during this session, we also extend our hearty thanks.

And, in conclusion, believing that this Assembly, in its aims, is in harmony with our work in this place, we hereby extend to it a cordial and hearty invitation to hold its next session here in the summer of 1884.

On motion of Dr. HARTZELL, a resolution was adopted on the Mormon Question. (See p. 146.)

The following resolutions were adopted:

Resolved, That we accept the invitation of the Ocean Grove Association, and hold our session for 1884 at this place.

Resolved, That we re-elect the members of the National Education Committee and its officers for 1883-84, and that it be instructed to prosecute its work with such modifications as it may think wise.

The Committee is as follows:

National Education Committee for 1883-84.

Bishop M. SIMPSON, of Pennsylvania, *Chairman.*

Hon. J. D. WILSON, of Washington, *Treasurer.*

Prof. C. C. PAINTER, of Tennessee, *Corresponding Secretary.*

Rev. M. E. STRIEBY, D.D., of New York, *Chairman Executive Committee.*

Rev. J. C. HARTZELL, D.D., of Louisiana.

Hon. J. M. GREGORY, of Illinois.

Hon. J. L. M. CURRY, of Virginia.

Gen. S. C. ARMSTRONG, of Virginia.

Rev. R. H. ALLEN, D.D., of Pennsylvania.

Rev. A. G. HAYGOOD, D.D., of Georgia.

BENJAMIN TATUM, Esq., of New York.

Rev. C. R. BLISS, of Illinois.

Hon. A. D. MAYO, of Boston.

Rev. SHELDON JACKSON, D.D., of New York.

On motion of Gen. EATON, the following resolution of thanks to Dr. HARTZELL was adopted:

Resolved, That, profoundly impressed, as we are, with the necessity for the education of every child of every race in our land, and that Christian influence should have its full weight in that education, we who have enjoyed this series of great and inspiring meetings of the National Education Assembly, at Ocean Grove, do most heartily thank Rev. J. C. HARTZELL, D.D., for organizing them, and for undertaking and carrying out the plan of establishing here a platform on which all Christian sentiment can unite and express itself in favor of the great measures required for the removal of illiteracy among all classes, that we may be forever one people, having one country, where all may serve God according to the dictates of their consciences.

Benediction by Bishop W. L. HARRIS, of New York.

——◆◆◆——

Fourth Day, Sunday, August 12.

Subject for the Day: "**Christ in American Education.**"

AT 9 A.M.

Educational Love-Feast, led by Rev. I. W. JOYCE, D.D., of Cincinnati, assisted by Mr. THORNLEY, of Ocean Grove. (See page 217.)

———

MORNING SESSION, 10.30 A.M.

Bishop W. L. HARRIS, LL.D., of New York, presided, and conducted the opening religious exercises.

Sermon, by Rev. LEMUEL MOSS, D.D., President Indiana University, "The Christian Element in Education." (See page 207.)

———

AFTERNOON SESSION, 3 P.M.

Gen. CYRUS BUSSEY, of New Orleans, presided, and spoke. (See page 211.)

Opening Religious Exercises, conducted by Rev. E. H. STOKES, D.D.

Sermon, by Rev. J. P. NEWMAN, LL.D., of New York, "Religious Education the Safeguard of our Nation." (See page 212.)

———

THE SURF MEETING AT 6 P.M.,

On the beach in front of the Pavilion, was largely attended, and several addresses were made. (See pages 227–230.)

———

CLOSING SESSION, 7.45 P.M.

Hon. JOHN EATON, United States Commissioner of Education, presided.

After introductory religious services, Gen. T. J. MORGAN, of Potsdam, N. Y., delivered an address: "Christian Education a Factor in our National Life." (See page 219.)

Address, by Rev. S. P. Hood, of Beaufort, S. C.

The closing address of the Assembly was made by Rev. A. J. Kynett, D.D. (See page 231.)

The Chairman called upon Dr. Hartzell for some parting words. (See page 232.)

Dr. Stokes, after speaking words of hearty congratulation, asked the vast audience to rise, and by waving of handkerchiefs to express a hearty "God bless you" to the speakers and all who had made the Assembly a success. The scene was one never to be forgotten.

Dr. Stokes pronounced the benediction, and the National Education Assembly for 1883 adjourned.

Henry F. Reddall, Secretary.

Ocean Grove, New Jersey, August 12, 1883.

The stenographic reports of the speeches and addresses at this Assembly were made by Mr. Julius Ensign Rockwell, Stenographer of the Bureau of Education, Washington, D. C.

The music at the several sessions of the Assembly was under the direction of Prof. W. J. Kirkpatrick, of Philadelphia.

The Brass Band, composed of twelve Indian young men from Carlisle Indian Training-School, added much to the interest of the sessions of Friday night and Saturday by rendering sacred and patriotic music.

XIII.

TABULATION

OF

ILLITERACY AND EDUCATION

IN THE UNITED STATES IN 1880.

―――――――――――――

THE following tables are furnished by Hon. JOHN EATON, United States Commissioner of Education, and Hon. H. R. WAITE, Special Statistician of the Census of 1880. Some of them are found in the speech of Hon. H. W. BLAIR, United States Senator from New Hampshire, delivered in the Senate June 13, 1882. The data given on national aid to popular education in foreign lands are from the same sources.

In these tables are found the principal facts concerning the illiterate masses of our country, and what each State and Territory is doing in the work of popular education.

HOW MANY, WHO, AND WHERE ARE OUR ILLITERATES.

Table Number 1 gives the population ten years of age and upward, and the number and per cent. of these ages in each State, who cannot read or write; also the same facts concerning the whole number of whites, the number of native and foreign-born whites, and colored persons. The summaries are as follows:

Total population in the United States, 50,155,783.

Total population ten years of age and upward, 36,761,607.

Number of these ages who cannot read, 4,923,451; being 13.4 per cent.

Number of these ages who cannot write, 6,239,958; being 17 per cent.

Number of *white persons* ten years of age and upward, 32,160,400. Of these, 3,019,008, or 9.4 per cent., cannot write.

Number of *native white* persons ten years of age and upward, 25,785,789. Of these 2,255,460, or 8.7 per cent., cannot write.

Number of *foreign-born whites* of same ages, 6,374,611. Of these, 763,620, or 12 per cent., cannot write.

Number of *colored persons* ten years of age and upward, 4,601,207. Of these 3,220,878, or 70 per cent., cannot write.

OUR ADULT ILLITERATES.

Table Number 2 shows the number of persons, male and female, twenty-one years of age and over in the several States and Territories who cannot write, and how many of these are white and how many colored.

The showing is: Total, 4,204,363; and of these the whites number 2,056,463, and colored, 2,147,900. The white and colored adults in the nation twenty-one years of age and upward who cannot write are about equal in numbers. The per cent. is, of course, much larger among the colored because of their smaller numbers.

NUMBER AND LOCATION OF OUR IGNORANT VOTERS.

Considering that the males and females are about equal in numbers, and deducting from the 4,204,363 the Indians and Asiatics, *the number of voters in the nation who cannot write* their names is about 2,000,000. As there are about 10,000,000 of voters in the United States, it follows that *every fifth voter in the country cannot write his name.* The ignorant vote of any Middle, Southern, or Western State is enough to control any political issue likely to arise for years. Our ignorant voters represent ten of our fifty millions. It can be easily seen by Table No. 2 where these ignorant voters are. Nearly three fourths of them are in the sixteen Southern States, where are only one third of our population. South Carolina, with a population of 995,577, has about 117,000 ignorant voters, while New York has less than 100,000 in a population of 5,082,871, or more than five times as many. Iowa has a population of 1,624,615, and Georgia has a population of 1,542,180, nearly the same. And yet Iowa has only 18,886 voters who cannot write, while Georgia has 169,505, or almost nine times as many. If the comparison be confined to white voters, Georgia has twice as many as Iowa, to say nothing of her 123,059 colored voters.

THE NUMBER OF IGNORANT VOTERS AND ILLITERATE MASSES INCREASING.

Table Number 3 is taken from a speech of ex-President Hayes, delivered in 1882, and shows that the illiterate voters of the South are increasing. The increase from 1870 to 1880 being 187,671, about equally divided between the races.

Another fact of great significance is that while, by the census of 1880, there had been an increase of three per cent. in the number of our intelligent masses, yet there had been a much larger relative increase in our illiterate population. The census of 1880 shows that there were 581,814 more people in the country ten years of age and over who could not read or write than there were in 1870. The work of education is not keeping pace with the increase of our population, to say nothing of removing the vast clouds of ignorance which hang over multitudes of our older masses.

ILLITERACY IN OUR CITIES.

Table Number 4 gives important data in eighty-six cities of the country. In these cities are 8,300,081 people, with 2,052,923 of school population. Of these, who ought to be in school, 1,302,776 are enrolled, while 750,147 do not attend school. This means that not quite 63.5 per cent. of the children of school age in those cities are enrolled at all in schools, leaving 36.5 per cent., or over one third, to grow up in ignorance. In Chicago 57 per cent., or more than half the children of school age, are not enrolled. In Wilmington, North Carolina, 82 per cent. are not enrolled. In 34 cities 50 per cent. and upward are not enrolled.

The facts given in this table are of vast significance. The population, wealth, commercial, social, and political power of our cities are all rapidly increasing. If one third of the youth in these great centers continue to grow up in ignorance, who can estimate the appalling dangers which the future may bring ? This illiteracy of our cities demands as serious thought and as immediate action as does the illiteracy of the South.

THE PUBLIC AND PRIVATE SCHOOLS IN THE UNITED STATES.

Table Number 5 gives a picture of the public and private schools of the country. The school population of the nation is 15,303,585. Of these 9,780,773 are enrolled in public schools, and 566,989 in private schools. The average daily attendance in our public schools is 5,804,993, being only about one in three of the total school population; 4,955,602 of the educable youth of the land are not even enrolled in schools.

The number of teachers in public schools is 280,753, and in private schools there are 13,105 instructors.

By this table it is seen that in proportion as the illiterate masses of a State are great, the number of schools is small. To continue the comparison between Iowa and Georgia, the former, with its 2.4 per cent. of illiteracy, has 11,084 public schools, with 21,598 teachers in them; while Georgia, with about the same population, and 49.9 per cent. of illiteracy, has only 5,916 public schools and 6,000 public-school teachers. This unfavorable comparison for Georgia is slightly relieved by the fact that there are 48,452 in private schools in that State, as against 12,724 in private schools in Iowa.

POPULATION AND PROPERTY IN UNITED STATES.
1860, 1870, and 1880.

Table Number 6 gives the population and assessed valuation of the property in each State and Territory in 1860, 1870, and 1880. This table is specially valuable as indicating the financial capacity of each State. The rule is that in proportion as a State or section needs education, it is financially unable to secure it. The Southern States had a property valuation in 1860 of $2,289,029,042, and of this $842,927,400 was in slaves. The Negroes were then productive property, being taxed. Now they must be educated, and as yet are able to do but little in helping to bear the burden of that work.

Since 1860 the increase of population has been great in every part of the country. In some of the New England States the increase has been small, but nowhere else has the increase been less than 31 per cent., and as a rule it has been very great. The South has held its own in this increase, and the Negroes of the nation have gone up to 7,000,000. Valuation of property has not kept pace with increase of population. Property, in twenty years, has increased 40 per cent.; while population has increased over 60 per cent. For example, Alabama is worth 72 per cent. less than in 1860, and yet has 31 per cent. more of population. Arkansas has nearly doubled her population, while in the twenty years her property value has gone down nearly one half. So in all the South. The necessities for educational facilities have increased enormously; while the financial capacity of that section has greatly decreased. This table affords a powerful argument in favor of national aid to common schools.

TAXATION FOR PUBLIC SCHOOLS.

Table Number 7 gives the amounts raised by taxation for public schools in each State and Territory in 1880. The whole amount raised from State and local taxation is $70,371,435.

Here, again, the rule is that in proportion as schools are needed, judging from the number of illiterates, the revenue for schools is small. Comparing Iowa and Georgia again, we have this: the former taxes its people $4,227,300 for public schools, while the latter taxes itself $471,029 for the same purpose. If, however, we remember the property of Georgia as compared with Iowa, the disparity is not so great.

The great reduction in real estate values in the South since the war, as shown elsewhere, must be taken into the account in comparing the South with the North.

PROPOSED DISTRIBUTION OF NATIONAL AID BY SENATOR BLAIR'S BILL.

Table Number 8 gives the amount each State would receive provided the general government would give $15,000,000 a year for common schools, and distribute on the basis of illiteracy.

INCOME AND EXPENDITURES FOR PUBLIC SCHOOLS IN UNITED STATES.

1881.

Table Number 9 gives a summary of annual income and expenditures in the States and Territories for education in 1881.

The total income was $88,142,088, and about the same amount was expended. The estimated value of sites, buildings, and all other school property for 1881 was $186,142,452.

The study of this table reveals an important line of facts, as already indicated. Where ignorance most abounds school funds are the smallest. The school income of Georgia was $498,533, while that of Iowa was $5,006,024, more than ten times as much, with about the same population.

PUBLIC SCHOOL EDUCATION IN THE SOUTH.

Table Number 10 gives a comparative view of education in the South in two parts: one representing 1880, and one 1881. Both years are given so that a comparison of years may be made, and the advance or the opposite be noted. The increase of school population among the whites during the year was 54,639, while the increase in enrollment was only 19,203, but little more than one third what it ought to have been, to say nothing of the vast increase demanded to remove, in the near future, the appalling illiteracy among the whites of that region.

The comparison among the Negroes is still more unsatisfactory. The increase during the year in scholars was 125,930, while the increase in enrollment was only 17,663. That is, but little more than *one seventh of the increase* of youth among the Negroes of the South were enrolled.

The Southern States expended for both races in school work in 1880, $12,475,-044, and in 1881, $13,359,784, being an increase of $884,740. This is more favorable. New York and Michigan have a larger income for public schools than the whole South.

NATIONAL AID TO POPULAR EDUCATION IN EUROPE.

The data submitted upon popular education in European countries will aid in comparing ourselves with others. As Senator BLAIR says: "The principle is fully recognized that when the general welfare demands, individuals and subdivisions must submit, if necessary for any cause, to receive compulsory blessings; coupled with which is the duty which implies the right of the whole to provide for the protection and safety of all the parts by the utmost exercise of its powers."

The foreigners who come to our shores have about 14 per cent. of illiterates among them, which is about the same grade of intelligence we have in America. So that immigration does not add essentially to our national illiteracy.

STATISTICAL SUMMARIES.

Table No. 1.

Illiteracy in United States, (Census of 1880.)

STATES AND TERRITORIES.	Total Population.	PERSONS OF TEN YEARS OF AGE AND UPWARD. Enumerated.	Returned as unable to read. Number.	Per cent.	Returned as unable to write. Number.	Per cent.	WHITE PERSONS OF TEN YEARS OF AGE AND UPWARD. Enumerated.	Returned as unable to write. Number.	Per cent.	NATIVE WHITE PERSONS OF TEN YEARS OF AGE AND UPWARD. Enumerated.	Returned as unable to write. Number.	Per cent.	FOREIGN-BORN WHITE PERSONS OF TEN YEARS OF AGE AND UPWARD. Enumerated.	Returned as unable to write. Number.	Per cent.	COLORED PERSONS OF TEN YEARS OF AGE AND UPWARD. Enumerated.	Returned as unable to write. Number.	Per cent.
Alabama	1,262,505	851,780	370,279	43.5	433,447	50.9	452,722	111,767	24.7	443,827	111,040	25.0	9,395	727	7.7	399,058	321,680	80.6
Arizona	40,440	32,922	5,496	16.7	5,842	17.7	28,634	4,824	16.8	15,300	1,225	8.1	13,434	3,599	26.8	4,258	1,018	23.7
Arkansas	802,525	531,876	153,229	28.8	202,015	38.0	393,905	90,344	25.0	384,060	97,990	33.5	9,845	552	5.6	137,971	108,373	75.0
California	864,694	681,062	153,229	28.8	53,430	7.8	569,235	26,763	4.6	374,772	7,600	2.0	214,463	18,430	8.6	91,827	27,340	29.8
Colorado	194,327	158,220	9,321	5.9	10,474	6.6	155,456	9,906	6.4	117,132	3,728	1.0	38,324	1,538	4.0	2,764	508	20.5
Connecticut	622,700	497,303	30,986	4.2	28,424	4.2	487,780	26,763	5.5	361,733	8,373	1.8	126,047	23,035	8.6	9,523	1,661	17.4
Dakota	135,177	99,849	3,094	3.1	4,821	3.1	98,348	4,157	4.2	51,229	933	1.8	47,119	3,224	6.8	1,501	664	44.2
Delaware	146,608	110,856	16,912	15.5	19,414	17.5	91,611	8,346	9.1	82,318	6,690	8.1	9,293	1,719	18.5	10,845	11,066	57.5
District of Columbia	177,624	136,907	21,541	15.7	25,778	18.8	91,672	3,988	4.3	75,025	1,960	2.6	16,847	2,038	12.1	45,085	21,790	48.4
Florida	269,493	184,550	70,219	38.0	80,183	43.4	99,187	19,763	19.9	91,749	19,024	20.7	7,388	739	10.0	85,513	60,432	70.7
Georgia	1,542,180	1,043,840	446,683	42.8	530,416	49.9	563,977	128,931	22.9	563,769	128,362	23.2	10,208	572	5.6	479,863	391,482	81.6
Idaho	32,610	25,005	1,384	5.5	1,778	7.1	21,481	784	3.6	15,011	341	3.0	6,470	341	5.0	3,524	994	28.2
Illinois	3,077,871	2,362,315	96,809	4.3	145,397	6.4	2,234,476	42,436	5.9	1,666,214	68,519	5.3	568,264	43,907	7.7	34,837	12,971	37.2
Indiana	1,978,301	1,466,095	70,006	4.8	110,761	7.5	1,438,955	100,308	7.1	1,297,159	87,786	6.8	41,796	12,612	8.9	29,140	10,363	35.6
Iowa	1,624,615	1,181,641	28,117	2.4	46,600	3.9	1,174,063	44,337	3.8	918,723	22,660	2.6	255,330	20,677	8.1	7,578	2,272	30.0
Kansas	996,096	704,297	25,503	3.6	39,476	5.5	673,121	24,688	3.6	568,360	17,825	3.1	104,711	7,063	6.7	31,176	14,588	46.8
Kentucky	1,648,690	1,163,498	258,166	22.2	348,362	29.9	973,275	214,497	22.0	914,311	208,796	22.8	58,964	5,701	9.7	190,223	133,995	70.4
Louisiana	939,946	649,070	297,312	45.8	318,380	49.1	320,917	58,951	18.4	268,600	53,261	19.8	52,317	5,690	10.9	328,154	259,429	79.1
Maine	648,936	519,669	18,181	3.5	22,170	4.3	518,011	21,758	4.2	463,158	8,775	1.9	54,853	12,983	23.7	1,658	602	37.0
Maryland	934,943	695,364	111,387	16.0	134,488	19.3	541,086	44,316	8.1	462,697	36,027	7.8	83,389	8,289	10.3	154,278	90,172	59.6
Massachusetts	1,783,085	1,432,183	75,635	5.3	92,960	6.5	1,416,767	90,658	6.4	990,160	6,933	0.7	426,607	82,725	19.6	15,416	2,322	15.1
Michigan	1,636,937	1,236,086	47,132	3.8	63,723	5.2	1,219,006	56,932	4.6	654,925	19,981	2.3	364,981	36,951	10.1	16,780	4,791	28.5
Minnesota	780,773	559,997	90,631	8.9	84,546	15.0	537,193	33,346	6.0	300,747	5,671	1.9	326,436	27,835	10.6	2,794	1,037	37.2
Mississippi	1,131,597	753,698	315,612	41.9	373,201	49.5	328,298	33,448	16.3	319,285	5,910	16.6	8,911	588	6.0	425,397	319,754	75.2
Missouri	2,168,380	1,557,631	188,818	13.4	208,753	13.4	1,453,236	152,510	10.5	1,244,738	137,949	11.1	208,500	14,561	7.0	104,363	56,244	53.9
Montana	39,159	32,919	1,530	4.8	1,707	5.8	32,396	631	2.2	19,598	272	1.4	9,368	359	3.8	3,063	1,076	35.8
Nebraska	452,402	318,271	7,830	2.7	11,388	3.6	316,312	10,926	3.5	224,841	5,102	2.3	91,413	5,825	6.4	1,959	94	15.8
Nevada	62,266	50,656	3,103	7.3	4,060	8.0	42,593	1,915	4.5	22,660	240	1.1	19,936	1,675	8.4	8,199	2,154	26.7
New Hampshire	346,991	284,588	11,932	4.2	14,302	5.0	285,595	14,208	5.0	242,811	2,710	1.1	42,783	11,496	26.9	593	94	15.8
New Jersey	1,131,116	865,591	39,196	4.5	63,249	6.2	833,385	44,049	5.3	200,093	20,093	3.2	216,444	23,936	11.1	30,206	9,200	30.5
New Mexico	119,565	87,966	52,994	60.2	57,156	65.0	73,760	49,952	62.2	72,219	46,329	64.2	7,548	3,264	43.3	8,199	7,559	92.2
New York	5,082,871	3,981,438	166,625	4.2	219,600	5.5	3,927,603	206,175	5.3	2,742,847	59,516	2.2	1,184,756	148,659	12.5	63,835	11,423	21.2

Table No. 1 (continued)

STATES AND TERRITORIES						
North Carolina	867,890	98.3	463,975	48.8	606,806	21.6
Ohio	60,751	3.6	131,817	5.5	2,389,528	4.9
Oregon	130,365	4.1	7,456	7.1	119,482	3.6
Pennsylvania	146,138	4.6	229,014	7.1	3,136,561	6.7
Rhode Island	17,456	7.9	24,793	11.2	235,158	10.9
South Carolina	331,780	49.2	369,848	53.4	272,706	21.9
Tennessee	291,385	27.7	410,733	38.7	790,744	27.3
Texas	226,223	24.1	316,432	29.7	808,031	15.3
Utah	4,851	5.0	8,899	9.1	95,876	8.5
Vermont	12,993	4.9	15,857	6.0	263,245	6.0
Virginia	360,495	34.0	430,352	40.9	630,584	18.2
Washington	3,191	5.7	3,880	7.0	49,203	2.9
West Virginia	52,041	12.1	85,376	19.9	410,141	18.3
Wisconsin	38,633	4.0	55,558	5.8	961,433	5.6
Wyoming	427		556	3.4	15,240	2.5
The United States	36,761,607		4,923,451	13.4	6,239,958	17.0

Number of persons, male and female, in the United States, twenty-one years of age and over, who cannot write, as shown by Census of 1880:

STATES AND TERRITORIES	White	Colored	Total
Alabama	60,174	206,878	267,052
Arizona	3,550	633	4,183
Arkansas	50,335	68,444	118,070
California	22,635	22,100	44,725
Colorado	7,025	465	7,490
Connecticut	23,339	1,497	24,836
Dakota	3,306		14,397
Delaware	6,462	7,935	14,397
Dist. of Columbia	10,585	19,447	23,016
Florida	71,053	39,753	50,638
Georgia	510	247,318	319,011
Idaho	10,397	943	1,453
Illinois	90,356		109,753
Indiana	77,076	8,806	85,882
Iowa	35,815	1,958	37,773
Kansas	17,095	11,498	28,593
Kentucky	194,123	90,730	213,401
Louisiana	34,813	178,789	213,602
Maine	10,234		16,569
Maryland	34,135	66,357	100,512
Massachusetts	81,671	2,221	83,892
Michigan	48,291	3,758	52,049
Minnesota	27,645	769	28,414
Mississippi	27,789	208,122	235,911
Missouri	89,924	40,357	130,281
Montana			207,052
Nebraska			4,183
Nevada			118,070
New Hampshire			44,725
New Jersey			
New Mexico			
New York			

Table No. 3

Number of voters in the late slave-holding States, twenty-one years of age and upward, who could not read and write in 1870 and 1880:

	1870		1880	
	White	Colored	White	Colored
Alabama	17,429	91,017	34,450	96,408
Arkansas	13,610	23,681	21,349	34,300
Delaware	3,405	3,765	2,953	3,787
Florida	3,876	16,806	4,706	19,110
Georgia	21,899	100,551	28,571	116,516
Kentucky	43,826	37,899	54,956	43,177
Louisiana	12,048	76,612	16,387	86,555
Maryland	13,344	27,123	15,132	30,873
Mississippi	9,357	80,810	12,473	99,065
Missouri	34,780	68,669	40,455	19,128
North Carolina	33,111	44,430	44,439	80,282
Tennessee	37,713	65,938	46,948	58,601
Texas	17,505	47,235	33,085	59,669
Virginia	27,646	95,948	31,414	100,210
West Virginia	15,181	3,146	19,055	3,830
South Carolina	12,490	70,839	13,924	93,010
Total	217,371	830,022	410,530	944,424

Total number of illiterates of voting age in the late slave-holding States in 1870	1,167,363
Total number of males of voting age in the late slave-holding States in 1880	1,354,974
Increase illiterate voters in South, from 1870 to 1880	187,671
Total number of illiterate males of voting age in the South in 1880	4,154,125
Total number of illiterate males of voting age in the South in the holding States in 1880	1,354,974

Table No. 4.

Showing the Total Population, School Population, Enrollment, etc., in 86 Cities, (Census of 1880.)

CITIES.	Population.	School population.	Enrollment.	Average attendance.	Total number of teachers.	Length of school year in days.	Number of pupils not attending.	Per cent. of school pop. enrol'd in sch.	Per cent. of pop. not enrolled in sch.
Mobile, Alabama	29,132	.....	4,639	4,014	125	172	.....	50	60
Selma, Alabama	7,529	1,757	882	717	14	...	875	50	60
Little Rock, Arkansas	13,138	6,169	2,503	1,655	33	180	3,606	41	50
Oakland, California	34,555	8,108	5,996	5,067	128	206	2,112	74	26
Sacramento, California	21,420	4,843	3,895	....	75	200	1,048	79	21
San Francisco, California	233,959	53,892	38,320	28,150	686	211	15,572	71	29
Denver, Colorado	35,629	5,770	3,310	1,933	65	190	2,460	56	44
Bridgeport, Connecticut	20,148	6,841	5,229	3,529	91	210	1,412	76	21
Hartford, Connecticut	42,015	9,452	7,312	4,886	140	201	2,140	79	21
New Haven, Connecticut	62,882	13,897	11,897	7,911	230	200	2,000	86	14
Wilmington, Delaware	42,478	.....	7,043	4,472	115	207	.....	..	..
Georgetown and Washington, D. C.	150,871	27,143	15,728	12,506	269	208	11,414	58	42
Jacksonville, Florida	7,650	1,011	804	....	17	176	207	79	21
Key West, Florida	9,890	3,415	1,138	828	17	240	2,247	34	66
Atlanta, Georgia	37,409	10,500	4,100	2,609	68	200	6,400	39	61
Augusta, Georgia	21,891	5,366	4,027	....	32	183	5,339	43	57
Chicago, Illinois	502,155	137,085	59,562	42,375	896	200	77,473	43	57
Peoria, Illinois	29,259	9,070	4,701	3,384	76	200	4,409	49	51
Indianapolis, Indiana	75,056	25,789	13,936	8,323	219	200	11,853	52	48
Terre Haute, Indiana	26,042	8,094	4,138	2,375	78	190	3,956	57	43
Des Moines, Iowa	22,408	3,570	2,332	1,505	41	190	1,254	65	35
Dubuque, Iowa	22,254	9,476	3,686	2,655	71	200	5,790	39	61
Leavenworth, Kansas	16,546	6,237	3,000	2,154	34	190	3,197	49	51
Topeka, Kansas	15,452	2,816	1,935	1,507	30	180	881	68	32
Covington, Kentucky	28,720	10,094	3,286	2,445	80	198	6,809	32	68
Louisville, Kentucky	123,758	46,587	19,990	13,498	325	215	26,597	43	57
New Orleans, Louisiana	216,090	56,947	17,886	15,190	407	208	39,061	31	69
Bangor, Maine	16,856	5,479	3,190	2,438	71	200	2,350	55	45
Lewiston, Maine	19,083	5,974	3,558	2,061	76	187½	2,410	60	40
Portland, Maine	33,810	10,960	6,707	4,347	128	200	3,953	64	36
Baltimore, Maryland	332,313	84,961	48,060	21,963	892	184	36,895	55	45
Boston, Massachusetts	362,839	57,703	58,708	46,130	1,201	200	2,065	*108	..
Lawrence, Massachusetts	39,151	6,865	4,800	4,212	118	200	2,065	70	30
Lowell, Massachusetts	59,475	8,121	13,211	6,045	160	...	5,090	*134	..
Worcester, Massachusetts	58,291	10,988	11,452	7,913	218	200	403	*104	..
Detroit, Michigan	116,340	39,467	15,719	10,415	350	200	23,748	40	60
Grand Rapids, Michigan	32,016	9,784	5,727	3,900	106	200	4,057	58	42
Minneapolis, Minnesota	46,887	12,956	6,112	4,348	130	200	6,664	48	52
Saint Paul, Minnesota	41,473	.....	4,338	3,036	96	200	.....	..	..
Vicksburg, Mississippi	11,814	3,000	1,196	....	21	...	1,804	39	61
Kansas City, Missouri	55,785	11,325	5,239	3,140	82	200	6,086	46	54
Saint Joseph, Missouri	32,431	8,908	3,820	2,579	58	200	5,088	43	57
Saint Louis, Missouri	350,518	106,372	55,780	36,440	1,044	200	50,592	52	41
Omaha, Nebraska	30,518	7,381	3,716	....	87	200	3,665	50	50
Dover, New Hampshire	11,687	2,350	1,880	1,436	46	180	470	80	20
Manchester, New Hampshire	32,630	4,774	4,350	2,818	86	190	424	91	9
Nashua, New Hampshire	13,397	2,072	2,526	1,830	52	180	454	*121	..
Portsmouth, New Hampshire	9,690	2,251	1,891	....	35	200	360	82	38
Jersey City, New Jersey	120,722	41,226	22,776	12,905	328	204	18,450	55	45
Newark, New Jersey	136,508	41,935	19,778	11,100	270	210	22,457	46	54
Paterson, New Jersey	51,031	13,072	7,901	4,759	142	190	5,571	58	43
Albany, New York	90,758	33,411	14,040	8,175	620	210	21,362	40	60
Brooklyn, New York	566,663	181,083	96,336	52,677	1,315	205	84,720	53	47
Buffalo, New York	155,134	56,600	18,850	14,555	439	201	37,384	53	47
New York, New York	1,206,299	395,000	270,170	132,720	3,337	204	114,834	70	30
Rochester, New York	89,366	37,000	13,809	8,250	230	200	23,141	37	63
Wilmington, North Carolina	17,350	.....	896	....	..	...	4,055	18	89
Cincinnati, Ohio	255,139	87,918	36,121	27,279	671	225	51,497	41	59
Cleveland, Ohio	160,146	49,256	24,262	16,807	508	196	24,994	49	51
Columbus, Ohio	51,647	14,662	7,902	5,953	149	200	6,760	54	46
Dayton, Ohio	38,678	11,000	6,114	4,527	125	...	5,546	52	48
Toledo, Ohio	50,137	14,898	7,415	4,730	125	200	7,983	51	49
Portland, Oregon	17,577	4,669	2,650	1,956	46	200	2,019	57	43
Allegheny, Pennsylvania	78,682	.....	11,810	8,287	202	198	.....	..	..
Philadelphia, Pennsylvania	877,170	.....	105,541	94,145	2,265	207	.....	..	..
Pittsburg, Pennsylvania	156,389	.....	26,437	17,387	620	...	.....	..	..
Scranton, Pennsylvania	45,850	19,800	10,174	6,801	169	220	9,626	41	19
Newport, Rhode Island	15,693	3,419	2,580	1,808	53	198	839	75	25
Providence, Rhode Island	104,857	19,108	13,993	9,030	289	...	5,115	78	27
Charleston, South Carolina	49,984	13,727	7,284	....	91	197	6,443	57	43
Columbia, South Carolina	10,036	.....	.....	....	..	...	.....	..	..
Chattanooga, Tennessee	12,892	3,061	2,185	1,382	30	180	876	71	29
Knoxville, Tennessee	9,693	2,100	1,509	930	26	200	591	72	28
Memphis, Tennessee	33,592	9,011	4,105	2,589	63	151	4,906	45	55
Nashville, Tennessee	43,350	12,460	6,098	4,208	96	190	6,362	49	51
Houston, Texas	16,513	2,740	1,776	1,172	28	160	900	64	36
San Antonio, Texas	20,550	3,022	1,584	934	22	205	1,438	52	48
Burlington, Vermont	11,365	.....	1,566	....	32	...	.....	..	..
Rutland, Vermont	12,149	.....	2,395	....	64	...	.....	..	..
Norfolk, Virginia	21,966	6,005	1,613	1,110	20	210	5,082	24	76
Petersburg, Virginia	21,656	7,417	1,985	1,404	29	174	5,432	27	73
Richmond, Virginia	63,600	21,350	5,821	4,778	129	198	15,715	27	73
Madison, Wisconsin	10,324	3,517	1,939	1,745	34	185	1,578	55	45
Milwaukee, Wisconsin	115,587	37,742	17,085	11,140	239	...	20,687	45	55
Oshkosh, Wisconsin	15,748	5,874	2,217	2,017	53	...	3,657	38	62
	8,300,081	2,052,923	1,302,776	856,533	21,672	...	750,147	..	..

* More than the school population. This is due to the fact that they are allowed to attend school after the age established by law.
Average attendance about two thirds of enrollment or one third of population of school age.
Thirty-four cities, 50 per cent. and upward not enrolled at all.

Table No. 5.

Public School Statistics of the United States in 1880, with Number of Teachers and Pupils in Private Schools.

STATES AND TERRITORIES	School age.	School population.	Number enrolled in public schools.	Average daily attendance.	Average duration of school days.	Expenditures in the year—per capita of pupils enrolled in public schools.	Number of public schools.	Teachers in public schools.	Teachers in private schools.*	Pupils in private schools.*	Amount of permanent school fund, including portions not now available.
Alabama...	7-21	388,003	179,400	117,078	80.0	$2 08	4,594	4,615	....	......	h$190,186
Arkansas...	6-21	247,547	70,972	......	....	....	1,837	1,837	....	......	h$190,186
California..	5-17	215,078	158,765	100,006	146.6	b17 17	2,803	3,595	....	14,953	2,104,405
Colorado ...	5-21	35,506	22,119	12,018	b89.0	17 80	....	678	....	......	....
Connecticut	4-16	140,235	119,694	k78,421	179.2	11 01	1,030	p3,100	512	13,000	2,021,346
Delaware...	6-21	85,459	27,623	......	l158.0	8 12	561	594	....	......	....
Florida.....	4-21	68,677	39,315	27,040	....	....	1,131	1,005	....	......	....
Georgia....	6-18	b483,444	236,533	145,190	....	1 09	b5,916	6,000	1,080	48,452	....
Illinois.....	6-21	1,010,851	704,041	431,038	150.0	9 61	14,064	22,255	1,497	60,440	9,049,302
Indiana....	6-21	703,558	511,283	321,650	130.0	7 96	9,383	13,578	l592	l12,112	9,005,255
Iowa.......	5-21	586,556	426,057	259,836	148.0	11 25	11,084	21,598	474	12,724	....
Kansas.....	5-21	340,647	231,434	137,607	107 0	7 85	5,233	7,780	979	b6,205	11,815,519
Kentucky...	a6-20	545,161	265,581	f193,874	102.0	3 85	....	6,764	....	......	1,755,682
Louisiana ..	6-18	273,845	68,440	44,620	118.0	b6 74	1,494	2,025	u247	u4,404	1,130,867
Maine......	4-21	214,050	149,827	103,113	120.0	6 53	....	6,934	....	......	....
Maryland...	5-20	d276,120	102,431	85,778	m210.0	8 64	2,300	3,125	....	......	....
Mass.......	5-15	307,321	306,777	233,127	177.0	f14 93	5,570	8,595	....	26,289	....
Michigan...	5-20	500,221	362,556	f213,898	141.0	b8 11	6,695	13,940	703	13,854	3,340,949
Minnesota..	5-22	e271,428	180,248	f117,161	94.0	b8 42	p4,004	5,215	....	......	15,000,000
Mississippi .	5-21	426,089	236,704	156,761	77.5	2 70	b5,307	5,509	....	......	....
Missouri....	6-20	723,484	476,370	f219,132	b100.0	....	8,641	10,447	....	......	....
Nebraska...	5-21	142,348	92,549	f60,156	109.0	12 29	2,922	4,100	....	......	f20,754,810
Nevada.....	b6-18	b10,295	b7,590	b5,108	....	....	....	b184	....	......	....
N.Hampsh'e	b5-21	bf72,102	b65,048	b48,010	b101.5	....	2,528	b3,582	....	b3,000	....
New Jersey.	5-18	380,685	204,961	115,194	192.0	9 48	....	3,477	572	43,530	2,516,785
New York ..	5-21	1,041,173	1,031,593	573,080	179.0	10 09	p20,500	30,730	....	w139,470	....
N. Carolina.	6-21	459,394	235,600	147,802	54.0	1 12	5,503	4,130	....	......	y531,555
Ohio........	6-21	b1,043,320	747,138	476,270	150.0	8 59	12,043	23,684	292	23,050	....
Oregon.....	4-20	59,273	37,583	27,435	80.0	8 37	b865	1,341	212	3,741	....
Penn'a.....	6-21	g1,200,000	937,310	601,027	147.0	....	b18,386	21,375	v947	v24,060	....
Rhode Isl'd.	5-15	52,273	44,780	20,065	n184.0	11 03	926	1,205	208	6,076	266,980
S. Carolina.	6-16	b228,128	134,072	......	77.0	2 42	2,973	3,171	....	......	....
Tennessee..	6-21	544,862	290,141	191,461	68.0	....	5,522	5,594	1,665	41,068	h2,512,500
Texas......	8-14	230,527	180,786	......	o73.0	....	6,127	4,301	....	......	e3,385,571
Vermont ...	5-20	c92,881	75,238	48,600	125.0	....	2,616	4,320	....	......	....
Virginia....	5-21	555,807	220,736	128,404	113.0	3 82	4,854	4,873	1,000	25,692	1,468,703
W.Virginia.	6-21	210,113	142,850	91,704	99.0	4 43	b3,725	4,134	....	......	423,989
Wisconsin .	4-20	489,220	290,258	197,510	102.5	7 51	5,984	10,115	804	25,938	2,995,112
Arizona....	6-21	7,148	4,212	2,847	109.0	....	...	108	....	......	....
Dakota.....	5-21	12,030	8,042	3,170	86.0	....	....	286	....	......	....
Dist. of Col.	6-17	43,558	26,439	20,637	103.0	14 87	p325	433	....	......	60,385
Idaho	5-21	....	0,758	....	...	....	155	r160	....	x5,000	....
Indiana	....	l11,444	j6,008	j3,944	....	....	212	h196	....	......	....
Montana ...	4-21	7,070	2,506	2,500	90.0	....	158	101	....	......	....
New Mexico	c7-18	d29,312	c5,151	......	c132.0	....	c138	c138	c61	c1,259	....
Utah	6-18	40,672	24,320	17,178	128.0	....	b373	b373	....	......	....
Washingt'n.	b5-21	b24,233	b14,082	b9,585	b87.5	b8 15	340	340	b31	b431	....
Wyoming ..	b7-21	......	b2,090	b1,287	....	....	....	....	....	......	....
Total....	....	15,303,535	9,780,773	5,804,908	....	....	188,701	282,753	13,105	566,983	....

a. For whites; for colored, 6-16.
b. In 1879.
c. In 1815.
d. Census of 1810.
e. In 1878.
f. Estimated.
g. In 1873.
h. In 1877.
i. In the Cherokee, Choctaw, and Creek Nations.
j. In the five civilized tribes.
k. For the winter.
l. In white schools only.
m. In cities; 116 in counties.

n. In evening schools, 61.
o. In the counties.
p. Approximately.
r. Number necessary to supply the schools.
t. Private schools in public buildings.
u. In 1879; exclusive of New Orleans private schools.
v. In 1879; exclusive of Philadelphia.
w. In academies and private schools.
x. Estimated average number of pupils.
y. Exclusive of 1,000,000 acres of swamp land made subject to entry sale by last Legislature.
* As far as reported by State superintendents.

Table No. 6.

The Population and the Assessed Valuation of Personal Property and Real Estate in the States and Territories, from Census Returns for 1860, 1870, and 1880.

STATES AND TERRITORIES.	1860. Population.	1860. Assessed valuation.	1870. Population.	1870. Assessed valuation.	1880. Population.	1880. Assessed valuation.	INCREASE PER CT. 1860 TO 1880. In population.	INCREASE PER CT. 1860 TO 1880. In assess'd val'n.
Alabama	964,201	$432,198,762	996,992	$155,589,735	1,262,505	$132,867,228	31	−72
Arizona	......	......	9,658	1,410,235	40,440	9,270,214	......	......
Arkansas	435,450	180,211,330	484,471	94,528,843	802,525	86,409,364	84	−53
California	379,994	186,654,667	560,247	269,044,108	864,684	584,578,036	128	319
Colorado	34,277	......	39,864	20,243,637	194,327	74,471,693	467	......
Connecticut	460,147	341,256,976	537,454	405,624,489	622,700	327,177,385	35	−4
Dakota	4,837	......	14,181	20,924,489	135,177	26,331,630	2,295	......
Delaware	112,216	39,367,233	125,015	64,787,282	146,608	58,463,643	31	61
District of Columbia	75,080	41,081,945	131,700	74,371,663	177,624	99,401,787	137	142
Florida	140,424	68,929,685	187,748	32,460,643	269,493	30,038,309	92	−55
Georgia	1,057,286	612,932,387	1,184,109	227,219,519	1,542,180	239,472,599	46	−61
Idaho	......	......	14,999	5,522,265	32,610	6,440,876	......	......
Illinois	1,711,951	380,207,373	2,539,891	482,899,575	3,077,871	786,616,394	80	102
Indiana	1,350,428	411,043,424	1,680,637	663,455,044	1,978,301	727,815,181	46	77
Iowa	674,913	205,196,988	1,194,020	302,515,418	1,624,615	398,671,251	141	94
Kansas	107,206	31,327,895	364,399	92,125,861	995,496	160,891,689	829	615
Kentucky	1,155,684	522,318,433	1,321,011	464,314,494	1,648,690	350,563,971	43	−34
Louisiana	708,002	435,787,265	726,915	25,591,000	903,946	160,162,439	33	−63
Maine	628,279	151,389,388	626,915	204,553,700	648,936	235,978,716	3	58
Maryland	687,049	296,143,239	780,894	423,834,918	934,943	497,307,675	36	67
Massachusetts	1,231,066	777,157,816	1,457,351	1,584,983,112	1,783,085	1,584,759,802	45	104
Michigan	749,113	163,331,005	1,184,059	272,242,917	1,636,937	517,284,359	119	217
Minnesota	172,023	32,018,772	439,706	84,133,332	780,773	258,028,087	354	706
Mississippi	791,305	609,472,512	827,922	177,278,890	1,131,597	110,628,189	43	−78
Missouri	1,182,012	205,585,851	1,721,235	655,199,969	2,168,380	532,795,201	83	100
Montana	......	......	20,595	9,943,411	39,159	18,609,802	......	......
Nebraska	28,841	7,426,939	122,993	54,584,616	452,402	90,585,782	1,469	1,120
Nevada	6,857	......	42,491	25,740,973	62,266	27,491,459	808	......
New Hampshire	326,073	121,810,489	318,300	149,065,290	346,991	164,398,531	6	33
New Jersey	672,035	298,682,493	906,096	622,124,047	1,131,116	672,343,801	68	93
New Mexico	93,516	20,838,760	91,874	17,784,074	119,565	12,363,406	28	−45
New York	3,880,735	1,394,461,638	4,382,759	1,967,001,185	5,082,871	2,651,940,466	31	91
North Carolina	992,622	292,297,602	1,071,361	130,378,622	1,399,750	156,100,202	41	−47
Ohio	2,339,511	959,467,101	2,665,260	1,167,731,697	3,198,062	1,534,360,508	37	60
Oregon	52,465	19,021,915	90,923	31,798,510	174,768	52,522,084	233	......
Pennsylvania‡	2,906,215	719,258,335	3,521,951	1,313,206,042	4,282,891	†1,683,459,016	47	156
Rhode Island	174,620	125,104,305	217,353	244,278,454	276,531	232,536,673	33	134
South Carolina	703,708	489,319,128	705,606	183,913,337	995,577	133,560,135	41	−73
Tennessee	1,109,801	382,495,200	1,258,520	253,752,161	1,542,359	211,778,538	39	−45
Texas	604,215	264,782,335	818,579	149,732,929	1,591,749	320,364,515	163	50
Utah	40,273	5,158,020	86,786	12,563,749	143,963	24,775,279	257	496
Vermont	315,098	84,758,619	330,551	102,548,528	332,286	34,600,776	6	−57
Virginia†	1,596,318	657,021,336	1,225,163	365,439,917	1,512,565	308,455,135	134	60
Washington	11,594	4,894,735	23,955	10,642,863	75,116	129,622,705	548	......
West Virginia†	......	......	442,014	140,538,273	618,457	233,610,663	......	......
Wisconsin	775,881	185,945,489	1,054,670	333,209,538	1,315,497	434,971,751	70	136
Wyoming	......	......	9,118	6,516,748	20,789	13,681,829	......	......
Total	31,443,321	$12,084,560,005	38,558,371	$14,172,996,732	54,155,783	$16,902,755,893	§63	§40

* Per cents. preceded by the minus sign indicate a decrease.
† Virginia and West Virginia are taken together, as West Virginia belonged to Virginia in 1860.
‡ In Pennsylvania occupations are also valued for assessment. This valuation for 1880 was $63,659,580.
§ Average for the United States.

Table No. 7.

Amount raised by taxation for support of public schools in each State and Territory during the year 1880.

STATES AND TERRITORIES.	AMOUNT RECEIVED FROM TAXATION.			STATES AND TERRITORIES.	AMOUNT RECEIVED FROM TAXATION.		
	From State tax.	From local tax.	Total.		From State tax.	From local tax.	Total.
1. Alabama....	$130,000	a$120,000	$250,000	27. N.Carolina.	(*314,719)		$314,719
2. Arkansas	b111,585	77,475	189,060	28. Ohio	$1,548,207	$5,155,879	6,714,086
3. California....	1,318,209	1,393,572	2,711,781	29. Oregon	133,477	79,562	213,039
4. Colorado....	....	c336,333	c336,333	30. Penn'a	....	7,046,116	7,046,116
5. Connecticut..	210,353	1,066,314	1,276,667	31. Rhode Isl'd	80,800	414,852	495,652
6. Delaware	....	d151,045	d151,045	32. S. Carolina.	....	....	440,116
7. Florida.......	(*104,530)		104,530	33. Tennessee .	....	....	j698,773
8. Georgia......	e345,790	125,239	471,029	34. Texas	k678,003	....	k678,001
9. Illinois......	1,000,000	5,735,478	6,735,478	35. Vermont...	113,173	304,318	417,490
10. Indiana......	f1,436,834	f2,168,302	f3,605,136	36. Virginia ...	596,516	665,459	1,261,975
11. Iowa.........	....	4,927,300	4,927,300	37. W.Virginia	212,753	490,432	703,185
12. Kansas.......	....	1,276,786	1,276,786	38. Wisconsin .	*25,000	2,198,581	2,223,581
13. Kentucky....	535,354	g382,038	917,392	39. Arizona....	....	....	167,028
14. Louisiana ...	356,000	h104,000	h450,000	40. Dakota	....	123,643	123,643
15. Maine.......	224,565	596,295	820,860	41. Dist. of Col.	....	474,556	474,556
16. Maryland....	491,406	721,571	1,212,977	42. Idaho......	....	48,017	48,017
17. Massachus'ts.	....	4,372,286	4,372,286	43. Indian Ter.	....	....	....
18. Michigan....	i379,758	2,074,073	2,453,831	44. Kansas	m64,645	5,256	69,890
19. Minnesota...	257,680	1,073,837	1,331,526	45. N. Mexico..	....	....	....
20. Mississippi ..	....	334,769	334,769	46. Utah	63,041	43,337	106,378
21. Missouri	....	2,163,330	2,163,330	47. Washing'n.	f102,201	f3,319	f105,520
22. Nebraska.....	73,808	713,155	786,963	48. Wyoming..	....	f7,056	f7,056
23. Nevada	....	....					
24. N.Hampshire.	....	....	f544,716	Total.....{	(419,249)		} n$70,371,435
25. New Jersey...	1,017,785	724,413	1,742,198		$14,287,570	$58,913,986	
26. New York....	2,750,000	6,925,992	9,675,092				

a. From poll tax.
b. State apportionment, which here probably includes the income of the State School Fund for 1880, and so much of the ordinary State revenue as may be set apart for the purpose by the Legislature.
c. From county and district tax, fines, etc.
d. This amount raised for white schools.
e. This includes rental of State Railroad, ($150,000.)
f In 1879.
g. Includes tax on billiards and dogs.
h. Estimated.

i. From township tax.
j. Includes income from permanent fund.
k. State appropriation.
l. Total income as reported for 1880, the greater part of which comes from Territorial, county, and district taxes.
m. From county tax.
n. Includes $1,750,630 reported as derived from taxation and given in the column of totals, but not appearing in the first two columns.
* Special for building purposes.

Table No. 8.

Showing how much each State and Territory would receive on the basis of Illiteracy, should Congress appropriate $15,000,000.

STATES AND TERRITORIES.	Proportion of $15,000,000 to each State.	STATES AND TERRITORIES.	Proportion of $15,000,000 to each State.
Alabama......	$1,127,869 88	Montana	$4,060 36
Arizona......	16,740 82	Nebraska.......................	23,830 18
Arkansas.......................	406,735 53	Nevada	11,270 84
California	147,983 82	New Hampshire........	36,497 17
Colorado	28,373 77	New Jersey....................	119,206 26
Connecticut....................	63,933 36	New Mexico....................	101,419 72
Dakota........................	9,424 32	New York......................	507,589 75
Delaware	51,514 96	North Carolina.................	1,120,602 94
District of Columbia...........	65,613 89	Ohio..........................	264,252 08
Florida..........	213,887 07	Oregon........................	16,875 30
Georgia........................	1,360,596 42	Pennsylvania.....	445,136 35
Idaho.........................	4,215 66	Rhode Island................ ..	53,170 98
Illinois........................	294,880 21	South Carolina.................	960,141 88
Indiana........................	213,244 37	Tennessee	1,201,290 71
Iowa..........................	85,644 38	Texas..........................	780,455 26
Kansas........................	77,682 14	Utah..........................	14,776 15
Kentucky	786,494 56	Vermont.......................	39,576 68
Louisiana......................	905,612 35	Virginia.......................	1,098,067 77
Maine.........................	55,379 33	Washington....................	9,719 79
Maryland......................	339,264 60	West Virginia.................	158,510 89
Massachusetts..................	230,384 21	Wisconsin.....................	117,858 88
Michigan......................	143,503 15	Wyoming......................	1,300 64
Minnesota.....................	62,598 35		
Mississippi	961,354 15	Total	$15,000,000 00
Missouri	422,839 63		

Table No. 9.

Summary of Annual Income and Expenditures in States and Territories.

STATES AND TERRITORIES.	Annual Income.	Sites, buildings, furniture, libraries, apparatus.	Salaries of superintendents.	Salaries of teachers.	Miscellaneous.	Total.	Estimated real value of sites, buildings, and all other school property.
Alabama	$337,479	......	$11,884	$384,769	a$14,037	$410,690	$285,976
Arkansas	710,462	$29,505	......	......	......	388,412	263,125
California	3,680,161	299,976	b48,330	2,340,050	401,573	3,047,005	6,998,825
Colorado	708,516	......	......	......	......	557,151	977,213
Connecticut	1,492,026	121,382	80,000	1,025,323	299,986	1,476,691	......
Delaware	147,300	......	c2,300	c138,819	c64,472	ed207,281	e450,000
Florida	c189,710	......	c8,021	c97,115	c8,557	cf114,805	c132,729
Georgia	498,533	......	......	......	......	498,533	......
Illinois	7,922,460	837,256	g72,977	h4,722,340	2,225,832	i7,858,414	j16,056,310
Indiana	4,480,306	616,450	......	k3,037,110	835,194	4,528,754	12,034,180
Iowa	5,006,024	870,334	......	l3,046,716	1,218,769	5,120,819	9,533,498
Kansas	1,740,593	365,159	25,200	1,167,620	419,409	1,976,397	4,884,386
Kentucky	1,194,258	......	......	......	......	1,248,524	2,305,752
Louisiana	486,799	m12,760	19,667	m274,127	34,930	441,484	u700,006
Maine	1,089,414	95,347	28,370	q965,097	......	1,080,414	3,026,305
Maryland	1,608,274	o174,684	p40,138	1,162,499	227,329	1,604,580	......
Massachusetts	r4,851,567	803,441	159,314	o4,130,714	425,713	f5,776,542	......
Michigan	3,615,328	730,611	......	l2,114,567	578,055	3,418,233	10,500,000
Minnesota	1,679,207	238,520	16,600	999,907	217,375	1,466,402	3,715,769
Mississippi	716,342	68,327	12,607	644,352	32,472	757,758	......
Missouri	c4,020,860	c137,894	......	c2,213,037	d673,820	cf3,152,178	c7,353,401
Nebraska	1,320,449	221,965	29,443	627,717	285,978	1,165,103	2,054,403
Nevada	138,610	pst11,510	......	859,194	s12,169	140,419	200,191
New Hampshire	586,139	......	14,373	408,554	154,095	577,022	2,113,857
New Jersey	1,914,447	172,942	38,557	1,510,830	192,118	1,914,447	6,275,061
New York	10,895,765	1,677,673	114,600	7,775,505	1,355,624	16,923,402	31,091,630
North Carolina	698,772	27,225	6,394	342,212	33,828	409,650	220,442
Ohio	8,120,326	843,696	154,805	5,151,448	1,983,673	8,133,622	22,103,982
Oregon	323,201	45,192	8,575	234,818	20,746	318,331	657,460
Pennsylvania	8,708,724	m1,207,011	o113,000	4,677,017	1,998,677	7,904,705	26,605,321
Rhode Island	582,965	50,834	10,376	408,993	79,734	549,937	1,954,444
South Carolina	452,965	17,334	18,445	309,855	......	345,634	435,289
Tennessee	700,152	58,852	13,076	529,618	86,403	638,009	868,713
Texas	c891,235	c27,565	c12,648	c674,860	c38,264	c758,316	......
Vermont	454,832	p32,613	......	366,448	42,117	f447,252	......
Virginia	1,335,984	137,230	44,927	823,310	94,763	1,100,230	1,199,333
West Virginia	855,466	102,858	g11,725	539,048	107,019	761,250	1,753,144
Wisconsin	2,178,219	274,846	61,075	1,618,283	324,999	2,279,103	5,522,657
Arizona	58,768	......	......	......	......	44,638	121,318
Dakota	f363,000	......	u8,616	......	......	814,484	t532,267
District of Columbia	555,014	120,533	10,800	205,608	100,251	527,312	1,326,888
Idaho	54,609	2,151	......	38,174	4,515	44,840	......
Montana	94,551	......	3,000	52,781	......	55,781	140,250
New Mexico	u32,171	......	......	u28,002	u971	u28,973	u13,500
Utah	198,876	54,859	......	30,637	199,264	415,186	......
Washington	127,609	v14,592	v2,883	v94,019	v2,885	v114,379	v220,405
Wyoming	u36,161	......	......	u25,894	u2,610	u28,504	u40,500
Indian:							
Cherokees	52,300	......	......	......	......	52,300	......
Chickasaws	33,580	......	......	......	......	33,440	......
Choctaws	31,700	......	......	......	......	31,700	......
Creeks	26,900	......	......	......	......	26,900	......
Seminoles	7,500	......	......	......	......	7,500	......
Total	$88,142,088	$10,502,036	$1,151,804	$55,291,022	$14,603,659	$85,111,442	$186,143,452

a. Includes expenditure of $13,500 for normal schools.
b. Paid out of the general fund for counties and not included in State expenditure.
c. In 1880.
d. Includes $1,800 expended for colored schools outside of Wilmington.
e. For white schools only.
f. Items not fully reported.
g. Salaries of county superintendents.
h. Includes salaries of superintendents other than county.
i. Exclusive of appropriations for normal schools and expense of State superintendency.
j. Exclusive of the value of normal-school property.

k. Total amount expended from tuition revenue.
l. Includes salaries of superintendents.
m. For rent, buildings, etc.
n. In 1878.
o. Includes miscellaneous expenditure.
p. Includes expenditure for repairs.
q. Supervision and office expenses.
r. Exclusive of receipts for school buildings, permanent improvements, and ordinary repairs.
s. Storey County not reporting these items.
t. Value of school-houses only.
u. United States Census of 1880.
v. In 1879.

Table No. 10.

Comparative Educational Statistics in the South.—1880 and 1881.

PART I.—1880.

STATES	WHITE School population	WHITE Enrollment	WHITE Percentage of the school population enrolled	COLORED School population	COLORED Enrollment	COLORED Percentage of the school population enrolled	Total expenditure for both races, a.
Alabama	217,509	107,468	49	170,113	72,007	42	$375,405
Arkansas	b161,799	b53,229	99	b54,332	c17,543	33	238,036
Delaware	31,505	25,033	80	3,651	2,570	70	297,281
Florida	46,410	18,671	41	b42,099	20,444	49	114,805
Georgia	c286,819	130,134	64	c197,125	98,399	45	471,029
Kentucky	c478,597	c241,670	50	c60,564	c23,902	38	803,490
Louisiana	c139,661	c34,032	92	c134,184	c31,470	24	480,830
Maryland	f313,660	131,210	63	f63,591	28,221	44	1,544,367
Mississippi	175,251	112,991	64	251,438	123,710	49	860,704
Missouri	681,995	454,218	67	41,489	22,158	53	3,152,178
North Carolina	291,770	136,481	47	167,554	89,125	53	$362,982
South Carolina	b84,813	61,319	73	g144,315	72,833	50	824,829
Tennessee	403,353	229,290	57	141,509	60,851	43	724,462
Texas	h171,326	138,912	81	162,015	47,664	77	753,316
Virginia	314,827	152,136	48	240,980	68,400	28	946,109
West Virginia	292,364	138,779	68	7,749	4,071	53	716,864
District of Columbia	29,012	16,634	67	13,946	9,306	08	438,567
Total	3,899,961	2,215,674		1,808,257	784,709		$12,475,044

PART II.—1881.

STATES	WHITE School population	WHITE Enrollment	WHITE Percentage of the school population enrolled	COLORED School population	COLORED Enrollment	COLORED Percentage of the school population enrolled	Total expenditure for both races, a.
Alabama	214,152	107,338	50	208,567	68,951	33	$410,690
Arkansas	b199,109	b74,384	37	b63,206	c24,360	33	388,412
Delaware	33,133	26,578	80	4,152	2,544	61	297,381
Florida	46,410	f53,156	67	b42,099	91,044	49	114,805
Georgia	c229,672	f53,156	49	c231,144	f39,223	39	498,533
Kentucky	c483,404	38,870		c70,331	33,560	17	1,248,524
Louisiana	c129,291	133,981	55	f142,190	24,028	34	441,481
Maryland	245,009	111,655	62	f74,192	125,633	52	1,604,580
Mississippi	180,530			239,433		53	757,738
Missouri	681,995	f454,218	67	f41,489	f22,158		3,152,178
North Carolina	283,450	140,311	48	174,292	100,405	58	$409,659
South Carolina	b94,450	61,389	65	b167,829	72,119	43	345,634
Tennessee	402,540	215,702	54	143,205	67,700	47	698,009
Texas	h171,435	162,087	51	262,015	76,930	77	753,316
Virginia	314,827	141,319		240,980			1,100,239
West Virginia	205,087	17,716	69	8,104	3,884	48	761,250
District of Columbia	29,612		60	13,946	9,583	69	527,312
Total	3,954,600	2,294,677		1,920,187	802,372		$12,329,784

a. In Delaware, in addition to the school-tax collected from colored citizens, which has heretofore been the only State appropriation for the support of colored schools, the Legislature now appropriates annually $2,400 from the State treasury for educating the colored children of the State; in Kentucky, in 1881, the school-tax collected from colored citizens was the only money coming from the State for the support of their schools—there was, however, in this year a growth in the movement to give to colored children of school age equal advantages with the white children in the common school fund of the State; in Maryland there is a identical appropriation; in the District of Columbia one-third of the school funds is set apart for colored public schools; in South Carolina the school moneys are distributed in proportion to the average attendance without regard to race; and in the other States mentioned above the school moneys are divided in proportion to the school population without regard to race.

b. Several counties failed to make race distinctions. c. Estimated. d. In 1879. e. For whites the school age is 6 to 20; for colored, 6 to 16. f. Census of 1870. g. In 1877.

h. These numbers include some duplicates; the actual school population is 230,257. i. United States Census of 1880. j. In 1880.

NATIONAL AID TO POPULAR EDUCATION IN EUROPEAN COUNTRIES.

1. FRANCE.

THE population of France is 36,905,788. The liberality of the government of the French Republic in providing for the education of the masses is without precedent in its history. At the close of the Franco-Prussian War, in 1871, popular education was in a backward state. According to the census of 1872 the total population was 36,102,921. Of this number 13,324,801, or 36.9 per cent., (including 3,540,101 children under six years of age,) were unable to read or write; 3,772,603, or 10.5 per cent., could read only; and 19,005,517, or 52.6 per cent., could read and write.

This lamentable condition of affairs was due to optional attendance at school, and to the neglect on the part of the government to provide ample accommodation for a school population of nearly 6,000,000.

Many communes were too poor, and some were unwilling, to establish new schools or enlarge the existing ones. After some delay a law was passed, March 28, 1882, making education obligatory for all children between the ages of six and thirteen, and authorizing poor communes to apply for government aid whenever their means are not sufficient to establish and maintain public schools. The government, however, does not always wait for departments or communes to apply for aid; it invites them to apply, and assures them of hearty co-operation. Letters were sent on the 3d of April, 1882, by the Minister of Public Instruction to the prefects of the departments of Morbihan and Vendée (on the western coast of France) on the condition of education in these two very backward districts.

In Morbihan, 60 per cent. of the conscripts for the army, and the same proportion of persons who present themselves at the *mairies* (city halls) for marriages, cannot read or write. A number of communes have already voted sums amounting to 500,000 francs for the purpose of increasing the number of schools, and the Minister of Public Instruction now offers them a further subsidy of 1,000,000 francs for the same purpose.

In Vendée, owing to similar causes, there also prevails a lamentable state of ignorance. Here 40 per cent. of the conscripts cannot read or write. In order to attend school hundreds of children would have to walk daily from eight to ten miles. The minister offers the department a subsidy of 600,000 francs for the purpose of increasing the number of schools.

Government aid to primary education. In 1860 the government aid to primary education amounted to 5,424,036 francs; in 1870, (under the empire,) 9,817,513 francs; in 1877, (under the republic,) 22,035,760 francs. In 1882 the government aid will be about 50,000,-000 francs, in order to enable all the communes to enforce the obligatory school law. In addition to the above amounts the departments spend this year 25,000,000 francs, and the communes 60,000,000 francs, for primary education. During the two weeks from April 15 to April 30, 1882, the government has spent 1,244,835 francs for new school-houses. The total amount spent by the government alone in 1881–82 for all phases of instruction amounts to 114,353,941 francs, or $22,717,880.

2. BELGIUM.

The following table shows the government grants to education from 1831 to 1882:

Years.	Francs.
1831	217,000
1843	466,000
1845	711,000
1852	1,230,000
1857	1,680,000

1864	3,707,000
1870	6,425,000
1878	11,500,000
1882	20,400,000

The population of Belgium is 5.403.006.

In 1830, when Belgium separated from Holland, there were only 1,146 public primary schools. In 1875. there were 4,152 public primary schools and 2,615 adult schools. In 1847 41.06 per cent. of the conscripts were illiterate ; in 1850, 35.35 per cent., and in 1878, only 19.59 per cent.

3. ITALY.

Italy has a population of 28,209.620, and a school population (6–12) of 4,527,582. Of this number 2,057,977 attend school, against 1,604,978 in 1870. The number of public elementary schools has arisen from 32,782 in 1870 to 41,108 in 1879. The annual grant to these schools in 1882 was 31,000.000 lire, ($6,200,000.) The 7,422 private elementary schools receive no state aid. In 1873 the government grant was 15,000.000 lire ($3,000.-000); in 1876. 20,000,000 lire ($4,000,000); and in 1878, 24,000,000 lire ($4,800,000.) This shows an increase of 16,000,000 lire, or $3.200,000, since 1873.

The above grants are made in addition to large buildings and gardens given for educational purposes in nearly every city and town of the kingdom.

According to the census of 1861, out of a population of 21,777,334 there were 16,999,701 who could neither read nor write—7,889,238 males and 9,110,463 females.

In 1871, out of a population of 26,801,154 there were 19,533,792 who could neither read nor write.

The present Minister of Public Instruction has taken energetic steps to provide accommodations for all the children of school age, and to enforce the law which makes attendance at school obligatory for all children between the ages of six and twelve.

4. ENGLAND.

The annual parliamentary grants to elementary schools in England and Wales was: In 1840, £30,000 ; in 1850, £180.110; in 1858, £668,873; in 1862, £774,743; in 1863, £721,-386: in 1866, £649.006: in 1867, £682.201; in 1868, £680,429; in 1869, £840,711; in 1870, £914.721; in 1873, £1.313,078; in 1875, £1,566,271; in 1877, £2,127,730; in 1879, £2,733,404; in 1882, £2,749,863.

The number of schools has risen from 10,751 in 1872 to 17,614 in 1880 ; the number of seats from 2,397.745 in 1872 to 4.240,753 in 1880 ; and the average number of children in attendance from 1,445.326 in 1872 to 2,750,916 in 1880.

The population of England and Wales is 25,968,286.

5. SCOTLAND.

Population, 3,734.370. The parliamentary grant to elementary schools amounts to £468,512 for 1882–83. The number of elementary schools has increased from 1,962 in 1872 to 3,056 in 1880: the number of seats from 267,412 in 1872 to 602,054 in 1880, and the number of children in average attendance from 206,090 in 1872 to 404,618 in 1880.

6. IRELAND.

Population, 5.159,839. Number of elementary schools, 7,522. Number of pupils, 1,011,-995. The parliamentary grants for popular education in Ireland amounted to a total of £2,948.669 in the ten years, 1860–69; in 1868 it was £360,195; in 1872, £430,390, and in 1882–83 it amounts to £729,868.

7. PRUSSIA .

Population, 27,251,067. The government expenditure for education amounts to $11,-458,856 in 1832, against $10,000,000 in 1881. As nearly all the Pussian schools derive income from endowments, the government grants are chiefly devoted to the establishment of new schools and the improvement of old ones.

8. RUSSIA.

Russia, with a population of 78,500,000 and a school population of 15,000,000, has only 28,357 elementary schools and 1,213,325 pupils. The annual government grant to all grades of schools amounts to $9,000,000. Of this amount only $475,000 is devoted to elementary education. The finances of Russia exhibit large annual deficits, caused partly by an enormous expenditure for war, and partly by the construction of railways. According to official returns, the total war outlay incurred by Russia during the four years 1876–79 amounted to $728,984,635.

The mass of the population of Russia is as yet without education. In 1860 only two out of every hundred recruits levied for the army were able to read and write, but the proportion had largely increased in 1870, when eleven out of every one hundred were found to be possessed of these elements of knowledge.

9. AUSTRIA.

Education until recently was in a backward state in Austria, the bulk of the agricultural population, constituting two thirds of the empire, being almost entirely illiterate. During the last twelve years, however, the government has made vigorous efforts to bring about an improvement by founding new schools at the expense of the state wherever the conveniences were too poor. A law was passed in 1868 making education obligatory for all children between the ages of six and fourteen.

The government expenditure for public education has increased from $2,300,000 in 1870 to $6,500,000 in 1881.

10. BRITISH EMPIRE.

As illustrating the educational impulse moving the whole British Empire, the follow data of schools in the province of Ontario is given:

The population of Ontario is 1,913,460, and the school population, 489,924.

In 1844 there were in the province 2,505 schools, with 96,756 pupils; in 1875, 5,058 schools, with 494,065 pupils, and in 1880, 5,245 schools, with 496,855 pupils. The total expenses for education were $275,000 in 1844, $2,297,604 in 1871, $3,258,125 in 1873, $3,433,210 in 1878, and $3,414,267 in 1880.

GENERAL INDEX.

Mutual Benefit Life
✤ ASSOCIATION ✤
—OF—
AMERICA.

THE OBJECT OF THIS ASSOCIATION

Is to provide for the beneficiaries of deceased members a *Perfect Indemnity* at the *lowest cost* consistent with the *greatest possible security,* with the absolute certainty of all its beneficent aid to widowed wife and orphaned children, and within the reach of men of very moderate means.

Our SYSTEM FURNISHES INSURANCE at exact cost upon the actual mortality, instead of upon an assumed death ratio.

Our EXPENSES OF MANAGEMENT are limited to $3 per $1,000.

Our POSSIBLE ADVERSE CONTINGENCIES (increased mortality) are *guaranteed* by the Reserve and Guarantee Funds.

By our system *all surplus and net earnings accrue to members only.*

Incorporated under the Laws of the State of New York.

OFFICERS.

President.
EDWARD HENRY KENT.

Vice-Presidents.
CHARLES B. BOSTWICK.
WARD B. SHERMAN.

Secretary.
WILLIAM L. GARDNER.

Medical Directors.
WHITMAN V. WHITE, M.D.
PROF. F. LE ROY SATTERLEE, M.D., PH.D.

Board of Finance.
WILLIAM H. OAKLEY.   JOHN H. REED.
CHARLES B. BOSTWICK.

Counsel.
GILBERT HOLMES CRAWFORD, 229 BROADWAY.

Board of Directors.

WILLIAM H. OAKLEY..........................President National Citizens' Bank, New York.
JOHN H. REED...Bates, Reed, & Cooley, New York.
Hon. BUREN R. SHERMAN..Governor of Iowa.
CHARLES B. BOSTWICK.............................Satterlee, Bostwick, & Martin, New York.
Gen. CLINTON B. FISK...Banker, New York.
GEORGE T. PATTERSON, JR............President Clinton Fire Insurance Company, New York.
ZACHARIAH DEDERICK...Dederick & Co., New York.
Hon. JOHN HARDY..Member Congress, New York.
Rev. SANFORD HUNT, D.D..............................Methodist Book Concern, New York.
ALBERT G. GOODALL.....................President American Bank Note Company, New York.
JAMES CRISSY PEABODY..Merchant, New York.
Rev. C. WINTER BOLTON, D.D...New Rochelle, N. Y.
Hon. HIRAM CALKINS...................Associate Editor "New York World," New York.
Hon. CHARLES BEARDSLEY.........Fourth Auditor United States Treasury, Washington, D. C.
EDWARD M. L. EHLERS.....................Secretary Masonic Grand Lodge, New York.
JAMES W. HORTON...Sewell & Erickson, New York.
BREWSTER MAVERICK.................................Maverick & Wissniger, New York.
SAMUEL MARSH...Lawyer, New York.
WILLIAM H. WHITON...Merchant, New York.
EDWARD HENRY KENT..Insurance, New York.

Depositary of Mortuary and Reserve Funds........The Farmers' Loan and Trust Co., of New York.
Depositary of Guarantee Fund......................The National Citizens' Bank of New York City.

Our Business

Is conducted upon the plan of mutual benefit by assessment, and as one assessment will eventually produce, according to the membership, a much larger amount than is necessary to pay a single death claim, no assessment will be made for subsequent death claims so long as there is money left in the Mortuary Fund from the previous assessment to pay them.

Our Future

Is provided for by a Guarantee Fund and a Reserve Fund, the latter being composed of twenty (20) per cent. of all sums received from assessments.

For full particulars send to

HOME OFFICE: Temple Court, cor. Beekman and Nassau Sts., N. Y.
RELIABLE AGENTS WANTED.

The Chautauqua Text-Books.

PHILLIPS & HUNT,

805 Broadway, New York.

www.ingramcontent.com/pod-product-compliance
Lightning Source LLC
Chambersburg PA
CBHW030635030726

47497CB00006B/1793